Vol. 1

THIS BLOOD THAT BINDS US

Books 1 & 2

THIS IS A WORK OF FICTION. NAMES,
CHARACTERS, BUSINESSES, PLACES, EVENTS, AND
INCIDENTS ARE EITHER THE PRODUCTS OF THE
AUTHOR'S IMAGINATION OR USED IN A
FICTITIOUS MANNER. ANY RESEMBLANCE TO
ACTUAL PERSONS, LIVING OR DEAD, OR ACTUAL
EVENTS IS PURELY
COINCIDENTAL.

COVER ILLUSTRATION AND DESIGN BY LUCÍA
LIMÓN.
LINE EDITING AND PROOFREADING FOR BOOK
ONE BY SAMANTHA PICO, MISS ELOQUENT EDITS.
UPDATED PROOFREADING BY DEE'SNOTES
EDITING SERVICES.
BOOK TWO LINE EDITING AND PROOFREADING BY
DEE'SNOTES EDITING SERVICES.

PAPERBACK ISBN: 979-8-9906188-0-0

FIRST EDITION AUGUST 2024
SLCOKELEYBOOKS.COM
OCEANSIDE, CA

This Blood That Binds Us

BOOK ONE

A SIDE

THIS BLOOD THAT BINDS US

▶ **I Found**
Amber Run
4:35

▶ **How Big, How Blue, How Beautiful**
Florence+ The Machine
5:35

▶ **Playing God**
Paramore
3:03

▶ **Leaving It Up To You**
George Ezra
3:37

▶ **Cosmic Love**
Florence+ the Machine
4:16

▶ **Ceilings**
Lizzy McAlpine
3:01

▶ **Daylight**
Taylor swift
4:53

▶ **You've Got The Love**
Florence+ The Machine
2:49

▶ **Dropout**
Lala Lala
2:50

Trigger Warnings

Don't let the cover fool you. This series deals with heavy themes that can be triggering to some readers including but not limited to: mental illness, graphic death, substance abuse, and more.

Please see the full updated list on my website.
www.s.l.cokeleybooks.com

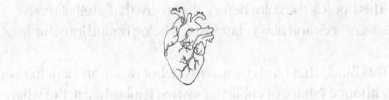

FOR THOSE WHO FEEL ALONE,
REACH OUT YOUR HAND AND FEEL MY
HEARTBEAT MERGE WITH YOURS.

Dear Reader,

There is something beautiful about innocence and beginning a story in blissful ignorance. That's what this book is. Just the beginning of a very long story.

This book is the calm before the storm that's full of fresh adventures and new relationships being bound into our lives.

This Blood that Binds Us was my debut novel, and it didn't come without its share of challenges when I published it. But when asked if I would rewrite it, I say no. I started TBTBU when I was nineteen. I had recently completed school and landed a fantastic job that I believed I would enjoy. But I didn't. I felt trapped, and I yearned for escape and to hold on to my creativity as I entered the workforce.

The person who wrote this book doesn't exist anymore. But there is a piece of her still lingering in these pages and she comes alive when I reread book one. This Blood that Binds Us is exactly the book I wanted to write. And it serves as a great intro to the story I wanted to tell.

Would I write it differently now? Definitely. Because I'm no longer the girl who wrote it.

That's why when building bonus material for this book, I realized I couldn't go back and try to mold myself back into that person. Writing the summer after the initial story was more natural. I didn't want to add my new voice to the old. For me, that feels like painting over old art. Because despite the flaws of a first novel, I'm proud of a messy first voice because we all have to start somewhere.

(Cont.)

I hope this reminds you to never be afraid to try. To push forward and do things without fear of failure, and to do them imperfectly. If I had never published this book, there would be no other books. No one else would have ever met these characters and it would still be sitting in my computer collecting dust to one day be deleted. I'd never have met all of you. Writing this book changed my life.

This is a love letter to my fellow creatives.
I've always been a bit of a daydreamer. I thought it was something I'd eventually outgrow. It wasn't till I started writing I realized it was a gift. Like all creative gifts, the more you practice, the better you get at it.

I worked on this book for six years and no matter how many revisions and rewrites I did, it never felt perfect. It still doesn't and I don't think it ever will. Eventually, you must set the paintbrush aside and admire your creation, flaws and all.
So if you're a fellow creative with any medium and you're afraid to start, or maybe you've been working on something and it's not quite perfect. I'm here to tell you it never will be. But do it anyway. Just try. Show your work to the world. It won't be for everyone, but it will be for someone. And they'll see it and wonder how the world could have ever existed without it.
New beginnings aren't perfect, but they're one of the most important things we'll ever encounter.

With love,

S.L.Cokeley
xoxo

ONE

AARON

That was my new life. Prowling through stupid trees in some stupid forest. I could have said stalking, but I hated that word. The night was stagnant as I waded through swarms of gnats and prickly cedar branches. It was like a scary movie—only I wasn't the idiot who decided it would be a good idea to investigate the noise coming from the basement. I was the bad guy. Next, I'd be a cameo in someone's shower.

My legs propelled me farther into the thicket. Twigs snapped with each step, sending a satisfying crunch into my ears. I wished nothing bad had ever happened. I wanted to be a typical college guy, playing shitty video games and getting too drunk on a Friday night, with my only real worries being money or failing all my classes. I wanted to be myself again, but as I walked and reflected, it was apparent my freedom would never come. I couldn't go back.

Up ahead, flickering fire illuminated the trees. Its shadows bounced and danced along the tree trunks. The fire whispered through incoherent crackling and popping. A pine scent hit me first followed by a strong aroma of burning wood. It was a surprise when I could pinpoint the smell of the dirt and decay orbiting my feet. I wasn't used to my stronger senses then.

My body moved forward despite my screaming heart. I was almost close enough to see the source. Warmth pooled in my palms, and I wiped my hands on my pants, anticipating sweat I no longer produced. Butterflies circled in my stomach as I bent over and crouched on my knees. A girl sat on a rock overlooking the cliff in the distance. The blinding, flickering fire highlighted her auburn hair, igniting the long strands that framed her porcelain face.

My stomach sank. It just had to be a girl. I cursed under my breath, wondering why anyone would even consider camping alone. I was the perfect example of what could go wrong. Though, I couldn't blame her for not anticipating a vampire stalking her in the woods. My shaky hands brushed against the rough bark on the tree beside me, my gaze unbroken as I inched closer.

Kill her.

The nagging voice was back. *It* popped into my head after the change, as if It had always been there. A part of me was glad I wasn't alone in my head anymore, but It only came out to antagonize me when I hadn't fed. Whatever It was.

The twigs crunched underneath my boots, breaking my focus. I wrapped myself behind the tree to hide from the warmth of the light. My fingernails dug into my palms, and I tried to get my hands to stop shaking. As I peeked from behind the tree, another branch cracked under my feet. I was really great at being stealthy.

She turned toward the tree line. The fire's reflection glistened in her soulful blue eyes, while her breath caught in her throat. Her heartbeat. It was fast, and growing louder by the second.

Get closer. We need her.

Fear struck deep in my chest. I took a step back, forfeiting a breath. My jaw tensed, and I moved my hands to my face, trying to regain focus. Pushing past everything physical, I walked into the open.

With eyes narrowed, she examined the tree line. "Hey. Private campsite, and I don't feel like sharing, so . . ."

Her voice was liquid nitrogen injecting into my veins. I was frozen. If I had contemplated it for more than one second, I would have run back through the trees.

You want to kill her. You need to kill her.

It took every bit of strength I had to shut out the voice and drag my heavy body forward. Not only was the voice annoying, but It lied. I kept my eyes glued to her shoes. She'd have a hard time running in those. More pain inflamed my chest as my beating heart hammered against my ribs. *Blood.* I had to stop thinking and think only about blood.

"Stay away from me."

The conviction in her voice made me trip over my feet.

I had to stop thinking.

That's right. Stop thinking. Let me take over.

I wanted to listen, but letting *It* take over wouldn't help me. It hadn't before.

Tracking her feet as she backed farther toward the cliff's edge, I took another step. Her heartbeat was loud in my ears. I studied the way it fluttered in a consistent rhythm. Darkness of the night overtook the warmth in her eyes, her terror tearing my chest open.

Something deep inside me lit on fire, igniting my body from head to toe. My brain shutdown, instinct took over. Her heartbeat. Her skin. Her blood. They called to me. I lunged, grabbed her shoulders, and pulled her closer. I needed her closer.

Before I went for her neck, she twisted my arm and pinned me into the dirt. I wasn't ready for her to fight back. I hadn't even thought of the possibility. One part of me wanted to tackle her, the other part wanted her to run. Her yellow coat flashed in my periphery before disappearing into the dense brush behind me.

Instinctively, I followed her reverberating footsteps. It took no effort to catch up with her. Everything was easy in my new body. I wanted her to run faster, to disappear into the trees where I could never find her. She should have pushed me off the cliff when she had the chance.

That was the last thing I remember thinking for a while.

The other part of me took over—the dark, scary, ominous part I liked to pretend wasn't there. The Thing I was sharing a body with begged me to feed *It*.

In seconds, our chase was over. Our bodies collided onto a rugged patch of dry leaves and dirt. I pinned her arms beside her as she thrashed for leverage. Her fingernails dug into the soil. I went for her neck. My body moved as if it was an instinct. An instinct born of something foreign. It took over every thought. Every nerve. Blood was all that was left.

The taste rocked me momentarily. It was everywhere at once. Everything I could ever want but better. The numbness took over. Her cries were silent in that weird in-between place. Dull was the pain and any physical senses. It felt good in a strange way, like I could get lost there if I stayed too long. The voice won, consuming me with its carnal desire for destruction and death.

Her heartbeat reverberated in my veins. Electricity shocked my body in the form of fear. The numbness subsided, and the feeling returned to my hands. Like being chiseled from stone, one by one, I could feel my limbs again. As I thawed from that dark place, fear and horror filled my stomach. With every second, I regained my sense of reality.

Her heartbeat caught my attention again. The rapid beating echoed in my eardrums. It was so loud it hurt. Cupping my ears, I stumbled to my feet, then wiped the remnants of blood from my lips. It smelled sweet but tasted bitter.

The forest was quiet, other than bugs buzzing in cadence with my victim's heartbeat. The voice was gone, thrust back into my head somewhere. My feet were moving without my permission. I backed away until a tree branch jabbed me. Only then did I take in the scene fully.

Her body was a few feet away. Her skin was pale, her warmth fading into the damp forest floor. Her bright hair dulled as she lay on the ground.

Instinct told me to run, but my feet were glued to that spot. She was dying. I couldn't leave her there.

Fear and guilt swallowed me whole. My stomach rumbled in pain. Nausea traveled up my throat, and I retched out loud, covering my mouth. Even as a vampire, my body reacted to stress.

I dry heaved until I willed my wobbly legs to move. I wouldn't let her die. She had to live. After rushing to her side, I leaned down to search her bright fleece-lined rain jacket. Carefully, I rummaged in her jacket pockets, praying to myself.

I grabbed her cellphone with shaking hands and pulled it in front of my face. Squinting from the light, I fumbled past the lock screen. The call wouldn't connect. I jumped up, holding the phone in the air until it rang.

Softly, I laid it back in her hand, making sure the connection remained. It was the best chance I could give her. I wanted to stay with her and hold her hand and see life return to her face until help came, but footsteps echoed from behind me.

I left my heart on the ground and disappeared into the forest. My mind still raced, looking for a better solution. I slipped between the trees, hiding just outside of the fire's glow.

An unrecognizable male voice rebounded through the thick tree trunks. "Honey, she's fine. She said she does this thing all the time."

A glimmer of hope sparked a tingling in my hands that traveled to my throat. I thrust a hand over my mouth to stifle the desperate pleas hanging onto my lips.

A woman whispered, "I have a bad feeling. She's out here all alone. I just want to check on her."

A bickering husband and wife, no doubt. I walked closer to them, staying just out of sight.

The man spoke again. "Louise, we can't just have a fun camping trip, can we? You always have to be worrying about something."

"Shut it, Ron."

They were close, heading toward where I had left the girl. The smell of her blood caught in the breeze, swirling around us, the light of the girl's fire still burning.

It was the best gift of fate I'd ever been given. In just a few steps, they'd find her.

Another set of footsteps tore through the forest floor in the distance.

Two more people came running, leaving a path of destruction in their wake. That's when I knew exactly whose footsteps they were.

I ran as fast as I could toward the melody, and a strong set of hands cut off my momentum. They would have sent me flying if not for the firm grip on the back of my shirt, pulling me onto my heels.

My two older brothers stared back at me. Their protective shadow engulfed me, making me feel small. They were still in their sweats and baggy shirts. They must have gone after me right after I had left the house.

"W-What are you doing here?"

"We couldn't let it go. We followed you," Luke said as he towered over me, much like he would when we were kids. His eyes searched me up and down with worry.

"Yeah, fuck this 'on your own' shit," Zach said.

His shoulders fell away from his ears, and he stuffed his hands into his pockets, waiting for me to speak.

Luke said, "Are you okay?"

I was surprised he couldn't smell the blood, but I couldn't either. I had run farther than I thought.

"I think so. I'm all right." I lowered my gaze.

"Did you do it?" Zach's eyes darted to Luke. "You know, drink blood?"

Two months into being a vampire, and that sentence still sounded wrong in my ears.

"Yeah, I did. It was fine. It's all fine."

I couldn't tell them about the girl. What would they think if I told them I had called 911? Would they be mad? We had to keep a low profile, and that was the exact opposite of a low profile. Soon, rescue crews would scour the grounds—hell, maybe even news crews.

"Can we go?" I blurted. "Please?"

They exchanged another twin telepathy moment, and I sighed.

I turned to Luke, knowing his vote was the only one I needed.

"Please. I-I just wanna go home."

Luke's eyes bore into mine. "Yeah, all right. Let's go."

With one final turn, I gazed through the trees to where the campfire's flickering light was, praying her light wouldn't fade.

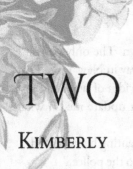

TWO

KIMBERLY

Everything was too bright. Too cold. Too loud. Nurses chattering accompanied the heart monitor's soft drum. It took me a few minutes to realize it was my heartbeat.

I opened my eyes. A large poster stared at me from across the room. The hospital. My brain rebooted like a 1990s computer. Pain shot through my arms and into my fingertips as I sat up. My fingers lingered on bandages that clung to my sore shoulder.

It all came back. The adrenaline. The black eyes . . . the fangs. It couldn't possibly be what I was thinking. There had to be another explanation. My thoughts betrayed my own resolve. What else could a man with fangs mean? Could there be another logical explanation? In a loop, I ran breathlessly through the trees until a man—who didn't look exactly human—pinned me down. That couldn't be possible. There was absolutely no way.

The heart monitor's rapid beating echoed as the nurse walked in. I wiped the sweat from the nape of my neck.

"Hello. It's nice to see that you're up. Kimberly Burns?"

She was fluorescent in her pink scrubs with her hair pulled into a clean ponytail.

"Uh, yes." I pulled my shoulders back, feigning a positive mental state. "I feel fine."

"Good, I just need to get some good information from you. Your belongings are right in that bag on the table. We don't have any emergency contacts on file for you in our hospital. Is there anyone you want us to call?"

"Oh, no, actually. I'm okay."

Her gaze lifted from my chart. "Are you sure, hun? We recommend at least a friend be here for emotional support and to pick you up from the hospital."

"I don't have anyone . . ." I shifted in my gown. The only person I could call lived more than two thousand miles away in New York. That disastrous phone call could wait until I had some idea of what had just happened to me. "Really, it's fine. Can you just update me on what happened?"

"You don't remember?" she said, a sharp line denting her forehead.

"I do. I'm just wondering when I'll get to talk to the police."

"The police—honey, you were attacked by an animal."

"No, I wasn't. Someone bit me. A man chased me through the woods and bit me."

She averted her eyes, her lips twisting into a grimace. "Let me go talk with your doctor for a moment. Hold on a second."

Her fluffy pink pen jangled as she left the room, leaving me with the television's low hum. I peeled the bandage from my shoulder and peeked at the jagged bite mark on my skin, a clear indentation of teeth. Oddly perfect.

Drawing in a quick breath, I closed my eyes. My body rejected the thought of it all. The black eyes, the teeth. The face of a man. The feeling of blood draining from my body. I had been awake for all of it. Up until the point my heartbeat pounded in my ears and everything went black for a while.

"Help is coming, sweetie."

I remembered the sound of that sweet lady's voice as she held my hand. She made me feel safe. I was incredibly grateful I had seen her and her husband earlier that day on the trail. She had even offered me some of their packed food. Despite the sickness settling in the pit of my stomach, the kindness of strangers made me feel secure, even while being alone in that hospital bed.

My eyes opened to the empty room, the walls too close. The four white walls felt like a prison. There had to be another explanation, but an animal attack wasn't one of them. I'd just need to tell them. They'd have to believe me.

With the crack of the door, I pulled my blankets to my chest, savoring the little warmth they held. Every soft breeze of the air conditioner only exposed the rigid vulnerability shaking my entire body.

"Kimberly, I'm Dr. Hendrix. It's a pleasure to meet you." A large man walked through the door.

His muscles pulled at the edge of his doctor's coat awkwardly as he swung the door shut with unnecessary force. His dark umber skin complemented his tight black curls.

I shifted under the force of his gaze. "Nice to meet you."

"How are you feeling? You're a very lucky young lady. You lost a lot of blood."

"That's what they tell me. I feel fine. But my shoulder is a little sore when I move it back and forth."

He offered a small accepting smile. "That's normal. It will feel sore for a week or two. There's some pain medication I'm going to send you home with, as well as some antibiotics. Infection can accompany these types of attacks."

"What do you mean by 'these types of attacks'?"

"Oh, yes, sorry. The nurse told me you were having some memory troubles. That is to be expected after experiencing a traumatic event. Animal attacks are quite common in the area where you were found."

I sucked in a breath. I hadn't anticipated that answer. The word I was looking for was a little more taboo, and I didn't dare say it aloud.

"Memory trouble? No, I was camping in the woods, and a man attacked me. He bit me. I remember it. I even remember what he looked like," I said, finding my voice despite my dry throat.

His hazel eyes panned over me one moment before he took a seat in the chair next to my bed. "Kimberly, you were attacked by an animal. The level of blood loss when they found you at the scene . . . there's no way a human could have caused that. Not with the wound you have."

The lump in my throat went down slowly. My life was disintegrating right before my eyes. One moment, I was doing everything to graduate college, and suddenly, a huge vampire-shaped truck wrecked my life. Was it possible I could have hallucinated the whole thing? Was I the crazy one?

"We didn't find any drugs in your system. Do you have any preexisting conditions? Any history of mental illness?"

"I'm sorry?" I choked.

"Is there anything else that could have caused your lapse in memory?"

His gaze pierced mine. We held a look long enough for me to recognize the emerald flecks in his eyes.

I steadied my voice, trying to quell my heavy breathing. "No, I'm just a little groggy, I think. I don't think I'm remembering everything correctly."

His shoulders dropped from his ears. "Don't worry about that. It's normal."

"Was there anyone else with me? I remember this older woman. She was really nice."

"Yes. This older couple was actually there with you when the paramedics arrived. They said they had seen you on the trail earlier and came to check on you"—the soft morning sun's beams shone through the window and warmed up his features—"and they've already called to check on you, actually."

"That's how I survived the animal attack, then? Because they found me and called for help?"

"We have already spoken to the police about this. Apparently, you were able to call 911 before losing consciousness."

"I-I was?"

I shuffled through the events again. My attacker's black eyes and the extended canine teeth were all that came to mind.

"Yes, you already had the paramedics on the phone when they found you."

I wished that were true. I wanted it to be. I single-handedly fended off my attacker and found the strength to dial the number. But it wasn't true. Everything after the attack was blurry, but everything leading up to the attack was plain as day.

My camping trip began like any other. A five-mile hike in the nature reserve located just a few miles out of town, a tradition I had started in the fall after I found out how truly abysmal finals could be. I prepared for every contingency: bears, unexpected rain, an assault of mosquitos. No bit of my fifty-point checklist could have prepared me for that night.

Once I heard the crackling of branches, I moved toward my tent to get my bear spray from my bag. Fear took over once I saw my attacker. The look in his eyes held me in place, infusing the darkest feeling of despair into me. Once my feet were moving, I hadn't even considered reaching for the phone in my pocket, since I thought I had left it in my bag at the campsite. I didn't call 911. "Right. I think I remember."

I forced out my best smile, pulling the blankets closer to my chest. Chills ran up my spine. I was thankful to be in the safety of the hospital.

"Well, I'm glad that's all cleared up. Your shoulder will be sore for a few weeks. We want to keep you for a few more days for observation, just to monitor for any lingering symptoms of shock or infection."

His words had me sitting at attention. The fear in my bones dissipated as quickly as it had come. "Is there any way I can be discharged sooner? I don't exactly have insurance, so if I'm doing well . . . I'd like to go home."

The corners of his mouth twitched. He wasn't going to find that an attractive option. I didn't either, considering a vampire could have been on the loose somewhere—or maybe I needed psychiatric help—but my brain flipped in cartwheels thinking of the hospital bill. A couple more days was going to set me back until I was at least thirty—and that was a generous estimate.

After some back-and-forth, he eventually agreed, though he had empathy in his eyes and a strong dad aura as he lectured me about the importance of taking care of my wound and looking out for any serious symptoms.

"Do you have any more questions?"

Those words snapped me back into reality. I had nothing but questions that begged to be answered. They danced on my tongue, pushing for my attention. But I wouldn't find them in that hospital bed, racking up a lifetime worth of debt.

I cleared my throat. "Uh, no thank you."

"The nurse will be back in shortly to discuss some follow-up care and instructions for your medication. You get some rest. No more hiking trips for a while—and bring a buddy next time." His voice echoed through the crisp white walls, leaving a deafening silence in his absence.

I was unbelievably confused. The urge to pull the covers over my head and hide expanded by the second, but I had an even greater urge to do that under my own cute strawberry-covered duvet. All I wanted was to nestle into my fluffiest pink socks and wrap my aching shoulder in my heated blanket. My first step was to get out of the hospital.

When the nurse came to talk to me, I sat up straight and softened my voice. I complimented the fluffy pen with the little silver balls. I put on my best fake smile, but I made sure to let some pain through, being a recovering patient, after all. The world was crumbling around me, but I needed to keep my feet steady, putting one very dirty hiking boot in front of the other.

My foot slumped into my thick-soled boot. Normally, I'd cherish strapping them on, but it was different. The usual strength and confidence they lent me was nonexistent as I struggled to pull my laces taut. Everything was sore, and my eyes were heavy. With no one to drop off some clothes, I had to wear out my hiking clothes. A few spots of blood lingered on my flannel, and my shorts weren't covering up my scratched-up knees. My hair smelled of bonfire as I pulled my yellow coat over my shoulders, little clumps of soil littered the floor around my feet. Jaw clenching with the movement, I let out a low groan. I needed more meds to survive the day. The only reflective surface in the room was an empty bedpan, and if I looked anything like I felt, it wasn't worth an attempted look.

The nurse led me out into the hallway, where I glimpsed my neighbors across the hall. Some were my age, asleep with a parent in the chair, their eyelids full with sleep, their arms draped across the armchairs. Others were older, with drooping faces and wrinkles settling into their frowns. I didn't know their stories. I wasn't sure I wanted to.

An older couple caught my attention, who reminded me of the couple I had encountered on the trail before my attack. Hair speckled with gray, wrinkled smiles. Love wafted off them in a way I could feel in the air. A tickle on my skin raised the hairs on my arm. The man lay in the hospital bed, his wife glued to his side. Children sprang from one side of the room to the next until they piled on to the hospital bed. Laughter reverberated through the walls. Their parents ushered them in for a picture, celebrating. Instinctively, I looked away, shielding myself from their light. Their love. My shoelaces snapped against the tile floor, and I stopped.

"Hold on a sec." I called the nurse, who was already a few feet ahead of me.

"Do you want me to take the picture so you can all be in it?" I said, pointing to their phone.

I knew I looked like I had been run over by a truck, but their moment was too special to pass up. The laughter's magnetism forced me to linger in the doorway. I almost hoped they'd say no, but the bigger part of me felt like a small child begging to be included in some way.

"Yes!" The woman's eyes lit up with excitement. "That's so kind."

Her warmth caught me off guard. The room radiated a euphoric energy of happiness and love. I swallowed the lump in my throat and took the phone. The kids clung to their elders, cheek to cheek. Their arms interlocked. Teeth flashed. The room erupted into a cadence of thank yous, laughter, and footsteps.

My nurse greeted me at the door, and we walked in silence down the hall. A hole had formed in my chest, and every time I inhaled, the hole expanded. I counted our footsteps as they echoed along the softer patterns of heart monitors and beeping machines. My phone was lead in my pocket. No one called. No one texted. After a deep, calming breath, I refocused. I wouldn't allow myself to think about it anymore, or I would explode.

Maybe the doctor was right. My memory loss caused some kind of wild hallucination. Meaning it would be safe for me to go back to my dorm without a care in the world. I could just go back to the way things were before. I could continue to work my butt off to get a good job. I could graduate college. It could work. If only my shoulder would stop throbbing.

THREE

KIMBERLY

All my life, I've never really been afraid of anything. I suppose when I was a kid I had fears but not the ones most kids do. I feared for my safety. Growing up in foster care was scary at times. Not all foster parents were created equal, and sometimes, just for a season or two, I'd keep my mouth shut to survive. But those times passed quickly in a child's mind. I always had something to occupy myself with. Things I could throw myself into that made unpleasant times pass quicker. But when I grew older, the fear that seemed to hold most others from achieving their dreams never frightened me. Most students fresh out of high school feared the world. It was different for me. I had already seen the world. Seen the dark. For the most part, I had come out unscathed. When I aged out of foster care, I wasn't afraid. When I became part of an annoying statistic and lived in my car, I wasn't afraid. When I got down to my last dime, I wasn't afraid. I wasn't ashamed of being a foster kid. I was proud I could get to where I was on my own.

So, it was no surprise I wasn't afraid of returning to a world where vampires might have existed. If it weren't for my wounded shoulder, I might have let my brain believe I'd imagined it.

Hallucination still seemed like the most likely option of all.

But the bite stared me in the face every time I looked in the mirror. Throbbing. Festering. Not in the normal way wounds would. Tiny blue and red veins bloomed, along with a bruising that grew with time.

I sighed and rubbed the bite's indentation. I had done an extensive Google search on the subject, but I was smart enough to identify humanlike teeth marks when I saw them. I had given up on the thought of it going away. I ruffled my hands through my messy mop of hair and went straight for my closet.

I liked to describe my dorm room as cozy. I used the word as an excuse to splurge for an extra fluffy comforter and twinkle lighting that wrapped around the bed frame, but it was just to atone for my lack of space. A few steps led me right in front of two warm wooden sliding doors I had decorated with Polaroids and book pages.

My heart sank as I looked at the little green plaid dress I had picked up at the thrift store just days before the accident. I had been so excited to wear it to school, pair it with some platforms and maybe a cute hat. That was out the window. The delicate fabric brought the gentle scent of wool and too much fabric softener embedded in the fibers to my nose. I loved that weird smell. Thrift stores were good for much more than finding old books, like furnishing the majority of my wardrobe and my dorm. I grabbed an oversized sweatshirt, denim jeans, and fluffy pink socks to wear with my Docs.

My phone vibrated on my desk across the room, which was only two steps away. My loft bed took up most of the space, leaving minimal room for my desk underneath and a small bookshelf. The plants on my windowsill cascaded down to a mini fridge and covered the tiny cat magnets holding up my reminder notes.

Excitement hummed in my chest as I unlocked my phone. Just a spam email. No new messages. Not even from Chris.

Chris was my suit-wearing best friend, whose dream led him away from the lush mountains to a concrete jungle. The only relationship that had truly stuck after aging out of foster care. I pulled the phone up to my ear, trying to call again. After a few seconds of ringing, I placed my phone into my pocket. Oh well. It didn't matter.

The clock on my desk caught my attention. I shoved my bag onto my good shoulder and left for class. The bag crackled with the new additions I added over the weekend. Taking my only known information about vampires, demons, and general bad guys, I prepped for two approaches. One practical: pepper spray and emergency key chain alarm. And the nonpractical: a wooden cross from the craft section and a wooden stake from the home improvement store. I was grateful *Buffy the Vampire Slayer* had taught me a few things, but I still wasn't completely convinced I was sane. Either way, the additions wouldn't hurt.

My hospital discharge landed on a Friday, a day when I had one class—luckily, it was Public Speaking. I had no issues with missing any curriculum in that class. My professors were more than understanding when I emailed over my doctor's note. I used the weekend to recover. Frantically calling Chris—with no luck—I did whatever I possibly could to convince myself I wasn't losing my mind. I scoured the internet for every animal attack forum and recovery page I could find, a disgusting chore. I did it to find some peace of mind, but there was nothing. No Google images of a bite mark with bruising and little blue veins.

My calves ached in sync with my throbbing shoulder. Every step hurt as I sped down the busy hallway of Johnson Hall, a long corridor with high arches and light peeking through the windowsill at the end. It was the longest hallway our college had, and the end of that hallway just happened to be my writing class. I glanced at my phone. I'd make it just in time. My body was still sore, and I cursed myself for not accounting for my slowness.

As I reached the end, dirty-blond disheveled hair caught my attention. A vague sense of familiarity set my nerves on edge. My feet stopped before I knew what was happening. Standing twenty feet away from me was the monster that had haunted my dreams since Thursday. He strolled with a group, two other guys at his side. One of them had to have made a joke because they were all laughing. His white teeth glistened in the morning light, and my stomach sank. Their laughter carried up the walls and up to the ceiling. His eyes . . . just brown. No hint of darkness from before.

It was him. That vampire was at my school. In my hallway. My heart kicked my ribs, and I ducked behind the person in front of me. My jagged breaths were getting me weird looks as I clawed my way against the flow of traffic. I wanted to run back to my dorm. But my class door was open, and I had already used up all my sick days when I got the flu that winter. Missing meant dropping a letter grade. That wasn't an option for me.

I spun, just in time to watch him disappear in the room two doors down from mine. He hadn't seen me. Just as the clock hit nine o'clock, I reached my classroom door and funneled inside. In a haze of exhaustion and wind-blown hair, I found my usual seat next to Mikayla. She wasn't someone I had considered a friend because we never hung out outside of class. I'd tried to invite her for coffee a few times, but it never amounted to anything. She always bailed at the last minute. But she was nice and praised me on my class presentations. Plus, small talk was her specialty.

"You look like you've had a rough day." A pointed smile played on her lips.

I ignored her, my eyes glued to the door. Every muscle in my body was on high alert, waiting to sprint out the door. I thought about saying something, but what would I say? He didn't look the same as he had in the forest. His cheeks were rosy, his eyes bright and full of life. Could I have been hallucinating again? Was I absolutely sure it was the same guy? I wasn't even one hundred percent sure there was a guy.

"Are you okay?" Mikayla watched me with a crooked thick brow.

I loved her Lily Collins-esque brows, and constantly gave her tips on how to enhance them.

"What gave it away?" I forced a smile, still short of breath. Blood pumped in my ears, and my hands shook. I willed my feet to walk to my chair and take a seat.

Our classroom was one of the least memorable on the campus. While some had stadium seating, wooden arched ceilings, and thick-framed paintings, this one must have been a broom closet at one time. It was smaller than my other classrooms, and the desks were old. Mikayla smiled. "Definitely the hair."

I chuckled. "Thanks. I woke up late this morning."

"Oh, I've been there. There's no shame in that. It's just unlike you. You're usually so polished," she said, reaching for her binder from her purple school bag hanging on her chair.

Mikayla eyed my university sweatshirt in her peripheral. She wasn't wrong. I loved dressing up for class and feeling confident. But confidence was miles away, floating down the river in the nature reserve.

Forcing my brain to focus on the present, I mirrored her movements. My fingers pulled the binder from my backpack and plopped my pencil bag on our table, the sound inaudible under the noise of the classroom.

Our professor had yet to arrive. I scanned the door. My forearms ached with tension, and I used my palms to try to get them to loosen.

"So, how was your weekend?" Mikayla said.

"My weekend?" My heart jumped into my throat.

"Jeez, too much coffee this morning?" Her voice was perky, but her eyes held no emotion as she flicked through each page in her binder. She stopped to point at the whiteboard.

In bold black letters, the board read, "Write a single page, front and back, explaining what you did this weekend."

I choked on the irony, covering my mouth for a cough.

"Didn't you say you were going camping or something?" She pulled her mechanical pencil out, clicking it a few times to move up the lead. "How did that go?"

"Oh, yeah. It was . . . great. Pretty uneventful. I read a lot. So, that was good."

My stomach twisted. At least it wasn't a complete lie. I pulled a piece of paper from my book bag, eyes still trained on the door, my only escape route.

"Well, that's way easier to write about than mine. I spent the entire weekend helping my boyfriend move into his new place. He was too cheap to pay for a moving truck, so we made, like, fifty thousand trips in my Fiat. Apparently, his brother stole his car, and his landlord wouldn't let him have an extension on the move-out date. It was so annoying." Mikayla groaned, resting her head on her hand. I was thankful for her long, detailed stories and lack of attention.

"Wow, that sucks. At least you guys can enjoy your weekend this week, right?" I gripped my pencil and concentrated on writing my name and the date in the left-hand corner.

She sighed, her brows pinching. "Maybe. I told him I wanted to go on an actual date. No more bars. He gets way too drunk, and I have to drive him home."

Our professor walked through the door and unloaded her materials from her rolling briefcase. "Good morning, class."

"Good morning," we both grumbled, along with just a few others in class.

I dug my pencil into the lines of my paper, leaving a little pile of lead. I could just jot down a quick lie for my warm-up, but my eyes kept floating to the door.

Out of all the places, the guy went to my school. What kind of hideous trick of fate was that? It was possible he wasn't a vampire at all. If it weren't a hallucination, he could be some kind of lunatic. For all I knew, there could be a cannibal cult running around, drinking blood. Somehow, that was the more likely scenario.

But something was still wrong with my shoulder. No amount of hiding could change that. It had no pus, no redness. Just these weird little veins that kept growing.

Before I knew it, the professor was doing her rounds, grabbing up our warm-up assignments. My page was still blank as I reluctantly passed it to her. The professor eyed me with disapproval. Warm-ups were meant to be an easy grade.

Not one word could I memorize or write during the class. I pretended to write most of the time, while violently scratching up my paper and glancing at the door every five seconds. The feeling rolling around in my stomach was confusing. On one hand, I was terrified. Obviously. A potential psycho was walking around my campus, and I still wasn't sure of how dangerous he could be. But another small part of me was relieved. If he was a vampire, then that meant I hadn't hallucinated, and maybe—just maybe—I could get a real answer about my shoulder.

My head hurt as much as my bite. That was the problem with fiction propelling itself into reality. Possibilities were quite literally endless. No matter which way I turned, I didn't have a good answer of what I should do, and I had no one to ask. No mentor. No parents. My only friend was still ignoring my phone calls. I could go to the police, but what good would that do? I'd be safe, but would I just be putting a bigger target on my back? Was my shoulder problem even something a doctor could fix?

I counted the tiles on the ceiling. One by one, I counted them until my shoulders dropped from my ears and I could take another breath. I glanced over at Mikayla, who was oblivious to my inner turmoil and picking dirt from under her nails.

The clock signaled five minutes till the end of class, and I prepared myself to go for the door. The only way I could make sure he wasn't some weird mirage or a figment of my imagination was to find him. I was already standing when the professor signaled the end of class. I shoved my notebook in my bag quicker than I thought humanly possible. My heart responded to another troubling thought. Could something be happening to me? Could I be turning into a vampire?

That thought was enough to set my feet on fire. I had to get answers. I had to know one way or another if I had actually seen him.

"I'll see you Thursday?" Mikayla looked up at me through her lashes, her eyes troubled.

"Yeah. See you then." I slung the bag over my shoulder and dashed to the door.

I was close. High on adrenaline, I crashed into a man who came out of nowhere. Stumbling back in pain, I clenched my jaw, my entire arm throbbing from the impact.

"I am such an idiot. Did I hurt you?" A smooth voice cut through the static of chattering students.

A man with dark-brown hair stood in front of me. His dark-green Black Forest University T-shirt stuck out to me. I focused on two little words under the bold black lettering. Swim Team.

"I'm fine." The words came out in one breath. My backpack had been unzipped, leaving my items scattered across the tile floor. Thankfully, the wooden stake hadn't found its way out, but everything else had. Pepper spray? Check. Small wood cross? Check. Taser? Definitely check.

"Here, let me help you." A broad smile danced on his lips before he hid it. With my only good arm, I shoved the scattered pieces of my disastrous life back into my school bag. "No, I got it, really."

He held up my pepper spray with two fingers. "You do not want to forget this."

His overall demeanor was calm, collected. Pieces of his brown hair cast a shadow over his dark eyes. The sides of his head were cropped but still had some length. He watched me with a worried expression, feet shifting in his high-top sneakers.

My focus moved to the door. The pain in my shoulder was so intense it made me forget about my vampire problem for a second. I feared I had let too much time pass. Tracking him would be impossible without catching him in the hallway.

"Are you sure you are all right?" he said, brows furrowing.

"Yes. Sorry, I'm really distracted today. Thanks for helping me with my stuff. I'm pretty sure I'm the one who ran into you."

"It's no problem. It's Kimberly, right?"

"Y-Yeah. Do I know you from somewhere?" I was taken aback, having no idea how he would know my name.

He was unfazed. "I sit right over there." He pointed to the chair in the far left of the room. "Don't worry. No one pays attention to who they go to class with. Well, usually. I'm William."

"Nice to meet you." I smiled, trying to mask the embarrassing arsenal he witnessed in my backpack. I didn't remember seeing his face, but I had never focused on memorizing my classmates' faces.

"I was actually coming to ask you if you had the notes on the final assignment. I was gone that day, and you are one of the only people I ever see taking notes."

"Oh, sure." I turned my bag around and dug for my binder.

My attention wandered back toward the door, where I caught a brief glance of the same tousled blond hair. The vampire was on the move. I dug faster, my sweaty hands struggling to grip the binder in one pull.

"I swear I'm not usually this flustered." I yanked the paper from my binder and handed it to him.

"Flustered? You? I don't know what you're talking about." A toothy smile sprang on his face.

"Thank you. I promise to be more normal. Next time we talk, let's just pretend it's the first time we've met, okay?" I stumbled toward the door, dragging my still-open backpack behind me.

"Next time? Sounds like a plan." He brought two fingers to his brow, saluting me as I left.

I didn't give it another thought as I fought my way into the crowded hallway. I lifted on tiptoes to see ahead. It couldn't have been more than thirty seconds. He was gone, and I was lost in the bustle of backpacks and tired faces, breathless.

Sparing only a moment for the frustration, I went to work on how to find him again. I could wait till next week to find him outside the classroom, but that was days away.

I made my way to the large window at the end of the hall that overlooked the courtyard. Thick walls of black-and-white stone stood like mountains, contrasting with the bright-green grass below. It was more populated than usual. Finals were coming up, with the end of the spring semester drawing near. Everything was lush green, and the campus bloomed with vibrance.

Black Forest University was an old college, which meant a lot of money went into preserving its rich history that was embedded in the gray stone and large windowpanes. Students ducked in and out of the stone archways at the edge of the garden, their books pressed firmly to their chests. Jaws clenched and heads down. The campus's undeniable warmth made me want to spend hours outside watching the breeze blow through the trees.

I contemplated where my vampire would go. Our campus was moderately big. Lots of common areas. Plenty of different classes he could be in. How could I ever find him? The clock tower above chimed, and I looked at the ceiling. It was muffled, but my fingertips vibrated standing directly under it.

I strained my eyes toward the common area across the yard that led to the cafeteria, and with sheer luck or fate, I saw him. He was still walking with the same group as before. Even with just a peripheral view, I was positive it was him from the shiver that ran up my spine. He was real. I wasn't crazy.

Every movement looked so normal. The way his backpack slung across his shoulder, the way he had a skip in his step to his walk. He looked like a regular college boy. Soon, he disappeared around a corner but not before I caught a glimpse of his smile. A smile like that was going to haunt me for more than one reason.

I had to get away. I wanted to run. To do something about the utterly disastrous and dangerous path my life had taken. But I had Biology labs at four. So, I'd need to reschedule my mental collapse until after finals.

Instead, I opted for the next best thing, running on the treadmill. It gave my fight-or-flight response the sedation it needed to get me through the day. Doctor's orders were for me to take it easy, but walking just wasn't cutting it. Within the following days, I'd done nothing but go to class, then run right back to my room. I spent hours and hours combing the internet for anything I could find concerning vampires or strange sightings, and the closest thing I found were online forums where people pretended to be vampires. Cool but not what I was looking for.

I hadn't seen the guy, a.k.a. the Maybe Vampire Psychopath, since that time in the hallway, but it was all I could think about. I couldn't get through the day without ibuprofen and noting all the emergency exits.

It was taking over my life. Every waking moment, I wondered and waited. Any second, he could show up again, and what would I do?

My mind went wild with different scenarios. I could turn him into the police. That option seemed like the safest, but it left me with one problem. What the heck was I going to do about my shoulder? The antibiotics weren't working. I could try to confront him, but that was the most dangerous option of all. Whoever he was, he attacked me. I couldn't trust him to tell me any form of the truth. There were too many variables, and even after writing every way it could play out in my notepad, I couldn't reach a decision.

My calves ached, and I glanced at the little dashboard displaying my run time. Three miles in thirty minutes. Crap. I did the same in twenty-four last week. I smacked the big red button, and my wobbly legs came tumbling to a halt. Still drawing in short breaths, I grabbed my water bottle and brought it to my lips. Empty. Strange. I thought I filled it back up after my warm-up earlier. I added that to the list of the things I wasn't doing at my usual rate of perfection.

I left the long aisles of treadmills and headed for the water fountain. A largely built man dripping in sweat blocked my path, and I stopped just short of ramming into him and falling into a rack of dumbbells. I expected him to say sorry—or anything—but he didn't. He stared at me with lifeless eyes, the muscles in his face completely relaxed. With annoyance and a strange sense of bubbling anxiety, I went to wait in the short line for the fountain, where only one guy stood ahead of me.

"Kimberly?"

My eyes shot up, and I was met by a nonstranger. "William?"

William's cologne hit me first. It was a soft punch that reminded me of rich men golfing at the country club. One of my foster dads loved golfing, and I'd tag along. He didn't look fancy, though. Standard board shorts and a tight-fitting Black Forest University swim shirt that looked one size too small. With his light complexion, he didn't look like he got much sun. If ever.

"You were supposed to act like this was the first time we met, remember?" He was all smiles as he eyed me up and down. "Here, let me get that for you."

He held his hand out for my bottled water, and I obliged despite my sweaty hands.

"Thanks. Did you just get here?"

Not an ounce of sweat gleamed on him.

I tried to wipe mine from my forehead casually.

"Yeah, I'm about to head to practice." He motioned toward the big glass doors that led to the campus pools. Our gym was the most modern-looking building on my campus, equipped with skylights, a new indoor track, and a swimming pool. My guess was that it was a recent build. How the alumni were ever able to survive college without a gym, I couldn't comprehend.

"I'm training for a marathon," I admitted. "It's over in Big Sur."

"Damn. That's impressive." His dark irises dug into mine, pools of dark ink and chocolate.

"It's just running." I grabbed my water bottle, breaking eye contact. "Just something I like to do in my free time."

"It's definitely an accomplishment, considering most college students won't even get up to get the remote to change the channel." He smirked.

I shrugged. "Eh, I do that too. But thank you."

"You seem to be in a much better mood today," he said, moving our conversation from the water fountain. The gym was surprisingly busy for the early morning.

"I am." I lied. My line of sight went toward the front doors. Thankfully, they were sparkly clean and clear, so you could see someone coming from down the street. "You caught me on a strange day."

"Strange?" His jaw clenched, highlighting the strong bone structure along his face. "Well, I hope things are better for you now. Your notes helped, by the way. You're very thorough. Mrs. Castilla talks fast. I have a hard time keeping up."

"That's what I like about her. She is extremely smart, and I love listening to her talk," I said.

The smile on his lips grew. "Listen, would you want to go get some coffee with me after practice? I can bring you back your notes." He propped himself up against the wall with one arm overhead. "I promise fun, interesting conversation."

I snorted. The nineteen-year-old girl in me couldn't help but be a little excited. Mr. Tall, Dark, and Handsome, with the infamous chiseled jaw, was essentially asking me out, but boys were the last thing on my mind. Well, other than one in particular, who, thankfully, I'd managed to stay clear of.

"I can't. I've got to study, so . . ."

He was unbothered, as if he was expecting that answer. "If you change your mind, you know where to find me."

William leaned down, lifting his bag easily with one arm, the trim of his shirt hugging his biceps. He waved before walking toward the pool.

My phone vibrated in my hand and kick-started my heart. I quickly checked for messages. Chris had managed to dodge my calls but sent a text message to me at three in the morning, stating he'd give me a call that day. I could finally tell him about everything that happened. I could let go of everything I'd been holding in and have someone help me decipher my mess. I had it all planned out. I'd start with small talk, a little back-and-forth to catch up, then I'd deliver the news and show him the bite on my shoulder.

I would be lying if I said I wasn't worried. Chris was a practical person. He never believed in things like Santa Claus or the Easter Bunny, even as kids. Once, when I had lost a tooth and did my usual ritual for the tooth fairy, he devised a plan to keep me awake all night so I could see that our guardian, whose name I'd long forgotten, was putting the change under my pillow.

But this would be different. What I was going to show him was actually real.

My heart sank into the pit of my stomach. The text was a coupon for five percent off at my local grocery store. It was helpful but not what I had hoped. The anxiety was getting to me. How much longer could I stand hiding in my room?

The walls of the gym were starting to close in around me. The weight of my secret threatened to pull me onto the sweaty mat flooring. I stopped just short of the front desk, looking back at the pool. William had just left the locker room—shirtless, with compression briefs. Maybe a coffee wouldn't kill me. It might actually be nice to get my mind off things for a minute.

I walked up to the glass doors and waved him over before chickening out. He left his huddle and waddled over to the doorway.

"Yes, madam?" His eyes glowed with expectation.

"Want to meet at Roomies later? Maybe three o'clock?"

He smiled from ear to ear. "I thought you'd never ask."

FOUR

AARON

The morning sun made me want to puke. Vampires couldn't get hangovers, but I swear my biological clock was still ticking somewhere inside my undead body, telling me it was morning and I needed to be in bed.

"Look, Aaron, these are handmade banana muffins!" Luke, the eldest by two whole minutes, thrust a fat, fluffy muffin right on my empty plate. "You used to love those, remember?"

I did remember. How could I forget when he dragged me and the rest of my brothers into the cafeteria every single morning to keep up with appearances? We'd walk through the same double doors, bicker, note the menu on the smudged whiteboard against the podium, bicker some more, then scan our school IDs to get a mostly empty plate.

Luke towered over everyone else in line. Not only was he the tallest of our group, but he was the bulkiest. His arms were the size of my head. I knew that because he loved flexing them in my face.

"Hey, Peggy. How are the kids?" Luke said, stopping at the end of the line to talk to one of the cafeteria workers. The edges of the hairs on his neck curled into a mullet, a ridiculous hairstyle he'd started growing since we left home, along with his beard.

Presley, the youngest, grinned and waved a pancake in my face.

"Dude, pass me the syrup."

"No, you're just going to waste it." I sighed and took another step forward, still waiting for Luke to stop holding up the line.

Presley leaned around me. He forced me into the bar, and his curly blond hair grazed my shoulder. "S'cuse me. Don't need that type of negativity in my life."

He proceeded to pour three different syrups all over his plate.

Zach groaned behind me and bounced on each foot, an empty cafeteria tray in one hand and the other shoved into the pocket of his sweat-pants. He was wearing his black sunglasses inside, which told me he was still a little drunk. It didn't matter. Vampire or not, Zach and I were dead men walking when it came to mornings.

Growing up, our mornings were chaotic. Lots of cereal and lots of arguing. Once Zach and Luke had graduated high school and moved out, I missed our mornings together. But under the circumstances, it wasn't exactly feeling like the good ol' days.

Zach pinched the bridge of his nose, speaking in a whisper only we could hear. "Luke, please, for the love of God. Can we go sit?"

"I second that notion," I whispered, grabbing a few pieces of bacon and moving them to my tray. I'd been sneaking them to the campus mascot—a big fluffy Great Pyrenees named Pretzel.

Luke said his spirited goodbyes, and we searched for an empty table. The lunchroom was on the second floor, with wide windows spanning the entire dining hall. Beige. Everything except the warm wood around the windows was beige—at least that's what it looked like to me. The sun made it hard to see across the room, but a small table next to the window was open.

Once we sat, my brothers broke into conversation, but my mind wandered. That girl was all I could think about. I'd been constantly checking the local news station but no mention of an attack. More importantly, no deaths.

I had to picture the girl alive. It was the only way I could get through every day. I imagined her as a traveler. A young backpacker, just passing through the area on a soul-searching voyage. She had a large loving family and definitely a protective dad who was worried sick when she turned up at the hospital, but they'd flown out to be with her and took her back home. The memory of what happened would be a distant one, maybe an interesting story she'd tell her kids. She wasn't dead. She couldn't be.

We'd only been in Blackheart for two months, and things were calming down. My brothers seemed happier—relaxed, even. Somehow, I'd ruined everything in the span of a couple of minutes just a few days beforehand. I expected the cops to come through the doors at any minute and arrest me.

Maybe that was why I looked over my shoulder. A strange sensation tickled my spine. Someone was watching me. I scanned the room with no luck. No one was looking at us, and no cops were around.

"Aaron, how are your classes?" Luke's voice snapped me out of my inner turmoil.

"Fine." I shrugged. I moved around the pieces of bacon on my plate, breaking them off into little pieces.

Luke sighed, and guilt bubbled in my stomach like old soda. Luke was trying his best to keep us all together—and happy. But it didn't change anything that had happened.

We weren't some normal, lucky group of brothers who'd decided it would be a great idea to go to college together. Back in Brooklyn, my older brothers never planned on going to college. But they spent all their time trying to ensure Presley and I did. From a young age, they "worked" and helped my mom stay afloat. They never explained what they were actually doing. I wasn't the only one who had a secret. My older brothers had kept the biggest one of all that led to my current plight. A vampire who couldn't eat food, sitting in the cafeteria thousands of miles away from a home I could never return to. We were on the run, and I didn't even fully understand why.

I had no idea how they dealt with the guilt or if they even had any. Judging by the smiles on Zach's and Luke's faces, I assumed everything was easier for them. I was just too soft.

A flash of red caught my attention in my peripheral vision, and I looked toward the line of students walking in and going toward the food bar. I don't know what I'd expected to see, but I never expected to see her.

Cascading red hair fell from her shoulders. Her cheeks were full of life again, and I identified the sound of her heartbeat. Loud and strong in her chest. With my mouth agape, she scanned her card, grabbed a tray, and walked toward the cafeteria line. She looked healthy—happy, even—in her workout attire. A black two-piece gym set, and earphones draped across her neck.

My chest expanded with relief. She was alive. I drew a small quiet breath to expel the erratic excitement that had bottled itself in my chest.

"What's up with you?" Zach said, his dark hair falling into his face. He pulled it behind his ears.

"Nothing. Nothing," I said quickly, stealing another glance in her direction. "I think I just need to go get Presley some more napkins."

She was almost done and heading toward the silverware area in the middle of the room. My body moved before my brain, and I snapped up and out of my chair. I had to talk to her. Just for a minute, to make sure she really was okay.

"Thanks, brother!" Presley chimed.

But I was already halfway to the center island. The girl and I reached it at the same time. She hadn't seen me at first. Her attention was on the silverware.

My heart was in my throat as I struggled to keep my voice calm and soft. "Hi."

She turned to me, and her eyes grew wide. Her heart stuttered, and she lost her grip on her food tray. It clattered to the floor in a mess of scrambled eggs and hash browns.

We both went for her tray at the same time.

"Hey, let me help you." I grabbed napkins and furiously wiped the floor.

"Come closer to me, and I'll scream." Her hands were shaking, her blue eyes filled with determination. "I know who you are, and I know what you are."

She picked up pieces of egg from the floor, and the cafeteria went back to its usual dull roar.

"I'm not going to hurt you! I-I'm so happy you're alive. Are you okay? Like, really okay?"

By talking to her, I knew what danger I was putting myself and my family in. She could belt out my identity at any time and have a mob full of people come to her aid. But at that moment, I didn't care. I had to know she was going to be okay and I hadn't completely ruined her life like mine.

"What kind of question is that?" She stared at me for a moment, looking me up and down. "I'm sure this is a surprise to you, considering you tried to kill me."

"No. No, I wasn't trying to kill you. I can see why you would think that. But that's why I called 911, to save you." Smearing mashed hash browns all over the floor, I attempted to clean up. "I didn't want you to die."

She dropped her fork onto her tray. "You called 911? That was you?"

"Yes! It was an accident. This is all a big misunderstanding."

Her eyes lit with rage. "Misunderstanding? You attacked me."

"You're right. I'm sorry. This is all my fault, and I'd love to explain everything to you if you would give me a chance to."

What was I doing? Explanation was the last thing I should have been doing. But real fear flared in her eyes as she spoke. I wanted to let her know she didn't have to worry. I wasn't going to hurt her again.

"Start explaining," she grumbled, snatching more napkins to wipe the food off her finger.

"This might not be the best place for me to talk about it," I said slowly.

She scoffed. "Why? Afraid someone might find out you're a vampi—"

"Don't say that word! Not here." I prayed my brothers weren't listening to me. We had a strict no-eavesdropping rule, but I wasn't going to take their word for it.

"Why?" she said, her eyes darting around. A small crease settled between her brows.

"Because my brothers are over there, and I don't want them to know about this."

My brothers could never find out what I was doing. Ever. We'd be packed up in thirty minutes flat and headed out of state to God knows where. I didn't want to run anymore. More importantly, I didn't want to run from her. If my older brothers had no problem keeping their secrets, neither would I.

"Are they dangerous?" She looked behind me, as if they were going to pop up any second.

"Protective is the word I'd use." I stood and grabbed her dirty tray for her.

She snatched it from my hand and headed to the trash can. I kept in step with her effortlessly. "Fine. But I have questions for you that need answered. If you try to bring anyone or warn anyone, I'm going straight to the police." She motioned to her shoulder. "I have proof."

"You name it. Place. Time. I'm there."

Her eyes narrowed. "Ten minutes. Courtyard by the fountain."

"Ten minutes?" I shifted, stealing a glance at my brothers. "Uh, yeah, I'll make it work."

"Good." She flung her food into the trash can before pulling her shoulders back and readying herself to go for the door.

"I'm Aaron, by the way." I smiled nervously. "I promise I'm much less of an asshole in normal circumstances."

A slow breath left her lips. "Nothing is normal anymore."

"You won't believe me, but I know how that feels," I said, soft and sincere.

I thought her being alive would rid me of my guilt, but it was the opposite. It grew every second we were together. I dragged a complete stranger into my mess of a life. "Ten minutes."

I was fucked. I glanced at my phone. Five minutes to ditch my little brother. I did have one thing going for me. Zach and Luke had already left for their classes. Luke was notoriously a master at detecting my bullshit. He said I have an obvious tell when I lie. I was inclined to believe him, since he and Zach were the best liars I'd ever known.

"I think I'm gonna skip Chem and go to the library to study." I kept my eyes forward as we treaded the sidewalk, a row of oak trees on either side. The fountain was just up ahead, passing the community vegetable garden on our way. A gated area where students could learn to grow their own produce. I'd never seen anything like it.

"Since when do you study?" Presley elbowed my ribs.

"Since I'm already failing Applied Algebra, I need to get my grade up before Luke ropes me into an hour-long lecture about responsibility."

"I don't know why you care. This whole college thing is a sham anyway." Presley walked on my other side, his hands behind his head.

"Well, it's the only thing I have going for me at the moment, so—"

"Ouch. Now you've hurt my feelings," Presley joked. "You spend too much time moping. Live a little. We literally have eternity to do whatever we want."

It didn't surprise me when we woke up after Zach and Luke changed us and Presley didn't have one bad thing to say about it. He made the vampire life look easy and fun. An exclusive thing only the cool kids got to do.

I sighed, bringing my attention back to the only important thing I needed to worry about. "I don't need your permission to go."

"It's your funeral." He smiled with a carefree chuckle.

"I won't be alone. I'll be in a public place in the middle of the day. Who is going to take me in broad daylight?"

"The big, bad, scary vampire mob. Oooo." Presley laughed.

"Yeah, and I doubt they'll even think to look for me in a library on a random college campus in California. I think we have some time."

The Family. My brothers' secret had a name but no explanation. Some kind of gang or cult they were a part of. Presley liked to joke it was like the Mafia. They were the ones hunting us, but I didn't know why. I also had no idea what they looked like or how many of them there were, but I did know they were dangerous. Only because my older brothers told me so.

Most of the time, I tried not to think about it. I couldn't do anything, and I didn't know what would even happen should they find us. It was all one big irritating mystery.

I glanced at my phone again. Any more talking and I was going to be late.

"I'm going and I don't want you to follow me. Can you keep your mouth shut for at least an hour?"

"Your secrets are safe with me." Presley gave me a wicked smile.

"Whatever. I'll see you later." I turned to leave, and guilt stirred in my stomach. I was about to do something insanely reckless.

"It was nice knowing ya!" Presley yelled behind me. "I call dibs on your PlayStation."

I ignored him, picking up my pace and glancing behind me one more time to make sure he was out of sight. The library was huge and, thankfully, surrounded by a plethora of trees. Right before entering the library, I turned left and made a beeline for the fountain.

There were two fountains on campus. I assumed she was talking about the biggest one located in the garden. My guess was correct, and it didn't take me long to spot her pacing on the cobblestone. The sunlight danced on the strands of her hair, and the florals blew in the breeze around her in an assortment of colors. "You're late." She stared at me, unimpressed, arms crossed, foot tapping.

I glanced at my phone to confirm. One minute late. "Sorry about that.

If you knew how hard it was to ditch my brothers . . ."

She may be the most intimidating woman I'd ever met. Her blazing hair matched the sense of fire she emitted. It engulfed me, stealing the breath from my lungs. Thankfully, I didn't need to breathe.

She spoke with strength, and her eyes narrowed. "Did you tell anyone you were coming?"

"Not a word." I ran my fingers over my lips, zipping them shut.

Her cool-blue eyes looked right through me, practically tearing into my soul. That's when I noticed police officers talking and laughing, with coffee in hand, not far from where we stood.

She came prepared. Of course she did. She was a fighter. Nestled between her white knuckles was a can of pepper spray.

My brain took it all in simultaneously. The Thing inside me assessed all possible threats without a second passing. Good thing I had the power to shut it up.

"Are you going to spray me with that? I promise that won't be necessary." Everything came out awkwardly, like the way people sing "Happy Birthday."

A strange pause lingered as she looked me up and down. I sensed her fear. It was weird. Definitely not a power superheroes had, as if I needed another reminder.

She didn't look scared, though. From the look on her face, she could kick my ass and eat me for breakfast. I liked that in a woman. But I shut that thought down quickly.

She finally spoke. "You talk. I listen. You'll answer my questions when I ask you, and I will decide if you are telling the truth."

I had no idea how that was possible, but I agreed. I couldn't hold back my urge to know one question. "Wait, can you at least tell me your name?"

"No."

Damn.

"What do you want to know? I'm an open book."

We stood like statues on the cobblestone path. Her arms were crossed, and she shifted her weight from one foot to the next. I guessed we probably looked like a bickering couple, since people mostly steered clear of us and the nearby solid granite fountain.

"You're a . . . vampire?" she said.

"Getting right into the hard questions first . . . Um. Yes. Technically. But I don't like that word."

"And you drink human blood to survive?"

"Yeah."

Her eyes hardened. "So, you kill people."

"What? No. No, I swear the drinking-blood thing is something we have to do, and I'm just not very good at it yet. I lost control for a minute. It doesn't usually involve anyone dying."

She eyed a couple as they walked past us holding hands, then whispered, "What do you mean by that? Be more specific."

"Well, I'm new to this. I haven't been what I am for more than two months. It's hard to control."

She wanted clear-cut answers for all of this to make perfect sense. Only problem was, I was completely in the dark about the whole vampire thing. On a scale of one to dumb, I was the dumbest when it came to knowing what was going on because my brothers had only told me what I "needed to know."

"I'm sorry. You have no reason to believe me when I say this to you, but the last thing I wanted to do was to hurt anybody. I didn't choose to be like this. I can't just drink the blood of squirrels or birds. I can't choose not to do it. I have to.

"We usually drink once a month, tops, and, usually, no one is seriously hurt. Most are drunks coming home from the bar, and they won't even remember. You were just a special circumstance because of me. I went up to the nature reserve because I wanted to try to do things alone, and it turned out to be a horrible idea. It's all because of me."

The word vomit poured from me like a gushing fountain. Something about this mystery girl made me want to reveal all my secrets.

Her expression softened. "Aaron, right?"

"That's me."

I prepared for a tongue lashing. For her to scream and throw the book at me. She'd never believe me. To her, I was just a monster who had attacked her, and I deserved that. I'd have to deal with whatever she chose to do.

"I'm not turning into a vampire. Am I?" She looked at me like cogs were turning in her head.

"What? Why would you think that?"

"Because of the scar on my shoulder. It's not getting better, and it hurts. I just assumed something was wrong."

I fought a smile. "I'm pretty sure you'd have to drink—"

A blonde chick dropped her book bag on the cobblestone with a thud and sat on the fountain two feet from us. Though I understood the reason for the public place, it wasn't ideal.

The fountain was large and well-kept. Celtic crosses were carved into the sides, with three cherubs holding jars that poured the water into the basin.

"Drink a milkshake. Drink a milkshake for that to happen. It's kind of a joint thing." I finished my sentence before turning my attention to the blonde. "Do you mind? She's kinda in the middle of breaking up with me. It's some sad stuff. Give me a few more minutes, and I might be crying all over the place."

I nodded toward the mystery girl, who looked like a deer caught in headlights.

She muttered, "Uh . . . yeah. Very hard . . . and sad." I stifled a laugh. Mystery girl was a bad liar.

The blonde stared at me for a minute before picking up her bag. "You probably deserve it."

"You have no idea," I said under my breath. I squinted, watching her leave in the midday sun.

The mystery girl sat in the blonde chick's spot. Her legs dangled as she took a deep breath and relaxed her shoulders. Every second, I could sense her fear settling.

I took a seat next to her on the deafening fountain. The gurgling water, the rippling waves, and the sputtering water pump all had distinct sounds. Tuning out all the stimuli was still practice for me. Lucky for me, the mystery girl spoke again.

"An infection. That's what the ER doctor said. If I had an infection, I needed to go see my primary." She sighed. "Did they know?"

"I'm not sure. Maybe. Maybe they knew it wouldn't heal and that you'd need to come back in. You don't need to worry, though. You're not gonna turn."

"Do your brothers know about me? That you saved me? Did you tell them anything?"

"No. It's not something they need to know."

She seemed to accept that answer, but I doubted she believed me.

"I can't believe this is happening. It doesn't feel real. How do I know this isn't some kind of fluke and you're not just some guy that calls himself a vampire and goes around biting people? I've seen the forums. I know it exists."

"Good point." I couldn't hold back my laughter this time. "I can show you one thing. I might be able to get away with it in broad daylight." I took a quick look around, making sure no one was intently paying attention to us. "What's your favorite flower?"

She eyed me suspiciously. "Peonies. Why?"

I was thankful she'd chosen one of the few flower names I knew. I took in a breath, and on the exhale, I let my instinct take over. I turned toward the stone archway at the garden entrance a few feet away and watched for my opening. The garden was a decent size, with tall hedges and stone statues that made it difficult to look clear across. I noted where everyone's line of vision was facing. Luckily, our campus wasn't completely open. Trees casting shade widened my window of opportunity. Once I had found my opening, I went for it. After running, I hid between tree trunks and dashed to the furthest end of the garden to pick her flower.

Within seconds, I was back, holding the delicate pink flower between my fingers for her to take.

Her eyes widened in fear, and the breath hitched in her chest, but her shoulders slackened from her ears, and she took the flower.

Her mouth stayed open as she analyzed every inch of the flower. "I know. It's weird, huh?"

Nothing I said would help. Nothing had helped me when I found out, certainly nothing my brothers said.

Her eyes were full of curiosity. "What else do you know?"

"Only what my older brothers have told me. Which isn't much." She was eerily quiet. Her face was hard to read.

"Where did you come from? I've never seen any of you here before."

"Um . . . we are new to the area. We moved from Brooklyn two months ago."

"How were you able to start in the middle of the semester?" Her voice sounded distant, but her eyes stayed trained on me.

"Kinda an unusual situation," I said, hoping she wouldn't push the subject.

"What do you mean by that?"

I didn't know what I was going to tell her, but I didn't want to lie. Not when I owed her the truth. The truth being: why her. Why I had moved was directly connected to why I showed up in Blackheart and attacked her in the nature reserve. Neither should have happened. But it did. Because of my brothers.

"There's a reason we left."

She raised her brows, waiting for me to say more.

"You see, the thing about that is . . . I can't tell you because I'm a little in the dark about it myself. My brothers didn't tell me anything, really. They just turned me and our little brother, and we left. They pulled some strings and got us set up here. I don't even know how they pulled that off either."

The familiar punch of anger hit my gut. It was a definite sore spot still aching two months later. My older brothers and I had countless fights that went unfinished for that reason. Why did they change us? Why were we running? Why wouldn't they just tell me more? It ended the same way every time. They'd never budge, and I'd always get angry.

"Do you expect me to believe that?"

Her tone didn't match her words. Her words were pointed, but her voice was patient.

I wanted her to have the answers, unlike me who was left worrying and wondering about what goes bump in the night. Maybe she could have the freedom I'd never have. She could have her answers—at least the best I could muster—and maybe she could move on and have a good life. Just like I'd imagined she'd have. "I didn't expect you to trust me, even after we talked. All I know is, it's dangerous, and I think I've already subjected you to enough of that."

She didn't miss a beat.

"Let's assume for a minute that I believe you. What kind of danger? Be as vague as possible without lying."

"Okay, people are looking for us."

"Can you explain people?" Her fingers gripped the edge of the fountain's stone wall.

The courtyard had emptied as the next classes started. The noon day sun was still high and bright.

I chose my words very carefully. "Um, a group of . . . nonpeople."

"So, there are more vampires out there."

"Yeah, apparently. And apparently, that's why we had to leave every-thing I loved and knew behind, and apparently, my older brothers think telling us nothing means protecting us. I think it's bullshit. Pardon my French."

"You don't seem like you know that much." A smile rested on her lips, and she sighed.

"Finally, you see it. I'm just here, trying to live my life and not kill people. And now, I've pulled you into our mess."

"I guess you do get the whole life-ruining thing." I did.

My hands would be sweaty—if I could sweat. "About that, there's a reason I wanted to talk to you alone . . . away from my brothers."

She eyed me suspiciously, her heartbeat picking up. "Go on." "You can forget this ever happened. Right here. Right now." I stood, hands to my side, looking toward the police officers enjoying their afternoon coffee. "I can walk right over there and turn myself in. I'll tell them I attacked you."

A wrinkle appeared between her brow again. "Why would you do something like that? You don't even know me."

"Because it's the right thing to do. I can't fix what happened. This is the only thing I can think of that makes any sense. Maybe I look great in prison orange?"

The words didn't flow like I wanted them to. I didn't want her to feel like I was guilting her into some situation. I wanted to want what she wanted. That was easier said than done.

The mystery girl was still watching me, though her eyes were glazed over in contemplation. She bit the inside of her lip and tapped her foot on the cobblestone.

I let her take her time and watched a group of students laugh in the distance. I couldn't help but think about how my life had completely catapulted into the sun. One day changed everything.

One minute I was studying and going to a community college close to my house. Presley had just turned eighteen, and he talked my ear off all year about how he wanted to go on a trip this summer. And then my brothers stormed in and ruined everything.

It wasn't all bad, though. I didn't miss the city. Surrounding our campus were redwood trees, and I never got tired of looking at them. I tried to soak in my last moments of freedom. The sounds of the birds and the breeze running through the trees.

"It doesn't make sense." She concluded. "You don't really mean that. You wouldn't do that. No one would do that."

I couldn't help but laugh. "You underestimate me?" I turned back toward the police officers and straightened my shirt. "I guess I'll just have to show you."

I started walking but stopped. "It was nice meeting you, by the way. Sorry again for everything."

Her eyes were wide as I turned back to the policemen. I didn't want to think too much about what I was doing. I had to right my wrong, and I hurt this girl. Her life would never be the same because of me and my mistakes. She was innocent. I had to protect her. That was the most important thing.

"Officers, I need to report a crime I committed." I cleared my throat, puffing out my chest and trying to look as threatening as possible.

They didn't flinch at my words or even stop sipping their coffee.

"All right, go on." One of the officers shared a playful smile with the other.

"I attacked someone."

Everything in my body was telling me to run. The Thing in my head was fighting for my attention. But I left my feet firmly planted in the grass. This was my choice, and I wasn't going to let anything sway me this time. This was my chance to right my wrong and make the decision I wasn't strong enough to make in the forest. It was her or me, and I should have chosen her over myself.

The officers stared at me for a minute, one of them lowering his sunglasses to his mustache. "You attacked someone? Like you got into a fight?"

"Not exactly. I technically bit someone." The officers exchange glances, looking amused.

The one with the deep voice scratched his beard, stifling a laugh. "Son, you want to make a report stating you bit someone? Do you have the name of the person you bit? Do they even want to press charges?"

"Well, actually, I don't know the name. I—"

"What are you doing?" Mystery girl's voice caught me by surprise as she walked in closer to the scene. "I didn't think you'd actually go through with it. I'm sorry, this is my . . . my friend. He's doing this as a dare for his YouTube channel." She held up her hand, showing her phone.

"You two are aware that filing a false police report is a serious offense?" The officer's deep voice boomed, but his expression was relaxed. He took another sip of his coffee.

"Yeah, I know. That's why I wanted to stop him before he actually said it."

I probably looked as confused as I felt. She narrowed her eyes at me before turning her attention back to the officers.

"Well, no amount of views are worth going to jail for. Kids these days." He chuckled under his breath.

"You are so right. I'm sorry. It won't happen again," she said before whipping me with her hair and motioning for me to follow her. We walked into a clearing away from earshot.

"What are you doing?" I said quickly.

"Me? What are you doing?! What was that?" she said through clenched teeth.

"I told you I was going to do it! I wanted to make it right. I thought this is what you wanted?"

"How could you possibly know what I want if I don't even know what I want?" She groaned and turned to look at the courtyard. "Just give me a second to think."

I stuffed my hands in my pockets and let the silence sit between us. She kept her eyes on the cars passing in the distance as she mumbled. Counting. One after another, she counted the cars. Not every one. Only the bright-colored ones as they drove up to the crosswalks and stopped for pedestrians before zooming down the hill.

"I don't want this on my conscience."

When she turned to me again, her eyes were softer than before, but worry settled in them.

"If you are telling me the truth, and everything just happened to you like it did me, then I don't want it on my conscience. I'm not done with my vampire questions, and if you go to jail, I'm never going to know if you were telling the truth about my shoulder or anything you just said."

I didn't know what to say, but she was clearly waiting for me to speak. I wanted to say thank you, then hurl myself over a bridge.

I didn't deserve the mercy she was giving me. "What do we do now?"

She crossed her arms. "We keep living our lives as strangers. You don't know me, and I don't know you. If I have more questions, then I'll come to you for help, but we're not friends. You don't approach me. You don't know me."

I rubbed the stress knot on the back of my neck. "Well, what if I want to be friends?"

She smiled. "You look like you have plenty of people to keep you company."

I laughed. She was joking. For the first time, she relaxed. "Fine. You're the boss. Can I at least get your name?"

"Kimberly . . . Kimberly Burns."

She looked down at her hand before stretching it out for me. A flash of excitement hit me, and I grabbed her hand a little too fast, but she didn't flinch.

"I'm Aaron . . . just Aaron. We're using a fake last name. Coleman. You know, because of the people following us. It even says it on my driver's license now. I should definitely not be telling you that, but I didn't want to lie. So, Aaron Coleman, I guess." A sheepish grin spread across my face.

I was breaking every single one of the rules my brothers had set in place. But I didn't care. For the first time since I was changed, I felt like myself again. The me before I turned into the guy who stalked girls in the forest.

The smile returned to her face. "So many questions, but for now, I have to get to my next class."

"I guess I'll see you around, then, Burns."

She straightened herself, fluffed her hair, and gave me a begrudging nod. Then slung her backpack over her good shoulder.

"Sure. We'll see." She waved at me awkwardly before heading back toward the lecture halls.

I stood, watching her leave, before strolling up to the library. I couldn't shake the notion that she may be the coolest person I'd ever met.

FIVE

KIMBERLY

"T hank you so much. Have a wonderful day." I faked a
smile at my barista as I reached for my favorite Pink Drink.

"Not a coffee person? Maybe I should have suggested somewhere else."

William's voice startled me, and I jolted forward, nearly spilling my drink over the counter.

He laughed. "Still jumpy, I see. Sorry."

William appeared beside me, wearing a black-and-blue sweater, fitted with a white collar, and khaki shorts that were snug around his knees.

"That's okay. I've had a long day, and I'm already plenty jumpy, so no coffee for me." I smiled sheepishly.

I had almost forgotten about agreeing to meet him.

He leaned against the counter, and we waited for his black coffee before choosing a table next to the window. The sun was setting, and ripples of peach and cream painted the sky.

Our café was small and filled with books, books on shelves, books stacked in every corner. It was my favorite spot on campus, and they stayed open late.

William let out a nervous laugh. "I'm afraid I've already made an ass of myself here."

"Oh, no." I placed the straw between my lips and sipped. "Thanks for meeting me today. I really needed company."

That was an understatement. After my run-in with Aaron, my thoughts felt so heavy I thought I might explode. I couldn't tell William anything, but just talking to another normal person helped.

He pursed his lips. "Do you come here often?"

"Oh, all the time. On Mondays, they have half-off croissants. They're to die for."

His expression melted, and the corners of his mouth twitched into another smile. "You don't say? Oh, before I forget"—he reached into his pockets and pulled out my notes—"I brought these for you. But don't worry, I don't plan on asking you to tutor me."

I smiled. "I'm happy to help you if you need it."

He leaned forward, putting his elbows on the table and taking a sip of coffee before saying, "No, I wouldn't dare waste our time with something so boring. Let's talk about you."

"Me?" I coughed. My throat was ice after a long sip.

He leaned away from the blinding sun on his right side. "Yeah, you don't think I invited you out for coffee to talk about myself, do you? What kind of gentlemen would I be? So, besides holing up in coffee shops and not drinking coffee, what do you like to do for fun?"

"I like hiking. I usually go up to the nature reserve, but sometimes, when I have a long weekend, I love going to the Redwood National Forest."

"You go with your family?" He took another long sip of his coffee.

"No, I usually go by myself. It's fun usually. This weekend— there was a bit of a hiccup."

He raised a pointed brow. "A hiccup? What happened?"

I hesitated, picking my words wisely. "I got bit . . . by an animal."

He moved his coffee from his lips. "Like a squirrel or something?"

"No . . . more like a bear or a wolf. I don't know what it was. It doesn't matter." I took another long sip of my drink.

"Wow, are you okay? You're saying that so casually. How bad were you hurt?" William's eyes grew wide, and I started to regret telling my half truth.

"I think I'm still a little in shock from it all. I'm okay. It's just a bite. I lost a lot of blood and went to the hospital, but I'm fine." My answer didn't budge the worry in his dark eyes.

"Are you sure? You need to take a rest. Maybe some time off. I can't even imagine what you went through."

I'll admit, the offer of time off sounded tempting. Even a weekend trip out of town would have been nice, but with upcoming finals, it made more sense to soldier through my suffering.

My phone vibrated in my pocket, and I leaned down to look. It was

Chris finally returning my phone call.

"Do you need to take that?" William eyed the phone in my hand.

"No," I said, placing my phone on the table.

I turned to face the window just as I set my phone on the table, and my body froze.

Aaron was walking across the campus, backpack in tow, wearing a large, slouchy football jersey and a backward cap. He was moving fast, like he was late for something. This time, there was no one around him.

"Do you know him?"

I must have been staring too long.

I snapped my attention back to William. "No. Definitely not."

"Except, clearly, you do." William chuckled. "What is he, an ex-boyfriend?"

"Oh, God no. No, he's just a guy I met recently."

Not even a day in, and I had already broken my own rule.

William swirled his coffee around in his cup, watching me as if I were the most interesting person on the planet. "Where did you meet?"

"We met in . . . the hallway. I, uh . . . dropped my books, and he picked them up for me. That's it."

The vibration on my phone sounded again.

"Are you sure you don't need to take that?" William smiled. "It's okay if you do."

His words reassured me, and I smiled. "I kinda do. I'm sorry."

"Don't be," he said.

I grabbed my drink and a few napkins, then made a beeline for the door.

"Kimberly, wait!"

My hand lingered on the door handle, and I stopped.

"Come with me to the Omega Beta Alpha party tonight. I can meet you there."

"Oh, I don't know . . ."

I felt cornered. On one hand, William was nice, but I didn't want to give him the wrong idea. My life was an actual tornado, and I didn't plan on dragging anyone else into it. Even if he was cute.

"Humor me. I'll make sure you have a great time. Don't you want to pick my brain?" William smirked.

The phone in my hand wouldn't stop vibrating, and it slipped from my grasp. William was quick to hand it to me, our hands touching. Suddenly, my head was in outer space.

"I'll meet you there," I said, betraying my previous resolve.

I wondered why I had just agreed to do the exact opposite of what I said I was going to do, but that could wait.

"See you then." He held the door open for me, and I bolted.

I walked out to the bus stop outside my dormitory. The clouds broke into pools of burnt orange above my head. The wind blew my hair in my face, sprinting the soft scent of my rose perfume forward. My heart was in my chest again. This was it. I was finally going to get to tell Chris everything.

The dirt whisked in a cyclone near the yellow bench I was sitting on. I swirled my heeled boots around in the dirt and kicked it on top of my laces. The sun was beating down, and my skinny jeans were sticking to my legs. The bus stopped to unload its passengers.

One by one, bodies trickled out of the bus. Why was I so nervous? I sighed and let my shoulders fall away from my ears as I leaned back.

I went to redial, and the shrill ring of my cellphone snapped me out of my trance. I shuffled around to bring it to my ear.

"Hello?"

"Hey!" Chris said, muffled. The roar of talking and laughter made it hard for me to hear him. "There you are. I was starting to worry."

I was surprised by the spark of annoyance that zapped right through me. I'd been calling him for almost a week.

I closed my eyes and brought my fingers up to squeeze the bridge of my nose. "I'm fine—"

"You don't sound fine. What's up? You said you wanted to talk to me." My fingers were sweating as I gripped the phone.

"I did. Something happened. Something big."

"Don't tell me. You got that scholarship for your sophomore year—"

"No. It was something bad."

"Hold on." A long pause followed by a click of the door came through. The roar in the background of his call vanished. "You're not pregnant, are you?"

Nervous laughter escaped my lips. I squeezed the phone, feeling the blood rush to my cheeks. Pregnancy would be so much easier to explain. "It's not that. I went on a camping trip, and . . . I was attacked by a man."

"Oh my God. How bad were you hurt? What happened?"

"I'm not finished. It was a man, but he's more than that. He bit me . . . and took a lot of blood. I had to go to the hospital."

"What the hell? Like some psychotic drifter?"

"Closer but not it. I'm going to tell you something, and you have to promise not to think I'm a crazy person."

"Okay . . ."

I took one big breath, filling my lungs and letting the words pour out on the exhale. "I think the person that bit me was a vampire."

A pause stagnated, and I wondered if the call dropped.

"Kim! This isn't funny. I thought something actually happened to you. You scared me." Chris laughed. "But it's a good joke. I didn't know you had it in you."

"I'm not joking! Something did happen to me. I have proof. I'll send the picture."

I quickly scrolled through my phone to send the picture I had snapped of my shoulder that morning. I was waiting to go back to the doctor to get my shoulder looked at until I showed Chris.

It was the only bit of indisputable evidence I had.

Another pause.

"Kimberly, when did you learn to do special-effects makeup? This is amazing."

"It's not makeup. I'm telling you. I. Got. Bit."

"That doesn't mean it was a vampire. I know you used to watch that Buffy show when we were younger, but come on. What did the doctor say?"

"That it was an animal attack." I sighed. "But—"

"Exactly. You can't even be sure of what you saw. You're probably just traumatized."

But I met him. The words lingered on my tongue, but I couldn't bring myself to say them. He was never going to believe me. Even if he was here, it wasn't in his nature to believe things he couldn't make sense of. It was our constant source of tension. When I said the sky was the limit, Chris had a way of weighing me down and keeping my feet firmly planted on the earth.

I got up from the bench and smoothed my wind-blown hair. "You're right. I'm fine. Don't worry about it."

He sighed. "I didn't mean to upset you. I just don't want you there alone, scaring yourself with weird theories."

"What does that mean?"

"It just means you're alone there, and you don't have anybody. I want to be there for you, but it's hard sometimes. I've got my own stuff going on here. I got a promotion . . ."

"I had no idea. That's amazing. You should be proud of that."

"I am . . . but sometimes, I wish you would have just moved up here with me."

"New York was your dream. The city . . . big business. That's so you. You were made for it. I'm not."

"I know. I can't be there for you like you need me to be. I'm—I'm only going to keep letting you down."

"Yeah, I know." With my shaky hand, I wiped a tear from my eye. "You don't have to worry about me. I don't need someone to take care of me."

"That's not what I meant—"

"I better go. It's getting dark here at the bus stop, and I don't want to get kidnapped, so I'll talk to you later."

"Kim."

"Congratulations on your promotion. I'm happy for you."

Tears flowed from my eyes, and I dug my fingernails into my palms. Every time I tried to hold on to our friendship, it seemed to slip further and further from my fingers. I kept holding on because I wasn't sure I was ready to let go. Letting go meant admitting our friendship might not last.

Chris always talked about moving to the city. I thought things would be different. I thought it would still be like the old days, where I could call him for anything, and he'd be there. But it was obvious to me things had changed. He was ready for that change, and I wasn't.

A lump settled in my throat as I made my way back toward my dorm.

I hated the word "alone." I didn't want to identify with that word, not when I was so many other things. But it seemed to follow me and show up at the worst moment. The moon lingering in the pink sky followed me with each step.

I took a deep breath and tried to steady myself. All those years of therapy had actually paid off. I glanced at the clock on my phone. I had planned to go straight to urgent care after showing Chris my shoulder. But it was that or the party. I couldn't do both.

My shoulder could wait till morning. What was a few more hours? The party could be fun, and I could even wear my new dress. As long as I wore a long-sleeved turtleneck under it, of course. That would definitely cheer me up.

SIX

KIMBERLY

M y stomach was in knots as I made my way up the stairs to the large wooden doors of the OBA frat house. The tall windows and white pillars loomed over me like an omen. Dark-red bricks blended into the trees surrounding it. The cool night air buzzed with the muffled music and laughter. It was dark, and I felt a lot less confident than I had just a few hours before.

My hand on the doorbell, I hesitated, adjusting the hem of my plaid dress. Was this a doorbell-type occasion? What if that was the most socially awkward thing I could do at this party?

Thankfully, a short blond-haired boy with curls, who greeted me with a smile, interrupted my back-and-forth. He was interestingly dressed with a pair of bright-pink swim shorts, a neon green-and-white-striped button-up and Croc slides adorned with emojis and icons. It was a chaotic look that reminded me of the '80s, but strangely, he pulled it off well.

"Hi." His voice was light and enthusiastic. "Nice to see ya. Come on in."

"Oh . . . uh. I'm sorry. I was supposed to meet someone here. His name is William. He's the one who invited me."

His wide smile turned down. "Uh, I don't know any William. Did he say he lived here?"

"Well, not exactly . . . I . . . uh." I was getting frazzled. It was a combination of the sound bursting my eardrums and the thought that I may have just made a fool out of myself. "I'm sorry. He invited me. I'll just go."

"Wait! I'm officially inviting you." He held out his hand. "I'm Presley."

I must have hesitated a second too long since he said, "I don't bite.

Promise."

Stifling a nervous laugh, I shook his hand. "I'm Kimberly. It's nice to meet you."

I relaxed as he led me through the front door and into what appeared to be a foyer. I didn't know what I had expected a frat house to look like, but this blew all my expectations out of the water. High vaulted ceilings, white crown molding, and dark-lacquered hardwood floors adorned each room. It was hard to notice anything other than the sea of people shuffling into the various rooms like schools of fish, but it was hard to ignore how expensive a place like that could be.

Presley led me toward the kitchen, walking in fluid steps, and had no trouble parting the crowd. He did so with a friendly smile, tapping people on the shoulder or striking small talk with them as we passed.

The kitchen had a huge stainless-steel fridge—bigger than any I'd ever seen—white marble countertops, and a center island occupied by a group of people doing body shots.

We stopped in front of a plethora of coolers littering the floor.

"What do you drink? We have every alcohol known to man."

"I'm good. I don't drink, actually . . ."

"No problem. We also have bottled water, sparkling water, and soda. Whatever you want, I'll go get it. Even if I have to drive to the gas station. Don't worry, my brothers and I aren't drinking tonight, you know, to keep an eye on things. Well, all except for—"

"Your brothers?"

I let my curiosity win.

Presley seemed nice and more than willing to talk to me. I wasn't sure what I was going to do once he left. The longer I could carry on a conversation with him, the better.

"Yeah. Do you know them? There's Aaron over there. Zach and Luke are playing poker, I think." Presley motioned over to the entry to a dining room.

And there he was, Aaron chugging something in a red SOLO cup. The room erupted in cheers as he threw his empty cup onto the floor.

All the cards fell into place. I had managed to find the one place on campus that Aaron happened to be, and it wasn't just him. His brothers were there too. How was it that the one time I tried to do something normal, vampires had to be there?

"No," I blurted. "Kind of. I know Aaron. Barely. We met once. It wasn't a big deal."

Presley's mouth stayed poised in a smile, his head cocked to the side. "Oh, yeah? What about Zach and Luke? I could introduce you." He wiggled his eyebrows playfully.

"Wait, you all live in the house . . . you're part of the frat?"

"Yep! It's a blast."

"Kimberly!" Aaron yelled, crashing into the kitchen like a tornado. SOLO cups on the ground scattered in his drunken wake, and he stumbled into one of the coolers. "What are you doing here!?" His smile beamed, red warmth peeking through his beige skin.

"It's kinda a long story. Boring one, though." The words came out slowly as he moved a little too close.

"All right, you kids have fun. I'm gonna leave you here. Kimberly, nice to meet ya. Let me know if you need anything." Presley snickered as he disappeared into the foyer.

Aaron was still beaming. "I was secretly hoping you'd show up, and here you are!"

Aaron was really drunk. That answered question one thousand and one. Vampires could drink.

"You didn't tell me you were part of a frat," I shouted over the loud frat boys entering the kitchen for their next round of drinks.

"You didn't ask." Aaron bounced on each foot to a beat entirely of his own.

"Aaron!"

Behind him, a large group of girls called to him, motioning for him to come over.

His lips curled up as he giggled and steadied himself against a wall. "I'm—I might have had a little too much. I usually don't drink this much, but it's just—the ladies keep giving me drinks. Like, what am I gonna do? Say no?"

I bit my lip, trying to hold back laughter. I could see why he would be popular with the ladies. No doubt, Aaron had a natural, boyish charm about him. Against my better judgment, I had to admit he was attractive.

"I had no idea vampires could drink things other than blood." He placed his fingers to his lips with a playful grin. "Remember, that's our secret. Just you and me know, okay? Don't tell anyone." His eyes lit up.

"I gotta give you a tour. Don't worry, I won't show you the whole thing. Just the highlights." He turned to lead without letting me answer.

My options were standing alone in the kitchen or following the drunk vampire. Surprisingly, I chose the latter. We stumbled through a wall of half-naked girls and boisterous frat boys. The bass from the stereo moved my entire body. My sweaty hands slid along the wall as I tried to steady myself. Too many bodies were packed together in the dim light, and I tripped on an empty beer can and fell backward. My shoulder slammed into the wall, inducing a sharp pain in my fingertips.

As I rubbed my arm, couples danced around me, and the occasional drunk threw a plastic ball into the liquid of sloshing red cups. Everyone was grouped together, as if they all knew each other.

We finally stopped in front of a large staircase in the hallway. It was pretty standard, same hardwood for the steps and thin white wooden guard rails.

"Now this . . . this is the staircase. Personally, my favorite part of the house." He pushed his hair out of his eyes and motioned to the ceiling with a smile.

A chuckle escaped my lips. "The stairs are your favorite part?" I ignored the prying eyes and tried not to block the flow of people moving around from room to room.

"Uh. Yeah. It's dark and has all these little swirls. It's so sick. It's oak—okay, that's a lie. I don't know what the different types of woods are. I'm just trying to be cool." He giggled to himself and stumbled backward.

I smiled. "Well, I appreciate your honesty."

Aaron's eyes locked with mine. "I'd never lie to you. No way. You'd never speak to me again. I'm going to tell you everything. Seriously, ask me anything."

"So, you're telling me that you haven't lied to me yet? Everything you've told me is the truth?"

"Yes! All of it." His eyes were droopy as he moved his hands over his face.

"So, you weren't lying when you said you hadn't told your brothers about me?"

Realistically, that was my biggest fear. Aaron seemed honest enough and kind. But I knew nothing about his brothers. They might not be so happy if they knew Aaron had willingly told me who and what he was.

His demeanor changed, and he hung his head but kept his eyes on mine. "Oh, no. They would kill me if they knew. I don't wanna talk about them. This is all Zach's and Luke's fault. It sucks, but I'm trying to be okay. I'm doing it. Look at me. Don't I look great? Don't I look happy?" Aaron paused before chugging the rest of his beer.

In the lighting, I could finally get a good look at his eyes. They were soft and warm. In his current state, he couldn't hide the hint of sadness pooling in his irises and the crinkle in his forehead as he spoke.

"You look drunk." I smiled. "Come on, I want to see the rest of the tour."

The night wasn't going like I'd hoped, but despite the strangeness of my circumstances, I was actually having fun.

"You do? Here, I'll show you the pool!" Aaron's pitch spiked like a kid's at Christmas.

I laughed at his silliness and followed him through the groups of people. As we got closer to the pool, the crowd was more dense and, surprisingly, more drunk. The sweaty bodies started closing in, making my heart beat faster. Aaron was unfazed as he pushed through people, politely telling them to move.

We stopped in front of a large pool that was glowing with different lights. The rock waterfall hid behind the crowd on the deck.

"Aaron, this place is huge. I've never seen a frat house look like this." I casually left out that I had never been to a frat house.

"Oh, yeah, there's a lot of money invested in this place." He got up closer, and we faced the pool's neon lights. "I heard the founder is the one who is sinking money into it."

"The founder . . . aren't all frats in this campus really old? This is an old town."

"Go, go, go!" Aaron cupped his hands over his mouth and yelled across the pool. A group of men held Presley up in the air, carried him to the edge of the pool, then threw him in.

"Aaron." I waved my hand in Aaron's face.

"What were we talking about again?"

"We were talking about the person who pays for all this."

"Oh, yes. That guy. I heard he's rich. Hey, do you think all vampires turn out to be rich like the movies? God, I hope so." A smile stretched across his face. "Wow, we need to come up with a new word for vampire. I really hate the word."

As my brain processed everything around me, Aaron made a beeline for the main house. "Come on, I want to introduce you to the girls."

"What? The girls . . ." I planned to plant my feet and not follow, but I didn't want to be left alone with all the people around. He led us through a glass door into a living room that was fit with a large lounge couch. It looked to be the common room where most people hung out.

On the leather couch sat a group of girls who were talking with a few guys standing and sitting close. A blanket of anxiousness fell over me as we neared it.

"Everyone, attention—attention. This is Kimberly. Kimberly, this is everyone else." Aaron fell back onto the couch.

"It's nice to meet you all." I took my seat across from them.

I was met with warm smiles.

"Hi, I'm Jennifer." A girl with brown hair and warm skin twirled her fingers at me in a wave. The other girls took turns introducing themselves.

"I'm Heather." Her neon-purple hair glowed in the dim lighting, the only one to stretch out her hand to me in a handshake.

"Chelsea," the only blonde said.

The most prominent thing about her was her smudged red lipstick and the subtle dirty look she was giving me.

Chelsea inched closer to Aaron. "Tell us about how you guys met. I've never heard your name come up."

Aaron and I exchanged a tentative glance. He opened his mouth, but I cut him off.

"We actually met in the hallway between classes one day. You know, the whole drop-the-book thing. He picked them up for me."

"Not surprising. Aaron's a gentleman." Chelsea traced her fingers along Aaron's arm.

"Yeah, I can tell he's pretty popular." Their eyes were trained on me. "Jennifer, I like your shoes. They're super cute."

If there's one thing I had learned about living with women in the group home, it was to compliment them to gain their trust. It worked on almost everyone.

Her eyes lit up instantly. "Thanks. I got them down at the boutique on Main Street."

"Your dress is so cute, Kimberly. Did you thrift it?" Chelsea said, wearing a black bodycon dress.

"Thank you! I did."

Chelsea eyed me up and down. "I could tell. You just have that vibe."

I couldn't tell from her expression if she was genuine or not, so I assumed she was complimenting me.

"That reminds me. I almost forgot to tell you about this new thrifting app I found." Heather ushered them into a new conversation.

I leaned into the couch, my shoulders relaxing away from my ears. Chelsea averted her attention away from us and talked to Aaron and some guys beside him. Every few seconds were met with her giggling laughter. Slowly, I started to feel like I always do in social situations. Like I was fading into the background. Every minute ticked by, and I imagined them all watching my every move.

"So, Kimberly, what's your major?" Chelsea's voice broke my concentration. The whole group hushed to listen. Their silence was deafening despite the loud vibration of music.

"I'm a Psychology major. What about you?"

"Oh, interesting. I'm in Criminal Justice." Her face was soft, but her tone was off.

"That's cool. Do you want to be a lawyer?"

"Yeah. I'm pretty good at arguing, so why not? Aren't I, Aaron?" She leaned her hand to rub his chest, but he wasn't paying attention to our conversation. When he didn't answer, she nudged him in the side.

Aaron's head spun around. "Yes to whatever you are asking."

"What about you? What's your big dream?" Chelsea uncrossed her legs and leaned in closer.

"I don't really know. I've never had a definite idea for a job I think I could do for the rest of my life."

I hated that question. Though I knew I wanted to graduate and be successful, I never felt settled into my major. I had already changed it once before. It was hard to narrow down one thing I was passionate about, but I was afraid to be left with nothing and crippling student loan debt. So, I settled at the end of the year with Psychology.

"Oh, I'm sorry. That sucks. Maybe you should talk to a counselor or something. I know there are a lot of people who can help you with that.

I could never do that. I like to know where my life is headed."

"Yeah, it's okay. I have time." I shifted awkwardly.

"Isn't that what everyone says? Then you spend all your money for a major you don't want?" Chelsea grabbed a red cup from the table and took a sip, her lipstick staining the edges.

"Probably. I try not to think about it."

"Well, my cousin didn't even go to college, and he makes so much money now. I wouldn't worry too much." Heather gave me a reassuring smile.

I turned to Heather. "What about you? What are your majors?"

"I'm in nursing. I've wanted to do it since I was little."

Envy bubbled in my stomach. I wanted to be one of the people who had a strong conviction of what they wanted to do. I had the drive, knowing I wanted to support myself, but I lacked the how. The passion behind something I could go to school for.

Jennifer smiled at Heather and grabbed her hand, pulling her in closer. "Me too. We actually met in one of our classes."

Jennifer got up in a flurry of excitement and pulled Heather from the couch. "Oh my God, Angie just showed up. I didn't think she was coming. Come on!"

They said their goodbyes and shuffled into the foyer.

"Bye." My voice sounded like a whisper.

Chelsea furrowed her brow as they left. "Aaron, come on. Let's go with them and get some drinks."

"Uh. Okay. Lead the way." He smiled as she got up and dragged him off the couch. "We'll be right back. You're staying, right?"

Chelsea didn't give me time to respond as she dragged him into the other room.

"Yeah, I'll be here." My body sank back into the couch before I sighed. "I guess."

I was close enough to the speaker that it was rattling my entire body. I grabbed my shoulder and winced with every vibration. The longer I sat there, the more relaxed I became. Scanning the crowd for any signs of activity, I noticed a large crowd huddled around a poker table. Every few seconds, the crowd would cheer and gasp. I had to fight the urge to check my phone as another song went by without them returning. I peered anxiously at the kitchen but couldn't see anything.

"Mind if I sit over here?" William slumped into the seat next to me, holding a beer, surprisingly a tad overdressed in his black blazer.

I couldn't fight the pang of annoyance resting in my stomach. "Oh, didn't expect to see you here, considering you invited me to crash a party."

"Now, now, I never said I lived here. Just that you should come." He was smiling again, watching my expression carefully.

"You got me." My attention floated back toward the kitchen.

A large number of bodies traveled in and out of the hallway, yet no one familiar was in sight.

"Well, I'm glad you came." He breathed through words easily and effortlessly. "Sorry I couldn't meet you here sooner. I got held up. I see Aaron kept you company in my absence."

I laughed. "Yeah, well. I didn't expect him to be here. Do you know Aaron?"

He grinned, his mouth twisting into an unusual expression. "Just in passing. Him and his brothers have thrown a lot of parties since they got here. Wild bunch, all right."

As we talked more, I leaned farther into the couch.

"Really? What makes you think that?"

"Well, they throw parties like this, for instance." He motioned up into the air, sloshing his beer around.

"Yeah, I've never been to anything like this."

He smiled. "Well, I'm thankful someone as pretty as yourself decided to grace me with your presence."

I wasn't used to the way he was staring at me. His eyes panned over my features, making my face hot with embarrassment.

"It's time for you to fess up. So far, all I know is, you're in my writing class and your name is William."

William never let his eyes wander from my face. "Ah, yes. Well, I'm currently studying Criminal Justice. I want to be a judge someday."

I took another look at him, analyzing his pressed blazer, clean-cut hair, and sable-colored dress shoes. He looked old enough to be a lawyer already. "Is that something you've always wanted to do?"

"Yes. My younger sister died when I was fifteen, and ever since then, I've wanted to dedicate my life to justice." His smile widened, his eyes scanning the crowd before sipping his beer.

"I'm sorry."

"Don't be. It was a long time ago." His eyes followed my gaze back to the kitchen. "Are you sure I can't get you something? Doesn't have to be a drink. They have food here too." I almost blurted out another rejection but stopped myself.

"You know . . . sure. I'll take some chips if they have it."

He smiled. "As you wish."

Excitement fluttered in my chest as he retreated to the kitchen. A sense of pride from my newfound people skills called for a celebration. Something good was coming out of one of the craziest days of my entire life. I was exhausted, and it was my way past my usual bedtime, but I was having more fun than I'd had in a long time.

"Hey, beautiful."

The words brought me back to reality. A tall, slender guy with moppy brown hair sat beside me, forcing me to move over. He was wearing a shirt I'd seen before, another BFU swim team shirt.

He didn't look coherent as he spoke again. "Wow, you're— you're so pretty."

"Uh, thanks." I squirmed back, the stench of alcohol on his breath stinging my senses.

He leaned closer. "No, you're like the prettiest girl I've ever seen."

"You're too kind."

"Would—would you like to come back to my place?"

"No, get away from me."

I got up and moved to the other end of the couch, looking toward the kitchen, but no one familiar surfaced. Everyone was drunk and stumbling into each other to the beat of the music.

He scooted beside me again. "But you're so pretty. I mean it. An angel."

"I'm not interested. Leave me alone."

He caressed my outer thigh, igniting rage in my chest.

I grabbed his wrist and twisted it. "Get off me."

"Ow, what the fuck!" he cried, weaseling himself away. "You crazy bitch."

His yelling shifted the crowd's attention. I got up and kept my head down. A dark silhouette cast a shadow over us. Two guys with broad shoulders came into view. It took one glance up at them to realize who they were.

Aaron's older brothers.

I could tell by how many of their features matched Aaron's. It was different for each of them.

The big bulky one, who was wearing a colorful button-down that hugged his huge biceps, had Aaron's soft auburn eyes. He also shared his warmer skin tone. The other—the shorter, dark-haired one—had Aaron's jaw and facial structure, especially right around the eyebrows. He was wearing a long '90s band T-shirt that swallowed him.

The larger, muscular one with the dirty-blond mullet looked at the guy. "Hey, Danny, do we have a problem?"

The other was a smaller build but no less muscular. His dark hair was long and curled at the edges of his ears. "Looks like someone is being rude to our houseguest."

Danny backed up with his hands in the air. "No problem. We were just talking, man."

"Bullshit," the dark-haired one spat with pure venom in his voice.

"You need to leave. Now." The large one grabbed him by the collar and shoved him toward the door, leaving the other brother standing next to me.

"Hey, where'd you learn that?" He motioned to his wrist.

A smile curled at the edge of his lips. He leaned casually into the leather armchair just a few feet away from me.

"I've taken some martial arts classes," I said, my heartbeat thrumming in my ears.

Cheers erupted as everyone watched Danny get thrown out, cutting my attention.

"Uh, I think I'm going to go."

"Are you sure? Fuck that guy. He won't bother you again. Promise," he said, his dark brows knitted together.

Before I could answer, the other brother walked up. "Are you okay?"

I couldn't take my eyes off them for a second. My brain was slowly rebooting, trying to comprehend how they could look and act so normal—and be vampires.

I didn't know anything about them. They could be dangerous. One slip up, and I could find myself in another tricky situation. I had enough for the night. I needed to do the smart thing and go home.

"Uh. Yeah. I was leaving anyway. Thanks." I sheepishly waved and made a beeline for the front door. My heart was in my throat, and I pushed my feet faster. With the slam of the door behind me, I breathed a sigh of relief. I think I've had enough embarrassment for one day.

Keys in hand, I searched for my car. Clouds covered the moon, making it hard to spot it in the yard. After weaving through the muffled maze for a few minutes, I found my car wedged between two large flatbed trucks, with another small white car blocking me from behind. I had to go back in there.

Pushing my hands through my hair, I turned my attention toward the campus. The streetlights were dim in the dark night. My dorm wasn't that far. It was against my better judgment to walk home alone, but it was a Saturday. Surely, there would be people around.

Making my way out of the yard and into the street, my heartbeat was loud in my ears. The streetlights were spaced far apart, leaving me to walk in the shadows. An unnerving feeling slowly overtook my train of thought.

My ears focused on the distinctive sound of my platform shoes hitting the sidewalk. With my purse strapped to my shoulder, I kept it close to my body, my hand gripping my phone. Behind my footsteps, another noise emerged, nearby tapping to the sound of my own steps. My heart jumped into my throat, and I spun around. There was nothing. Drizzle misted in the illumination of the streetlights. I took a deep breath and headed toward the campus's glowing lights, reassuring myself of my own paranoia.

Keeping my head up at all times, I moved faster. No one revealed themselves. Counting my steps, the tapping started again. It was almost undetectable, partially concealed by my own footsteps.

It didn't matter. I was almost to campus. I finally reached the courtyard, and my anxiety deflated. I checked my phone and kept my hand firmly on the lock button. It crossed my mind to call for help, but I hadn't seen anything at all, only heard the sound.

As I turned to leave, the flick of a lighter caught my attention. It was close behind, not even fifteen feet away. My body froze, and my breath caught in my throat.

Slowly, I turned to the empty air behind me, digging in my purse for my Taser. The wind blew burning embers into the air. I forced my feet to move, jogging back toward my dorm. I could feel a nearby presence. Every second felt like I was taking a step back. Goose bumps erupted on the back of my neck.

My momentum came to a halt. With my hand on my Taser, I squeezed the button, ready to go. The lights were too far, and whatever was pursuing me was too close. With my eyes closed, I drew in a breath. My whole body shook with adrenaline. For the last time, I turned to face the darkness behind me.

I was knocked off my feet, and my body braced for the fall. I placed my hands in front of me, but they never reached the ground. A strong set of arms stopped my tumble, and pressure engulfed my neck. I couldn't see anything.

My attacker's hand pushed my face in the other direction and covered my mouth, too strong for me to struggle under their grasp. Their arms were stone, tightening every time I tried to move.

We tumbled to the ground. Something knocked him off me. This time, I landed onto the freshly mowed lawn. I opened my eyes in just enough time to see the shadow of my attacker. Whoever it was had a hat covering their hair and a thick black leather coat. "Are you okay?!"

It was Aaron. Aaron saved me from someone—or rather, something—and I had a pretty good guess of what that something was. I couldn't feel my body. I sat up and focused on the scrape on my leg. It should have hurt, but it didn't. I didn't feel anything.

Aaron's hands were warm on my face. "Hey, talk to me. It's okay. You're safe." He frantically looked me up and down. "You're bleeding a little bit. It doesn't look bad, though. Do you want me to take you to the hospital?"

He was talking to me, but I couldn't take my eyes off the light pole right next to us. Raindrops fell, leaving fuzzy streaks in the glow of the light. Everything was a swirling blur. My mouth still wouldn't form words.

"Kimberly! Please say something."

Slowly, I held out my hand to touch the raindrops. The water dissolved into my palm, and I felt myself coming back to my body. Aaron's warmth helped as he rubbed my back.

"All right, that's it. We're going to the hospital." Aaron lifted me to my feet and moved his arm around me to make sure I didn't collapse.

"No. I'm okay. No hospitals."

I didn't let go of his arm at first. I was convinced if he were to let go of me, I might turn into a puddle on the sidewalk.

"What happened? D-Did you see who that was?" I said.

"No. I couldn't tell. They were too fast. I pushed them off you, and they bolted."

I blinked a couple times, letting the cool raindrops run over my face. Every moment, I was more aware of where I was and what had happened. "Someone bit me . . . They bit me. Oh my God. Check me."

Aaron pulled my hair over my shoulder, and I wrapped my arms around my waist to steady myself.

"It doesn't look deep. I think I got to you pretty quickly. I don't think they took much blood."

"You got to me right on time. What were you doing? Following me?"

I scanned the courtyard, expecting someone to jump out from behind a tree. Everything was eerily quiet for a Saturday night.

He let out a nervous chuckle. "You made that sound weird. Technically, I was, but I heard about what happened at the party, and when I saw you leave your car, I wanted to catch up with you and make sure you made it home safe. I was worried about you . . . for good reason, apparently."

"You seem sober." I finally released the iron grip I had on his arm and dusted off my plaid dress.

The rain had picked up, and I was getting soaked. My body was still shaking with adrenaline, and the cool breeze wasn't helping either.

"Well, to be honest, I'm still a little drunk. But it wears off pretty quickly for us. Plus, I sobered up a lot when I saw someone jump you. I didn't even think—I just went."

I gasped. My attention turned to the empty sidewalk ground. My purse was gone.

"They took my stuff. What the heck? What kind of vampire steals women's purses? What am I going to do? My keys and everything are in there. Without my keys, I can't get into my dorm or my car." I buried my head in my hands. "What is going on? I thought this was over. Why does this keep happening to me?"

"It will be okay. I promise. We'll figure this out." Aaron smiled, and I could see how he was a little drunk; he was a little too excited when he delivered his next line. "In the meantime, it sounds like you need a place to stay. You know, a safe, warm place. With plenty of vamps to protect you."

I opened my mouth to protest but quickly shut it. I needed help. I couldn't do it alone, and I didn't want to. I was exhausted. I needed a place to sleep, and no other place around was offering vampire body-guard service.

I sighed. "All right. Lead the way."

SEVEN

AARON

The windows of the OBA frat house loomed ahead just as the rain picked up. Kimberly was next to me, teeth chattering and arms wrapped around her body. I'd have offered her the shirt off my back if it wasn't also soaked. But I felt bad for her sloshing around in her platform shoes. I'd offered to vampire run us to the frat house, and she declined. I was only slightly disappointed.

I tried my best to keep Kimberly calm and distracted as I scanned for any signs of danger. The rain made it hard to hear anything and left me blind. But I was determined, drunk or not. Nothing was going to hurt her with me around.

I still hadn't fully processed what had just happened. I never imagined Kimberly and I would ever talk again, let alone that she'd come to one of our frat parties and get attacked on the way home.

We trudged up the steps until we stood in the porch light, the rain around us creating a roar under our covered patio.

"Welcome to my humble abode. Yes, you've already been on the tour. But there is still lots to see." I put my hand on the door handle.

She grabbed my shirt and yanked me back a few steps. "What? No, I can't walk through there. I don't want you to march me up there like one of your—your conquests."

"Who do you think I am? I totally don't do that. Plus, I told my brothers you're just a friend. If I told them what happened, minus the vampire part—"

"Aaron, you don't understand . . ." She looked at me with beads of water dripping from her hair to the ground below. "I don't exactly want everyone to know. You trust them, but I don't know them."

"It's okay. I get that." A sly smile curved my lips. "I have a plan for an alternative, but I don't think you're gonna like it."

"What is it?" She sighed and crossed her arms, her weight shifting from one foot to the other.

"I'm going to carry you up there, like, through my window. Now just come here and wrap your arms around my neck." I inched closer to her and patted my back.

"Oh, no."

"You don't have any other options. It's either the door or the window."

She kicked the air sheepishly and walked in closer. Her arms wrapped around my neck from behind.

"Don't say I didn't try to do it the normal way." I chuckled, effortlessly lifting her legs. "Ah, okay. I got you."

Nervous laughter escaped her lips as we stepped into the rain. The tall three-story house loomed above our heads. Her heartbeat radiated through my skin, the sound of her pumping blood flooding my ears.

"What's wrong?" I said, walking us over to a wall, where water was running like a waterfall over the red bricks.

"Not trying to be that girl, but I'm kinda afraid of heights." She buried her head in my shirt, shielding her face from the rain. Her legs squeezed harder around my waist, and I forced myself to think only about the wall in front of me and not the cute girl hugging my back. I definitely didn't want to think of how warm she felt or the feeling of her breath on my neck. No. The brick was a really nice shade of red, and the rain made the color pop away from the mortar. "I can't believe this is happening to me." Kimberly sighed, strengthening my resolve to keep focused.

I glanced behind me to make sure no one was looking, scaled the building in two seconds, and plopped us onto the steel fire escape near my window. Being a vampire was fun sometimes.

"You can't believe what? The vampires or scaling a three-story building in the rain?" I said, attempting to lighten the mood.

"How did I end up in some angsty teenage novel?" She looked up at me through wet eyelashes. "This is not what I wanted to do today."

I couldn't help but smile at her expression, and I led us to my window around the corner of the house. "Well, don't fall in love with me, and there won't be a problem."

We reached the window, and she swayed anxiously, waiting for me to open it. My window was locked but pulling it up and breaking the plastic was no harder than picking up a pencil.

"Don't worry. I won't," she said, teeth still chattering.

I offered my arm to her and motioned toward the window. "Oh, it's so easy for you, then?"

She turned her head to the side to look at me before putting her feet through my window. "Yeah. Simple. I don't have time for that."

I couldn't hold back my laughter as I stepped in after her into my dark room. "I'm pretty sure it doesn't work like that."

A small lamp on my nightstand illuminated a small corner of my room. Kimberly stepped forward and tripped over something in the darkness.

I grabbed her arm and steadied her. "Shit, sorry, hold on."

I dashed across the room in a split second and hit the light switch. My dorm was nothing special. It was a reasonable size, not much smaller than my room back in Brooklyn. The corners were still bare. Nothing but old nails hung on the white walls. My bed was pushed up close to the window, fixed with a cheap white bedspread I had bought on Amazon. On the other side of the room was my TV, accompanied by a tangled pile of wires and a large stack of video games. The TV stand was a different color than my desk, which was littered with textbooks and loose papers.

In Brooklyn, my room was filled with knickknacks. My mom had a love of collecting things and passed it on to me. I had shelves filled with my childhood action figures I wouldn't part with and energy drink cans I thought looked cool. The blanket on my bed was a hand-me-down from the twins' room. A large quilt of different-colored patches. It was a chaotic space filled to the brim with color, including the walls that my mom let me paint neon green when I was in middle school. It contrasted with the stop sign hanging above my bed that Presley and I stole in high school.

My new room didn't feel like home, but it would do.

"Wow," Kimberly said.

"I know my room is dirty. You don't have to rub it in." I went to work, picking up various dirty clothes off the floor, being extra quick to pick up my old underwear first.

"I have to admit, I'm a little surprised." She leaned down and removed her soaked shoes. "Your room isn't what I expected."

I chucked my dirty clothes into a huge pile in my closet. "What do you mean?"

She marveled at the walls. "It's so empty . . . and boring."

"Yeah, uh, when we moved, I didn't get to bring anything, even my rock collection, which was like my prized possession. I just haven't felt like decorating—it hasn't been my top priority."

That was an understatement. I missed all my things from home. Everything I had collected as a kid, I would never see again. All my Pokémon cards and the coolest rocks I had spent every summer combing local ponds for were gone. It was stupid, and I should have been too old to care, but I did.

She opened her mouth to speak, but a yawn took its place. Her wet clothes swallowed her.

"Way ahead of ya." I turned around and rummaged through my small dresser, picking out what I thought would be most comfortable: sweatpants and the freshman orientation T-shirt I was given when we arrived. I then headed back toward the window.

"What are you doing?"

"You didn't want anyone to know, remember? If I don't come back, it's going to be pretty obvious I'm with you. I'll get you some food too." I opened the window and moved my legs out first.

"You don't have to do all that." She shifted nervously, clothes still in hand.

"Well, considering you're a guest, and I don't want to listen to your stomach grumble all night, I'll take one for the team." I winked before shutting the window and dropping out of sight.

Within seconds, I was down the wall and through the front door. My mission was simple. Get Kimberly a sandwich from the leftover party platter without my brothers noticing. It seemed simple enough, but it wouldn't be. Because my brothers were nosy.

Presley peeked his head around the corner. "Hey, how'd it go? Is she okay?"

I forgot I had mentioned to Presley I was going to check on Kimberly before I left.

"Yeah, she's fine. I walked her home. She got locked out of her car."

I went for the kitchen but stopped my foot before it hit the ground. Luke and Zach were in the kitchen cleaning up. I stood still and moved behind the wall. As I turned, I found myself face-to-face with Presley.

I mouthed for him to be quiet, and he grinned. He clasped both of his hands together and pretended to shout for them. With the quietest motion I could, I hit him in the arm.

He mouthed a string of words slowly so I could understand.

"What's the big secret?"

I need them out of the kitchen, I mouthed.

Presley's eyebrows raised, and a wide smile stretched across his face. "I'm not telling you."

He shrugged, and I knew what he was waiting for.

I got closer. "If you do this, I will write your English assignment."

I constantly questioned Presley's decision to major in Journalism, considering he hated anything that involved writing. I didn't think he fully understood that becoming immortal had axed his dream of becoming a TV talk show host. It was a nightmare trying to keep him off social media.

His eyes lit up, and he gave me a big thumbs-up before heading to the stairs in the foyer. The party was winding down, with the occasional human straggler passing through to get to the living room. Presley grabbed an empty beer bottle on the way and stopped midway up. He winked at me before dropping himself off the side of the banister. The shattering bottle and the loud thump of his body weight hitting the hardwood floor was enough to make some girls rush into the foyer and scream for help.

Like clockwork, their cries brought Zach and Luke into the foyer, and I could already picture the annoyed look on their faces. I snagged the sandwich and watched them help Presley, who was faking a sprained ankle, to the couch.

"Hope you like turkey," I said after softly knocking on the door.

To my surprise, she smiled upon seeing me, and her wet hair was perfectly combed away from her face. "Thanks. I found your hairbrush . . . and a semiclean towel to dry off. Hope you don't mind."

"What's mine is yours." I casually walked over to my desk and plopped down in my spinny chair. It felt good to be dry. I'd snuck into Zach's room and borrowed one of his band T-shirts and his favorite flannel pajama pants.

"I take it you don't sleep?" She took a big bite of the sandwich, her eyelids still heavy.

"I wish. I don't even get tired, so I'm up all night. It's not as cool as it sounds. I mostly just play games all night to help me pass the time."

"What kind of games do you play?" She motioned to my console. "I used to play before college."

"I like anything I can get my hands on at the moment. It's shocking how fast you burn through games when you're up for twenty-four hours." I leaned back, propping my feet up on the desk. "Why don't you play anymore?"

"I can't afford a console. The one I used to play wasn't mine." She took one last bite before scooting back into bed and getting more comfortable, but she didn't relax. Her hands moved to her shoulder, and she winced.

"We should check that bite again."

"Oh, no. I'm sure it's fine." She pulled the sheets up to her shin.

"I think we're a little past being shy, aren't we? I mean, this is as vulnerable as it gets." I smirked. "You're in my room. That's a huge step for me. Clearly, I'm the one who is suffering the most." She smiled, and I was thankful she understood my humor.

I sat up a little straighter. "I want to help."

She contemplated for a minute before nodding and scooting toward the edge of the bed. She moved her hair out of the way and revealed an imprint, similar to the one on my shoulder. It was a clean imprint but not deep.

"That's weird. It's like they bit you but didn't take any blood. It doesn't hurt at all?"

"Nope. Just my shoulder. Thanks to you. I planned on going back to the doctor tomorrow, but I've been dreading it because it didn't go well last time. Another joy of vampires existing, mention them one time, and everyone wants to ship you to the looney bin."

I chuckled. "You seem to be taking it well. I was completely mute for the first couple of days."

"That must have been hell, not knowing what's going on and being changed." Her eyes beckoned me to say more.

I contemplated how much I should say. Every bit of information I gave her would push her further and further down the rabbit hole. She'd be lost in wonderland.

The bite on her neck was a visual reminder it was too late for that. Besides, it was not like I knew that much, anyway. She deserved to know after everything I had put her through.

"What you need to know about my older brothers is that they have their own little secret life they don't like to share with the class. Not sure if it's a twin thing or an older brother thing, but it's been that way since we were kids. I never thought much about it until it was too late."

"How did they change you without telling you?" Her eyes softened.

"Since it's late, I'll give you the cliff-notes version. They came home one day, looking frantic. Told us to get in the car and wouldn't say why. Just that someone was after us. There wasn't time to grab anything or even call my mom. We threw away our cellphones, got these weird fake IDs. We drove for hours and hours without stopping until, finally, they took us to some safe house they knew about and then changed us. Just like that. It was kinda a trust thing."

Saying it out loud only reminded me how stupid I sounded. Blind trust was something expected in my family. Family over everything else. I used to think it was cool, and being so close to my brothers felt like we were part of some secret club. But since, I've been regretting ever trusting them.

Her eyes traced the lines on my bedspread. "What about your mom?"

"She's safe. They took care of her somehow, and she's somewhere they can't get her. I don't know where she is, though."

I missed my mom. Her traits reflected in each of my brothers, and I couldn't go a day without thinking about her. Presley got her humor, Luke her warmth, and Zach got her endless determination and fiery spirit. Despite everything my brothers had put me through, it was hard to want to be away from them. They were the only thing I had.

"I'm sorry." Kimberly's voice brought me back to the present. "That must have been hard."

There was no ounce of sarcasm in her voice. She was genuinely being kind.

"Not as hard as being bit by a vampire twice in one month." I chuckled, hoping the new heaviness of our conversation would disappear.

A crooked smile played on her lips. "You're right. Tonight is all about me. I'm the only one in this friendship that's allowed to have problems."

I sat up in my chair. "Did you just say the F-word?"

"I wouldn't say that."

"You definitely said it. Admit it, Burns, you want to be my friend."

"Help me with my shoulder problem, and maybe we'll talk," she said, an extra sharpness lacing her words.

I didn't need to be told twice. "Yes, ma'am. I've got just the thing."

I opened the small wooden drawer in my desk. Within seconds, I held up a long sewing needle. "This."

Kimberly's eyes grew wide. "Oh, no. Absolutely not. What would you do with that?"

"It's for your shoulder. The way it works is younger, inexperienced vampires—a.k.a. me—have trouble controlling their . . . venom. Uh, yeah, let's call it that. It's supposed to numb everything, but if you can't control it, then it gets trapped under the skin, and it hurts."

"So, you use that needle to get it out?" She grimaced. "Are you playing a joke on me right now?"

"What? No. See, look." I grabbed the collar of my shirt and pulled it down, revealing my shoulder. "It should look like this. I'm just going to make small pricks, and it will help release all that pressure."

"I don't know . . ."

"Hey, if you don't want to, I understand." I turned to face her, making sure I could get to her at eye level. "I just want you to know that I'm indebted to you. I dragged you into this. I can't change that, but I can try to make your life better, and hopefully . . . you'll trust me after that."

She watched me for a minute. "Aaron, if I didn't trust you, I wouldn't be here. Besides, I think if you were going to kill me, it would probably have been easier like a week ago. And now, you've added my DNA into your room, so you're screwed."

I joined her in laughter. "Damn, I didn't think this one through. Now my master plan is ruined."

She took a deep breath and blew it out slowly. "Okay, let's do this shoulder thing."

"You sure?"

"Yeah. I'm tired of it hurting. Plus, I'll save money, so win-win. I have to warn you, though, I have a low pain tolerance."

"This will be quick. Okay, I'm going to move your sleeve over, so just don't freak out."

"Wait." She pulled away.

"Yes?"

"I just don't want this to be weird. You know, with vampires in the movies, it's all like . . . sexual." She grimaced, forcing the last word out.

"Whoa! You're the one bringing the S-word in here. I'm just trying to relieve the pain in your shoulder." I held up my hands.

"I'm just double-checking."

"This is a move-free zone. I'm going to touch your shoulder in the least sexual way possible. I'm just going to poke around your scar and then I'm going to gently press on the skin to massage it out."

"You never said that. You're going to have to milk it out of me like a cow?" She groaned before placing her head in her hands.

"Now you're just being gross. Hold still. I'm about to touch your arm, but it's just a friendship touch. F-R-I-E-N-D."

"Oh, shut up and just do it." A nervous laugh escaped her before she pulled her hands to her lap and squeezed them together.

I rolled up her sleeve. She looked a thousand times better in my shirt than I did.

"Ow!"

"Kim, I haven't started yet."

"I'm sorry. I'm nervous."

"I know, it's okay. I'll be quick."

I had to concentrate fully on the amount of pressure I was putting on her skin. Tiny little pinpricks brought little beads of blood to the surface. I wiped it gently with a napkin.

Her blood smells good. Do you remember the taste?

My hand slipped, and she yelped. I quickly apologized and readjusted my focus. The voice could talk all It wanted to. I'd just have to drown It out.

Kimberly's soft counting distracted me. I peeked up to figure out what she might be looking at. My guess was she was counting the hangers in my closet.

"Why do you do that?" I asked before pricking her with the needle again.

She grunted. "Do what?"

"Count. I can hear you under your breath." I pressed my hand harder into her shoulder. "Almost done."

"I don't know. I've done it since I was a kid. It calms me down."

"Take a deep breath." I waited for her to fill her lungs with air before I applied more pressure to her shoulder on her exhale.

"Ow. Ow. Ow. Ow. Ow."

"Done!" I got up from the bed and went for the first aid kit.

Luke insisted we each have one. Just in case someone in the frat needed help.

"You were right. It feels way better."

I placed a large bandage over her shoulder. "Told ya. You should listen to me more often." I winked and retreated for the trash can.

She groaned, pulled herself under the blanket, and propped herself up on the headboard. "I'm not so tired anymore."

I plopped down on the floor next to my scattered video game controllers. "Well, good thing you have me to keep you company."

After everything she'd been through that night, I was happy she seemed so relaxed. For a moment, it felt like we were in our own little world. A weird world. But one where no one else was watching us.

"Yeah, I guess you're, like, thirty percent my friend now." She smiled.

Silence introduced muffled music coming through the door.

"Uh, you gotta give me more credit than that," I said.

She sighed. "Fine, forty percent."

"Fifty."

"Forty-five."

I smiled. "So, does that mean I get to ask you questions now?"

"Sure. What do you want to know?"

I thought hard for a second on a good starter question.

"Do you have any friends? I'd kinda assume you'd want to tell someone after you got attacked."

"I do. His name is Chris. I've known him since I was, like, eight or nine. But I didn't tell him. Well, I did, but he didn't believe me."

"Does he go to BFU too?"

"No, he moved up to New York. He was the forward-thinking one." She turned her attention to the fluffy pillow on my bed.

"Is that a bad thing?"

"No, I'm happy for him. It's just not the same. He's basically moved on with his life, and he's the closest thing to 'family' I have," she said, hooking air quotes.

I leaned in. "What happened to your family? If you don't want me asking that, feel free to tell me to go to hell."

"Well, my mother abandoned me on the side of the road when I was four. There were no other living relatives to take care of me, so I grew up in foster care. I aged out when I was eighteen."

"Oh shit, I'm sorry—I don't know what to say."

"It's okay. Most people don't, but that isn't something I go around announcing to people. I've made my peace with it." She smiled, the warmth coming back to her cheeks.

My made-up life for Kimberly, back when she was still a mystery girl, must have been wishful thinking. It only added to my guilt. I couldn't imagine what her life must have been like. There wasn't a time when I was ever alone. But she had to face everything by herself.

"Yeah, we were in a group home together on and off until we both aged out."

"And you wanted to stay here in the mountains."

It was easy to tell how much Kimberly loved the mountains and not just because of the camping trip I had ruined. Everything about her screamed local, especially the various trail patches and enamel pins I had seen on her backpack.

"Yeah, this is my home. It's the only constant I've ever had. I wasn't ready to leave."

I was lost in her blue eyes and the way she was looking at me. She was opening up to me, and we were clicking. Talking with her felt easy. Easier than it had been with any girl I'd ever met before. The more I thought about it, the more my heart kicked my rib cage.

"Well, I'm glad you're here. Not glad you got mugged by a vampire or that I clearly ruined your life but happy that I'm talking to you now."

"Yeah, me too." She smiled at me, and a brief silence followed. Her heartbeat accelerated just like mine before she spoke again. "You sure I didn't interrupt any fun plans?"

"Ha. If you call sitting in my room studying and playing video games fun. I mean, I guess it is, but this is way better."

She rested back onto the pillows. The sleep was back in her eyes.

"You can get some sleep. I'll probably just go hang out in the living room all night."

"Okay. If you still want to play video games in here, I don't mind. I'm a deep sleeper, so you won't wake me up."

I was already up and headed toward the door. "Really? Okay, but when you wake up in the middle of the night because of my violent button mashing, don't say I didn't offer a solution."

"Aaron . . ."

I stopped just short of turning the knob. "Yeah?"

"Thanks for this." Her heartbeat was still beating in a steady rhythm.

"Anytime."

It was three in the morning. Walking around in the middle of the night was something I'd often do to curb my midnight boredom. I searched for Zach and Luke in hopes I might be able to kill some time with them for a few hours. I also needed to keep tabs on them and make sure my cover wasn't blown. When I couldn't find them, I cocked my head toward the ceiling and listened as far and wide as I could. It took a minute to sort through unwanted sounds—talking, laughing, the grunting from upstairs . . .

My best guess was that they were somewhere outside. I found a wall in the back of the dining room and pressed my back against it. The hum of the electricity buzzed under my fingertips. I pushed my attention further, listening intently until I could make out one of their voices. It was challenging to keep my full attention on the vibration of their voices, but I had a lot of experience eavesdropping on them as a little kid. My new vamp powers were just a cool, new extension of what I used to call my super spy persona.

"So, what now? I think we are down to plan, like, X." Zach exhaled sharply.

"He just needs time . . . just like we did." Luke's voice was softer and, therefore, more muffled and harder to hear. Despite being fraternal twins, they couldn't be more opposite.

I knew they had to be talking about me. No one gave them more grief than I did.

"Look at how good that turned out for us," Zach said.

Luke replied, "Well, he doesn't exactly have the best role models."

I could hear liquid sloshing, hitting the glass in waves. Luke was drinking. It made sense, since the party had died down, and he didn't have to worry about driving anyone home. But something about it never sat right with me. Luke never used to drink. "Okay, then. Plan Y, it is—to let our brother become a drunk. Sounds good to me," Zach said.

A brief silence wedged itself in.

"Oh, come on, I'm kidding."

Luke didn't laugh. "I know. It's not that. I'm just having a bad night." The sloshing of liquid continued, followed by another sip.

"Well, I'm all ears. Shoot."

"Can you promise not to hate me after?" Luke's voice came out more clearly this time.

Zach laughed. "You know that's impossible. You can tell me . . . however fucked up it is." Another pause.

"Do you ever . . . miss . . . her?" Luke whispered, and I almost missed it.

My mom was the first person to come to mind.

"Fuck no," Zach replied.

"Oh," Luke said, deflated.

"You want to know why? Because that's what she wants. She wants to pin you and me against each other, and she wants us to fight over her because she's a sick, twisted bitch with a twin fetish. So, no, I don't miss her. She doesn't care about us. Fuck her."

It was definitely not my mom they were talking about. But who else could it be? They shared a lot of things as twins, but women weren't one of them. Zach had been with a girl named Ashley for more than five years until she moved to San Francisco and they decided to separate. I'd never seen him look at another woman since.

Zach spoke again. "I know it's different for you but, Luke. It's not real. The way we feel about her isn't real because it's been a lie the whole time. She fucked with our heads from the start. They all did. The sooner we forget them, the sooner we can all move on."

They definitely weren't talking about Ashley. Luke didn't actually date in high school, but he did have a girl he was interested in: his best friend, Sarah. Luke and Sarah had been inseparable since kindergarten. They did everything together. When Luke joined the football team, Sarah joined the cheerleading squad to cheer him on. They even ended up as prom king and queen their senior year. But it couldn't be Sarah . . . because Sarah went missing a year prior and was never found.

"I just wish this feeling would stop. Sometimes, I feel like it would just be easier if they found us."

They weren't talking about girls at all. Well, they were, but it had to be someone I didn't know. Someone in The Family. Their gang.

At least that's what my best friend in high school, Enrique, called it. But even he was vague about what he knew.

Back in Brooklyn, our family had to be strategic. It was easy to get pushed around, so my older brothers grew up hard. Learned to fight. Covered our ass and kept us from getting in trouble or bullied. That's all I thought it was at first. That was—until I ran right into Damian in the hallway right before a sophomore year pep rally. Damian was someone everyone knew not to mess with because his family was big in the crime world. I heard a lot of stories, none I was interested in figuring out if they were true. I ran into Damian by accident, one that was entirely my fault. I was carrying Presley's mascot head, "Axe the Alligator," and I didn't see Damian rounding the corner in the hallway. Presley was always forgetting it at home, and I'd have to run to get it for him.

"Oh shit, sorry about that, man." I stumbled backward. I wasn't afraid of him beating me up because I knew my brothers would never let that happen. But I was afraid of what might happen to them if they did.

"No. I'm sorry. I shouldn't have ran into you. Please don't say anything. Let's just forget about it," Damian said.

I stammered in agreement and he scurried off behind me. I'll never forget his wide-eyed stare, like he'd seen a ghost.

After running to give Presley his alligator head, with two minutes to spare, I found my place in the gym stands next to Enrique. I told him everything that had just happened, casually yelling over the sound of the drumline.

Enrique's eyes grew wide. "You don't know?"

"Know what?"

After a little back-and-forth, he finally spit it out. "Well, don't tell your brothers I was the one to tell you, but Luke was gunned down two weeks ago. He was shot in the shoulder. Had to be admitted to the hospital and everything."

I let out a laugh. "You're kidding." I looked across the gym to where the seniors sat, and there sat Zach and Luke, casually leaning against the bleachers. They had their usual smiles and were talking as the cheerleaders performed. It wasn't uncommon for them to be out at night or for me not to see them for a couple of days. I thought back on the last few weeks and noticed how they had been gone longer than usual. My mom worked long hours as a nurse, so it was easy for them to come and go unnoticed. Plus, they were so close to graduating, she gave them more freedom. I guessed it could be possible, but could something like that happen, and they wouldn't tell me? They didn't seem like everyone else I knew in gangs at my school. They never dressed differently, and they didn't run around with other groups of people. It was just the two of them all the time.

"Dude, I wouldn't lie to you about that. It happened, and the talk is . . . whoever your brothers are hanging with is no joke. Their retaliation was brutal. It's got Damian's family scared. It's got everyone here scared."

"What retaliation?"

Enrique put his hands up defensively. "Nope. I'm not saying it. I shouldn't have told you. Your brothers have obviously tried to keep it a secret. Don't bring me up. I don't want them knowing my name."

"They already know your name, dumbass." I waited for him to say more, but he turned to watch the pep rally. And that was the first time Enrique had ever kept a secret from me. It was also the first time I ever suspected my brothers were a part of something sinister.

"I am literally the worst person in the world for saying that." I heard Luke's heavy sigh, and I leaned into the wall, drawing my attention back to the present.

"If you're the worst person in the world, there is truly no hope for me." Zach kept his tone light.

"Shut up."

"It's true. Plus, you're thinking too much about it. You can't trust your feelings, remember?"

Luke stayed silent, and a sharp clink of glass hit the concrete. "Relax a little. I'm going to get you another beer."

I stumbled away from the wall, and thanks to there being no humans in the kitchen, I was able to run back up the stairs to my room. I couldn't risk my brothers catching me listening to them. My mind raced with the new information, but I didn't have anywhere for it to go. It didn't make any sense. But it did strengthen my resolve. My brothers had their secret life, and I had mine. I could pull it off, just like they did. Kimberly needed my help and, in a way, so did my brothers. Kimberly needed to stay as far away from my brothers and their problems as possible, and Zach and Luke needed me to figure out this vampire problem. Knowing would only add to their stress. If there was another vampire in town, I'd need to be the one to track them down and figure out their motive for everyone's safety. I was doing the right thing.

EIGHT

KIMBERLY

After waking up, my hands searched for my phone under my pillow. Nothing was there. I had forgotten all about the night before and was reminded when I sat up and surveyed the room. Aaron's TV was dimly lit with a video game save screen on pause. A cool breeze hit my face, and birds chirped close to the window.

The door clicked, and Aaron appeared, looking cheerful as ever, holding a purple drink. "Wow, you look like hell."

"Thank you." I scoffed before turning my attention to the drink in his hand.

"Is that for me?"

"Yeah, I got you a smoothie. Thought you might need nutrition, considering you need food to not die."

"Thank you for that thorough explanation," I grumbled, my whole body sore.

He strolled over to sit on the edge of the bed. "How's the shoulder?"

I brought my lips to the glass to drink a bit of the cool liquid. "A lot better. I slept all night. It usually wakes me up a couple times."

"Good. Are you happy?" He was watching my reaction closely. "Uh, yeah, I'm happy. Why do you ask?"

"I was hoping your happiness might soften the blow of the mistake I made just now." Aaron flashed a sad puppy dog expression.

My smile dropped. "Uh-oh."

"I might have let it slip that you were up here in my room." He held up his hands in defense. "But I told them what happened, and it's cool."

"What?! Aaron, I knew you couldn't keep a secret. Is that all you said? Do they know how we met?"

"No, of course not. I said I met you at school and that we are just friends."

He tilted his head toward the door, his expression hard to read. "Would they be mad? I mean, if they knew who I was?"

My imagination went wild, wondering how they'd react. I still had no idea what kind of family I was dealing with. They all seemed nice, but I had a hard time believing a family on the run from other vampires could be normal.

Aaron must have heard my heartbeat pick up.

"It's nothing bad. I think they would be really lecture-y about it. They're just protective."

I put my smoothie down on the nightstand and scooted closer to Aaron. "You keep saying that. I don't get it. Are your brothers some kind of mobsters or something? Who are they running from?"

"I have theories. They fit the profile for gang members, I guess. They got matching tattoos before they turned eighteen. People started treating them differently—"

"Different how?"

"People in town were scared of them. But I know my brothers are good people. They just made shitty decisions growing up."

I couldn't fathom trusting someone as much as he trusted them. But something in his voice made me believe him every time he'd mention them. He cared about them in a way I'd never cared for anyone. If I trusted Aaron, I'd have to—at least for the moment—trust the people he cared the most about in the world.

"You said you had theories. What theories? What do you know?"

He hesitated, kicking one of his college textbooks on the floor.

"Aaron, do you trust me? I know I'm just some girl that you met and attacked, so you probably don't yet, but our paths are directly linked now. You're literally my only hope in figuring out what is going on and who this vampire that attacked me is. We have to work together if we're going to get to the bottom of this. I need to know everything you know."

"I do trust you." He sat next to me. "I know that we're running away from something called The Family. I think it's a vampire cult. Presley calls it the Mafia. That's how my older brothers were changed. I don't know anything about it, their purpose, or what they do. I just know there's a lot of them, and they could be anywhere and that they're dangerous. So dangerous that we had to leave behind our life and go into hiding."

"What do they want with you?"

Aaron raised his brows without a response.

"Got it. You don't know. Do you think it's possible my attack could have to do with them?"

"Anything is possible at this point."

A large thump on the door broke our concentration.

In the blink of an eye, Aaron was pounding his fist on the door. "Presley, get away from the door."

I sucked in a breath, still completely enthralled with his abilities. It was going to take a while before I was used to anything that was going on.

"Sorry, they are normal, I promise. Let's head down before they pitch a tent outside. Remember the story. We are just friends who met at school."

"Well, don't forget you're only a percentage," I teased. A permanent crease settled between Aaron's brows since I had mentioned his brothers, and for reasons I couldn't yet explain, I wanted to see it disappear.

"Oh, ouch. Okay, mathematician, do you even remember what percent that is?" Aaron laughed as he watched me frantically brush my hair to look halfway presentable.

"I think it was something like twenty percent or some low number like that," I said.

"All right. All right. Stop mocking me. Let's go."

Aaron opened the door, and we walked to the edge of the stairs. I caught a glimpse of them as they disappeared into the living room. It was at that moment every lofty idea I had about vampires being elegant disappeared right along with them. Aaron should have been my first clue.

"Yep, those are my brothers." Aaron chuckled as we descended the stairs. The smell of wood polish filled my nose. I placed my hand on the smooth guard rail. "Look, Aaron. This is your favorite part of the house."

He flashed his teeth right before we reached the hardwood floor, and he ushered me into the living room. I expected to see a war-torn room filled with beer bottles and trash. Instead, everything was clean and pristine. Suddenly, I was contemplating how long I'd been asleep.

"Well, well, the infamous Kimberly Burns."

One of the twins met us in the entryway. He was the more muscular one, wearing what looked to be a Hawaiian button-up and gray sweat shorts. His mullet was curly and his beard looked recently trimmed and tamed. When he smiled, I was taken aback. He smiled just like Aaron. A big out-of-this-world smile brought a sense of warm safety to my chest.

"I'm Luke. It's a pleasure to officially meet you."

I held out my hand promptly. "Nice to meet you. Thanks for saving me from that guy yesterday."

"Happy to do it. He causes a lot of trouble here. He tried to fight Zach last week. But, you know, I've never seen someone try to break his hand before. That was pretty sweet—Hey, come over here." He turned around and pulled his other half out from behind the wall.

"I'm Zach. And you are Kimberly," Zach said with an unamused tone.

His hair was much darker than Luke's and longer. He, too, was muscular but much slimmer than his twin. What stood out the most was the dark circles under his eyes, making his ivory skin look hollow.

"You look nice in my brother's shirt," Zach said.

Everything about him was darker than his twin, including his entirely black outfit that consisted of black joggers and a Nine Inch Nails T-shirt.

"Uh, thanks?" Like clockwork, heat rose to my cheeks.

"Really, you're going there? Even though we just talked about this two seconds ago." Aaron's eyes were like daggers.

Zach chuckled, holding his hands up. "Hey, I thought it was a compliment. I was being nice."

With sweaty palms, I rubbed my hands together, looking for the exit.

"He's kidding," Luke said with a boisterous confidence and toothless grin.

"And I'm the cool one. Obviously." Presley walked in and propped himself against the wall. His clothes were even louder than the day before.

"Oh, you're the guy that got thrown in the pool." I smiled and held out my hand to shake his, hoping he would get the joke.

He squinted with a mischievous smile before shaking my hand. "Oh, you saw that, huh?"

He pulled up a chair, closing an awkward circle around the couch, leaving me on the outer edge.

"We all saw it," Zach said.

"Well, Kimberly, we're happy to have you. Is there anything we can do to help? Aaron told us about what happened to you last night. We'll accompany you to the police station if you need help."

Zach leaned over the couch's arm. "Or better yet, we could track them down for you and beat them up?"

"Again, he's kidding," Aaron blurted nervously.

But something in Zach's eyes didn't convince me. His posture was rigid, his shoulders back. He looked on edge, but his apathetic look told me he was good at hiding it.

"No, he isn't." Presley laughed, and Zach kicked his chair.

The wood splintered, causing Presley to crash to the floor. Their group shared a collective look. Aaron and I stole a glance at each other, while a strange silence sat between us all.

"Wow, these chairs must be cheap." Zach scoffed.

Presley picked himself up, dusting off his shirt. "That, or Zach's legs are freakishly strong . . . you know, because of the martial arts thing?"

They definitely weren't great at blending in. I decided to hand them a way out.

"I think I'm okay. Thanks, though. I probably need to get going and figure out my life." I turned to Aaron, shrugging.

"Yeah, hold on. I'll go get your stuff!"

"Maybe you can come over again sometime?" Zach was still leaning over the couch's arm. "Luke and I want to see some more of those martial arts skills you have."

I chuckled. "Yeah, I don't have that much skill in it. I just take a self-defense course every month. It's free on the first Monday of every month at the W. I take it you guys are pretty involved?"

"Yeah, we used to compete." Luke smiled proudly and crossed his huge arms across his chest.

"We miss it sometimes," Zach said.

I silently wondered if their martial arts had anything to do with The Family. Martial arts could be a useful skill, but I was pretty sure gangs didn't learn hand-to-hand combat. But a vampire cult might.

"Did you guys ever win any trophies or awards?"

"Zach did. He was the best in class," Luke said.

I concealed my surprise. Due to the sheer size of Luke, I'd thought he'd be the better fighter.

I turned my attention to Presley, who was sitting casually on the couch. "What about you? Did you and Aaron ever . . . ?"

"Oh, no. Definitely not. We did a lot more dormant activities growing up. Usually including staying home and playing video games until three a.m." Presley leaned back to talk to Aaron, who was coming down the stairs. "Isn't that right?"

Aaron sighed, a plastic grocery bag in his hand. "What are you telling her about me? I bet it's embarrassing."

"Just solidifying your laziness and love of video games. You know, to let her know what she's signing up for." Presley smiled just before Aaron elbowed him in the ribs.

I grabbed the bag from Aaron, waving to the group. "It was good meeting you guys. See you later."

"Likewise," Zach and Luke said simultaneously.

"Looking forward to it." Presley winked.

Aaron guided me to the door, and I followed closely behind. The house was bustling with other frat guys. Button-up shirts and khaki shorts everywhere. I'd almost forgotten there was an event on campus that Saturday. A lot of the fraternities and sororities were having their last get-togethers before summer.

He walked me to the edge of the stairs. "Are you sure you don't want me to walk you home or drive you?"

"No, I'm fine. I can handle it. I'm going to go talk to my RA. Have her help me get some things figured out."

"Well, I put my flip-flops in there for you. That way you don't have to wear your wet shoes back." He smiled, but it quickly faded as his attention shifted to the street.

"Thank you . . . thanks for everything."

I didn't have words for how I felt. Not only had I stayed the night in his room, I felt safe doing so. I'm not sure who was more surprised. Even more than that, I enjoyed our time together. It was confusing, to say the least.

Aaron's brown eyes glowed in the afternoon sun.

"Yeah, anything you need. I'm here for you."

I grabbed the too-big flip-flops from the bag and slipped them on. "So, what are we going to do? If there's another vampire out there, we need to know who they are and what they want. Do you think your brothers would be open to looking for the guy that mugged me? Maybe they can find him quicker than we can. We wouldn't have to say anything."

"Oh, no. I don't want them anywhere near this. If they think for a second that there's another vampire here, they're going to bolt."

"Like leave Blackheart?"

"Yeah, they're on edge." The little crease returned to Aaron's forehead.

A wave of anxiety washed over me. That was the last thing I needed. To be there, alone, with a vampire problem and no way to defend myself.

"Don't worry. That's not going to happen," Aaron said, rendering it almost believable. "We'll just have to deal with it ourselves."

"If it was someone from The Family, why did they bite me and not drink my blood? Why would they want my stuff? I don't feel like it makes sense. It doesn't fit the profile of some dangerous vampire super mob."

Aaron sighed and ran his fingers through his hair. "You're right. That's weird. I mean, I guess there could be a vampire using their abilities to steal stuff from people."

"How are we supposed to know if someone is a vampire? Is there a way you can tell? With a heartbeat, maybe?"

He shook his head. "No. We have heartbeats too. Maybe I can pick one of the twins' brains about it and see if they'll tell me anything useful. I doubt it, but I'll try."

"That's a great place to start. I'm going to cancel my debit cards today, and I'll be able to see if my attacker actually used them or not. That might help us figure out a motive."

I sounded like a crime detective. One look at Aaron in his scruffy bed hair and pajamas told me there was no doubt we were amateurs. But we were amateurs with combined brain power and similar goals. So, that had to count for something, even if the only thing Aaron contributed so far was an overly optimistic disposition.

"I'm going to go get my stuff. And when I pick up my car, do you want to hang out . . . maybe?"

The sun was higher in the sky than I would have liked it to be. I had overslept. I had a lot to do, including getting the locks to my room changed and picking up the spare car key in my dorm room.

Aaron beamed with a raised eyebrow, his disheveled morning hair almost covering it. "You're asking me? You want to hang out with me?"

"Yeah, I do. Unknown vampire on the loose. Probably best to stick together. Plus, I kinda want to see what video games you have."

"So, this means you and I are officially friends, then, Burns?" "Yeah, it does . . . Coleman," I teased.

A wicked grin spread across Aaron's face, and he held out his hand. I took it, and he leaned in closer to me. "Calem. That's my real last name. Aaron Calem at your service. Let's add that to our secrets list."

NINE

AARON

"Earth to Aaron. Hello." Presley waved a hand in my face. "You keep doing that."

"Doing what?"

I sat up in my chair. I was in the frat house's dining room with my books and assignments scattered around me. It was the middle of the week, which meant many people weren't around.

"Zoning out like that. Where do you go, and why can't I come to your planet?" Presley said, pulling on a highlighter-yellow pullover.

I hated that sweatshirt. Mostly because it was blinding but also because he insisted on pairing it with the weirdest clothes possible. Presley hated matching, but once he was in second grade, we pretty much gave up on trying to get him to dress any differently. Zach resolved to beat up anyone who made fun of him for it, and Luke didn't stop him.

"Where are you going?" I said, removing the papers stuck to my arm.

"I met some girls who invited me over to their sorority party. You should come. They have a pool."

"We have a pool," I said.

"Yeah, but this pool has women in it." Presley ruffled up his curls, eyeing himself in the big over-the-top mirror hanging on the wall opposite of me. "Unless you know any hot guys with an ounce of personality, then I'll swing over there instead."

"Aren't there plenty here?"

"Yeah, but they're all aggressively straight and not nearly as cool as me," Presley said, putting on his shades. "You wanna come?"

"I'm not going. I have to study." I turned back to the books sitting in front of me.

I had numerous finals to keep me busy, and that's all it was. Just to keep me busy. I wasn't exactly excited to start a career I could never advance in. Back in Brooklyn, I wanted to become a veterinarian. I didn't have much hope for that future anymore.

Plus, the newfound information of an unknown vampire on campus had me on edge, not just the immediate threat to Kimberly but also the possibility that, should my brothers find out, they would flip. All the effort we'd put to settling in and making a home here would fly out the window.

Presley laughed. "Whatever. Do your thing. We can all play Warzone when we get back."

He had truly never worried about anything, but I wasn't sure if I admired that quality or if I hated it. Nothing ever fazed him. Not even the sudden realization he was a vampire. Not moving across the country. Not having to hide from people who wanted to hurt us. He was still right as rain.

"All right, I won't be gone long. Three hours tops. Tell Mom and Dad I have GPS on my phone, and I'll check in every thirty minutes," Presley said before he disappeared toward the foyer.

Glass clanking against stainless steel broke my concentration. The sun was going down, and it cast a shadow into the kitchen where a few of our housemates were cleaning up their dishes. I looked down at the mechanical pencil in my hands. Somehow, I hadn't even noticed.

I adjusted my sore butt in my chair. Piles of notes buried my textbooks. The grandfather clock chimed from the living room, and I looked at my phone. How long had I been studying? It didn't feel long, but hours had passed without my recollection.

I tried to focus back on my textbook when a soft cry rang in the air. The sweet scent of blood flooded the room. The smell slapped me in the face. It was easy to identify, not only because of how potent it was but also in the way it lingered in the air, sucking up the potential for any other odors. Once it hit the air, I'd be smelling it for a week.

I got up quickly to follow the scent to the kitchen. A housemate stood with a bloody towel in hand, drops of blood dripping onto his flip-flops.

"I cut myself," he said, a little too calm.

His face was familiar, but I wasn't recalling a name. To me, he was the guy who loved to wear tank tops.

He checked his hand again. "It's not that bad."

The water drained the crimson smudges. I was frozen. Not because I couldn't control my thirst but because I didn't have a lot of experience with emergencies.

Within seconds, Luke pushed past me, and grabbed another towel, coming to the tank top man's aid.

I almost didn't realize he was dripping water all over the kitchen and in swim trunks.

"You're definitely going to need stitches, man."

Luke's voice was calm. Reassuring. My frozen muscles thawed, and I walked over to help.

"W-What do I need to do?" I said.

"Just hold pressure here while I wrap this." Luke smiled at me and grabbed the clean towel before wrapping it around the guy's hand.

Tank top guy's teeth ground with each bit of pressure, his heart rate skyrocketing as he let out a slow breath.

Luke turned to the guy's friend, who was still looking at us dumbfounded. "Are you going to take him, or do I need to?"

"Well, the thing is, I'm a tiny bit drunk, so . . ." the friend responded.

A crowd had gathered, gasps of horror and awe amalgamating in an awkward shuffle.

"I'll take him!" Another housemate swooped in and dragged him away from Luke.

Bodies shuffled toward the front door, leaving Luke and me alone. Specks of blood littered the floor, stains of swirling red glued to the stainless-steel sink. I was thankful being a vampire wasn't like the movies. No burning throat or uncontrollable thirst. If that were the case, I was almost one hundred percent sure Presley would have accidentally killed our diabetic housemate.

I grabbed a towel to clean up but stopped when I saw Luke's face. His calm, collected smile was gone. His eyes bore a hole into his hand, where blood still lingered on his fingers.

"Luke? A-Are you okay?" I said.

He couldn't have been having a reaction to the blood. Luke was overly meticulous about feeding. He even had a calendar reminder on his phone.

I stepped in front of him and waved my hand in front of his face. "Luke, come on."

His body stood stiff, his eyes vacant.

My stomach turned. Something wasn't right. I'd never seen Luke react that way to anything.

"Zach," I said, barely audible. I knew he would hear me from inside the house. "I think something is wrong with Luke."

Within seconds, Zach was right next to me. One mention of Luke being anything less than fine always sent Zach into panic mode.

"What happened?" His eyes scanned the blood on the floor, like the wheels were turning in his head.

"This guy cut his hand, and Luke helped him. Everything was fine. But he just shut down or something. He won't answer me."

"Hey, look at me," Zach said slowly, grabbing Luke's shoulders.

I thought we might have been causing a scene, but everyone's attention had shifted to the bleeding guy outside.

"Come on." He dragged Luke to the counter and washed Luke's bloody hands. "It's just a little blood. You're okay. See? It's all gone. Everything is okay. We're safe. You're safe."

Without looking to see if anyone else was watching him, Zach snatched a towel from the other side of the room and wrapped Luke's hands up.

Luke responded to Zach's touch by blinking as Zach toweled off his hands for him. It reminded me of the shocked, unresponsive state in which I had found Kimberly in the courtyard, with the same vacant stare.

Luke's voice was unusually quiet. "S-Sorry. I just—I'm fine."

"You don't have to explain," Zach said, his voice sharp. "I'll take you back up to your room, and we can chill, watch one of those dumb comedy movies you like."

Luke shrugged him off. "No way. You have to go tonight. I'm okay."

He straightened himself, using the towel to wipe himself off.

He ignored me completely.

"No, I'm not going. I'll go tomorrow."

Zach was still giving Luke a head-to-toe protective scan, raising a brow.

It had been just two weeks. Zach hunted more than the rest of us. When I asked why, he'd say, "Because I have to." And that was that. Zach hated repeating himself. It wasn't worth the argument to ask him about it any further.

"No. You're going." Luke slapped Zach on the shoulder reassuringly.

Luke had spoken. And when he spoke, we listened. Even Zach. Something about the way he talked made us fall in line. Luke had been our natural-born leader since he came into the world two minutes before Zach. It was a role only he could do because he was great at it, and the rest of us sucked at it.

Presley, Zach, and I proved to ourselves repeatedly that our decisions either got us in trouble, or they were just plain stupid. Luke, on the other hand, had great ideas, and he had a good way of speaking to each of us in a way we understood. We didn't follow his lead because he was the oldest. It was because he was a great leader.

"I'll keep him company," I said quietly.

Zach gave me a disapproving smirk. "Can you keep your attitude to a minimum, Your Highness?"

"Yes." I gritted my teeth before forcing a big fake grin. That was my least favorite nickname.

Zach's expression softened, and he let out a sigh. "All right. I'll be quick."

He took a look around before grabbing one of the towels and speed-cleaned the rest of the blood from the floor and the sink. "There. I'll see you guys later."

He turned to leave but stopped before he rounded the corner.

"Be good."

I groaned. "I got it. I got it. Jesus, just go." Luke was already making a beeline for the stairs.

"Where are you going?" I followed close.

"I'm going to lay down for a minute." He peered over his shoulder, forcing a smile. "Don't worry about me, though. Nothing I can't handle."

Luke's weight shifted with each step. His invisible burden rested on his shoulders. I guess it was the worst part of being the leader. He had to be the strongest person in the room.

We reached his room, and he slumped onto his pristine bed despite still being in his swim trunks. Everything in his room was in order. Not a pen out of place. Sheets pressed, pillows perfectly symmetrical.

Luke would have done great in the military. It's all he ever talked about when we were kids. He wanted to save people. Fight for his country. All for the greater good. I scanned the empty shelves over his desk and contemplated how different life would have been if he had enlisted.

"You don't have to stay." Luke sat up and pulled his hands through his hair.

The mullet was a new style for him. Growing up, he'd sported a short military cut. It wasn't until we left Brooklyn that he started to let it grow.

There was no way I was letting what had happened in the kitchen slide.

I plopped down next to him. "I know. But I figured I'd annoy you for at least forty-five minutes before I go back downstairs to stare at my textbook for three more hours and get absolutely nothing done. Then I may play some games till my brain rots out of my skull and the sun comes up."

Luke smiled. "Sounds like a wild night."

"I like to live on the edge."

My attention drifted to the hardwood floors. The silence between us grew, and footsteps passed by outside the closed door. Just normal people doing normal-people things.

I wished that could be us. I wanted to be like them, and it would just be me and my brothers going to college together.

"Just ask." Luke watched me with a raised brow.

"What's going on with you? I've never seen that happen before."

I didn't look at him. I kept my eyes on the small little lines of the wooden floor.

A pause expanded before he answered.

"Look, I know that probably looked weird, but it had nothing to do with me losing control. It's nothing like that. I promise."

"Is this about The Family?" I blurted. "Did they . . . do something to you?" Luke sighed.

"Why won't you just tell me? I don't get it. Why do you have to keep this a secret still? Halfway across the country, and you still won't talk about it."

"Did it occur to you that maybe I just want to protect you?"

Luke's sincere gaze made me sink into the bed like a stone in water.

"From what? From them? I don't even know who they are because you won't tell me a single thing about them. I'm starting to wonder if they're even dangerous."

"They are," Luke said, his words cutting me. "The less you know about all of it, the better."

"How does that protect me from anything?" I scoffed.

The familiar anger swelled, and I was already eyeing my escape route.

"Not just from them but from me. I'm not the person you think I am. I'm a lot worse," Luke said.

"You're the best person I know. You've been my go-to hero for all my essays since kindergarten."

He shook his head. "Not anymore. I'm no one's hero."

"I'd say you're doing pretty good. We're all alive. Mom is safe, at least. All this other stuff is just growing pains."

It wasn't enough. I wished he trusted me more to tell me, but it was the most real talk Luke and I had had in months. It felt good.

He nudged me. "When did you get so mature? I can't believe you're trying to make me feel better." I couldn't believe it either.

Kimberly shot into my mind, with her reassuring smile and her grace. She was undoubtedly the most patient, understanding person I'd ever met. The least I could do was to pass on some of her magic sorcery to my brother.

"What are brothers for?" I said, lying back on the bed to stare at the ceiling.

He smiled half-heartedly, but he didn't say another word.

I knew it wasn't that simple. We were brothers. But he and Zach had been much more to me. My only stable male figures, mashed together, made up a pretty good dad. Because of that, I'd never be able to be there for him the way he was for me. There would always be things he'd want to keep from me.

"Can I ask you something that's kind of random? And you can't ask me why I'm asking."

I proceeded with caution. If I was going to get any information, it would be from Luke.

He nodded.

"How would one identify other vampires around? Like, say someone in our frat was a vampire, could you tell?"

His eyes narrowed. "Well, you wouldn't. It's easy to hide. Unless you can catch them not breathing, but it's rare. Now, I don't think I'd need to tell you that if you suspect someone you should come out and say it. Vampires around isn't a good thing. It's not like the movies, where they are everywhere and anyone can change whoever they want. Vampires are few and far between. They come from . . . places of power. I'm not even sure you could turn someone if you wanted to."

"What? Why not?"

"I'm not one hundred percent sure, but to put it simply, the blood that changed me was powerful and then you took mine. My blood wasn't as powerful as the last, and yours won't be as powerful as mine."

I started thinking out loud, trying to understand. "You're saying this isn't like *Twilight*, where there are little covens all over the place?"

Finally, a wide smile returned to his face. "*Twilight*?"

"Presley made me watch it." I chuckled, remembering that time.

Presley made me watch a week-long marathon of vampire movies and TV shows when we were first turned. It felt like torture at the time, but admittedly, it was kinda helpful.

Our conversation didn't ease any of my worries. Kimberly was definitely bitten by a vampire, which meant whoever it was could be the big bad. There were so many questions I wanted to ask him, but I had to choose my words carefully.

"So, you haven't suspected anything, then . . . about vampires in the area?"

Luke hesitated, watching my expressions like a hawk. "I haven't. Have you heard anything . . . seen anything?"

"No—"

"Because The Family is dangerous. They'll hurt you. They've killed people. People I know. So, if you know something, you need to tell me."

"I know. There's nothing. I'm just curious."

I held my tongue. Any more talking and I was going to blow the secret. This conversation wouldn't go unnoticed by Luke. He'd definitely tell Zach about it when he got home.

They kept their secrets under lock and key. I would too. I reminded myself of that every time I felt guilty. They had a lot on their plate. All I was doing was easing their burden and following up on a lead. That was it. They didn't need to be involved.

After a few seconds of silence, I sat up and said, "Want to watch me play Final Fantasy?"

Luke hated video games, but when we were kids, he'd watch me play. I wondered if I had blown my cover.

Finally, his shoulders dropped, and he chuckled. "Hell yeah."

TEN

KIMBERLY

With labored breaths, I ran along the busy roadside. My feet followed like a magnet. I checked my watch, squinting in the glare of the morning sun. I had been slowing down and needed to pick up the pace.

I pushed harder, staring straight ahead. My lungs pushed against my rib cage, begging for air. Finally, I went downhill. I jogged on and felt a rush of relief. My headphones drowned out the noise of passersby, and I kept pushing, leaning into the pain. All I had to do was make it to the end of my song.

A gentle tap on my shoulder stopped me in my tracks. I turned and ripped my headphones out of my ears. Nothing. Just the steady stream of cars on one side of me and a white wooden fence on the other. Thoroughly confused and extremely out of breath, I assumed I had imagined it.

I replaced my headphones and picked up my feet. They tried to find their rhythm again, but my body was slow and heavy. I turned my head to make sure no one was following.

Dizziness came over me, and I had barely stopped in time before tripping over my feet. I placed my hands on my hips and leaned down to try to catch my breath. Even though I was still, my eyes couldn't focus on anything. I tried concentrating on the cracks in the sidewalk before finally closing my eyes for a second to get ahold of myself.

"Hey, are you okay?"

A hand touched the middle of my back, and I shrugged it away.

I opened my eyes, and William was combing me over with worry. He looked like he had raided the campus merch store, with his BFU dark-green shorts and baseball tee.

"Yeah. I just felt dizzy for a second." I blinked a couple of times. The feeling from before was completely gone.

"Shouldn't you be taking it easy?"

He was kidding, but I could hear a hint of conviction in his voice.

He reminded me of what the doctor had said. I should be taking it easy. My body was still under stress, and I hadn't given it much time to adjust. I must have gone a little too far.

"Maybe I should walk you back to your dorm," he said. His hair was wet, with beads of sweat, his face flushed.

"Oh, no, you don't need to do that. I can walk by myself. I feel better, really. Were you out running too?"

"Yeah, endurance helps with swimming. Here, you can have my water."

He held out a flask of water that had been buckled to his hip, and I wondered if it was hygienic to drink after a practical stranger. I took the sip of water anyway and closed my eyes for a second to ground myself.

I thanked him, trying not to feel bad about another chance at getting my three-mile time back on track.

"Let me walk you up to the shops up there. I'm heading that way." William motioned up ahead.

I nodded, and we started walking. Our campus was located a short distance from the main town square. I picked my running location for that exact reason. It was populated, usually bustling with bike riders and students walking between classes to get lunch at one of the outdoor patios or an ice cream sandwich from the parlor on the corner.

"I missed you at the party after I came back from the kitchen. They told me you left."

My heart sank. It had been more than two weeks, and I'd completely forgotten about leaving William in the kitchen at the frat house.

"Oh my God, I forgot. It wasn't on purpose. It was a whole thing with this creepy guy, and I left early. I'm so sorry. I should have said something."

It had been two weeks since the night of the party, and in those two weeks, I hadn't seen William in my writing class once. I was starting to wonder if it was because of me.

"Please don't apologize. I was just checking to make sure everything was okay."

His smile seemed sincere as he pulled his hands through his hair.

"I did look for you in class, but I didn't see you. Is everything okay with you?"

"Oh, yeah, I was sick last week, and this week, I had another class to cram for. I'm pleasantly surprised you noticed my absence, though." A smile tugged in the corner of his lips.

"Hey, Kimberly!"

Aaron's voice was coming from up ahead. He bounded toward us in his white socks, flat sneakers, chest held high. Aaron's outfits were casual. Simple tees, and if I were to guess, he had a few different-colored pairs of the same shorts he cycled through. He wore a long-sleeved baby-blue sweatshirt layered with a white shirt underneath.

"Sorry, I got here early. I had nothing to do today, and I was excited."

He looked at William and immediately stuck his hand out. "Hey, man. I'm Aaron. Nice to meet you. I didn't know you knew Kim."

William grabbed Aaron's hand firmly. "I'm William. Kimberly knows me from class. I was just helping her up the sidewalk. She nearly fainted back there."

Aaron frowned. "What? Are you okay?"

"I'm fine. It was nothing. I think I just got dehydrated or something," I said before turning to William. "Thank you. Sorry again about the party. Maybe we can have a raincheck?"

"I'll hold you to it. I'm sure Aaron here will have another party soon. Then we can pick up where we left off. Right, Coleman?" William's dark eyes glistened.

"Uh, right. Sure. I'm sure we will. At my place. The perfect place for you guys to . . . bond. Great idea!" Aaron said at a mile a minute. "Anyway, Kim, are you ready to go?"

"You two have fun today." William cast a lofty expression at Aaron before jogging back down the hill we had just come up.

I shook my head. *Boys.*

"Someone's got an admirer." Aaron nudged me.

"Hardly. He's just a friend."

The sun was high in the sky, and the light reflected in Aaron's dirty-blond hair. I couldn't help but stare at him for a second. Aaron was light, and the sun's rays enhanced every one of his features. It reminded me of that early-morning feel, when I'd wake up in the mountains, the sun catching my skin. It was warm, and it woke me up and invigorated every cell in my body.

"You think he's cute."

Aaron skipped backward in front of me, his hands stuffed into his pockets. Despite the amount of people on the sidewalk, he had no trouble dodging them.

"No."

The words rolled out quickly, but I didn't want to lie.

"Maybe. But that doesn't mean anything. It means I have eyes. Just like everyone else."

"Should I expect wedding bells in the future, then?" Aaron said.

"Wedding bells? I think as far as life events go, right now, I'm a lot closer to a funeral."

Aaron laughed. "Whoa, dark! It's way too early in the day to be talking like that."

We stopped in front of my favorite boutique. It was painted pastel pink and had little hearts on the windows. It displayed the cutest clothes I'd ever seen, and if I could save up long enough, I could afford the block-colored long blazer in the window.

"Do you think I'm cute?"

Aaron's tone was still light and airy.

I wasn't prepared for the sudden rush of heat in my face.

"Why would you ask me that?"

"You're blushing, Burns."

"Can we focus? Please?"

He shook his head. "Right! You're right. I'm focused, and I have news."

We took a seat on one of the concrete benches that had a view of the street and the horseshoe drive across from it. A grassy park was just behind it, with kids playing and a couple having a picnic.

In the two weeks since the night of the frat party, Aaron and I had found zero leads for the vampire in town. Nothing in the news about animal attacks or any other attacks on campus when we had checked the sheriff's log. I had suspected someone had been in my room when I went back for the first time, but I didn't have any evidence other than an out-of-place sticky note and a shirt on the floor I didn't remember wearing. But I wasn't one hundred percent sure I was thinking clearly, considering everything that was going on at the time. I was thankful for the change of locks, though.

"Well, I had an opportunity to ask Luke some stuff. I guess vampires are a pretty big deal if there is one stalking you. They aren't very common, I guess. Not like the movies. He said they come from places of power."

That sentence could have meant so many things. Places of power could refer to anything. Government, money, religion.

"So, the chances of me being attacked by a random vampire are pretty slim, then?"

"Slim but not impossible, I don't think. There are probably outliers and strays. Take me and my brothers, for example. I doubt we're the only exception."

"Yeah, you're right. Did he mention any kind of spidey sense for vampires?"

"I asked about that too. Apparently, nada. And honestly, maybe it's wishful thinking, but I don't think it's The Family. Luke said something yesterday he's never mentioned before. He said they've killed people he knows. It just got me thinking . . ."

"Yes?"

"I just have a hard time believing a member of The Family would go through the trouble of stalking you on campus and not take your blood. Wouldn't they just kill you? And if they're so powerful, wouldn't they just come right out and take us? I mean, we're right here, in broad daylight. It doesn't add up."

"Good point." I kicked at the concrete. "At least we have a good place to start."

If Aaron was right, then that could be a good thing. One vampire we might be able to handle without getting anyone else involved, at least in the beginning. A straggler vampire made the most sense, and that made me feel better. One was better than a mob, and I was sure I didn't want to get involved where The Family was concerned.

"You don't have to worry, though. I won't let anything happen to you. I know that's the most ironic statement of the year, coming from me, but you can count on me."

His smile was warm again, doing that thing where it made me feel like I was floating. It came with no strings attached. No pressure.

"Yeah. I know," I said.

I trusted Aaron in a way I knew he wouldn't hurt me, but I wasn't sure I actually trusted his protection. But that wasn't his fault. I wasn't sure if I'd ever trust anyone else for my own protection other than myself.

"All right, I have to ask you something that's been bothering me, and you have to answer honestly." Aaron hung his head, and I nodded for him to continue. "Do you think I abandoned you at the party? Because, looking back, I'm annoyed that I got too drunk, and I feel like if I had stayed with you, then none of this would have happened."

"No. I don't think that."

"You're sure?" Aaron creased his forehead. "I didn't make you feel bad or . . . lonely?"

There was that word again, haunting me, even in the daylight.

I swallowed. "You don't have to worry that much about hurting my feelings."

"Why not?"

"I'm a big girl. I don't need you to worry about stepping on my toes. I can handle it."

"That's not even a question. I know that. But if I'm being an asshole, I want you to call me out on it. Because I'm stupid, and I'm going to make mistakes. Promise me you will?"

I was speechless at first, surprised by the seriousness in Aaron's eyes and the conviction in his voice.

"I promise."

Aaron slapped his legs and popped up off the bench. "Good. Now, what are we doing? I know we said the library was the move, but now, I'm thinking that sounds extremely boring and my attention span is not there today." A smile danced on my lips.

"Well, that's okay. We don't have to. We can do anything. I was going to head to the grocery store after."

"Can I come!?"

Aaron's eyes were wide.

"You want to come to the grocery store with me?"

"Yes, I want to go. Do you know how long it's been since I've been to the grocery store? Months! It's funny—when you don't need food anymore, you kinda miss the mundane."

Pure excitement radiated through every muscle in his body as he bounced.

I exhaled right before he grabbed my arm and pulled me from the bench. "I can't believe you want to do something so boring."

"It won't be boring with me."

"I don't mind. Come if you want to."

"Yes!" Aaron skipped around me like a kid. "Sorry, I am feeling really good today."

"Hm, you don't say."

"You've never noticed this place?" I said, pulling my car into park.

"Kim, grocery stores are the least of my worries right now." Aaron wasted no time bolting out the door.

I took my time gathering my things and my door opened beside me.

"For you, madam."

Aaron's voice carried and echoed from the mountains around. The grocery store was tucked off the side of the road and looked like every other building in town. They were all made of the same materials. White slatted wood panels and brown shingled roofs. It was one of my favorite things about town. It made everything feel cozy.

"Well, thank you, sir."

Butterflies soared in my stomach momentarily. I'd never had someone open my car door for me. Ever. There was a first for everything.

I grabbed my backup purse and swung it over my shoulder. "Now, don't get too excited. I have to eat pretty healthy because I'm training for a marathon, and I live in a dorm, so I don't have a lot of room."

"You eat healthy? Kim, you're in college. Live a little." He grabbed a cart from one of the outside racks and hopped on the back. "Away we go!"

Aaron was like a kid in a candy store, zooming around, looking over every display. I casually walked around with my cart, waiting for Aaron to come up to me and display some item he loved. To my surprise, I didn't find it annoying. It was endearing and fun.

For thirty minutes, he didn't get tired of showing me new items. "Kim, you have to get these. Please."

I turned around, and Aaron was holding not one but two packages of blueberry waffles.

"I don't need waffles. You're just trying to live vicariously through me."

"Yes, yes, I am." He threw both into the cart. "Oh my God— and these! I lived on these."

He grabbed a package of Oreos. "Double Stuf!"

"Aaron, they're going to kick us out if you keep yelling." I laughed.

Aaron gasped. "I need to go get you some milk for these!"

In a flurry, he threw the Oreos into the cart and left. I sighed, looking at all the junk food in my cart. One junk grocery haul wouldn't kill me.

I kept walking through the aisle and combed through oatmeal flavors. The hair stood on the back of my neck as I looked up expectantly. No one was in the same aisle as me. Looking back, I noticed there weren't many people in the store, just the overhead lights' green, fluorescent glow, which was unusual for the middle of the day.

An eerie feeling poured into the atmosphere like a fog. In all of Aaron's excitement, I had let my guard down. Something I had never done before.

I searched around for the threat my body perceived, but it was nowhere to be found. A weight settled on my chest. Gripping the cart, I pulled myself through the aisle. I glanced behind my shoulder once more. An empty aisle mocked me. Someone was watching me, but who?

I picked up my pace. Every few aisles, I skipped and peeked around corners. The large, circle mirrors on the ceilings revealed nothing. I couldn't put my finger on what I felt or why.

A man walking toward me on his cellphone caught my eye. I ducked into another aisle, hoping to conceal myself. I gripped my cart but kept watch on the bottle of wine on the display next to me, imagining how I could use it to beat the crap out of my attacker. It seemed unlikely that a vampire could be following me in broad daylight, but like Aaron and I said, anything was possible.

The man dressed in a lounge sweater and button-up collar turned the corner, following me into the aisle. My heartbeat was strong in my chest as I hunkered myself closer to the food shelf. I squeezed my fingernails into my palm as I grazed the white wine bottle. I was ready for anything. To my surprise, he passed me quickly, not even looking in my direction.

I relaxed my shoulders and did another quick sweep. The man was one of the only people in the store. No one was following me. I was truly just being paranoid.

"Hey, are you okay?"

I jumped at Aaron's voice behind me, surprised by the sudden relief I felt at his proximity.

"Your heart is beating really fast."

His warm, chocolate eyes panned over me, looking for any sign of danger.

"Oh, yeah. It's nothing. I'm not used to shopping with someone else. It's taking a little adjusting."

Aaron smiled before observing our surroundings. "You don't need to worry. I won't let anything happen to you here, and new things are good."

His words hit me like a ton of bricks, but I kept my reaction neutral. I fought an inside voice that wanted to tell him I didn't need his help. It was true I didn't trust anyone else to protect me, but another part of me—that was growing larger and larger by the day—did. I wanted to trust in the way Aaron did.

"New is really good."

Aaron cradled a giant red gummy bear in his hand. "Here. I got you something." He waited expectantly for my reaction. "Look what I found. Isn't it great?"

"It's . . . a giant gummy bear."

"Awe, you're not as excited as I'd hoped. Come on, let's keep looking."

We continued walking together down various rows before landing in front of the beverages. I grabbed a liter of Diet Coke and handed it to Aaron to put in the cart.

"You know that stuff will kill you, right?" Aaron smirked.

"Is that more probable than me being killed by vampires?"

"You've got a point."

I pushed the cart but stuttered to a stop. "Speaking of which, I've been kind of curious about something."

"Oh no." He raised his brow. "It's a doozy, isn't it. What is it?"

I checked to make sure no one was around us. "I was just thinking about how it's been a few weeks since you . . . you know. Do you have a plan for drinking more blood?"

Aaron groaned. "I knew it. Do we have to talk about that? I was having fun." He tried to push the cart away, and I quickly walked in front, blocking the aisle.

"Come on. You don't think about this stuff? What about your brothers? How do they do it?"

He kicked a dusty wrapper that clung to the floor. "Of course I think about this stuff. All the time. I get it, though. I would be curious too."

Hanging on the cart, he averted his attention, cleaning the dirt from under his fingernails. "I don't have a plan right now, I guess. I'll just tag along when my brothers go out again. They like to go together but I don't know. It feels too casual. Too weird. I don't like it."

I tried to imagine myself in Aaron's position. What it would be like to have to attack the innocent for their blood. The fear. The guilt. It hurt to even imagine. Despite being one of Aaron's victims, I knew it was harder to imagine him having to do something like that. As I got to know him, I could see how completely devastating it must have been for him to have to make those choices.

I nudged him to try to get him to perk up. "Come on, let's go check out."

Upon reaching the checkout counter, the cart was full of junk.

"What is all this stuff? How did you even get it in the cart without me noticing?" I hoisted the groceries onto the conveyor belt.

"I have my ways." Aaron snickered. "Don't worry, I'm paying for it all."

"Uh, no, you're not. I can pay for it myself." I leaned into the cart and fumbled for my purse.

"Kim, I'm paying for it. I put like eighty percent of the stuff in here."

Ignoring him, I continued to search for my wallet in my cluttered purse.

He walked around me to stand in front of the cashier. "Don't listen to her. I'm paying."

I snatched my wallet from my purse. "Don't listen to him. I'm paying."

The young cashier stood frozen, dumbfounded with our banter.

"Ah ha!" I grabbed my card and held it in the air.

Aaron spun around me, blocking the card reader. "Nope, nope. Not happening."

"Aaron, no, you're not paying for my groceries." My frustration was building as I sighed and folded my arms. "What are you doing?"

He held up his hands in surrender, his voice soothing. "I promise I'm not trying to win by trying to assert some weirdo dominance over you. I'm your friend, and I want to pay because I picked all this stuff out. I. Feel. Bad."

"Okay, I get that, but I don't need you to do that. I can pay for them."

Aaron smiled again. "Then, I'm sorry."

I raised a brow. "Sorry?"

"For this." In one fluid motion, he swiped the card from my hand and chucked it as far as it would go.

I could hear the distinct snap of the plastic as it landed two aisles away. I dashed after it with a grunt. As quickly as my anger came, it was gone. It disappeared as I combed through the dusty tile floors. Upon reaching the corner aisle, a girl with long brown hair greeted me.

"Thank you so much. I'm so glad you found it."

Her eyes were glossy, vacant. None of the muscles in her face other than her mouth moved.

"Here you go."

I slowly reached out to grab the card, observing her blank expression. "Okay, thanks again."

"Here you go."

Something about her didn't sit right. Her unblinking expression never left mine as I turned to leave and headed for the front door.

Aaron was casually leaning against the cart, waiting for me.

"You're a jerk." I crossed my arms.

"Sorry, Miss Independent. It had to be done." He watched me, probably expecting me to smile, but I turned back toward the aisle I had come down.

"What's wrong?"

"Something weird just happened . . . and it's happened before."

I had to turn away from him to think back to why that interaction felt so familiar. The blank stare on the girl's face. The lifelessness in her features reminded me of the guy from the gym, the one I had bumped into on the way to the water fountain. He had the exact same look in his eye.

"Kim? You're freaking me out."

"Tell me every vampire power you know about." I moved out of the way to the entrance and just outside the sliding doors.

"Uh, okay. Super strength, killer hearing, good sense of smell, speedy—"

"What about any type of psychic power, anything to do with the mind?"

Like the flip of a lightbulb, Aaron's face lit up.

"You know . . . my brothers did tell me about this thing. I can't do it yet. Kind of like a memory lapse thing."

I frowned. "And you're just now telling me? Tell me how it works."

"I forgot! Presley and I are too young to do it, and my brothers can only do it for a few seconds. So, it's pointless. Basically, I was talking to them, then, two seconds later, I noticed my arm hurt. They told me it was because they punched me. But I didn't remember. I still don't."

"When you said you're too young . . . do you mean that, the older you are as a vampire, the more psychic ability you might have?"

"I think that's a good assumption. Why? Tell me what you're thinking."

"It may be a good way to find our vampire. Think about it. The vampire who attacked me was likely watching me at the frat party. I bet there's evidence somehow at the party. Maybe he compelled someone there."

"Compelled? Like wiped memories, you mean?"

"Yes, or what if it's more . . . what if they can make people do things?" I ran my fingers through my hair and tucked it behind my ears. I desperately wanted to keep my train of thought going.

Aaron bounced from one foot to the other. "I don't know if I'm following but keep going."

"All we need to do is think back to the party and figure out if anything strange happened, anything out of the ordinary."

Aaron frowned. "Shit. I'm not going to be any help. I was drunk off my ass the whole night."

"I know. But can you remember anything weird anyone said or did at the party?"

Aaron rubbed his forehead. "What about that guy? That guy that grabbed you at the party. Uh, Danny!"

"He was probably just a creep."

"Maybe, but he did cause you to leave the party."

"You're right. Maybe when he touched me, it did something or maybe he was setting everything up to make me leave. You're a genius!"

"Me? No, don't give me the credit for your great ideas." Aaron moved us out of the way before an old lady was about to ram us with her grocery cart. "What do we do now?"

I smiled. "We find him."

ELEVEN

AARON

"This is a bad idea." I paced back and forth, my sneakers squeaking on the gym court.

Kim sat with her legs dangling over some dirty wrestling mats. It was the first time I'd seen her hair up. It was pulled into a ponytail, with soft wisps caressing her face.

For days, we tried to track down Danny. I had talked to all the guys in my hall and tried to find any mutuals, but no one knew him. Zach and Luke didn't know anything other than he wasn't welcomed back to the house for any reason and to tell them if I saw him. I didn't even bother asking Presley, since he would want to know why.

I thought we might be at another stall until Kimberly called me in the middle of the night. She remembered that Danny was on the swim team.

"Maybe, but we don't have another choice. If we want to know if Danny is our guy, then we have to get closer to him. This is the best way."

Her blue eyes were fixed, set on her intention. She wouldn't be taking no for an answer.

"Plus, it's the perfect setting. There are tons of people here."

"Fine, but we need a code word, something we can work into the conversation if we're feeling uneasy and need to bail." I cast a quick glance at the glass doors in the lobby.

Danny would be there any minute, according to the swim schedule posted on the school bulletin. "Good idea! What about . . . pineapple?"

"Why pineapple?" I smiled.

"It's the first thing that came to mind. Plus, it's my favorite fruit."

Learning one of Kimberly's favorites felt like a privilege not a lot of people got. I swallowed, the butterflies in my stomach fluttering. Luckily, the footsteps outside distracted me.

Danny strolled in on time, duffle bag in hand, and he headed toward the locker room. The way he walked and breathed all seemed normal to me.

Kimberly and I decided not to talk, in fear it might give us away. If he was a vampire, he'd be able to hear us in the lobby.

She raised her eyebrows at me, waiting for my approval. Another look toward the locker room, and I gave a thumbs-up. We started walking. A singular force.

Danny spotted us immediately and turned on his heels. Kimberly and I exchanged looks before running in front of Danny and blocking his path.

"What's up, Danny? Got somewhere to be?" I stuffed my hands in my pockets. I tried to take every note on how to be threatening from what I'd seen Zach do. Step one: be casual.

"I'm not talking to you. I don't want to be seen with you. Leave me alone."

Danny moved to go around us, but Kimberly and I had our hands firmly on the glass doors that led to the pool.

"What? Why?" Kimberly said.

Danny met my eyeline. "Your brothers made it very clear that I need to stay away from you guys. Especially you." He stepped back, eyeing Kimberly. "Zach threatened to break my arms if I didn't. Plural. That dude's a psycho, so I don't want to see if he's bluffing."

He probably wasn't. It looked like Zach had done enough threatening for the both of us, but I wasn't going to let him off that easily.

"We just want to talk to you."

I kept my shoulders pulled back and chest out. Step two: stay calm and act like the coolest guy in the room.

"Listen, I'm sorry I grabbed you, okay? Won't happen again. I was really drunk. I don't even remember being in the living room." He went for the door again, but Kimberly stepped forward, and he flinched away from her proximity.

I wasn't getting any good reads on the guy other than the fact that he genuinely seemed scared of my brother.

"You don't remember?" Kimberly said.

"No. One minute, I was out by the pool, the next, I was sitting next to you. I was really drunk."

I understood what Kimberly was getting at.

"What about after my brothers threw you out? Where did you go?"

Danny reared his head. "I called an Uber to get home. Why?"

"Can we see your Uber receipt?" Kimberly said, her eyes daggers.

The gym bag dropped from Danny's shoulder onto the ground, and he sighed. "Will you stop talking to me if I do?" We nodded.

We waited for Danny to take his phone out and scroll to his previous Uber transactions. Other teammates of his strolled in for practice. All three of us were met with weird looks as they weaved past us behind the glass doors.

After a few minutes, Danny shoved his phone in our faces. His story checked out.

"Now what?" Kimberly said.

We walked toward the weight section. The smell of sweat was everywhere. In every direction I turned, it was all I could focus on. The high ceilings and the echoing amplified the ambience. I could hear everything. Every splash of the pool, the girls sparring in the boxing room, and the clinking of weights hitting the floor.

The front lobby doors opened, and William appeared.

My chest tightened, and my stomach felt like lead.

William spotted us instantly and waved at Kimberly. He didn't look in my direction.

Before I could say some kind of joke, Kimberly's eyes grew wide, and she grabbed my forearm before ushering me out and onto the school lawn.

"What? What's happening?"

"William! William was at the party with me. He got up to get food, and once he was gone, Danny came over. He's the only other person it could be." Kimberly paced back and forth in the freshly mowed grass. "I didn't even want to go to that party. I was going to say no, but I dropped something, and he touched my hand. And suddenly, I wanted to go. I never suspected him because . . . because I thought he was my friend." She went silent, blinking a few times.

"How could I be so stupid?"

I hated hearing the hurt in her voice and seeing the disappointment on her face.

"Whoa, whoa, whoa. I never want to hear you say that again. You are the smartest person I know. Who wouldn't want to be your friend? Plus, we don't know if he is our guy yet. We'll have to test him first."

Even though my dislike of William was growing by the minute, I didn't want it to be true. For her sake, I'd have to hold on to the hope that he wasn't the guy, which was the opposite of what I needed to do, since we needed to find the rogue vampire.

I was surprised when a soft smile returned to Kimberly's lips. I tried not to focus on it, but something about her smile drew me in. Hanging out with Kimberly made me happier than I'd felt in a long time. She was genuine. Strong. Brave. Everything I wanted to be.

Kimberly spoke, crossing her arms. "Well, if he's the guy, then he's smarter than I thought. We have to be careful. He could have been planning this from the beginning . . . from the first time I met him. That means he's cunning, and it sounds like he has some kind of plan."

"Shit." I spied my brothers walking toward the gym.

Luke and Zach strutted with their sparring gear in tow, mostly for show, Presley with a basketball under his arm.

Kimberly followed my line of sight. "Oh, no. Are we still sure we shouldn't tell them anything? I don't want them to know who I am, but at the same time, I keep asking myself if we're in over our heads here."

"I'm sure. If I tell them anything, we'll be on the road in the next hour. I'm not risking them leaving you here."

She looked relieved, and I swear she leaned into my arm a smidge.

"Besides, if our theory is right, and he isn't part of The Family, then one vampire shouldn't be hard for us to handle. Maybe there's a reason he's doing what he's doing. Once we know more, we can tell them."

"Hey!" Luke shouted, his voice booming between the stone buildings. "You guys should come with us to the gym."

Luke was back to his usual self, and I hadn't seen him so much as frown since his incident in the kitchen. He wrapped his arm around me and shook me with delight. "Zach and I are practicing some Krav Maga drills today."

Kimberly's eyes lit up as she smiled. "Really? I've always wanted to learn Krav Maga."

"Hell yeah. We'd be happy to teach you." Zach stuffed his hands in his pockets.

I elbowed her softly. "We can't, remember? We . . . have . . . stuff."

"Oh, right. We have stuff."

Zach smirked. "Stuff, huh? Presley, what was it we were talking about earlier?"

"I know! The formal. You're coming to that, right, Kim? Aaron already asked you, I'm sure. It's like three of the frats on campus coming together to throw a huge party at The Conservatory."

Kimberly looked at me for direction, and I shrugged. I had completely forgotten about the formal in all the madness.

"Uh. Yes. I'm going. When is it again?"

"Saturday night. We'll pick you up." Luke smiled. "It will be fun!"

"So much fun," Zach said flatly.

My brothers smiled.

"We'll meet you guys there in a minute, okay?" I made eye contact with Luke and motioned toward the gym.

"All right, we're going," Luke said.

My other brothers, thankfully, followed suit without too much of a fuss.

I turned to Kimberly and slowly let out a breath. "I was going to ask you. I—"

"I just had a really bad idea." Kimberly looked up at me with big innocent eyes. "You're not going to like it."

"Uh-oh."

"What if we got William to the formal somehow? It would be the safest place because we'd be close to your brothers if anything went wrong. We could get William to expose himself somehow and then we'll find out what he wants. Maybe I can ask him to go with me?"

I grimaced. It was a great idea but way too risky. Kimberly was in enough danger as it was. "Oh, absolutely not."

"How else do you expect us to get close to him? I can be his 'date,' and we'll just see what he does. If he's trying to get me alone, we'll be in the one place it's almost impossible to do so. I've been to The Conservatory before for a local concert. It's not that big, and you could stay close by. We'll be able to see if he tries to compel me, and maybe we'll be able to catch him in the act. If our lone vampire theory is correct, we can get his motive and then turn him over to your brothers. He'll be done and dusted and then we can finally be done with this."

"Kim, that idea makes so much sense, but there is no way I can possibly agree to let you do that." My stomach turned.

"I know it's risky, but this may be our only chance to do this. Especially if he doesn't know that I've caught on yet. It will look like we're directly playing into his hand."

She was right. Of course she was. It was clear from the look in her eyes she wasn't going to take no for an answer. But I didn't have to like it.

I sighed. "Does this mean, we need to go crash swim boy's practice so you can ask him to the formal?"

She nodded, and we walked toward the gym. Her breathing hitched in her chest when we reached the entrance. I left to walk out of sight, my heartbeat matching hers. Erratic.

Once again, I found myself eavesdropping. I sat where Kimberly had been sitting on the mats and put in my headphones, with no sound. The gym was loud. On top of all the TVs and workout equipment, I had to tune out the sounds of the basketballs hitting the court in front of me. Thankfully, Presley wasn't on the court. In the next room over was a spin class. And, once again, the horrible echo of the pool room. I listened for Kimberly's heartbeat. I found it quickly. The night in the forest must have etched its unique rhythm into my brain. I would definitely not be telling her about that creepy, newfound information.

"Are you okay?"

William's voice made her heart kick like a horse, the faintest sound of water dripping almost masking his words.

"I'm okay. I just wanted to ask you something that couldn't wait." An edge tinged her voice. "Would you want to go to the big fraternity formal on Saturday? Aaron said I could bring someone, and I thought of you first."

"I have to say I'm surprised. I heard of the formal, but I thought for sure Aaron would ask you first."

He was smirking. I could hear it in the way he said my name.

Vampire or not, I did not like the guy.

"He did, but he's just a friend," she said in one breath.

I swallowed. A burning sensation filled my stomach. The edge in Kimberly's voice remained, and I hoped William would pass it off as nervousness.

"And I'm?" William said.

"Someone I'd like to get to know better," Kimberly said, this time with confidence. "It's Saturday at eight."

"Okay, I can pick you up at your dorm—"

"Oh, no, that's okay. I can just meet you there," Kimberly said, the words tumbling out too fast.

I buried my head in my lap. He had to be on to us by then.

"Are you sure? I'd be happy to," William said.

"I'm sure. I will see you there." Her tone wavered as she turned to leave. "Did you have a number I could reach you at?"

"Actually, my cell is currently broken. But don't worry, I'll be there on time this time, and I'll find you. It shouldn't be a problem, seeing you already know how to find me." He laughed, as if it was perfectly normal to not be reachable by cell phone.

In this day and age, it was less and less likely.

Kimberly's heartbeat was back to doing kick flips.

They said their goodbyes, and as Kimberly and I joined, still not talking, we shared a look. This was about to be our best idea yet, or our worst—I couldn't tell. But if the sick feeling in my stomach was any indication, I was going to regret it.

TWELVE

AARON

"Are you sure you're ready for this?" I whispered in Kimberly's ear, holding the car door open.

"I'm ready." She smiled at me, and I marveled at her in her red dress. It hugged her in all the right places. It was short but not too short. She looked comfortable and confident, and I really needed to think about something else. Anything other than how amazing she looked.

"Why are you looking at me like that?" She narrowed her eyes.

"Your hair is fluffy," I spit out quickly. It was beautiful and fluffy. She went to smooth it down and I laughed. "It looks good. Don't worry."

Party buses were pulling into the narrow driveway, tree branches scratching the windows. Fraternity guys and their dates piled out onto the gravel drive, most of whom were already drinking.

An industrial building tucked into the tall pine trees greeted us. A soft, warm glow radiated from the two-story compound, showing the red bricks and iron architecture. A long line stretched all the way to the back of the building. The more people, the better, as far as I was concerned.

"Let's get this party started!" Zach yelled, practically bursting my eardrums.

I followed my older brother's lead on what to wear for the night. Luke and I had on black blazers, matching slacks, and a simple white shirt underneath, but Luke's blazer barely fit over his shoulders, and he had to leave it unbuttoned. Zach, of course, opted for an all-black look.

Presley groaned. "I think your party started way too early. You guys gotta sober up. You promised to get my drinks at the open bar."

Presley found a black-and-white-checkered blazer and opted for a pink bowtie, and thanks to Luke, we were almost late because of his drunken tutorial on how to tie a bowtie.

"Don't worry, little brother. We are here for you! You can count on us." Luke flung an enthusiastic finger at Presley, jabbing him hard in the chest.

"Ow!" Presley rubbed his chest. "You guys should just go and do your loner-twin thing, and we'll catch up later."

"Got it!" Zach and Luke said simultaneously, leaving us in peace. They disappeared into the growing crowd together.

I heard through the grapevine multiple sorority girls had been dropping hints for them to accompany them to the formal, but since we'd been in Blackheart, I hadn't seen either of them do anything more than flirt with a few girls here and there.

"They seem excited," Kimberly said.

"They were in a weird mood today and started drinking early."

I stuffed my hands in my pockets. I'd stopped trying to figure out the reasons for their moods a long time ago. Whatever the reason, it would stay locked away along with all their other secrets.

"Now that's an understatement." Presley chuckled under his breath, pulling out a pack of cigarettes, then popping one in his mouth.

"If Zach sees you smoking, he's going to freak out." I sighed.

"Please, it's not like it matters now." His eyes switched to Kimberly. "Besides, he's way too drunk to notice." Presley exhaled a large puff of smoke with a pleased sigh.

Kimberly and I exchanged another glance as we started for the back of the line.

We'd spent the last few days preparing the best we could. Our hearts beat together in our collective spiral of anxiety. I had to keep a watch on my brothers and make sure they didn't get too close, while also keeping an eye on Kimberly and William.

"Are we going to stand in this line?" Presley whined. "I'm already bored."

Outside, the crowd surged at the doorway, with more people than I had thought. A wall of cologne and perfume hit me like a freight train. My throat was instantly dry from the inhale.

Heightened vampire senses weren't always a good thing.

"What do you suggest?" I said.

"Well, I did have one idea. The thing we used to do to sneak into the movie theater..." Presley shot me a wicked smile. "We even have a damsel now. It will be way more convincing."

I frowned. "I'm not subjecting Kim to our stupidity. I mean, not unless she wants to be subjected to it?"

Her eyes searched us. "I have no idea what you're talking about. But I guess I'm open to it."

"You heard the woman. Follow my lead." Presley put his cigarette out on the ground and threw it into his pocket. He pointed out into the trees. "Oh my God. What is that?"

Innocent Kimberly fell for his trap, like I had hundreds of times growing up. She turned to look for the signs of dangers in the trees, and in one fluid motion, I leaned down to pick her up bridal style.

"What are you doing!?" she yelled.

"Shhh. Be chill. Act like you're dead or something," Presley whispered to her before cupping his hands over his mouth. "Everybody, move! Out of the way. We have a fainter over here! She needs to get inside!"

To my surprise, she played along, leaning her head into my chest and relaxing. Her warm skin emitted electricity against my chest, and I hoped she couldn't feel my heart beating like a hammer.

I did my part in maneuvering us through the crowd. "Everybody, please move! We need to get her inside to get some air!"

A slurry of voices talked around us, most whispering their concerns and wondering if she was okay.

"Do we need to call an ambulance?" someone said close to my ear. "She'll be okay. We just need to get her inside." Presley sounded so reassuring.

She was a natural, with her eyes firmly shut, her body limp in my arms.

We stepped through the entrance, and the music hit me even harder than the perfume had. I thought navigating large crowds was bad, but loud music would take some getting used to. I slowly tilted her out of my arms, letting her stilettos hit the floor. The venue held high steel beams strung with lights in every corner. I had imagined a sort of club with dance floors shifting colors, but everything was warm-mahogany wood. The bar was tucked off into the corner, and the stage stood front and center. The DJ was already in place. Next to him was a winding staircase that led to the second floor.

The smooth groove of the music vibrated into my feet and up my spine. It felt powerful, igniting my senses.

I glanced at Presley to see if he was feeling as disoriented as I was. His wide-eyed smile told me he wasn't. It was going to be a long night.

"And here we are. A fast pass to the fun." Presley smiled, looking proud of himself.

"Do you guys do that kind of thing often?" Kimberly brushed off her dress and readjusted her hair.

"More than I care to admit." I chuckled.

The venue wasn't packed yet, and I didn't see any sign of William.

"I'm going to go try to steal a drink from someone. Do you guys want anything?" Presley said, mid-sprint for the bar.

"No, we're good." I waved him off.

I turned to Kimberly, speaking louder. "A little birdie told me that you don't drink."

She smiled but never stopped searching the crowd. "No, I don't."

"Do you mind if I ask why?" I shifted my stance closer to her, letting our shoulders touch as we watched the door.

"I just don't know what my tolerance is, and I've never had anyone I trusted enough to drink with. You know, in case I got so drunk I couldn't drive home or something. Is that stupid?" She bit the inside of her lip.

"Definitely not stupid. You know . . . you do have someone you can trust now, though. I'd take good care of the drunk you. I'll even hold your hair if you throw up." I nudged her.

"Maybe when we aren't on an important mission." She looked up to me, her blue eyes sparkling in the twinkle lights ahead.

I wanted to drown in them, but I had to focus. I reminded myself of not only the task at hand, but the fact that the girl in front of me had been attacked twice in the last month, once by me. That made thinking of her as anything other than a friend off-limits. She needed me to help keep her safe, not have feelings for her.

Her attention shifted back to the door, and her face dropped. "There he is. You're going to stay close, right?"

"Don't worry. I'll be right here." I winked at her before William intruded into our circle.

"Good evening." He smiled in his crisp black blazer. Everything about him was well-put together. He pulled a red rose from behind his back, handing it to Kimberly with a short bow. "You look breathtaking."

Her voice caught in her throat, and her heart sped up. "Uh, thank you."

I wasn't prepared for the heat that rose from my chest into my face. Loosening my balled-up fist, I swallowed the lump in my throat.

Wipe that smirk off his face.

The voice was back with a vengeance, and I had a feeling It was here to stay. It only came up sometimes, and usually, I could push It away, but despite my resolve, the heat traveled up my throat.

"She likes peonies, by the way." I tried my best to force a wide, toothy smile. "Don't worry. You'll get it next time."

William chuckled, the whites of his teeth taunting. "Noted. Thanks for keeping my date company. Much appreciated. Say . . . where's your date, Coleman?"

It took me a second to realize he was using my fake last name.

Kimberly looked up to me, chewing the inside of her cheek, and I gave her a reassuring wink.

"Didn't bring one. Thanks for the reminder."

The events of the night would have been much more fun if Kimberly was my date. I imagined twirling her around on the dance floor, dancing like maniacs, and maybe even . . . slow dancing. Maybe in another life that would have been possible, but in the one where vampires existed, I was doomed to go stag.

William placed his hand on the small of Kimberly's back. "You ready?"

The proximity of his skin next to her felt wrong. Not just because he was potentially a brainwashing vampire, but something else made me want to snatch her away from him.

She nodded, and they made their way into the crowd. The music was loud, making it hard to hear where they were. I'd have to keep her in sight while not making it obvious. They slowly moved toward the bar.

As people piled into the building, the volume in my ears kicked up a notch. The smothering conversations everywhere were a dull roar. Announcements were just about to start, and I was already feeling sensory overload.

"Whatcha doing?" Presley appeared next to me, holding a Jack and Coke. His favorite. I diverted my attention to my shoes, but Presley caught my line of sight. "W-What's she doing with that guy?"

"That's her date," I said.

"I thought you guys were going together. That sucks. You must be mad jealous, huh?" Presley laughed before sipping his drink.

"No, we're just friends."

They were still standing next to the bar, due to the crowd, and William had Kimberly pressed against a wooden pillar. His arm was placed casually over her. He'd lean in closer to her every time someone passed behind him. I coughed a little, diverting my attention, before the voice started up again.

Presley smiled. "Whatever you say. You look jealous, though."

"I'm not. And, no, I don't," I snapped.

It couldn't be jealousy. If I were jealous, that would mean I liked Kimberly more than a friend, and I couldn't do that to her. Not after everything she'd been through. We couldn't be together. So, it was settled. I didn't like her.

"You don't have to get all defensive. If one of us was going to fall in love with a human, it was definitely going to be you. Zach and I already placed a bet on it. A thousand dollars says you admit it by the end of the month. Zach thinks you'll cave earlier than that."

"Where'd you get a thousand dollars?"

There were so many things wrong with his statement, so I homed in on the less offensive one.

"Betting, duh." He took another sip of his drink.

"You're one to talk," I snipped. "You also invited someone who happens to be human."

Presley's date for the night was Ellis Finch, but he hadn't arrived yet. A guy from Presley's Art History class who was at least six foot two with warm-brown skin and a thick mustache. He was a mellow dude who seemed way too smart to be into my brother.

"Oh, that's different. You've been giving her 'I love you' eyes since I first saw you guys together. Me and Ellis are completely casual. You look like you might propose any minute."

"All right. I'm done talking about this."

Presley snickered with his lips pressed to his glass. "Truth hurts sometimes, I know."

The announcement commenced, and we listened to the speaker, who was the president of another frat. He was tall and lanky and cussed like a sailor, which Presley found hilarious. I periodically diverted my attention back to Kimberly and William, who were also at a standstill, watching. Kimberly looked to be perfectly fine. Every so often, I'd tried to find the rhythm of her heartbeat or tune into their conversation, which was mostly small talk. Mentions of the weather. Nothing important.

Kimberly fluffed her hair, and her eyes searched for me. I reached up, acting like I was yawning, and caught her gaze.

My mind started to wander. What if William wasn't the vampire but just a charming guy who was into Kimberly? What if she ended up liking him too? The rage bubbled in my chest. I tried to stifle it, but the thought of them together kept bringing it to the surface. I didn't like William. Vampire or not. He wasn't good enough for her. I wasn't either.

She's ours.

The voice was a mere echo as the music picked up. The announcements faded and the partygoers broke out into dance while the lighting dimmed. Warm twinkle lights turned cool, and pools of blue and green hues flooded the dancefloor. A light fog poured from the stage, covering our feet.

I sighed. That was going to make my spy adventure much easier.

Presley had emptied his drink and chewed the ice. "I don't get the big deal, anyway. If she was your girlfriend, couldn't you just tell her you were a vamp and then maybe she could donate her blood to you? That would solve a lot of problems."

"What!? No, no I wouldn't tell her," I said quickly.

"But you'd drink her blood?"

Presley was clearly buzzing, and he loved to stir the pot. He was the cause of almost all our fights at home when drinking was involved.

"No! Can you go away so I can enjoy my night, please?" I moved into the crowd, keeping my peripheral on Kimberly.

"Fine. Ellis is almost here, anyway. I gotta go get another drink. I think I see Chelsea over there. I'll be sure to tell her you're going stag." He patted me on the shoulder, and before I could turn around to protest, he was gone. I rolled my eyes. *Little brothers.*

I caught sight of my mark in the fog. William had his arm locked with Kimberly's, and he led her into the crowd. Still looking nervous, she played it off well and let him coax her into dancing with him. William looked up, catching me watching them. The smile returned to his face, and he kept dancing.

I shook my head. I had to regain my focus. Keep William in a safe proximity to the rest of my brothers and wait to see if he made any kind of move. We outnumbered him, four to one. No way was he going to leave with Kimberly.

A hand grazed my shoulder, and I knew who it was by the smell of her sickly-sweet perfume. Chelsea was a beautiful blonde from Sigma Sigma Xi, but she wasn't my type. For one, she couldn't take a hint.

"Aaron, oh my God. You clean up well," she said, looking me up and down. Her dress reminded me of a disco ball, adding to the sensory overload.

"Chelsea, this isn't a good time." I patted her on the shoulder. "Cool dress, though."

I didn't actually like her dress but thought it might make her happy enough to leave.

She followed my line of sight. "You look lonely and a little sad. Dance with me."

Chelsea grabbed my hands and pulled me closer toward William and Kimberly, walking us into their direct line of sight. I exchanged looks with both of them while Chelsea pulled me closer. She put her hands to my chest before sliding them down my body.

I stopped her. "What are you doing?"

"Just having fun. You should try it." She winked.

Having fun was out the window. I glanced back at Kimberly, who was watching me. When our eyes met, she raised her eyebrows, and I shrugged. Chelsea and I continued to dance, while William spun Kimberly around. My heart jumped every time his hand met hers.

Every so often, I would see Zach and Luke fist pumping, drunkenly dancing, and jamming to the music.

Each song passed slowly, and I was relieved when Kimberly pulled away from him and excused herself to the restroom.

I mirrored her movements, stopping Chelsea from dancing on me. "I gotta head to the restroom. I'll be right back."

"Do you just want me to wait for you here?" Chelsea said, moving her body to the beat of the song.

"Uh, sure. Sure. That works."

Kimberly and I reached the hallway to the bathroom at the same time. A large red velvet door led into a hallway. The muffled noise felt like a warm blanket over my ears.

I opened the door for her, and we could finally talk despite the music shaking the walls.

"Are you good?"

"I'm doing okay." She grabbed my arm, ushering me toward the quiet corner. "He hasn't said anything definitive yet, but he keeps talking about what we are doing after this. I think he's trying to get me alone."

"Well, that's not happening," I said. "Do you think this is our guy?"

"I'm still not sure. I feel like I'm getting closer, but he keeps noticing you watching me. Maybe you should back off a little and stay out of sight? That way, if he is the guy, he'll be more likely to slip up."

"Kim, that seems like a horrible idea on top of our already risky plan. I don't like this guy."

She looked down, calculating. "I know, but there's something weird about this. I can feel it. It has to end tonight, or we may not get another chance. We have to draw him out. Once he does, I'll give the signal, and I'll make an exit and then you can get your brothers. Do you think you could stay in earshot enough that you could hear the code word?"

"I don't know. It's so hard to hear in here, but I think one word I can listen for."

She looked so sure of herself. It infused me with confidence. He couldn't take her anywhere I wouldn't see and couldn't hurt her in public without exposing himself. She was right. Our time was up. Everything had to end that night.

I accompanied her back through the crowd, returning her to her date, and I returned to mine.

Chelsea placed her hand on my chest. "Now, where were we?"

Kimberly and William disappeared farther into the crowd and into the fog. It was going to take a lot of mental power to listen for her signal, while also entertaining Chelsea. Not to mention, the music had picked up, and people grew wilder. Sweaty bodies moved me in every direction, while the music drummed in my ears.

"Chelsea, I don't know. I'm not in a dancing mood," I blurted.

"That's okay. Maybe we should get a drink instead?" I hesitated, and she caught it. "I know your mind is elsewhere, okay? But I still don't think you should be alone tonight. We can have fun."

Her words cut deep. From the moment I met her, I felt for her.

Her ex-boyfriend had tried to push her down the steps in front of our frat house when I stopped him. I stayed up with her all night as she cried off all her mascara onto my white shirt.

She could be pushy at times, but she also gave me the impression that she'd been through some things. At the same time, I knew the more attention I gave her, the harder it would be for her to let go of her image of me. I wasn't the man she envisioned. I wasn't even a man, really. She wanted something I couldn't give.

She didn't wait for my reply and dragged me by hand toward the bar. That was my cue to listen hard for Kimberly's voice.

Kimberly's voice rang through the crowd. "Are you having fun?"

"I'm having a marginal amount of fun," William said. "Are you?"

"I am. I just don't feel like I'm getting to talk to you," Kimberly said.

"Well, this was your idea." William laughed. "What do you want to know?"

"What do you want to drink?" Chelsea's voice cut my concentration.

"I don't know. My stomach kinda hurts, so I'm not sure if I want to drink."

"Two AMFs please." Chelsea slapped down her ID. It hadn't occurred to me that she was older than me.

I hid my face, hoping the bartender wouldn't see me lurking nearby, not that I had planned on drinking, anyway. Leaning against one of the large wooden pillars, I tried to listen again.

"What are you doing all the way over here?" Kimberly asked.

He chuckled. "The sunny views in California were calling my name. There are so many interesting people."

A longer-than-usual pause gave way, and I wondered if I had somehow lost their voices in the crowd until William said, "I'd love to tell you all about it. Would you accompany me upstairs, where it's a little quieter?"

Heat rushed to my face again, and before I could contemplate what I was feeling, Kimberly spoke again. "Uh, sure. I'd like that, but I think I'll take you up on your offer. Do you think you could get me a pineapple margarita?"

Shit. I spun around and searched for her in the crowd. As the night went on, the music was louder, the lights darker, and more people swarmed the dance floor.

"You don't drink, sweetheart. Why don't you tell me why you really invited me here?" William's voice was sharp.

Ice ran through my veins. He knew. She was right. He was the vampire.

"Here you go. This should help your mood." Chelsea thrust a tall glass of blue liquid into my hands.

My mind was going a million miles a minute. I needed to ditch Chelsea, and any attempt to get her to go away was bound to lead into an argument I didn't have time for. Kimberly needed me.

William's voice was a small whisper in the crowd. "You don't know what you've gotten yourself into."

Chelsea's white sparkling dress caught my eye. It was the way the lights from the disco ball danced and shimmered on the sequins. I knew what I needed to do. I brought the drink to my mouth and pretended to chug it. A few streams of the alcohol trickled down my neck, and I pretended to fall into a coughing fit. The liquid sprayed all over her dress. The blue glowed neon against her white dress, and Chelsea cursed under her breath.

"What the hell? Are you okay?" She placed her drink on the bar, grabbing mini towelettes to clean herself.

"I'm so fucking sorry. I'll get you more paper towels!" I said, knowing full well I would not be doing that.

I found myself in the middle of the dance floor. Kimberly's voice wasn't coming up. I couldn't tell if she wasn't replying or if I just couldn't hear her.

I peeked over the wall of bodies, then the bass exploded into a never-ending pulsing that wouldn't stop rattling my eardrums. The crowd thrashed from side to side, nearly knocking me to the ground. I cupped my hands over my ears, my eyes darting for the faintest sign she was near. With every second, fear crept into my mind, and I tried to search faster. Every corner ended up empty. I couldn't find my brothers, and I couldn't find Kimberly. The light show continued, and my heart beat faster in my rib cage. I stumbled into the crowd. The rhythmic thumping boomed harder and harder. Every sense that had once made me feel invincible dragged me down with it. No matter how much I tried to focus on anything else, I couldn't. I was drowning.

"What's wrong?" Luke towered over me. He grabbed my forearm and pulled me away from the view of the dance floor. Relief washed over me.

"Please help me. I've got to find Kimberly. Something's wrong."

I pushed my way through the crowd with a newfound confidence, caring less and less how hard I was pushing. I searched continually for any sign of her red hair.

Luke was hot on my heels. "Tell me what's going on."

"I will. I just have to find her first."

I called out her name, knowing it was futile with the whole dance floor pulsating with movement.

"There she is!" Luke pushed me in her direction before I could even see her. His height gave him an advantage I didn't have.

When I spotted her, she was moving toward the edge of the dance floor close to the stairs.

"Wait, stay here! I'll be right back, and I'll explain everything. Okay?" I said.

Luke nodded and I left him in a haze of bodies in the middle of the floor.

When I reached Kimberly, she was stumbling around on her heels, her eyes hazy and confused.

"Kim! Are you okay?" I couldn't hide the desperation in my voice. I scanned her shoulders to check for the faintest mark or bruise. There was nothing. She was unharmed. The world slowed, and I pulled her close to me. "Don't scare me like that."

She blinked a few times before speaking. "Yeah, I'm okay. It was just . . . I don't know what I was doing. We were dancing, and . . ."

The groggy look in her eyes didn't leave immediately, and my throat tightened.

Her head snapped up. "William! He went to get me a drink and never came back, but I saw him go up the stairs. Then it was like I couldn't control my body. But I wanted to go up there."

She pointed to the tall winding staircase next to us. Black iron all the way to the ceiling.

"You don't remember what he said to you?" I said.

The blue lights accentuated the worry in her eyes. Kimberly frowned. "No, what did you hear?"

"Don't worry about it. I'm going to take you to Presley and don't leave his side, okay? I'm going to go up there."

She grabbed my wrist as I turned to lead her. "Aaron, wait!"

I glanced down at her hand and then back up to her face. "Kim, you're going to be okay. I'll be right back. I'm just going to see if he is still here."

She kept a firm grasp on my wrist. "No, it's not that. You have to be careful."

A smile tugged at the edges of my mouth. "Are you worried about me?"

"Do you even know how to fight vampires or fight anyone?"

"I guess you have a point, but I have to go see if he is still here."

"Aaron, something doesn't feel right. I don't know."

Her blue eyes swallowed me whole, longing woven into her voice . . . for me. I wanted to bathe in the feeling.

"I'll have Luke come with me. We'll finish this."

Her eyes grew wide, and she squeezed my arm. "Don't tell him anything. Don't tell him about me. Promise me you won't. Please."

She was backing out of our plan. I opened my mouth to protest. Her desperation flooded my senses. I was pathetic, absolute putty in her hands.

"I won't. I'll be very vague. You will have to let go of the death grip you have on my arm, though." I motioned to my wrist, where she had been white knuckling it.

She let out a breath. "Okay. Yeah, that's a good plan."

I snuck her through the crowd, leaving her with Presley, who, to my surprise, wasn't too drunk . . . yet. He wrapped his arm around her, promising to keep her safe.

As I made my way back to the dance floor, Luke walked in step with me. "Are you going to tell me what's going on with you?"

"Kimberly has a stalker. He's been around all night, and I need to go and check and make sure he's gone. Will you come with me?"

It was a bold move, saying a lie directly to Luke's face. He wouldn't buy it, but he would come with me. That's all I needed.

Luke stared at me for a minute, looking completely sober.

"Why can't you just tell me the truth?"

"I don't have time. We have to go now."

I walked toward the iron steps looming in the distance.

Luke followed behind me, and my confidence rose. I didn't want to admit to Kimberly how nervous I was. If her theory was true, William was dangerous. Questions had to be answered.

As we neared the top of the steps, Luke slapped me on the back. A pat of reassurance. Guilt ruined any ounce of comfort it brought me. I hated lying to him despite every lie he'd ever told me to my face. This was different. He had those secrets to keep me safe. I was putting us all in danger.

As we reached the top of the stairs, I slackened. There didn't appear to be anyone up there. The lighting was dim, and the stage lights cast a light show over the ceiling above us, the cool blues and greens long gone. The ceiling was red, and the lights above danced a warm orange. We stepped out onto the wooden floor that made a distinct sound with every step.

"Is that him?"

Luke, the more observant one, spotted him leaning into the corner almost completely disguised by darkness. "To what do I owe the occasion?" William's voice was cold.

"I've seen you around before." Luke took a step forward, and I followed close behind.

"You have. I've attended some of your fancy parties," William said.

"What do you want with Kimberly?" Luke took another step forward, keeping a protective stance over me. "Whatever it is, I think we can come to an agreement here. You need to leave her alone."

I matched his stance. "He's right. This ends now."

"Oh, so he does speak? Hiding behind big brother, are we? Typical Aaron," William said.

"I'm not the one hiding," I said.

"You're right. How rude of me." William stepped into the red light, only half his face showing. Something dark lurked in his eyes.

Luke must have sensed the shift. He leaned in closer to me. His shoulder pushed me back a half step.

"Now, I thought this was a party? Why so serious all of a sudden?" William smirked, his eyes never leaving Luke.

"You're one of us."

Luke's voice was the one that was icy cold this time. I wasn't used to it.

William scoffed. "I'm nothing like you."

Luke talked through gritted teeth and looked at me. "This was your secret. You knew what he was, and you didn't say anything."

"Well, technically, I had an idea, but I wanted to be sure." William took another step toward us.

Luke's voice was shrouded in worry. "We need Zach."

"Too bad he's all the way across the building. I don't know much about you, Luke, but I do know that you'd never leave your poor little brother up here to fight alone." William's eyes bore into mine.

"Who are you? What do you want?" Luke said.

"Isn't that obvious? I want the girl," William said.

I shook my head. "If that was true, why didn't you take her before? You had plenty of opportunities."

William's pointed teeth peeked behind a confident smile. "Are you sure you're not just jealous you weren't the only one to taste her?"

I wasn't prepared for the wave of anger crashing into me.

Within seconds, I was shaking from head to toe.

Kill him. Kill him. Kill him. Kill him.

The voice seeped into my skull, making it harder and harder to think clearly.

"What's he talking about?" Luke gripped my forearm, but I couldn't feel it with the heat pulsing through my body. "Kimberly? The girl you've been hanging out with?"

William tilted his head, laughing at me. "Maybe I just like messing with you."

Killhim.Killhim.Killhim.Killhim.Killhim.Killhim.

The voice was getting louder and louder.

"You shouldn't have brought big brother, Aaron." William sighed. "Now I have to complicate this a little."

I wanted to comprehend what he was saying, but I couldn't get a grip. Every time I tried to hold on, it felt like a rope pulling me out to sea. My body was rigid, writhing with anger.

"Aaron, what's wrong with you?" Luke's voice sounded faint.

William's eyes locked with mine. "She tasted good too."

I lunged forward, letting rage take me. William moved toward us. A millisecond later, I found myself on the floor. Luke had pushed me behind him, and William was standing in the middle of the floor, bathed in crimson light. Luke stumbled backward slowly.

As quickly as it came, the rage and the voice were gone. I rushed to Luke's side, with my heart in my throat. His eyes were hazy and confused, just like Kimberly's, only they were cloudy and black. He looked right through me, as if I weren't there.

William's eyes stayed locked on Luke. "Now that was interesting. Just when I thought there was nothing you boys could do to surprise me."

"What did you do to him?" I said.

"He'll be okay. Just needed to jog his memory a bit. Oh, and I did you a favor. He won't remember any of this. Neither will you." William grabbed my wrists. His face just inches from mine. "You're not ready yet. But you will be soon, and when the time is right . . . you won't be able to save her."

He let go, and the world fell away. The floor opened up and blackness took over.

THIRTEEN

KIMBERLY

Waiting for Aaron was impossibly long. Every minute that passed felt like an hour. Presley was getting more drunk by the second, and I felt less and less secure. I had no view of the stairs, and all I was left with was a worried pit in my stomach.

My brain didn't feel right. I replayed the formal over and over again in my head to try to find the hole, and there was something I missed. I just couldn't put my finger on it.

Had I found out William's true identity? Was he actually dangerous? Signs still pointed to him being the vampire, but I had no clue why. I was missing something crucial.

The stairs were still empty, and my manicure was trashed. I had chipped off almost every single speck of paint in the span of five minutes.

"So, Kimberly, seen any good vampire movies lately?"

I turned my attention back to Presley, who was casually swaying with a drink in his hand. His date, Ellis, was at the bar, getting them more drinks.

"W-What? That's really random." I scratched my neck.

A smile spread across Presley's face. "Is it? Come on, tell me your favorite."

"Uh, I'm not sure. I don't like vampire movies."

"Hmmm. That's interesting because you're into my brother, and he's one, so I figure you must have a thing for vamps."

A lump caught in my throat. "He's what? I-I don't know what you're talking about."

Presley's curls bounced when he laughed. "Come on. Cut the shit. I know."

Terror filled my body in a way I never felt before. My mind went over anything I might have done to reveal the secret.

I stole a look back at the crowd. "How did you find out?" I spoke in a whisper, knowing he could hear me. My hand was shaking at my side.

"What?! You know?" Presley yelled. "Aaron told you, didn't he? I knew it!"

Despite the loud music, he had gained a few sideways glances.

Shushing him, I said, "Presley, please be quiet. You can't tell anyone."

"I can't believe I was actually right! I knew Aaron couldn't keep a secret." He bounced.

"He didn't tell me. I found out . . . another way."

"You found out another way . . ." His head popped up. "What, did he bite you or something?"

The nightmare continued. I couldn't believe it. How could he guess? How could he figure it out?

His eyes were wide, and he bounced again. "I'm right, aren't I? He bit you! Holy shit."

"How did you figure it out?"

He held up his hand matter-of-factly, counting down. "Well, you're a bad liar, for one. Two, you didn't even flinch when Zach broke that chair in the living room. Let alone question it. Three, you guys have been sneaking around and giving each other the eyes. It was not that hard to decipher."

My face was hot, and my stomach was doing somersaults. It was too much. I wasn't ready for Aaron's older brothers to know about me yet. Something deep inside me was directly opposed to that idea, but I didn't know why.

"Presley, please don't say anything to your brothers."

He wouldn't let it go that easily. Like a five-year-old who just discovered the best secret in the world, it was written all over his face.

"Come on. This is the secret of the century. It explains so many things!"

"Please. I'm literally begging you not to tell them."

I spotted a familiar face making his way through the crowd. Luke beelined for the bathroom, only he was alone. Aaron wasn't following him. I turned my attention back toward Presley. "I have to go. Just don't say anything yet. Please."

His smile softened. "Don't worry, your secret is safe with me."

I had no idea if I could trust him enough to believe a word from his mouth, but it would have to do. I had done enough begging for one night. I pushed through bodies, much slower than I'd hoped. Sweaty people were packed together like sardines closer toward the stage. I made an exit for the hallway that led to both bathroom doors.

"Luke?" I peeked my head in, trying not to startle him. "Is everything okay?"

He stopped at the sound of my voice but didn't turn to face me. I moved in, trying to get a good look. Luke's once-warm complexion was cold. His expression had turned into a blank slate. His hands were shaking. The blue neon sign above us cast a dark shadow on his face.

He was silent as he stared off into space. His forehead creased, the reflection of pain registering into his frown lines.

"Hey, what's wrong? Are you okay?"

Luke closed his eyes for a second and took a step back. When his back hit the wall, his eyes were forced open. "I don't know. I'm sorry. Just give me a second."

Immediately, his reaction registered. He was having a panic attack. I'd seen it many times growing up in foster care, though I'd never had one myself.

My heart sank, and panic grew on his face. He crumpled to the ground, pulling his back up against the wall.

"Hey, it's okay. You're okay," I said softly.

He gripped his chest and cried in pain. "I'm okay. I'm okay. I'm sorry." He exhaled sharply, as if he were struggling to force air out of his chest. "I-I'm sorry just—just give me a second."

The creaking door let in a flood of music, and Luke laid his head on his knees, covering his ears.

I blocked Luke from any prying eyes. "Hey, can you give us a minute?"

The group of sharply dressed, sweaty men met me with blank faces.

"Seriously, give us five minutes, please?"

They finally retreated, and I leaned down next to Luke. "It's going to be okay. You're safe."

He pulled his hands to his head and covered his eyes. His body rocked with each stifled sob. "I'm sorry. I can't do this . . ."

I was careful not to touch him.

"Do you want me to get Presley? I think I saw him—"

"No! I just need a second. I need a second." He buried his head into his knees, exhaling. "I just need it to stop."

"You're okay. Everything is okay," I said. I tried to keep my voice low, but the music echoed in the hallway.

"I need my brother. I need—"

The door swung open, the thumping of the music shaking the walls. Zach appeared, his eyes full of panic. "Hey, I'm here. I'm here."

I backed up and let him sit next to his brother. He sat on the floor, and Luke held out his hand for Zach to grab.

"I saw her. I saw her." I could barely make out Luke's voice among the sobs. "She was here. She's in my head again."

"She isn't here." Zach dug his hand into his pocket and pulled out a piece of gum. "Come on, chew on this. Focus on the taste."

Luke pushed his hand away, but Zach persisted. "Come on. It's going to help. This will pass."

Luke took the piece of gum and buried his face into his knees. "She was here. I felt it. Maybe they're here somewhere. We need to check."

Zach gripped his hand and whispered, "They aren't here. We're okay. She can't find us."

I'd never seen Zach so soft or Luke so vulnerable. It reminded me of the feeling I got when I'd taken the picture of the family in the hospital. Their love for each other felt tangible, so strong I could reach out and touch it.

Zach looked up, as if he had forgotten my existence. "Thanks for keeping him company. I think I've got it from here."

The dark circles under Zach's eyes revealed a man worn beyond all recognition. They told thousands of stories all at once. I didn't know what the twins had been through, but I knew it was something that must have never touched Aaron or Presley. I was starting to truly realize why Zach and Luke had kept secrets from their little brothers.

Zach gave me a shy smile before the door swung open again. A few guys and their girlfriends stopped to stare at us.

"Hey, give us, like, ten minutes, okay? Then we'll be out of your hair," Zach said.

One random guy huffed. "We've been waiting. You can't—"

"Dude, does it look like I give a shit? Get the fuck out!" He grabbed an empty beer bottle and chucked it at the door. Its shattering spilled all over the floor, leaving remnants twinkling in the hallway's dim lights.

He sighed, turning his attention back to me. "Sorry."

"Let me know if you need any help." I smiled and walked back toward the door.

As I opened it, the same group tried to walk past me.

"I swear to fucking God, if you try to walk in here again before that ten minutes is up, I will kick your fucking ass. Stay the fuck out!"

I eased past them, and they reluctantly closed the door.

"Ugh. I hate that guy," they complained, planting their feet firmly by the door.

And I thought my life was complicated enough with a vampire trying to kill me. I couldn't even contemplate the things Luke said. The questions kept bubbling up in my mind. Who was the girl Luke was talking about? What happened to him to make him so scared? All of that was overcome by the growing fear that I needed to find Aaron as soon as possible.

"Hey! Sorry about that. I cleared everything up."

Aaron's voice startled me. Relief washed over my senses, seeing him perfectly fine next to me. I did a quick once-over to make sure he was still in one piece. His hair was a little wild, but he looked fine.

"What do you mean? What happened to Luke?" I said.

"Luke?" Aaron looked behind me and responded like he was citing a well-rehearsed speech. "Luke's fine. He got upset before we talked to William and left."

"I saw him come down the stairs," I said.

Aaron shrugged. "If he did, then it must have been after I left."

"That doesn't make any sense! None of this is making any sense," I said.

Something in Aaron's expression didn't look right, and every time I tried to dig into my memory to try to investigate, I couldn't pull anything up.

"There's nothing to worry about at all. He is not the vampire. I'm one hundred percent sure." Aaron smiled, but it didn't match his eyes.

His words didn't comfort me like I'd hoped. I looked back toward the stairs, and as I did, William descended the stairs. Without a word to Aaron, I pushed through the crowd. I had no idea what I'd say, but I knew he had the answers I needed. In the blink of an eye, I lost William in a sea of dark-haired boys.

Aaron was hot on my heels. "Where are you going?"

"To find him. There's something we're missing. I know it."

As I made my way through the crowd, yelling outside the building stopped me in my tracks.

"Come on." Without any explanation, Aaron grabbed my hand, leading me through the crowd and toward the back door. I knew I should have been more focused on the surrounding chaos, but I couldn't focus on anything other than Aaron's hand on mine. It was warm. Comforting. Heat flushed my cheeks.

Despite the music, the sound of commotion grew louder and louder as we neared the door. One by one, people funneled outside to look at something.

Once outside, we arrived at an open circle in the mob. Guys were mauling Presley, at least ten of them. In the midst of his shuffle, Presley lay on the ground, protecting his body with his legs and arms.

It was a relief knowing he wouldn't be seriously hurt, but that didn't stop my stomach from churning. Aaron left me at the edge of the circle and went in to pull the group off his brother. A gasp of horror escaped my lips as they relentlessly punched and kicked Aaron as he tried to pull Presley off the ground.

A fire ignited under my feet, and I went to step in. For a moment, I lost all sense of reasoning. He didn't need my help, yet my body leaped into action.

Chelsea grabbed my arm. "You don't want to get in the middle of that."

I wanted to push her off, but I knew she was right. The two were becoming overwhelmed. Probably too afraid to fight back in fear of exposing themselves.

"What happened?! Why are they fighting?" I said.

Chelsea grimaced. "I don't know. Some guy just punched Presley out of the blue and then everyone started jumping on him."

Ellis tried to jump in and help but was also punched and thrown to the ground a few feet away. I ran to his aid.

I pulled him from the gravel driveway. "Are you okay?"

He dusted himself. "I don't know what happened. We were walking to the car, and this guy just sucker-punched him. They won't let me through."

Ellis wiped the blood from his chin with labored breaths. This looked bad. I wished I could tell him he didn't need to worry about Presley. He looked like he was about ready to jump back in.

"Wait here. I'm going to get help," I said.

The music was still blasting from inside, and I went for the door to go get more help, when Zach appeared.

"What the hell is this?" Zach barreled through the crowd, wasting no time flinging people off Presley and Aaron.

His body was fully alert, with his shoulders back. With two hands, he flung the guys into the dirt with sheer force. They flew back, knocking bystanders down in the process. When one would go to punch him in the head, he'd easily counter and shove them to the ground. He was a natural. This time, the guys didn't come back for more. Once they'd picked themselves off the ground, they disappeared into the crowd.

Zach picked a guy up from his white collar and pulled him close to his face. "Want to tell me what the fuck happened here?"

"I don't know! He just made me so angry, so I punched him." The guy struggled beneath Zach's grasp, but there was no escaping the iron grip he had on his shirt.

Zach turned to Presley. "What the fuck did you do?"

"Nothing! Ellis and I were just talking outside."

Zach's eyes caught fire as he turned back toward the guy, who was still trying with all his might to get Zach to let go of his shirt. "Please, don't tell me you just punched my brother because you're a homophobic asshole, or I swear to God—"

"No, no, no, no! That's not it. I don't know why I did it. I just got angry."

A guy in the back got up, bloodied from Zach's assault. It took me a minute to recognize him as the guy from the party. Danny.

Zach dropped the other guy to the ground and met Danny face-to-face. "I should have known this was you. You better get to talking. Fast."

Danny's face twisted in horror. "Okay, I know what this looks like, but I didn't mean to do this."

A light bulb went off in my head but illuminated an empty room. Something about this was strange. Danny was terrified of Zach when

Aaron and I questioned him earlier that week. There was no way he would have done this on purpose.

Zach's expression turned sinister. A complete deadpan with a lifeless look in his eyes. "I'm in a really bad mood. So, I'm going to say this once. You hurt my brother. I will fucking kill you. I don't care about your reason or why you did it."

"Zach." Luke appeared next to him, putting his hand on his shoulder. "Let me talk to him." Danny's whole body was shaking.

"What was this about?" Luke said.

Luke looked worn, but that didn't make him look weak. He towered over Danny.

"I-I just was angry. That's it. I'm sorry."

"Sorry isn't fucking good enough," Zach spat.

"Stop." Luke stilled Zach with his hand before turning back to Danny. "I don't want to see you around us anymore. If I see you, we'll have a problem. This is the final warning. Understand?"

Danny nodded and tore off into the crowd. Aaron appeared, looking freshly untouched, with only messy hair and a dirty blazer to show for his fight.

He looked worried. "Are you okay?"

"Me?! What about you?" I reached for his forearm, but I caught myself just before my fingers touched his skin.

He leaned in, whispering in my ear. "Vampire, remember?" He pulled back and winked.

Aaron's brothers were huddled in a group, all looking mentally thrashed. The fact that there wasn't a scratch on any of them didn't bode well for their cover.

"I think we should go." I tugged on Aaron's blazer, and he nodded.

I peeked at the dance floor inside. As the night wound down, the crowd dispersed, and it was easier to see. William was nowhere to be found. My stomach felt empty but not from the lack of food. Our big experiment had come up inconclusive. If anything, there were more unanswered questions. Aaron's answers about William didn't add up. Nothing made sense.

Presley took a few minutes to check on Ellis, and Chelsea pulled Aaron aside to make sure he was okay. "Hey, Kimberly, can we talk for a sec?" Luke's voice startled me.

I nodded and followed him to a light pole that illuminated a portion of the pine trees. The music was still going inside, but some people were stumbling back into their buses and getting ready to leave for their after-parties.

"I, uh. I'm sorry about earlier. Truth be told, I don't even like showing my brothers that side of me, so I feel weird that you had to see that."

"Oh. Please don't feel that way. It's nothing to be ashamed of. I understand."

He laughed nervously and rubbed his neck. "I'm glad you feel that way. Maybe someday I will too. Thanks for being so cool."

"Well, thanks for raising your brothers to be the way they are. You've done a pretty good job. I'm sure you've dealt with a lot. It's not easy being the example, I'm sure."

His eyes lit up, and a huge grin spread from ear to ear. "That's probably the best compliment I've gotten in a long time. Thank you. Glad to have you around. I gotta go check on everyone, but you're riding with us, right?"

I nodded, and Luke disappeared toward the car as I waited for Aaron.

The night's events repeated in my head. I couldn't shake the feeling I had forgotten something important, but I couldn't put my finger on it. I thought of the look on Danny's face and how strange his behavior had been, then went back to Presley. Presley knew my secret. I had to warn Aaron as soon as possible.

After a few minutes, Aaron was done talking to Chelsea, and we walked toward the car. He was oddly quiet.

"Presley knows," I said. "He knows I know you're a vampire."

Aaron went to open his mouth, and I continued. "It slipped out. He tricked me, and it doesn't matter. He knows, but he promised not to tell."

Aaron sighed, and the car was fast approaching.

"Well, that's not good because Presley is notoriously bad at keeping secrets."

"There she is!" Presley jumped with a beer bottle in his hand. "Guys, I found her!"

The alcohol must have finally caught up to him. Luke put his hand over Presley's mouth to keep him from talking further.

"Yeah, Pres, we see her." Zach groaned. He sat on the hood of the car and ran his hands through his hair before taking a pack of cigarettes from his pocket.

"Can you get off the car so we can go?" Aaron snapped. His shoulders were rigid as he struggled to pull the keys from his pocket.

"Here we go." Zach took a drag of a cigarette. "What is it now?"

"Did you have to cause a huge scene like that?" Aaron said.

"I didn't cause a huge scene. The people trying to beat Presley to a bloody pulp did."

"Bloody." Presley snickered in his own little world.

"Yeah, I know, but do you always have to come in and do the thing where you walk around like some psychotic asshole?" Aaron said.

Zach groaned. "Please. Spare me. I don't want to hear your holier-than-thou monologue today."

Aaron shook his head. "Typical."

"You're both being rude." Luke's voice cut the tension. "We still have a guest. Your bickering can wait till we get home." Luke smiled at me and put his large arm around me. "Sorry, about that, Kimberly. I thought I taught them better."

Luke's half hug was oddly what I needed at that moment. My previous reservations about him had disappeared. He radiated a sense of safety and warmth, yet the thought of telling them who I was flooded me with pure terror. I didn't know why, other than the obvious reasons. Something felt different.

We piled into their car, and I laid my head against the cool glass window and breathed in the scent of the vanilla air freshener hanging from the rearview mirror.

My brain was still playing wrapped up in what I was missing. No matter how close it felt, it was out of reach.

Should I have just believed Aaron and what he said about William? We came to the dance to put everything to rest, but somehow, I found myself back in the car with no answers.

"Aaron, crank it up!" Presley was the only loud one. Zach and Luke sandwiched him in the back seat.

Aaron was driving and hadn't said anything since his conversation with Zach.

"Shhhh. Kim is trying to sleep," Luke said in a hushed voice. "No, she isn't. Come on, I just want a little music."

"No." Aaron groaned.

"Fine, I'll just sing, then."

"No!" they all said simultaneously.

My eyes fluttered open. I loved being in the car at night. Something about it was so calming, seeing lights in a blurry haze. But they didn't give the same comfort this time around. A deep, unsettling sensation had crept its way into my body, and I had a feeling it wasn't leaving anytime soon.

"Presley, if you're quiet, I'll get you a present tomorrow," I said, without moving my head from the window.

"Really?! Okay. I'll be good, I'll just hum." His voice trickled with excitement between slight slurs of speech. "Hmmm. Hm, hm, hm, hm."

"Oh, she's good at this." Zach chuckled.

The car's roaring blended with Presley's loud humming. I took a deep breath, compressing all that had happened. My eyes opened just enough to watch the lights pass by in the window again. Sparks of light in the infinite dark sky.

FOURTEEN

AARON

The carnival lights' buzzing only strengthened the nervous energy pulsing from head to toe. I walked in step behind my brothers as we strolled the boardwalk. The ocean breeze was comforting, along with the nostalgic scent of fried Twinkies and turkey legs. I wished we were there for the carnival.

It was late, and the full moon hung overhead, lighting our path between abandoned stands at the edge of the carnival. We were following a group of four guys, who were drunk and belligerent. We'd spent the better part of two hours scouting the perfect group, pretending to be normal people. Zach smoked a cigarette and shared a casual conversation with Luke, while Presley tried his best to beat every carnival game we walked past. He carried around an empty fountain drink container, which he would loudly sip on occasionally. I, on the other hand, had not uttered a word since we got there.

The events of the dance loomed over us like an omen. Zach and Luke were particularly stressed about the brawl's unneeded attention. Their strict rules were even more rigid. I was constantly trying to find time away from them and meet with Kimberly, who seemed just as fearful as Zach and Luke. I couldn't get myself to feel much of anything. A strange sense of numbness chilled me when I remembered the dance.

The Ferris wheel stood in the distance, and my mind wandered back to Kimberly and her fear of heights. I imagined how different the night would be if I had come with her. Her red hair blowing with the cool night breeze as we swung from high up. She might have grabbed my arm and told me how scared she was by the swaying, and I could have said something cunning, like, "Do you think there is any universe in which I'd let something happen to you?" Yeah. Something cool like that. The dance was a steady blur but had one shining moment I couldn't stop replaying. Her hand on my wrist. The way she looked up at me. The heat from her body as she begged me not to go.

You just want to kill her. You don't really care about her.

The voice had been nagging me all day. Every time I tried to think of Kimberly, the Thing would turn it around.

We need her.

I tried to focus on her face and the way she laughed. How much I enjoyed her company.

Her blood. Think only of her blood.

The Thing wouldn't go. I looked across the lot at a group of people chatting. I focused on their pumping blood. Their hearts were beating in unison, but the voice didn't respond, almost as if It wasn't interested in them at all, just Kimberly.

I tried to put the thought out of my mind and focus on the task at hand. The drunken group continued to walk on by themselves, and as fate would have it, the large crowds in the carnival stayed away from the outer edges. It was good for us, bad for them.

"How are you doing, Aaron?" Luke nudged me.

He hadn't been the same since the dance. Kimberly told me about his panic attack. I'd already asked him. He wasn't sure what triggered it. Only that he thought he saw someone, but he wouldn't say who.

I should have been worried about it and figured out the thing Kimberly insisted we were missing from the formal. But I couldn't focus on anything other than what was in the present. The night I'd been dreading all month had finally come. It was time to hunt.

"Peachy. I'm having a great time," I said.

"It will be better this time. We're right here with you." Luke placed a firm slap on my back.

"Yeah, we'll knock this out in just enough time to ride the Tilt-O-Whirl!"

Presley's enthusiasm was annoying, but I couldn't help but be a little envious. I wanted to puke, and he was already thinking about what he was going to do after.

"All right, there they go. Let's do this." Zach watched them disappear down an alleyway made up of large steel storage containers. He flicked his cigarette on the ground.

"You're really going to litter, huh?" Presley said.

Zach scoffed. "I think as far as moral dilemmas go, I've got bigger problems. But go ahead and add litterbug to the list."

Anxiety buzzed in my body. We picked up the pace and went completely silent. I hated that hunting people was so easy. It was easy to hide the sound of my footsteps. Easy to move out of the way when they looked behind them. It was too easy.

Kill. Kill. Kill.

That voice stopped me in my tracks. Luke stopped up ahead and motioned for me to come. I walked in closer, trailing the back.

Blood. We need blood.

With every step, the voice got louder and louder.

It happened like we had planned. Zach went first, taking out the lead and blocking the way, in case any others tried to run. They were too drunk to run. Luke grabbed two and pushed one in Presley's direction and the other to me.

Kill him.

It was impossible to drown out. I grabbed the guy by the collar and shoved him up against the wall. He was blackout drunk. There was no struggle, and he was easy to overpower. I just needed to drink a little blood. That was it. I brought my lips to his neck, the blood pulsing along the jugular vein so close I could almost taste it.

We need to drink him dry. You need more than that. Kill him. Kill him, now.

I pushed him away, knocking the guy into a pile of trash. He groaned, flailing on the ground. I couldn't do it. I was going to kill him by drinking his blood.

"Aaron, what's wrong?"

Luke was next to me, his face already clean, the scent of blood smeared across his forearm. My eyes focused on the red, and my body shook. I was about to lose it. My control was slipping.

"I'm fine. I'm done. Can we just go?" I sprinted out of the alleyway and toward the nearest streetlight.

"What the hell happened?"

Zach was hot on my tail and was the first to reach me. If it wasn't for his speed, I would have kept running.

All three of them waited for me to speak, watching me with worried eyes. I thought the feeling would stop, but a boiling rage was coming to the surface. Whether it was the Thing inside me screaming for attention or my own emotion, I couldn't tell anymore.

"I'm going home. I'm done."

I stepped toward the carnival, but Zach grabbed my jacket from behind. I thrust him off me, tearing my sleeve in the process.

"We can't go yet. We still have to hunt more."

Presley was right. Because we hadn't killed our victims, one wasn't enough blood to sustain us for a month. I knew the consequences of that too well. I was living it.

"No, fuck this. Fuck all of you and your ability to be okay with this."

The words spilled out, and I couldn't stop them. This time, I wanted to hurt them. Every one of them.

"Not this again." Zach sighed.

"Fuck you. You want to talk about me staying in line and being a good brother when you're the one who betrayed me?! You did this to me, and you didn't tell me. You didn't prepare me. I'm fucked because of you and your selfishness!"

Zach grabbed me by the collar and forced me back against the light pole. "You are such a prick. What would you know about sacrifice!? What do you know about being selfless?! Absolutely fucking nothing because all you do is sit around and bitch and moan."

"Zach," Luke cautioned.

"No, he needs to hear this." He turned back to me, our faces deathly close. "I've sacrificed everything I've ever wanted *for you*! So you could fucking live and have a decent life. I'm not perfect, but I'll be damned if I'm going to sit here and let you call me selfish."

I pushed him off me, my mind spinning. I wanted to stop talking, but the rage poured out of me. "Well, it was all for nothing. This is your fault. You ruined our lives."

"Eh, don't bring me into this." Presley had his arms crossed and looked to be inching farther and farther from our group.

"Of course. How could I forget? You don't care about anything! This is all easy for you. So, fuck you too."

"Aaron, come on. I thought we were past this." Presley looked defeated. "Let's just finish and—"

"Past it!? I'm just getting started." I snarled. "You have no idea how I feel. How could any of you? You only care about us. But what does that make us? It makes us monsters! We're bad people, and I used to be a good person, but I can't be anymore because of you and shitty decisions!"

I couldn't convey the betrayal I felt since the day I was changed. They were the reason I was forced to hunt people in the first place and risk killing them. I was tired of the burden. Tired of the fear.

Luke's solemn face washed over me, pulling me out of the flames and straight onto ice.

The pain in their eyes felt like an ice bath after a dip in the hot tub. It looked different in each of their eyes. Zach was pissed at me. Presley desperately wanted peace, and Luke just looked disappointed. I hated the bond we had sometimes. I wanted to be mad at them. To hate them for all the times they let me down, but I couldn't. No peace came from loving or hating them.

"Are you done?" Luke waited in silence, the carnival sounds playing an amalgamation of melodies in the background.

I didn't say anything, and turned back toward the carnival lights. They didn't try to follow me. I fought the knot in my stomach and the urge to turn back. For the first time in my life, I wanted to be alone.

FIFTEEN

KIMBERLY

I tapped my foot as the clock on the wall ticked by in an achingly slow crawl. The professor proceeded to overexplain the requirements for our finals. His monotone voice only made my eyes heavy with boredom. I rubbed my sweaty palms together and counted each tick of the clock. A change had taken place in me. It was as if a hidden part of me was coming alive. Things grew more important than school. I wasn't spending all my time thinking of the next thing. I was completely present in my own life.

"All right, class. You're dismissed." He furrowed his eyebrows.

I got up and fought my way to the door. Once in the hall, I barreled toward the exit. The courtyard was booming with a flurry of activity. It was the week before finals, and students who were previously less invested started to show up again.

"Boo!"

Aaron's voice startled me.

"Jesus! Be careful. Don't you know there are dangerous vampires afoot?" I joked.

"How could I forget?"

Aaron was dressed in his hiking boots and flannel shirt. He had a tattered canvas bag strapped across his shoulder that looked almost exactly like the one I had thrifted years ago. I'd since decorated it with various patches from all the places around the mountains I visited and hiked.

"I can't believe I can't go camping alone now because of vampires." I sighed as we walked toward my dorm.

I had just a few more things to pack for our trip up the mountain. We were planning on staying all weekend, and Aaron had convinced Luke to let him go despite the seclusion.

"You should probably get used to that, seeing as you're a vampire magnet and all." Aaron smiled.

My phone vibrated in my backpack pocket, and I checked it.

It was Chris. Again.

I turned it off and put it back.

Aaron raised an eyebrow. "Are you ever going to answer him or keep him in suspense?"

"I don't know. I'm not his biggest fan right now."

It was easier to ignore him and focus on more important things like dangerous mystery vampires.

"Well, you did try to convince him vampires exist. Maybe the guy needs some time. You can't ignore him forever," Aaron said as we passed through the school garden. The smell of fresh flowers and pollen drifted in the air.

"Why are you being so levelheaded right now?"

"You're right. That's your job, and I'm truly the last one who should be giving you advice right now." Aaron stopped to pluck a huge white peony. He brought it up to his nose to smell it before handing it to me. "You're doomed to receive flowers from me now until the end of time since I know which is your favorite."

Butterflies swarmed my stomach, and I sniffed the delicate flower. The petals were ivory, velvet between my fingers. "I think I can live with that."

There was goodness growing among the darkness and confusion. My relationship with Aaron had brought me more joy than I wanted to admit. Something about his internal optimism

quelled the fear of opening up. He relentlessly pursued me and my happiness. That was more than I could say for anyone else in my life, including Chris.

It made the world easier to take. Even the most confusing parts.

"Have you seen William anywhere?" I asked, peeking over my shoulder.

Worry had settled permanently in the pit of my stomach since the dance. I was afraid to go anywhere by myself anymore. I felt delusional again. Nothing indicated William was our vampire, but I couldn't shake the fact we had missed it at the formal. I was having trouble remembering our original plan and why we even thought it was William in the first place.

"Kim, how many times do I have to say it? He's not the guy."

Aaron didn't know, but I noticed his change in demeanor when he came back to find me in the crowd that night. Since the dance, he looked more troubled than usual. I noticed the weird shift in his voice every time he recited the same monologue back to me of what happened when he left.

It was the same each time. They went to find William, then something triggered Luke, then he left. Aaron swore he had talked to William and concluded there was nothing to worry about, but when trying to get direct pieces of dialogue from him, he'd repeat the same thing back to me.

Yet, I still trusted Aaron's cloudy judgment. At least I trusted that he felt he was telling the truth.

"I just think there's something we are missing about the dance. He never came back, remember? And we haven't seen him since. That's weird," I said.

Aaron and I had done a few "covert ops missions," as Aaron liked to call them. We'd checked the swim team schedule posted on the bulletin in the gym and waited for William to show up for practice, but he never did.

I kept replaying the same scene in my head. When I started to feel nervous because William wanted to get me alone, I used the code word. Everything after that wasn't clear. I remember walking toward the steps, and Aaron looked panicked.

"You're right. It's weird. We shouldn't rule anyone out." Aaron nodded matter-of-factly.

I loved Aaron's refusal to gaslight me despite the doubt in his eyes.

"What are we going to do about Presley?" I said.

Aaron shrugged. "He swears he can keep the secret this time."

"And your brothers—how have they been since the fight?"

"They're fine," he said quickly. "Kim, come on! It's a beautiful day. Can we just go enjoy it? I'm kind of looking forward to our little getaway, just to have a break from everything." Our getaway. The butterflies were back.

"You're right. Why worry about dangerous, life-altering events when you can ignore all your problems and sleep in the mountains?"

The grin returned to Aaron's face. "Exactly."

"Hey, wanna see me climb that tree over there?" Aaron bounced in step with me, pointing to the tallest tree on our horizon. The giant redwoods surrounded us and kept us company on our journey up the trail. It was magical.

"Uh, no, actually." I laughed.

The wind sang through the trees in the distance and stirred the pollen and petals. I took a deep breath and admired the aroma. There was still a good bit of daylight left.

"Do you need to stop to rest? Tell me if we're going too far." Aaron walked beside me, casting a long shadow over my face.

"You're too worried about me. I'm not made out of glass."

"I'd say humans are pretty fragile. Hey, I can carry you on my shoulders if you want." He wiggled his eyebrows, tempting me.

"No thanks, I can walk by myself." I snickered.

"Suit yourself, then." He looked up, admiring the sun peeking through the trees.

"I didn't know you liked to hike. I can't imagine there are many places to hike in Brooklyn."

"In Brooklyn, no, but my brothers would take us hiking upstate for special occasions when they could."

"Your brothers were very charming at the dance." I slid slowly back into a conversation Aaron refused to have with me.

He apologized for how he acted after the dance. I told him he got a pass after spending five minutes being kicked and punched in the head. But I wanted to bring it back up to get a read on Aaron's true feelings on his brothers.

"Oh, yes, they were *so* charming, weren't they?" Aaron's voice oozed sarcasm. "Was it Zach threatening to kill someone or maybe Presley figuring out our secret and blackmailing me to do his homework *again* that screamed gentlemen?"

"That's not what I meant. I just saw a different side to them that I wasn't expecting."

We picked up the pace and headed for higher ground. Thanks to my long-distance running, I wasn't out of breath yet.

I spoke again. "When Luke was having his panic attack, Zach came in a few minutes later to comfort him. It was sad . . . but sweet. If I hadn't seen that, I might have a different opinion of what happened."

He eyed me curiously. "And what was your opinion?"

I shrugged. "I get it. If I had a family I loved that much, I'd probably act the same way."

Aaron's laughter carried through the canyon walls. "I find that hard to believe."

"You've got a lot to learn about young Kimberly. You'd be surprised. I once hit someone over the head with a lunch tray for taking my diary."

His mouth fell open, and I continued. "These girls liked to steal my stuff, and I had to show them I meant business. So, I attacked this girl, and Chris had to pull me off her. I wouldn't let go of her hair."

"Holy shit! You're hardcore, Burns. I had no idea." Aaron was smiling from ear to ear.

I savored that look, knowing everything that was going on. His natural state was this carefree, fun person—only, lately, he never had the opportunity. Neither of us did. But there, in the shadow of the trees, it felt like we were completely alone for once. The world was falling away and our worries along with it.

"Tell me a good memory you have of your brothers."

We pushed farther into the ravine. The rocks greeted us with an assortment of colors. Steel grays and blues mixed and contrasted with the dark-chocolate dirt beneath our feet.

"Well, they never missed a single one of my baseball games. Don't be too impressed; I was the worst one on the team." Aaron laughed. "They also never missed any time Presley appeared as a mascot, and I truly mean not one. Even when they moved out after they turned eighteen, they picked us up from school every day because my mom was always working."

Aaron kept his gaze ahead, a sense of sadness lingering in his words. "I could count on them for everything. If I got too drunk at a party, they'd drop everything and come get me. My dad left when Presley and I were young. He was never there for them, so they wanted to be there for us."

"They sound pretty great, and I can't believe you played baseball."

I smiled, thinking about what his childhood must have been like. Very different from mine. Filled with family Christmases and fun high school memories. When I was younger, I might have felt jealous. But I just felt bad for him. It was one thing to never have it and another to have it get ripped from you.

"I give them a hard time now, but I know they didn't mean for any of this to happen. I've been kinda an asshole to them lately, and I feel bad about it. I'd still do anything for them . . ." Aaron turned to me. "Sorry, I'm getting cheesy again."

"No, it's okay. Cheesy is good." I kept my eyes trained on the rocky path spread out before us. "Wow, this is some rough terrain."

I was partly joking, though I had never hiked in that part of the mountain before. I normally picked grassier areas closer to the woods. I analyzed the assortment of rocks all around our feet and spotted a grayish-blue one, entirely unique from the rest. I picked it up. It was smooth and had small golden flakes.

"Too rough for the greatest hiker that ever lived?" Aaron's wide smile was back.

"Ha! I wish. If I could just stay up in the mountains all day, I would."

Aaron chuckled. "Why don't you? It's not too late to change your major."

The dirt clumped beneath our feet. The sound of my soles hitting the ground brought a comforting melody to my ears.

"I just don't see myself making a lot of money in that. You have to make a lot of money here to support yourself, and I don't want to struggle. Doesn't it seem smart to choose the option that makes more money?"

Aaron shrugged. "Not if you'll hate it. Don't get me wrong, you'd be a great psychologist, but you won't find this in an office."

He gestured to the expansive wilderness around us. Tall pines and redwoods stood like giants and complemented the canyon walls. The rushing waterfall roared in the distance. Its echo beckoned me forward into the wonderland. He was right. Fresh air was hard to beat.

"You've got a point." I paused. "Here. For your rock collection. Maybe we can start a new one." I placed the rock in Aaron's hands.

He looked at it, turning it over a few times. "You've got a good eye,

Burns. Thank you. I like that idea."

We peacefully walked in cadence until a huge stream separated us from the other side of the trail. The water rushed in and out, covering almost all the rocks. There was no definite way across.

"Uh-oh, maybe we should go around." I peered down the bank. "I bet if we head down, it won't be as rough."

"Nonsense." Aaron rushed toward me, and I found myself suspended in the air. He grabbed my legs and pulled me to his back. I had no choice but to hold on to his neck. "Is this necessary?"

He was steady as he waded into the rushing water. The cool water splashed up and hit my exposed legs, sending a shiver down my spine.

"Probably not." He chuckled.

The atmosphere was still and tranquil in the wake of the setting sun, the sound of the water peaceful and smooth.

He was right. It was easier. My body relaxed into his, and every muscle melted in his warmth. The soft breeze brought a whiff of his mint shampoo to my nostrils. It wasn't an uncomfortable place to be.

Soon, we made it to the campsite. Aaron helped me unpack everything and set up the tent. He cooked me some hot dogs and cracked jokes. I wrapped a blanket around me as we settled by the fire. The fire lit up his face in a warm glow that complemented his eyes.

"Ah, nice, warm fire. One might say it's a little romantic." Aaron rested his back against a tree stump.

"Yeah, I'm sure that's what you say to every girl by the fireside." I raised my eyebrows, taunting.

"Oh, please, you're exaggerating my skill with the ladies. Plus, I'm not putting 'the moves' on you. I'm just stating a fact."

My face felt hot, and I blamed it on the fire. "Ouch. I'm not good enough to put moves on?"

Aaron sat up. "Whoa, whoa, whoa. That's not what I meant. I just don't want you to see me as some creep."

"Well, I don't think you're creepy. I'm happy you're here."

His eyes twinkled in the shadow of the fire. "Wow, someone's feeling open today. I'm happy too. You're fun to hang out with. Kind of a stubborn pain in the ass sometimes—but fun."

I was convinced every word Aaron spoke was true. Even his jokes had a level of truth, which was rare in a person.

I leaned back and listened to the sounds of bugs chirping in the night. Our silence wasn't hollow. A warm feeling surged in my chest. It was calm yet exhilarating. A sense of familiarity came with the smell of the pine. Warm. Comfortable. Happy.

"What are you thinking about?" Aaron's gaze was heavy with curiosity.

"I think this is as close to home as I've ever felt."

My heart skipped a beat at the thought. The moment was perfect, but I couldn't put my finger on why. I had been out there so many times before. What made this time so special?

"Does this include me?" He narrowed his eyebrows expectedly. "Yeah, I think it does."

The smoke twirled up and disappeared into the night sky above us. I inhaled the smell of burning wood and savored it.

Aaron spoke again. "Have you ever had anyone hike with you? Did any of your foster families take you?"

"Chris used to come with me sometimes, but no one has ever enjoyed hiking as much as I do. Some of my foster families brought me with them, but you'd be surprised how many take in kids but exclude them from the rest of the family."

"They excluded you? I find that hard to believe. You're like the most perfect rule follower I know."

"I wasn't always that way. I was put in a lot of homes when I was younger, but they weren't good. One of them even accused me of stealing. Which I didn't."

"Jesus, that's harsh. Do you have any good memories of it?"

"There are a few. Once, when I was around maybe ten years old, I got put into a home with another little girl my age. Her name was Dusty, and she was like a sister to me. Probably the closest I ever got to feeling like I had a sibling. I stayed with them for a little more than a year. We still write to each other sometimes."

"Wow, maybe she can come and visit, or you could go visit her. Hey! We could go on a trip. It would be fun."

"She lives in London now."

"London? All the more reason to plan a trip. Do you not ever think of traveling?" Aaron scooted closer as the wind blew the smoke nearer to his face.

"I guess I didn't. Not alone anyway."

Aaron's smile widened, and I knew what he was going to say. "Well, you're not alone now, are you? You have me . . . and my brothers. Not sure if you want them, but they are there."

I contemplated the truth in his words. I wanted to believe them. But Aaron's brothers didn't know about me, and I doubted Zach and Luke would be happy about me knowing their secret. But the small hopeful part of me dared to imagine a life where they did.

If we were to have told them, then they'd find our rogue vampire a lot easier. Best-case scenario: once we solved our mystery, we'd get to move on. We could continue to go to Black Forest University together and go to football games in the fall. Maybe the people following Aaron and his brothers would give up eventually, and we could all be safe . . . together.

I shuddered at the thought. That was the first time I had allowed myself to contemplate a future with anyone else for more than a few seconds. I sat for a minute and allowed myself to think on it and hope.

Aaron's laughter turned cold as he stared into the fire. "Kim, I need to tell you something."

I hugged the wool blanket wrapped around me a little tighter. "Okay . . ."

"If we have to leave, I promise that I'll come back for you. I would never leave you here alone, and I won't just leave without telling you. So, if I disappear because something happens to me, I just need you to know how important you are and that I wouldn't abandon you."

"You're leaving?"

"No! Just. I don't know how this is all going to play out, and I wanted you to know that just in case."

My heart was beating harder in my chest, and I couldn't look away from Aaron's gaze. No words would form on my lips.

"I'm sorry I dragged you into all this." He smiled softly, little bits of his blond hair resting on his brow.

"Come on, no more apologizing. I think we are past that, aren't we?"

"I guess you're right." He was close to me, our knees touching. "W-Would you be okay with telling my brothers? I'm kinda wondering if that needs to be our next step here. We're out of leads, and I don't want you to get hurt. It's harder and harder to get my brothers to keep you safe without telling them anything."

"I've had the worst feeling about telling them ever since the formal. I don't know why. But I think it logically makes sense to tell them. Do you think they'll get really mad?"

Aaron grabbed a twig and drew a smiley face in the dirt. "Mad at me, definitely. But you, no."

"Okay, let's do it, then," I said, my heart beating faster at the thought.

"Cool. We'll tell them tomorrow, then." Aaron studied me. "I still don't get why you're not totally freaking out and running away from me after everything I've put you through. You're so calm."

"I'm just happy with my choices. I don't want to run away from this . . . from you."

Aaron's eyes pierced right through me. Crickets echoed in our silence. "You don't want to run away from . . . me?"

"Yes, believe it or not, Aaron, I enjoy your company." I pushed out a laugh, feeling a little breathless.

"I enjoy yours too, Burns." He smirked, closely watching my face.

I admired him for a moment, and the way his eyelashes touched the wisps of his hair. His golden-brown eyes sparkled in the glowing flames. My heart thumped louder in my chest. Aaron had an incredible magnetism to his soul. I often struggled to get out of his gravity, but my attempts were futile. Aaron's warmth was inescapable, unavoidable . . . inevitable. I wanted it close. To warm up the coldest parts of my soul.

A smirk danced on his lips. "You know, the dance was a disappointment for a lot of reasons, but it disappointed me for another reason entirely."

I waited in the silence, still not fully understanding.

"Will you dance with me?" He stood and brushed the dirt from his pants. He beckoned to me graciously, holding out his hand.

"You're kidding." I grimaced. "With no music?"

"Humor me."

With his signature wink, I took his hand. He waltzed me away from the ground and into the glow of the fire. He wrapped one hand around mine and the other on my waist. We swayed, and as we took our first stride, Aaron stepped on my foot.

"Ow." I giggled.

"I'm sorry." Aaron exhaled nervously. "I never said I was good at it, just that I wanted to."

"That's okay. I'll show you." I rested my hand on his shoulder and gave his other hand a reassuring squeeze. I imagined what it would be like to dance with a boy growing up. I hoped it would be at prom, but I never went to mine. This was better than that.

"Now you just feel the rhythm and sway."

Chirping crickets played our symphony. The soft silence between us didn't matter.

For a few minutes, we were just present. Enjoying every step of our dance. Our eyes met at the same time. It was almost like we were the same person sometimes. Like puzzle pieces, we just clicked.

"So, Aaron . . . crayons or colored pencils?"

He narrowed his eyes. "Uh, what?"

"If you could pick only one to use for the rest of your life, which would you pick? I'm just curious."

"Is this a test?" A wicked grin spread across his face.

"No. I'm just trying to get to know you better. There are a lot of things to learn about a person. Technically, I could start anywhere."

"Hmmm. Okay. Colored pencils, definitely."

His hand was firm on mine as we continued to move to the music of the forest. Everything around us fell away. Aaron's feet would bump into mine every so often with his off-rhythm swaying. "Oh, bad choice. Crayons are way better."

"Yeah, whatever. You lose all color choice with crayons. There are a million shades of colored pencils."

"I guess you're right, but crayons are dark and more opaque."

"Okay, I'll give you that one for using the word 'opaque.'"

I knew it was ridiculous to talk about something so trivial, but somehow, it was fun. All our conversations were so heavy. This one was light.

"What about food?" I said.

"Oh my God, I miss food so much!" he exclaimed. His voice mixed with frustration and excitement.

I laughed. "Hamburgers or hotdogs?"

"Um, I'm a true American, so hamburger."

"I think you could make an argument for both there but agreed. Hamburger."

"Hamburgers were so good . . ." Aaron's eyes glistened as he talked. "What about icing. What's your favorite?"

He opened up to me like a book, pouring out long-forgotten quirks and lost loves. I loved every bit of it. Not just hearing his, but also getting to share my favorites with someone who was interested in hearing them felt nice.

"Cream cheese. I love red velvet cake," I said.

"Me too! I'll have to make you one for your birthday. I used to love cooking and food. Luke taught me most of everything I know."

"I didn't know you cooked? Did you want to be a chef or something?" I tilted my head up to look at him.

"Nah, I just loved to cook for my mom back home. She loved it."

"Your mom. What is she like?"

We had never talked about it. I bit my lip, hoping I wasn't prying too much.

"She's the most amazing, supportive, strong person I know. I miss her a lot . . ."

I caressed his shoulder. "We don't have to talk about it if you don't want to."

"No, it's okay. I like talking about her."

He gave me a half smile as we swayed to the rhythm. Calm washed over me. With each step, everything felt right with the world. It was late, but I didn't feel tired. I didn't want to break away from him.

"I wish I could see her again." Aaron's tone grew more serious, and his grip tightened around my hand. "Do you think she could ever forgive us for this? We can't call or visit—we just left. She's probably worried. Sometimes, I wonder if I will ever get to talk to her again, and if I do . . . I wonder how mad she'll be." His shoulders tensed at the thought.

Mothers were not usually my favorite talking point. I often teared up in movies where the mom would tear down the world to get to her kids. I'd never felt such love, but Aaron had. Aaron had a mom who was probably doing everything in her power to get back to her boys. If Aaron had love like that, then I knew it would find him again. Nothing could stop it.

"Well, even though I've obviously never had any parental figures, I've always believed moms have sense when it comes to their kids. She knows you love her, and when you see her again, she'll take you back with open arms."

"R-Really?" His eyes searched mine. A sudden desperation appeared in his voice like I had never heard before. "You say the most perfect things."

"I don't think so."

I was taken aback, left breathless by the way he was looking at me.

"You do. It shouldn't be a surprise. You're perfect." Aaron's eyes locked on mine for a moment, and our dancing came to a pause.

We stood close to each other, completely still, waiting for the other to move away or to say something. But for some reason, I couldn't avert my eyes. We couldn't look away. The fire lit up his glistening brown eyes and the flecks of amber in his irises. My breath caught in my throat, and my attention shifted to Aaron's lips and his to mine.

"You should probably go to bed. We've got a big day tomorrow." Aaron released my hands and stepped away from the light.

I let out a breath, forfeiting any hope that had been building in my chest. "Yeah. Okay."

Hot disappointment prickled my face. What was I doing? What had I expected to happen? Aaron was potentially leaving—not to mention he was a vampire. We couldn't be together. What was I thinking by allowing myself to get close to a person who, in every scenario, would be destined to leave me in some way?

My neck stiffened. The once cuddly, warm air turned hard and frigid. One crack broke the dam, and all the worries I kept out came back with a vengeance. My mind flashed to me, alone in my room. The old, familiar pain and envy radiated in my chest. I felt so different from that version of myself. I hated her. I didn't want her back. I swallowed the lump forming in my throat.

"What's wrong?" Aaron was next to me, giving me puppy-dog eyes.

I wanted to collapse into his arms. I wanted his comfort. But I didn't know how. Every minute I spent getting attached would lead me down the same path as before. One where I'd end up alone.

"Nothing." I spat, retreating into myself.

It didn't matter. None of it mattered if he was just going to leave, anyway. I didn't know why I envisioned a future where things could turn out or where his brothers might accept me. Even if they did, things wouldn't end the way I wanted them to. It was always going to end in a goodbye of some kind.

Aaron frowned. "Don't lie."

Genuine hurt welled in his eyes, compounding my guilt. I squeezed my mouth shut to lessen the damage.

He stood in front of me, lightly grabbing my shoulders. "Talk to me. Please."

"I just misunderstood. I thought . . . I don't know what I thought. It doesn't matter! Because you're going to leave and everything that has happened will just be some wild memory. I shouldn't be here with you. I should have just gone alone like I wanted to do. I shouldn't have done all this stuff with you. I don't know what I was thinking."

"What did you misunderstand? I never said I was leaving. I just wanted to warn you of the possibility, so you wouldn't think I abandoned you or something." Aaron pressed in, but I pushed him away and gathered my stuff. "What are you doing?"

"I'm going to bed. I don't want to talk about this." My old wounds had split open, leaving me sore all over.

"Come on. Fight with me. I'm an idiot. Just tell me what I did, and I'll fix it." Aaron stayed by the flickering flames.

His compliance and yearning only made my head spin harder. I just wanted to do what would hurt less, and being alone hurt less.

"No. There's nothing to fix. It's fine. I can handle it."

"You promised you'd fight with me." Aaron walked closer to me, and I stepped back.

"I don't want to fight with you. I don't want to talk about it. This was all a mistake. We'll tell your brothers tomorrow, and once the vampire is found, we'll go our separate ways again. I just want to be alone."

Aaron's eyes widened, his brows furrowed, and his mouth was agape.

"What? I don't und—"

"Tsk. Tsk. Tsk. Are the love birds fighting?" William's voice crashed into our conversation.

My breath caught in my throat, and before I could blink, Aaron grabbed me by the waist and pulled me behind him. I couldn't see William in the dark, but I knew Aaron could hear him. His gaze was fixed on the tree line.

"What are you doing here?"

Aaron's voice shifted into an aggressive tone I'd never heard before.

"Aaron, just the man I was expecting to see."

Though he was far away, I instantly recognized a change in William's voice. My memory sparked. He had an accent. Irish. I faintly remember talking about where he was from at the dance, but any specifics of the conversation were blurry.

"You didn't answer my question," Aaron said.

"Do I need a reason to come see you?"

William was standing next to the tree line. Leaning against a large pine tree, he was hiding just out of sight from the light of the fire. He wasn't the same guy. He no longer sported his pretty white shoes and striped preppy sweaters. Instead, he wore thick-soled boots that he had tucked his high-waisted trousers into. He was layered in a mixture of different hues and patterned shirts and a long black jacket that went to his knees. Nothing like what I'd seen him wear before. His eyes were dark as he pulled out a cigarette. With the familiar flick of the light, I stood, frozen. The flame flared across the bridge of his nose.

We were right.

William was the vampire.

"Will you cut the bullshit? What do you want with her?" William's attention turned to me. "Ah, the leadin' lady." He spoke with venom in his voice that made my skin crawl.

"Kimberly, you're looking lovely, as always." He kept his eyes solely on Aaron as he took a puff of his cigarette.

"What do you want with her?" Aaron repeated, still standing in front of me.

"How'd last night go? Rumor has it, you left early on your hunting trip." William smirked and pushed himself off the tree before stepping into the light.

Aaron's body stiffened. "How would you know that?"

"Your brothers are a lot of things, but subtle isn't one of them," William said. "They're easy to keep tabs on."

Hunting? Aaron never mentioned hunting. The last time we'd talked about it was at the grocery store. William straightened himself back up, regaining his posture and blowing out another puff of smoke.

His black eyes finally settled on me. "How ya feeling? Last few times I've seen ya, you haven't looked so good."

That's when I remembered the thing I had forgotten. Only I hadn't forgotten. William made me forget. He made Aaron forget. The reason Aaron and I suspected Danny. The very person who made us suspicious of William. William compelled us.

With a new fire under my feet, I said, "Because of you! Aaron, we were right. He is the vampire."

"I've gathered that one, Kim."

"No! We figured it out! At the dance. But he made us forget. He wiped our memory. You still don't remember?"

William clapped a long, slow clap. "Wow, I'm impressed. I knew it wouldn't last long on you. You're too strong-willed and smart. Aaron, on the other hand . . ."

"I still don't remember." Aaron looked back at me.

"You will, eventually. I can't place permanent blocks on your long-term memory. I'm guessing you won't remember our little conversation at the top of the stairs for a while either."

"Why are you here?" Aaron's voice was cold.

William moved forward, advancing with a calculated shuffling of his feet. "I'm just having a bit of fun . . . enjoying nature."

With a flick of his fingers, his lit cigarette flew to the ground, and he stomped it out. Aaron grabbed my hand, pulling me back behind him. My heart was beating out of my chest. I could sense something shift in Aaron. His whole body was shaking.

"You know, I'm curious about you, Aaron. You didn't tell your brothers about this secret you've been keepin'. That's an interesting choice for someone like you."

A brief silence followed, and I squeezed Aaron's shoulder.

"Come on, you don't want to talk? It's not fun that way." William chuckled, his jaw set and serious. Hatred flashed in his eyes with the flames of the fire.

Aaron scoffed. "I'll answer you if you answer me."

"Why am I here? Isn't that obvious . . . vampire. She's got blood." He pointed to me. "Come on. Ask me a hard one."

"You're not going to touch her." Aaron snarled.

William took another step forward. "Do you think you could protect her from me? Don't you think if I wanted to take her right now that I could?"

Crunching the leaves with another step, I flinched, and my heart leaped in my chest.

"Wanna bet?" Aaron moved away from me, taking a step toward

William, until they were inches from each other. He was acting like another person, his hands shaking uncontrollably.

William smiled with his black eyes shimmering in the light of the fire. "Can you feel it? Your blood is boiling and rising to the occasion."

Aaron glanced down, looking at his hands, watching them silently.

"Aaron, you have so much to learn," William said.

I couldn't see Aaron's face, just his clenched, shaking hands. His eyes locked with William's. I stepped back toward the tent.

An aura wafted off Aaron. It wasn't fear. It was dark, sinister, pure evil.

The feeling made me quiver. William emitted the evil too. The menacing aura radiating off them tainted the air, and everything around me grew colder, darker.

"It's because you know you can't fight me. You cannot win. So, you let that thing take over." William's lips pressed together. "You don't look so good, Coleman."

"Stop." Aaron's voice sounded far away.

"What are you doing to him?" I clenched my fist.

For the first time, I couldn't think, fear seizing my thought process. I was frozen like a frightened, cornered deer.

"I'm not doin' anything. This is all him." William had a grin plastered on his face, and he turned back to Aaron. "You can't control it, can you?"

Aaron moved his hands over his face and groaned. I kept careful watch on William's proximity. It wasn't looking good. I couldn't protect Aaron, and I couldn't run. I fought the negative voice in my head and my stiff muscles. I'd fight with whatever I could.

"Shut up!" Aaron groaned and placed his hands on either side of his head.

"How long has it been since you've tasted blood? I'm guessing it's been quite awhile," William said.

Aaron's hands shook harder at the mention of blood. His body stiffened as he glared at William.

"I just love the young ones. You are so easy to mess with." William was speaking to Aaron in almost a whisper until his gaze landed on me. I clenched my fist to stop them from shaking.

"So reckless."

White-knuckling, Aaron pulled his hands through his hair. "You need to leave."

William's lips curled with insidious laughter. "You're making this too easy. Maybe I should just go ahead and—"

As William turned to push Aaron, I stumbled back. In the blink of an eye, Aaron placed his hand on William's chest, stopping him completely. His once-slumped shoulders pulled down and back. Aaron's head no longer swung low, as he was fully alert. He didn't look like the same man I knew as he stared William down.

"Stay away from her, or I will fucking kill you."

A shiver went down my spine. The words came from Aaron's lips but sounded nothing like him. He stood like a statue. His once-violent shaking had stilled.

The forest went silent.

William stepped back, keeping his eyes on Aaron. His face was more serious. "Now, now, no one has to die today."

He placed a hand softly on Aaron's shoulder and leaned in close to his ear. With black eyes, he stared at me, whispering something unintelligible to Aaron. Aaron stepped backward, his rigid body relaxed. He deflated before my eyes until he seemed small in comparison to William.

William licked his lips with a chuckle. "This has been fun, but I think it's time I leave you two to enjoy the rest of your night. Just wanted to pop in for a quick hello." He walked toward the trees and paused right by the tree line. "I will see you guys around." He turned to me with a crooked smile before disappearing into the brush.

Relief washed over me, and I let out a breath.

Aaron stood by the fire, staring at the ground with hunched shoulders. I rushed over to him.

"Aaron! Are you okay?"

The warmth returned to his skin. His face was a mixture of confusion and worry.

"Talk to me. Come on," I said.

He grabbed my arm to steady himself.

"I'm sorry. I don't know what that was." He stared past me into the trees. "That was . . . weird."

"Aaron." I waved my hand in front of his face and looked behind me, fearful William would come back any second.

His head snapped up, and I could tell he was really looking at me again.

"I'm sorry. I'm so sorry. Are you okay?"

"That's the question I'm asking you!"

His fingers were soft as he held my arm. "No, I'm okay. Are you hurt?" He frantically searched me, squeezing my shoulders.

"Do you not remember?" I said.

"I do. It's just . . . my head feels foggy."

The color returned to Aaron's eyes, and my wobbly legs stilled. He looked like himself again.

"Was what he said true? You haven't been hunting?"

"Kim. I've got it under control." He pulled away from me.

"That didn't look like control," I said.

"We need to go. Now. I can't protect you up here." His words still sounded harsh. Too cold for his own lips.

"What? What's happening? Tell me what he said to you."

"No. It's better if you don't know." He went to the tent, pulled out my stuff, and stuffed it in my bag. "We're going back to my house. You can stay with me. I thought I could protect you here but I can't. I have to get you somewhere I can figure out what to do."

"You're really not going to tell me?"

The breeze made me shiver as I took my bag. I searched the trees behind him, nervously expecting something to pop out. My stomach was still in knots. A fog was settling into the forest and weaved in out of the darkness.

"Kim, can you promise me you won't say anything to anyone about this? I'm going to figure this out. I'll make sure you get to go back to the life you wanted, and you won't have to talk to me again. This will be over for you."

Sadness stung my eyes. I instantly regretted my flare up of emotion and our argument. I didn't want to stop talking to Aaron. That was the problem. I wanted to be near him.

After our run-in with William, I was more sure than ever that I was scared of losing Aaron. I opened my mouth, the words lingering on my tongue. But I didn't say them. "Yes. I promise."

SIXTEEN

KIMBERLY

"**A**re you okay?" I eyed Aaron as he held a frying pan to the stove's flames.

The smell of hot oil and butter loomed in the air. We were back in the frat house kitchen, using an old cooking pan that had seen better days. The kitchen was nice and fully stocked, but it was clear no one had been taking care of the cookware.

"I've told you. I'm fine," he grumbled as he flipped a perfectly made grilled cheese sandwich. "Please stop asking."

He wasn't his normal self. He hadn't spoken much since the campsite. Since we'd met, a day hadn't gone by where he wasn't laughing—at the very least cracking a joke or two. I never thought I'd say it, but I wished Aaron was talking more. Our argument was long gone, and my sudden urge to bolt was a bad memory. I wanted to take back all the things I had said, but it never felt like the right time.

I leaned onto the counter. "Are we still telling your brothers?"

"No. Just give me some time to figure this out." His voice cut through me.

Aaron was still refusing to tell me what William said. He said it was because he didn't want to involve me anymore than he already had. It was so unlike him. Even when I insisted, because it involved my life, he stayed silent.

I sighed and moved to sit at the table. The room bustled with people. Tons of boys I didn't know passed by me, dismissing me as if I was another piece of the modern art deco furniture that littered the house.

"You just couldn't stay away from us, could ya?" Presley tapped my shoulder from behind and startled me. He grabbed the chair beside me and twisted it around to sit.

"I thought I smelled Aaron cooking in here." Luke was suddenly on the other side of me. I hadn't seen him come into the room.

The smell of food was thick in the air. The sizzling oil on the griddle filled our small silence. Their energy breathed much needed life into the room. They even seemed happy to see me, which was oddly comforting.

"So, Kimberly, you and my brother seem to be hanging out a lot. What are your intentions with our boy?" Zach laughed at his own personal joke, leaning against the doorframe.

He watched me with cautiousness. Though it sounded like a joke, the conviction was apparent in his voice.

"Is it the muscles or the hair?" Presley nudged me.

"Don't listen to them. They are just trying to be funny, as always." Luke greeted me with a big toothy grin and sat across from me.

"Hey, assholes, Kimberly is our guest. Let's not bombard her with questions." Aaron dropped a bowl of tomato soup in front of me, then placed a grilled cheese in my hand. "And we should probably let her eat first."

Luke leaned back in his chair and folded his arms with a wide grin. "I think Zach had something he wanted to say."

Zach bit his bottom lip before pulling up a seat next to me. "I'm . . . sorry about the other night. I had a little too much to drink and then the fight—"

"A little?" Aaron rolled his eyes.

Zach pointed at Aaron. "Don't interrupt me." He looked at mc again. "As I was saying, Kimberly. I'm sorry if I made things uncomfortable."

"You didn't hurt my feelings at all. It was nice hanging out together," I reassured him.

"Is it good?" Aaron watched me as I sipped my soup.

Everyone's eyes were on me. I wanted to say so much and even more needed to be said. But I couldn't say any of it, so I picked the first thing off the top of my head to talk about.

"Yeah, thanks. Did you tell them that we went camping in the ravine?"

"Whoa, whoa, wait. You guys went camping together?"

Presley's face twisted into a wicked grin.

"That sounds . . . secluded." Zach exchanged glances with his brothers.

"Oh, shut up." Aaron groaned.

"So, like, what did you guys do up there . . . you know, with all the free time?" Presley asked, steering the conversation in a completely different direction than I intended it to go.

"Okay, that's enough, Luke?" Aaron motioned for his help.

"He's right. We don't want to make Kimberly feel uncomfortable. Right?" Luke stared down Zach and Presley.

"Right," they said in unison.

"Are you still feeling grumpy today?" Zach nudged Aaron, who was standing right next to him.

Aaron turned back toward the kitchen. "I would love it if everyone stopped asking me that."

Clanging pots and pans startled me as Aaron threw them into the sink to wash them. I took a bite of my sandwich, enjoying the toast's crunch. With every minute that passed, I doubted Aaron's judgment. His brothers needed to know something. What if William showed up again at their house? What if he was already trying to trick them into being friends with him or something?

"Well, I do have something interesting to report to you guys," I said midchew.

"Oh, yes, do tell." Presley was excited again.

"I think I have a stalker."

Aaron turned to glare at me. I tried ignoring it and turning my chair toward the others. "Yeah, do you guys remember William? He's come to a few of your parties."

No recollection crossed Luke's eyes. He must not have remembered anything either. I secretly hoped it would jog his memory, but if it's like William had said, it would be a while.

"Dude, yes!" Presley smacked the table. "I think he's on the same swim team as that Danny guy."

Zach added, "That fucker gave me a bad vibe."

"Why do you think he's stalking you?" Luke said, rubbing the stubble on his beard.

"He keeps popping up in weird places. He was even camping in the same ravine we went to."

Aaron's gaze was heavy on my face. I hated lying, but a lot of truth meshed with the lie. If William was dangerous, they needed to know.

"We can say something to him if you want." Zach motioned to Luke.

"Oh, no. Definitely not. It was just weird, and I wanted to tell you, just in case you saw him around. Be careful." I stuffed the rest of my grilled cheese in my face to avoid any further questions.

Zach scoffed. "Careful? I think it's him who would need to be careful."

"Now you've done it." Aaron sighed as he finished up the dishes and returned to the table.

"You knew she had a stalker, and you just didn't say anything?" Luke said.

"Hmm. Wonder why that is? Maybe because I knew terminators one and two would overreact," Aaron said.

The group turned to face him.

"He's been like that all day," I said softly.

Guilt crept into my chest. I couldn't tell them anything without betraying Aaron's trust. But something was seriously wrong with him. He was acting like another person entirely. My stomach turned with worry.

"Oh, no." Aaron groaned and buried his head in his arms on the table. "I don't want to hear it."

"Uh-oh. Aaron's in trouble." Presley snickered.

"I'm fine! How many times do I have to say it?" Aaron lifted his head, his eyes foggy. But his voice was full of aggression.

Luke got up from his chair, walked over to Aaron, and put his hand on his shoulder. "Why don't we go talk about it in the other room?"

"Let go of me," Aaron warned.

"Nope, family talk. Come on." Luke grabbed Aaron by the shirt, forcing him up.

Aaron eyed me as he made his way to the other room. I gave him a half smile and watched him walk away.

"Don't worry. She is safe and sound," Presley called into the other room. "Now onto the good stuff. Tell us about you. What do you like to do? Aaron tells us you're a bit of a loner."

I was actually relieved with his question. I expected Presley to blow the secret any second. But he leaned back in his chair and put his hands behind his head.

"You're not supposed to tell her that," Zach said.

"Who cares if Kimberly is a loner? Lots of people are like . . . uh, that lady who writes poetry . . . or wrote poetry," Presley said.

It occurred to me they have probably never had to deal with loneliness. From Aaron's stories, it was safe to say they always had each other. From morning until night, they were stuck together.

"Shut up. Don't try to act like you know things." Zach placed an elbow on the table and rested his chin.

"Aw, don't be jealous. Some of us actually paid attention in high school," Presley mocked.

Zach opened his mouth like he was going to argue more, but I cut him off. "It's okay. It's the truth. I kinda stick to myself." They directed their attention back on me.

"All right, all right. I'm asking the questions here. So, what is your favorite thing about Aaron?" Presley's eyes narrowed.

That's when I knew things were getting serious. I expected it sooner or later, seeing how close they all were. They were definitely grilling me.

"What kind of question is that?" Zach groaned.

"Hey, I wanna know! We have to weed out the gold diggers and self-centered broads." Presley smiled. He leaned in closer, waiting for my answer.

"How could she be a gold digger if we aren't rich?" Zach rolled his eyes.

"My favorite thing? Aaron's a good person. He's got a kind heart. I can tell. I'm sure you all had something to do with that," I said, still nervous.

My voice hung in the air. The house was oddly quiet for a Saturday.

Zach smiled at my answer but laughed under his breath.

"Actually, despite us, I'd say. But yeah, he really is."

"Is there anything we should know about you?" Presley said, wiggling his eyebrows.

"Um, I'm a pretty reasonable, forgiving person. I like reading . . . hiking—"

"Oh, Aaron told us you were an orphan too," Zach said.

"Zach!" Presley shouted.

I was beginning to understand their dynamic.

Zach pressed his lips together, annoyed. "What? I'm just trying to make conversation."

"Ignore him. We all do." Presley ruffled up his hair, leaning back.

Zach stood abruptly and moved toward Presley, his shoulders squared.

It was obvious they'd all spent copious amounts of time together. They were closer than any family I'd ever encountered, not that I'd had many good examples.

Presley almost fell backward out of his chair. "Ah! No, sorry, sorry!"

"It's okay. Yes, I'm technically an orphan. But that doesn't mean much to me anymore. The only thing you need to know is I'm good at reading people. So, don't lie to me."

"A threat. I like it." Zach took his seat again, relaxing his shoulders.

"Looks like she'll fit right in," Presley said, a sly smile spreading across his face.

The doorbell's loud chime broke our conversation, and we all turned our attention to the entrance.

"Who could that be?" Presley jumped up and ran toward the door.

Aaron rushed out of the room. "No, don't open that!"

"Too late." Presley swung the door open. "Hey, Chelsea!"

"Oh, there he is! Aaron, your girlfriend is here." Presley motioned for her to come inside.

Spit caught in my throat, and I wondered if, somehow, I had missed something. She walked into the room slowly and stopped once she saw me sitting at the table.

Her once calm demeanor turned sour. "Oh, hey. Kimberly, right? What are you doing here?"

I finished chewing the last bite of my grilled cheese, then answered. "I'm just hanging out." I smiled and waved.

"Oh."

She stood there and stared at me for a moment, and our awkward silence grew. I glanced over to Aaron, who was still glaring at Presley. Presley's muffled laughter echoed in the foyer.

Chelsea turned to Aaron. "Are you still going with me to buy my new car today or not? I know we planned it a while ago, but you said you would. I've been trying to get a hold of you."

Aaron and I shared a look before he answered. "Uh . . . yeah. Just let me get my stuff. Can you wait out in your car?"

She squinted. "Yeah, sure."

"Oh, wait, Chelsea, we are all still going to that thing tomorrow, right?" Presley called to her before her thick-soled heels clomped with another step.

"It's going to be great. We invited Kimberly too." Zach nudged my elbow.

"It's out in the woods. There is camping involved," Presley said.

"We heard a lot of college students go the weekend before finals. And our tests don't come until after Tuesday, so . . ."

"Um." I stood out of place, not knowing what to say.

On one hand, it seemed completely reckless for me to agree, with William on the loose doing God knows what. But technically, finals weren't going to stop because of my vampire problem, and being with Aaron's brothers was the safest place we could be. I just had to get Aaron alone and convince him that telling his brothers was the smartest thing to do.

The fear I felt about telling them dimmed, and I was wondering if William had planted the idea in my head, that telling them was a bad idea to buy himself more time. But why would he need to do that?

"Great! It's going to be so much fun." Presley wrapped his arm around my shoulder and stared at Aaron. "Chelsea, you're coming too, right?"

"Of course I'm coming." Her eyes met mine as she spoke. "I'll be in the car."

We waited in an awkward silence for her to leave. As soon as the door shut, Presley went running.

Aaron chased after him. "What was that!?"

They ran through the kitchen and all over the living room, knocking things over.

"I couldn't help myself!" Presley's voice echoed by the stairs.

"Hey, this looks fun!" Luke appeared at the side of the room, leaning against the wall, holding a beer.

"Are you kidding?" Zach laughed and headed to the fridge.

"What? What did I miss?" Luke asked.

"The opportunity was staring me right in the face! It was worth it—Ow!" Presley groaned.

Aaron had grappled Presley into a headlock. Presley grunted with the tight grip. Aaron maneuvered him around to punch him a couple of times in the arm. When he let him go, Presley skipped away with a smile.

"All of you are to blame for the drama that is about to unfold," Aaron said through clenched teeth.

"I didn't know she was your girlfriend . . ." I smiled, keeping my tone light.

I didn't want to think about Presley's comment, not when there were so many other things going on, but I couldn't help it.

"She's not. She's just been telling people that," Aaron said.

Presley laughed. "She knows it's not true either. I just thought I'd humor her."

"Well, I don't think she likes me very much." I gave Aaron a sheepish grin.

"Oh, don't worry, she doesn't like anyone." Zach placed his beer bottle up against the counter and hit the top of it. The bottle cap flew to the other side of the room.

"Yeah, even us sometimes." Presley rubbed his arm.

Aaron sighed, searching for his keys. "Kimberly, I will come pick you up in an hour, okay? Two hours, max."

Our eyes met, and I wondered if he could see the fear in my eyes. Being split up felt wrong.

He gave me a reassuring look before turning back toward his brothers. "Will one of you walk Kimberly home?"

"You don't have to do that." I got up from my chair.

"Oh, of course." Presley smiled. "Allow me. I'm a perfect gentleman."

"Do you think we'd let you do that after you just got mugged? What kind of men would we be?" Luke strode toward the front door, beer still in hand.

There was no use in arguing with them. All three of them walked me to my dorm, and I spent the next two hours in the common room where there were plenty of witnesses.

Luke put the car in park and placed his hand on the passenger seat's headrest to look at me and Presley. "All right, we're here!"

In a hurry, we piled out and pulled our stuff from the back of their car. It was an older Honda that had seen better days. Once we were in the parking lot, I knew exactly which park they were talking about. I had seen it in passing.

Large billboards lined the roads, coaxing us to come visit. Though I had lived in the town all my life, I'd never been. It was a one-of-a-kind adventure park geared toward adults. There was normal camping, rafting, swimming available but also common areas where you could eat and drink. I could see why it was a favorite spot for finals-fatigued students.

It was in a different part of the mountain from what I was used to. We traveled on long winding roads farther away from town. It was more secluded than I had expected, and also less kitschy. I expected an amusement-parklike structure, with huge gaudy signs and maybe a few animated animals. Instead, it was the mountain itself that greeted me. The park appeared to blend into the scenery, as if they were made together.

"Hey, guys."

Aaron's voice came from behind me. He had his arm wrapped around Chelsea's shoulder. She stumbled over her long, flowy cover-up. Her long blonde hair was perfectly curled underneath her sun hat. They rode separately, and I was having a hard time gauging how I felt about the whole thing. Aaron was acting more and more strange by the hour. Despite staying the night in his room again for protection, he left me alone all night and only said a few words when he came in to check on me. It was safe to say I didn't get any sleep.

Aaron met my eyeline. It was brief, and he averted his gaze to Luke. The look in his eyes was unsettling, and it left me with a cold chill.

"Trying to turn a few heads, I see." Presley chuckled, looking Chelsea up and down.

She smiled and moved herself to take Aaron's hand. "Always. I'll probably need to borrow one of Aaron's hoodies later. Are we ready to go inside?"

I caught myself in a troubling thought. Was I . . . jealous? It was the same feeling I had at the dance, watching them dance together. But there was no reason for me to be jealous. Aaron wasn't mine, after all. He was free to do whatever he wanted and date whoever he wanted. But it was still strange seeing him interact with her, even stranger that it came out of nowhere. If I didn't know any better, I would have guessed he was doing it on purpose.

Still, I found myself averting my eyes from his hand on hers.

"Kimberly needs to change!" Presley grabbed my shoulders from behind.

I examined our group, realizing I was the only one not ready. I packed so fast I forgot to change into my bathing suit. The boys were already wearing their board shorts and shirts in different colors and patterns. Presley's were the brightest.

"Uh, no, that's okay. I can wait until we get inside." I shifted my feet uneasily.

"Yeah, but the faster you get changed, the faster we can get to the fun," Luke said.

"Fine." I caved and grabbed my bag from my shoulder. It wasn't hard to find the changing area. A little building in the corner of the parking lot hosted a swarm of girls hanging around the entrance.

I caught a few glimpses of the river flowing through the trees in the distance. Loud, thumping music coming from the cars in the parking lot drowned out the rushing water.

"I'll come with. I need to check on my hair." Chelsea was hot on my heels and wrapped her arm around mine as we made it through the door.

I knew it had to be a trap. My heart was in my throat when she led me next to one of the dress stalls.

"Okay, let's cut the shit. Do you like Aaron?"

Warmth pooled in my cheeks. "I—why are you asking me that?"

Chelsea sighed and ran her black acrylics through her hair. "Because I'm not an idiot. I can see it going on right before my eyes. I just want to clear the air because I'm not trying to step on anyone's toes. If you like him, I'll back off."

"I-I . . ." I desperately wanted an out. I wasn't ready to answer that question.

Not when my world quite literally felt like it was falling apart, and the last real conversation between Aaron and me had ended in an argument.

Aaron meant more to me than I wanted to admit. He was definitely my friend, but did I want more? I thought back to the forest, to us swaying in the moonlight, crickets chiming their symphony. For a moment, I wanted more. In a fleeting moment, I wanted his lips on mine.

But he pulled away. He pulled away, and I pushed him away. That's how I needed to leave things. It would be a lot less messy for the both of us. I'd just had to forget about that fleeting moment. Forget I ever allowed myself to get sucked into that fantasy.

"We're just friends." I saw myself in the reflection as I said it. My eyes were hollow, and my cheeks tugged into a tight-lipped smile.

"Good." Chelsea turned to the mirror and pulled her hair into a high ponytail with her sparkly scrunchie. "Because I thought he liked you. That's the vibe I got from him at the formal, anyway."

My heart steadily beat against my ribs. I had no idea what she was talking about. I hadn't noticed anything. Aaron actually went out of his way multiple times to make it clear everything was platonic. I was the only one who slipped up for a second and thought I was feeling something more, or at least that's what I thought.

"Well, now that that's out of the way"—Chelsea dragged lip balm across her lips—"I'll let you get dressed, and I'll wait outside with the boys."

She sashayed out of the changing rooms with a new pep in her step, and I stood silent for a moment.

I had to stay focused. None of this was going to matter if we were all dead. I wasn't sure what William was capable of, but I knew he was an older vampire, and I knew he was strategic. I wasn't one hundred percent sure of his motive either. He stated I was his only goal, but he'd had so many opportunities to take me before. Like in the coffee shop. But maybe he was playing a game in which Aaron and I posed as his little pawns. Maybe he liked to see us squirm and suffer. I had to convince Aaron to tell his brothers, and to do that, I needed to know what William whispered to him.

I quickly changed my clothes and headed out. It definitely wasn't a place I wanted to be for a long time. Something about the crowded changing room made me nervous.

To my surprise, as I walked out, my friends were waiting by the front. The boys' faces all twisted into smiles.

"Are those board shorts?" Presley smiled bigger than I had ever seen.

"What?" I opted for board shorts and a long-sleeved shirt. It seemed more practical to me. Plus, I had a scar to cover. "There are rocks and stuff . . . you know?"

"Totally. Makes perfect sense." Luke held up his thumb.

"You look great!" Presley and Zach said simultaneously.

But I was starting to pick up on their cues and their mischievous tendencies. "Are we going to go in, or what?" Aaron avoided eye contact and turned toward the entrance.

Chelsea giggled and squeezed herself closer to Aaron. She smiled in my direction, more relaxed. I was thankful there wouldn't be any more animosity between us.

"We aren't trying to make fun of you." Zach walked around to my other side. "Promise."

I stumbled around awkwardly and let them lead us through the parking lot and up to the ticket booth. Aaron and Chelsea walked ahead, and I tried not to stare.

I scoffed. "Oh, I know exactly what you were doing."

"Do tell," Zach said.

"You wanted me to come out in a skimpy bikini to make Chelsea jealous." I smiled a little at the thought, then shoved it deep down inside. It wasn't a competition.

"Holy shit. She's a psychic." Zach chuckled, sounding almost proud.

"Or she's already getting scary good at reading us," Luke said.

"You guys just want a front-row seat to a real-life soap opera," I said.

"Yes. Definitely, that's it," Presley said.

Aaron and Chelsea walked hand in hand ahead in front of me. "Is that why you invited me?"

"Oh, no. We invited you because we like you." Luke sandwiched me between him and Zach.

"I don't know. It seems like you guys just worship chaos," I said.

Zach smiled. "I can see why you'd think that. But sometimes, chaos must ensue for the greater good."

"She gets it! Damn, Kimberly, you're already fitting in perfectly." Presley nudged me.

Happiness bubbled up in my stomach, but I tried not to let it show too much on the surface. It was comforting to be included in their group. But also guilt-inducing. I wanted them to know the whole truth and rid myself of the heavy weight in my chest.

The air was warm as the breeze hit my skin. The trees swayed, their branches bending softly with each gust. I was stopped abruptly by Aaron's back.

I stumbled backward apologetically. "Sorry, I wasn't paying attention." Aaron ignored me and stared straight ahead. His shoulders were rigid, his fists clenched.

"Is that the guy?" Presley leaned around Aaron.

"What guy?" Chelsea's voice chimed.

I peered around Aaron, where William was casually buying a ticket at the counter. He had a big bag and a tent strapped to his shoulders, and he was back to wearing his school attire.

"Yeah, that's him." Aaron's voice was cold.

"What do we do?" I muttered. My heart started beating faster as I remembered the night before.

William turned around and spotted us. He smiled nonchalantly and waved at our group.

"Oh. He is definitely following you, huh?" Presley's voice was concerned. "Isn't that the guy you were dancing with at the formal?"

"Uh yeah, he turned into a stalker."

The words came out awkwardly, the simplest definition I could muster.

"Stay behind me," Aaron said.

"Uh-oh, someone's getting protective." Presley snickered.

Luke and Zach huddled in closer, shielding me from my surroundings.

Aaron propelled forward, and Chelsea stayed closer to the back of the group.

I struggled to keep pace as we pushed forward indefinitely. Just when I thought my life couldn't have been more complicated, William had to show up.

SEVENTEEN

KIMBERLY

"What the hell are you doing here?" Aaron's voice echoed in the canyon walls. He stopped in front of William with a straight spine. William and Aaron were virtually the same height, but Aaron had a slightly smaller build. That didn't stop him from getting in William's face.

"Oh, hello, I just noticed you guys over there." William peeked behind Aaron to speak to me. "Traveling with the pack today, I see."

He was flipping a coin between his fingers. His lingering accent was long gone. He was back to hiding and playing the role of a regular college student.

"Yeah, you could say that." I forced a smile.

I was thankful Chelsea was there. Things might have gotten a little messy if she hadn't been.

"Are you following Kimberly?" Luke said.

"Why would I do that? You must be Aaron's brother, Luke. I've heard so much about you." The smug smile never faded from William's face.

I watched Luke's face closely. I wanted him to remember what happened on the stairs, but after a few seconds, I gave up on that hope.

"From who?" Zach studied him.

"Come on, you're holding up the line!" a random guy from behind yelled.

I hadn't noticed, but we were standing right in front of the entrance booth.

"Oh, don't worry. I already paid for them." William held up the passes and flailed them in the air. "Here, keep the change." He took the coin and flicked it toward Aaron with his thumb.

In the blink of an eye, Zach grabbed the coin before it reached Aaron's face. He held it tightly in his fist before letting it drop. His shoulders grew stiff, and his frame moved to protect Aaron.

I couldn't see his face, but the tension grew.

Luke placed his hand on Aaron's shoulder. "Come on, Aaron—Zach, let's go inside."

William's smile grew, and his eyes darted between the three. Aaron grunted but let his brother push him forward and away from the booth. Zach loosened his stance but kept his eyes firmly on William.

We entered the park, and I nearly stopped in awe. I had seen the mountain but not like that. A lush enclosure towered above, casting shade over us in front of the walking area. The canyon walls surrounded us on both sides. Somehow, the park was wedged right between the entrance of the canyon. As the walls expanded, so did the park. There was tall iron fencing stretching along the border that disappeared into the trees.

We followed the walking trail and stopped in front of a large tree. Vines wrapped around its trunk and covered it in little pink and white flowers. A division forked the trail, and we huddled at its crossing. I could finally get a good look at William. His hair was smoothed back, and he had on dark long sleeves and black board shorts that displayed the university swim logo in big white letters.

William's dark eyes ran through me. "I think camping is this way."

Aaron stepped in front of me again. "Why are you here right now?"

William matched his distance. "Same as you. Just a little fun."

"It's okay, let's just keep going," Luke said, watching Aaron.

"You don't know him like I do," Aaron spat back.

"Yeah, I don't know about this, Luke." Zach kept his eyes trained on William.

I shifted my feet. I was safe among the group, but I wasn't confident in their ability to stay calm. We were on the edge of causing a scene when the park guide spotted us.

"Hello, are you new to the Mountain Top Park?" A burly man with a blood-red park T-shirt interrupted us. "Sorry to startle ya. I just noticed you guys are packing some luggage. Are you here to camp?"

"Totally!" Presley cleared his throat and placed his hands in his pockets.

"All right, everyone who is camping, come over this way! Be sure to have your ticket stubs ready." He guided us through the trees and closer to the riverbank's soft trickling water.

Other guides were ushering in the strangers, and their voices carried in the echo of the canyon walls. The scene at the riverbank was pure chaos. Guides waded knee-deep in the water, pushed off its banks, then filed into the blue rafts.

Our guide gathered his hands in a single clap. "Okay, bros, this is how this is going to work. I'm going to need to do some bag checks. Don't worry, I'm not here to judge. Just gotta make sure you're not here with any illegal substances."

His voice was mellow as he continued explaining the list of illegal things. Our group was still staring daggers at each other. We weren't paying attention. "All right, enough talking. Place your bags on this cart here. We will get them checked out, and they will be left for you to pick up at the campsite location. You can locate your assigned campsite by the number on your ticket."

Afterward, we followed instructions and handed over our bags before he ushered us toward another table of life vests and helmets.

All the nervous energy was getting to me. My stomach dropped as I stared at the blue being tossed about in the rushing water. "Are you guys needing any help with your gear?" The guide stopped in front of us.

"No, we got it. We've been rafting tons of times," Presley said as he grabbed his helmet from the table.

Luke grabbed another one and handed it to Aaron. He leaned in to whisper something in his ear.

"Uh-oh," I mumbled. I held up one of the neon-yellow vests and tried to watch the others around me put theirs on.

"Have you never been before?" Zach was in front of me, putting on his vest. "I figured you had since you've lived here so long."

I had moved my vest to my shoulders, fussing with its buckles. "Uh. No, I think I got it, though."

"I can help you." Zach watched me with amusement. "Or watching you struggle is pretty funny too. I could continue doing that."

He grinned despite the deep indentation between his dark brows.

I threw my hands up in defeat. "Fine. Yes, I need your help."

"Ah, you broke so easily. Here." He helped me put it over my shoulders. "Then these straps will go under you. That's the only real difference. I'll get you a helmet. Hold on."

"Hey. Zach?"

He stopped and turned around to look at me. "Yeah?"

"Can you just watch Aaron? I'm worried something is off." I motioned to William, who was also getting his gear on.

I wanted to tell him everything. The danger. The fear. The uncertainty.

Zach smiled sincerely. "I'm way ahead of you. And don't worry about that guy. He won't get near you. That, I can guarantee."

With those words, he turned around and headed for another table. I waited and tightened my vest, looking around. Presley was playing around, with his vest already on.

Chelsea had her stuff on and was standing by Aaron and Luke.

The boys were talking too low for me to hear.

William stayed on the other side of them. He stayed casual but caught a glimpse of me and winked.

I sighed aloud and turned away. There was no relief from the stress I was feeling. I was about to start my counting when Zach appeared.

"Here it is." Zach appeared next to me and put on my helmet. I moved the strap under my chin and clamped it loosely.

"All right, you guys all check out. Are you ready to board?" The burly guy came back up beside us. I could barely see his lips hiding behind his unruly beard.

"Yeah, we are!" Some of the boys let out excitedly, mostly Presley and Luke.

We moved closer to the rafts, and I fell behind. Luke and Zach were leading the way toward the roaring river, and Chelsea was busy asking the guide about summer jobs. A hand grazed the middle of my back. Aaron was ushering me forward. He didn't say a word and kept his eyes on William. I longed for us to find a place alone. To slow down and figure everything out . . . together. We all stopped in front of a rubber raft that was beached on the thousands of small rocks covering the water's edge. The water was clear and smooth underneath the calico rocks.

"Hey. Wait." Aaron moved his hands to my helmet and pulled the strap tighter. His finger grazed my chin, and my heart jumped in my chest. Somehow, he felt like him again. Our eyes met, and despite the cloudy skies, his eyes burned like liquid honey. "There. That's better. Safety first."

My cheek was on fire where his finger lingered. "Thanks . . ."

"All right, your group is next." Our guide was knee-deep in the water, holding our raft steady for us to enter.

"Looks like we will all be able to fit. Perfect." William smirked as he turned to Aaron.

"We're not going anywhere with you," Aaron spat.

His brothers were instantly at his side. Zach and Luke took to his shoulders, and even Presley flanked him.

It was shocking to me how quickly their body language changed. "Come on. What's he going to do with all of us here? It's just a raft ride. We're here to have fun, remember?" Luke grabbed Aaron's arm, but Aaron didn't lose determination.

"Why's he acting like such an asshole, then?" Zach scoffed.

"Guys, I don't think this is the place to be doing this. We have some lovely ladies with us, who I'm sure didn't come to see us fight." Presley's voice was soft.

"Really, come on." Chelsea huffed. "He seems like a normal guy, and he paid for our tickets."

"There, listen to their reasoning. You wouldn't want to cause a scene." William smiled and stepped onto the raft.

"That's right, come aboard. Watch your step. I need strong rowers to come right over here." Our guide was still extremely energetic despite sounding like he was reciting from a well-rehearsed script.

Aaron's brothers filed in the boat after William, and I followed Chelsea.

Aaron stayed on the shore, watching us with disgust.

"Come on, bro! We don't have all day. These waters are moving with or without you." Our guide flashed him a toothy smile, moving the raft into position. Aaron moved reluctantly to the raft without saying another word.

"All right, guys, my name is Jared, and I'm going to be your guide today. Someone told me that you guys have done this before, so I'm sure you're familiar with our movements. I'm going to be in the back, steering and telling you guys what to do. So, follow my lead."

The boys chattered excitedly as we started to move. I grabbed my paddle, pulled my elbows in, and braced for our journey.

As the sun beat down, it became blatantly clear my day's struggles were not over. I sat casually next to Chelsea, who was much more interested in talking to me, and told me about her studies and expressed her readiness for finals. I was pleasantly surprised that we had some things in common, but I couldn't enjoy the small talk.

Aaron and William sat on opposite sides of the boat, right in the very front. They were in competition with each other from start to finish. Our guide constantly had to stop and talk to them about working as a team. Though, it didn't help us from spinning our raft around and hitting things. Zach and Luke were busy watching William like a hawk, while Presley was constantly poking me in the back, telling me jokes. It was amusing, though, and after a while, I was ready to get off the hot piece of plastic.

It took us twenty minutes longer than the rafts around us to reach the shore.

"All right. Your stuff should be available to check out with your ticket stub. Thank you, guys." Jared sounded much less excited.

Our first step on shore introduced us to an open area, where food carts created a small food court with wooden tables and benches and an area leading to a couple of swimming holes.

"I guess this is where we part. Thank you, guys, for having me. Enjoy your time." William collected himself, and my "bodyguards" shuffled me toward the back. Despite being smothered by them, William continued to make eye contact with me. "See you around."

We watched in silence as he disappeared toward the swimming holes. A lump settled in my throat.

"Nothing we can't handle." Luke spoke slowly as he ushered our group in the opposite direction.

"I don't like him." Zach wiped the tip of his nose and rocked back on his heels.

"The guy did buy our tickets. That's a couple hundred dollars." Presley moved around excitedly.

"He had money. Does that make him a good person?" Aaron's emotionless expression never faltered.

"He's gone. Kimberly's safe. So, for now, I don't think we should focus on him anymore." Luke walked over to Aaron.

"Besides, I think he is just trying to get under your skin."

"Oh, it's working." Presley chuckled with a mischievous smile.

"Food. Did anyone bring food? I'm starving," Chelsea said from behind.

We shook our heads.

I still felt a little sick from rafting, not to mention the constant emotional whiplash of dealing with William.

"Aaron can take you to the food court. We can take Kimberly to the water." Presley's voice raised in excitement.

I tapped my foot and looked around. I didn't want to split up. Splitting up meant one or both of us were in danger.

Chelsea smiled. "Come on, Aaron, let's go." She dug her other arm into her bag and pulled out her wallet.

Aaron stared at his brothers as if they were talking telepathically. "All right. I'm coming."

After one final look behind me, we walked toward the springs, and the boys erupted into casual conversation.

"Hey, do you think something is wrong with Aaron?" I turned to Luke. "He has been ignoring me all day, which I assume is because of Chelsea, but he is just acting strange."

Luke's gaze floated to Zach and then back to me. "Yeah, we noticed that. It's not just you. He's been—"

"An asshole," Zach reassured.

"Well, I just don't know what to do." I kicked the dirt as we walked toward the springs. "It's so unlike him."

"I grilled him in the kitchen, but he wouldn't tell me anything," Luke said.

"Did something happen at the campsite?" Zach walked next to me with his hands in his pockets.

I paused a little longer than I should have. "No, everything was . . . fine."

"I just ask because when you guys came back, he seemed off."

"But he's been off in general, so . . ." Presley said.

"What do you mean?" I said.

Echoing laughter, splashing, and yelling rang through the mountain's walls as we continued on.

Something shifted in Luke's voice. "He just hasn't been our biggest fan lately."

"Well, all families have issues." I tried to sound as nonchalant as possible.

"Yeah, that's us. Normal family with normal family problems." Presley walked a few steps ahead of us, but he turned around to share a twitch of his eyebrows.

"I was hoping this trip would cheer him up, but I think it's having the opposite effect." Luke smiled at me half-heartedly, his gaze straight ahead. "Speaking of, are you okay being here with that guy walking around?"

"Um . . ."

I wanted to scream. I wasn't okay. I had a vampire stalker who was probably there to kill me and possibly anyone else that planned on getting in his way.

"It's not ideal . . ."

"Are you sure you don't want us to say something to him? We could probably manage to get him to leave you alone," Zach said.

"No," I said a little too quickly. "That's okay. It's probably nothing to worry about."

I didn't want them digging. Digging could be dangerous. My mind flashed back to William's black eyes as he whispered in Aaron's ear. I just need to get Aaron alone for a second.

My thoughts were interrupted as we reached the beach area. Natural pools of water blended into tall weather-painted cliffs. The water was an array of blues blending into a deep green. In the distance, I spied various waterfalls and water slides. More than a hundred people were scattered around, but there was room for more.

"I don't know about you guys. But I'm ready to actually have fun today." Presley's smile beamed. "Let's go!"

Presley ushered me toward the springs. I stumbled forward, almost losing balance. The others followed in a roar as they charged toward the water.

The water was cool on my skin. I let my hair down, immersing myself completely.

A cold silence rejuvenated my body. I enjoyed my one moment of peace. Upon returning to the surface, chaos ensued.

"Oh yeah, that's the stuff." Presley let his body float on the water's surface.

"Finally."

Luke waded in, and the rush of water hit me in the face, causing me to lose my footing.

"Kim, you can hold on to me if you want to." Zach was a few feet away. He swam effortlessly in a backstroke. His obnoxious splashing stirred the water.

"Wow." I laughed, letting my legs do the work of keeping me afloat. "You can talk to me like a normal girl, you know? I'm not some delicate little flower."

"Yeah, I know, but we can't let Aaron's special friend drown." Zach submerged half of his face under water, only revealing his eyes.

"Nah, I think Kimberly can hold her own. Right, Kimberly?" Luke chuckled.

I nodded in agreement. "See? Someone believes in me."

"Fine, but how else are we supposed to annoy Aaron? He's so protective of you." Presley spun in circles, letting his arms trail around him like an octopus.

"Trust us. Aaron hasn't brought any woman around that he gets jealous with," Luke said.

"I don't think I've ever seen Aaron get like this." Zach cast a look in Luke's direction.

"I mean, Aaron's had girlfriends . . ." Luke started.

"Quite a few, actually," Presley yelled enthusiastically.

"He's also had girls that are friends. But never has he brought someone around like you," Luke said.

I swam around to hold on to a rock. My shirt bubbled up as I moved half of my body out of the water, and I shook it out of my ears. "What are you talking about. What's so different about me?"

Luke smirked. "I don't know. What is so different?"

"I don't know." I leaned back, letting the water wet my hair again. Anything to avoid full eye contact with either.

Zach appeared on my other side. "Hm. You seem to be telling the truth. But . . ."

"We don't buy it." Zach and Luke talked in unison.

"We know there is something you guys aren't telling us. We can feel it." Zach moved in closer, closing the circle around me.

I dared to glance over at Presley, who was silently enjoying my struggles. He bit his lip, and his face was red from holding back laughter.

"Point is we need details. What are you guys hiding?" Luke leaned up against the rock I had propped myself on, his wrist visible.

Three parallel black lines that extended three inches onto the forearm. They were slender and wobbly and a little uneven. I peeked over at Zach's wrist that held the same ink. I'd never noticed them before.

"Nothing."

I kept my tone calm, but internally, I was screaming. There was no way I could convince them I was telling the truth.

Zach relaxed. "Don't worry, we will figure it out."

"They're really nosey, huh? You get used to it." Presley propped his elbows up on the rock and let his body hang. He turned and looked behind him. "Quick, get on my shoulders."

"What? Why?" I said.

"It's that game, you know . . . Marco Polo."

"What?" Zach said.

"Not even close. It's called Chicken." Luke laughed.

Presley shook his head. "No, that's not it."

"How would you know?" Zach splashed Presley, causing an outpouring of chaos.

I leaned farther into the rock as they splashed and pushed each other under the water, once again failing at their job of looking human.

Their special bond engulfed me. Being with them made time pass quickly. They made me feel comfortable and accepted, even if they'd spent half the time grilling me. I knew it came from a place of love and protection.

Aaron walked up to the water bank with a perky Chelsea at his side. "What are you doing?"

His heavy gaze penetrated our carefree circle.

"Nothin'," the boys said simultaneously.

A strange silence settled among us. Happy, young adults passed with their yelling and splashing. I wished that could be all of us. Carefree. If only Aaron and I had met in another life, maybe things would have turned out differently for his brothers too. Maybe they wouldn't have ever gotten mixed up in bad things, and they would have never had to suffer as much as they had. Maybe I wouldn't have spent so much time alone. We could have been at the Mountain Top Park just like normal college kids.

"All right. Let's go cliff diving." Presley practically sprinted out of the water.

"Cliff diving?" I fidgeted.

"Yeah, it's right over there." Zach pointed to a tall cliff nearby, a rocky ledge. Some guy in hot-pink swim shorts hurled himself off the edge and past the rocks below.

"Are you afraid of heights?" Luke said.

"Um, a little," I admitted.

I waddled to the shore. My clothes stuck to my skin, the hot sun beating down on my back.

Luke took off his wet shirt and wrung it out. "Don't worry. It's perfectly safe." Easy for them to say.

That was my first chance to get Aaron alone. I went up behind him to try to tap on his shoulder, but he was already leading the charge up the cliffs. I sighed. I'd just have to wait till we got up there. I looked around, making sure my vampire stalker wasn't following.

Water sloshed around in my shoes, and they squeaked with each step. The sun was high above the trees and peeked through the branches and dried the beads of water on my skin. I followed behind the shirtless group of men—and Chelsea, who still looked as perfect as the moment she stepped foot in the park.

My attention drifted to Aaron and Chelsea again. It might have been good for Aaron to stay focused on someone completely normal. A normal girl. Completely removed from our world. I didn't feel like a normal girl anymore. I couldn't be. Once I was bitten, my life had changed forever.

Chelsea stumbled forward every few seconds and cursed her shoe choices. Aaron patiently helped guide her up the path. I didn't like the feeling settling in my stomach as I watched his hand graze her back.

Presley trailed behind me, and I slowed down to meet his pace. "How did Aaron meet Chelsea?" I tried to keep my voice low.

I couldn't help my curiosity. Chelsea was the polar opposite of Aaron. My brain couldn't handle them being so close.

Presley watched them with amusement. "They met when we first moved here. We have a lot of sorority girls over for parties. I guess some guy tried to push her down the stairs after the party was over, and he stood up for her. She's been obsessed with him ever since."

My heart fluttered uncomfortably. "Wow, I could definitely see Aaron doing that."

"Welp, the story is—or at least I've heard—Aaron was the first guy to ever be nice to her." Presley shrugged.

Chelsea stumbled again, and her shoe flew off beside her.

"Hey, hold on!" I called, and the boys came to a halt.

"What the . . ." Chelsea stood unevenly with one foot bare. Her flip-flop was broken and wedged between some rocks. "That's just great."

"What's the holdup?!" Zach's voice carried through the trees.

"We've had a blowout!" Presley said.

I pulled my bag from my shoulders and rummaged for my water shoes, figuring we would be the same size.

"What kind of blow out!?" Luke chimed.

Presley chuckled. "Like flip-flops!"

"Oh, okay . . . Hey, Presley, tell those ladies to hurry it up!" Zach's voice echoed in the canyon.

"Ugh, we can hear you! Just shut up." Chelsea's voice was so shrill, even Presley covered his ears.

I skipped up the trail. "Here. You can have these."

It was my pair of old, tattered water shoes I used for my camping excursion when I needed to get close to the water. It wasn't much but better than nothing.

She held the shoes with her mouth agape for a moment before the corners of her mouth curled up into a smile. "Thanks."

"It's okay. Better than walking through the dirt and rocks," I said, thankful she'd taken my olive branch.

"All right. The princess has been tended to. We may resume the procession!" Presley yelled.

It didn't take us long to reach the cliff. The trees gradually became sparse, and people gathered all in one place. One by one, boys and girls danced their way to the edge and took a big leap. My stomach dropped as their bodies disappeared out of sight. I made my way to the edge, my feet inches away from the drop. The water rippled in a perfect circle as one person plunged their body straight into the water. I let out a slow breath as they swam over to the embankment.

"Kim, over here," Presley called before disappearing into an opening in the trees.

I reluctantly followed him through the small opening. Pine branches pricked and scratched my skin.

We walked out into a more secluded spot, where no one was jumping. The grass was lush, and there was plenty of room to get a running start.

"We're the only ones here." Chelsea folded her arms.

"Yeah, that's the point. One of our friends told us about this spot. Don't worry, it's perfectly safe, just a little more rocky." Presley's smile beamed, and he flung his flip-flops off to the side.

"Will we get in trouble?" I said, knowing the boys probably had no problem doing something that might get us all kicked out.

"I think we'll be fine. Live a little, Kimberly." Presley nudged me before walking closer to the cliff. It was the most ironic statement, coming from someone who was practically invincible.

"Don't you trust us?" Zach shot me a wicked smile as he moved his arms around his body and limbered up for show.

"Absolutely not," I said, smoothing a smile over my lips. "Someone go first, then I'll follow."

I stayed close to the trees and kept my attention on Aaron, who appeared to be in a different world. He stared off into the trees, his body not moving an inch.

"Suit yourself." Zach ran for the water without hesitation and did a front flip.

"See, the trick is to run, squat with your knees, and throw yourself into the air." Presley demonstrated the flip extremely close to the edge.

"Are you sure you want to jump?" Luke was watching my face. "You don't have to. I can walk back down with you if you need me to."

"No, that's okay. I'm just scoping it out. Don't worry about me," I said.

"Luke!" Presley jumped up excitedly. "Do the back flip."

He pointed out into the vastness of the water below. Up on the cliffs, we had a view of the top of one of the water walls. A series of alternating rock ledges were smooth and flat enough for some people to slide down.

Luke gave me a soft pat on the back. "See you down there." He went over to the edge and flung himself backward, easily missing the rocks below. A feat that might not work for someone who didn't have superhuman strength.

A large splash sounded below, followed by an uproar of cheering. Music blared and echoed up the mountain walls along with the constant smell of a burning campfire.

"Come on, Aaron, let's jump together," Chelsea said, with more pep than I had anticipated. She grabbed his forearm. "We can head back to the campsite early."

He was turned away, his body completely still, looking into the woods. Chelsea nudged him to get his attention, but he didn't reply.

I strolled over to Presley seconds before he was about to bound off the cliff. "Presley, can I ask you for a favor and you not ask me why?"

His brows pressed together curiously. "Sure, but it will cost ya. For friends, it's free. For family, it costs."

"What? Presley, you just met me."

"I know, but I only trust the people in my family. I trust you. So, therefore, you're family. Therefore, it costs."

I sighed. "Fine, can you distract Chelsea for a few minutes so I can talk to Aaron . . . alone?"

He chuckled. "You got it, boss. Just remember, I'm going to collect one of these days."

I didn't have time to think about what that meant, but knowing Presley, it probably meant I'd be doing his schoolwork, or he'd be asking me to do something embarrassing.

Presley playfully waved to her. "Hey, Chelsea, let me show you something over here."

She spun around. "Do you think I'm stupid? You're going to push me off."

"Me? No, never," Presley said. "Come on. I'm having a girl problem, and you're the only girl I trust to give me an honest answer. No offense, Kim."

Chelsea reluctantly followed him closer to the ledge, the fringe of her white cover-up soiled.

I made a beeline for Aaron and wasted no time grabbing his arm and pulling him between an opening in the trees, just out of sight from the others. He didn't resist. It was a tight fit, with only a couple of feet between us. Our backs pressed up against the trees, and we faced each other.

"Aaron." My voice was firm. "Tell me what's going on."

A small wrinkle separated his brows, and he spoke slowly, his eyes distant. "I feel kinda weird . . . foggy."

"We have to do something. I'm serious. We're getting you help."

I tried to hide the fear from my voice, but I knew I couldn't hide it from my face. I never contemplated the burden Aaron had to bear. He had a side he didn't want me to see. A side he couldn't keep from bubbling to the surface. It was eating him alive, and that made me unbelievably angry.

There was something different about being angered for the protection of others. At fifteen, the embers of anger were red-hot in the pit of my stomach. Longing for malice and revenge. This kind was different. It was a fire that lit up my entire body, which made me want to run to get help. It sprang my feet into action.

I'd keep pushing for whatever it took to get him better.

"I just want it to stop," he said.

I gripped his shoulders to steady him. Our bodies pressed together. "Come on. Let's just go down there and tell your brothers everything."

"No." His voice grew cold again. "We're not doing that."

"Why not?"

"We just aren't." He tried to divert his gaze, but I held him in place.

"What did William say to you?"

He stared at me, lips pressed together. After a few seconds, he shook his head. "Kim, I can't . . ."

His voice softened. Then he was the man I knew again. Soft, enticing smile and rich, warm-brown eyes. Less than a day without it, and it felt like a lifetime. His cute, fluffy hair and blushing cheeks were a sight to see.

I wrapped my arms around his neck and hugged him. "It's going to be okay. I promise we'll figure this out. You don't have to do this alone."

He hesitated, his arms pinned to his sides. His entire body felt like a rock, but after a few seconds, he wrapped his arms around my waist and buried his head on my shoulder.

He melted into me, and I nuzzled into his neck. My chest pressed firmly against his, and the world went silent. His heartbeat stayed in a steady rhythm with mine.

In the shadow of the trees, it was just the two of us. Aaron was just like me. Alone in the darkness, trying to find his place in our new world.

From the very beginning, that's who we were. We were the same in so many ways I'd never seen before.

No matter the consequences, I was going to stick it through till the end. Even if his skin on my skin felt like the most comforting, perfect thing in the world, and it would soon be a distant memory. It would be worth it.

Soon, another splash sounded below, and Chelsea's voice was close. "Come on, Aaron, Presley was just—"

I pushed away from Aaron, but it was too late. Chelsea was already staring at us with her big blue eyes.

"This isn't what it looks like," I blurted.

"I knew it. I knew something was going on." She snarled. "Just friends my ass."

She bolted for the cliffside, and we followed.

"Chelsea, wait!" I said, my voice echoing in the trees.

She turned on Aaron. "Here, you had me fooled. You like to play like the cute, innocent type. But you're just like the rest of them. Some loser who has nothing better to do than to get drunk and fuck with women and their feelings."

His eyes darkened, and his voice cut through the warm spring air with a cold shill. "Maybe you were the delusional one. Why would I like someone like you? There is nothing special about you. You're controlling, and you can't even take a hint. I never wanted you around. I just felt sorry for you."

Chelsea's face fell, her mouth agape. She was completely unguarded, astonished at the verbal assault. Her pain washed over me like fresh gasoline, igniting the guilt in the pit of my stomach.

She was an innocent bystander left in the wake of our mess.

"Aaron, stop," I said.

He ignored me, his gaze searing into hers. He cast a shadow over her petite frame. "It's sad. All the things you do for my attention. Pathetic." His lips curled into a smile. He was enjoying her pain.

If I hadn't seen him say the words, I never would have believed they were capable of coming out of his mouth.

With lips trembling, she held her head high. "Fuck you."

Her hair whipped around as she made a dash for the trees, and I followed. "Chelsea, wait. He didn't mean that. He—"

She turned with a slap to my face. "Never speak to me again." Her eyes glistened with tears. I knew the pain in my cheek was nothing compared to the pain Aaron had inflicted on her. Chelsea leaned down to remove my shoes and threw them at my feet. I rubbed the warmth in my cheek as she disappeared. The sting imprinted the truth on my face for the world to see. What we were doing was reckless. Dangerous. It was time to tell the truth.

I turned around, expecting to see Aaron. He was nowhere in sight. The only sounds came from below. The splashing carried into the trees behind me, and carefree laughter fluttered like a songbird.

"Kimberly!" Presley's voice was easily identifiable. I followed the sound to the cliff's edge where our group was waiting near the beach area.

I waved back to Presley. My stomach was still in my throat. Would Aaron's brothers accept the truth? Would they still allow me to hang out with them? Maybe they would leave without a word. Without a trace. Leaving me here. Alone. I pushed the thought out of my head. None of it mattered. I couldn't think about myself anymore.

As I turned to look for Aaron, his frame towered over me, stopping me. His eyes still looked hazy and lost. "Are you okay?" His hand touched my cheek, and I flinched. The warm amber still wiped from his irises.

"I'm fine," I said.

"You look . . . scared." His voice still sounded far away despite our proximity. I could smell his cologne and feel his body heat.

"Aaron, there's something very wrong with you." I watched Aaron's footsteps as he moved closer, forcing me back a step. The cliff's edge loomed in my mind. He closed the distance between us. My feet stuttered backward, and he grabbed my waist, pulling me closer to him.

"W-What are you—?"

He brushed my hair from my shoulder, bringing his lips close to my neck. I stood, frozen. Swallowing a breath. "You smell so good."

His words dripped with longing, the sound foreign to my ears, his breath hot on my skin. He twirled his fingers in my hair. Judging by my sweaty back and damp hair, he wasn't talking about me or the sunscreen I had put on that morning.

Placing both hands on his chest, I tried to force him back. His muscles were stone. Tense and rigid.

"What's the matter? I thought you'd like me like this?"

His breath was still hot on my neck as I shoved his chest again, this time much harder.

"No. I don't. You're being an asshole."

I fell back. Only, this time, there was no ground left to catch me. I fell into the open air. My only thought was on the rocks below.

Something firm hit me and wrapped me up before I made impact with the water. I flailed around, feeling trapped as I submerged deeper into the spring water. My hand stung, and I pulled it close to my body. With no effort of my own, I found myself pulled to the surface of the water. Water filled my throat, and I coughed, struggling to swim. Somehow, someone had pulled me up, as if I had a life preserver.

Upon opening my eyes, Aaron was pulling me toward the shallow end of the water. When I got my bearings, I pushed him off to swim by myself. Cheers and applause erupted around us. My stomach dropped as their eyes weighed me down.

Aaron didn't stop walking toward the shore as countless people applauded and patted him on the back. I swam, then walked till the water hit my knees, pulling my hair out of my face and wringing it out. A stabbing pain radiated from my hand. A large cut lined my palm. I closed my hand and wrapped it around my waist. That was the last thing we needed right then.

As I struggled to get my bearings and tried to comprehend what had happened, Aaron's brothers circled me.

They talked in a flurry around me, their voices running into each other.

"Are you hurt?" Luke's jaw was set and serious.

"What happened?" Zach said.

"Dude, you scared me." Presley grabbed my shoulders.

I couldn't help but chuckle at the sound of worry in their voice.

"Funny to hear you guys being so serious."

They relaxed with sighs of relief and nervous laughter.

"Well, if you wouldn't be so dramatic and throw yourself off a cliff, we wouldn't be in this mess," Presley said.

"He's right. What were you thinking? Who does that?" Luke placed his hand on my back, guiding me to the shore.

"Wait, where's Chelsea?" Zach said.

"It's kinda a long story," I said as Aaron barreled past us and out of the water.

Luke and Zach shared a look before following after him, not speaking a word.

Presley and I stood dumbfounded for a second. The breeze filled the silence, and we watched as college students ran around in hoards. Their laughter and screams carried through the air.

"Uh-oh, you're bleeding." Presley motioned to my hand that was still wrapped around my waist.

I released my grip, revealing the long gash oozing across my palm. It looked worse than it felt.

"I better go clean this up."

"I'll come with you!" Presley gave me a sheepish grin. "And you can explain to me this long story of what happened with Chelsea."

I reluctantly agreed and told him the bare minimum of truth, skipping the part where Aaron's eyes had turned black, and he looked at me like he wanted to eat me. I was so close to telling him. The words were right on the edge of my tongue, yet I held back.

We had to tell Zach and Luke what was going on. Everything had gone too far. But Aaron was serious about them not knowing, and I didn't know why. Would he stop me if I tried? I just needed to get Aaron alone and talk some sense into him. I was so close to getting him to open up.

Presley and I reached the restroom, and I went inside to clean my hand up. My shoes squeaked in the water that wove its way between the tiny tiles. The sick smell of dirty toilet water motivated me to quicken my pace. I grabbed a few paper towels and walked to the sink to examine my hand. The cut wasn't as deep as it looked. I put my hand under the cool water, searching for something to cover it with. My only option was my shirt. I pulled it over my head and held it in front of the hand dryer.

After ten minutes of awkward stares, I wrapped it around my hand and over my wrist. I left the bathroom with a sigh and kept my attention on the wet floor to keep from slipping.

"Guess you decided to take that shirt off after all." Presley nudged my shoulder with a carefree smile.

Thankfully, my wet hair provided a good scar cover-up.

I couldn't fight the look on my face. I was drowning.

"What's wrong? You know, other than the obvious bleeding hand you have there and getting slapped in the face."

His frown didn't suit him. If Aaron was the sun, Presley was the wind. Always moving. Free. The drooping corners of his lips tied him down in an unnatural way.

"There's something wrong with Aaron," I said.

"Yeah, I know he's been on one lately."

I stopped him. "No, you don't get it. There's something seriously wrong. I don't know what to do, and I'm freaked out. Your brothers are going to freak out, and . . . and . . ."

Presley squinted, waiting. "And?"

"I don't know what to do. Help me!"

"Okay, okay. Chill." Presley steadied me. "I think you're overexaggerating Zach's and Luke's reactions. Sure, you lied, but it's not like they haven't. I don't get why you're so scared for them to know. The sooner you rip off the Band-Aid, the better. For the record, I'm happy you know about us, and you don't hate us. That's pretty badass."

I smiled at his sentiment but quickly overwhelmed myself again with thought. "I just need to talk to Aaron first."

Presley leaned in and whispered, "The truth is, they're actually big softies. Zach, especially. Underneath that hard outer shell is a man who used to write poetry to his high school sweetheart. The long sappy kind."

"Wait, Zach had a high school sweetheart? What happened?"

It didn't shock me he had a girlfriend. He was attractive and seemingly athletic, so, of course he did. But I was curious about the details.

"They ended up breaking up when she went off to college. I think she wanted to stay, but Zach basically told her he couldn't be with her because of . . . you know." He shook his head. "Anyway, Aaron will cool off eventually. He always does."

"He's been like this before?" I said.

"Yeah, kinda. Standoffish—and not to mention the big fight he got in with Zach just a couple days ago."

"He didn't say anything about a fight."

Just like he hadn't mentioned anything about going hunting.

"That's not surprising. It was intense. He yelled. Zach almost broke a light pole. Then he just stormed off. He hasn't been right since."

"Was this on your hunting trip?" I said, lowering my voice a bit.

"Oh, so you know about that kinda stuff, then, too? Sweet. Yeah, it was."

"Did Aaron drink blood on your trip?"

The words felt weird coming from my mouth, but there was no way around the question. I had to follow the thread.

Presley eyed me suspiciously. "Yeah, we all did. We don't kill people, though. You know that, right? He told you?"

"Yeah, yeah. He told me." My mind spun in circles.

Was it possible William lied about Aaron? At that point, anything was possible, and it explained a lot. Aaron did seem off on our camping trip. Maybe this was just a trickle-down effect and not as serious as I had thought, or more likely an idea William had compelled in some way.

If that was the case, Aaron might never agree to tell his brothers, and I'd need to be the one to do it. I hated the idea of doing something like that without Aaron's agreement or help, but I couldn't wait anymore. Whatever was wrong with him, his brothers had to know.

"You don't need to worry about Aaron. He'll come to his senses. As for Zach and Luke, I don't think it will be a big deal. I mean, it's not like you guys did anything dangerous. You're obviously not going to tell on us."

A lump caught in my throat. If only we had just one secret. They were all dangerous.

I spotted the twins in the distance, who were walking over from the food court. My hair was drying and falling away from my shoulders. One swift breeze, and the scars on my neck would stand out. Dropping the bomb on them in the middle of the park with tons of bystanders was probably not the best idea.

"I have another favor to ask you."

I couldn't hide my fidgeting, and Presley spun to see where I was looking.

He smirked. "You're running up quite the tab. Remember, you owe me."

The twins were closing in.

"Okay, fine. I owe you. Give me your shirt." I tugged on his blue shirt that had a little embroidered logo on the sleeve.

He laughed. "Weird request but okay."

I wrestled the thin cotton number over my bathing suit. After a few moments, Luke and Zach appeared, looking less solemn.

"There you are. Wait, why are you wearing his shirt?" Luke searched for the missing link between us.

I held up my wrapped hand. "I had to sacrifice mine for the greater good."

"Yeah, and Kim's embarrassed of her bathing suit." Presley's voice had no hesitation.

"Why didn't you just say that earlier?" Zach said.

"Aaron's calmed down a lot. He told us about what happened with Chelsea. We tried to catch up with her, but it looks like she took her stuff from the campsite and left. I know we haven't made this all that fun for you, but we promise no more slapping." Luke's grin radiated eternal optimism.

"Except, if you want to slap us to let go of all that pent up anger, go ahead." Presley leaned his face close to mine.

A soft laughter escaped my lips. "Yeah, I'm up for anything at this point."

Their attempt to lighten the mood worked, and for the first time that day, I could see things working out. I just needed to get them alone. I resolved to tell them at the campsite. With or without Aaron, I was going to come clean. They'd be upset, but maybe they would understand. We could figure out the William problem. We could do it all together.

Dark pools of purple and red filled the perfect portrait above. I never grew tired of seeing the sunset over the mountain treetops. I loved watching the sun disappear out of view, entrenched in silence. It made me feel small but secure at the same time.

The calm sound of the sleeping forest came out to play shortly after. I sat alone by the campfire and Presley and Zach argued about how to set up the tent a few yards away. I sighed and let the warmth of the fire wash over me. The cloth felt heavy on my hand. I removed the shirt and stretched my hand open and closed.

We had two campsites reserved about fifty feet apart. The other camp-sites were full, and it was oddly quiet and calm. After a long day of swimming and rafting, everyone must have been too tired to keep the party going. My whole body ached from the jump, and all I wanted to do was crawl into my sleeping bag.

A branch crunched behind me, followed by Luke's voice. "Can I get you anything? I was going to make dinner."

"Uh, sure, I could eat. I'm not picky."

"Great, um . . . I just wanted to tell you that I'm happy you came today. I know it wasn't the best day, but it was good to see Aaron smile again. I know I have you to thank for a large part of that." Luke smiled, watching my expression.

"I wouldn't say . . . large."

"Oh, I would. It's been hard for us lately, and since you came along, Aaron—he just seems happier. So, thank you."

His words warmed me with the fire. "Thanks, Luke. That means a lot."

"Don't mention it." He patted me on the shoulder and walked back toward the others.

I allowed my legs to bring me to my feet. It was right then or never. I hoped I could get through the whole conversation without puking.

I spied Aaron walking across the yard toward me, and I stopped. He had left to get us some more firewood and to scope the place for any signs of William.

"Hey, can I talk to you?" Desperation leaked in his voice, his mouth twisting into a deep frown.

"Okay, sure," I said slowly.

He didn't speak another word, and I followed after him. I expected him to stop at the tree line, but he didn't. He kept walking farther and farther into the forest. I stumbled over a few branches and unearthed roots, wading through the twilight.

"Where are we going?" I asked, trailing behind.

"Just to where they can't hear us."

After a few more minutes, Aaron stopped abruptly and turned to face me. His features surprised me. His eyes were soft and filled with worry. Pieces of his dirty-blond hair fell into his face. "Kim, I'm so sorry about today. I-I don't know what happened."

I walked a few steps closer. "It's okay. Are you feeling better?"

"No, there's something wrong with me. I don't know what to do." His voice caught in his throat.

Seeing him in pain, hurt. It blindsided me. All I wanted was to make it better.

"Come on, we're going to fix this. We're going to tell your brothers."

"No!" Aaron called out desperately. "You don't understand."

"Then, tell me. What is it? What did William say to you?" My voice echoed through the trees in sync with the birds, who were singing their last song of the day.

His eyes searched mine. "I can't—I'm scared. I don't know what will happen. I don't know what to do. This is all my fault. First, dragging you into my shit, and now, my brothers . . ."

"William mentioned them, didn't he?" I closed the distance between us and took his hand. His skin was cold, and I placed my other hand on top of his to warm it.

"He said if I told my brothers, he would kill you. And if I told you, he would kill one of them. I just needed some time to figure out what to do, but I can't think straight. I don't know what's happening to me."

"I know. That's why we need your brothers' help."

"Kim, I can't protect you. I thought I could. I want to, but—"

"You don't have to protect me. I'm not scared."

I surprised myself with how true that statement was. All the fear I'd been working through since figuring out I was being stalked by a vampire, paled in comparison to the thought of losing who Aaron was.

The world needed people like Aaron, someone who could find the good in any situation, someone who risked everything to save me twice. I couldn't let his light go out.

His eyes never left mine. The hints of warmer-lighter brown had come back into his irises. It was comforting, just like his presence always was. He shook his head. "You're never afraid."

"That's not true. I get afraid all the time." I cupped his shaking hands in mine. "I need you. You have to get better."

"Okay." Aaron's voice was stronger. "We'll tell them. We can still fix this."

Relief washed over me as the color returned to his face. Everything that had once fallen into the darkness had come back to the light. We could fix this. We still had time to save Aaron and keep his brothers safe. After all, there were four of them and one of William. This nightmare could soon be over, and I could experience the relief of coming forth.

"Come on, let's go back to the campsite." I pulled away, but Aaron had a firm grip on my forearm. I tried again to break his rock-hard grasp. "What is it? What's wrong?"

He stayed silent for a moment, his gaze settling on my hand. "You're bleeding . . ."

I looked down at my hand, only then realizing I had taken off my makeshift bandage. My wound had reopened, and the tiniest bit of blood smeared onto his hand.

"Aaron . . ."

My heart leaped into my throat as the color drained from his face. In the blink of an eye, his skin was lifeless. Hollow. The whites of his eyes black. Gray rings glowed around his irises. Void of any color. His canines sharpened into fangs.

He tilted his head, licking the tinge of blood from his fingers. It was quick, so quick he thrust me into the tree with a hand over my mouth before I could scream. The bark tore through my clothing, and I groaned in pain. Every part of my body vibrated. Aaron was shaking uncontrollably.

I shook my head, my muffled screams of protest hidden with me in the shadow of the trees. Aaron bit down on my wrist, and a white-hot searing pain tore through my forearm. Every attempt to wiggle made it hurt worse, but I managed to free my mouth.

"I know you're still in there. You have to stop." I winced as the pressure increased on my wrist. "Aaron, let me go!"

Without warning, the pressure and pain were gone. I fell against the tree and pulled my bleeding wrist to my body, holding it with pressure. The surrounding area was still, save for my staggered breath. In a matter of seconds, it was over. Aaron had disappeared into the night.

I crumbled to the forest floor. Every movement made my wound sting, and the throbbing wasn't letting up. Inhaling through my nose, I took in a long breath and let it out slowly. I knew what I had to do. Getting back to the campsite as quickly as possible was imperative. For me and for Aaron.

My adrenaline helped me get back to my feet, but the dizziness had taken over. Taking another deep breath, I attempted again, only this time, I flew forward into a tree, knocking the air from my lungs.

It was completely dark out, and I found myself walking in circles. My head was spinning, and the more I walked, the more turned around I felt. I stopped, my eyes darting in every direction, everything unfamiliar.

"Can anyone hear me?" My voice wasn't as strong as I wanted it to be. Nothing but silence followed. I made my way to the ground and cried out at the pain in my wrist. Blood trickled down my arm, and I hugged it close to my chest. My rapid breathing was the only sound in the quiet trees.

Rustling leaves and cracking of twigs broke the silence.

"Aaron?" I said.

A silhouette emerged through the trees. It took a few seconds for me to make out the face in the dark. My heart dropped.

William was standing in the clearing, looking at me with black eyes.

"I'm afraid not, love."

EIGHTEEN

AARON

A strange ringing filled my head. It wasn't just loud. It was everywhere. I grabbed my head and pulled my hands down over my ears. Incessant ringing filled every corner of my mind. The pressure that came with it was intense. Internally, I screamed for it to stop.

Just like that, the ringing was gone. I blinked a few times and tried to get my bearings. The area didn't feel familiar to me. I was walking through a clearing in the trees. It was dark, the glow of the fire casting silhouettes on their trunks. It was a campsite. No. It was our campsite.

The fog in my head lingered. I blinked, trying to focus. Somehow, I still felt like I wasn't in reality.

"Hey, Aaron." Presley jogged toward me. He met me with a smile, but it quickly turned to a frown. "Where's Kimberly?"

My body moved in slow motion. "Kimberly?"

"Yeah, short, red hair . . . our friend?"

His tone didn't match his words. Worry had dispersed in his eyes, and he panned to the woods.

I still had no idea who he was talking about. My mind was still playing catch-up. I strained my brain, trying to push back the fog and think harder.

"Guys. Get over here. Now," Presley called out.

"What? What's wrong?" Zach appeared, and I stumbled back onto my heels.

"Something's w-wrong with Aaron . . ."

Presley had only stuttered a handful of times in my life.

"Luke. Get over here," Zach muttered.

"What?" I said slowly.

Their seriousness was unsettling.

"Aaron, where is Kimberly?" Luke pulled me close to his face.

"Kimberly . . ." I closed my eyes, trying to remember. Kimberly. Of course. Kimberly Burns. How could I have forgotten her?

Luke shook me. "Can you hear me? Where is she?" His grip was firm on my shoulders.

"Why do you keep asking me that? I don't know! What's happening?" I pulled away from them. I didn't like the wide-eyed stares they were giving me.

"Aaron." Luke's voice was strong, and he stood in front of me. Time was passing quickly, and I didn't even see him appear. "I need you to focus. What happened?"

"Wha—what happened, when? Why are you looking at me like that?"

He shook his head and got closer to my face. "You left with Kimberly. What happened to her?"

Like the snap of a rubber band, my thoughts fell into place. Everything came back at once. My dull senses kicked back into overdrive, and I could smell the sweet scent coming from my shirt. I'd know that smell anywhere. Blood.

I looked down, afraid of what I would find. Red stains shining brightly in the dark night smeared my hands, almost as if it were glowing. Shock hit, and I threw my hands in disgust.

"No! No, no, no. This isn't happening. What the fuck!?" I fell backward, but Zach stopped me.

"Tell us what you remember," Luke said, his voice sharp.

They crowded me, and I closed my eyes. "I-I walked with her, and we were talking . . . I think it was getting dark and . . . I don't remember."

Her blood was so sweet it was almost repulsive. I couldn't take my eyes off my hands.

Luke and Zach were staring at each other. "You smell that, right?"

"Blood," Luke said as he peered back toward the forest again. They weren't talking about the blood on my hands.

"We have to go get her." My voice shook with fear that was consuming me. I had hurt her. I was sure of it. Nausea erupted in my stomach.

"Okay, show us." Luke moved us out of the circle, and we headed for the forest.

As I ran farther into the trees, memories resurfaced. I followed the familiar feelings until we reached an opening. The stench of blood was all over the ground.

"Kim . . ." I meant to say it loud, but it didn't come out as more than a whisper.

"Kimberly!" Presley yelled, his voice echoing in the trees.

Zach and Luke searched around in the trees, but my feet were frozen. Blood spatter littered the ground. It confirmed what I had already known.

I attacked Kimberly. This was her blood, and it was everywhere.

The weight of those words hit me, and my knees buckled. Fear paralyzed me. My head was pounding, and my body ached all over again. It was too much.

"Hey, we didn't find her. The trail of blood cuts off not far from here." Zach's voice was barely registering.

The ringing came back, and I buried my head in my hands.

Their voices were blurring into a cacophony, and I couldn't tell who was saying what anymore. I didn't care to know.

"What does that mean?" a frantic voice called out.

"I don't know. But we didn't find her . . . you know, so that's good."

"How is that even remotely good?"

"It means she's alive."

"We don't know that."

"Or something . . . or someone carried her off."

"Or maybe she just got away on her own!"

I opened my eyes, and Presley was leaning in front of me.

His voice was far away. "A-Are you okay?"

The ringing was getting louder every second. I couldn't hear the breeze flowing through the trees or the crickets chirping. My vision was darkening, as if the moon was dimming.

A strange presence crept forward. Evil radiated from the dark figure that kneeled beside me in my peripheral view. White hair was falling down, almost touching my hands. It was an apparition of a woman. I refused to look in its direction. It put its face right next to mine, and smelled of rotten flesh. Her eyes were pure white.

"Are you ready to give up?" a dark, morphed voice spoke from the apparition next to me.

I opened my mouth to speak but couldn't. My fingers had no feeling as I laid my hands in my lap. The vision in my right eye blurred. Everything around me was cast in red, slowly fading to black.

My brothers' voices were barely audible in the darkness.

"H-Hey, what are you doing?!"

"Stop! Stop!"

"Come on, get him off!"

"I can't. He won't let go!"

Deep rage bubbled within my stomach. I was about to explode. It was spreading to every cell in my body. "Are you . . . trying to . . . kill me?"

The voice of my little brother soothed the flames of rage.

Everything snapped back into reality once again. I found myself leaning over him, my hands squeezing his throat. If he were human, he would have definitely been dead.

"Pres?" I said in barely a whisper.

He smiled as he coughed. "Hey, welcome back."

"I'm sorry. I don't know what that was." I jumped off him and grabbed my chest.

My heart was hammering against my ribs, and I was seconds away from a full-on mental breakdown.

"Okay, what the fuck was that?" Zach's voice was close behind me.

Luke forced me to sit up, and he leaned on his knees in front of me. "I need you to tell me the truth. Have you drank blood in the last month?"

This time, I didn't hesitate. "No, I lied at the carnival. I couldn't do it. I couldn't control it, and I was afraid. I should have just said something."

I ended up hurting the one person I most wanted to keep safe. The irony wasn't lost on me. Nausea shot up to my throat.

"I've never seen anyone not drink." Zach directed his conversation toward Luke.

"But he just had blood when he bit Kimberly." Presley was back to his feet, combing his hands through his hair. "Why is he still all . . . scary?"

"That probably only helped him regain a little control." Luke frowned. "He needs more. A lot more."

"I'm done. I can't do it anymore." I shook my head, wanting to wake up from the nightmare I was living.

"Aaron—"

"No. I'm done. This is too much. If she's dead. I'm dead. If I killed her, it's over for me. I can't keep killing people . . . especially the ones I care about." I touched my hot face. "You're just going to have to go on without me because I'm done. I can't live with myself anymore. I want this to be over."

"Look at me." Luke pulled my hands away. "You didn't kill her. You want to know how I know? Because you are you. You are still Aaron. You care about her. I know you do. So, that's why I also know she is out there somewhere, and we're going to find her." I searched for doubt in his eyes. There was none.

"But . . . how . . . how do you know? How are you so sure?" I choked back tears.

I felt five years old again. Begging my brother to help show me a way to get back on my feet. But out of all my rock bottoms, this was the lowest. I didn't think there was a way to keep going.

"Because I'm your older brother. It's my job to be sure. We need you." He gently held out his hand, palm facing up.

But I knew it wasn't meant to help me up. I placed my hand on top of his, and he sandwiched it with his other hand. I completed it with my left hand. It never failed. When Luke held out his hand to me, it felt like he was giving me some of his strength.

"No one is dead. We're going to find her. I promise." Luke smiled.

I wiped the wetness from my eyes. Luke always kept his promises.

"What if she ran away and went to the police?" Zach said.

Presley was next to him, still rubbing his neck.

"Then, we will figure it out." Luke pulled me up from the pile of dry leaves and prickly branches.

"I-I don't think she would do that." Presley shifted nervously.

"She just discovered vampires exist. It's probably her first instinct," Zach said.

Presley talked through gritted teeth. "I was going to keep this secret for longer, but considering the circumstances have changed, I feel like I have to say it . . . Kimberly knew we're vampires." My older brothers both turned to me.

"You told her?!" Zach snarled.

"No, I didn't! Well, I did but not like you think." I interjected.

"Aaron bit her." Presley gave me a sorry expression. "I'm just trying to help."

"What? So, she's known this entire time?" Zach said.

"I called 911 that day in the forest when you guys found me. I never thought I'd see her again and then I found out a few days later that she went to BFU. It was like fate. I don't know! I apologized, and after talking, she didn't want to press charges or anything. Then she got mugged, and it just progressed from there."

"Aaron, what the hell were you thinking?" Luke sounded more disappointed than angry.

Zach was on the verge of blowing a gasket.

"If you're taken to jail, they will find us and our location immediately. You could have gotten us all killed."

Presley stayed silent but went to stand beside me for moral support.

"I know! Okay, I know. I was just so happy that I didn't kill her, and I wanted her to know she was safe. I messed up. A lot, apparently." I sighed, pulling my head into my hands again. The ringing was ever present. "And . . . you're about to get a lot more mad at me."

Zach was giving his death stare. "There's more?"

"Kimberly's mugger was a vampire . . . and that vampire is named William. He almost attacked me and Kim on our hiking trip, and I couldn't say anything because he told me if I said anything about it that he'd kill her."

"I fucking knew it." Zach snarled and threw his hands up.

"Okay, Aaron's giving me a run for my money for the most reckless brother award, and I don't like it," Presley said.

"That could be where she is. Maybe he took her." Luke perked up.

"Wait, he's here?" I tried to think back on the day, but I couldn't reach it. I could make out small moments with Kimberly, mostly, but they were all a blur.

Luke nodded. "Yes, he followed her here. You really don't remember?"

I shook my head.

"What else do you know about him?"

"He's smart, and I think he's got some kind of plan. He's had a lot of opportunities to take Kimberly and me, and hasn't. We figured it out at the formal, and before we could say anything, he did some kind of mind trick and made us forget. When Kimberly was attacked, I was afraid you guys would just want to leave, and I didn't know if he was after her, and I didn't want to leave her without any help. I'm sorry . . . I'm such a burden."

"Do you really think that little of me? We wouldn't have left her to deal with a vampire on her own. I'm sorry you felt you had to do this all by yourself. I know we haven't exactly inspired trust." Luke grabbed my shoulder. "But now. Please. No more secrets. Okay? Zach, want to add?"

"You're an asshole, and you almost got us all killed," Zach spat.

Luke eyed him, waiting for him to say more. "Five-words-or-less apology."

Zach groaned, holding up five fingers on one hand and counting. "I. Don't. Think. You're. A"—he held up his middle finger on the other hand, counting six—"burden." Surprisingly, it was one of his best apologies.

Luke cracked his knuckles. "All right, let's assume that William took Kimberly. Zach and I will go back through the camp and check for any sign of her. I'll be calling hospitals and feeling out the police stations to see if she has appeared anywhere in town. Pres, you stay with Aaron, and you guys circle around to the front of the park and search for clues. Watch for William and, if you see him, do not approach. Call us."

"So, you don't think he's a part of . . . The Family?" Presley was pacing back and forth between tree trunks.

Zach shook his head. "No, we'd know. This guy sounds like a loner. Which is unusual. He's been playing the long game. Definitely not The Family's MO."

I turned swiftly at the sound of laughter ringing through the trees. I blinked, trying to peer farther into the dark, but a fog set in. It couldn't be real.

"Did you guys hear that? Sounds like someone laughing." My brothers all stopped talking to look at me.

"Buddy, there isn't anyone laughing out here." Presley sheepishly smiled.

"He's hallucinating," Zach said.

"Presley, keep him sane?" Luke said.

"Roger that!" Presley pulled my head back around to focus on the group. "Please don't start talking about some little creepy girl following you or something."

My entire body was weak. I decided to focus on moving one foot in front of the other. I lost my balance a few times and almost landed on my face. Everything was exhausting. I had almost forgotten what exhaustion felt like. Zach and Luke grabbed my shirt to keep me upright.

In the tree line, I saw a flash of white hair again. The same haunting apparition of the woman in a long-slip dress appeared. She turned around to wink at me. A giggle escaped her lips, and her eyes taunted me.

"Oh, no, this is much worse," I said.

"Right. Okay. Call if you find anything. And, Aaron?" Luke stopped just short of the tree line. "I promise. We'll get her back." He gave me one final smile before disappearing with Zach into the fog.

"I don't feel good," I said as we started walking. I forced every muscle to bend to my will. My feet were cement blocks as they pushed through branches and debris. I sniffed the air, constantly searching for the scent of Kimberly's blood.

I was emotionally numb, and I could only focus on the possibility of finding her.

"I can tell. Considering you are shaking." I turned to look at Presley, and he smiled. "What sort of things are you seeing right now?" He locked arms with me and dragged me through the trees. "Well, it's a lot scarier than your fear of little ghost girls." *You're weak. That's why you will die.*

"Doubt it. Don't knock it because you haven't even seen half the scary movies I've seen."

"I don't think I need to watch any more for the rest of forever, considering I'm basically living in one." *This is all your fault.*

As we walked on, the voice was harder and harder to tune out.

"Thank God you never workout, Aaron." Presley held onto the other side of me. "It's way easier to carry your scrawny body."

"You're one to talk." I closed my eyes, feeling sleepy.

The trees morphed together in a big blob. I blamed it on the blurry vision slowly drawing my attention. Footsteps scurried between the trees, and I sensed someone was watching us, but I had enough sense to know it was just another hallucination.

Kim came to mind. Light bathed her. Her skin glowed, and her hair was always in her face. Guilt was quick to snatch my warm feelings. I couldn't believe I had let her down.

We quietly made our way through the forest. Despite me slowing us down, Presley was helping us make great time.

After a few minutes, he spoke again. "I'm sorry I've been such a shitty brother. I should have listened to you . . . I should have listened to her. She tried to tell me something was up with you."

I shook my head. "It's not your fault. This is all me."

"You don't get to play the martyr here. I think we can all take a share of the blame in this one." Presley kept his gaze firmly ahead.

I sighed. I didn't want them to take the blame. I wanted to drown in the guilt. I wanted to take the pain of it all. I deserved it.

"Well, I don't think she is out here. We should check the front and the parking lot. They have staff we can ask," he said.

I nodded, and I was thankful Presley's navigation skills had always been better than mine.

I felt the strangest urge to look up at the sky. I obeyed the quiet voice and tilted my head. I couldn't see anything on the ground, anyway. But it was also because this voice sounded different from what I was used to. It felt good and hopeful. The beauty of the night sky was overwhelming. Little sparks of light lighting up a blue sky. Kim would have loved it.

Chirping crickets came back, as well as the wind whistling through the trees. The breeze tickled my cheeks, bringing a smile to my face.

"Look, there's the fence," I said.

An iron fence was interwoven in the trees, massive as it towered over us.

"You think it would have electricity or guards or something." Presley scoffed.

"Well, I doubt they accounted for the undead scaling the twenty-foot fence." I walked up and placed my hand on the bars.

Barbed wire lined the top.

"Let's go. I've wasted enough time."

I imagined a clock slowly ticking. Kim was out there somewhere. I knew the longer it took me to find her, the worse things would be. As I pulled myself over the barbed wire, pain stung. I knew there would be no blood or cuts. With each moment, I was stronger. I turned to look at the park behind me. In the darkness, the gloom faded, or at least I hoped it would. I pushed my feet away from the fence and thrust myself to the ground. I didn't land gracefully, and neither did Presley.

"Oh, hell." Presley cried in pain, and he grabbed his ankle before falling over me.

I grabbed him and stumbled to pull us to our feet. My body still ached, but I wanted to hurry.

"Come on, I think the parking lot is to the right."

We jogged through the trees with a new determination. It wasn't long before the gleam of streetlights revealed the hoods of cars littering the parking lot, but it was sparse on the edges. I searched the empty lot for any sign of movement. A couple leaned against an old red Trailblazer. They turned with annoyance, and their red eyes seared into ours. Their skin was sunken in, and their thin arms grabbed at each other.

"Uh. Have you guys seen a red-headed girl come by here?" I smoothed my hair down in my best attempt to look like a normal college kid.

"If we did, I wouldn't tell you, kid." The male snarled, showing the gaps in his teeth.

I turned to Presley with an unamused expression. "So, I'm going to take that as a no."

"How much money do you got?" The slender woman stretched out her hand.

"Yeah, that's a no." Presley sighed.

"Okay." I pushed past them, looking out into the empty parking lot.

The moon was high in the sky. I had no idea what time it was, but judging by the lack of people, it was late.

I sighed. "There isn't anyone out here."

"What if we went by the front gate? There has to be a security guard or something. Come on." Presley hit my shoulder, and we jogged toward the ticket booth.

As we got closer, none of it felt familiar. I didn't remember the signs, the colors, the smells. Nothing. How much did I miss?

What else had I done that I didn't remember?

"There's someone over here."

I followed the sound of Presley's voice to an alleyway located in the back of the entrance.

A security guard with a thick gray mustache and olive skin was tucked into a small room. He didn't appear to be paying the slightest bit of attention. His eyes were glazed over, watching the surveillance monitors. Deep dark circles added to his hollow, sickly appearance.

I caught up to Presley, and we ran up to his window. "Hey!"

The man turned his head to face us.

"Have you seen a red-headed girl come through here? Or maybe she's on one of the cameras? She's my friend, and I . . . I lost her in the forest."

"We have reason to believe something bad has happened to her," Presley said.

"What is your name?" The security guard's voice was cold. His words came out slowly.

"I'm Aaron."

Our eyes locked onto each other, and my heart sank.

His face was void of expression.

He moved his hand across the desk to hand me a business card. "Here you go."

His voice was monotone, his eyes unblinking.

"What? No. I don't need that! Have you seen her or not?"

"Here you go." He moved the card toward me again.

"What is this?"

"Here you go."

"Is he possessed or something?" Presley leaned in, watching the man's face.

"What? That doesn't make any—oh."

"Here you go."

I took the business card. Underneath the guard's name read a scribbled address. *113 Chesapeake Rd. Come alone.*

"Oh." I turned back toward the parking lot.

My stomach knotted at the thought of her alone with him . . . bleeding. There was no telling what he might do with her.

I had to find her.

"What does that card say?" Presley followed me into the car lot. I stumbled back and shoved it in my pocket.

"It's nothing."

He sighed. "Let me guess, it says to not bring anyone with you."

I ignored him and moved my hands to my thighs, searching for my keys.

"I don't have to tell you that this is a trap," Presley said.

"Nope." I grabbed my keys and headed for my car.

Presley stepped in front of me. "You don't think I'm going to let you go by yourself, do you?"

"I think we're going to talk about it for a minute and then you will inevitably realize I'm right and let me go."

Presley didn't smile back. "If you go there alone, if he could do that"—he motioned back to where security was—"that means—"

"It doesn't change anything. I'm going."

"It changes everything! If he can do that, then there's no telling what he could do to you . . . what he might do to her. We gotta talk about it. You need someone to go with you. Let's just think of a plan."

"You know as well as I do, the moment Luke and Zach catch a whiff of this—if they ever saw this address, no matter what—they would go busting in. There's no plan with them. I can't risk that, and we don't have any leverage."

"So, you just want to walk in there and do what? What if he is a psycho and just wants to kill you?"

"If something happens, if I don't come back. At least it's just me. It's not everyone we care about. I just have to get her out of there, and I have a much better chance if I go alone."

"Don't even talk like that," Presley said.

"You know this is the only option. You are the only one who would let me go." I walked in closer, suddenly feeling heavy.

"If Zach and Luke found out I knowingly let you go, they would kill me. Literally."

"No, they wouldn't."

I moved forward to pat his shoulder. "Just take care of them, okay?"

He smiled and reached in to hug me briefly. "See you later?"

I patted him on the back, fighting the lump in my throat. "Hey, it will be so quick you'll hardly know I'm gone."

We moved away, and I nodded before turning to my car. It was too much to think about. I didn't let myself ponder for more than a second.

Twenty minutes from the park, a small dirt road led to an opening in the trees. A complete dead end. There were no lights and no cars around.

From my years of watching crime movies, I knew I was walking into a trap. "Come alone" always means there's someone waiting to kill or torture you. I just didn't have any other options. To my surprise, there was no convenient stroke of genius that happened seconds before I arrived. I had no plan. No stroke of luck. No fancy way to talk my way out of this.

I arrived at the address with my heart in my throat. My heartbeat felt fifty pounds heavier. I flung the car door open and stepped out into the grassy green area. My headlights illuminated the night in a limited space. I searched for any sign of movement.

"I'm here. Just like you wanted!" I didn't let the fear show in my voice as I took another step. "Come and get me!" Only silence answered.

"Kim, are you out there?" I walked closer to the trees, trying to peek around the branches.

It was strange walking alone. With each step, it occurred to me I had never had to feel true isolation. What I wouldn't give to have one of Zach's classic "Hey, asshole, get behind me" lines.

As minutes passed, my nervousness faded and I wondered if I was in the wrong place. There was no way I could have typed it in the GPS wrong.

I sighed and turned back toward the car. When it swung open, I stopped.

"Sorry, I'm late." William watched me with a wicked smile, seated and leaning over my steering wheel. "You're alone, smart boy."

I didn't have time to think before he touched my hand.

NINETEEN

AARON

M y eyelids were heavy as I fought past my disorientation. I blinked a few times until my vision focused on an ugly piece of art on the wall. It was colorless, just like the wall it was hung on. I was in a small room that reminded me of a funeral home with an old, faded carpet. The strange scent of dead flowers and wax cleared my brain fog. I had no idea where I was or whose ugly painting I was staring at. The smell of rain was faint in the air, and my clothes were just barely damp.

Finally, my senses came back, and my eyes landed on a patch of red lying on a cream couch a few feet in front of me.

"Kimberly." I sprang from my chair and ran to where she was draped across the couch.

Her heartbeat was identifiable, thundering. It was beautiful music to my ears. The best sound in the entire world.

I sighed and collapsed at her side. A joyful relief washed over me as I stroked her hand. "I'm so sorry. I'm going to get you out of this. I'm going to fix this. I promise."

She was breathing peacefully. A bandage wrapped around her hand and forearm with a tinge of blood coming through the cloth.

My stomach dropped, and another lump settled in my throat.

What I feared most had happened. I lost control. I hurt her. "Oh, you're up! It took ya quite awhile."

William's voice was laced with arsenic as he entered the room looking like a combination of a school professor and zombie killer. His thick-soled boots crunched the dirt on the hardwood floors and matched his plaid waist coat. "Don't worry. She's fine. I can assure you the only marks she has are from your dirty work."

"What is this?" I got up and stepped in front of her.

His eyes scanned me. "I've finally got you in a place where we can talk."

"I'm here, just like you wanted. Now, can you please let her go?"

"Please? It's a little early to start begging. You're not so tough now without your big brothers." The menacing air compounded around him, and I could tell he was sizing me up.

I was in no way prepared for a fight. I had to stay calm. Talk my way out of it.

I opened my mouth to say something witty.

"Shut up."

In the blink of an eye, he was sitting next to her, stroking her hair. I sucked in a breath. He could kill her in an instant if he wanted to. Whatever I did, I had to make sure she made it out of that room alive.

"You can't protect her in the state you're in. When you don't drink, you get weak." He got up and circled me like an animal circles its prey.

I hated that he was right. My body was slow. I could normally take in the scene in eighty different ways in a matter of seconds. But even my mind felt slower. I couldn't think of anything other than the fear I had for Kimberly.

"What is this about? What do you want with her?" I couldn't take my eyes off her. Her heartbeat was the only bit of comfort I could find.

"Don't you get it yet? This isn't about her. It's about you. She's here because of you." He was suddenly behind me, almost breathing down my neck.

"Me? What about me?" I turned around with nothing but a gray wall staring back at me. "I don't understand what you want."

He pushed me from behind, and I moved deeper into the room.

"Come on. I want to see that anger you had earlier. Show me that anger, Aaron." He pushed me again as he appeared in front of me, and I stumbled back into a small wooden table.

Come on. Fight him. Kill him.

"I don't have it anymore. It's gone," I said slowly, choosing my words.

Kill him.

"Don't lie. I know it's there." He started pacing back and forth, coming closer to me each time.

He's mocking you.

"Shut up," I tried to say under my breath, but I knew William heard me.

His smile stretched wide. "You're not talking to me, are you?"

"If you don't want her, what do you want with me?"

He stepped forward, and I shuffled back. "Tell me, what do you know about The Family?"

Shit. I wasn't surprised. I had a feeling that, one day, everything would come back full circle. All my secrets had come out. It was only natural my brothers' would too.

"Uh, I-I don't know anything."

He tilted his head curiously. "You expect me to believe that? Your brothers are part of the biggest criminal cult in America, and you're . . . innocent?"

"I don't know anything about it." I backed away. "They've never told me anything."

"That's what you're claiming? Oh, Aaron." William's brows pressed together, and malice wafted off him in waves. "Don't. Lie."

"What? We haven't done anything."

William pressed his lips together. "I can feel the guilt radiating off of you. You're practically sweatin' it."

Come on. Do something.

"I-I . . ."

My head was spinning. Every muscle in my body felt stiff.

William moved in closer to me. "You can't even say it, can you?"

A flash of white caught my attention, and the haunted apparition appeared again. Her long hair dangled around her face, and she floated from one end of the room to the next. I swallowed the lump in my throat.

"Your brothers have to pay for their crimes. For centuries, The Family has done nothing but spill blood and brought the plague of evil. That includes you."

My attention snapped back to him at those words. "What crimes?"

"They've been linked to a number of deaths in the Brooklyn area. Not to mention various crimes of stealing, their involvement in money laundering . . . I could go on," he said with a stupid smirk still on his face.

"I don't believe you. My brothers don't kill people. The other stuff . . . maybe. But they wouldn't kill anyone."

His eyes bore a hole into mine. "You don't sound so sure about that."

The apparition appeared next to his shoulder, and I fell back a few steps. It traced its fingers across his shirt. The white hair was blinding.

"What are you lookin' at?" His face was only inches from mine. A smug smile danced on his lips. "Seeing things, are we?"

"No."

I flinched as it stalked farther into the room to sit next to Kimberly, who was still lying peacefully on the couch. Its skin was hollow and translucent.

"It's that thing in your head. You're losing it. That's what happens when you don't feed. You get weak. It found your weakness. Now it's here to collect."

"To collect what?" I said, still watching my own hallucination.

The white-haired apparition sat over Kim and moved its hands over her hair. Panic hit me instantly. I knew in my head it wasn't real, but everything about it looked that way. It felt like reality.

"Your body. Your soul. It doesn't matter. You won't be alive much longer to feel it. Who knows, maybe I'll leave you alive long enough to let you suffer."

Numbness traveled up my hand. The apparition was gripping my arm. I pulled my hand away. She was closer than I had ever seen her. Her white eyes pierced, and I jerked away in panic, but William grabbed the sides of my face and forced me to look straight ahead. Searing hatred and a wildfire of rage behind his irises.

He pushed me into a floral lounge chair that was situated in the corner. A layer of dust flew up into the damp as he spoke. "Stay with me. Don't pay attention to it."

He pressed his palms into the sides of my face. I struggled to turn my face away, but his grip was strong.

"Don't struggle. It will be over soon."

A disorienting feeling washed over me. A thick film filled my vision. And then everything was black. My world faded in an instant.

The room was gone. Like being hooked into an amusement ride, my mind flew off. Flickering light induced pain in my head. I knew I had no control as flashes came up in my mind.

At first, my head was throbbing, but in seconds, it turned into searing pain. Whatever the flashing was, it flickered too fast. Heat flushed my body. A range of emotions hit me all at once, over and over in a reel, making me nauseous.

My limbs tingled. Electrical pulses surged through my veins. It felt as if my body was being torn apart from the inside out. William was in my head. It wasn't a subtle occupation. He was stomping around and turning up the mattresses. I couldn't feel my body anymore. I was completely in my head. His searching made me frantic. My brain couldn't take the intruder.

William's voice was close. "The more you struggle. The more pain you will feel."

The floor dropped out, and my chest ached with that familiar pain. I could feel my fingers again. I tried to pull my arms away from the chair with all my might. My eyelids were heavy and refused to open, and I was locked in my own body.

A wobbly image pulled into my vision. Everything was tilted back and forth. Everything was too vivid. Too sensitive.

Something caught my attention. Flowing locks of white hair, bending and blowing in the light. It was a woman. She felt oddly familiar.

"No need to be upset. You can relax."

Her voice sucked me back into the image. It wasn't the words she said but the way they affected me. Her voice was magnetic.

I was in my old living room. It was all there. Our mismatched couches, the pencil we broke off into the ceiling, and the smell of cheap vanilla candles my mom loved.

The comfort of that nostalgia didn't last for long. My hands were restrained behind me. The muffled sounds of Presley's groaning came from somewhere. The muscles in my arms burned as I struggled to get free.

It looked like a memory, but it wasn't anything I recognized happening before.

"Don't worry, he won't be harmed. I just need to see your face. I need to look into your eyes."

Her cool hands traced my chin and up to my brow. My entire body was shaking in fear.

The full image still wasn't coming into view. But I could hear my ragged breath. "W-What do you want with us?"

Her face was beautiful porcelain, her lips flushed with red. But it was her eyes that froze me into place, white and glossy. Void of any hope or light.

It was the woman who I'd been seeing in all my hallucinations. Was she a real person?

"Aaron, you have so many good qualities. So innocent. I can see you'll be a valuable member of The Family one day."

"What? Who are you?" My hands were still being held down by something as she moved over to Presley. "No, stop! Leave him alone."

She ignored me and ran her fingers through his curls. Her white dress, almost see-through, dragged along our shag carpet. It was flowy, elegant, and clung to her hips. Around her were men with cloths covering their faces, adorned in all black. Slacks and blazers with pointed loafers. They watched the woman like a hawk. Her every movement. Every word.

"Such handsome boys. No doubt your older brothers will be much happier with you by their side."

Her face almost reflected sadness, her eyes fell to the floor, admiring her soft, sheer gown.

Who was this woman? I didn't remember meeting her, yet she knew my brothers. And then it hit me. This was the girl they were talking about outside the frat house, the one Luke missed, the one he wanted to go back to.

Her eyes fell back on mine, and fear swallowed me. Her presence felt otherworldly. Bloodlust fell from her lips. *What* was this woman was a better question.

In the blink of an eye, she was in front of me again. Her lips grazed my ear. Despite her beauty, a feeling radiated off her I couldn't explain. Impending doom swallowed me as she caressed my skin. The room started to slow. My body was wobbly, and I couldn't move my head up. A smile appeared on her red-stained lips. She brought a pale finger to her lips and bit down. A stream of black tar-like blood flowed down in droplets. In one graceful sweep, she brought that finger to my lips. The bitter taste of iron landed on my tongue.

"Copula quae numquam solvi potest."

My world spun once more, and my old living room dissolved. I awoke to William biting into my neck. My hands were glued to the armrests of the floral chair. Kimberly was, thankfully, still resting peacefully. Weakness carried itself through my upper body until my arms were numb. It was a struggle to keep myself upright. I couldn't catch myself from falling forward. I squeezed my fingers on the armrests to try to catch myself, but my body weight was too heavy. Everything hurt.

William reached my chest just in time to stop me from sliding out of the chair. "There. Now let me look at you."

He grabbed my face and brought my chin up to look at him. "That's as close to death as I'd like you to be."

He was such a fucking prick. I wanted to say something, but I couldn't stop replaying the scene I had just seen over and over again. That was the first glimpse into my brothers' secret life I'd ever seen. I had imagined so many different possibilities, but I never imagined . . . her.

"W-Was that a memory? I don't get what's happening."

"The body has a hard time adjusting to the mental recall. Reliving old memories is like experiencing them for the first time. When you experience moments, they pass without a second thought. It's only when you are forced to relive them that you see and feel everything as it should be."

None of the words he said made any sense.

"Oh, yeah, I forgot you enjoy being a cryptic asshole." My eyes drifted back to Kimberly, who was still unconscious on the couch. I squeezed the armrests, trying harder to pull myself up. My body shook as I forced my muscles to bend to my will.

"Still making jokes, I see." William's smirk softened as he placed a hand on my chest and held me down. "Don't struggle. Your pain will be over soon."

"Don't say that like you care," I spat.

"I don't relish makin' a kid suffer the agony of a torturous, slow death, no. But there's no other way to kill vampires. It can't be helped."

Said the guy who just bit a hole in my neck.

"I take it you do this often." I fought hard to keep my eyelids open. But every so often, my head would fall. I still didn't know who William truly was or if that was even his real name. And I was growing too weak to care.

"I specialize in killing vampires, yes." William looked far away as he analyzed a fresh set of flowers on the table next to me.

"But you're a vampire . . ."

His fingers grazed the petals on a white rose. "But I'm nothing like you. The easiest way to kill one is to be one. A fitting sacrifice to make for the greater good."

"Hmm." I closed my eyes for a second and reopened them.

William was watching my face closely, but his face was devoid of anger, expressing sympathy.

"You made it easy for me, though. Without you, none of this would be possible. I'm sure your brothers will come after you."

"Exactly like you planned." I groaned.

His words hit deep in my chest, only adding to my physical pain. My heart leaped into my throat. A strange but familiar sensation bubbled into my stomach. Of all my fuckups, this was my worst. There was a lot I should have done differently, and I couldn't change it.

He motioned to Kimberly. "You are a lucky kid, though. I've seen thirsty vampires rip off limbs and break bones of humans when they lose control. They kill their own husbands, wives . . . children."

My body lurched forward, and my chest wouldn't stop heaving. Another wave of pain hit me, and I leaned forward, resting my body in my lap. The nausea was back with a vengeance.

"Is this normal for ya?" William was beside me with a hand on my back.

I shuddered between the muscle spasms. "When I was a kid . . . I used to—to throw up when I was stressed." I groaned, bringing my arms close to my body. "Vampire me"—I lurched forward again, feeling the burning muscles in my chest—"hasn't gotten the . . . memo."

I used my hand to cover my mouth and braced for the next round of nausea.

"Just relax. Here, lay back." William gently helped me move my head to the back of the chair.

I didn't have any choice but to receive his help. My body was spent, and my eyelids kept drooping. A soft brace supported me as he placed a plump white pillow underneath my head. "W-Why?" I closed my eyes, unable to keep them open for a second longer.

"Well, I can't have you dying before your brothers get here." He laughed, grabbed my arms, and placed another pillow on my lap. "Now, just rest for a minute. Stop talking and just rest."

Every second, the spasms in my chest lessened and the nausea faded.

"I'm tired," I whispered.

The soft sounds of rain hitting the rooftop were the loudest thing in my ears. I tuned into the soft symphony. I didn't have any other choice.

"Then, sleep." William's voice was far away as I drifted off, and for the first time in a long time, I slept.

TWENTY

KIMBERLY

My eyes opened, and the fog cleared. It took me a few minutes to get my bearings and assess where I was. My wrist was wrapped in gauze and tape, and to my surprise, I no longer felt any pain.

None of it mattered when I saw Aaron draped over a wooden chair with black blood staining his shirt like dark pools of ink. Droplets littered the floor around him and stained the ornate fabric he was sitting on.

I leaped to my feet. "Aaron! Please wake up. Please."

His eyes were shut, his body motionless. My heart kicked my ribs, and I put my head to his chest, checking for a heartbeat. I couldn't hear anything other than the blood throbbing in my own skull.

"Wake up. I need you to get up." I wrapped my hands around his arms, shaking him.

We were in an empty, windowless room with dusty wooden floors and stone walls painted in thick gobs of white paint. The room was large enough to be a decent size bedroom, with nothing to signal what type of building we were in. Thunder cracked overhead, and the faintest taste of salt lingered on my lips. We were by the coast, if I had to guess.

Aaron's eyes fluttered open, and he blinked before focusing on my face. For the first time, I felt like I could take a full breath. I kneeled at face-level, taking his blood-soaked hand.

"Oh, thank God. You're awake. I was so worried."

"Yeah, yeah. I'm fine." His tone wasn't convincing, and he struggled to keep his eyes open. He looked to be glued to his chair. Every movement of muscle didn't move him an inch. "Ah!"

Aaron's cries brought a lump to my throat. I fought back the threatening tears. Things weren't looking good for him. Even if I had any idea what was going on or how to get help, no help was coming.

"You're bleeding." I touched his shirt close to his neck, where a bite mark was still wet with fresh blood. I didn't have to guess who did it.

"Oh, that? Just a scratch." He tried to straighten himself but any attempt to move was futile.

"We have to get out of here." I struggled to get back on my feet. My own blood loss was still apparent.

"Don't worry about me. I don't think I'm going anywhere anytime soon."

"What? No. I'm not leaving you here. Now, get up." I grabbed his arm, trying to pull him up and onto my shoulder. He winced with each pull.

"Kim, you gotta get out of here before he comes back." Aaron groaned.

His defeated eyes only ignited the fire under my feet.

"Don't get all noble on me now. There's no way I'm leaving you here." Pure determination fueled my muscles to try to pull Aaron up again. He was deadweight. I groaned in frustration. "Why are you so heavy?"

"Kim—"

"No." I dropped to my knees beside him. "I won't leave you."

I sucked in a breath and put Aaron's hand in mine. I wanted to warm the cold slowly overtaking his skin. His light, usually glaringly bright, felt dim.

Aaron's voice was soft. "Why?"

It made sense to me why he would ask me that. For the majority of our relationship, it had been about me. He had done everything he possibly could to right his wrongs and put my wants ahead of his. But something had changed. I had changed.

"Because, if this is the end . . . at least we won't be alone. I won't leave you here alone to die. No way."

Tears streamed down my cheeks, and I squeezed his hand.

He squeezed mine back. "I'm sorry for everything. I really screwed your life up."

I smiled, wiping a few tears. "No. You didn't. I'd do it all again. All the good. The bad. To meet you."

He chuckled. "You're delusional. You lost too much blood."

Every minute that passed, I knew it might be our last. But I was at peace. I looked at Aaron, soaking in his features.

I could say one thing that could describe the way it felt to be in Aaron's wake. The warmth. The laughter. The undeniable happiness. It felt like love. Love that showed in the way he cared for his brothers and they cared for him. And I was there, in the wake. Engulfed and enamored with it. I didn't want it to ever leave me, and I wanted to hold his hand forever.

The door clicked, shifting our focus.

Aaron's eyes glued to its frame. "Get behind me."

I looked at Aaron's utterly defenseless posture. "Oh, hush."

"Oh, you're up? That's a surprise."

William wasn't the only one to file into the room. Two others followed. One was female, the other male, all wearing fitted black cloaks that touched the floor.

I didn't recognize their faces.

"Leave her alone." Aaron tried moving again with no luck. "Fuck!"

William didn't say anything else, and they encircled us.

"Aaron, it's okay." I kept my voice steady. My hands shook slightly, but I clenched my fists.

"Don't touch her." Aaron strained again as he desperately tried to stand.

A cloaked figure came up behind him and wrapped fingers over his mouth. In the blink of an eye, I was met with the same fate.

A set of stone hands clamped my mouth. Another set of hands grabbed my waist to keep me from moving.

"Settle down, kids. I've got good news and bad. Good news is, your terrified waiting is over. Bad news is, Aaron has to come with me." William nodded once, and chaos ensued.

The man dragged Aaron from his chair. A trail of black blood smudged the floor with each kick of Aaron's sneakers.

If he was still fighting, I would too.

I shoved my foot down onto my captor's foot with no luck. No amount of pressure was being taken off my ribs. I used every ounce of strength in my muscle to try to wiggle free from the iron grip. I exhausted all the air from my lungs.

Aaron disappeared through a wooden door across the room, our eyes meeting one last time. A scream curdled in my throat. I threw my head back in anger, and pain radiated through my skull. Dizziness hit me, and for the first time, I relaxed, letting the hands keep me up.

"You're goin' to give yourself a concussion if you don't stop. Give her to me," William said.

As they passed me off, I bolted for the wooden door I'd seen Aaron disappear into. I slammed into it with my body weight and fell to my knees.

The smell of dirt and old cedar wood greeted me from the darkness. Candlelight flickered throughout the room.

With a groan, I pulled my aching body from the creaking floor. It was running on empty. A large wooden cross loomed in front of me. We were in a church. It was small, with only about ten wooden pews lining an aisle adorned with white candles. The walls were made of stones, and they went all the way to the ceiling, only stopped by a small worn mural.

Lightning struck outside and rattled the floor beneath me. The large stained-glass window in the front of the church illuminated the room.

"Aaron!"

My voice echoed into the high ceilings. His black blood smeared across the floor, marking his location next to a pew, where someone was shoving a gag in his mouth. My forearms stung from the impact as I went to run for him. Someone grabbed me from behind, and I flinched forward in a last-ditch effort to reach Aaron on the floor. Aaron and I collided, our heads smacking onto the dusty hardwood.

I groaned and held my head on my way back up. My world was a vivid blur. Aaron was still unable to move, so I removed his gag.

"What are you doing?" Aaron's eyes searched mine in desperation.

"I don't know!" I blurted as something blocked the dim light. We looked up to see a cloaked man staring at us inquisitively. He was beard-ed, with salt-and-pepper hair, some of his natural dark brown peeking through. It was short and cropped. His robe was white and ornate, adorned with gold embellishments and crosses.

My heart stuttered, and I leaned into Aaron. I found his hand and squeezed a little too hard.

"I'm not going to hurt you."

The cloaked man's voice was pure steel. Sharp and cold.

William was at the door, bowing before entering. "I'm sorry. That was my fault. I can take her."

"No, leave her. For now."

"Kim, I think we're officially fucked." Aaron squeezed my hand back.

I swallowed. The air was unnaturally dry, considering the rain pelted the stained-glass window.

The robed man crouched in front of us. "My name is Kilian. You must be Kimberly and Aaron."

Up close, I could see the crow's feet by his gray eyes. His hands rested on his knees casually. He had large gaudy rings and long scars on the backs of his hands.

Naturally, I took the lead. "What do you want with Aaron?"

"You were right. She's definitely strong-willed." Kilian smiled.

But it wasn't warm in the way Aaron and his brothers smiled— it was solemn. A smile that came from someone who bore great responsibility and had seen some things. I didn't want to know what those things were.

"Kim, don't let him touch you! Be careful." Aaron struggled to get onto his elbows. His arms shook with the weight of his own body.

Kilian turned his attention to William, who was standing at attention with his hands behind his back. "How much blood did you take from him?"

William smirked. "Only what was necessary."

"Prop him up," Kilian said.

William and another girl in a black robe grabbed Aaron on both sides, pulling him up from the floor. They scooted him back and leaned him at the foot of one of the wooden pews.

"I'm sorry you're so uncomfortable. It's not how I like to do things." Kilian stood. His long thick robe dragged on the hardwood, nearly missing a few candles.

"Can you please tell us what's going on?" I said.

"In order for me to do that, I must know what you know. How much do you two know about The Family?"

William stepped up and opened his mouth to speak, but Kilian held up his hand. "Please. I want to hear it from them."

I looked at Aaron, who seemed to be putting all his energy into staying conscious. I wasn't surprised to hear the name come up. The Family felt like an omen hanging over the Calem brothers. Therefore, it was hanging over me as well. It was only a matter of time before it caught up. I just didn't expect it would be so soon.

"Kimberly doesn't know anything. Just what I've told her, and it's not much. So, you can leave her out of this," Aaron said.

"I repeat. I'm not going to hurt you." Kilian stood in front of the cross.

Despite his calm disposition, he wasn't very convincing.

Aaron scoffed. "You know, I might have believed you if I wasn't bleeding all over the floor of this nice church."

"If there was ever a time when this church was nice, it was long ago," Kilian said.

"What choice do you have?" William walked next to Kilian, his arms still poised behind his back.

He reminded me of a soldier. His shoulders were pulled back and waiting at attention.

"Fine. I know that The Family is dangerous. I know that . . . my brothers are somehow involved in all this, but I don't know how. They never told me anything. Probably to prevent situations like this."

"William informed me that he pulled a memory for you. Tell me about it."

"Memory?" I squeezed Aaron's cold hand. "What's he talking about?"

"Yeah, it was back in Brooklyn. At my house, some lady was there, with these weird eyes. They had me and Presley tied up, and she gave us her blood, and they said—"

"Copula quae numquam solvi potest. It's Latin. It means a bond that can never be broken." Kilian kneeled in front of us again with what appeared to be a handkerchief he had wetted from a bowl on the altar. With the linen cloth, he moved toward Aaron. "May I?"

Aaron hesitated. "I guess."

Without another word, he sponged the blood that was stained across Aaron's neck.

I never let go of Aaron's hand.

Kilian spoke again. "You don't remember because you were touched by a queen. She's the purest, strongest form of what we are. The history of The Family is a long insidious one, so I will tell you only what pertains to you.

"The Family began in the Renaissance Age, when politically influential elites would practice necromancy and try to summon demons. They wanted to use their power to obtain riches and knowledge not known to humans. After many attempts, they were successful in the transferring of a powerful demon into the body of a woman. They used women, usually orphaned or poor, as their test subjects and tried duplicating the transfer in men but were unsuccessful. The men did not predict the hold that the demon would have over them. They found themselves enthralled with Her.

"Their devotion turned into an obsession, and thus the first Queen was born. From there, the Queen made Her Guard, and the Guard made up their lower members. The original is long gone, and only six other Queens remain in existence, and it looks like you've met one." Aaron and Kilian locked eyes.

I cleared my throat. "Wait, so if you're not The Family, who are you?"

The double doors at the end of the aisle burst open. Zach and Luke stood with fire in their eyes. Soon, Aaron and I were being dragged backward. William grabbed both of our shirt collars and hurled us at Kilian's feet next to the altar. My bones ached as I crashed into the wooden block. Two robed figures placed a gag in our mouths and quickly tied our hands behind our backs.

"Stop right there. Unless you want the rest of your dear little brother's blood to be spilled." William tugged at Aaron's shirt.

Five robed figures, including William, surrounded Zach and Luke. The last two filtered in from behind, limping.

"I'm surprised you were able to get through our watchers. You are skilled," Kilian said, holding his hands in front of himself patiently. His face was unreadable.

The two guards rushed them, and I braced myself for their impact, but combined, they worked like a well-oiled machine. They stood back-to-back and fought them off one by one. When one twin dodged, the other one countered with a punch.

Kilian raised his hand, and the fighting ceased. The robed guards stood a few feet away with their hands behind their backs.

Zach wiped his chin. "Who the hell are you?"

"We are Legion. A movement founded a little more than a century after The Family. Our true purpose is to bring balance back to the world by exterminating members of The Family and exposing them for crimes they have caused."

William's voice cut the air. "Someone had to hold them accountable."

The twins shared a tentative look.

"How did you find us?" Luke asked, making eye contact with me and Aaron, his jaw set and serious.

"How do you think? Little brother right here. He attacked a girl and sent her to the hospital. We search constantly for places with abnormal activity and places where idiots like you may be stupid enough to feed." William smiled. "But it was our leading lady who did most of the work for me. She led me right to him, and from there, you can imagine how easy they made it for me."

Luke puffed out his chest with an eerie sense of calm. "Well, then, you know that Aaron doesn't know anything and therefore Kimberly either. So, why don't you just let them go?"

"They're not going anywhere."

William's voice was cold. His grip tightened on my shirt collar.

"Cut the shit. This is about us. If this is truly some overly right-eous cult hell-bent on rallying for justice, then why do you even need hostages?" Zach spat.

William tilted his head. "Justice? There will not be justice until you're wiped from Earth."

"Oh, really?" Zach squared his shoulders. "Why don't you come over here and do it, then? I'll let you get the first punch."

"My apologies for William's behavior. He has more reason to hate members of The Family than most," Kilian said. "The Family's actions are often overlooked by many government agencies, so justice often never comes for their victims or their families."

William's eyes bore a hole into Zach's skin. "We have no interest in bartering with you. We have you outnumbered. We can take you right now."

To my surprise, Luke smiled. He reached into his pocket and pulled out a switchblade. "I thought you might say that."

He threw the knife into his left hand before plunging the knife into his forearm and pulling it down toward his wrist. Black blood sprayed the floor.

My body felt cold, and a scream curled in my throat, muffled under-neath the thick cloth in my mouth.

Aaron's muffled groans sounded next to me.

Luke chuckled to himself as he passed the knife to Zach, and Zach repeated the same on his arm. A long ribbon of blood dripped to the floor and spread to a puddle soaking into the dry wood. The determined smile never left Luke's face, though his scrunched nose told me he was in pain. "See, I think you're bluffing. You need us."

"You didn't think we'd come prepared to die, did you?" Zach moved his hair, revealing a bite mark.

I connected the dots. Vampires needed to be drained of blood before their skin could be pierced. That's why the blade would penetrate their skin. Losing blood meant they'd grow weak, just like Aaron.

Luke's body convulsed. "You want us. Let them go. It's a fair trade. We die, and everything we know dies with us."

"Better make your decision quick. We're bleeding out over here." Zach squeezed his hand, and more blood fell.

"You'd leave little brother and Kimberly here alone?" William tightened his grip on my collar once more, and I groaned.

Luke turned to Kilian. "You won't kill them. If you're who you said you were, then you wouldn't kill innocent people."

The scene was surreal. Just hours before, we looked like normal college kids, enjoying our time and swimming in a natural spring. Afterward, we'd stepped into a horror film.

The robed figures stood around the room like statues, most of whom were hidden by the dim light.

"I'll barter with you." Kilian looked intrigued. "But you can only choose one. Kimberly or Aaron. The other must stay here."

Aaron and I shared a look. Aaron squirmed under his restraints and tried to scoot forward.

Luke shot him a smile, blood still oozing from his arm. "Don't worry. I got this."

Another crack of thunder vibrated the walls.

Zach and Luke shared a look. Silently reading each other's minds. My heartbeat was in my ears again as I contemplated what it meant. The thought of one of us being left behind took the breath from my lungs. Let alone the thought of only one of us was making it out of the church.

Luke watched Kilian. "How can we know you're going to keep your word?"

"You're still alive, aren't you?" William said.

I couldn't see his face, but I could tell he was smirking.

"Let Kimberly go." Luke's eyes met mine.

William grabbed me by my shirt, lifting my feet from the ground. I struggled against his grip, but I wasn't allowed to look back at the altar.

"As you wish."

William dragged me toward the double doors. The two other guards grabbed Zach and Luke and pulled them toward the altar in my place.

"Can I talk to her first? Please." Luke shrugged them off with his big shoulders. "Just for a second."

"I'll allow it," Kilian said, a barely there smile appearing on his lips.

William didn't remove my gag and just flung me in front of Luke without a word while Zach was gagged and dragged toward the altar to join Aaron.

"Kim, Presley will come and find you. If you want to, you can go with him and get away from this place. I won't be there to protect you guys, but you're smart, and I know you'd be able to make sure he doesn't do anything stupid. But it's up to you. Whatever you want to do. Thank you for keeping our secret and caring about my brother. If I don't see you again, I'm happy to have met you."

Luke smiled in a way that made my stomach turn. Despite his world crumbling, he was still trying to give me some of his strength. To instill me with hope, that I would carry on.

All I could focus on was their blood falling to the floor, the same way Aaron's was, and the sinking feeling this may be the last time I would ever see them. Tears formed in the corners of my eyes, and I made eye contact with Aaron one last time. In the dim light, I could see the glistening reflection in his eyes. Relief. "All right. Goodbyes are said. Dominique. Come with me."

William brought us through the doors and to a hallway. A dusty, abandoned space with nothing but old, tattered paintings hung on the walls.

The tears kept falling, and William removed my gag once we rounded the corner.

"Let go of me!" I screamed, and it echoed in the empty hallway. He chuckled. "Gladly. Once you're out the door."

A wooden door was just up ahead, with an oil lantern illuminating the brass fittings.

I struggled to free myself again, only causing more pain and bruising to my already sore arm. The one named Dominique was right on my heels.

"What are you going to do with them?"

I didn't want to know the answer. I couldn't save them. Tears ran from my eyes, and I fought with everything I had to refrain from sobbing in front of them. I didn't want to give him the satisfaction.

We reached the door, and he stopped. "Kimberly, I understand this has been hard on you. I do. So, I'm going to give you an option. The deal was, you get to go and find Presley, but I could make you forget this ordeal for a while. You won't remember what happened here for at least a couple weeks, even with your strong will, and by the time you remember, they'll all be long gone. You'll mourn them, but it will be easier. You can move on with your life. Let all this go. With no more connections to the Calem brothers, The Family won't have any reason to come find you. You'll be free."

I was dumbfounded by what he had offered. Something so unbelievable and out of this world, even for a world where vampires existed. Forgetting would be bliss. The blood on the floor, the fear in Aaron's eyes. The pain ripping through my chest.

The thought of Aaron and me swaying in the forest came to mind. The soft scent of pine, and Aaron constantly stepping on my foot. His smile and his laughter changed me. It made me believe in a life I had given up on. Aaron's brothers were part of that too. I didn't want it to be easy. I wanted it to be hard and messy. Because that's how love and family were.

"No. I want to go with Presley."

His jaw tightened, and his dark eyes pinned me against the wall. "If you go with him, we will hunt you both down. Not to mention, if The Family doesn't find him first. You will be on the run. Come on, you and I both know Presley won't get very far without his brothers. You're condemning yourself to a life you don't belong in. Don't let them drag you further into their mess."

"Presley won't have his brothers, but he'll have me." I smiled through gritted teeth. "Their mess is mine now."

William sighed and grabbed the sides of my face. My breath caught in my throat. His eyes were cold. In them, anger burned, bubbling under the surface, waiting to explode. "Fine. As you wish."

TWENTY-ONE

AARON

E very minute passed strangely, consciousness slipping and returning. Some moments I felt alert and scared. Then my eyes would close for a few seconds and something else entirely was happening.

My older brothers chatted, and every once in a while, they'd attempt to wake me up again.

My head lay on the floor that smelled of old cedar. The candles around me were starting to drip puddles of wax onto the dry wood. The assortments of colored wax swirled together into streams. Zach and Luke were chained just a few feet away. Rusty chains hooked into steel rods underneath the floorboards. This place was a prison.

It took me a minute to remind myself where I was, which was, apparently, on the floor of an old church, about to bleed out. My brothers looked like they were going to suffer the same fate.

But Kimberly was safe, and so was Presley. Somehow, my mangled body didn't hurt as much with that truth. The two people I needed to protect were safe. No matter what happened to us, at least I could die knowing that fact.

"How did you find me?" It took more effort than I anticipated to speak. The cloth from earlier was gone.

"You left your phone location on, dumbass." Zach smiled, but his eyes were still scanning me and the trail of blood I left beside me.

"How bad is it?" Luke's voice was more secure and, somehow, made me feel a little less worried about our situation.

"Pretty bad." I groaned.

Kilian and the other robed figures were setting up what looked to be some type of ceremony, with a large silver bowl full of some kind of liquid, set by the large cross. That's when I realized how tall Kilian was. He had to duck every time he walked past the corners of the cross.

One of the girls in a black robe motioned to me, white hair peeking beneath her hood. "Does he need to be chained?"

"No. He's lost a lot of blood. He isn't going anywhere." William's eyes bore into mine.

In the dim light, I could see his expressionless face. His eyes were glued to Kilian, awaiting his instruction.

"Can we get this over with?" Zach groaned. "If you're so holy, why drag it out? Don't you want to be merciful?"

Kilian turned to Zach after lighting another candle at the altar. "You see, this isn't an execution. While it's true, we are dedicated to finding and hunting down members of The Family. William has discovered something very interesting in your case that I think may be useful. Therefore, this is your trial, a place for your sins to be laid out before our council. Then we will decide what to do with you."

"That's fucking fantastic." Zach sighed. He turned his attention to me. I could feel his worry.

Luke's voice was softer. "Why does Aaron need to be on trial here? He hasn't done anything."

"I know. But he has been marked, meaning he's of great value to The Family." Kilian's robe dragged behind him as he paced the floor. The wooden boards squeaking and the occasional flicker of the flame were the only things heard in the otherwise silent room.

I sighed. My head was pounding, and all I could think of was getting on with our impending doom. "What does that even mean?"

Zach's eyes were wide. "That's impossible."

"Our brothers never met anyone we knew in The Family. How could they be marked?" Luke said.

"Aaron's memories revealed something he did not remember. A memory of . . . Her."

The twins sat up straighter, their eyes trained on Kilian, who was still slowly pacing the floor. "In this memory, She offered your brothers Her blood. We believe She planned to turn them herself and induct them in The Family, but it sounds like She was waiting . . . for what, we don't know."

"Does She have a name?" I asked.

"Since the Renaissance Age, they have been called many names. None are accurate. Her worshippers don't sully her with a name."

He stopped pacing and stood directly in front of Zach and Luke. I wondered what She had to do with my brothers. In my memory, She was haunting. Terrifying. Not exactly someone I imagined you could actually have any type of relationship with. Were they obsessed with Her too?

Luke spoke. "No. She was going to kill them. That's why we did this. That's why we ran away."

"Is that why you changed us . . ." I met Luke's gaze. "You thought The Family was going to kill us?"

"We didn't think, we knew! We've fucking saw it happen! It was all bullshit. Everything they ever taught us and showed us when we were kids was a lie and manipulation." Zach's face was red with rage. "That's what they do. If anyone has a family, they kill them. Because they want your loyalty. But we didn't know that, and when we found out, we left."

"And you played into their plan all along and sentenced your brothers to death." William was no longer smug. I couldn't see his face, but I could hear it in his voice. He was dead serious. "How does that feel?"

If looks could kill, William would be a dead man.

"Come closer, and I'll show you," Zach said deadpan.

"I don't believe The Family's plan is to kill you. Though, historically, you're correct. That is why I believe, even now, though, you have defected and therefore have committed treason against them. They're still looking for you. Not to kill you. But to take you back . . . the reason for that we will hopefully find out." Kilian stopped passing and stood in front of the cross, shoulders back and head high. "We will begin the trial. The results of this trial will determine the fate of your entire family."

I knew I should have been scared, but I couldn't bring myself to feel anything at that moment. My attention drifted to the puddle of my blood on the floor again. Black liquid soaked into wood grain. Tingling and numbness bled into my fingertips. I spat black blood onto the floor while trying to keep my balance sitting up.

The sleepy feeling was settling into my muscles again. I shook my head. "Let's just get on with it. Let me guess, you'll push your way into my head too?" I reached out my arm for him to take.

"Go ahead."

"Aaron, don't," Luke said, stirring in his chains.

"I like to give everyone a chance to plead their own case. The Family specializes in the mind manipulation of their members. They often mess with their memories and experiences, making it very hard to decipher the true intentions of the individual. That makes solely looking at memories quite difficult. I'm also opposed to pressing into the minds of others without consent, especially those like yourself, who have undoubtedly suffered a great deal," Kilian said.

"If we tell you what we know and you think we're innocent . . . We'll go free?" Luke said.

A crack of lightning illuminated the room and Kilian's face when he spoke.

"Precisely."

William pulled us to our feet. I swayed, and William caught my arm. Kilian walked to the front of the altar and grabbed the silver bowl. Placing his hands in the dripping water, he then marked a cross on Luke's forehead.

Luke flinched away as Kilian grabbed his face and hands and recited a prayer. "In this judgment, may you find peace, and your soul be set free."

"Amen." The robed members, who stood at the edges of the room, all spoke at once.

"Jesus, out of one cult and into another," Zach said, as Kilian placed the holy water on his head and repeated the same phrase.

Kilian walked up to me last, placing the cool water into two lines on my forehead. His gray eyes bore into mine as he repeated the prayer. "In this judgment, may you find peace and your soul be set free."

"Amen." The echoes of their voices rang in the dark room, solidifying their ceremony.

"Aaron, I will be addressing your brothers for most of the trial. It's important that you do not speak out of turn. I will address you directly if I need to." William placed me back on the floor, where I sat on my knees near my standing brothers. Probably to prevent having to hold me upright for the entirety of the trial. I was thankful, nonetheless.

"Luke and Zach Calem, you've been brought here under our council in your involvement in the death of the Hogert family and the disappearance of Sarah Garanger."

"What the fuck?" The words flew out of my mouth before I could catch them.

William clasped his hand over my mouth and leaned close to my ear. "Do not speak."

He kept his hand securely over my mouth, and I had no energy left to struggle. My stomach turned with anger and fear. Fear that my brothers were truly exactly like William claimed they were. My heart refused to believe those accusations. Luke would have never hurt Sarah. They were inseparable. She was like my Kimberly. He'd never lay a finger on her. I knew that. The room full of total strangers knew more about my brothers than I did in my nineteen years with them, and for a moment, I doubted my own conviction.

I was alert again.

"Zach, tell me what you know about the Hogert family."

Kilian stood tall. His shoulders pressed away from his ears, his body fully alert.

The Hogert family. Despite the brain fog from the blood loss, I was still certain I didn't know who that could be. The name wasn't ringing any bells in my memory.

"Raymond Hogert is the one who shot Luke our senior year of high school . . ." Zach's eyes panned to me, then back to Kilian. "Luke was in the wrong place at the wrong time, and he almost fucking killed him."

I sucked in a breath. It was true. Everything my best friend told me had actually happened.

"I see. I can imagine that made you angry."

"I didn't kill him. But believe me, I wanted to . . ." Zach's voice shook. "I wanted to kill him for what he did, and I probably would have if Ezra hadn't told me not to."

"And who is this Ezra to you?"

"He was a member of Her Guard, but to us, he was like a mentor. He's the one who helped us escape. That's how we were able to get all of our fake documents and shit and hide in Blackheart."

"A member of the Queen's Guard helped you escape?" William scoffed.

Luke spoke. "It's true. Ezra was the closest thing to a father figure we had. He helped us a lot."

"When Luke was shot, he promised they would handle it. They didn't want Luke and me involved in certain things. The Family worked like a real family. Someone hurt us, we hurt them. What did they do to them?"

"You don't know?" William scoffed, still sitting on the pew beside me, holding my mouth shut.

"Honestly, I don't. We never saw Raymond again. We never heard anything. After I cooled off and Luke got better, I let it go." Zach's voice was more solemn. "That's the truth. We didn't kill anyone."

Kilian cleared his throat. "The Hogert family were massacred in their own home. In that event, Raymond was killed along with his three siblings and his mother. The only survivor was his ten-year-old sister. The Family often leave survivors to send a message to another family member and give them an option for retaliation. Most don't."

A lump caught in my throat. How could my brothers be involved with people so sinister? I racked my brain, combing through old memories. All I could see were the smiles of my big brothers. Every time they picked me up from a party because I was too drunk or every Father's Day we spent celebrating just having each other. They couldn't be killers. They couldn't be the same as these people.

Zach gritted his teeth. "We didn't know."

"Of course you did," William spat. "Don't lie here." The robed figures stirred, whispering together.

"Check my memories, asshole. We didn't get a choice. They never let us see all the awful shit they did. All they had to do was make us forget. And they did. Over and over. Until we finally figured it out one day. That's why we left."

Kilian put his hand up, and the room stopped stirring. "I want to hear from Luke now."

He walked over to Luke, who was staring a hole into the floorboards.

"What happened to Sarah Garanger?"

I never knew Raymond. I didn't even know what he looked like. But Sarah I'd known for almost my whole life. She was funny, inquisitive, and she treated me and Presley like her little brothers. She had long shiny brown hair and a dimpled smile. She made the best chocolate chip cookies. When she went missing, the whole town was littered with her face. My mom cried. We all cried.

It never occurred to me that my brothers might have something to do with her disappearance. But they refused to talk about it. I just assumed it was too painful for Luke, and I didn't want to make him bring it up.

Luke's eyes fluttered at her name. "I didn't hurt Sarah."

"Do you know where she is?"

I waited anxiously for Luke to speak.

He looked over at me with solemn eyes, then back to Kilian. "She's dead."

It was like the wind was knocked out of me. I thought knowing the mystery would make me feel better, but it just made me feel like I was going to vomit. Sarah, who made Presley and me cupcakes for every birthday, who loved her big family more than anything else in the world, was gone. Why would anyone want to kill her?

Anger ignited under my feet, and I stirred, but William kept a firm grasp over my mouth. His other hand was resting firmly on my shoulder. How could my brothers let anything happen to her?

She was practically family.

"She died because of me," Luke said.

"Stop saying that." Zach was quick to correct him. "We didn't kill her. She did."

I swallowed. A cold chill ran down my spine. I was starting to truly understand how deep my brothers were in over their heads.

It only made the anger in my chest burn hotter.

William's hand tightened over my mouth. "They're lying."

"You weren't fucking there!" Zach yelled.

"Would you rather show me than tell me?" Kilian reached, and Luke flinched away. There was no anger or judgment in his voice.

Just pure patience.

"No. No, I can't," Luke said. "I can't go back there. I can't."

Kilian spoke again. "Then, tell me what transpired."

Luke's face grew red, as if mentally recalling it was physically painful. "Sarah meant everything to me. I wanted to save her. I tried to keep her away from me so she'd be safe, but it didn't matter. She killed her right in front of me . . . to punish me because I cared about someone more than Her. She wanted to teach us a lesson."

The anger I felt was short lived. I was right. Luke would do everything in his power to keep her safe. That's probably why they never actually got together. Luke had tried to protect her, but it wasn't enough.

I couldn't imagine the pain Luke must have been in, unable to tell me or just unwilling to. Kimberly came to mind. If I lost her, especially like that, I don't know if I'd be able to recover. Let alone keep on with my regular responsibilities. I wasn't much different from my brother. After all, I'd done the exact same thing with Kimberly. I tried to keep her safe but ended up dragging her down with me. Something that had almost killed her multiple times.

William scoffed. "We need to confirm his story. We can't just take his word for it. How do we know he didn't lead her there as a trap?"

"What benefit would we have from killing her?" Zach was growing more and more angry. "Come over here and confirm the story, then. I volunteer. I can show you what happened to Sarah. I was there too. And you can look back in my head as far as you want to make sure we're telling the truth."

Luke's head snapped up. "Zach, no."

Kilian's features softened. "You don't need to be afraid. I won't mess with your minds the way they did. Only with your permission will I look upon your memories."

Zach hands jangled in his chains, and he held up his bloody arm. "Do your worst."

A smile appeared on Kilian's face. He moved in closer, closing the gap between them. "I can feel your fear. You don't need to be afraid. Just relax."

Zach opened his palm, and the man cupped his hand. Immediately, Zach's chest heaved inward, and he closed his eyes. I never took my attention off his face. He was calm at first, but he stifled sobs. One by one, tears fell from his eyes.

William tightened his grip on my shoulder. He probably expected me to react in some way. The joke was on him. My legs were completely numb, and I was about eighty percent sure I was about to lose consciousness.

Kilian let go of Zach's hand after a few minutes. "So much pain. A terrible thing to witness."

I didn't need to know the exact story. The look on Zach's face was enough. It all made sense. The reason Luke was having panic attacks, the reason they kept everyone a secret. I thought I was the one who was in way over my head, but my brother's had me beat by a long shot.

Luke looked at me across the room, the candlelight flickering light on his face. "I didn't want the same thing to happen to you and Presley, and I didn't want you to ever know about this. I'm so sorry. Zach and I just wanted to help Mom with the money. That's why we joined when we were young. We thought it was harmless. Just stealing and pickpocketing in the city."

Zach sounded more melancholy. "We met Ezra when we were ten years old. He caught us stealing groceries. He promised us a life that didn't exist, one where we would never worry about money if we just did what he said. We didn't know what he was or who he was. They lied . . . a lot."

William released his hand, and I could finally speak. "He didn't tell you he was going to change you?"

"No," they said.

"We didn't know that was part of initiation. They drug you beforehand. We just woke up different. That's when we learned that She shared Her blood with us," Luke said.

And there it was. My brothers were manipulated into joining a vampire cult. The answer I'd be waiting months to hear, and it wasn't all that surprising for some reason. I think a part of me knew it because they cared and wanted to take care of us. They'd do anything for us, but I was seeing how far they'd go and the toll of what their decision meant. Zach and Luke had protected us, mostly, but it cost them everything. All their hopes and dreams. The girls they loved. They gave up everything they wanted for me.

"She is the one who turned you?" Kilian walked to the center of the altar. "You're sure?"

They nodded. A strange silence settled into the room. Everyone was more alert. More interested.

"Why? What does that mean?"

My days of keeping my mouth shut were done. Sadist swim boy be damned.

"The Family has a hierarchy of power. Lower recruits are not fed Her blood for the change. It's too sacred. Too important." Kilian was pacing again. His robe was gathering a layer of dust. "You must not be lower recruits to them . . . you must be much more precious to them."

"Precious . . ." Luke repeated under his breath, his eyes on the floor.

"How would you describe your relationship with the queen?" Kilian said.

He leaned forward with a string of prayer beads rolling between his fingers anxiously.

"Didn't I just show you that?" Zach snipped.

"This question in particular is for Luke," Kilian said as he watched Luke's face.

The room turned dead silent, other than the rain rushing along the stone walls.

I was reminded of what Luke said when I was eavesdropping. He said he missed Her. His voice dripped with longing. But how? After killing Sarah, how could he not hate Her like I hated Her?

Luke shook his head like he didn't want to answer, but after a few minutes in the silence, he did. "She's important to me. I'd be lying if I said I didn't feel connected to Her. But it's not real. It's just because we shared blood. But I never let the way I felt about Her come between what I knew was right. It's like Zach said. It's all just . . . manipulation."

His connection to Her was all blood, which meant that's all mine was too. The reason she showed up in my hallucination was all because of that tiny speck of blood.

I knew there was more to their story. There was no way all their stories could possibly be told in the course of one trial. I didn't know the extent of how deep their ties to The Family were or who She was to them, but I knew who my brothers were to me. I knew the extent they'd go to keep us safe, and in the end, they chose us. That was enough. It was finally enough for me.

"Gentlemen, I believe we've reached the end of the trial. You will now be able to say your final pleas."

My heart pounded. I leaned forward involuntarily, and William grabbed me to sit me up. The light of the flames blurred, causing haze to fill the entire room. A metallic taste lingered on my lips. I was scared. Yes. But also, I was barely holding on. If this was the end, at least we'd all die together.

Kimberly danced back into mind, with her fiery hair and laughter. I was going to miss her. There was so much more I wanted to do with her. Things I wanted to say. But her safety would have to be enough. She was with Presley, and they were safe. My job was done.

"I've collected sufficient information to make my final verdict and deliberate with the council. Please tell me your final plea." Kilian stood in line with the robed members who lined the walls, his hands outstretched as if he were worshipping.

Luke turned to me. "I'm sorry we can't get you out of this one. I wanted to tell you everything, but now you see why I didn't. I didn't want you to see how bad we messed up. Just because we didn't kill Sarah or Raymond doesn't mean we aren't guilty. We are. If I could go back, I would."

Zach sighed, watching Luke. "We're not guilty."

Kilian finally turned to me. "And you . . . What do you plead?"

I cleared my throat. The small movement hurt my chest. "I can't speak for my brothers . . . You'll probably say I'm biased, but they are good people. But in two months' time, I lied, put my brothers in danger, and then attacked an innocent girl twice because of my own stupidity. So, I'm guilty."

Zach put his head in his hands. "How did I know you would say some cheesy shit like that? You two and your morality really pisses me off sometimes."

I smiled. "What can I say? It's kinda been my job since birth." To my surprise, Zach laughed. In a strange way, I felt at peace. I'd finally fixed my mess. I righted my wrongs. That alone was enough to keep me calm. Kilian held up his hands, and the robed figures followed him to the altar. With their backs turned, they deliberated. I tried to remember every detail of my brothers' faces, hoping that, if death wasn't swift, I could have that as my last comfort. I thought we'd have eternity together, but forever turned out to be pretty short.

My voice was barely a whisper. "I'm sorry I was such an asshole. I think I get it now, why you kept all those secrets."

"We know. You don't have to apologize," Zach said.

"No, I mean you literally joined a cult when you were ten, so we wouldn't go hungry and then, somehow, you were able to escape that cult despite some weird connection to a vampire queen and try to save us. Granted, it didn't exactly work out but . . . Zach, you were right. I don't know anything about being selfless, nothing that you haven't taught me. Thank you both for everything. Maybe in another life we'll stay clear of the cult thing."

Luke's eyes glistened, and he held up a fist to Zach, who bumped it, then held up his fist to me. Our unspoken bond could never be broken. Not even in death. I was convinced wherever I went after death, they'd find a way to get to me. It was our unspoken promise to never go alone.

As the meeting adjourned, two more robed people each came to stand by us. William stayed next to Kilian. The candles were little wax stumps on the floor, the large candelabra dripping wax in little red pools next to the cross.

"Our deliberations have been made. Through the majority vote of council, you have all been found guilty for your involvement with The Family," Kilian said swiftly.

My heart sank as the room stirred around me.

"However, it is by my decision your final verdict is made. I was quite moved by your displays of affection earlier. I did not expect you to choose someone other than your family to live. To condemn your innocent brother to death is your ultimate fear, and yet you looked it in the face and accepted it because it was the right thing to do. I've met many members of The Family. I've been battling them for centuries. Many of them are cold and unfeeling. Their obsessions are forced into them at a young age, and they are loyal only to their queen. I see that is not the case here. Having seen the memories . . . I was quite moved by your resilience to evil and your love for your family."

He turned to Luke. "I do not know Her plans for you, but I do see what She saw in you. Someone valiant, innocent, and virtuous. The Family loves corruption. They need people like you, Luke. They chose you because you are good."

"And, Zach, you as well. Your loyalty to your brothers is what they ultimately want from you for them, but you would not give it freely. So, they take."

"Despite your failings, I've concluded that your connection to The Family is by blood only. This manipulation, along with the tragedy it would be to convict the rest of your family of your past crimes, has made it very clear for me. Your final verdict is not guilty."

My brothers and I shared a joyful smile. Relief washed over me.

"Does this mean you'll let us go?" Zach said, stirring in his chains.

"You are wanted by one of the only six queens left in existence. We will require your help to bring Her down. You and your family will be allowed to continue on with your normal lives on campus with . . . supervision. I must stress the importance of your involvement with The Family. In all of my years hunting them, I have never seen their queen show such interest in Her disciples. They want you for something. We can use this to draw them out of hiding."

"You want to use us as bait?" I chuckled, my body wobbly.

"You will be protected. You will not be allowed to go anywhere that members of The Legion cannot. The Family will hunt you whether we are involved or not. We can use this opportunity to bring down the last queen in the western hemisphere. It will not be easy, but I believe you all have great potential to be productive and valuable members of society once more."

We had babysitters. It was better than waiting around for The Family to find us and do God knows what with us. This was a major upgrade. The tightness in my chest loosened when Kilian spoke again.

"With that conclusion, we must start with the removal of your tattoo. We cannot risk you being identified in public."

At the sound of his words, the two members closest to Zach and Luke unchained their hands. Without another word, they pulled small silver blades from their robes and took it to my brothers' skin. Carving out the little black lines tattooed on their wrists. My brothers didn't fight it, but their cries of pain echoed up into the walls of the stone church.

The shock of what was happening hit me like a train. My brothers' screams of pain echoed in my ears. Dizziness hit me, and it took me a moment to realize what was happening. The ringing was back in my ears, and the room faded. I brought my hands up to my head, trying to get it to stop.

"Stop. Please. Stop," I said.

My own words felt far away. The room spun, and I no longer felt any evidence of reality. Pain was my only reality and an unreal feeling of terror took over my entire body. I couldn't find my way back. That Thing in my head was clawing its way out of my head and taking over.

"Aaron, you need to drink blood."

William's voice was my only companion in that dark place.

He pulled me back into the world, and he placed something in my hand. "Drink this."

"I-I can't. I don't need it."

"Oh, you don't? The look on your face is telling me otherwise." He raised a blood bag in front of me. The red liquid made my mouth water. "You're spiraling. You need to drink if you want to live."

His face was blurry and hard to see. I could feel other eyes on me, but I couldn't focus on anything but William.

"Drink. It."

I moved the plastic around in my hand and watched as the wave of blood crashed inside. A deep longing surfaced within. My eyes trained on the red color, and it took over my vision. I brought the bag to my lips and bit down. The first drop on my tongue sent my mind racing. I squeezed the bag harder and tried to get more. Blood was the only thing I could think about. It was everywhere all at once. It was everything. Time passed quickly, and I snatched the other bag from his hand without a second thought. Blood. Blood. Blood.

A carnal thirst ripped open my chest, and every drop filled an infinite void. I opened my eyes, but all I could see was deep red. My hands shook as I squeezed harder until the bag went limp in my hands. It dropped, and I stared at the smearing of red covering my hands. More. More. *More.* I needed more.

The fog lifted, and I could finally see where I was. I had been brought back to the empty room Kimberly and I had been in. William and another robed man watched me with worried expressions.

The longing I had for blood wasn't fading. My muscles moved on their own, and I flew out of the chair. The men grabbed my arms and held me down.

"I need more." The words escaped my lips, and I shut my eyes and glued my back to the chair. I wouldn't dare let my body move another inch.

"No, you don't. You don't need more. Listen to my voice."

William's voice was calm, and I tried to focus on that despite the strange numbness traveling up my body.

"Don't think about the blood. You have to focus on something else."

That was easier said than done. Panic was setting in, and I couldn't think of anything other than the fear in my head. I was losing control.

"Here." William grabbed my hands and dug his fingers into my skin.

The pain sent a shock wave through my body. The sudden jolt was enough to stop the numbness from traveling farther and for my mind to prioritize.

"There. It should be stopping. You're okay. This is your body. You're in control of it."

"This is my body. I'm in control." I repeated the phrases until I believed it.

"You feel that? That release? It's letting go of ya."

The numbness disappeared completely. The empty room came back into view. Somehow, everything seemed brighter. I looked at the chair next to me. Kimberly's absence felt like a gaping hole. But soon, I'd see her again. I couldn't wait to get out of that godforsaken church.

I wiped my mouth and tried to still my trembling body. "Thank you."

"You need to get yourself under control. Honestly, waiting this long to feed . . ."

Kneeling beside me, he sighed. "But I suppose I have to give you a pass, considering your idiot brothers turned you themselves."

"Yeah, they meant well. I know they did," I said, every muscle in my body aching and fatigued.

"Must you always defend them?"

I shrugged. "I think they did all right with what they had."

William scoffed. "Well, remember this. When you drink, you can't think about the blood. The blood isn't for you. It's for that Thing you share a body with. It's dark and evil. So, you drink, but only to shove it back into the hole it came from. You got that?"

"Yeah." I cleared my throat, my body feeling like a truck had run me over.

"This is just the beginning. We have blood bags to help you, but you're going to need to feed more now for the rest of your life because you let it get this bad. Surely, you've learned your lesson, finally."

I nodded. My mind couldn't comprehend what he was saying. There would be consequences. That much I gathered.

"You will be weak for a few days. It's normal to be sleepy. Just rest. You'll need more blood, but we can help with that," William said.

He turned his attention to the robed girl with white hair in the hallway.

"They're causing a fuss again." She motioned back toward the hallway.

"Tell them he's fine." William growled. "Thanks to me."

William pressed his fingers into the bridge of his nose. "You guys are going to be a handful. I can already tell."

"I guess I'll be seeing you around a lot more."

He smiled as he placed his hands on his knees and hoisted himself up. "Yeah, guess so. It's a shame, though. I really wanted to kill you."

I mustered up the strength for a laugh. "Sorry to disappoint you, psychopath."

"Good night, Aaron." William smirked, reaching to touch my forehead, and everything deteriorated again. But no pain followed.

Only rest.

TWENTY-TWO

KIMBERLY

Excitement bubbled up in my chest as I walked up the sidewalk toward the frat house. The sun peeked through the trees in the most beautiful way. Rays of sunshine painted the bricks. Warmth hugged my entire body, and I danced up the steps with a decadent bouquet of wildflowers in my good hand. My left hand was still wrapped up and would stay immobile for a while. I'd already gotten used to doing a lot of my daily tasks one-handed. As the doorbell rang, I pressed my head against the thick wooden door, listening to the stirring inside. The muffled sounds of yelling and laughter.

Aaron answered the door, wearing his khaki shorts and soft cotton button-down, his socks impressively rolled and complementing his white Converse.

He greeted me with a warm smile and grabbed the bouquet from my hand. "Hey! Are you ready to go? Let's go."

"Wait. I wanted to say hi to the guys before we leave."

Little lines appeared on his forehead. "Eh, right now isn't a great time."

My curiosity instantly piqued. "Why? What's happening?"

I pushed the door open, and Aaron led me inside. Zach's loud yelling was identifiable and coming from the living room. Aaron's brothers were all gathered there with a scattering of other guys I couldn't identify. William was leaning over the couch, watching Zach with a bored expression. All The Legion members had the same clothing aesthetic. Plaid, beige, and trouser pants.

"Fuck you." Zach's words echoed in the empty frat house. His shoulders were hunched as he glared at William.

"Kimberly's here!" Aaron jumped in front of me.

"Hey, Kimberly!" Everyone greeted me with excitement and smiles.

Even those in The Legion were starting to get used to seeing me around. It was going to take time to learn all their names and faces, but the summer break would be the perfect opportunity.

Presley wrapped me in a hug and spun me. We had quite a lot of bonding time in the car after I was let go and we needed to get out of town. We talked about strategy, future plans, and cried together. We were overjoyed when we got the call and we didn't actually have to become runaways.

"Oh, Kim, I was just explaining to William how excited I am that they will be living here with us." Zach forced a smile in my direction. A small gust of wind blew his hair, and he ran his hands through it to tame it.

A long faint scar replaced the spot where the tattoo used to be. Luke had the same one. A reminder for all of us of the lengths they would go to keep us safe.

All the windows in the living room were open, and the summer air was wafting throughout the room, and the smell of freshly mowed grass was everywhere.

Finals were over. Aaron and I had to ask for an extension due to medical reasons and ended up taking our tests a week late. I passed all my classes with flying colors. Thankfully, my classes for the last semester had been pretty easy. Aaron struggled a bit but passed with mostly Bs and Cs. Luke was proud.

Luke was beside him. Laughter escaped his lips. "Yeah, we are super excited, if you can't tell. How's your hand?"

"You know you don't have to ask me that every time you see me?" I joked.

"He can't help it. It's his dad instincts." Presley shot Luke a wicked grin as he balanced himself on the back of the armchair.

Luke grabbed Presley by his hood and pushed him off the chair. "Shut up."

"Where'd you get the flowers? Are you guys going on a date?" Zach nudged Aaron playfully.

"No, they're actually for someone else." I smiled. "Another girl, actually."

"Damn, Aaron, what's wrong with you?" Presley crawled on his stomach toward us. "Don't worry, Kim, I'll get you some flowers."

"Thanks, Pres. You're the best." A playful smile danced on my lips as

I turned to Aaron.

"Do you guys ever shut up?" William rolled his eyes, turning his attention back to Zach.

"Don't worry, you'll get used to it." I smiled.

William winked at me as he leaned against the wall. I didn't completely trust him. But neither did Zach, and I knew I could trust Zach to keep an eye on him.

Zach and Luke filled me in as Aaron recovered, leaving out no details. Even ones they didn't need to tell me. I wouldn't be forgetting anytime soon how The Legion actually felt about the Calem brothers and how they had been found guilty. I was thankful for Kilian, though, and his ability to see a fraction of what I saw in them. It made me a little more willing to trust them, but I wasn't fully convinced.

"Where is everyone? I know it's summer break, but it's really quiet," I said, eyeing the empty staircase and kitchen.

"That's the problem." Zach scoffed.

"They relocated all other frat members and are moving in all of their people." I could tell Luke was choosing his words carefully.

By the look on Zach's face, I guessed it was to avoid another fight.

"Whoa, you can do that?" I said.

"We can do a lot of things. It will be a new chapter. One no one has ever heard of before." William smirked.

Aaron reached the door and quickly turned the handle. "We should probably get going."

"Wait! Kim, you're still coming over later, right? Luke was going to cook you one of his old favorite dishes," Zach said.

"Wow, thanks, Dad." Presley joked.

"Oh, I'm definitely coming." I dashed over to Aaron's side.

"See you guys later."

Their voices ran into each other in a loud roar as they said their goodbyes. Aaron quickly shut the door behind me.

"Oh, thank God. Sweet freedom!" Aaron jumped from the stairs and spun in the yard.

"You were eager to get out of there." I chuckled at the exasperated look on his face.

"They've been driving me crazy. They cannot agree on a single thing, and Zach and Luke are constantly arguing back and forth with them.

I cannot go *anywhere* without them needing to know an exact location and for how long. I don't know how I'm going to last the summer, not to mention the next school year."

I imagined all the parties Aaron and his brothers loved that year. From the looks of the members of The Legion, I didn't peg them as the partying type.

"Oh, it will definitely be interesting."

Aaron sighed. "I'm sorry. I just had to get that all out."

"I thought we agreed you weren't allowed to say that word to me anymore." A small smile tugged at the corner of my lips.

"Shit. You're right. I'm so happy to be here with you and don't want to ruin it by talking about my brothers."

It felt good seeing Aaron back to his fun, happy self. I hadn't been allowed to see him for the first five days since he was so blood deprived.

The sorority house was coming into view. Giggling laughter escaped my lips as our feet peddled along the sidewalk. I turned to the bright bouquet of wildflowers Aaron had bunched in his hand. The smell was intoxicating.

Aaron's sunbathed face turned white in an instant. "Kim, I'm scared."

"Oh, hush, you'll be fine." I tried to stifle another laugh.

"You don't think it's a little early? She's probably still pissed. She only slapped you, like, a week ago . . . Wait or was it two weeks? Shit, I need a calendar for this stuff."

We stopped in front of the Sigma Sigma Xi sorority house. It was a beautiful tan color with white shutters that blended nicely with the greenery behind it. The entryway had long, thick pillars, and we hid out of view.

I leaned in. "No, this is perfect. She's had time to cool off but not so much that she can completely resent you yet."

"You are the smartest, most cunning woman I know. How do you do it? Tell me in extreme detail," Aaron said.

"Stop stalling."

"I know. I know. But does this apology even count if I don't remember saying what I said?" Aaron looked up at the house, the crease returning to his forehead.

"It will matter to her. Trust me." A smile danced on my lips, my eyes gazing at the muscles on his forearms. "I don't think I've ever seen you look so . . . dashing."

He squinted and tried to hide a slight blush in his cheeks. "This is a trap. I know it."

He took a deep breath before bouncing up the marble steps. I followed close behind and moved over to the edge of the porch. He rapped his knuckle on the large door, and my heart jumped in my ribs. Aaron flashed me a worried expression before the door opened.

"Hey, is, uh, Chelsea here?"

I couldn't see anything on the inside as I hid my body next to the wall.

"Yeah, hold on. I'll get her for you," some girl said.

I tried to keep a brave face for Aaron, but even I was a little worried. Butterflies fluttered around in my stomach, making it harder to wait. The sound of heels clicking against hardwood echoed in a rhythm.

"What are you doing here? Come to yell at me again?"

Aaron cleared his throat. "Uh, actually I wanted to bring you these and apologize."

He flung the flowers a little too swiftly, causing some petals to fall to the ground.

"I don't need an apology. I'm a big girl. I can handle it."

"Of course you can, and if you never want to talk to me again, I understand. Just know, who I was on that day . . . It's not reflective of who I am. I never wanted to hurt you. I'm sorry for all of it. I really am."

A long pause followed by the swing of the door. "Goodbye, Aaron."

He turned toward me, letting out a long breath. "Well, that could have gone better."

I smiled softly and patted him on the shoulder.

"No, you tried. You apologized. That's all that matters. Now, it's my turn." I reluctantly grabbed the bouquet from his hand and walked toward the door. It was a lot more fun being the one who was hiding.

I knocked on the door, only this time, seconds passed before a very distraught Chelsea opened the door. Her hair was wild and out of place, but her makeup was well-kept.

"Great. Have you come to plead for Aaron. Because it's not going to work."

"Actually, I just wanted to see how you were doing. I, uh . . . hated how things went, and I just wanted to check on you."

She leaned against the door, watching me. "Why? I'm the one that slapped you in the face."

"Well . . . just . . ."

My chest tightened. I glanced over at Aaron who motioned for me to continue. "I'm not good at this. So, I'm just going to say what I'm thinking."

"This should be good."

"I know we haven't gotten along very well, and we had a misunderstanding, which was my fault. But I'd love to hang out with you sometime because I feel like we have a lot in common."

Her face was unmoving, and her dark circles had overtaken her prettier features.

"I know I'm awkward. I don't have a lot of experience in this type of thing." I held out the bouquet to her. "Whatever you choose. We are good in my book."

She sighed as she eyed the flowers in front of her. "Yeah, this is kinda weird." Her expression softened, and she grabbed the bouquet from my hands. "But that's okay. Thank you."

For the first time, she smiled at me. Really smiled at me with her sparkling white teeth. It looked good on her despite it being a rarity.

"You're welcome." I flashed her a smile before turning back to Aaron, who was hiding behind the pillar.

"Kimberly. You live in Rogers, right?"

"Yeah, I'll be here through the summer."

"Okay. I'll come by, and we can go shopping or whatever. I've noticed you have pretty good taste."

"Uh, yeah, that would be awesome."

She turned to leave but stopped. "And no, you can't come, Aaron."

"I know. I know." Aaron winked at me.

"Bye, Chelsea." I waved, and Aaron and I returned to the pavement.

Relief washed over me as I let out a breath into the wind. The weight of guilt was lifted.

"Looks like someone made a new friend." Aaron nudged me, causing me to stumble off the sidewalk.

"Yeah, it's kind of cool. I've never outright asked someone that before."

"If only I had similar good news. I get it, though. I wouldn't forgive me either." He kicked a tiny pebble, and it skidded between fault lines.

"She'll forgive you. She just needs time."

The smell of freshly cut grass rode the breeze. Every gust gave way to that sweet scent again.

"So, what do you want to do with the rest of our day? Frolic through the mountains, read a book, talk about how utterly doomed this life is?"

"Actually, I kind of want to stay in. Do you have any good movies?"

"Ha! Please, do I have any good movies? I'm the smartest of my brothers and have much better taste when it comes to the cinema." His words curled together in a melody.

"Yeah, I believe that."

My phone buzzed in my pocket, and I let it go to voicemail. It was Chris again, but this time, I had guessed he was just calling to check in. I had called him and cleared the air, leaving out all vampire-related details. He wasn't a perfect friend, but he had been there for me growing up. Letting all that go would be a mistake. After nearly dying, I realized how life was too short to hold a grudge. Our friendship changed. That didn't mean it had to end. The distance between us was a blessing. I didn't want to risk bringing anyone else into the Calem brothers' wake.

It was too late for me, but I wasn't complaining. Aaron's smile warmed me again. It was even brighter than the sun. The weight of darkness was gone . . . mostly.

"You seem better. How are you feeling?" I said.

My words stopped his fluent walking.

"Yeah, I'm dealing. Slowly. But I've been talking to my brothers about it. I think I'm going to get a few more blood bags from William, then they are going to help teach me how to control it so I can feed on my own. You know they have the mind-control thing that should help."

"That's a relief. We can't have you turn Mr. Hyde again. That was . . . ."

"Scary. I think I'm always going to struggle with it a bit, but I've got all the time in the world to figure out my inner torment." His grin returned to his face.

"Yeah, you're already a little too much." I smiled. "But seriously, I'm proud of you for putting in the work. I honestly can't imagine how hard that would be."

"You're giving me too much credit." Aaron chuckled and wrapped his arm around me as we carried on. "Come on, I want to show you something. I hope there are no vampire hunters following me!"

I put my hand on Aaron's mouth. "What are you doing?"

"I just don't want any of those guys following us." His teeth gleamed in the sunlight.

"Where are you taking me?" I said as he steered us off the sidewalk.

"To show you all the mysterious wonders of BFU."

We walked through the grass in the parking lot behind building C, the same one with the clock tower and the high arched windows.

"Isn't this where they keep all the garbage bins?" I joked.

Aaron's walking turned into a skip. "That's what everyone wants you to think but really . . . "

We rounded the corner to some trees that cleared a way onto a path, a little sign hung loosely that read, "Twisted Oak Point."

"What is this?"

"Well, I thought to myself, what's a unique location I can bring the girl who has lived here her whole life, and after rigorous searching and, by that, I mean asking a few random people on the street, they told me about this old trail."

"Wow." I stood in shock for a moment. "Yeah, let's go."

My sundress and strappy sandals didn't stop me. I ran up to him, and we locked arms.

He chuckled. "Don't worry. It's short."

We'd only grown closer since our near-death experience, and I found myself relishing every minute together. Time was precious. "I may have scoped it out beforehand. I had to see if it was lame," Aaron said.

"Why did you go through all this trouble?" I looked up at him, squinting into the bright sun.

He patted my hand as I wrapped it around his forearm. "Because. Because it makes you smile. You get this look on your face. I love it."

I couldn't take my attention off the feeling of his hand on mine. His touch was warm and sincere, but most of all, it felt natural. We reached the clearing into a wide-open space. A little pond was set ablaze by the setting sun. An old bench was perched right on the water's edge. The golden sunshine hit the water at just the right angle, and the peach sky reflected in the soft ripples.

"Well, what do you think?" Aaron was watching my face.

"It's so beautiful—come on." I pulled him to the bench. Its bright, tattered blue finish caught my eye instantly.

It was the perfect picture. The perfect gift. I wanted to drink it all in. Aaron's expression melted into one of peace, and we sat close together. My mind wandered back to our meeting place in the campus cafeteria. If anything hadn't lined up perfectly, I wouldn't have been sitting there. I would probably be in my dorm alone.

My chest tightened at the thought. I turned my attention to Aaron, and the light tinged every feature on his face an ambient pink. Even the pale-blond streaks in his hair were tinted like a glow from a fire. He turned to me without any words. His winning smile took over his lips.

"Aaron, what are you doing?" I chuckled. "You keep looking at me like that."

He let out a quick breath and averted his eyes. "What are you talking about? I'm not doing anything."

"That look . . ." I said, with a wide smile.

"Well, you're nice to look at, Burns. What can I say?" He wiggled his brows.

Nervous laughter escaped my lips, and I kept my gaze out on the water. I pulled my hair behind my ear as heat rose to my cheeks.

"You're blushing again." He grinned.

"Well, so are you."

He tilted his head back and laughed. "So what if I am? I think it's you that's giving me the eyes. It's like you're secretly in love with me or something."

If I wasn't blushing before, I was right then. My breath hitched in my chest, and my heart beat faster.

"So what if I was . . . hypothetically. Would that be bad?"

There were a handful of reasons why it would be bad. The most glaring one was the fact that Aaron was immortal and I was not. But in the crux of the prettiest sunset I'd ever seen, I didn't care. There was no way to deny the way I felt when he was near me.

Aaron looked shocked by my seriousness and was instantly nervous. "Uh, no. I'd be really happy if that were true. Even though, hypothetically speaking, it might be a bad idea. Probably not the smartest thing we could do. But I might say that . . . I felt the same way."

I smiled. "All hypothetically, of course."

He smirked. "Totally."

His attention was on my lips. The air buzzed between us with electricity. Fireflies were starting their night. Slowly floating around us. He leaned forward, and my heart responded. After a long pause, he reached over, grabbed my bandaged wrist, and softly traced his fingers over mine.

He wouldn't forgive himself easily, if he ever would.

"We have time," I said, leaning my head back and letting what was left of the sun warm me.

But we did have time. I didn't need to rush it. I could let it burn. Grow. Enjoy the moment and not think too far ahead. Every minute that passed, my heart grew softer and more used to the idea of him being around for good.

"Oh, I've got all the time in the world." Aaron was all smiles again. Our expressions were a perfect reflection. The longer I stared into his eyes, the more it hurt to turn away.

Aaron stretched his arms and let out a big yawn. "Gosh, I'm just so tired. Must be leftover trauma."

He placed his arm around my shoulder, and my heart leaped in my chest.

"Yeah, yeah." I scooted closer and rested my head on his cotton shirt.

Every muscle in my body relaxed. Our hands touched in the amber light, and the soft echo of Aaron's heartbeat reverberated in his chest. I knew there was one truth I would always hold on to.

Everything was better when we were together.

EPILOGUE

THE FAMILY– THE GUARD

"California? What the fuck are they doin' there?" Akira said, sitting on a table from the French Revolution.

His thick-soled boots scuffed the finish.

The queen's Guards were sitting in the library, every wall filled with towering book shelves that went clear to the ceilings. The shelves were lined with century-old reads with tattered spines and old parchment. A large lavish rug brought warmth to the velvet couches. The soft glow of the fireplace lit up their brief reunion.

"They're being protected by The Legion." Sirius walked the length of the room, his hands shoved into his high-waisted trousers, his warm skin contrasting the white sweater that covered his neck. Dark-brown locks covered his ears. The gears turned in his head like a well-oiled machine. As third in command, his smarts kept the Guard in line.

"Legion? Protect? Who the fuck are they going to protect? They're weak bastards." Akira pulled his hands through his jet-black hair, his arms covered in tattoos. His style always changed, but he'd found a love in tech wear. He loved the overlapping fabric jackets and the large over-the-top baggy shorts he could tuck into his boots.

"You're awfully quiet." Sirius looked over at Ezra, who still had his nose in a book.

"Just thinking," Ezra said, wearing a fitted black blazer and a white undershirt. He preferred to wear something less fussy.

Akira's eyes bore a hole into Ezra's neck. "I'm still trying to figure out how they got out in the first place? Eh, Ezra?"

Ezra set his jaw and didn't let an ounce of emotion show on his face. He knew Akira suspected him. If he ever had a minuscule piece of evidence, he'd turn him in for treason. Akira, though a bit of a wild card, was the second in command for a reason. He was fiercely loyal to the queen.

"She needs to know right away." Ezra placed his book down on the end table Akira had been sitting on.

"Then, let's go." Akira jumped up. They knew their assignment at once.

They followed Ezra down the hall. One on either shoulder. The hallway was lined in an ornate flower rug that moved when they walked on the dusty hardwood floors. The walls were laid in gray-and-red brick, framed by a warm wooden trim. The Family's young members stopped as they passed by, averting their eyes and bowing their heads. They clung to the edge of the walls to leave more than enough room for the Guard to walk. At the end of the hallway was a long winding staircase that disappeared into the ceiling above. They ascended, heads low and shoulders back. Every muscle held a level of discipline and reverence.

They stayed silent. Each of their minds in another place entirely. Until they reached Her room.

They opened the door to Her chamber, a place only they were allowed to go freely. It was crafted to Her liking and had all the furnishings She could want, including a white canopy bed and a handcrafted vanity She would use to comb Her hair. Velvet couches and soft rugs from all over the world. She stood staring out the window to central Manhattan. Long black curtains blocked the sun's rays from Her skin. Her long white hair stretched down to Her waist, and Her porcelain skin contrasted with the red bricks that stretched to the ceiling. A thin veil grazed Her translucent cheeks, shielding Her eyes.

She turned to greet them, Her satin white dress dragging across the rich hardwood floors. Her fingers danced on the top of the sleeping grand piano in the corner. There was always an occasion of great importance when all three guards were gathered in the same place.

They stood in front of Her and took a knee. One hand reached for the floor while the other hid behind their backs. The Guard always waited. Always willing.

Ezra, the leader of the Guard, spoke. "We've found them. The Calem brothers."

The other Guard members dared not speak a word. Ezra was the only one freely allowed to speak with Her. He was Her ultimate protector. Not just Her physical body but of Her will.

"I knew you would." She smiled beneath Her veil. "It's far, but I can go—"

Her voice pierced them. "You will not. Akira will."

"May I ask why?" Ezra swallowed, his mouth suddenly dry. "Zach and Luke were my responsibility. Having been the one to recruit them and train them, I believe I could bring them home."

"I need you with me. The time is coming where the old Guard will pass away, and the new shall take its place." She walked in closer and ran Her fingers through Ezra's brown hair, noting the bits of silver. "Our time together wanes, and I need to make sure you'll be here to lead them."

For the last hundred years, the Guard had known their time was ending. Her prophecy stated the change and that two Gemini twins would secure Her Guard, with the addition of two more.

"I understand. I'm happy to stand by your side." Ezra closed his eyes, savoring the feeling of Her skin on his.

She smiled, Her lips perfectly pink. "Akira, are you able to complete the task? I want them all brought back here. Alive."

"Yes. I'll see that it's done." Akira pulled his arm tightly to his chest and nodded.

Sirius lifted his head, signaling he needed to speak.

"Yes, dear Sirius?" She walked forward and kneeled before him before placing a delicate hand against his cheek. His body shivered in Her proximity.

"They are being protected by The Legion. I saw it with my own eyes."

The smile left Her delicate lips. A silent rage burned. "I see. That will make your journey more treacherous, Akira. But I have full confidence in your abilities. Please bring members of your squadron with you."

"Of course." Akira kept the excitement bubbling in his chest at bay. He loved a challenge.

Sirius raised his head again, waiting for his permission to speak. "There is one more thing. The Calems appear to be with a girl. Possibly a girlfriend to the younger brother, Aaron."

A long silence stilled as She paced. Sirius tried to avert his eyes from Her face, but he couldn't. He admired every inch of Her skin. Every strand of hair that flowed from Her head was a sight to behold.

She stopped and removed the veil from Her eyes to face Her Guard. Jealousy laced in beat with her cold heart. Her Guard stood at attention, the ecstasy of seeing Her washed over them.

A sinister smile crept on her lips, and Her venomous voice filled the room. "Kill her."

The Summer Chronicles

Chronicles

"I can still recall our first summer."

"Now or Never"

Aaron

I'd planned it for weeks. It had taken me that long to summon the courage to ask her.

For a date, but not *a date*. We couldn't date, but as I watched her, lying on her stomach engrossed by her book, red hair glimmering in the sun, I knew it was now or never.

All summer she'd worn sun dresses. Some longer that went to her ankles, but this one was short and bunched up around her upper thighs.

She was too beautiful to be sitting with me, but she was with me almost every single day we weren't working at the waterpark. And sometimes even there too.

Giving me her arm to doodle on with a pink paint pen, I drew a little fat cat with vampire wings and fangs, accompanied by tiny hearts that went up her forearm.

I liked the way goose bumps ran up her arm and she wiggled when I traced my fingers along her skin.

"You're tickling me." She smiled up at me with the summer sun in her eyes.

I moved to block the rays. Lying in a grassy patch on the lawn of BFU, the soft smell of pine mixed with the scent of her perfume and the garden permeated the air. The cool thing about California was that something was always blooming there. Even though there were summer classes, the campus was empty.

"I thought you weren't ticklish," I said.

"I guess I'd never had it put to the test."

I lay back on the grass, watching the blue sky, and she put her book aside to lay next to me.

"You're always watching me," she said.

I rolled on my side to face her. "I'm kinda afraid you'll disappear."

Her nose crinkled. "I think that's my line."

I moved a piece of hair from her eyes. I could stay with her forever, in our eternal summer, where we had nothing to do but see each other. Some days felt untouchable when it was just us—and I could almost forget about all my vampire cult problems.

As I grazed her cheek, I savored the soft rhythm of her heartbeat growing faster.

"I have the greatest idea," I said.

"Hm?"

"We should go to the carnival together."

"The one on the boardwalk? It's too far, they'll never let us go."

The Legion was strict. Work and campus were the only places we could go freely.

"That wasn't a no." I smiled.

"Are you asking me on a date, Aaron Calem?"

Did I detect flirting?

"I mean . . . would you want it to be a date?"

Her face flushed. "That's probably not our best idea."

"No, it's an amazing idea, I think. You and me. Lots of food. Rides. Smell a little of the salty sea air."

"We go as friends. And no kissing." She folded her arms over her chest, but her gaze lingered. She *was* flirting with me. Did she know she was flirting with me? Because that wasn't fair.

"You say that like I'm going to try to kiss you."

"You might. You keep giving me that look."

"Okay, well you give me the look all the time. You're doing it right now."

Her mouth fell open, and she tossed her paint pen at me. "Am not."

"Fine. Normal"—I couldn't bring myself to say the word friend—"hang out. Totally not a date."

"It's not a date," I whispered to Presley as we walked. "She specified no kissing."

"That just means she's thought about kissing you. It's totally a date. Look around."

We walked along the boardwalk toward the carnival. The smell of the fried food and sweets drifted in the ocean air. Its lights were enough to block out the stars around us.

It was not how I imagined our first date—with my brothers. William wouldn't let us go alone, and they didn't want to split up their security. So group activity it was. Will lurked somewhere close, along with some other Legion, but I couldn't see them . . . thankfully. After the broken window in OBA—Presley's fault—I think William learned it was better to let us out to blow off some energy.

When we reached the entrance, I attempted to create distance between them.

"Okay, see you guys later. Kimberly and I going to go wherever you aren't."

"You won't even know we are here," Luke said. "You guys go have fun, and we'll hang around."

It was like being back in high school when my mom or my brothers had to take me on dates before I could drive. Embarrassing didn't cover it. I was a grown man forced to stay next to them for all eternity.

"Good. You guys go the complete opposite way," I said.

"We get it." Zach pulled out a cigarette and lit it.

I wrapped my arm around Kimberly and led her away as quickly as her legs would allow.

"You didn't want them to come?" she asked, eyebrows furrowed.

"Uh, no. I spend every moment with them now and not nearly enough with you . . . alone."

"Well, we're alone now."

She fluffed her hair, seemingly as happy about that as I was.

My daydream had come true. The sparkling carnival lights lit up in her eyes, and the breeze from the sea blew her hair away from her face. We were here.

"What should we do first?" I asked.

She shrugged. "I don't know. I've never been."

"Like ever? I'm sensing a pattern here. One where you need someone to drag you from your room and tell you to live a little."

"You wouldn't have to drag me, and I have seen movies. So I know how they work. I know there are games and food, and rides that make you throw up."

"But you've never rode any amusement park rides or played the games?"

She pursued her lips. "No."

"Come on." I grabbed her hand and took the lead.

I knew exactly where I needed to take her first.

The bustling crowd was relentless. Which, in hindsight, was probably one of the only reasons William agreed to it. They were watching in the distance. I couldn't see them, but I could *feel* them. *Just* out of sight, hiding between the bodies of parents and their crying kids jacked up on too much sugar.

We stopped in front of the duck game. Fun and easy. A classic.

"It's a rite of passage for you to play this game. All you have to do is pick a duck and you win."

Her eyes lit up with excitement as she pulled a plastic duck from the flock, which resulted in a small pink bear, and an ear-to-ear smile formed on her face. I was on the right track.

"How do you get those big ones?" She pointed to someone holding an adult-sized teddy bear.

From then on, I made it my life's mission to win her a huge teddy bear.

"Most of these games are rigged and designed to make you pay lots of money. Good thing you have a vampire to help you."

Something human Aaron would have spent a lot of money to do, but vampire Aaron was much cooler and didn't need money to win games.

"What about that one?" I pointed to a huge pastel-pink bear with heart eyes tied to a pole in the distance.

Her eyes widened, and the lights sparkled in her eyes. *Bingo.*

"You don't need to get me that. I don't need anything. Plus, where would I put it?"

"Does it matter? It's the thrill of winning it, then staring at it in your room for at least a year."

Presley used to have an army of his victory stuffed animals he'd hoarded in his closet along with his clothes.

I led the way to the game, and she held onto my shirt while walking

through the crowd. Buzzing from the excitement of our first game together, we reached the next one. A test of strength. A long lighted pole
that stretched high into the sky. A couple finished their turn and brought
home a medium-sized stuffed monkey. The man had swung the hammer
against the target on the ground, and it flew up halfway.

"Sir, you look like a man on a mission. Wanna see if you are the
strongest and win a prize for your girlfriend?" A man smiled at me as he
leaned over a large hammer.

"Absolutely, I do." I winked at Kimberly.

The corners of her mouth tugged, and she shook her head.

I grabbed the large plastic hammer from his hand. "Do you have a
heavier one?"

"I do. Are you sure you want to try it?" The man had a long, thick
brow that wiggled when he spoke.

"Positive."

With the hammer in my hand, I pretended it was heavy. Human
Aaron would not have been able to lift it over his head.

Okay, Aaron, let's not break this game.

If I wanted, I could send the bell flying into the night sky. I gripped
the mallet in my hand, got familiar with the weight, and focused solely
on not breaking it. Slamming the hammer on the target with a crack, I
hoped it wouldn't fall apart in my hands.

The lights traveled up, the bell hitting the top and ringing out among
the carnival music.

"Wow. That's the highest I've ever seen it go." The man's mouth fell
open.

"I want that one." I pointed to the hulking pink bear.

"You got it, dude. Want to take a picture for the Winner Wall?"

I agreed and pulled Kimberly in for a picture with her new prize.

When the bear was in Kimberly's arms, the excitement passed over her
face. My favorite thing in the entire world. There was a lot for her to see
and experience still.

"It's so soft." She beamed.

I imagined her as a child watching everyone else win their toys and her
never having one. She deserved all the bears and someone who would
win them for her. I wanted to be that person.

Grabbing the bear, I slung it over my shoulders. "Let's go find my brothers so they can hold it while we ride rides."

"Oh no. I don't want them to do that."

"Zach wants an excuse not to have to ride." Further explanation that Zach was a fun hater.

Presley's laugh was a dead giveaway where they were in the carnival. I spotted them on the carousel. Zach looked bored. Presley rode with his hands in the air, and Luke chatted with some random stranger.

I waved at Presley, and his eyes lit up. "You won that?!"

The carousel was fast, so I had to wait for him to come around each time.

"Can you hold it for her?"

"Sure!"

As I went to hand it to him, William came up beside me.

"Done already so we can go home?"

"No. Just handing this off. Can you give it to him?"

"Nope. You got it."

"Thanks for the help." I sighed.

William was a constant antagonist in my life, even after we'd buried the hatchet in the church. I tried to get to know him, but he was uninterested. Kimberly still wanted nothing to do with him, and every time I talked to him, I was reminded why.

"Aaron, pass it to me!" Presley came around, so I chucked it at him, and he swung it in the air like he'd won it himself.

I pulled Kimberly off her feet to climb on my back. "Hurry, lets go!"

She wrapped her arms around my neck, and her giggling warmed my neck. "What's the hurry?"

"If we're there when that ride is over, we're never getting rid of them."

After a few more games, I'd convinced Kimberly to try a fried Twinkie. She loved it but turned down my plea for her to try the fifty other sweets displayed. The smell brought me back to childhood when I'd spend all my ticket money on trying each of the chocolate-dipped foods.

We walked up the lighted steps to a circular ride where everyone sat on the edges with no seatbelts. Its main function was to spin and make people crash into each other. It had been my favorite growing up. Though this one was different, with a space mural painted on the back.

"There are no seatbelts," she said with her brows drawn inward.

"You just hold on."

I had her place one hand on the bar next to my shoulder.

The ride was a lot more fun when I wasn't a vampire. I had some of my best memories on that ride, unable to hold on and falling all over the place. My brothers and I would see who could hold on the longest.

When the speed picked up, Kimberly let go of the bar with one hand and gripped my upper thigh.

"You're trying to kill me." She squealed as she squeezed her eyes shut.

She fell into me, other people did too, but I focused on her, not letting her stray too far or let anyone else run into her.

The ride shifted, and her other hand let go of the bar. She flew forward, but I caught her before she fell to the floor. With one arm around her waist and the other on the bar, I hoisted her up and into my lap.

Her scent was everywhere. Her hair in my face. Her neck close to my lips. She shifted her hips back, digging into my lap. My mind emptied, and all I could think of was the pressure of her. *Friend. Friend. Friend.*

I forced the words into my head to try to distract myself from the way my body was reacting to feeling her. Hot. Confused. Irrational. I hadn't thought any of it through. How it would feel to have her warmth pressed up against me. She latched on to me, digging her fingers into my thigh. It felt good. Too good.

I was flirting with danger. I wanted to kiss her and bite her. I just wanted her and her intoxicating scent. My grip on her tightened.

Mine.

The voice was suddenly back in my head.

"Isn't this fun?" I asked, wanting her voice to steady me.

"You did this on purpose." She huffed as the spinning sputtered to an end.

I helped her back into her seat and could hear everything again. The ride. The music. People screaming and laughing. The electricity buzzing through the entire park. People eating. The overload of stimulation was a great distraction.

Kimberly's hair was wind swept and wild. She looked less put together now—messy even, but she shined radiantly as we walked down the lighted steps and back into the bustle of the crowd.

"You're not following the rules." She was still flirting. *God, help me.*

I stared at the outline of her lips in the shadow of the broken streetlamp overhead. The cascading of lights around us illuminated the side of her face.

"I haven't kissed you yet."

"Yet?" Her breath caught in her chest, and she licked her lips while staring up at me. "Rules."

"Rules," I said.

We agreed, lingering there for a few more beats, letting ourselves draw a little closer with each passing second. I'd never been much of a rule follower, but I'd do it for her.

She pulled my hand into hers. "Let's go ride more."

I let her pull me until we were in the middle of the crowd where we found a stand of cotton candy. I tried not to think of the fact I'd never get to eat it again—the soft, fluffy goodness—but it was hard to be sad next to her.

"Take me somewhere else," she said, scooping a fluffy pinch of the candy in her mouth.

"Oh, you're demanding me now."

"Yes." She smiled, looking at me through her lashes. There was want there and, dare I say, a hint of mischief?

"You got a little . . ." I brushed away the faintest amount of cotton candy hanging under her lips.

She sucked in a breath.

Be good, I had to remind myself, but I'd already taken a step closer to her. What would it be like to tilt her chin up to kiss her? Would she let me?

"Are you sure you want to be a rule follower today?" I was holding on by a thread.

"The rules are the rules," Miss Matter-of-fact said, still looking at my lips. "Do you have a problem with authority?"

"My last name is Calem, so the answer is hell yes." I wanted to linger there, staring at her lips, feeling her breath, but I promised myself I'd be good. More importantly, I promised her I would be. "Come on."

We walked past a few rides. Nothing looked safe enough to take her on until we got to the Ferris wheel. It had a line of little kids and couples waiting and was bigger than the one I was used to. The gondolas were large and covered, and they were covered in pink and blue lights.

"Let's go up there." I pointed to the top.

Her smile disappeared. "I don't know . . ."

"Don't worry. I won't let you fall."

She nodded, and we headed for the line.

The air blowing off the ocean got colder as the night pressed on. I took off my jacket and laid it over her shoulders. She fidgeted and bit the inside of her cheek so hard I could smell the blood. Wrapping my arm around her, I rubbed her arms.

She was trying to be brave. It was cute.

"The view will be worth it." I reassured her.

When it was finally our turn, we were ushered into the gondola. Kimberly took one side, and I took the other. The cart rocked and swayed, and her knuckles whitened as she squeezed onto the pole. Our world below disappeared as we ascended into the sky. Thousands of little lights on one side, and the darkness of the ocean on the other side.

"Oh my God." She grabbed my hand on the pole this time. "Why does something so pretty have to be so terrifying?"

"I'll protect you." I put my hand on top of hers. "I'm right here."

"I'm glad." Her smile was brief. The wind picked up and rocked the cart from side to side.

"Here." I pat the seat next to me.

"I-I can't stand."

The salty air blew the car again. Sitting at her side, I pulled her into me. She wasted no time scooting until she was almost in my lap. Her arms wrapped around my waist.

"Hey." I squeezed her. "You're totally safe. Do you really think I'd let you fall?"

"No, never. But what if the whole thing crashes down and takes us both out."

"You ran into a room with a bunch of unknown vampires but a little height gets you?"

"That was different. I was saving you."

I smiled and pressed my face into her hair.

"And you did such a good job at it. No matter which way this hunk of metal breaks, I'll catch you every single time."

Her whole body relaxed. "I know you will."

The crack of fireworks rang through the air, and Kimberly's hands tightened around me. The light exploded in front of us. Sparks of pink and red fading into orange. Then purple into blue.

She leaned into me, and we soaked it in. This moment was ours, and no one could ever take it away.

I liked that thought. *Ours.*

When we stepped off the ride, I floated next to her. Thinking about her. Thinking about the future. How I needed to do this again with her, and a little bit about how I didn't want her to do it with anyone else. How could I make this work? There had to be a way.

Those thoughts disappeared when she led me out of view of the crowds and to a secluded spot where you could see the ocean. Fireworks continued to pop overhead and reflect in the water.

The weight of her gaze fell onto me. I couldn't look away. She opened her mouth like she wanted to say something, but she stopped and rested up against a light pole.

I waited but she said nothing. Her heartbeat grew ecstatic.

"I think you're the one who has a problem with rules, Burns." I leaned over her and placed my hand above her. She crossed her arms over her chest.

"No. Never have."

"Hm. Interesting." I leaned in a little more, and I swear her breath caught in her chest. "You sure?"

"Yes."

"You look like you might want to suddenly rebel."

The edge of her mouth tugged into a smirk. She loved a challenge. "Despite the Calem influence, I'm very resolved."

Oh, what I wouldn't give to have just one night where we weren't confined to those roles. One where we forgot about those unspoken rules and the spoken ones. Where I might be able to let go and actually flirt with her how I wanted to.

I moved a piece of hair from her forehead, and her heart responded.

She grabbed my hand, and I expected her to push me away. Instead, she held onto me.

"Come on. You've still got to take me to the tower."

"The tallest ride here?"

"Yeah, suddenly, I'm feeling quite brave."

I let her take the lead, knowing I'd follow her and that auburn hair forever if she'd let me—and I hoped she would.

"THE BIRTHDAY GIRL"

KIMBERLY

I opened the door, and a flurry of pink heart balloons pushed me back inside my dorm room.

"Happy birthday!" The Calem boys were staring at me with their warm-brown eyes full of excitement at seven in the morning.

"I've never told any of you the exact date of my birthday."

It was somewhat intentional. They had a lot on their plates, and we'd all been busy over the summer working. My birthday wasn't important to me. Why should it be important to them?

Presley walked past me and plopped on bed. "I might have snooped in your wallet once."

"Where's Zach?" I asked.

"He's flirting with the RA that let us come up here." Aaron's smile was more radiant than it had been lately as he handed me a fresh bouquet of pink peonies, this time in a heart vase.

He wore warmer colors that only made his sunshine disposition more prominent. Plus, he was holding flowers for me. On my birthday. Grabbing the flowers, I turned before he could detect the redness in my cheeks.

I couldn't resist a quick sniff before placing them on my desk. Thankfully, I'd spent some time tidying up when I woke up. Making plans on my birthday wasn't something I put a lot of thought into. I'd learned as a child it was like any other day. Most of the time, I was the only one who remembered. Sometimes, I'd forget and remember days later.

"We hope you've got your bathing suit ready." Luke tied the balloons to the edge of my bed frame. So many balloons. Way too many. They were filling up my very small room.

We worked at the waterpark all summer, of course I had one.

"You guys don't have to do all of this. I work today, anyway."

"No you don't. I spoke to Cary, and I got your shift switched." Presley rummaged under my bed and pulled out my hiking boots. "You'll need these."

"Camping, lake, delicious cake. What do you say?" Luke could barely fit in my room with the balloons and was forced into the corner.

"I—did you say cake?"

"Yeah, Luke baked you a red velvet cake," Aaron said next to me.

"Completely made from scratch," Luke added.

I can't remember the last time I had a homemade cake for my birthday. Or one I didn't pick up myself at the grocery store. But no candles. My only rule.

"What do you say?" Aaron picked up my hiking backpack and dusted it off. "It's been a while since we've all gotten to go on an adventure."

"Is this allowed?" I crossed my arms.

"We might have all sacrificed greatly to make this endeavor happen." Presley frowned.

"Uh-oh."

"Don't worry about it! Let's go." Luke opened the door, signaling our time to leave was now.

Aaron nudged me. "Come on, birthday girl. Let us celebrate you."

I'd never been celebrated before, but it wouldn't kill me. I was fairly certain with the Calem brothers around that nothing would.

Two minutes was all I had to pack my bags before the boys practically pushed me out of my door.

"No talking."

"Was that one of the conditions?" I whispered to Aaron.

We walked on a dirt trail, and the sun illuminated the warm-brown bark of the trees that towered overhead.

"Shush." Willam smiled like he was proud of his idea for peace and quiet.

Aaron nodded and smiled too, practically skipping along the path with not a care in the world.

A decent breeze blew through the redwoods. Just enough to keep sweat from building on my neck. The trees still held a lush green, but much of the grass had died from the drought.

Zach rolled his eyes and grabbed Presley in a headlock to ruffle his hair. It was good to see him loosen up. The twins had grown increasingly stressed all summer over working nonstop and being trapped. Luke hardly ever let it show, but Zach showed it often. There was nothing fun about being old enough to be on your own and still stuck in everyone else's plans, unable to do anything for yourself.

Luke seemed the most content, even with the large backpack strapped to his hulking frame. He carried a small plastic cooler that held my cake—and I wasn't allowed to look.

He walked next to William, taking the lead and scanning everything.

Things were perfectly safe. There had been no word on The Family over the summer, and I doubted they'd find us all the way out here.

We were hiking in an area I'd been to before. Though, it had been a while.

It was a trail that was mostly thick forest and dirt. Not a lot of views or rock formations, but it was worth it because there was a waterfall I'd like to visit and eat my lunch by before heading back.

I didn't mind the silence and couldn't imagine a better birthday than soaking up the sunshine and listening to the forest.

It was different alone. There was a solitude to it that was peaceful. As the Calem brothers snickered to themselves and pointed out things along the way, I realized there was peace in this too—being together.

Out here, I forgot about The Family. None of those things existed in the coverage of the trees. A false sense of security I welcomed, fighting to stay present with them. None of them looked worried, so I wouldn't be.

A harmonica playing came from ahead. I guessed Presley but wasn't sure. I didn't see anything in his hands, but he was smiling.

"What the hell?" William spun around.

"What? We didn't do anything," Presley said.

"You promised."

"Yeah, and we're keeping it," Aaron chimed in.

I shook my head, knowing how this scene would play out because I'd seen it before at OBA.

When William turned back around, Zach pulled a harmonica out of his pocket and played a few notes before passing it to Luke, who was now walking beside him.

"For fuck's sake. I do a nice thing and let you all take Kimberly out for her birthday, and this is what I get," William grumbled. Everything was up in the air about William. In my book, he couldn't be trusted, but he was part of The Legion, and they'd spent the entire summer protecting Aaron and his brothers. That counted for something, but I just wasn't sure how much.

"We're not doing anything," Zach snapped.

Presley's voice got higher. "Yeah, it's gotta be a bird or something."

"Mockingbird," Luke added.

Will kept his eyes ahead, and Luke played a quick note before tossing it behind his back to Aaron. It was so fast I almost didn't see it.

"I'm not humoring you. Let's just get to the lake," William said.

"You got it, boss," Luke shouted.

William didn't turn back around. "No more talking."

We walked a few more minutes, and I tried to focus on the trees, but instead, I thought of Aaron as his feet hit the dirt next to mine and his hand brushed my fingers as we walked

My hand was sweaty—too sweaty to try to hold his hand—but it was my birthday and he didn't care about stuff like that. I grabbed his pinkie and ring finger. Then he curled my hand into his, shifting me closer. My whole body warmed, as his skin felt good against mine, and my body sang.

Aaron smiled while he pulled the harmonica from his pocket, played a note, then threw it to Presley, who caught it behind his back. When his part in their game was over, he pulled me even closer, lacing his fingers in mine.

Presley brought it to his lips to play a note, and in the blink of an eye, William was there grabbing it from him and chucking it into the woods.

"Hey, we're doing leave no trace!" Presley whined.

"Will, do you have anger issues, buddy? Because we can work on them together." Zach snickered.

"Yes, you're all the issues making me angry."

Aaron and I shared a look, and I bit my lip to stop from laughing.

We filled the silence by kicking dirt on each other's shoes. The waterfall roared in the distance, but we walked past my usual turn and went farther into the thicket of trees.

I took a deep breath, filling my lungs with crisp air, and on my exhale, another harmonica sounded. This time, Zach played a full-on tune, long and loud.

William turned around, giving Zach the finger and a you-win smile.

We'd spent most of sunlight at a lake so secluded we didn't see anyone else even boating around. Crystal blue spanned for miles. Stopping by a dock, a short and simple thing not too scary to walk across barefoot, we jumped off it at least fifty times. After, Presley found a rope swing a little up the shoreline, and we spent the rest of the daylight swinging into the water. Then Aaron had to carry me to our camping spot because of the exhaustion.

I'd coached the boys on how to make a fire, as my human body ached from head to toe. I couldn't take another step or even form full sentences, but the Calem boys were all full of energy. Zach, Presley, and Luke were passing around the harmonica. Aaron sat next to me, letting me lay my legs over him, and gently squeezed my aching feet.

"Okay, time for cake," Luke said as he reached for the cooler and pulled out a slightly melted red velvet cake covered with red icing and a white border covered in red glitter. On the front were messy white letters: Happy Birthday Burns.

"Aaron did the lettering." Luke nudged Aaron.

"I wanted to help, but Luke is the best at cakes," Aaron said.

Presley waved something colorful in my face. "I brought the candles!"

"I don't do candles on cakes," I said, mostly out of reflex. "I'm not big on making wishes on my birthday."

"That's the best part," Aaron said, watching me. Always looking at me with that same sweet, contemplative expression, like he really saw me.

Birthday wishes weren't all that good for me. More like a constant stream of disappointment, but I didn't want to bring the mood down.

"Well, there's a first time for everything," I said.

Things were different now, and making a little wish wouldn't kill me.

They covered the cake in so many candles that I worried for the safety of the forest.

As they sang "Happy Birthday," my face got hot and, surely, red. Zach and Luke sang the loudest and off key. William did not participate and ignored us completely by sharpening a stick with his knife.

I concentrated on the candles. The burning turbulent red and orange against the cold of night.

"Okay, Burns. Make your wish," Aaron said.

They were all staring, waiting for me to blow out the candles with a wish on my breath, but nothing came to mind right away. So I wished for the night to last longer. For another hour or minute, whatever the fates would allow, before my body gave out.

They cheered, and Luke handed me a fork and the entire cake. "For the birthday girl."

From the moment the cake entered my mouth, I knew it was the best I'd ever had. Moist, with cream cheese frosting in the middle.

Zach drank from a liquor bottle, and Aaron motioned for it.

"I'm going to need a little more to drink for what comes later." Aaron winked at me.

"Should I be worried?"

"Yes, be very very afraid."

"Okay time for your gift. Presley, would you like to take the lead?" Aaron smiled with flushed cheeks.

"Uh-oh." There was something mischievous in their eyes.

"Oh, brother, I thought you'd never ask." Presley pulled out his phone.

Aaron scratched his forehead and avoided eye contact. "This is about to be the most embarrassing thing I've ever done."

I waited for him to explain, chaos and energy building in the air.

"I wanted to get you something else. Something better. But you don't keep a lot of objects or jewelry, so I went with a sentimental-memory-type gift. I agonized over it for weeks . . . I hope I guessed correctly."

I was taken aback that he'd noticed at all. "You guessed correctly. But what else could it be? You've already taken me on this trip."

"It's our kitchen routine. A song we memorized and made a routine for when we were young. We haven't done it for *years*. But we're going to perform it for you. All of us."

"No way!" I inhaled complete elation.

"Way." Presley had snagged his sunglasses from his bag and popped up the collar on his jacket.

"Please, take our collective embarrassment as the greatest gift we could ever give you." Aaron's face was close to mine. Really close. I enjoyed it a little too much and tried not to think about the way his eyes glowed like molten honey in the firelight, or the softness of his lips.

Zach was the only one still sitting. "I'm not doing this shit."

"Nonsense. It's for Kimberly," Luke said.

"I'm too sober to pull off the kitchen routine. Plus, I don't remember the lines." Zach crossed his arms and leaned back in his lawn chair.

"Oh, that's bullshit." Luke handed him a liquor bottle. "You've got the smallest part anyway."

"Fine. You guys start," Zach said, putting his hood up.

Presley turned the volume up to full blast in the middle of the most quiet night. It had to be illegal to be that loud in nature.

Once the music started, I picked up on the song quickly. *"Blue (Da Ba Dee)" by Eiffel 65.*

That's when I knew it would be the best thing I'd ever seen.

Presley started first with a dramatic spin, saying his part in the song, then he passed an invisible microphone to Aaron, who said his line, then he passed it to Luke. They knew every word.

My mouth was on the floor, begging my brain to absorb every minute of this performance so I'd never forget it.

When the chorus came, they held onto each other and started spinning. Which should have been fine, considering they were all vampires, but they were drunk. Therefore, the spinning sent them all in opposite directions. Presley hit a tree. Luke fell into Aaron, and they were laughing. Unstoppable, bubbling laughter that was almost louder than the music. I could imagine them as little kids hearing this song, crafting this routine, and doing it over and over again. Spinning each other around in their kitchen in Brooklyn. Four boys stuck in a house with nothing better to do than to try to be some kind of boy band. It was the most ridiculous thing I'd ever seen or would probably see in my lifetime.

"Okay, let me show you how it's done." Zach left his hood up and grabbed Presley's sunglasses.

Then my jaw dropped again, as Zach shimmied around the fire—smooth and suave—reciting his parts to their number, which he obviously had no trouble remembering. The other boys jumped around him like hype men.

Somewhere in their chaos, my amusement turned into awe. These boys had something others never got. Something people like me searched their whole lives for. And as I watched them spin and fall and laugh till it looked painful, I couldn't look away. I'd never felt anything so visceral and real. I was happier than I'd ever been and wanted to weep because of how much they loved each other, and I was sure they didn't realize how special it was.

William caught my attention from my peripheral vision. I expected his expression to be flat, unamused, or even angry, but he looked at Aaron and his brothers with the same awe as I did. I wondered then if he could feel it too. His eyes were soft and held longing as he admired them. Nothing I'd ever seen in his eyes before. It almost made me sad.

I'd done everything in my power to avoid that man. I didn't want him here any more than he wanted to be here. He made it easy to hate him, and now I wondered if that was on purpose. Maybe we weren't as different as I thought.

He spotted me, and I averted my gaze, shaking the thought from my head.

After they were done spinning and singing and laughing—lots of laughing—Aaron pulled me to my feet and gently twirled me around before sitting down and pulling me next to him.

"Now she's got real embarrassing dirt on us. She knows our deepest darkest secrets."

Presley and the twins stayed dancing by the fire while singing different songs, and William begged them to shut up.

"Are you getting tired?"

I nodded, still watching them.

The boys were drunk and dancing and falling all over each other. Their voices echoed in the woods. Laughter that etched its way into the bark and up into the stars. They were infinite, swirling and pulsing with energy you could feel in the warmth of the fire. Bathing in the coziness of their affection, I watched every step of their feet onto the earth, a mixture of swirling dirt and dry pine needles.

"Yeah, a little." I didn't want the day to end, but my eyes were closing, and every so often, I found my head dipping.

"Come on." Aaron held out his hand, and I let him pull me off the lawn chair.

"Wait! Kim!? You're going to bed?" Presley yelled across the fire.

"I know, I'm sorry."

"Don't make her feel bad for being human," Aaron grumbled.

"Sleep well!" Luke waved, stopping dancing. "We're going to hit up the lake one last time before we leave tomorrow. So get some good rest."

"Night." Zach tried to stop too, but he found himself on the ground. Their bubbling laughter erupted again.

"Fuck me. It's going to be a long night." William didn't look up from sharpening his stick with a knife.

Aaron led me behind a row of bushes that kept us in camp but far enough away I could at least hear the crickets amid the Calem brothers' giggling.

It was lit with a small lantern, and a tent big enough for two people came into view. Blocked on the sides with a small clear roof on top. Inside, there was a thick pile of blankets and a soft pillow.

"We wanted you to be extra comfy. You know, since it's your birthday."

Aaron led me to the entrance and stopped like he might just say goodnight. Like he might just leave me here in the cold.

"Maybe you could ... stay? We could watch the stars for a little bit." I don't know why I was nervous to say it. Aaron didn't make me nervous in the slightest, but the thought of him saying no did.

"Yeah. Whatever you want, birthday girl." Aaron smiled from ear to ear.

I crawled in first, afraid to shed my coat but knowing I needed to. The fleece was thick with the smell of bonfire. A smell I usually invited, but when Aaron crawled in next to me, I realized I preferred the smell of his cologne.

He scratched at the nape of his neck. Was he nervous being up against me? I couldn't help but laugh .

"Take off your coat."

"You want me to strip for you?"

"Just your jacket."

"You're sure?" He smirked.

"Oh, I'm sure."

I pulled myself into the fluffy blanket, but it was still chilly with the night air, and my teeth chattered.

"Here." Aaron had nestled his way under another blanket and invited me next to him.

I pulled myself in beside him. How was he warm so fast?

Resting my head on his arm, everything in me relaxed, and I lost myself in how good it was to have someone warm me. This was what everyone was always going on about in the movies and the books? I'd been missing out. I snuggled closer to him. He was the sun, and I was the battery soaking up his rays and relishing in the way it felt to be near him.

"You'll stay?"

"If you want me to."

"I want you to if you want to."

"Then I'm yours."

He looked down at me, and I lifted my chin. Our faces were close. His hand traced along my hairline, like a feather grazing the top of my forehead, along my ear, then the nape of my neck. Warmth pooled in my gut, and goose bumps raised on my skin.

Every touch was an experiment, and each time we each gave a little more. I wasn't cold anymore and traced his bicep with the tips of my fingers. He shifted slightly but didn't move away. Exploration at its finest. Slow and methodical. I touched the inside of his forearm, analyzing every curve and burning it into my memory. His touch seemed as if he was memorizing me too. Like any moment, the other might disappear into thin air.

"I know you have to be exhausted," he said.

His touch leaving me made me sad.

"A little."

Not wanting my eyes to close, I fought it with everything else I had.

Hundreds of stars peppered the darkness. It was hypnotizing watching the thick blanket of shimmering light. A star tore through the dark velvet sky.

"Oh my God. Did you see it?" Aaron said.

"Yes, I saw it. Have you never seen a shooting star before?" I asked.

"Never. They didn't have night skies like this in Brooklyn."

"Well, go on. Make your wish."

"Did you make one?"

"No." In that moment, I already had what I needed.

"Let's make one together."

"I don't know if it works that way."

"We both saw it at the same time, so we get to share a wish," he said.

"Okay, what should we wish for?" I asked.

"Well, if we say it out loud, it won't come true."

"What's the point of wishing together if we don't say it out loud?"

"It's the intention. We're hoping together. Believing together. It makes it more likely to come true."

"You're making this up."

"No. It's perfectly sane logic for making wishes."

Making wishes wasn't something I was accustomed to. I believed in myself and the things I could accomplish, like graduating college and supporting myself. Wishing wouldn't get me there, though. The world didn't work that way.

Aaron watched the sky in amazement. I wondered what it was like to live in that world, where you could dream up anything and believe it with your whole heart. A world where dreaming, wishing, and hoping decided the fates. Suddenly, I wanted to be there too, riding on the backs of dragons and floating and using fairy dust.

"Okay, let's make a wish," I said. Unbundling my hands, I found his and laid them on his chest, just over his heart, squeezing. Then he moved one hand over mine and squeezed back.

"Okay. Just close your eyes."

I closed my eyes and breathed in. Hiding in his warmth and smell, felt like balm to my soul.

What did I want?

I wanted this warmth to never leave me, his hands to stay on mine, and for his brothers' laughter to keep me up and echo in the forest just as it was. My life needed more nights gazing up at the stars.

I squeezed my eyes harder. Hoping. Wishing. Asking the stars for the first time . . .

Please let us all stay together. Let this work out. Let us be free of all our fears and anything that would want to tear us apart. Please let him stay with me. It's all I want. The only thing I've ever asked for.

"Did you make a wish?" Aaron asked.

"Yes." Scooting closer, I rested my legs against his. My brain wasn't working like it normally did. I was tired and he was *so* warm.

"Me too. It was a good one too."

I didn't have the strength to open my eyes again. Sleep was finally taking me.

"You're . . . going to . . . stay?"

"Yeah, Burns."

"Like you'll be here when I wake up?"

It was selfish to ask him to stay next to me all night, clinging to his arm, when he couldn't sleep. But I wanted desperately—more than I wanted to admit—for him to be the first thing I saw in the morning. For his smell to fill up my space and him to warm me up before the morning sun had a chance.

"I promise. I'll be right here."

The morning sun woke me first, and the smell of crackling bacon wafted into the tent. I reached for him before I registered where I was.

"Morning, beautiful."

I breathed a sigh of relief, still lying on his arm.

Bonus
Alternate Ending

"FALSE PROMISES"

KIMBERLY

* *Author note**

    Have you ever wondered what might have happened if Aaron pulled an Edward Cullen and left at the end of Book One? Now you don't have to. Admittedly, I wrote this scene as an alternate universe for myself and never intended for it to see the light of day. But it showcases something very important in this series. How one choice could cascade this cute little story into misery and hopeless despair. All their choices are important and have been so from the beginning. That's what this is—a bad ending to haunt your thoughts and poison your dreams. I advise caution and for you to play "Right Where you Left Me" by Taylor Swift.

Excitement fluttered in my chest as I walked up the sidewalk toward the frat house. A sprinkle had turned into a downpour, deepening the red of the bricks. I danced up the steps with my umbrella in my good hand. My left hand was still wrapped and would stay immobile for a while. I'd already gotten used to doing a lot of my daily tasks one-handed. Ringing the doorbell, I pressed my head against the thick cold wooden door, listening for the stirring inside, but I couldn't hear anything.

Aaron answered the door, wearing sweats and a dark-gray hoodie with white Converse. "Hey."

He shut the door behind him and took the umbrella from my hand, but he wasn't smiling. Not his usual smile that warmed me from the inside. This one was forced and didn't meet his eyes.

"Are you hungry?" Aaron asked as he looked out the window and into the rain.

"Well, I could eat. But I thought we were going to go to Chelsea's to apologize."

"Right." He looked down at his shoes. "Sorry, I forgot."

My stomach turned. There was something wrong. "Did something happen? You seem off."

"You're sure you don't want me to take you to go eat?" he asked, more desperate this time.

"Why do you want me to eat so badly?"

His eyes softened. Something flickered in his pupils, but I didn't understand it. "Because I just want you to be taken care of."

"Fine. Let's go."

He led the way with the umbrella.

We sat at a table in the corner of the coziest diner in town. A fan favorite in Blackheart that had been there for at least fifty years. The original owners greeted us as we took our seats. Normally, I'd make small talk about the dated décor or let Aaron talk my ear off about the different choices and his old favorites, but he wasn't talking, just fidgeting with the sugar packets on the table.

"Aaron, what's wrong?"

"Nothing. You should eat."

The waiter had brought my food, but I wasn't hungry. Not with my stomach doing somersaults and my heart pounding out of my chest, waiting on what Aaron would say.

I lowered my fork. "I know you well enough now to know when something is wrong."

He was still burning a hole in the tablecloth with his gaze. When his eyes finally met mine, he couldn't hide the emotion passing over his face or the flush of red in his cheeks.

My heart dropped. "Aaron . . ."

"We're leaving."

I swallowed. "Wait, what do you mean? I thought—"

"I know. I know. I—" He pressed his hands into his eyes. "But The Legion wants to move us somewhere else, they say it's safer."

"Oh." I stared at him while the waitress poured me more water.

I wasn't naive. I knew what this meant. "You're going alone, aren't you?"

He looked up at me. "Kilian doesn't think it's a good idea for you to come. We all argued for it, but he might be right. Dragging you along with us might put you in more danger, but I promise I'll come back one day. When this over, I'll come back for you."

My face was hot. My stomach churning. That could be years. That could be never.

A single tear fell from my cheek, and I tried to wipe it before it fell on the fresh linen.

"Kim . . ."

"You promised."

He leaned in with pleading eyes. "I know. And I will keep it. I'll come back to you. I'll find a way."

Tear after tear fell.

"When are you leaving? Don't I get to say . . . to say goodbye?"

I didn't want to say the word. Another tear fell that I couldn't catch.

"They're packing the car now. I thought it would be easier if they didn't. I just don't want to hurt you any more. I want you to be happy. I want you to have a good life."

I wanted to hit him. I wanted to hug him. I wanted to walk out. I wanted him to stay.

I needed him to stay.

"Aaron, just wait. Let's talk about this."

We could work it out like we'd worked out every issue before. Together.

"I can't. That's just going to make this worse." Aaron shook his head. "I'm so sorry, Kim. I promise, I will come back for you."

He was up on his feet before I could move, and his lips pressed to mine. Then, in a blink, he was gone.

The napkin fell from my hand onto the floor, and, in my emotional flurry, I knocked my glass off the table, and it shattered. All eyes were on me, but I was frozen. My mascara stung my eyes, and the water from my glass soaked the soles of my shoes.

All of my plans had changed, and everything I'd silently hoped for was gone. Just like that.

I don't know how long I sat there. Long enough for the sun to set and the waiter to ask if they needed to call someone for me. Long enough for all my mascara to melt into linen napkins and the candle on the table to melt into nothing.

Two months later, I was still there. Still sitting in that restaurant, replaying that moment, wondering when I'd see him again and if that memory would fade before I did. *Was there something different I could have said to make him stay?*

I snuggled into my comforter in the calm of my own bed while the rain pelted the window. The summer would be a wash, but I wanted it that way so I'd have an excuse to stay locked in my room. I'd recover, eventually. This pain would end. I'd move on and forget Aaron Calem and his brothers existed.

I told myself that over and over again. What was wrong with me? It was like I had the flu that wouldn't go away. The memory of him wouldn't leave me alone. His teeth marks were etched into my skin, and his laughter in my brain. When I thought of them, I came back to one conclusion: I'd let something rare slip through my fingers, and I'd never have it again.

Why did I care so much?

I sighed. A knock at the door caught my attention and stilled the rising tears that threatened to surface. I glanced at my clock. Almost midnight. Probably an RA telling me to stop playing Taylor Swift on repeat.

I sniffed, smoothed my hair, then opened the door.

"Well, hello." A man with dark slicked-back hair, pale skin, and tattoos was propped up in my doorframe.

For the second time, I froze.

Vampire. No obvious tells, but that smirk and the way he effortlessly pushed himself into my room and locked my door, told me so. And this wasn't just any vampire either. There was power there. I could feel it filling the space.

"I'm surprised you didn't scream. Most would," he said, smiling.

He enjoyed this. I tried to keep my voice steady. He'd suspect a scream. I had to do something else. Anything else.

"There's no use in screaming, is there?"

His eyes sparked with excitement. "I like you. You're brave, Kimberly Burns."

"How do you know my name?"

"I know everything. I know you're an orphan who used to get in trouble a lot as a child. And I know that you're very close to the Calem brothers."

"And you are?"

"Akira." He took another step closer and stopped to look around my room.

The Family. They found them, like they thought they would.

Stepping closer to my speaker, I ran my finger along the wall to keep myself upright. I needed to focus on getting help, but who was coming? Who could save me from this fate now?

"You're part of The Family," I said, taking another step back.

That made him look at me again, the smile on his face grew. "They told you?"

"Yes." It didn't matter now if he knew.

"Do you happen to know where they went?"

"No."

"If you're lying, I'll know." He didn't say it like a threat but matter-of-fact.

I took another step. My hand rested on my speaker—*just a little farther*.

"I'm not lying. He didn't tell me."

"Aaron, right? I heard you guys were quite smitten."

My heart stuttered.

I shook my head. "We weren't . . . intimate. It wasn't like that."

I didn't want to finish this conversation. My hand found the switch to my stereo, and I turned the dial to full blast, but Akira was quicker and pulled the cord from the wall. In a last-ditch effort to bring someone to my aid, I grabbed the speaker and tried to force it on the ground. Akira caught it inches from the ground in one swift motion and forced me against the wall with a hand over my mouth.

Akira clicked his tongue. "You are fun. I can see why Aaron liked you so much."

His body was stone against mine. I couldn't stop my body from shaking, but I willed myself not to cry.

"Now. I promise to remove my hand if you let me in that cunning little head of yours."

He wanted to search around in my head like William had done to Aaron. My body tensed at the thought.

"I'll be gentle. Promise. It won't hurt. As long as you don't fight me." He removed his hand.

"Why ask, then, if you're going to do whatever you want?"

Playing with a strand of my hair, he licked his teeth. "I'm not here to torture you. I'm just searching for the truth."

"Fine. If you let go of me."

He did, and I sat on my bed. It didn't matter. I knew nothing that would help him find them. Maybe he'd find what he was looking for and leave . . .

Who was I kidding? I wasn't getting out alive.

I hadn't fully realized it yet but my body had. A sense of doom threatened to pull me into my bed.

"At least you'll get to see him again." His voice was remarkably soft for the sharpness of his features. Akira leaned in front of me and reached his hand to cover mine.

At his touch, I was back there again, in the restaurant, my face hot from tears and Aaron's apologies. This time was different. As if I couldn't hide any of the pain from that memory under numbness.

Tears streamed down my face, and when Akira pulled away, he reached up to wipe them. I flinched away, feeling hard all over. Now I was crying and couldn't stop.

"Alone again. I'm sorry Kimmy."

"It doesn't matter."

It didn't. I'd never get to say goodbye. I wouldn't be here when Aaron came back. If he ever did.

"I promise I'll make your death quick. It will be like falling asleep. Gentle. Easy. I'm not really supposed to do it this way, but I'll make an exception for you. It's more peaceful to drink your blood than to snap your neck."

I faced him, staring deep into his irises.

"Just tell me why. Why do I even matter? Why are you here?"

He pulled a hand through my hair until it rested on my neck. This time I didn't fight it.

With his index finger, he stroked my cheek. "Because he will come back for you. And I can't allow that to happen. This is cleaner. No loose ends."

He would come back for me.

I shouldn't have been surprised. He promised.

I smiled.

That was my last thought before he grabbed me and caressed me like he might kiss me. There was an easy pressure in my neck as we fell back onto my bed.

Akira kept his promise too.

Death felt like sleep pulling me under the earth, and as heaviness and coldness took me into the dark, I remembered Aaron's smile warming me one last time.

I hoped he'd run as far and fast as he could with his golden hair gleaming in the sun so this darkness would never reach him or his brothers. *Run.*

AARON

It wasn't easy, but it was the right thing to do. At least, morally, it felt right, but not when I thought of her face. Not when I imagined her crying. Not when I spent everyday away from her thinking of our time together or what she could be doing.

I think I'd convinced Kilian to let me go see her soon. Or at least write. Something. Every day, I'd imagined going back to her, and I would have if I thought it wouldn't put her in danger.

We'd moved to some place on the Canadian border. It was cold and snowy and nothing like the place Kimberly was at. I headed in for the night. A night spent training with The Legion. I had my own cabin because I needed the privacy to wallow in self pity-and guilt, but it was always cold. Too cold.

As I walked up the snowy steps, I noticed my door was cracked open. Odd but not alarming. Could be an animal. Or maybe I forgot to lock it. As it creaked, I noticed a trail of candles illuminating the floor, along with flower petals. *What the hell?*

I picked one up, instantly recognizing it—peonies.

I followed them until they stopped at the door to my bedroom, then turned the knob. It took me only a moment, the equivalent of a small breath, to register what I saw.

Kimberly laid across my bed. Pale. Dead.

Gone.

She was gone.

I rushed to her and felt the cool of her skin. No heartbeat. She was cold. So cold.

No. No. No.

It wasn't real. It couldn't be. I was hallucinating again, but she was in my arms and cold, and despite my attempts to warm her, her pulse wasn't coming back.

I'd never hear that sound again. Her laughter. See her smile.

I didn't know what happened after that. I sobbed for what felt like hours but was probably only a few minutes.

It was my fault. I'd ruined everything. I knew it, deep in my bones, that I chose wrong. I should have stayed. She'd be alive if I stayed.

It had to be The Family. I never should have left her there with no protection.

My brothers' feet pounded to get to me to the sound of my cries. Was

I yelling?

"I'm sorry. I had to." A man I'd never seen before crouched next to me in the dark. Dark hair. Tattoos. The Family was here.

There was relief in that thought, like my agony would be short-lived. I needed to warn my brothers, but I wasn't leaving her alone again.

I should have been mad, but all I felt was emptiness as I wondered what she felt in her last moments.

"This will make it better. She can take all your pain away." He thrust a blood bag in my face with black blood.

I ran my fingers over Kimberly's pale skin. She was gone, and I wanted to be gone too.

My brothers hadn't reached my door in time. I took the blood bag from his hand and drank every last drop, hoping Her blood would take me far away from this place that held my own nightmare and failings. A reality I didn't want to be in anymore.

It worked.

My world of pain passed away, and I turned to my brothers with Her blood in my veins.

This was our destiny, and soon, they'd see it too.

This Blood

That Burns Us

BOOK TWO

THIS BLOOD THAT BURNS US

Between Two Lungs
Florence+ The Machine
4:09

What Once Was
Her's
4:16

Evergreen
Richy Mitch & The Coal Miners
1:27

I'm Not Calling You A Liar
Florence + The Machine
3:05

First Love/Late Spring
Mitski
4:39

Howl
Florence + The Machine
3:34

Would That I
Hozier
4:29

Rabbit Heart(Raise It Up)
Florence+ The Machine
3:53

Run Boy Run
Woodkid
3:34

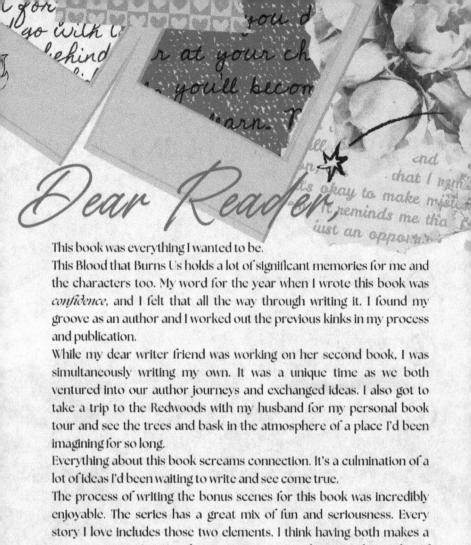

Dear Reader

This book was everything I wanted to be.

This Blood that Burns Us holds a lot of significant memories for me and the characters too. My word for the year when I wrote this book was *confidence*, and I felt that all the way through writing it. I found my groove as an author and I worked out the previous kinks in my process and publication.

While my dear writer friend was working on her second book, I was simultaneously writing my own. It was a unique time as we both ventured into our author journeys and exchanged ideas. I also got to take a trip to the Redwoods with my husband for my personal book tour and see the trees and bask in the atmosphere of a place I'd been imagining for so long.

Everything about this book screams connection. It's a culmination of a lot of ideas I'd been waiting to write and see come true.

The process of writing the bonus scenes for this book was incredibly enjoyable. The series has a great mix of fun and seriousness. Every story I love includes those two elements. I think having both makes a story stronger. Love and connection get to thrive in the midst of challenges.

This book is the definition of warmth. It's that feeling you get when you're falling in love. It's when something grows into more than you anticipated—in a good way and a bad way. Like popcorn kernels on a hot skillet, the heat can't be contained.

This is a warm up for what's coming. So enjoy your time by the fireside.

Lots of love,

S.L. Cokeley

ADMIT ONE

CINEMA

VOID IF DETACHED

$1.25

062895

PROLOGUE

???

I hated everything about them. Their twin theology—*and* physiology, for that matter. The lowly, filthy clothes they were always roaming around in. That ignorant smirk Zach wore with pride, and the way his brother Luke walked around with his chest thrust out like he hadn't a care in the world. Disgusting, overrated scum. Yet I could not treat them as such. They were *special*. Special to Her.

I walked along the corridor with my hands tucked in my pockets, and my boots were silent with each step. Ornate rugs gave color to an otherwise lifeless, dusty hallway. The warmth of the bricks wasn't enough to keep out the winter chill or the breeze that came from the ocean. I was told our home had stood there in Manhattan for more than a hundred years. No one ever ventured close. They knew the stories and heeded the warnings. We were criminals, but not peasants on the street killing each other over nothing more than pieces of paper or chemical compounds. No, we were more than that. Infinitely superior. Doing the work that needed to be done to keep Her safe, secure, and comfortable. We built a life to serve Her every need.

"Hey, Connery. Come here," Akira called.

"Yes, sir." I bowed, though he preferred a less official presence. He was one of the highest-ranking members in our family. One of The Guard. Showing him respect was imperative, even if he didn't rejoice in it. When he accepted my bow, I straightened myself and pulled my blazer collar taut. All-black attire, including dress shirts and slacks, were required for all members. We had a reputation and a standard to uphold every time we ventured out into the city.

"You're coming with me." He leaned against the wall with his sleeves rolled up and lit a cigarette. "I'm gonna need you to be on your best behavior."

I inhaled in surprise. Never had he asked me to accompany him.

He blew the smoke slowly in my face. "Hello? Is this fucking thing on? Answer me when I speak to you."

"Who is we?"

"The Guard, Zach, Luke . . . Her."

The mention of Her sent my skin ablaze, and the hairs on my arms stood on end. "S-She'll be there?"

"Yep." Akira took another long drag. "I know you have some choice feelings for the twins, but I mean it when I say I need you to stay in fucking line." His voice was deadly serious as he stared into my eyes, but he remained leaning against the wall.

"Why are we all going?"

"Well, I actually asked to take you along." He nudged my shoulder.

I tightened my fist to shield myself from the disappointment. She didn't ask me to be there. Which meant She didn't care if I was there. But She wanted *them* there—Her precious Zach and Luke.

"Oh, lighten up. Just be happy you're coming along. You're the only one I've asked because I trust you."

I beamed with pride under my mask of stoicism. Akira was my mentor, and he had been for more than a century. I hadn't been worthy enough . . . until now.

"But that fucking mouth gets you into trouble." He laughed, coughing out smoke. He motioned for me, and we walked toward the basements.

"I'll be on my best behavior, sir. I mean it." I was jittery inside, though annoyed with having to see them with Her. I knew the jealousy would remain, but at least I'd be in Her presence. Being in the same room was a gift, and I wanted to sprint there.

"Good." He took one last drag of his cigarette, then put it out on his skin. He didn't even flinch as the ashes smeared onto the black ink of his tattoos.

We walked in silence down the corridor until we reached the steps that led down. As we passed several other members, they all stopped to bow as Akira walked past.

Akira spoke again. "You know . . . it's not everything to be the favorite."

I took a second to decipher his words. "What?"

"I know you think you want to be Her favorite, but there are better things to be."

It seemed blasphemous, but I knew a member of The Guard would never speak ill of the one they were sworn by blood to protect. Especially not Akira. He was Her most loyal companion and had been with Her almost the entirety of Her time here on Earth. She was the reason for The Guard's existence. For mine.

"You'll learn." He winked at me as we turned the corner leading toward a wide set of double doors. They were thick dark mahogany carved with Gothic embellishments. We stopped in front, and he pulled me against the door and held me by the shoulders. "Don't embarrass me here. Do as I say. Only speak *if* you're spoken to. Am I crystal fucking clear?"

It wasn't usual for Akira to be so serious. I squirmed under his grip. "Yes, sir."

A smile stretched across his face, and he relaxed again before opening the door.

I didn't know what I expected. Perhaps the twins being doted on with Her hands twisted up in their hair while She beamed at them like they were the brightest things to ever walk the damned Earth. That seemed pretty on par with my experience with them thus far.

My expectations were shattered as I took in the scene. Zach and Luke sat against the far side of the room with their backs pressed against the concrete wall. Each with a bite mark on their necks and black blood smudged on their cheeks. They had bled onto their street clothes and were filthy as always.

Then fear penetrated my body, but it wasn't mine. One ordinary-looking girl with long mousy-brown hair, stood shivering in the center of the room. She was wearing pajamas, which made me wonder if she'd been pulled from her bed in the night. Sirius, another member of The Guard, had firm watch on her. There was no scent of blood. Her crying was the only sound in the underground room. I didn't feel pity for her, only the undying urge to end her suffering. The pulse in her neck reverberated through my body. The basement was a place for sparring and training. This human wouldn't be leaving alive—that much I knew.

Akira and I took a spot on the opposite wall where we could see it all. I realized then I was only meant as a witness—to watch what was about to unfold. It was a few minutes before the door opened and I saw Her. Our queen.

I only glimpsed Her white hair before I fell to my knees in a bow. My body buzzed from Her proximity. As we all stood, I tried to remember every detail of Her. The way Her long white hair fell on Her shoulders in soft bouncy waves, or the slight tinge of red on Her lips, and Her pale cheeks. Her fingers were slender and perfect. Two ethereal legs peeked between the slit in Her long white dress, and I was certain my knees would give out if I watched Her any longer. She was beautiful, amazing, perfect—the greatest thing I had or would ever see in my long lifetime.

Her bare feet made no sound as She walked along the concrete to kneel before Zach and Luke. She caressed their faces and ran Her hands through their hair. One at a time, they awoke, groggy and disoriented.

"W-what the fuck?" Zach was the first to speak. After blinking a few times, he tried lifting away from the wall, only to find himself too weak to move. He jerked his head to the side. "Luke!?"

His sigh of relief when he felt his brother next to him was short-lived. Their little friend came into view, and their eyes grew wide.

"Sarah . . .?" Luke said, and I relished the betrayal and sadness in his eyes. Zach's attitude made him intolerable, but Luke was the one I wanted to see fall to his knees in anguish. Maybe then he'd break and be out of here and away from Her.

"Why is she here? What are you doing?!" Zach's voice wasn't as strong as it usually was. He was scared, and I liked that.

"Please don't do this." Luke tried to move from the wall, but his limbs were immobile.

The queen put Her hand up to silence him. "I'll be doing the speaking, my love." Her words were a knife to the heart. She loved calling him that. "I've brought you a familiar face. One...lover."

Her words spun with venom on the last word, and chills ran through my body.

"She's not. She doesn't have anything to do with this. Please just let her go." Luke's voice was soft as he pleaded. The way he talked to Her filled me with silent rage. It differed from the fury I had when Zach spoke. Luke talked to Her as if he knew Her. As if they were . . . close somehow. That couldn't be true. It wasn't, and yet the look he was giving Her through red eyes said otherwise.

"I can't do that. It hurts me to punish you both . . . but it must be done. You have committed an unthinkable crime against your family."

Finally, they were being punished for something.

They glanced at each other. Guilty, of course.

"We didn't—"

"Don't lie. You've already hurt me enough." Her voice was colder now.

Luke spoke again. "That wasn't what we were trying to do. We don't want to leave you. We just wanted to keep our family safe."

"*We* are your family." Her eyes lingered on him. "And you want to leave . . ."

I could hardly believe what I was hearing. They wanted to leave? The favorites wanted to run away. How could they have chosen such a foolish plan? No one leaves The Family. There was no need to. Everything they could ever want was here.

"I hope this helps you understand the importance of your family a little more." With those words, She grabbed a long dagger sheathed to Her leg and held it to the girl's throat. She used it to make a tiny cut, and the twins let out a cry of desperation.

"Stop! What are you doing?" Zach said.

"Please don't do this. We'll do whatever you want. We'll stay. Just stop," Luke pleaded.

"Like hell we will! We don't owe you anything! You crazy bitch!"

Zach's words echoed throughout the halls. It wasn't forbidden to speak such words to Her, but no one had ever done so. My foot moved forward, ready to make him hurt for ever uttering something so foul in Her direction, but Akira grabbed my shoulder and raised an eyebrow at me.

She smirked at Zach, unfazed by his words, and pulled the girl by the arm closer to Zach.

"Zach, what is this?" The girl known as Sarah spoke between muffled sobs.

"I'm sorry. I'm so fucking sorry. It's going to be okay. We can fix this." Zach shook with rage, but fear leaked into his voice.

"Sarah." The queen spoke close to the girl's ear. "What's the name of your friend? Ashley, is it? Maybe I should have brought her along for the reunion."

"N-No. Stay away from her." The girl said, with no hesitation. She had guts. I'd give her that.

The queen smiled, while shifting Her attention to Zach. "Fine. Should we play a game? You kill her now or I'll bring your lover next."

"Fuck. You." Zach spat.

She moved toward Zach, put Her hands on his face and leaned in close to his neck, whispering where even I could not hear. He squirmed away from Her grasp, but it was futile. Without a word, She walked back a few steps, and Her tight lips stretched into a smile.

"Zach?" Sarah called to her once-dear friend, and I waited for the show.

Zach's eyes were replaced with black puddles. He lunged forward as the girl scrambled backward.

"Stop! Please stop." Luke was forced to sit and watch.

The queen held up Her hand stopping him just before the attack. She grabbed Zach by his face, and pulled it close to Hers. "This is connection. Never forget you're *mine*." She pushed him to the ground, and he fell back in to unconsciousness. Her gaze veered back to Luke.

The girl's muffled crying was the only noise left in the room. I didn't like the sound of women crying; something about it made me nauseous. But She had a plan for this girl, and I was eager to see it.

"Now, for you." The queen circled the girl like a viper cornering a mouse.

"Why would you do this to me? Why? I've given you everything. How is it not enough?" Luke sobbed while shaking uncontrollably.

The queen frowned at his words with real sadness in Her eyes, and I felt sick again.

"It will never be enough."

She walked up to the girl, pulled her by her hair, and stood in front of him. He was still too weak to stand. Too weak to do anything.

"I never wanted this to happen. I-I . . ." Luke stammered.

The girl spoke, her eyes red from crying, but she smiled. "It's okay. I know this isn't your fault. I know everything. You don't need to say it. Luke, I lo—"

The queen slit her throat with Her teeth before she could finish. Blood sprayed everywhere, and Luke was frozen. All sobbing ceased as he stared down at the blood splatter covering his hands.

She walked up to him, the blood gloriously complementing Her white dress. The crimson only enhanced Her elegant beauty. At the touch of Her hand to his face, he crumpled to the floor, unconscious once again, with his arm outstretched to his dead lover, and hers to his. The girl's blood pooled on the floor, and I shifted from foot to foot. Partly because it was reaching my time to feed again, but the other was more unexpected. It didn't feel as good as I thought it would to see them tossed from their throne. I hated them. We didn't agree on a single thing. I envied them and wanted to be desired like they were, but seeing them broken on the floor wasn't something I would soon forget.

She scanned the room, making eye contact with The Guard. "Clean this up." Ezra wasn't there yet, but if I had to guess, he'd be there in a few seconds to collect the twins.

She left while licking Her lips, and Her gown trailed behind Her.

As the doors shut, I followed Akira's lead. One question lingered in my mind.

"Go ahead. Ask your questions," Akira said.

"Will they remember this?"

"No."

"Why do all this to make them forget?" I surveyed the carnage that lay before us.

"They will forget until She *wants* them to remember." Akira stopped dragging the girl's body to look at me.

And that's when I finally understood what it meant to be Her favorite.

ONE

Aaron

I'd never been a big believer in destiny. I hated movies where the hero was doomed by the fates above, but meeting Kimberly Burns felt a lot like fate. The good kind, where there was one person in the world you were meant to meet, and everything had to go right for your paths to cross at the perfect time. I wished I could change the circumstances of that encounter, but I was thankful, nonetheless.

The true significance of meeting her may have forever been out of my reach, but as I stood in the middle of our fraternity mixer, I wondered if I'd still be right here if I hadn't. Something in the pit of my stomach told me life would be shitty if I hadn't met her. I probably wouldn't be slightly tipsy at a college party enjoying my Saturday night like a normal college student. Maybe The Legion would have killed us in that church . . . or maybe The Family would have already found us. I'd never know. But as I caught sight of her across the backyard, all the fears I'd had about the future disappeared. She saw me and smiled with rosy cheeks, and my heart kicked my ribs. She was magic like that.

The mist on the mountain sent a chill into the air. The dusk was upon us, and the light warmed her features. The scattering of trees around, painted in hues of orange and yellow, gave way to the most beautiful fall I'd ever seen. Brooklyn couldn't hold a candle to the beauty here. I could see why she never wanted to leave. Trading these views and these smells for concrete slabs and high-rises seemed criminal.

"Come on, let's go over there!" Presley said while he dragged me in the opposite direction, past the steaming pool. I groaned my reply, cursing the fact that our hands were zip tied. The sun disappeared over the horizon, casting an orange glow on the pine trees that surrounded the backyard of the OBA frat house.

We passed our fellow fraternity members, mostly comprised of The

Legion's plants that rushed at the start of the fall semester. They, too, were subjected to our current mixer with the Sigma Sigma Xi sorority. Which required each guy to be zip tied to a girl until they both drank a fifth of alcohol, but Presley thought it would be hilarious to have me linked with him all night. It was annoying, but I was a little thankful. The one girl I wanted to be linked with wasn't part of the sorority, but she was here. If only I could get to her.

We passed William scowling in our direction. He was linked to a blonde talking his ear off, and I guessed it would be a matter of minutes before he compelled her to think they'd met their requirements. Drinking parties were prohibited at William's request at the first of the semester. I suspected it had something to do with his disdain for drunk college students' untidiness and messing with his precious plants he'd filled the house with. But since we were required to participate in school events and mingle with sororities, he didn't always get what he wanted. Presley had put in extra effort to pull some strings with the sorority president to ensure the theme.

The Legion's quiet occupation of our frat house over the summer was part of a bigger plan. OBA was always a smaller fraternity and paled in comparison to some of the larger ones on campus. With more than half of our members graduating last year, it made The Legion's invasion easier. Especially with Kilian's connections in the big wide world of academia. He wasn't very forthcoming with details, but I'd heard he knew a guy who knew a guy that could ensure any dealings in the fraternity were met without trouble. It also helped that the elected president of the fraternity transferred schools, leaving his spot open for a revote. Luke was able to get on the executive board, considering on his fake transcript he was technically a junior, and he was elected president. He took his job very seriously.

I'd finally understood what William meant about a new chapter. OBA would never be the same after their occupation, at least not the chapter in Blackheart.

Presley brought us to a group of girls who had been unlinked, and I couldn't help but stare off into space while remembering the first of the summer.

It was the day right after the night in the church. Due to the blood loss, I'd spent most of my time in bed sleeping, but I never got any good rest since I was constantly waking up because of nightmares. I'd desperately wanted to see Kimberly, but it wasn't safe for her to be around me until I'd gotten my thirst under control. It was torture.

"You want us to stay in Blackheart?" Zach had said.

I'd rubbed my tired eyes and tried to keep myself upright while we'd had a meeting with Kilian in the study. The tension in the air could be cut with a knife. Luke's foot tapped relentlessly as Kilian sat at his desk across from us, and we were forced on the velvet couches. I felt like I was back in grade school being scolded by the principal.

"I mean. I don't wanna leave, but if The Family knows where we are, shouldn't we get out of here?" Presley said.

My heart sank. I couldn't leave Blackheart. I couldn't leave her.

"They don't know where we are. We'll know when they do. Trust me," Luke said, leaning back and pushing his hands through his hair.

"You really trust that Ezra won't tell them where ya are by now?" William said as he paced behind Kilian. He was always with Kilian, clinging to him like a lap dog.

"He wouldn't." Luke shook his head. "He could have easily prevented us from leaving, and he didn't."

Kilian spoke with strength in his voice. "Running puts you more at risk. They have the numbers. If they want to find you, there's nowhere on this Earth you can run."

"So, we're fucked." Zach groaned. "You want to wait here for them to find us?"

"No. We can't outrun them. But we can outsmart them. They will come for you, and we need to be ready when they do. They will not march armies and drag you. The Family must adhere to human laws just like us."

"I don't get it. If they're ultra powerful, can't they just overthrow the government or something? Take control of stuff. Why would they need to worry about laws?" Presley squirmed next to me.

"The Family has no interest in that. Each coven is different, and the only thing they care about is their queen. Some live quite peacefully within their communities, only killing a few locals a couple times a year. They may outnumber us . . . but they've learned from experience that creating unlimited amounts of members only brings them grief. The more bodies vying for Her attention, the more they fight. It always ends in bloodshed and the annihilation of Her coven."

"What's your plan?" Luke squared his shoulders and furrowed his brows.

"There will be three phases. One, the set up. Two, integration. Three, defense. You will stay here, and we will integrate into the fraternity. Here, you are surrounded by witnesses, and you will be safe to continue your education. Next, you will learn our ways while we teach you what we know. We will put all our resources into defending you. I can make some calls and get some people to help."

"Why?" It was the only question I had. The most important one. Why would they go through the trouble? What angle was he playing? There had to be more he wasn't saying.

"Because, figuring out why you are so important to them is the most vital thing. For years, we've been waiting for a way to bring down the North American coven, and it looks like you might be the key."

I didn't much like being a key. Something about being referred to as an object didn't inspire confidence. What use was a key once the door was unlocked?

There were other issues. A major crux of his plan hinged on me and my brothers adhering to The Legion's rules and learning how to blend into the world. But over the summer, I'd found it mostly meant they wanted us to listen as they bossed us around. I was thankful for their help, but the events in the church were still fresh in my mind. Trusting them had been out of the question, but my older brothers were oddly on board with Kilian's half-baked plan, and I hadn't complained because there was one beautiful redhead I hadn't been ready to say goodbye to.

"Aaron." Presley waved his hand in my face. "Uh, dude. She asked you a question." Presley motioned to the girls in front of me.

"Uh . . ."

"She wanted to know what your major is." Presley took a sip of our drink as he watched me squirm.

"General Studies." When we arrived at OBU, I stared at the list of majors for over an hour and had to choose something. So, I picked the only one that meant I didn't have to actually make a decision. There was still time to change it, but my career choice was the last thing I was concerned with.

Presley finally got the hint after I tugged on his wrist for five minutes, and we retreated into the crowd.

"Are you okay? You sure you don't need to . . . you know . . . feed?"

He said it almost like a joke, but I knew he was being serious. I had to feed more often, and it wasn't something I wanted to discuss with him in the middle of the party.

"I'm fine."

"You're doing that head-in-the-clouds thing again. I wanted to make sure." He pulled up his hands which pulled up my left arm, and I sighed. "I know what you want."

He handed me our bottle. I took a drink, wanting to get out of my predicament with Presley as soon as possible.

He turned toward the house where two fraternity members were mingling by the sliding glass doors. There weren't many humans left in our frat, but there were a few, including tank-top guy, who I'd discovered was named Jackson. He'd been in our pledge class in the spring, and I was surprised he'd survived his time on academic probation.

"You see that? He's eyeing your girl." Presley wiggled his eyebrows at me, and I tried to hide the heat that built in my chest when he said it.

"She's not my girl," I said, watching him study *my* girl. And he was way too drunk to be looking at her like that. I could see why, though. She wore her BFU sweater paired with these cool plaid pants that hugged her hips and legs. She made everything look good.

I tried not to let it bother me. If she wanted someone, she should pursue them. I wasn't her best option. Why shouldn't she be with a normal guy?

There might still be a way for her to have some sense of normalcy, but not with Jackson. Anyone but him.

Kimberly sat with Chelsea, who had been unlinked, across the yard. Earlier, she bribed Zach to drink some of their bottle when her date wasn't looking because she couldn't stand him.

I couldn't hear what the girls were saying over the music, but it seemed like Kim was trying to force some water on her.

"Why not? All you gotta do is ask."

He said it as if that were simple. As if I hadn't hurt her more than once. As if I wasn't immortal. As if it were truly that easy.

I opened my mouth to speak, but Presley dragged me across the yard before I could say anything. I wanted to snap that little zip tie and be rid of him for the night, but he hauled me to the one place I wanted to go.

"Kim, Aaron isn't feeling good." Presley slung me toward her, and I steadied myself with my hand on her shoulder.

She stared up at me with her brows drawn together while clinging to my shirt. "What's wrong?"

"His stomach hurts," Presley said before chugging more of our fifth.

Her nose crinkled, and her eyes narrowed. "Oh, really? And when did this start?"

"Couple of minutes ago, actually."

"Well, Aaron's a big boy. Maybe he just needs some Tums." Chelsea snickered, and I flashed her a fake smile. Despite her friendship with Kim, she still hated my guts, and I didn't blame her.

"I don't know. He looks pretty sick to me. I think we better take him inside the house before he starts puking everywhere."

"I'll take him," Kimberly said, grabbing my hand and sending a shiver down my spine, which felt weird while being tethered to my little brother. She let Chelsea know she'd be right back, and I shot Chelsea a weak smile, and she replied with a middle finger. Okay, maybe she had warmed to me a little.

She guided us through the crowd of people on the lawn and through the open glass door where Jackson got an unobstructed view. I finally understood Presley's plan all along, and I couldn't help but smile at the pinched expression on Jackson's face. She led us to the kitchen where Zach and Luke were still cuffed to their dates, making them laugh so loud it echoed through the house.

"My party people!" Presley said, pulling our hands up in the air.

"Hey, losers." Zach smirked, and he waved his free hand while his other pinned his blushing date to the wall. He was tipsy enough to be having a good time.

Luke was playing cards with his date, and from the wide smile he gave her, I'd have guessed he was losing. He loved a challenge. When he saw us, he chuckled. "Who told you guys you could link together?"

"Come on, Aaron's my buddy. My pal. What would a night of drinking be without him?" Presley passed me our bottle, and I swallowed a few gulps.

"What about that *thing* tomorrow?" Luke said, furrowing his brow.

And I pressed my finger to my lips.

Kimberly grabbed my forearm and whispered into my ear, "You didn't tell them?"

"We . . . have not mentioned it. Tomorrow is all about you," I said, and she squeezed my arm. "Don't worry about it."

A worry line settled between her brows before disappearing with the most adorable nose scrunch. She stayed pressed to me, her fingers grazing my arm, and I inhaled her rose perfume. After our near-death experience in the church, her hand found mine more often when we were walking on the street. She'd rub my back when I got too stressed out and clung to my arm when we watched scary movies. It was easy. Simple. Like breathing. Back when I used to have to do that.

Though we hadn't mentioned anything more since that yellow bench in the park, something about our relationship had changed. I'd be lying if I said I wasn't happy about it.

"Assholes," William said as he burst into the kitchen. "Pool. Now."

"Can't, officer, I'm a little tied up." Zach lifted his hand still zip tied to his date.

"Yeah, my hands are tied." Luke chuckled.

"Fine. You three"—William pointed to Kim, Presley, and me—"pool. Now."

We followed him, and I led Kimberly with my free hand. As we opened the door to the backyard, foam filled the yard and pool.

"What the hell is that?" William said as he flicked the foam that had settled on his sleeve.

"Uh, looks like a foam machine, sir." Presley smiled.

"No shit. Which one of you stole the money for that?"

"We didn't!" Presley and I protested.

"The sorority girls rented it," Kimberly said. "They wanted to surprise the boys."

"Jeez, we get in trouble for stealing one time, and now you think we're criminals." Presley folded his arms in a pout.

At the beginning of the semester, Kimberly had been a little short on money for her textbooks. We talked about it briefly, not expecting my older brothers to show up the next day with five hundred dollars cash for her. She'd tried to refuse it, but Luke convinced her to keep it, stating he would figure out what book it was and buy it if he needed to.

Gradually, over the summer, their guard came down. They'd started to show little parts of themselves I'd never seen before. Suddenly, the small crimes William accused them of seemed much easier to understand.

"You are criminals," William growled before heading around the growing pile of foam in front of us.

Presley bounced up and down, and I knew it was only a matter of time before he pulled me headfirst into the foam.

Things were changing, and nothing with The Legion was easy, but Zach and Luke were determined this was where we needed to be. And wherever Kimberly was, I wanted to be there too. But like the weight of Presley on my arm, we were chained to The Legion, and I wondered how long I could stand the pain in my hand as we pulled each other in the opposite direction.

One thing I knew was that if they hated us today, then tomorrow they really wouldn't be happy.

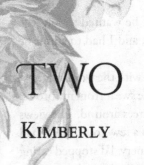

TWO

KIMBERLY

W hen I imagined running the marathon a year ago, I imagined I'd awaken in my dorm with the sun still waiting to greet me. I might have had a hot shower and given myself enough time to dry my hair and read a few pages of a book. I'd watch the soft light come up as I bit into a piece of buttery toast and listened to the bird song coming from my window. It would be a peaceful day for me. But that's not what happened.

Instead, my morning started with a loud knock on my dorm room door. Early. My RA begged me to get up and answer my phone before the boys woke everyone from the lobby. Thankfully, my RAs were used to the boys showing up. The Calem brothers being extra charming and handsome helped their rapport with them. The boys brought me breakfast, made special by Luke and Aaron. Which I ate while Presley and Zach used red face paint and colored hair spray to paint themselves and then destroyed my room in the process. I prayed their laughter didn't wake my neighbors.

The morning of the marathon wasn't what I'd imagined. It was better.

The four-hour long car ride with the Calem brothers was spent listening to everyone fight for the AUX cord, and Luke gave me many pointers for how to prepare myself mentally for the twenty-seven-mile run.

And I remembered his words of encouragement when I reached the final moments of the race. After rounding the corner, I finally saw the bright-yellow finish line in the distance. My feet were hot and throbbing with each step on the asphalt. Fire burned in my lungs with every inhale. I'd never been in so much pain all at once. I'd have taken the vampire bite again if it meant I could stop running.

"Come on! You're almost there! God, you're impressive." Aaron jogged in step with me, unfazed and practically skipping. I loved the glowing smile on his face when I asked him if he wanted to join the marathon with me. I knew he wanted to come, and I had to admit he was a good cheerleader.

"You're . . . not . . . blending." I mocked Aaron with the words he most hated to hear. Keeping my eyes ahead, I wiped the sweat from my brows. The roar of the crowd echoed through the tall trees around. The views were beautiful, and I'd seen more of the ocean in a few hours than I had in my entire life. But I was over admiring the scenery. I'd stopped caring at least fifteen miles ago. I wanted to stop the burning in my legs and the pressure in my toes that made me think my toenails might pop off any second.

Aaron laughed. "Come on. Blending is what we do. Look!" I followed Aaron's point to a bright-red speck in front of us. The red face paint was hard to miss. Aaron waved his arms, and his brothers yelled louder. It was a nice distraction from the exhaustion.

I coughed at the phlegm building in my throat, and Aaron returned to his cheerleading. Distraction was useless. The only relief would come from stepping over the finish line.

"Come on, Burns. This is nothing for you! You're doing amazing!" He checked the time on his phone. "You're making great time! But you gotta keep going if you want to hit your goal."

I had a reasonable goal for the marathon. Beat my best running time. I never cared much for placing in anything. I didn't even want a medal. I just wanted to finish. His words pushed me harder, and I picked up my pace. The burning rose in my chest until I was certain I'd die any second. The shouts from the crowd were loud in my ears. My little speck of red was now fully visible.

Zach, Luke, and Presley were all adorned in their "Go Kimberly" shirts. Presley's idea. Zach had black shades pulled over his eyes, and his hands stuffed in his pockets. While Luke had Presley's camera near the gate, fighting for the best angle to take a picture. Their cheering got louder as we passed them. It pushed me toward the finish line. Their motivation was the final push I needed.

"Go, Kimberly!"

"Go! Go! Go!"

Once one chant ended, they'd pick up another one.

Once my feet passed the finish line, I came to a halt. My legs gave out beneath me, but Aaron's arms were fast around me.

"You did it! You beat your time!" He held me in an embrace and helped me to my feet. Blood rushed through my veins, and a smile crossed my lips. He pulled away, but I didn't let go, and my hand lingered on his arm for support. I was happy, unbelievably so, but not just because I reached my goal, also because Aaron's touch was warm and it made my skin buzz with excitement.

"Dude! You did it!" Luke scooped me up in a bear hug. The boys proceeded with their chanting, and to my surprise, the crowd around us didn't mind.

Zach stayed cool and collected with his hands in his pockets. "Now all we need is some Gatorade."

"Come on. Let's go celebrate. I'm thinking . . . dive bar?" Presley said, red paint still smeared across this face.

"We can't get in, remember?" Aaron laughed.

"Oh, I have my ways,"Presley said.

My legs were like Jell-O as Aaron propped me up. I leaned into him, letting him do most of the work. The tall trees greeted us with a scenic beauty, and we walked in ecstasy at being in each other's company. My days of being alone were long gone, and as I listened to their chatter, I knew I didn't miss the quiet. Not even a little.

To my surprise, Chelsea was making her way through the crowd. The backs of my ankles were raw, and my feet were still throbbing, but that didn't stop me from limping toward her.

"God, you were like superwoman out there," she said, embracing me in a brief hug.

"You drove all the way here? I told you not to!"

Chelsea had been busy at a sorority event all day, and I didn't want to burden her with the driving it required to see me at the finish line. Over the summer, Chelsea and I had only grown closer. A few thrift store trips turned into constant texting and phone calls. A lot of her closer friends had graduated last year, and she'd needed company. I did too. Aaron and his brothers were great, but sometimes I needed girl time.

"Please, it's nothing. I arranged to meet some close friends nearby, anyway." Chelsea smiled and handed me a bottle of water before turning back toward the boys. "None of you brought her water, I see."

"We were thinking of Gatorade." Presley chuckled.

"Well, I'm glad you made it." I smiled and leaned back into Aaron to get some pressure off my feet.

"Wouldn't miss it." She winked at me while narrowing her eyes at the boys. "I hope Aaron will take good care of you tonight and help you ice your feet."

She said it with such a flat tone the other boys snickered. Chelsea still wasn't a fan of Aaron, but she tolerated him for me, and I appreciated that. I expected him to banter back, but he was still staring at me with bright, glossy eyes. My cheeks flushed.

"Chels, you still coming to the house tomorrow to help me make some stuff for the charity event?" Presley put his arm around her, and she rolled her eyes.

"Yes, I'll be there. Can't believe I got roped into being a sweetheart for the killjoy fraternity. OBA used to be fun."

Zach leaned forward to whisper in her ear, "There will be alcohol."

"Suddenly, I'm excited again," Chelsea said, perking up.

We soon said our goodbyes, and she left to meet her friends, and we made our way to the parking lot. I stared up at the trees and drank in the wilderness. The faint scent of bark and cedar filled my senses. The summer brought on a drought for almost the entirety of California. The oak tree leaves had been scorched on the ends, and the dirt underneath our feet was a dry powder. But that didn't stop the colors of fall from painting the leaves.

Aaron's gaze was heavy on my face. "How are you feeling? Do you want me to carry you?"

I smiled with a nod and climbed onto his back. I nestled my chin on his shoulder, enjoying my new view and the feel of his clean cotton shirt. It was our group's first moment alone in months. Something about it felt right, like the world was in perfect harmony when the five of us were together.

A dark shadow in front of us leaned against the trees, and we came to a halt. Like a singular rain cloud on a perfect sunny day, William and two other Legion members appeared from the trees.

"Uh-oh. The fun police are here," Presley joked.

"Do you know how long we had to look for you? You all had your GPS turned off." William's jaw clenched as he approached our group. "Not to mention the drive alone to get to you."

Kilian assigned us all our own respective "bodyguards," and William oversaw Zach and Luke. A task that turned out to be his own personal hell, as far as I could tell.

That was all Zach needed to square his shoulders and get in his face. "Come on, we've been talking about this for weeks. You knew where we were."

"Why must you always make it more difficult than it needs to be?" William sighed, his gaze landing on me, then Luke and then Aaron. "I expected more from you."

A pang of guilt fluttered in my stomach. It wasn't my responsibility to make sure the boys followed the rules, but I needed to encourage them in the right direction. The Legion weren't my favorite people, but they were protecting the boys, and that was the only thing that helped me sleep at night. If there was one thing I could count on them for, it was their obsession over keeping the Calem brothers in their sight. Which Aaron and Presley resented, but I was a little thankful for. The Family was out there somewhere, and the boys had all been marked with the queen's blood. The Legion, though a little unconventional and uptight, was our best hope.

"Maybe we wanted to hang out . . . alone. You know, just the fam. One day without randoms breathing down our necks." Presley still had a smile plastered on his face.

"Do you think I like following you all around? Nothing would please me more than to see you all wiped from the Earth because of your own misfortunes, and yet, here I am. Stuck watching over all of you."

Presley fake yawned and Zach spoke. "No one asked you to. You can fuck off, for all I care."

It had been months, but the tension between us lingered. It was hard to trust someone who once tried to kill you. I remembered the firm grip on the collar of my shirt and the hate in his eyes when William slung me up against the altar in the church. Proximity didn't make that go away. I squeezed tighter around Aaron's neck at the thought.

Sparing their lives in the church didn't come with no strings attached. They were tethered to The Legion, which unfortunately meant I was too.

"Alright. That's enough. We're sorry. Won't happen again," Luke said. He was mostly the voice of reason, but he'd had his moments with

The Legion too. He picked his battles more carefully than Zach did.

"Why do I feel like that's a lie too?" William groaned but turned toward the parking lot, and the other members of The Legion followed without a word. "We can split you up between cars. Thane, you're with me. Dom, can you ride with the others on the way home?"

He nodded. Dom was tall, taller than Luke even, and the most stoic man I'd ever encountered. He had short stick-straight black hair and green eyes. The best dressed in all The Legion, and no matter the occasion, he loved to wear beige slacks and tops that accented his copper skin.

I'd heard him say little since being assigned as Presley's guard over the summer, and the most expression I'd seen from him was the side-eye he'd give Presley when he wouldn't shut up.

"We can't even drive ourselves home now?" Zach said.

"So, you can run off and take Kimberly out to eat and get drunk? No."

"Damn, he's good." Aaron looked back at me with a smile. "Don't worry, we've got food at the house. And I might have packed a few snacks in case you needed it."

My chest warmed at the sentiment. Aaron thought of me in ways I wasn't prepared for.

Zach pulled white-knuckled hands through his dark hair, and his shades reflected in the sun. "God, you guys are such a fucking buzzkill."

"And you're all petulant children. Now get your asses in the car." William motioned to the cars in the parking lot.

"Fuck, I'm not going anywhere with you. Luke and I will ride with Dom."

"Fine," William said.

"Good." Zach always wanted the last word. He and Luke averted course toward their car while Presley, Aaron, and I sauntered toward William and Thane.

"Come on, guys, a little road trip will be fun." Thane's smile was radiant. His dimples barely showed under his groomed beard and medium-brown skin.

Thane oversaw Aaron, and his personality had won him over quickly. He was one of the only members of The Legion who didn't look like he hated being around us. In fact, he blended in well as a college student.

We stuffed ourselves into their black SUV that smelled of thick cologne.

"Which one of you was it today, gentlemen?" Presley hopped in the very back while William and Thane piled into the front seat.

Thane turned with a shy smile, his straight dark hair brushing past his shoulders. "What do you mean?"

"Which one of you bathed in the cologne?" Presley chuckled to himself in the back seat. "I'm not knocking it. I like it. I'm just curious as to why my eyes are always on fire when I sit back here."

Thane didn't seem at all phased. "Hey, it's my signature scent."

"Presley, let's not make the car ride home awkward. Please, just this once." Aaron sighed.

"Fine. Fine. I can't believe it's the only day we are all off work, and we're being forced to go sit at home."

The summer brought a host of changes we weren't expecting. We all became broke. My scholarship money dwindled, and Aaron's brother's stack of cash they had saved had gone faster than they thought possible. Aaron and I believed it was due to Presley's addiction to gambling, but he denied it. Instead of everyone getting separate jobs and The Legion being spread thin, we all worked at the same place. In the summer, that wasn't an issue. The water park's busy season was in full swing and had numerous openings. Since college students were their main customers, getting a job there was easy. Chelsea even snagged a job there too.

I worked in the gift shop with Presley and Chelsea, while Zach and Luke got stuck with the concession stand, and Aaron got the best job of the group being the person who greeted everyone at the front and told them where to go. While we slaved away at our respective jobs, Aaron talked to people all day long, and he enjoyed every second of it.

It was a great job, and we could have kept working on the weekends during school if it wasn't for Zach making a scene and getting us all escorted out. I couldn't help but recall that memory and the very event that led us all to being fired on the spot.

I had held a stack of shirts, preparing to refold the entirety of the clothing rack for the fifth time that day when I had heard something coming from outside. "What's that noise?"

I had turned to the back of the store where an open archway led outside to the courtyard. The roar of a crowd had pulsated in my head and rivaled the pop music that gave me a headache almost daily.

"Oh, shit. Come on!" Presley grabbed my arm, and we tore off through the clothing racks.

"We'll be right back!" I said to Chelsea, who was manning the register.

"Where are you going?" she called as we reached the archway.

Looking back, I was glad she didn't follow us. It wasn't planned she'd end up with the same summer job, but more like fate. And it aided in growing our friendship.

Presley and I went through the back section of the store and ran past Aaron's post next to a sign and a map that explained every route in the park. He had the best view of us all and could see the mountain ridges encircling us, but he was already at the food bar across the courtyard. Even without super vision or hearing, I could hear and see a crowd forming.

"I told you that wasn't what I ordered." A man who looked to be our age held up the line in front of the food stand Zach and Luke were managing.

"And I told you that's exactly what you fuckin' ordered. You're just being a dick. So, fuck off." Zach's eyes were set to kill, and he motioned for the next person in line.

"No. Like I said, you're here to serve me." The man put both of his hands on the bar, and his friends backed him up with laughter.

"Fuck. Off," Zach growled.

A spray of soda soaked Zach, and he took one inhale to wipe the liquid from his eyes and hair out of his face before jumping across the counter and punching the man in the face.

"Uh-oh," Presley said, pushing me behind him as chaos broke out in front of us. Luke slid over the counter, only looking disappointed for a split second before he went into backing up Zach. There was a wildness in his eyes like he was having fun catching the punches of anyone who thought they'd be able to land one on him. Presley and Aaron had joined in to stop the fight. Even with Zach holding back, it had earned the guy two black eyes and a bloody nose. As we got escorted, Zach had chuckled and licked the blood from his knuckles—way too pleased with himself.

I'd been disappointed at first, but working at the movie theater in town was closer and all around a better job. Our summer bled quickly into the new school year. It turned out when you had to work almost every day, the days flew by.

I groaned, leaning into Aaron. My feet were still hot in my running shoes, and I didn't want to imagine the week ahead at work. I couldn't imagine standing.

"Hey, tomorrow is Monday!" Aaron exclaimed. "Hell yeah."

I smiled, and a heat flushed my cheeks. There was one good thing about Mondays. Aaron and I closed together at the movie theater. He'd practically bribed our manager to make our schedules coordinate on certain days. It was fun to stay after hours and take our time cleaning and locking up. Our only true alone time together.

William and Thane went on talking back and forth in the front seat like we weren't there, and a restlessness had me shifting in my seat. How long would we be stuck under their thumb? And when—if ever—would The Family find us.

The smell of burning popcorn and butter stuck in my nostrils. I scooped another bucket and passed it to a customer. My aching feet were still at the forefront of my mind. The fluffy socks I'd slipped on did little to help.

One of the best places of entertainment on the mountain was the theater, which meant it was often busy. Monday nights were easy and slow, and I enjoyed the peace from the weekend rush. The theater was a place I could get out of my head. It felt safe to be among the public, in addition to The Legion waiting outside for our shifts to end.

In the center of town, our theater was moderately sized and had decent upkeep. New fixtures and red velvet carpets made it seem more upscale than it was. But I was thankful it didn't smell of musk and dirt like the old bowling alley in town.

"Wow, you make that look easy," Aaron whispered close, and I jumped.

Aaron leaned against his broom. He loved to pull his collar up on our all-black uniform shirts to make me laugh. It wasn't a color that suited

Aaron, but he didn't look bad in it either. The best sweeper in the whole dang theater.

"How's the shift going?" I said, grabbing a rag to wipe the counters to look busy.

"Great! I found a watch in theater three."

My phone buzzed in my pocket, and I held it under the counter.

Chris. He was back to being interested in my life again. At one time, that might have brought me joy, but now it brought me guilt. Chris and I could never be friends like we once were—for many reasons, but the biggest one being I could never tell him about the Calem brothers and what they were.

"Anything you want to share with the class?" He leaned on his broom while fluttering his lashes at me.

"Chris wants to come next month. The second to the last week of October."

"That's great." Aaron's voice went up an octave. "He can come to the Halloween party."

"What Halloween party?"

"You know, the one we're inevitably going to throw. The biggest one on campus in years. It's gonna be crazy."

"And who will let you have this party?" I said, knowing it was easier said than done.

"We're working on it."

I sighed, returning my phone to my pocket. "Well, I think Chris is worried."

"Smart man."

"Is right now a good time, though?"

The nagging thought of danger lingered. There was no indication The Family knew our location, but I couldn't shake the gnawing fear it might be inevitable.

"What better time than the present?"

Aaron's smile deterred that negative line of thinking. I couldn't think like that. My two worlds meshing left my head spinning. Chris was tucked safely away in New York, and that thought made me feel better. He needed to stay away from me and whatever was going on in my life. Yet I couldn't drop everything because of a bad feeling.

Our manager eyed Aaron, and without a word, signaled for him to go back to his post. Aaron and I shared a look, and I had to bite my lip to keep from laughing. We'd gotten a warning already for Aaron's "excessive trips to the concession." Aaron saluted her and gave me a wink before leaving to sweep the main auditorium.

"Excuse me." A soft voice caught my attention at the edge of the counter. A woman around my age stood with a heavy aura.

I walked over, and she placed a sheet of paper before me. It was a missing person's flier. A boy with soft features and a rounded nose. His brown hair was cut off at his shoulders, and he looked young. Old enough to go to BFU, but not anyone I recognized.

"Do you have a bulletin board I can hang these up on?" She, too, had the same soft-brown hair and similar nose. Siblings, I ventured to guess.

"Of course." I motioned over to the board at the left side of the lobby. Mostly filled with local ads and fliers, but one stood out stark white among the rest. Another missing person from earlier that summer, still not found.

They'd found strong evidence she may have been fleeing a dangerous situation at home. That was the story, anyway. Our town had only had one other missing person in my lifetime—a six-year-old girl found safe a few hours after a domestic dispute.

When she left, I read the bottom of the poster. He was last seen two days ago around 9:00 p.m. at a local bar. The missing girl had disappeared in broad daylight after lunch with her friends. *There wasn't a connection*, I told myself, but my heart would never believe it. There was no evidence to suggest anything. Yet I knew something most didn't, vampires were real, and they could be here right under our noses.

THREE

KIMBERLY

I t took a week before I was able to walk correctly. I'd limped to class for the better half of the week. Now that the marathon was over, I'd need to find something else to keep me busy.

Keeping myself occupied stopped the black cloud of worry from settling over me. It was harder and harder to imagine my life before I'd had worry as a companion. Back when the only thing I cared about was graduating college. Something about being lonely was easier in that regard. Worrying was easier to handle when it was just myself. Caring about someone else walking around in the world, unable to protect them, was worse. At any moment, things could be taken from me. How could anyone stand it?

I'd promised Chelsea I'd spend the day with her on Saturday. It was my first Saturday off in weeks, and she had a way of keeping me out of my head and in the present. We met in my dorm in the morning, and I hadn't changed a single thing about my room since last semester. Other than it was less kept because I spent less time there.

"Tell me on a scale of one to kill me now how bad is calculus this semester. I'm already getting stress wrinkles, and I don't think I can take the anticipation." She paced my room while looking at the photos I'd added to my mini fridge—a couple polaroids Presley had taken of us over the summer. The calculus professor had a reputation for being a brute, and I could attest to that fact with the mountain of homework I still needed to complete.

"It's . . . fine."

"Kimberly, the scale. Use the scale."

"Probably somewhere between 'holy crap, I hate this' and 'this isn't so bad.'"

She perked up. "Oh, alright, doable. You're smart, though, not sure how well that bodes for me."

"Are you kidding? You're going to be the most badass lawyer there ever was." It was easy to compliment Chelsea. She was good at everything. Naturally talented and charismatic in a way I looked up to.

Her smile let me know she didn't need to be told. She already knew.

"God, let's do something fun today." She plopped down on my bed and shielded her eyes from the sun peeking through my window.

"We're not going to a club," I warned.

Chelsea would love nothing more than to dress me in the skimpiest dress she owned and drag me out onto a dance floor.

"No, I'm feeling something athletic. Rock climbing?"

My mind wandered about as my attention panned back to the polaroids on the fridge, and I thought of the boys. Things had been tense with The Legion since their stunt last weekend. The ones who weren't working were undoubtedly stuck in the frat house, and with no events or games this weekend, they were probably restless. If only there was something I could do to bridge the gap between the boys and The Legion. If they got along, things might run smoother. Maybe we could all work together to get out of our mess. Maybe then the constant worry in the pit of my stomach would cease.

A rogue idea sparked in my mind, and I perked up.

"Do you mind if I invite someone?"

"Aaron can't come."

"No, not Aaron. Someone else I think you might get along with."

"Hm. Fine. As long as they're fun."

I didn't know yet if this person was fun. I, too, had someone assigned from The Legion to protect me—Skylar. I'd scarcely put in the effort to build a relationship with her. I didn't even know her last name or where she was from. She often stayed out of sight, but I'd seen her from across the campus yard watching me in case there was trouble. But like the changing leaves outside, there was a shift in the air. I needed to trust them. That might be the only way forward, and if so, I'd have to be the one to make the first move.

We pulled into the parking lot of the rock-climbing gym. A tall building stacked with warm wood at the entrance and black stone. It resided on the edge of Blackheart. I'd been alone a couple times, but it could be expensive, so it was something I considered a treat. It was as good a day as any to celebrate.

"I didn't know if you'd be into it since you've been such a busy bee lately. The marathon, the job, the boy . . ." She rolled her eyes, and I knew it wasn't an invitation to talk about Aaron. She never would forgive him, but since we'd become good friends, she tolerated him, and that was enough for me. It was no issue for her to pretend he wasn't there.

I side-eyed her, and she smiled. "I just mean, I bet you're . . . tired."

My cheeks turned red, and I gave her a look for another reason entirely.

"Please do not tell me another story about how you guys are just friends. You're not fooling anyone but yourselves. Now, come on." She wrapped her arm in mine while carrying a gym bag on her other arm.

Living in a mountain town resulted in having one of the largest climbing gyms in the state. The ceilings were at least forty feet high, and inside, the walls were ivory concrete splashed with assortments of color all the way to the ceiling. Chelsea ushered us in like she owned the place, and gave an affectionate wave to the receptionist before smacking down her debit card and membership on the wooden counter.

Before I could protest, Chelsea cut me off. "I got it, hun. My treat today."

"What do you do again?" I joked, knowing full well Chelsea talked nonstop about day trading. She was hooked and promised I'd never find her doing retail ever again.

The door opening caught my eye, and Skylar walked in with a gym bag in tow that looked like it could topple her over. Her straight white hair that grazed her shoulders was pulled up into a half ponytail with a few pieces framing her porcelain skin, and she was dressed for working out. I wasn't sure what to expect from her, and I was surprised when she agreed to come. Especially at such short notice.

"Chelsea, this is Skylar. Skylar, Chelsea."

Skylar reached her hand out to Chelsea, her cool-gray eyes sparkling with unbridled joy. "Oh my God, I love that bracelet."

Skylar motioned to the bracelet on Chelsea's arm. A thin delicate charm bracelet Chelsea never took off. Her mom had given it to her, whom I could tell was her best friend in the whole world.

Chelsea arched a brow with an approving smile, and I relaxed a little. Inducting her into our friend group might be easier than I planned.

"Come on! Let's go." Skylar scanned her membership ID and linked arms with me.

"You have a membership?" I said.

"To one of the best climbing gyms in the country? Duh!"

I balked at the words coming out of her mouth and the ease with which she'd said them. I'd never heard Skylar speak more than a few words, and I'd guessed she was as stoic as her brother, Dom, Presley's guard.

She led us to the belay area where we suited up in our harnesses and got on our shoes.

"Where'd you meet Kim? She tells me about her whole day, including what she has for lunch."

"That was one time!" I said, stepping into my climbing harness.

"We met at OBA." Skylar didn't skip a beat.

"I take it you're dating one of the boys, then?"

"I'd rather die." Skylar smiled as she tucked her hair behind her ear. Her eyes panned to me for the briefest of seconds.

Chelsea laughed. "Oh, I love her already."

Skylar and Chelsea continued their chit chat while we took turns going up the wall and repelling down. Skylar matched Chelsea's energy, and I was thankful I didn't have to do much to keep our conversation flowing. I had no idea Skylar was so impressive. Why hadn't I thought of this ingenious plan sooner?

After an hour, we switched gears, and I picked Skylar's brain while Chelsea was in the bathroom.

"I didn't know rock climbing was one of your hobbies."

Skylar's voice was like dark velvet. "It's not. But it is for Chelsea."

I stared at her in disbelief. "Wait, you did that for show?"

She smiled at me, but not the same smile she had before. This was more reserved, a nontooth variety. "She pegged me as the type that might take better to a bubblier personality. Looks like my assessment was correct."

"Assessment? Have you been spying on us or something?"

"No. Just observing. It's my job to keep you safe, and it's easier when I know everything about everyone you interact with. I was happy to take this opportunity to get to know her better, and you. The more I know, the easier it is for me to move around and adapt to what's needed."

I didn't know whether to be freaked out or impressed, but something about her held a sense of calm. She handed me a water bottle, motioning for me to drink. I was still slightly scared of the power she held over me. *Who is this woman?*

"Don't worry. It's all harmless. I'm not stalking you guys. Chelsea's bracelet was a good guess."

I steadied myself and took another sip of the water bottle. "Is Skylar even your real name?"

"It's the name I go by, and have for at least twenty years now. I like it. I think I'll keep it for a while."

I wondered if this was a terrible idea. I didn't know Skylar. She could be anyone. I had no idea the things she had done in the past or even if she was truly a good person I could trust, and yet I'd invited her straight into the lives of people I cared about. I was suddenly aware of all The Legion surrounding the Calem brothers. How far had they dug into their lives? For all I knew, they were building case files on each of them, noting their strengths . . . and weaknesses.

"Are you okay?" Skylar watched me with her head tilted and brows drawn together, and I hadn't noticed my heart leaping out of my chest.

Chelsea emerged from the bathroom just in time, and I took the opportunity to get a little space.

"I think I'm going to go to the bouldering wall. I'll catch up with you guys in a little bit."

I left them behind, hoping neither of them would follow me. With each stride separating me from them, my shoulders relaxed. I counted my steps on the way to the wall, savoring the distraction. Chelsea would be safe with Skylar for a couple minutes. There was no reason for me to believe The Legion would have a reason to hurt her.

I stared up at the wall, placed my hands on the colored grips, and took a deep breath before pulling myself up. The world fell away, and it was just me and that rock.

Was it naive to think the Calem boys could get along with The Legion when there were things we still didn't know? Their relationship was transactional and relied on the boys giving The Legion exactly what they wanted. But who were they?

I moved up the wall, taking my time to think and move.

There were a few things I knew. The Legion liked to keep the boys occupied. They'd insisted on the jobs. On the surface, there could be an angle, but the most obvious one was the boys were broke, and The Legion weren't exactly swimming in money. I also knew they spent a lot of energy and manpower to protect us. They weren't doing it for no reason. Their reason was obvious. The real question was what did I know about them? Truly know.

The muscles burned in my wrists as I walked up another step and then another. I placed my hand into the silky chalk on my hip. I focused on a notch on a slight overhang.

With a deep breath, I leaped, and my hand reached its target destination. Both hands gripped the notches, but my foot slipped. I hadn't accounted for my momentum and fell backward. Way backward.

I inhaled on the way down. All the lights in the building were dim, and I fought slow weight pulling me down onto the floor. My back slammed against the mat, and pain radiated in my skull. When I breathed in, every ounce of air was gone. A feeling of dread and uncertainty threatened to overtake me, so I counted the movements in my chest. After a few seconds, every breath didn't feel out of reach. I didn't know how long I lay in darkness, but it only felt like seconds before I heard a voice beside me.

"Kim! Don't move." Chelsea's voice was far away, but her pointed acrylics dug into my palm. A few more ragged breaths later, the lights came into view.

"Where am I?" Nothing close felt familiar, especially not the scent of sweat lingering in the air.

"You're at the climbing gym. You're safe." The voice sounded slightly familiar and then I caught sight of the white hair swaying above my head. Skylar was there. She squeezed my free hand.

"What happened? My head . . . Why are these mats so hard?" I got feeling in my limbs again and tried to reach up to my head, but someone held me in place.

"You fell between the mats, but you're going to be fine. Someone already called 911, and the ambulance is on the way." Her voice soothed me as she stroked my arm.

Chelsea's voice was harsh as she guarded me. "Hey, no, unless you're a doctor, back the hell up. Do not move her."

"It's okay, Chelsea." I held up my hand to calm the fear in her voice. "Please, no ambulances. I'm fine."

"You're bleeding. It's nothing to panic about, but I don't think we should move you in case something happened to your neck." Skylar was letting down her guard, and her bubbly persona dissolved.

Normally, I'd protest more, but since she'd brought notice to it, all my attention rushed to the throbbing in my head. My eyelids still felt heavy. Skylar kept one of her hands on my head, applying a firm pressure. I worked my way through each body part. First, I moved my feet and then squirmed to make sure I could still feel my legs and nothing was broken. There was some soreness, but nothing felt fractured.

"Noted."

"I already called Aaron. We'll meet them at the hospital," Skylar said.

"Oh no. They're probably freaking out."

Chelsea stopped me. "They'll be fine."

I mumbled in agreement, and the more my consciousness came back, the more my head hurt.

She directed her words toward Skylar. "We have to keep her conscious."

"Alright Kimberly, tell me—"

"No, you tell me something. Tell me a story."

Skylar blinked. "A story?"

"I'm a shit storyteller, Kim," Chelsea said. "You got any ideas?"

"Anything." I wondered if Skylar heard my heartbeat still throbbing against my ribs. I didn't want to think about my head. Or the fact I could be bleeding internally. Instead, I focused on the lights above and the rising and falling of my chest.

"Well . . . did you know that Dom is my adoptive brother? My family, we used to foster."

We were more alike than I thought. I couldn't be shocked with the amount of adrenaline already pouring through my veins, but it made sense. They looked nothing alike.

She continued. "We didn't get along at first. But one day, when I was a little girl, I snuck out in the pouring rain because I wanted to see this building in town. It was tall and beautiful, but it lit up at night, and our mom was strict, so she never let me go anywhere. Especially not at night. I thought I was so smart and climbed up onto the rafters of some construction in the city, but I slipped—"

"This is the story you chose?" I wasn't looking at Chelsea, but I could feel her side-eyeing Skylar.

Skylar sounded unfazed. "Let me finish. I slipped and remembered thinking I was alone and I was going to fall and no one would be there to help me. But my brother was there, he had followed me, and he caught me before I hit the ground. We landed in this puddle, and he just said, 'Next time, ask me to come.' And that was that. He didn't bring it up again. Point of the story being, I was okay, and you will be too. Because we won't leave your side."

"Okay, yes, what the Disney princess said." Chelsea's grip on my arm tightened.

I laughed, and that made my head throb. Her story seemed genuine, and I could work with that.

FOUR

AARON

"Can you drive faster!?" I pressed an invisible gas pedal, willing the car forward.

"I'm at a stoplight," William said through gritted teeth as he white knuckled the steering wheel.

"We're almost there. She'll be okay, Aaron." Luke's usual calm wasn't helping the anxiety swirling in my chest.

"Plus, Skylar is with her, and she said she's stayed conscious, which is a good thing, right?" Presley rubbed my back.

"Yeah, unless she's got bleeding or something on the brain," Zach said.

"Not helping," I spat.

"For what it's worth, she's in good hands. Of everyone, I'd trust Skylar the most to take care of her," William said.

"Ouch," Thane said from the passenger seat.

Rock climbing. Of all the things Kimberly could have gotten hurt doing, rock climbing wasn't on my list of worries. It didn't even make the top ten. None of it was fair.

A shift happened when I'd realized my brothers and I were immortal. Half of the things I used to worry about in life meant nothing anymore. I'd never have to worry about my brothers dying or getting hurt. I used to be extra cautious when driving in high school. After one of our classmates died in a car accident, it kick-started the thought in my teenage brain that we weren't invincible and guaranteed a long life. One of us could get some deadly disease or die in some freak accident. It was a weight I never knew I carried until it was gone. All of that flew out the window once I met Kimberly, and the weight was like a boulder.

William skidded into the parking lot. "We're here!"

My brothers and I tore out of the car and into the emergency room lobby, leaving William and Thane to park. I spied Skylar through the window, sitting and reading a magazine.

"Our friend was in an accident. Kimberly. Kimberly Burns." My voice shook.

"Okay, I can give you a visitor badge, but only one of you can go back right now. You'll have to switch out."

"We'll figure it out. Go." Luke didn't wait for me to reply before ushering me forward.

I walked the empty halls. Monitors beeping and the stench of blood hung heavy in the air. The familiar smell of antiseptic brought me back to Brooklyn and visiting my mom occasionally on her lunch breaks. It was a rare occurrence, but I remembered them clearly. I'd always given her a hard time about the smell and joked about how she'd bathed in cleaner. But now it was a comfort. My mom would have taken great care of Kimberly . . .

I pushed away the thought and the longing to turn the corner and see my mom in her colorful scrubs. I didn't need to add to my inner turmoil.

I found her room on the corner. I took it all in quickly. Chelsea was draped over her bedside and then I glimpsed her face. Kimberly was laughing. Relief washed over me.

I composed myself, waiting by the doorframe, before I knocked. "I've come for the girl."

Chelsea rolled her eyes. "Fine." She turned to Kimberly and whispered, "I'm going to be outside. But I'll be close if you need me to kick any of them out." It was funny how she didn't think I could hear her.

She smiled. "Thank you . . . really."

Chelsea stared daggers at me and bumped me on the shoulder on the way out.

"Well, well, well, someone's had quite the adventure today." I walked over to her and took her hand without another thought. I wanted to feel the warmth in her skin and the blood pumping underneath its surface to double-check she was alive. There was a bandage over her head, and I could smell the faintest scent of dried blood.

She smiled while eyeing me up and down.

"Are you sure you're okay?"

"Wait, who are you again? Starts with an A, I think . . . talks *a lot*."

"Yeah, that's right. I'm Anthony. We met in class and have been friends ever since. Nothing bad has ever happened, and you're trying not to fall in love with me. Just a normal guy with normal issues."

I contemplated those words, and I wanted them to be true. She deserved normal issues.

Kimberly giggled. "Shut up."

I didn't let go of her hand, and she never pulled away. Instead, I pulled up a chair and watched her tired eyes as she traced the veins on my hand.

"I'm glad you're here."

"I'm glad you're alive."

There was a long silence between us, and I didn't need superpowers to know what she was thinking because I thought the same thing since I got the call. This had turned out fine, but she wasn't safe. She would never be safe as a human, which meant our time together would be short. Short in comparison to the eternal life I faced.

"Does your head hurt?" I moved the hair from her face. My fingers lingered on her ear before grazing her cheek. Her heart jumped.

"No, they have good drugs. They said I can go home if the results from my scans come back okay."

"You're definitely coming home with me, then."

"I'm not sure how The Legion would feel about me spending the night in your dorm."

"I *really* don't care," I said, pulling away from her hand, but she held onto my arm, not letting me move away. "Come on. It would be fun. I make a great concussion buddy because I don't sleep."

"Do you ever wash your sheets?"

"Uh, yes?" I laughed. "Back to the important stuff, you're saying you want to sleep in my bed?"

She huffed. "Are you going to make a brain-injured girl sleep on the floor?"

"Of course not. But, then, where am I going to sleep?"

"You don't sleep."

"Yeah, but I lounge."

"Fine. We can lounge together, then."

I perked up. "You want to . . . share a bed?"

Her cheeks pinked. "I mean . . . we could lounge and watch movies. That sounds fun, right?"

I studied her face, trying harder and harder to get the image of us lying in bed together out of my head. She didn't look away from my gaze, and the world dissipated. My attention landed on her soft pink lips, and I thought back to our camping trip together in the spring. I wanted to kiss her. More than anything, I wanted to lean in and take hold of her heart, but I couldn't because once our lips touched, I'd be done for. I'd never be able to pull myself away from her without it destroying me. The string pulling our hearts would tie us together forever. So I stopped. For me, but mostly for her.

Now I wasn't sure I could stop. All I could think about was her hand on mine and the way her breathing had changed. Nothing else in the world mattered than the beating of her heart and the life in her features.

"Ding dong!" Presley jumped in. "Oh, wait, are we interrupting?"

Zach walked in with his hands in his pockets. "We're definitely interrupting."

Kimberly and I pulled away, and I cleared my throat. "No, you're not."

God. I'm so weak.

"Well, scoot over. You've had your time." Presley pulled up a chair next to me and moved me over a few inches, and the screeching of the chair legs broke our awkward silence.

Luke came in last and shut the door behind him.

"What are you doing? We can't all be in here at the same time," I said.

Presley leaned back in his chair. "I think we're fine. We snuck in."

"Please don't tell me you did something that will get you arrested," Kim said with a sly smile. She was way too used to us.

"No," Luke said. "I mean, probably not. We snuck past the security, nothing major."

Luke stood behind me with his arm on my shoulder, and Zach leaned against the wall on the other side of the room. The room was small, and we crowded Kimberly's bed, but she didn't look uncomfortable, even with us all staring at her.

"Dude, you look like shit," Zach said with a smile on his face.

"He's right. How far did you fall?" Presley's eyes widened. "Did you go to that place on Walker Street? Totem? I love that place!"

Luke surveyed the whole room. "Got any broken bones?"

"Yeah, it was supposed to be a fun girl's day. I was on the bouldering wall and fell at least fifteen feet, between the mats, but no broken bones." Kimberly raised her forearm and flexed her fingers. "Just have to make sure I don't have any internal bleeding."

"Sick," Presley said.

"You know Luke and I had a pretty severe concussion once—" Zach started.

"Please don't tell us about the time you voluntarily got the shit kicked out of you to join a blood cult," I grumbled.

Presley leaned onto Kim's bed. "You should have seen Luke's eye. It was bloody for weeks."

"I think what Zach is trying to say is . . . you shouldn't worry," Luke said with a confidence that put a natural ease into the air. "But it sucked. I got really nauseous, threw up everywhere."

"Sounds fun to look forward to," Kimberly said, watching them all closely. She scanned the room every couple minutes. Her jaw was set in an unreadable expression.

"Are they annoying you? I'll tell them to leave."

"Tell me?" Zach arched a brow at me, practically begging for a fight. We hadn't bickered in weeks. Probably because he had William as his new torture buddy. But Zach had been at work all day, and I was overdue.

"No!" she said. "Really. I was thinking . . . I'm happy you all came to visit me. This is nice."

We all felt the weight of her words. I realized that this was the closest hospital to Blackheart, and this wasn't her first trip. She'd been in this hospital before, only completely alone. I pressed into her and put my hand on her leg to comfort her. That wasn't even the worst part. She'd been hurt because of me. I'd begged her to let me help her pay off her medical bills, and she'd only said, "Maybe." Absolutely no elaboration. Two syllables. She was so stubborn . . . It was cute most of the time.

A brief silence threatened the room but then Presley said what none of us would dare say aloud, "So, like why don't you just become a vampire so we don't have to worry about you anymore?"

I hit him. "Presley!"

"What?! Come on. This sucks. And we have an obvious solution."

Zach leaned against the wall with a sigh. "He's got a point. Less work for me. I'm for it."

"What!? You're not serious," I said.

"Just one less thing for me to worry about, honestly. The sooner she's less fragile, the easier it will be to protect her if anything happens."

He *would* say that. I hadn't received an exact answer from my older brothers, but I was almost certain the idea to change Presley and me came directly from Zach. It seemed like he would be the one to have the idea.

"You guys are serious?" Kimberly spoke slowly.

"Luke?" I turned, looking for a sensible perspective.

He didn't respond right away; he looked to me and then back to Kimberly. "That's completely up to you. If that was something you wanted . . . hell yeah, we'd do it."

I opened my mouth but stopped when I saw Kimberly's face. In that moment, I had forgotten the most important part. Kimberly's choice. It wasn't mine to make. And I wanted desperately not to ever say goodbye, but the thought of her becoming like me was a foreign concept. I'd daydreamed about it a few times, sure, but I never thought the option was even on the table. The guilt of knowing I was truly the one who took her away from having anything resembling a normal life made my stomach turn.

"Wow." She eyed the cotton linens on her bed. "That's a huge decision."

The click of the hospital door had us all shuffling out of the way.

"Kimberly, long time no see." A muscular man with brown skin and tight curls entered the room. He wore way too tight of a white coat, and he matched Luke's height and stature.

Kimberly's eyes were void of recollection, and I wasn't sure if it was because she didn't remember him or she wasn't able to focus due to our conversation.

"I see you've got a lot of family here. Are these your brothers?"

"Totally," Presley said. "You must be the top doctor. Tell us, is she dying?"

Presley's tone was too nonchalant. I didn't have to be a mind reader to know what he was thinking. If she was, no problem. We'd change her. Simple. Only, he didn't realize how complicated it was.

"Far from it." The doctor spoke directly to Kimberly this time. "Your scans look great, no broken bones. You do have a mild concussion, though. That will take some time to heal, but overall, with how well your body took that fall, you're going to be fine."

I squeezed her. We got lucky this time, and I was thankful Skylar had been there to help her—and even William for breaking his rigid rules and speeding toward the hospital.

"Tough as nails." Luke looked at Kimberly. "When can she go home?"

"Today. I'll get everything settled in with the nurses, and you guys can take her. You'll have to go wait in the lobby, I'm afraid. I don't mind a crowd, but these nurses will bust ya."

"No problem." Luke gave Kimberly a fist bump before heading toward the door.

Zach and Presley left too, and Presley whispered his excitement about our conversation we'd just had all the way down the hall.

I hesitated by her bedside. "Are you totally freaked?"

She chewed her lip for a moment. "Kinda."

"Same."

"I've thought about it, but I never thought your brothers would ever offer . . ."

"Don't feel any pressure. This is your life."

"I know. I just . . . I need time to think about everything. Giving up my mortality is a lot."

Time. She needed the one thing I wasn't sure we had. I had no clue how long we'd be able to stay in Blackheart. And when we finally left, would she come with us? Would it ever be safe enough for her to stay?

Now everything was even more confusing.

"Do you need me to back off a little and leave you alone?"

"No." She gripped my arm. "That's not what I meant. Just turning into a vampire wasn't exactly in my five-year plan."

"Me either. That's why I'm glad you're going to think about it. I'll be here regardless of what you choose. I'm not going anywhere."

She relaxed and the smile returned. The smile I was always after. I had to do whatever it took to make sure she'd never set foot in this hospital again. I needed to step up and protect her, but I couldn't be with her at all times. That meant I'd have to trust The Legion to keep her safe when I wasn't around. I didn't like that option, but I had to try.

"Alright. I better go before one of these scary hulk nurses comes to throw me out of here."

She giggled at my goofy-ass joke, and it gave me hope despite the feeling that was becoming apparent. Things would change whether I wanted them to.

FIVE

AARON

After another hour, Kimberly was free to come home, and surprisingly, William didn't give me much trouble regarding her staying over. I hated getting his permission for things, but with Kilian only being around occasionally, The Legion needed a leader. William seemed to fill that role with pleasure. He never smiled unless he got to boss us around.

It was late by the time we got home, and I let Kim use my room to get changed after we'd picked up her things.

"What . . . are you wearing?" I said, stopping dead in my tracks.

Kimberly was posted up in the doorway to my bedroom with her head still bandaged, and she clutched her toiletries. "What?"

My gaze lingered on her legs covered only partly by her knee-high socks. She wore an oversized T-shirt tucked into her checkered night shorts. It was the hottest thing I'd ever seen.

God was torturing me again. I had the prettiest girl in the world in my room. The only one who was purely off-limits and I could never touch.

I averted my gaze. "Whoa, Burns. Are you trying to flash the whole frat house? Put some clothes on, will ya?"

She pulled her hair to one side and rolled her eyes. "You're being ridiculous."

"Okay, Knee Socks. Have it your way. I . . . I'm gonna let you get settled into bed. Relax. Have alone time. Rest your head, and I'll go . . . go talk to everyone downstairs for a bit. You know, check in with the guys."

She smirked. "Fine."

I practically sprinted out the door and down the stairs. I had to get far away and think about anything other than her being in my room in those shorts.

"What's up?" Thane peered around the corner in the foyer.

"Nothing. Nothing. I'm good. Everything is good."

"How's Kimberly?"

"I think she'll be okay . . . thanks for asking."

Thane wasn't someone I'd trust with my deepest, darkest secrets, but he tried to get to know me, and I appreciated that.

He smiled. "No problem. You want to join? We're playing poker."

"N—" It wouldn't hurt me to build a relationship with some of them. It may make them more willing to actually protect us. "Sure, I've got a few minutes."

"Did I hear someone say poker?" Presley was next to me in seconds. That was one good thing about The Legion moving in. We had more freedom. The vampire-to-human ratio was balanced in our favor. Plus, it was Saturday night and, though I wasn't one hundred percent sure, most left on the weekends. Either to stay with their girlfriends or travel home.

"You guys play?" Thane said.

"Just a little." Presley winked at me when Thane had his back turned.

"Great, come on! We've got plenty of room." Thane ushered us through the kitchen and into the hallway. In the back of the house, next to the library, was the pool room. It was the official living place of the pool table, but during parties, we usually moved it to the living room or kitchen. A group of four Legion members were already playing. Their scowls as we entered told me we weren't welcome. The thing about The Legion was despite having to protect us, none liked doing so. Except Thane . . . and maybe Skylar.

Thane pulled up two chairs, and the screeching on the hardwood broke the silence.

"Man, you know what would make this better? Beer." Presley ran to the kitchen and plopped down with a freshly cracked can and another next to it for when he chugged that one. "Ah, better. Want any?"

The death glares ensued. Seeing as how The Legion were opposed to anything fun, alcohol was off the table.

"I'll deal," I said. I found it was a good way to observe other players. See if I could identify their tells, but more important, I could stack the deck. Presley sat across from me beaming. We played poker a lot growing up. Only, we played it the Calem way. We all cheated in any way we could.

"Sweet." Thane kept his cheerful demeanor while eyeing Felix.

"Are we really gonna play with them?" Felix's voice was deep. He sat back in his chair, and his muscles bulged out of his shirt. Felix and Halina were fraternal twins. Their only similarities were their pinkish pale skin and blonde hair. That's about all I knew about them, other than they were from Russia and had a particular dislike for my older brothers. It was easy to steer clear of the ones who didn't like us. I guessed they were ordered by Kilian to play nice, but I had to wonder what was in it for them? If they were miserable, why did they agree to stay?

"Come on. It's your chance to completely obliterate them in poker." Thane winked at me, and I dealt cards after peeking at them while shuffling.

"Yeah, I'm sure he wants to beat us in something." Presley laughed as he chugged the rest of his first beer. The one and only time we'd gotten Felix to interact with us was at our frat recruitment when we'd hosted a Smash Bros. contest. Presley and I dominated with no cheating required. Poker would be the distraction I needed, and hopefully I could get a better read on some of The Legion members.

The Legion weren't watching me too closely, and I guessed they were amateurs. Thane explained the chip amounts before we started, and we agreed. Not that I had a lot of money to gamble away, but I didn't plan on losing much. Skylar and Dom were to my left and started the bids.

"How is Kimberly?" Skylar asked, and her eyes softened when they met mine.

"She seems okay . . . thanks for taking care of her, by the way. It helped knowing she had you."

A dimple appeared on her chin as she eyed her cards. "I did nothing. You shouldn't be thanking me."

She said it in a flat tone, as if I'd offended her somehow.

"Come on, Sky, you can't be everywhere at once." Thane sighed, and his brows wrinkled.

"Yeah, what were you going to do? Catch her mid free fall from across the room?" Felix said, already folding.

Skylar tucked her hair behind her ear. "You underestimate me."

Thane smiled before relaxing back into his chair. "Wouldn't dream of it. I know how you are, but you can't blame yourself forever."

Dom cracked a smile. "Sure she can."

Hearing Skylar felt bad for not being there made me feel a little bad for cheating at our poker game. But Zach and Luke taught me it wasn't personal. I looked to Presley, waiting for him to raise.

As kids, Presley and I spent many late nights researching how to stack cards. We practiced repeatedly in the dim glow of my TV into the early morning hours. It was a skill we used to cure our boredom, but also to beat Zach and Luke, who always won at everything. I'd learned sleight of hand from videos, and I was somewhat better at it, but the vampire advantage made it that much easier. Hence Presley's newfound love of gambling.

Felix eyed me while tapping his finger on the table. *Did he already suspect me?*

Presley slammed his hands on the table in a fit of laughter with Thane, dividing their attentions for a millisecond. I kept my attention on the cards and noticed Felix moving his hands from his cards to his lap and then back to his deck. I smiled. A game of cheater against cheater was a lot more challenging.

We played for more than an hour, and I'd been able to signal to Presley about Felix. We tried to remain inconspicuous, but as the pot grew higher, Presley couldn't help but to claim his victory despite already having a winning hand the last time. I fought the urge to kick him under the table.

"I don't play with cheaters." Felix smacked his hands on the table and stood.

I smirked. "What's your problem? Mad you lost at your own game . . . cheater?"

Thane threw his cards on the table. "Felix! I knew there had to be a reason you were always taking all my money."

He ignored him, his eyes ablaze and honed in on me. "No, I'm thinking we should have killed you when we had the chance. Saved us the trouble."

Thane frowned while taking his feet off the table. "Come on. Let's all be friends."

"Friends?" Halina ran her fingers through her hair, nudging Dom, who stayed stoic. "What do you think about that?"

"Nothing,"Dom said.

Skylar tossed her cards on the table. "Don't be so dramatic, Felix. It's just a game."

"Oh, come on, Sky. You can't love them that much."

"Don't engage," Dom said, standing up and leading his sister toward the door.

Felix pushed his hands through his hair. "Whatever. I'm sure his little human girl will be dead soon, anyway. Save us all the trouble of looking after a human who is doomed to die."

My body went rigid, and my attempts to help clean up the table stopped.

"What?" The word came out so low I didn't recognize my own voice.

"Is that a threat?" Presley said.

"Whoa, no, it isn't. Let's take it down a few notches." Thane's voice felt far away.

But my body wouldn't still. Anger bubbled in my chest and moved into fingers. My hands tensed, and my face warmed.

"You know as well as I do, Thane, that humans don't last in our world. Especially not ones with a target on their back from The Family." Felix's voice was soft when addressing Thane, but it cut like a knife when he turned to me. "A bump on the head is the least of your worries. Might as well start planning the funeral."

"Felix." Skylar clenched her jaw and stopped by the doorframe.

"You know I'm right, Sky. You just won't admit it to yourself."

"Let's let them kill each other in peace." Dom whispered to Skylar.

I gripped the table, and the wood splintered under my fingers.

You're in control. You get the final say in what you let shake you.

I tried to recall every pep talk Luke had given me, but it wasn't working. I couldn't tell what was getting to me more: the threat in his voice or the truth behind his words.

"Pres, come on, let's get Aaron back upstairs." Thane's hand on my arm felt more like a breeze on my sleeve with how the blood surged through my body.

"No way! Kick his ass, Aaron!"

"Yeah, try to kick my ass. Too bad you can't. You're just a child. You have no idea what you're up against, but I do." Felix smirked, no doubt enjoying every minute of watching me squirm. "Since you won't be able to protect her, maybe I should show mercy . . . put her out of her misery now."

I lunged. No longer feeling anything other than rage in my body. I was numb and only saw red.

I didn't get more than an inch or two before a set of strong arms pulled me back into my chair and held me down.

"What the hell is going on here?" William emerged, bringing the scent of cigarettes into the room. "I left you in charge and someone breaks the fuckin' furniture."

"Hey, I kept them from killing each other. That was my job." Thane rubbed the back of his neck.

"Barely," Skylar said as she and Dom sauntered out of the room. Her eyes flickered to me, and I detected a hint of sadness there. My head felt like it split in half, and with each beat of my heart, my head pulsated.

Luke, Zach, and William all looked worn. I'd wondered where they were, but they were all standing with their arms crossed watching me and Felix like disappointed dads.

"Can't leave you fuckers for two seconds," Zach said, and William nodded in agreement.

The divide between us was bigger than I thought, yet, if I didn't know any better, it looked like my older brothers were getting along with William. It was a miracle.

"What was this about?" William said.

"We just got into an argument . . . about cheating." Felix was watching me from across the room.

Presley waited for me to speak. Now that the anger had passed through my body and I had the worst headache ever, I realized I had given Felix exactly what he wanted. He was a dick, but I got his message loud and clear, and he was partly right. I didn't know what we were up against. Not really. I'd never personally dealt with the horrors of The Family. Everything I knew was secondhand, and even though I still missed Sarah, it wasn't the same as being there and watching her die.

I had no idea what the members of The Legion had endured at the hands of The Family. I didn't know their pasts and the things they experienced or the things they lost. To them I was a kid playing a dangerous game, and they knew the odds better than I did.

"Yeah, cheating. Presley and I got caught cheating," I said, standing, and the wood splinters crunched under my feet.

Luke's eyes were boring a hole in the side of my face.

"Why am I not surprised?" William sighed.

"Yeah, wonder where they got an idea like that." Zach smirked and nudged Luke.

It was after midnight when I opened the door to my room. Me, Presley, and Felix had to clean up the broken table and put it in the dumpster outside. We didn't say much, but Felix thanked me for not mentioning to William the things he'd said before we went our separate ways in the house, and I took that as we were cool.

I expected Kimberly to be asleep. Instead, she lifted her head with a sleepy smile to look at me. And just like that, the distraction was useless because there she was in my bed.

"Hi."

"Hi," she said with sleep in her voice.

I thought about telling her about my run-in with Felix but resolved to tell her in the morning. Her eyes might shut any minute, and I wanted her to rest.

"Do you still feel okay? Do you need any water? More pillows . . . Shoulder to sleep on?"

I knew I shouldn't say it, but it was Kimberly, and she was in my bed.

She sat up, lifted the cover, and revealed a set of my sleep pants. "Movie buddy?"

Seeing her in my pants was worse than the shorts. So much worse. I didn't say a word as I took her up on her offer. I slid under the comforter of my twin bed that was already toasty warm. I expected Kimberly to scoot over to her side of the bed, but she didn't. She stayed close and snuggled into my arm. I was thankful she couldn't hear my heartbeat, because it was bursting out of my chest.

Her heartbeat was a soft, comforting pattern. She was relaxed.

"Uh, what should we watch?" I said as I scrolled the streaming service I bummed off one of the guys in the house.

"I don't know, master of the cinema, you tell me."

"How about this one?" I moved the cursor over a western because

I knew that was the one type of movie she hated. There had been a resurgence of women adoring men with gray beards and cowboy hats after a western had played in the theaters for six weeks straight and hit box office records. I think she was tired of college boys in town calling her "little lady" when she served them popcorn at the concession stand.

"Oh, with Ryan Gosling?"

She said that about every movie.

I looked at her to see if she was serious, and she smirked. "You're a real comedian, Burns. You know that."

"Mhmm, hm." She pulled herself snug to me and closed her eyes on a sigh.

My arm and chest were burning where she rested her hands, and I tried to keep my attention on the TV. I'd picked some random romantic comedy. She loved those.

Only fifteen minutes into the movie, she spoke again. "Do you think your brothers were serious about what they said?"

I hesitated, but I knew the answer. "Yeah. I do. They don't normally lie about that kind of stuff."

Her eyes opened, and I turned my head to face her.

"Why do I feel like you're disappointed? Like you didn't want them to ask me."

"I'm not. It's not that."

"Do you . . . not want me to be part of your family? I mean, I know that's kind of a lot to ask."

"What?! No. That's all I want. It's just, after everything that went down a few months ago, I know how hard it is to have a demon in your head and having to hunt. You have to attack people, Kim. You know better than anyone what that feels like . . . and there's no way around it. I still hate it. I don't want you to go through that."

Her breath was hot on my face, and it smelled like bubblegum toothpaste. This girl would be the death of me.

She sighed. "That's why I don't know if I want to . . . that, and should I choose to be immortal at twenty years old? Seems like a huge life-altering choice I can't take back."

I chuckled. "Yeah, talk about committing yourself to a lifetime of dead-end jobs where you can never move up the ladder."

"Or there's a never-ending list of things to learn and do. I love the idea of that. Or places to go see." Her eyes shone with optimism before darkening again. "But I don't want to hurt people. I don't want to choose to do this at the expense of others. That seems . . . selfish."

My fingers found their way to her cheek, and I moved a piece of hair from her eyes. "I wish my brothers had been so self-aware."

I loved this side of her. Her opening up to me was the greatest gift I'd ever been given. Unknown to the rest of the world, Kimberly Burns had soft skin under that armor she put on every day. She tried to hide it, but when she was this close, she didn't hold back those inner fears. Instead, she relied on me for comfort, and I knew that wasn't a privilege many got from her.

She spoke again. "On the other hand, you guys are the closest thing I've ever had to family, and I don't know where this business with The Legion will take you. What if me choosing not to become a vampire was the only thing that kept you from taking me with you? Or even worse, what if me becoming one was the only reason for you to take me along."

I was still shocked and reeling by her words when tears formed in the corners of her eyes.

"Hey, hey, hey. What are you talking about? I want you with me every day. Vampire or not. I'm not going anywhere. I promise. And if you want to stay human, who cares. That doesn't change anything. You're still family." I relaxed my palms on her cheeks. "You can grow old, get married, and have kids, and do all those things, and I'll still be here. We can be those weird uncles who stay mysteriously young and handsome. I'll watch you fall in love, grow old, and . . . die if that's what you want. And it would be the most horrible, heart-wrenching thing I'd ever do, but I'd do it for you. I don't want you to choose this life because you feel like if you don't, you'll be alone."

I could imagine it all. After a couple years had gone by and college was over, Kimberly would work in whatever exciting career she chose. She'd be a CEO or a scientist, something astounding because she was amazing and hardworking. There, she'd probably meet a guy. We'd be introduced, and I'd struggle to like him, but she had good instincts, and we'd become good friends eventually. As time went on and they got married, he'd have questions, but she'd vouch for us. Maybe we'd all get along well enough and we could tell him. They might have kids and we'd be the cool, fun uncles that never aged. But she would. From an athletic twenty-year-old, to a very spritely ninety-year-old who would probably still do pool exercises. And then we'd have to watch her die and live with the fact that we'd have to continue on without her, with only her family left behind as a piece of her memory. The whole thing would be weird. It would be horrible. But I'd do it in a heartbeat for her.

Her gaze was heavy on mine. I had been consumed by my own thoughts, so I didn't notice the shift in her breathing and heart rate. She leaned forward, and her lips, like a magnet, pulled me closer.

I knew if I allowed myself to kiss her, everything I'd done to build the wall between us would crumble. One kiss and it would be over for me.

I hesitated one moment longer before our lips touched. A bolt of electricity jolted me forward, and I grabbed her face and pulled her closer. Of all the times I'd imagined it, the real thing was *so* much better. Her lips tasted like bubblegum, and the scent of her shampoo was everywhere. She was everywhere.

She tugged at my hair and invited me to move closer. I let her pull me till I leaned over her. I was careful not to grab her like I ached to. Partly because she was concussed, and the other, much more prominent, reason was because I felt the need to hold her so forcefully against my body and I was certain I couldn't do it without hurting her. Every kiss left me hungrier, and the ounce of logic still lingering in my brain held on for dear life. Our tongues entangled, and with every motion, my body burned hotter. Her breath was hot in my throat. I wanted her. All of her.

Finally.

I pulled away, stilling the dark voice in my head. I hadn't heard it in days, and I couldn't take any chances. I needed to hunt.

As that guilt set in, another stronger feeling took its place at the image of Kimberly's bloody arm and the terror in her eyes when I'd bitten her in the forest. What was I doing? I kissed the one person I shouldn't. Because I was immortal, and she was not. I hurt her. Her life would be better without me in it.

"I'm sorry. I shouldn't have done that," I said.

Her eyes met mine again as she leaned back, letting out a soft breath. "Aaron, I kissed you . . ."

"Right."

I couldn't take my eyes off her. My body yearned for her and her perfectly pink lips swollen from kissing.

"But we probably shouldn't . . ." she said. Her gaze held firmly on my lips.

"You're right . . . we shouldn't. You're concussed. Confused."

"Right. It never happened." She shook her head, as if it would shake away the evidence like an Etch A Sketch. But I still felt her on my lips.

"Agreed. You should sleep. That would be great . . . for your head. I think I should go—"

"No, please stay. I-I still need my movie buddy."

Her big blue irises were really convincing. Going was smarter. It was nobler. I should have gotten up and walked out and pretended that kiss never happened, but I promised I wasn't leaving, and as her grip tightened on my arm, I knew it was pointless for me to try. It was already done. I'd kissed her, and there wasn't a rewind button. I hooked myself into a ride with no exit, and I was certain I didn't want to get off. But as I nestled myself back into bed with her, I couldn't think of anything other than how I would never be able to go back to being just friends after a kiss like that.

SIX

AARON

O ne thing I liked about hunting with The Legion was the complete silence.

William and Thane could walk in silence without uttering a single word to each other. As if it was something to be done in reverence, not a casual stroll in the park. A skill I hadn't yet learned.

It was three in the morning before I wrestled myself from Kimberly's grasp and left her sleeping peacefully in my bed. And for those hours, I'd fought with the voice in my head and the feel of Kimberly's warmth. I'd exclaimed in the foyer I needed to hunt immediately, or I would go crazy. Which prompted Luke to come to my aide, but to move toward goodwill with The Legion, I decided it might be a good idea to go with them alone. I just hoped it wouldn't be Felix because I still wasn't sure I could trust him not to kill me.

Thane, William, and I walked along the outskirts of a nearby town farther down the mountain. It was far enough away from Blackheart where I wasn't worried about running into anyone I knew. We walked next to a road with tall redwoods shielding us on either side, and the stars above covered almost every inch of the obsidian sky. It probably would have looked like we were up to no good if it weren't for how well dressed William and Thane were.

"Why do you dress like that?" I literally couldn't stop myself from saying the words.

William chuckled. "I could ask ya the same thing? You're always runnin' around looking like a bum."

"Yeah, we're *stylish* and comfortable. The ladies...and some men dig it." Thane ran his fingers through his hair.

"Can you guys even date? Seems like Kilian would be strict about that kind of thing," I said while dodging a trash can.

"Kilian doesn't enforce any rules relating to our personal lives."
William lit a cigarette and snapped his lighter shut, and the smoke trailed
up into the night.

"But, I mean we're always moving around. Not like we can date
anyone, really. Shoot, I haven't dated anyone for at least a hundred years.
. . though I've met a few people I really wished I could have settled down
with . . . it never really works."

I sighed, thinking again of Kimberly just when the cold pine air was
finally taking me far away from my room and the memory of us in my
warm bed.

Thane must have read my mind because he backpedaled. "Maybe, it
could have, though . . . Will keeps me busy. You know, fighting the good
fight and all. We've been traveling since the day we met. This is the first
time we've been in one place for longer than a week in years."

It was hard to believe Thane was a century old. He blended in well
with everyone at college, even in the way he spoke. From day one, he was
there participating in our frat events and doing it with a smile.

"How did you guys meet?"

"We met at a pub, and he was plastered," William said.

"I had troubles to drink away." Thane winked at me before putting
his hands behind his head casually. "Good ole Will here stopped some
big oaf from killin' me."

I noted Thane's slight accent, probably picked up from William in
their many years together. Or maybe he was from Ireland too?

"You two aren't like the others, then? You've been together a long
time?"

William rolled his eyes and took another puff of his cigarette. "You
really can't stop talkin', can ya?"

"Nope. It's a curse."

"We've been together ever since that day. The Legion . . . Will . . . they
pulled me off my ass. The Legion is the best lot I've ever had in life, and
everyone I've met . . . may not be the easiest to get along with, but they're
good people through and through," Thane said with a smile.

I smiled, knowing exactly what he meant. He trusted them and saw
the best in them. Just as I did with my brothers. Something in me shifted
when I thought of them all. Maybe we all could get along? They could
get what they wanted, and we could get what we needed. Our freedom.

That's why we were all here. We had common interests. We just needed to work together.

William stopped me with a hand on my chest. "There. That's perfect."

A lone silhouette of a man sat at a wooden picnic table off in the distance. The large park was dimly lit with only three lights placed at the very edge of the tree line. A familiar fear traveled up my limbs, and I shivered.

William stood in front of me. The smoke from his cigarette swirled in my face. "Alright, I'll go in, knock the guy out, and then you feed. It will be quick."

My heart started beating in my ears, and my hands got sweaty. Two seconds in and I was ready to run back the way we came.

"But we won't let you kill anyone." Thane shoved his hands into his trouser pockets. "I swear it."

I nodded to them and started what felt like an eternity to close the distance. The man was sat on the bench, scrolling his phone, not paying attention or seeming to care about the late hour. But he was huge, he probably didn't think he had to worry.

Kill, kill, kill.

The voice was a sad mockery in my ears, but I was getting better and better at tuning it out. The more fed I was, the less scared I felt. The less scared I felt, the more control I had. But as we got closer, I stopped. The voice in my head swirled around too fast, and the panic set in.

"Aaron . . ." Thane's brows furrowed. "It will be okay. You can trust me."

I believed him, and his words were enough to keep me walking. I wished Luke were there with his added optimism and strength in case they couldn't pull me off this guy.

William shot behind him in a second, and with the cigarette still on his lips, he touched the guy's cheek from behind, and he slumped forward.

Stay calm, I told myself. My hands shook at my sides.

Kill him. Kill him now.

I stopped again on the other side of the table. They stared at me, but I froze, this time because the stability in me shifted. A surge of something primal ran through my body, and I feared if I kept walking, I might tear out the guy's throat. It hadn't been that long since I'd fed, but suddenly it felt like it'd been weeks.

"I can't do it," I whispered. My attention locked on his neck where I imagined the blood pumping beneath his skin.

"You can." Thane was next to me. "Remember, you're in control every step of the way. Try to think of the person you're biting. Imagine their life and who you think they are . . . what they do for a living . . . the people that want them to come home. Anything that makes you remember to keep them safe."

That sounded great in theory but implementing it when I felt only wildness coursing through my brain was the challenge.

"We don't have all day." William motioned to the guy again, but my feet were unwilling to let me move.

Seconds passed, and William grabbed the man's wrist and bit down, leaving blood stringing from his lips. I focused on the red blending in the moonlight. That was enough to make my feet move and take the guy's wrist from William. His heartbeat was steady under my fingertips. Finally, I gave in.

Blood filled my mouth, and I was gone again. Purely in a world of my own. But I knew I couldn't stay there. I had to move away. I had to stop . . . eventually. I wanted to linger there in the warmth.

No, I didn't. *It* did. This guy probably had a family like I did. He had to be messaging someone. Someone who knew him and loved him. I had to stop. Stop before he couldn't return to them.

I pulled away. It felt like only a few seconds, but I wasn't one hundred percent sure. My muscles were mine to use again. The man was still out cold, lying oddly peacefully at my feet, but his heart still beat steadily in his chest. Harder now, but not like Kimberly's had been that night in the forest.

I did it.

Thane and William picked him up and laid his head across the bench and then dusted off the dirt of their clothes.

"You did good," William said.

He smiled at me the way Luke did, and I felt a pang of sadness. I couldn't wait to tell him about tonight.

"We should get out of here. I think they're going to bring their search party in this area." William motioned to the road, and I followed.

"Wait, search party?" I said.

"Yeah, for that missing guy. They've found evidence to believe that he's dead. They're trying to find his body."

My blood ran cold. "Well, what about that guy? Should we be leaving him there?"

"He'll wake up in five. Don't worry," William reassured me.

"But—"

"Don't worry, Aaron." Thane was beside me. "We're keeping an eye on it."

He was scary good at reading me.

"But what about The Family . . ." I instantly regretted saying the name out loud, as if they would pop up out of the trees at the mere mention of them.

"You don't need to be thinkin' about that. What's that little song and dance Luke always tells you? Really inspirational stuff," William said.

I couldn't tell if he was mocking me or not, but I answered, "He says he doesn't want us to always be running."

Among other things, like focusing on school, so when everything was over, Presley and I could finish our degrees and maybe even use them. He loved talking about building memories and enjoying the here and now. He was basically a certified life coach at this point.

Luke made it clear he wanted us to keep our eyes on the future and leave all the worrying to him. Something about it never sat right with me, though.

I let William and Thane take me away from the scene, thankful they were keeping an eye on things in Blackheart. I didn't know what to think of the missing people popping up, but I knew what I feared. We weren't alone, and I started to believe that no matter what was coming, we could face it.

SEVEN

KIMBERLY

It was a long crawl down the mountain. A blanket of red and orange leaves peppered the tree line. The scent of pine drifted in my car window as I let my fingers dangle in the air. My whole world disappeared in my rearview just when I thought I'd never know the sound of silence again.

Chris needed me to pick him up from the airport. Only, driving two hours away was not permitted by anyone, including The Legion, but since I'd be in the car the entire journey and had Skylar protecting me, I'd been able to argue my way into going alone. Aaron wanted to come, but I decided easing Chris into the boys was best. Especially since it had been so long since I'd seen him.

Our last interaction had ended in the same place—a hug at the airport with me holding back tears that begged to stream down my face as he left. I swallowed at that old, familiar ache of sadness in my chest that I hadn't felt in a long time.

Gripping the steering wheel, I followed the curve of the road. Skylar was in my rearview, driving the SUV and looking stoic as ever. I wondered what type of music she liked to listen to. I'd offered her a ride in my car, but she preferred to be "more available." I didn't argue. It had been like pulling teeth to get any real information out of her. But since the rock-climbing incident, she seemed . . . softer.

It didn't take long being out of town before I saw traces of smoke in the air. Wildfires burning hundreds of miles away. The summer drought continued into fall, and fires were popping up everywhere. Thankfully, Blackheart had not yet had any scares. I couldn't think of my beloved hometown being evacuated and turned to ash. I'd been lucky to never live through any. Every fire that ever got close was snuffed out just in time.

I rolled my window up and set my focus on Chris. How was he going to function in my world? My future and the past were at odds and there was no middle ground. I just needed to survive the weekend long enough to show him he didn't need to worry about me and then he could go back to New York and forget my existence. Is that what I wanted? To lose my childhood friend? To never see him again?

I wasn't sure what I wanted, but I knew the facts. Bringing Chris near the Calem boys was bound to cause trouble, for more than one reason.

It had been a little more than two weeks since Aaron and I kissed. Or rather I kissed Aaron. Thankfully, he hadn't made anything awkward. He didn't even tease me about my impulsive decision. A decision I should have regretted, and I *did* regret that now every time I saw him my stomach swarmed with butterflies, and when he smiled, I remembered how soft his lips were.

All because of one reckless decision. When had I ever done something without thinking it through? Even when I'd confronted the vampire problem, I'd had a plan. But in the dim light of Aaron's TV, I didn't even second-guess it. I just kissed him. Because he was sweet. Because he was a little too attractive when his hair fell into his eyes. Because he was shining so brightly I couldn't look away.

Because I wanted to.

It changed nothing that mattered. Aaron and I couldn't be together, and any future in which we ended up together was bound to end in disaster. I couldn't just let go of everything I'd planned on doing and run off and become a vampire. No. I needed to dig my heels deep into my reality and stay at school. And when the business with The Family was done, The Legion would leave and we could all move on. I'd graduate college and age. That's the way it was supposed to be.

My two-hour drive was made in solemn silence. Each passing mile had my stomach turning, and it was made worse with each gnaw of hunger. But meeting up with Chris felt like a move in the right direction, something normal.

I circled the airport pickup lanes and awaited a text from Chris with his flight and gate number.

I spied him across the way with his sunglasses tucked in his mousy-brown hair. He wore slacks and a blazer, and I wondered if he'd gone to the airport straight from a meeting. I greeted him with a hug, and we made quick work of getting his things in the car. My nerves were a mess.

There were the normal exchanges, at first. The catch up. It had been more than a year since I saw him last, and he'd grown in stature and confidence. I hadn't thought that was possible, but he talked like the world was already in the palm of his hand. Chris was driven—like me. We both longed for something more than we had. Maybe that's why we became best friends.

Everything was coming back, and after picking up a bite to eat, I finally loosened my grip on the steering wheel.

"So, frat boys, huh?" He turned his whole body to look at me this time.

"Don't start. They're nice. You'll like them," I said while trying to push back the image of Zach flying off the handle and causing another scene. The image of him licking the blood from his knuckles at the water park stayed at the forefront of my mind.

Chris wasn't afraid to say what he thought, and while that didn't bother me, I wasn't sure all the Calem boys would cope the same.

"If you say so. I just think it's a little weird you're hanging out with all these guys all of a sudden. You never did before."

"I didn't hang out with anyone."

"There's nothing you aren't telling me? Are you involved with one of them or . . . all of them."

I hit the break a little too hard. The traffic on the highway had crawled to a standstill. Skylar was unfazed in her shades as we made eye contact in my rearview mirror.

"No! I mean . . . yes, I am. But just one and we haven't decided on what we are just yet."

I knew immediately what he would think. I sighed, wishing I could have just lied.

"Oh?" His brow lowered. "Can't wait to meet him, then. Make sure he's up to par."

At one time, I'd welcomed his protectiveness. Chris looked at me like I was his thing to watch over. Lost and alone. But I wasn't her anymore, and I hadn't been for a long time.

I adjusted the vents as my neck dampened at the thought.

"Whoa, what's that?" Chris eyed my wrist. The scar from Aaron was an eyesore, to say the least.

"Oh, I got bit by a dog." I hurried and covered it with my sleeve. I didn't like anyone staring at it too long because it was an obvious indentation of human teeth.

"You never told me about that."

"Well, you didn't ask," I said matter-of-fact and gripped the steering wheel tighter. The traffic jam in front of us dissipated, and my lungs felt lighter.

"I'm sorry." He sighed. "I've been distant. But that's why I wanted to come see you. I missed you . . ."

His gaze softened and his lips pressed in a tight line, making me nervous. There was a time when I'd wanted nothing more than for him to look at me like that. But now, everything was different. I thought back to the bus stop when I'd talked to him. How different things would have been if he had reacted differently. I'd spent the better part of my youth trying to get him to stop seeing me like a little girl, and now that I wasn't anymore, I wasn't sure where that left us.

"Didn't you miss me?" He smiled, his perfectly straight teeth on display.

"Yeah, of course I did."

"Good, because I was thinking about next year and how cool it could be if you came to New York and transferred."

Spit caught in my throat. "W-what?"

"Well, I was going to wait to ask you later this weekend to surprise you, but now seems like as good a time as any."

"You know I can't afford to go to your university."

"Yeah, but what if I said there were better scholarship opportunities and I could help pay your rent."

I couldn't believe what I heard. The Chris that lectured me about being my own person and making my own way was asking me to give up everything I worked for and let him take care of me.

"Why are you doing this suddenly? I don't get it . . ." I kept my voice neutral and eyes on the road.

"Because I'm worried about you here . . . alone. I make enough money that I can help you. And what's here for you, anyway?"

So many things. So much I couldn't say. I didn't know how to respond, but I wanted the cars in front of me to move faster. The only thing coming to mind was the warmth of Aaron's smile and the thought of saying goodbye. I imagined it all. His smile fading brought a wave of sadness I'd never felt before.

"Well, we can talk about it more this weekend. We have plenty of time." He said it with finality, and I could have sworn I'd seen him pull up his calendar on his phone and pencil me in.

We exited the elevator, having shared it with a few girls and their parents. The campus was crawling with people all dressed in dark green. Even I had taken to the game-day spirit and wore the school colors.

Chris trailed behind me with the phone pressed to his ear on a work call. I walked ahead without him, resolving to make sure everything was spick-and-span before he came in.

My plan was to show him my dorm first and give the guys some time to prepare.

I opened the door and wondered why the light was on, then Aaron lying on my bed gave me my answer.

He waited for me, legs crossed, enthralled by one of the squishy plushies from my desk.

"What are you doing here?!"

"You said to meet you here at twelve!"

"Not here in my room! Chris will be here any second." I spun around to survey the hall. Chris would be up the stairs any minute.

"I'm sorry! This is our usual meeting spot." Aaron jumped up and closed the distance between us. "Are you afraid of what Chris is going to think about you having a boy in your room?"

Aaron wiggled his eyebrows.

"I-I . . . Because I want him to like you."

Aaron leaned closer, our faces a few inches apart. "Why do you care what he thinks of me?"

"I-I don't know."

"We're just friends. Right? No pressure."

"Right," I said breathless. I leaned out of the doorway, and Chris rounded the corner from the stairwell. I quickly shut off the light.

"Then there's nothing to worry about." Aaron adjusted his shirt and squared his shoulders.

"Hey, Kim, slow down!" Chris said.

Aaron opened his mouth, but I covered it with my hand and pushed him toward the wall next to my door. He beamed as he stood quietly, just out of sight.

"All that running is really paying off for you."

"I changed my mind. I forgot my room is dirty, and I need to clean it first." I said everything too fast.

Aaron placed his hand over mine, and his fingers caressed the skin on the back of my hand and then slowly down my forearm. I gasped.

"What?" Chris said, his eyes narrowed.

My hand muffled the chuckling from Aaron's lips.

"Nothing. Let's go straight to OBA, and we can check out my room later."

The wrinkle between his brown deepened. "Come on, we're right here."

"I know, but the guys are ready for us, anyway. They just texted me."

He shrugged. "Whatever you want, I guess."

"You walk ahead, I gotta grab something."

Chris narrowed his eyes at me. "Alright. I will meet you at the car."

I waited for him to round the corner before disappearing into my room and closing the door. Without a word, I crossed my arms and waited for Aaron's explanation.

"Sorry. I really couldn't help myself that time." Aaron plopped down on my bed, and I tried not to think about how handsome he looked in his football jersey and backward ball cap. I'd never seen him in a hat before.

The room was dark still. The only light coming through my window.

"I really want this weekend to go well. I want everyone to get along."

"We will! That's what my brothers and I are good at."

"Yeah, I know, but . . ."

I stopped just short of the glaring elephant in the room. Aaron looked up at me through his lashes and smirked, and heat rushed to my cheeks.

"But . . .?" Aaron popped up and practically skipped next to me.

My foot faltered at his proximity, and I kicked one of my potted plants. I needed to focus. I couldn't be caught up in what was happening between us, but all I could think about was the smell of Aaron's new cologne and the shiver that ran up my spine when he'd touched my hand.

"This is complicatedI don't know how Chris is going to react. He's very protective."

"Like I don't have experience with that." Aaron smiled.

My body hummed with his proximity. "You need to hurry and get back to OBA, and please tell Zach to behave."

"On it."

With one hand, he reached for the door, simultaneously pinning me closer to his chest. I stumbled back, but he steadied me.

"You should be careful." He softly touched the cut on my head that was healing nicely and twirled a strand of hair in his fingers.

My breath hitched as he leaned for the doorknob while staring down at me. He could hear my heart beating. He had to know what I was thinking. I hadn't been able to think of anything but his lips on mine. The feeling was maddening.

He leaned in close to my ear. "I'll be good. I swear."

The door opened and he winked, leaving me breathless.

EIGHT

AARON

I'd wrangled my brothers to the front lawn being overtaken by the tailgating party spilling in from the road. A sea of dark green filled every bit of free space. It was good for our cover, but The Legion wouldn't be too happy about the hordes of drunk college students fluttering on and off the lawn.

"Are you all drunk!?" I eyed the lineup before me.

Zach, Luke, and Presley dressed in their BFU jerseys. Luke had a backward baseball cap on and a forty in his hand that he tried to hide behind his back. Zach was in his final drunken state—Giggly Zach. He'd never been able to hide his late-night parties from our mom because of that. When he came home after prom, he'd laughed his way into being grounded for a week. Luke was generally better at keeping a straight face. He'd actually convinced Mom he was sober.

But Presley . . . he was dancing in place. Which meant he was also very drunk. *Fuck.*

"No, no, no. I told you guys Kimberly's friend would be meeting us all today! He's going to be here any minute."

"Who is it again?" Presley said as he continued to dance in place.

"His name is Chris," I said, growing increasingly worried by the minute. I spun around, peering through the sea of people, hoping I wouldn't spot them. "And Kimberly specifically told us to be on our best behavior. Especially you."

I pointed at Zach, and a wide smile spread across his face. He tried to stifle his laughter with a hand over his mouth. It didn't work.

Luke took off his hat to smooth down his hair and compose himself. I guessed he was bolstering himself to do most of the talking. "Okay, where is he? I'm ready."

"This is important. Don't fuck this up for her."

"We won't!" they said simultaneously.

"Is this her boyfriend in New York she never told you about?" Presley said while Zach snickered.

"See, those are the topics I don't want you to bring up while he's around . . . and he's not her boyfriend."

"Right, that's you? Oh, wait, you're too chicken to ask her," Zach said.

"We're really not getting into that right now." I took another nervous glance behind me. I had a new mission. Get my brothers off the front lawn so they could sober up a bit before Kimberly got here. How had they gotten so drunk in the first place?

I grabbed their drinks from their hands and threw them on the lawn.

"Hey, you're littering!" Presley said.

Luke crossed his arms, making an attempt to appear sober, but it didn't stop him from swaying. "I say bring him here. We'll give him the warmest welcome BFU has ever seen."

"Yeah!" Zach and Presley cheered in unison. I'd had enough. I scanned the lawn for the closest Legion member. Luckily, William crossed the lawn with a clenched jaw and narrowed eyes as he dodged college students. At least he attempted to blend in with his too-small university T-shirt.

"I'm going to start making you guys wear flashing collars or something," William said.

"You're supposed to be watching them. Look at them! They're plastered!"

William pointed his finger at me. I knew my tone would not get my desired outcome. "I'm not a fuckin' babysitter."

William's good-boy routine was long gone. He cursed as much as Zach most days.

"Sure look like one to me!" Presley chuckled.

"Hey! Don't point fingers at my brother," Zach said.

Only he got to do things like that.

I didn't see anyone else from The Legion and hoped they were just so good at blending in they were all hidden, or hopefully there was a good reason they were out of sight. Maybe they knew more than they were letting on. I didn't have time to worry about it.

"Yeah, what are you going to do about it?" William smirked.

I stepped between them; I couldn't spare a second for their bickering.

"Can you take them inside and dunk them in the pool or something? Literally anything to sober them up?"

"I'm supposed to make sure they don't get killed. Your college-boy drama isn't my problem," William said.

"Well, what if it suddenly becomes your problem when an inebriated Zach takes a swing at a civilian for looking at him funny?"

"Hey!" Zach protested.

When William didn't say anything, I was forced to beg. "Please? I promise this is saving you more trouble in the long run."

I grabbed his sweater, and he shrugged me off. "Fine. Just quit grabbing me."

With a fluttering of his hands, William shooed my brothers back into the frat house, and I finally relaxed.

The noonday sun was warm amid the cold breeze blowing in. Living in Blackheart was quite the change from living in Brooklyn. The number of trees and the lush earth consistently littered with pine cones instead of concrete never seemed to surprise me. It was a nice change, but what I loved most was the sense of quiet. That even when the town and college would fill to the brim with college students, the air still had a sense of peace.

Kimberly made her way through the crowd. A man at her side looked to be about my height. And muscular. Shit, he was cool. A little orange from what seemed to be a fake tan but cool.

Kimberly was radiant with her hair pulled into a high ponytail that showcased the warmth and softness of her cheeks. As it got colder, she'd opted for sweaters more often and always paired them with skirts that, even when covered by leggings, accentuated her goddesslike legs. It was torture in the best way. As I stared at her a little too long, I realized I'd lied. My favorite thing about Blackheart was her.

When she spotted me, her eyes lit up and her nose crinkled with the perfect smile. Kimberly was my friend. Never mind that we kissed, or that less than thirty minutes ago I was in her bedroom and had been close to locking the door and kissing her again. I had to keep my shit together and be her friend. That's what she needed. We agreed the kiss never happened.

"Hi!" Kimberly greeted me. "This is Chris. Chris, this is Aaron."

She didn't say friend. That much I noted.

Chris reached out to me in the way businessmen in movies usually did. A strong squaring of the shoulders and a firm look in the eyes as he squeezed my hand unreasonably hard. "Hello, Chris Anderson. Nice to meet you."

I responded with a little extra squeeze to ensure he'd be feeling it a few minutes after. Handshakes made an impression on the mind, right?

"Hi! I'm Aaron Coleman. Kimberly's told me lots about you." We hadn't talked about him much at all since last semester, and he hadn't called her much over the summer. My feelings about Chris were twisted. On one hand, I needed this guy to like me, but he wasn't exactly the nicest person to Kimberly all the time, so I didn't care if he liked me or not. This trip would determine which hill I wanted to die on.

He smiled, and he opened and closed the hand I had shaken, as if to relieve a little of the pain I'd inflicted. *Mission accomplished.*

"I have to say Kimmy hasn't really told me much about you, or her time in college. But, then again, she doesn't tell me much nowadays."

Great, they had pet names.

Kimberly's cheeks reddened, and she stole another glance in my direction. Her eyes told me she needed me to be nice no matter what he said.

"Well, here it is in all its glory, good ole BFU. Did you ever tour with Kimberly before you left for New York?"

He shook his head. "No, I knew I wanted to get on the first plane out of here, and I took off right after I graduated."

The first plane out, huh? I imagined that was hard for Kim. Her only source of family and connection not just deserting her but in a hurry to leave.

"Make yourself at home. As you can see, it's game day, so it's a little more rowdy than usual. Especially here at OBA."

"Right, you're in a fraternity. Kimberly was telling me about that. I never really felt a draw to Greek life." He looked back toward Kimberly. "I never pegged her to be someone who would be friends with frat guys either. This is all new territory for me."

I expected her to say something, to stand up for herself or assert her typical sense of dominance. Instead, she averted her eyes to her feet, folding under the pressure of Chris's remarks—only, I didn't understand why.

I decided I'd have to be the one to take the lead here. "Alright, well if you want to come inside, I can have you meet my brothers. We're all good friends."

He smiled. "Yeah, somewhere a little quieter would be great."

I tried buying time by showing Chris the house. Thanks to The Legion, the house was in great condition. Normally on game day, we'd have had an all-out rager in our foyer. That wasn't an option anymore. I had to carefully lead them through the wall of leaves that were William's houseplants in the entry hall. He brought at least twenty house plants with him, and that wasn't counting the ones in his room. Presley had been helping him tend to them for a while until he accidentally killed one by watering it too much. The fight lasted days.

We passed by Dom and Thane in the kitchen, deep in conversation, and they gave friendly enough greetings. I didn't see her, but I could feel Skylar lurking. Her very distinct perfume smelled like luxury. It'd always signaled when she was close. I assumed she remained close for Kim's sake but was staying out of the meet and greet with Chris. I couldn't blame her.

We rounded the corner of the kitchen into the hallway and passed Kilian's haunt, when he was in—which wasn't often. The door was closed, and I was thankful we didn't have to go over that situation, until I spotted William and Kilian coming from the study at the end of the hallway. It was too late to go back, we were trapped. I'd have to grin my way through the awkwardness.

Kilian was a tall, slender guy. He had the same dated look that the other members of The Legion wore. Brown high-waisted trousers with those damn suspenders. He always looked otherworldly and smart. His obsession with the library told me he loved to read, and it was confirmed over and over again during my nightly roam arounds in which he'd pace from one end of the frat house to the other with his head in a book.

He stopped, taking in the three of us blocking his way. William sighed.

Probably bored and inconvenienced by my presence.

"Uh, Chris, this is Kilian and Will."

"William," he said, wearing a scowl I tried to ignore.

Chris extended his hand and greeted them with his name and another set of firm handshakes. Kimberly and I shared a tentative look. As the mood had lifted, the wet blanket crew came to smother it with their stoic gazes.

"Kilian is ... William's dad." I slowly pieced together a believable story as to why this old pair was in a place where there should be a flourishing of frat guys with SOLO cups in their hands.

Kilian lifted his eyebrow with a slight smirk on his face. It was the most emotion I'd seen cross his face since that day in the church, but I tried my best to avoid him at all costs. His eyes felt like little lasers searing into the deepest parts of my soul. I couldn't help but get the sense he wanted something from me during every conversation, as if he was waiting for me to reveal something about myself. Something he could use, but for what, I didn't know.

"It's a pleasure. Truly." Kilian nodded while gazing at me.

"He's visiting from New York for the Halloween party."

To my surprise, Kilian laughed. "I see."

Chris eyed them from head to toe.

"Is this ...William ... the guy you went to the formal with?" Chris said.

Kimberly nodded, and her cheeks flushed as we shared another look.

William gave me a sideways glance. "Right, we had such a great time. Didn't we, Kim? You should have seen her. She got wild—a complete drunken mess."

Chris cleared his throat. "Wild? Kim?"

"Oh yeah. Then she ditched me, and this guy stole my date." William winked at me.

I steered the conversation before Kimberly melted William with her eyes. "Have you seen my brothers?"

"They're out by the pool. Waiting for you guys, I think." William tilted his head with a stupid cocky smile perched on his face.

I led us to the patio, not sparing a moment for anyone to get another word in. What used to be one of my favorite spots, when it was filled with girls and parties that would go on till the morning, had now become the equivalent of an abandoned wasteland, especially since it was getting colder outside. But there they were—my brothers—shirtless but wearing their regular pants while sitting in the pool. William took my pool comment literally.

"Hey!" they exclaimed as we walked closer to the water's edge, and I waited to see if they had at least sobered up a touch.

They filtered out of the pool one by one, soaking wet with their pants clinging to their hips. I pinched the bridge of my nose to hide my embarrassment as Luke, with his large muscular body, went in for a bear hug after extending a handshake. The brief exchange left Chris's feet soaked and his shirt speckled with water droplets.

"How did you guys meet Kimberly?" Chris said, bunching his thick eyebrows together, and his posture was more rigid as he leaned in closer to Kimberly.

I opened my mouth to speak, but Presley was too fast.

"It was Aaron! He introduced us earlier in the year, and we've all been good friends ever since."

"Gotcha, well, I hope you guys are taking good care of her while I'm away."

Fire erupted in my belly.

"Oh, we protect her, all right. You don't need to worry about that." Zach had that wild look in his eye. He was sizing Chris up, and I knew I needed to step in before letting him talk too much. Making friends wasn't Zach's thing. He had a few in grade school, but they were just people who found him cool and knitted their way into his circle.

"Sure do. But Kim doesn't really need our protection. She's tough," I added.

Kim smiled but didn't say a word. What was with her? Had I messed this up so bad she was mad? Or was she embarrassed to be seen with us?

"Well, that part is true," Chris agreed, turning to Luke, who, despite his wide smile, looked the most intimidating due to his size. "Aren't you cold?"

"Nah, we do this type of thing all the time!" Luke said as he slapped Chris's shoulder, but it didn't budge that pinching in Chris's brow.

"Cold plunges are great for you. Zach and Luke do martial arts. It's supposed to help with muscle recovery." I pulled that bit of remembered information so far out of my ass I forgot it was there. "They're great teachers if you're ever interested. They've taught Kim a few times."

Zach shook his head, signaling he would not be teaching Chris anything. I needed to dial back the friendliness a notch or two.

Presley shook the water out of his hair. "Yeah, but not since she went to the hospital."

"Wait, you went to the hospital?" Chris said.

"I was going to tell you, but it wasn't a big deal . . . I fell while rock climbing. I got a minor concussion, but I'm doing better."

"That's two hospital visits in less than a year, and that's not counting the dog attack."

Chris sounded sincere, and for that, I was thankful.

"Dog attack?" Presley yelled. I signaled for him to shut up, and he nodded. "Oh, right. The dog attack."

"Well, I'm fine. So, we can drop it." Kimberly looked at me again, her eyes wide.

"Right. No need to worry. She wasn't alone." I motioned to my brothers. "Good thing she's got a lot of people who care about her."

Chris nodded with his mouth settling into a frown. I had to save this somehow and end our meeting on a good note.

"Luke, how's that haunted house plan coming along?" I asked.

Luke came up with the idea to earn money for the frat. I think that's why William agreed to the party, but I still had trouble believing that was the only reason.

"It's going to be sick." Luke beamed, and he wrapped his arm around Zach. "Chris, you're coming, right?"

"Yeah, I'll definitely be there."

The roar of the stadium echoed in the night air. The drumline played, and the stadium lights illuminated the night sky. It burned out any proof of the stars. Kimberly and I sat on the roof of the OBA—our safe haven. Somehow it became a habit. Kimberly in the frat house late at night turned into us disappearing into my room and stealing a blanket to sit on the roof and watch the stars.

She looked up at the sky, and pieces of her red hair fell on her cheek while her hands fidgeted in her lap.

"Are you going to tell me what's wrong?" I asked.

She turned to face me. "Do I give the impression that something is wrong?"

"Well, yeah . . . you're quiet. But not in your contemplative peaceful way . . ."

She turned to look back up at the sky for a moment, and I let her gather her thoughts. "Something about Chris makes me feel like . . . like I'm competing for his attention. Or I'm trying to impress him all the time. Like if I'm not interesting enough, then he'll just get tired of me."

"How could anyone get tired of being with you?" The words slipped out.

Her cheeks reddened as our hands intertwined. It was effortless, and I didn't argue. Friends could hold hands.

"I didn't think I cared anymore but when I saw him, it just brought everything back." She paused, but I could tell she would keep going. "It's like a small piece of me is still clinging to the person I used to be. I can't tell if it's good or bad. He asked me . . . he wants me to transfer to New York with him next semester."

I swallowed. "And is that what you want to do?"

She hesitated. Her silence answered my question.

"New York could be nice." I forced out the words.

"You want me to go?"

"No, of course not. I'm just saying it's up to you. I want you to have a choice."

"You always say that."

I smiled. "I'm smart sometimes."

Her eyes sparkled, and she took a moment before speaking again. "I-I used to want that. I had the biggest crush on Chris growing up, and I'd dreamed he'd whisk me away like a princess. Protect me. But I was a child then. I don't need him to do that, and I . . . don't want him to. There's nothing for me there. Everything I have is here."

I hid my relief. I knew a thing or two about clinging to the past. I'd spent my first months at BFU doing only that. Thinking, meditating, and even scheming on how to get back to Brooklyn, as if I could have just returned to my old house and life and nothing would have changed.

I squeezed her fingers. She was close with a blanket wrapped around her shoulders.

"Sometimes I think about the past and if I could go back and be who I was in Brooklyn again. Go to college . . . still live at home. It seems like my answer should be obvious. Even if I completely remove you from the equation, I always hesitate. Everything that's happened here has made me better . . . mostly. I don't really want to go back to the person I was before."

"Me neither." She smiled at me, and her gaze lingered on my face a few seconds too long. "But I'm still not sure if letting go is always the way forward. I keep thinking about what it would mean to become a vampire and all the things I'd have to give up. Things that you had to give up."

I sat up straighter. "You're still thinking about that?"

"Of course, I haven't been able to think of anything else. Did you think I'd already made my mind up?"

The butterflies in my stomach were back, but I pushed them away with a quick clearing of my throat. "It's just . . . I prepared myself for you to say no. I never thought you might actually consider it."

Saying it out loud, I realized how ridiculous it was. Of course she'd consider it. She always weighed every option carefully before deciding. It was a skill I didn't think any of my brothers had. Including Luke, who was the brains, but he was still marked with the same impulsiveness we all were. Just less.

"Do you want me to consider it?"

I hesitated. The words I most wanted to say, I kept to myself. How could she ask me that? Everything I said would be a betrayal. A friend would say no. But a lover would say yes.

"As a friend . . .?"

"As . . . everything. For a minute, let's pretend there is no vampire cult, and there is no Legion. We both make it out of this alive. It's just you and me and the possibility of . . . whatever this is. Would you want me to consider it? I mean . . . have you even imagined life beyond all this?"

Laughter escaped my lips, and I threw my head back at the absurdity of her question.

"What's funny?" She crossed her arms.

I reached in my pocket. "I have something to show you."

"Are you saying this so you don't have to answer the question?"

"No, just wait. I think you'll like it."

She nodded, and I loved the fresh excitement building in her eyes.

I pulled out a wad of cash held together by a rubber band. It was only about two hundred and fifty dollars, but it's all I'd been able to save.

"Don't tell me you stole it," she said, smiling.

"Nope. This is all hard earned, it's our stash. I've been putting back whatever I can . . . for you and me."

Her eyes widened. "Really?"

And there it was. That giddy excitement she usually concealed well behind her eyes. I'd do anything to put that look on her face every day.

"Yeah, I thought it would be nice to save some money that was just ours."

"Well, what would we use it for?"

"Whatever we want! A trip somewhere far away where no one can find us, like Fiji or Indonesia. And we can do whatever we want, whenever we want. I figure after The Legion get what they want from us, and they take down The Family, we'll be free and then possibilities are endless."

I stopped myself from saying more. As crazy and selfish as it was, when I looked to the future, I saw her, and sometimes, she wore a white dress, and I was in a tux waiting for her at the altar. An unbelievably selfish daydream, but it was my favorite one. I'd always thought the men in the movies were overexaggerating when they'd bought the girl a ring the day they met them because they knew they were the one.

But I'd never been more certain of something in my life.

I'd never be able to tell her that without scaring her off. Not to mention we're still strictly in friend mode and the likelihood of us ever being together hinged on her giving up her mortality. But I could still dream and maybe save a few dollars, just in case.

She leaned into me and rested her head on my chest as we sat staring at the stadium lights. I took that as a signal to wrap my arm around her to keep her warm.

"I love that idea." Her voice was soft and light. I laid my head on hers and savored her warmth in the night and the sound of her heartbeat.

"Does that answer your question?" I whispered close to her ear.

"Yeah, I think it does."

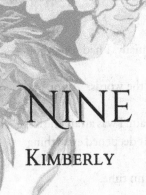

NINE

KIMBERLY

C helsea hacked away at a large tangle in her blonde hair with her rhinestone hairbrush while standing in front of my floor-length mirror. I was convinced she loved sparkle almost as much as she loved the color black. Luckily, she didn't mind being crammed into my tiny dorm room. I watched in complete silence, locked away in my own head, as she wrapped one of her thick strands of hair around her curling wand.

It felt like a fifty-pound weight had been placed on my chest as I re-played my night with Aaron repeatedly in my head. What was I supposed to do? Was I supposed to keep pretending I was just friends with Aaron or talk about it? It was getting hard to hide.

"Come over here, let me curl your hair," Chelsea demanded.

I obliged. My skin was crawling with the need to get up and move. Some of it was nerves, but the other was the itchy fabric of my Halloween costume and pinching of my platform leather boots. Chelsea and I had raided the thrift stores for the perfect outfits for our Daphne and Velma costumes. We nailed it.

"How's your head doing? Has Aaron been treating you like a queen while you recover?"

Under different circumstances, I'd have laughed at her choice of words, but I'd sworn off using the Q-word.

I straightened my shoulders. "He does. I dealt with a headache for a while, but I feel fine now. It was nothing."

I couldn't think of my concussion without thinking about that night. Aaron's lips on mine . . .

"You seem distracted."

"It's nothing."

"Come on. Don't treat me like some two-bit stranger. Spill."

I didn't know how she would react, but I trusted her to listen just as

I had listened to her dramas over the summer. Finally, I had something interesting to contribute.

There was a brief silence as I struggled to find the words. "Aaron and I kissed."

I left out the part about it almost happening again. I was afraid the kiss would have made things awkward, but it didn't. It deepened everything. Like it connected us in this new way.

She stopped curling. "Holy shit. It's about damn time."

"I'm kind of freaking about it . . . internally."

"Why? I honestly thought you guys were already a thing and you just hated labels."

"No. No. That's not it."

"Okay, spit it out. I'm not judging. You know I hate Aaron, but he obviously treats you well, so I'm for it."

"It's just complicated because . . ." I turned to look at her face. I wanted to scream. I wanted to tell her. Keeping these secrets was hard. "Because I don't want to lose him as a friend, and things in his life are just . . . complicated."

"You keep using that word."

"Well, it is!"

Chelsea put her hands on my shoulders and shoved me in front of the mirror. "It's not. You guys have been making lovey-dovey eyes since you met. Don't think so much. Have your smooches."

We watched our reflections. Chelsea wore a very short red leather skirt paired with knee-high orange socks, and an equally as orange long sleeve shirt. She opted not to wear a wig, but she got the glasses. I'd found the perfect purple dress and painted one of my headbands to match.

"Now, come on. Let's go get drunk."

I smiled. It was my first night drinking, and I was ready. All the criteria I had for keeping myself safe were met. I'd be with a trusted group of friends who had superhuman strength, hearing, and speed if anything went wrong. I was ready to let loose. Everything in my life was up in the air. The Legion kept most of their known information under lock and key, and I was tired of lying in wait for what was to come. I didn't want to think about the future anymore, only enjoy the night with the people I cared most about in the world all in the same place.

When they said the party would be huge, they weren't kidding. I'd never seen so many cars littering the campus streets. People were parking blocks away and walking down to the house. The autumn leaves danced in the night breeze, and laughter echoed in the air. As we reached the sidewalk that led to OBA, the crowd that overfilled the lawn drew us in toward the door like a siphon. The Legion would have their hands full tonight, but they got what they wanted. There wasn't a safer place for us to be than there in front of at least a hundred witnesses.

The bodies packed in tightly, but most seemed oblivious to the autumn chill in their assortment of costumes ranging from short to shirtless and everything between. A string of jack-o'-lanterns lit our way to the door. I recognized the ones Aaron and I made. Mine had long and hollow eyes with its mouth already drooping, while Aaron's cat face still looked pristine.

"Just remember who spent the majority of their day making sure this place looked like a damn horror movie." Chelsea signaled to the purple and black spider webs laced around the front columns.

I smiled, knowing there was no way I could forget listening to her complain about how the boys could never survive in a world without her. Also, how they were terrible at following her instructions. Aaron shot me a few "kill me now" texts throughout the day.

The door sat wide open, and we slipped inside. I texted Aaron to let him know we were here and that we'd be waiting by the stairs. Chris let me know he'd be here soon.

I gasped. An orange glow from the ceiling string lights was the only light in the foyer. It was held up by a blanket of webbing. Somehow I knew the boys had a great time hanging all of that on the ceiling along with the bats that covered the wall and made their way up the stairs. Under the stairs was a chalkboard sign held by a skeleton with a red SOLO cup taped to his hand, and in neon words, it signaled to the entrance of the haunted house in the backyard. It was occupied by a long

draping of fabric and fake candles. An ominous purple glow signaled the
way outdoors, and fog rolled in from outside.

"I think Monica is going to be here." Chelsea adjusted her bra and
scratched at the skin on her neck.

"Oh, right . . . there she is!" I waited for my vision to adjust before
pointing to the empty entryway.

She spun around and grabbed my forearm before sighing in relief.
"Those boys are wearing off on you."

"Why are you nervous? You guys have a lot of chemistry," I said.
Nervous was not a word I thought could even be in Chelsea's vocabulary,
but there she was, carefully watching every entryway and exit as her eyes
sparkled with anticipation.

"Duh. I know, but she's cool. Really cool." Her rhinestone black
talons fiddled with the rings on her fingers.

"*You're* cool," I said, knowing she didn't need the reminder.

Monica might be the sweetest person I'd ever met, and it amplified her
soft, sweet voice. We hadn't had the opportunity to hang out a ton, but
we all loved fashion, and that created a bond between us quickly. Monica
had a nineties-inspired style that leaned a little on the grunge side, and
I was jealous of her shoe collection. Chelsea had been obsessed with her
since they met in one of her classes.

Skylar walked across the kitchen and waved at us, back to her bubbly
persona for the night.

A flash of red caught my eye at the top of the stairs. "Oh. My. God."

"What!? You see her?"

"No . . . I see them."

Aaron and his brothers descended the stairs. They'd told me their
costumes were a surprise, and that they were. All were dressed up as
vampires. Luke's outfit was the most prestigious and well thought-out,
with his cape and dated-period wear. Zach took another approach. He
too had a cape on, but it was red, and he wore his normal clothes with a
big "Hello, I'm a vampire" sticker taped to his chest. Presley dressed in
a baseball uniform with his curly hair slicked back, and I instantly knew
he was Carlisle Cullen. Aaron wore a dated white long sleeve shirt with
a deep V and black pants, and it took me a minute to guess, but with the
added attempt to put curls in his hair, I knew he was Lestat de Lioncourt.

My pulse rose at the sight of him and his bare chest. He looked like a cutout of a male love interest in a period drama—only fifty times more adorable. I hadn't prepared myself for that. Why did he have to be so . . . attractive?

They joined Chelsea and I at the bottom of the stairs, and the crowd grew wilder at their presence. Five seconds in, they were already turning heads.

"Well, if it isn't the women of the hour!" Presley said as he ambled down the stairs. He stopped in front of Chelsea to bow. "And our Lord and Savior, Chelsea. What would we have done without her?"

She shooed him away and rolled her eyes. But I think she secretly enjoyed the acknowledgment. Aaron greeted Chelsea with a close-lipped smile, awaiting her beratement.

Zach came off the last step with less flourish. He stopped and stared at me before saying, "I promised Luke I'd wear this cape for *one* picture and then it's coming off."

Luke grabbed him by his shoulders for a squeeze. "And what a great picture it will be!"

I could feel Aaron watching me, and when I turned, he was staring at my legs.

I cleared my throat. "You guys just couldn't blend in, could you?"

"Never!" Presley, who was clearly eavesdropping, said.

"Not really our style." Aaron beamed with a brilliant smile that glowed in the black lights.

Presley yelled, "Come on, let's get a picture!"

He ushered us to a photo booth area with a gradient of orange-to-purple lights and tinsel. A camera with a thick lens wobbled in his hand. He'd shown it to me for the first time over the summer when we'd all gone on a hiking trip and visited Greenridge Lake. It was a gift from his mom and the only thing he'd found important enough to take with when they left Brooklyn. I'd never seen him take such good care of anything.

"Do you want me to take the picture so you can all get in?" William's dark eyes settled on us as he leaned against the wall. He wasn't dressed up, but his dark-academia style blended in like it was a costume. Something about him just looked older. Dated.

"Oh, the stalker," Chelsea whispered in my ear, and I smiled, knowing William could hear her. She disliked William even more than Aaron. I hadn't thought that was possible.

"That's ... nice of you." Aaron eyed him with furrowed brows.

"Where's Thane and Dom?" I asked out of pure curiosity. I wouldn't be able to find anyone in there with all the people, and I was curious how The Legion was faring during such an occasion.

"Manning the haunted house." William clicked his tongue, but he hid a smile. Probably just happy he never had to be roped into something like that; a perk of being a leader.

He moved his attention back to the boys. "Do you want me to take the damn picture or not?"

"Sure, but you have to be careful with it." Presley placed his camera in William's hands but stopped. "Wait, you're not gonna break it to get back at me because of the dead plant, are you? Because I already apologized for that a thousand times! It was an accident."

William sighed. "Keep talking and the answer is yes."

Luke grabbed Presley by the collar and huddled next to him and Zach. "Come on, Chelsea, you can get in too!"

"Absolutely not. I don't want anyone to know I was ever associated with any of you." She smiled at me, signaling she didn't include me in that.

Luke was in the middle with his arms around Presley and Zach. He scooted over to accommodate Aaron and me. I hesitated only for a moment before I grabbed onto Aaron's arm and pulled him close to lay my head on his chest. The flash blinded us, and I blinked to get my bearings.

"Alright. Drinks table. Now!" Presley led the charge to the kitchen.

"Kimberly's never had a drink before. We gotta make this good," Aaron said, putting his arm around me and motioning to William. "You should come to."

Zach groaned while he snapped the cape off his shoulders and left it on the floor.

Chelsea's gripped my arm. "There she is!"

Monica had entered the building with a flourish of beautiful fairy wings and glitter around her eyes. Her tight dark-brown curls rested on her shoulders, and her dress was floor length, a light sage that contrasted her dark skin.

I was still being pulled in two directions. "Invite her to come with us."

"The more, the merrier!" Luke was now the one eavesdropping. Unsurprisingly, Luke was Chelsea's favorite. He was never fazed by her insults. And she was rarely snippy with Luke since he made one of their housemates kiss her shoes for giving her attitude.

After Chelsea greeted her, we moved into the pool room. It, too, was decorated to the nines with spiderwebs and orange string lights everywhere—only, this room had a noticeable ghost theme. Presley pushed piles of empty SOLO cups onto the ground. We all pulled in chairs, and the boys placed various types of liquor on the table.

"Alright. We're making all our favorite drinks and letting Kimberly try them and rate them out of ten."

I groaned. Something about having everyone make a big deal of my first night of still underage drinking wasn't something I was proud of. But the boys were excited, and that somehow made me excited too.

They took turns preparing their drinks, making one for them and one for me, while everyone who already knew what they wanted to sip on for the night had one in their hand. Chelsea and Monica shared a chair—a little intimately, I might add—and I anticipated it wouldn't be long before she disappeared with her into the bustling crowd.

"Try mine first! Jack and Coke. Classic." Presley shoved a plastic cup in my hand.

I took a sip, the carbonation hit before I could taste the whiskey sliding down my throat.

"I didn't make it too strong, don't worry."

"I like it!"

"Hell yeah! Five points for me."

"Pres, we're not having a competition, what are you talking about?" Aaron rolled his eyes.

"Me next." Zach laid out two large shot glasses full of whiskey. "A double on me, baby."

Aaron grinned, watching my face. "This is going to get interesting."

"Pour us one too." Chelsea winked at me, and all four of us brought our glasses into the air at the middle of the table. The haunting Halloween music played in the background, a mix of EDM and a church organ was the perfect backdrop to our night.

We threw our shots back, and my throat caught fire. The liquid burned a path to my stomach.

"Bleh." I shook my head to stifle the burn.

"You didn't even let her have a chaser!" Presley said. I had no idea what that meant.

"Alright, me next." William stood and headed to our makeshift bar.

Zach's brows knit together. "I thought you were too good to drink."

William shrugged. "Maybe some of us are more rebellious than you think."

Zach shrugged, but his smile lingered.

Luke had a bright smile on his face that said he knew he was cool all along. "Hell yeah!"

William pulled out vodka and cold tonic water and poured it into two glasses.

"I want one!" Presley said, leaning over the table with his hand out. William must have been in a good mood because he made him one too.

I grabbed the glass garnished with a lemon and took a quick sip and swished it around in my mouth. "Eh. Kinda gross."

William seemed to like that answer. "Good. More for me, then." He took my glass and downed both.

"Alright. Alright. Back it up, because I know exactly what she's going to like best." Luke pulled two cold beer bottles from under the table.

Zach rolled his eyes. "You and that damn beer."

"She's gonna hate it," Aaron said.

"What? It brings back memories of simpler times." He cracked both open with the edge of the table and handed me one. "Cheers!"

We drank and the sour taste filled my mouth, but I didn't hate it. I wanted to keep drinking it. I drank and drank and drank until I popped the empty bottle on the table. And that's when I realized I might be getting a little tipsy.

"That's really good! I think I want another."

The group exploded in laughter.

"We've created a monster." Zach leaned back with his feet on the table.

Presley was up on his feet now, bouncing. "Move over to the dark side, muhahaha."

"I'll get the guest of honor her next beverage." Luke sauntered off.

"What did you bring her, Aaron?" Presley said.

"I'm not drinking tonight."

"Why not The Le—the other guys are keeping an eye on things. We can relax."

"Unlike you, I don't need to drink to have fun," Aaron said.

Presley flipped him the finger before downing the rest of his drink.

"You just didn't want her to know your favorite drink." Zach snickered as he poured himself another drink.

Monica smiled, and the glitter on her face glistened from the orange glow around us. "Go on, tell us. Now you've got to say it."

"I really like . . . piña coladas, okay? Sue me."

"You're not gonna tell her the whole story!? He doesn't like them. He *loves* them. I've seen him drink five in the span of an hour," Presley said.

"It was fun until I threw them all up on my mom's couch." Aaron's ears grew red at the mention of it. "She made me clean it up."

"Your friends are fun." Monica leaned into Chelsea, and I was grateful she was having as much fun as I was.

"Friends is a loose term for the boys." Chelsea smirked.

"Wanna go dance?" Monica's arms wrapped around Chelsea's neck and pulled her closer.

"Thought you'd never ask. Kimberly, wanna come?"

"No, you guys go ahead. I'll catch up in a little bit."

Their absence reminded me to check my phone. I hadn't received a text from Chris yet. I wasn't surprised. I was never surprised by that anymore. He could show up or he couldn't. It wouldn't matter. Nothing would ruin my night.

"So, William, what made you want to be rebellious all of sudden?" Zach's gaze was turned down now with his elbows on the table.

"I thought you hated us," Presley said.

"Well, I had a revelation. You're all soft."

"Soft?" Zach spat.

"Yeah, you're all harmless. Members of The Family are typically . . . motivated in other areas. They're ruthless. Smart. Now, what I'm doing, just feels like I'm supervising toddlers who do nothing but drink and pick fights." William said it with spite and a dash of humor.

Zach looked like he was about to hit him, but the worry I'd had was gone, as if it never actually existed. They could throw punches in front of me, and I was confident it would be fine.

"You're such a cocky bastard. Let's test it. You and me. Let's spar."

William smirked. "You're that confident, huh?"

"I'm that confident I'm strong enough to kick your ass."

"Not here, I hope," I said.

Zach relaxed his shoulders and leaned back in his chair. "Not right now. But soon."

"You think you can best me? I've got more than a hundred years on ya."

Zach knocked back his drink, and a darkness glazed his eyes. "You don't know what I'm capable of."

Presley jumped out of his chair and sprinted to the door. "I think Thane needs some help in the back! I'll catch up later."

I liked how close Presley and Thane seemed. All I'd wanted this whole time was for us all to get along, and now it felt like that wish was coming true. The weight of that emotion hit me harder than I'd anticipated, and I had the strongest urge to tell everyone about it, but Luke spoke first.

"Have you given more thought to our offer, Kim?" Luke's voice cut my concentration. A cold bottle of beer found its way into my hand, and I was pleased to see he'd already opened it.

"Uh." My brain felt slow all of a sudden. Like I needed to think harder to get words out.

"What offer?" William raised a brow.

"We offered to change her."

"Ah." William chuckled. "I can't say that I'm shocked."

"I'm sure you have an opinion on it. And I'm sure you'll tell us." I snickered. The words poured out of me more easily. Like a dam breaking, all my hidden thoughts were released. I couldn't stop it, or maybe I didn't want to.

William sucked on his lip. "You know, I already told your boyfriend over there this would happen. Either you'd end up dead or turned. There's not much alternative. Humans who hang around our kind don't tend to live very long lives. Especially the ones you hang around with."

Aaron and I shared a look. His hair uncurled and fell into his eyes again, and I had to tear my gaze away from his bare chest.

"We're not dating . . ."

We should be. I wanted to be. Wait . . . did I mean that? I did. If he wasn't a vampire, we would be together. If he was a normal guy, everything would be much easier.

Zach rolled his eyes. "Bullshit."

"It might be easier to keep her safe if she's like us." William shrugged.

And I remembered that look of rage in his eyes from when I'd left him in the church. That had to be the one and only time he'd cared about my fate. I was a lost cause in his eyes now. Not that I cared for his opinion.

"Either way, the queen will want her dead." Zach said it as if it were absolute. This time he watched me like he was trying to solve an impossible puzzle.

Luke narrowed his eyes at him. "Now *you're* being the buzzkill."

"Let's do more shots." Luke patted me on the back, drawing me out of my trance, and wrapped a big thick arm around my shoulders. "You don't have to worry about that stuff."

I let his presence hug me like the warmest, fluffiest blanket. In a place like that, what did I have to worry about?

After another shot, my body felt numb. In that fuzzy world, there was no pressure. No vampire cult. No vampire problems of any kind, really. It blended away into the background, like a beautiful milky sunset over the ridge on a foggy morning. And I was happy to enjoy my little slice of paradise for once as a normal college girl.

TEN

AARON

B utterflies filled my stomach, and not in a good way.

Chris's entrance was met with an excited, tipsy hug from Kim where she stood on her tiptoes and wrapped her arms around his shoulders, and his hands dropped way too low on her waist. I had to look away and pretend to be interested in one of William's plants currently struggling under the weight of pumpkin lights. Two seconds passed before I glanced again. He noticed and waved. The guy was friendly enough, and I didn't have a reason not to like him. Though, he wasn't in costume, which wasn't a good sign. He could be a fun hater like Zach, and Kimberly loved fun.

He danced near Kim in the flashing black lights in the living room. Our projector painted them in orange and purple dots. It wasn't their proximity but the way he looked at her. His eyes lingered on her too long as he took in every twist and twirl while she danced next to Chelsea and Monica. He'd shown up an hour later than he said he would, and that didn't sit right with me either.

What was wrong with me? Shouldn't she be talking to a normal guy? Shouldn't she be with him tonight instead of me? He was the guy she was supposed to be with. Last night, I had to sit through way too many stories of just how perfect for her he was when he'd stayed for dinner. The guy was going to be loaded. Heck, maybe he already was. He'd made Presley ooh and aah with all his stories of the people he'd met in New York—a few celebs and even a CEO of a popular tech app. Chris was a guy with connections. A guy who could give her everything she'd ever wanted. Plus, he knew her. He'd grown up with her. He had all the best stories from her childhood. Lots I hadn't had the chance to hear from her yet.

She laughed loud enough for me to hear over the music, and I was already picturing their wedding day. It would be in the city, and she'd hate that, but she'd have everything else she'd wanted like a big beautiful dress and her hair fixed in a long veil. He'd get her all of it. The huge rock on her hand, the caterer, any flower she dreamed of. I imagined that's what she'd like the most. I hoped she'd tell him about the peonies and have a huge bouquet of the freshest things you could buy.

He'd wanted to stay in the city, but she'd convince him to take her to the mountains, eventually. Hopefully he'd buy her the house she'd always dreamed of as a kid. She wouldn't be alone. He would take care of her, and that's all I needed to know. She needed to go to New York and leave me and all the problems behind.

"Checking out the competition?" Zach appeared out of nowhere to my left, surprisingly still sober. He joined me in my quiet corner. The only place where there weren't people standing around.

"Chris is a pretty cool guy. He may give you a run for your money." Presley was now on my right.

I gripped my stomach and keeled over. "Go away. I'm not in the mood."

"Aw, it's no fun if you're actually sad." Presley nudged me with the annoying plastic baseball bat he'd been carrying around.

"Don't you have someone else to annoy?"

"Come on, you know I'm riding solo right now." Presley frowned, obviously pissed I'd brought it up.

I think Presley had liked his formal date, Ellis, a little more than he'd let on. He'd moped about him graduating all summer.

He'd say, "*He just got me, you know.*" After every. Single. Story. I couldn't complain, though. I wasn't any better, and I felt bad for him. Especially when he got really attached to the girl he'd rebounded with and then she cheated on him. They both worked in the gift shop. It was an awkward summer.

Zach placed his arm around me and gave me a firm squeeze, which almost never happened. He explicitly saved his hugs for special occasions, like my dog dying in second grade. "What's actually getting you down, little brother? You can tell me anything."

There was a lot of sarcasm mixed in there, and I wondered if he was more drunk than I thought.

"Why do I feel like this? It physically feels like I'm dying," I said, having almost died before.

"You're in love." Zach said it like it was the easiest answer in the world.

"I thought I cared before, and I was jealous then, but this . . . this hurts."

"You're at the point of no return. You liked her before, you're in love with her now."

I covered my face and groaned. "How can I get it to stop? I can't watch them over there together."

Presley leaned next to us with our backs against the wall, watching everyone else dance in the living room. "What's that guy have that you don't?"

"Oh, I don't know. Money. Muscles. He's known her forever. Should I go on?"

"So, you haven't seen the way she looks at you. She's head over heels for you, dude," Presley said.

"According to Chris, they kissed in like fifth grade," I said.

That damned story. He loved telling it too. There was an extra pep in his voice when he said it.

Presley busted out laughing. "Ooh, he really got you there. Who cares about fifth grade?"

"Pres is right, plus Luke and I scoped him out yesterday. Definitely not her type," Zach said.

I scoffed. "Really, what's her type, then, geniuses?"

Zach smiled. "Uh, looks like it's scrawny, soft boys who reek of innocence and sunshine."

"Hey!" I protested.

Presley's eyes got huge. "You should go over there. I'll start karaoke!"

"Wait!" I started, but Presley was already up and across the room whisking her away from Chris and toward the corner where we had the karaoke machine hooked up. A deep-red glow lit up a tiny rug, and the dry ice added to the stage effect. Chelsea really did a great job with the decorations. I tried to tell her, but she yelled at me to get back to work midsentence.

"What should we sing?" Presley asked as he hooked in another microphone.

"The 'Monster Mash'!" Luke yelled from across the room while pumping his fist. I hadn't even noticed he was in there, probably chatting up the whole house and doing his job as the head of our house.

"Ooh, I love that one!" Kimberly practically jumped for joy in her drunken stupor and white platform boots. It was adorable.

Before the singing started, I spotted Zach whispering into the neck of some girl before leading her upstairs. I hoped he might be finally moving on a little since Ashley. He never brought it up, but he didn't have to. If he felt anything like what I felt for Kimberly—I knew he did—then I knew he missed her.

Presley and Kimberly drunkenly sang the "Monster Mash" in different keys, then inevitably moved into a few Taylor Swift songs. Some of which caused me to have to put my fingers over my ears, but it was fun to watch. Kim twirled around in her costume without a care in the world, and I cheered her on from the sidelines. The night felt like it belonged to her, and she deserved it.

Once they were done, Kimberly pranced into my arms, having me hold her up. "That was fun! Where is Chelsea?"

She turned around frantically, whipping me with her hair at every turn. I had to readjust her headband slipping off her head.

"Will you go look upstairs? I have to talk to her, it's important."

I agreed despite knowing I was the last person Chelsea wanted to see coming for her up the stairs. I started up, only to see Zach rushing down.

"What's wrong?"

His body went rigid. "Hey . . . uh . . . I'm fine. It's nothing."

With a pat on the shoulder on the way down, he left, and I continued my search, not entirely convinced. Thankfully, I saw no signs of Chelsea, so I made a quick trip to my bedroom to change into a hoodie and sweats. I wasn't sure how Luke went around with his chest exposed all the time. Too drafty.

I turned to go back and find Kimberly but stopped when I heard two girls conversing in one of the empty rooms about Zach.

"That's so sad."

"I know . . . he was shaking. He kept apologizing. I told him I completely understood . . . and we didn't have to do anything. We agreed to just go back to the party."

My brain broke into a fog as I descended the stairs and tried to process what I'd heard. The house and the people were suddenly suffocating. I didn't completely understand, but I could guess if I had long enough to think about it. I hadn't thought it was possible for anything to puncture the safety of our party, but that thick lead feeling was back, eating a hole in my stomach. My immediate instinct was to find Luke and ask him, knowing Zach wouldn't ever tell me anything personal about himself.

Bickering between Kimberly and Chris caught my attention. I'd gotten better at tuning out the loudness of music and pinpointing something specific when I wanted to, and I was always listening for her. The crowd parted for me as I moved toward her sounds of distress.

"You need water." Chris's voice was firm and easier to detect.

I reached them in enough time to see Chris's hand around Kimberly's wrist.

She pulled away and adjusted her dress. "I told you, I'm fine."

It took everything I had not to push him through the wall.

"Hey, is everything okay?" I only looked at Kimberly, fearing I might punch Chris in his perfect face if I glanced in his direction. I didn't want to be my brother. This was Kimberly's supposed oldest friend, and I needed to be cool. I grabbed my hand to still the slight tremor.

She let out a sigh, and her whole body slackened. "He keeps trying to get me to drink water. He won't leave me alone."

"Because you're acting like a child," Chris said.

"Well, you're being mean." She huffed and crossed her arms.

In the next few seconds, Luke and Presley gathered behind me. They, too, had been listening for her, and for that, I was thankful. Skylar watched from a few feet away, and looked ready to jump on Chris's back if he took a step closer.

"What's going on?" Luke said in an eerily nice-guy kind of way, but the muscle in his jaw flexed, and his shoulders were pulled back. That was his ass-kicking look.

"She's just freaking out for no reason," Chris said.

"I can take her to go get water," I said.

Chris's jaw clenched. "No, I'll take her."

"Why don't we ask Kim who she wants to take her?" Presley's tone was light. "Kim?"

Kimberly wasn't paying attention to our conversation. She was gawking at me. Her blue eyes sparkled in the lights and examined me from head to toe.

"What is it?" I asked.

"You . . . just look *really* good in hoodies."

I couldn't stop the smile that came to my face or the flush of heat in my cheeks. My brothers chuckled.

She put her arms around me, hugging me close. "I want Aaron to take me."

Presley laughed when he said, "That settles it, then!"

"We'll keep Chris company, don't worry!" Luke called as I steered Kimberly away.

Kimberly leaned into me as we walked. We neared the kitchen and her hands slipped beneath my shirt to touch my skin. She didn't shy away from the touch either. Her palms brushed my abs, as if it was normal . . . or allowed.

I grabbed her hand softly. "Hey, hands off the merchandise, Burns. You'll have to buy me a drink first."

She giggled and eyed me as I reached in the ice chest and handed her a water bottle.

She sat down on one of the coolers, and I kneeled in front of her. "You should definitely drink this before you have any more beer."

Without a word, she grabbed the bottle and chugged it. *What a woman.*

"Technically, you could probably use two." I laughed. "How many beers have you drank?"

"Lost count." She said it without a care in the world. I loved that for her.

"Have you been coming in here and getting them yourself?" I asked.

"No, Luke's been bringing me some. Different kinds too!"

I bit back a laugh. "Of course he did. He's a good big brother like that."

When we rejoined the others, Chris looked like he had cooled off, though he still gave me a death glare. Luke had even gotten him to drink a beer with him. He was good at diffusing. He got a lot of practice from being Zach's twin.

Kimberly finally found Chelsea, and they banded together with Monica for another dance in the living room. Thane stopped by a few times to get me to go to the haunted house, but I didn't feel like being haunted today. I'd had enough of that to last a lifetime.

I'd normally retreat to my room for some quiet or video games, but I didn't want to go too far where I couldn't be near if Chris started to be a jerk to her again. So, I stayed in the living room and pretended to look busy. There was still no sign of Zach, and the feeling in the pit of my stomach was still there. Dark. Brooding. Waiting.

"Why are you being weird?" Presley caught the Ping-Pong ball I bounced on one of the end tables.

"I don't know what you're talking about."

"I saw that in the kitchen, by the way, Kimberly had her hands all over you."

"We're just friends," I said, like a knee-jerk reaction.

"Why are you stuck on that? It gets tiring watching you look at her like a helpless puppy and her look at you like you're the coolest guy in the world. Which we all know isn't true." Presley plopped down on the couch next to me.

When I didn't answer, he kept talking. *Typical.*

"You never answered, why are you being weird?"

Luke came up behind us and leaned into our conversation. "I think I know the answer."

"Oh, you know the answer?" I rolled my eyes.

They couldn't just let me sulk on the couch.

"Yeah. You and Kimberly kissed."

I spun around, and Presley's eyes were wide, and his jaw had dropped to the floor.

"How did you know that!? There's no possible way you could know that," I said.

"Brother, I've been taking care of you since you were in diapers. I know everything about you. You both have been dancing around each other all day."

"I don't get it. Isn't this exactly what needs to happen? Why is this still such a weird thing?" Presley was still way too excited. I had to put my hand on his leg to stop him from bouncing.

"Oh, I don't know, maybe it's because I didn't meet her in the hallway like we love to tell everyone. I met her in the forest when I almost killed her, and that wasn't even the only time."

Presley groaned and leaned his head back on the couch. "It's almost been an entire year. She doesn't care. We're all past it. Why can't you let it go?"

"Because it's not something you just get past and let go of. You're acting like I'm not the reason she had to take physical therapy so she could use her hand again. That was because of me."

I didn't think I could ever forgive myself for that.

"But none of those things matter if she becomes like us. Don't you want that?"

Presley was always shortsighted. There was anticipation in his eyes. A world of possibilities. He didn't see obstacles. Ever. He lived in a different world than the rest of us. One where he could ignore the check engine light on the car by covering it up with a piece of paper.

"Of course I want that, but what is best for her? Is that what she wants? I don't want you guys pressuring her into anything. I know how you are."

"We don't pressure," they said simultaneously.

"Yes, you do. Let her make her own decision, and we'll just have to live with whatever it is. I promised her no matter what the decision was we'd be here for her."

"We will. She's family through and through." Luke hit me on the back, and I almost fell over.

"Have you seen Zach?" I asked before he left.

"Yeah, he's with Will in the library right now. Why?"

I wondered if I'd missed the memo that said we were calling William 'Will' now. He still bit my head off when I tried to say it.

Before I could ask, Presley's voice broke our conversation. "Uh-oh."

Chris and Kim were arguing again in the corner of the living room. I glanced over for a second to scope out the situation. Kimberly had the karaoke microphone in one hand. Next to her, Monica had the other, and Chelsea plugged in another. Chris had pulled Kimberly to the side and whispered back and forth with her.

"Why do you keep wanting to leave early? I'm having fun."

"A little too much if you ask me."

I'd already turned back around, but I could feel his eyes on the back of my head.

I shouldn't listen to their conversation, but he'd passed a boundary before, and I needed to make sure he kept his hands off her. I'd listen until I knew he was calm.

"What's that supposed to mean?" Kimberly huffed. She'd sobered up a bit since the water, but I could still hear it in her voice.

"You've done nothing but drink and dance around with a bunch of frat guys all night."

"They're my friends."

"Yeah, right."

"I don't like what you're implying. I have friends now. Why does that bother you? You're acting like such a jerk."

"*I'm* the jerk? I came all the way out here for you to ignore me and then run off and get drunk, and I'm the bad guy?"

"You were supposed to come multiple times before this and never did. This is the first time I've seen you since graduation."

"Kim, I have a real job. I can't come down here every time you feel lonely. I have a life! A good one."

My whole body burned with rage. I swallowed the lump in my throat and the urge to rip his head off. She could handle it, but my hands were shaking again.

Kill him.

The voice was back too. *Shit.*

I steadied myself and dug my fingers into the fabric of the couch. I needed to let her fight her own battles. She could. But God, did I want to go over there.

"The problem isn't your awesome job or your great life. The problem is you make promises you can't keep." Her voice had lowered in pitch.

"I already apologized for that!"

I stole another glance. His nostrils flared, and he raised his voice enough for Chelsea to look over too. Kimberly stared at the floor. He hurt her. I wanted to go over there. To hold her. To kiss her, but I couldn't.

He sighed. "I just don't know who you are anymore."

"A lot can happen when you're not answering texts."

"I'm sorry, okay? Do you want me to say I'm the bad guy? I guess I'm the bad guy. Can we just drop this? I'm tired of arguing. Come on . . . we're leaving." Chris had Kim's purse in his hand and motioned for the door.

"I don't want to go."

My immediate reaction was to go help, but Kimberly wasn't alone. She had Chelsea and Monica on either side of her, plus Skylar waiting undetected in the hallway. They were all within ass-kicking distance, and they looked ready to do it.

"We'll talk about it on the way back to your dorm."

"No, I don't want to go anywhere with you." Kimberly planted her feet.

Chelsea and Monica were beside her now asking her if everything was okay and if she needed help. They appeared to be at a complete stalemate in the middle of the foyer. Chelsea and Chris bickered back and forth for a moment, but he wasn't giving up.

"I'll diffuse!" Presley said.

I tried to protest, but he'd already hopped the couch and was halfway across the room. Luke and I shared a collective "this should be good" raise of the eyebrows, and I followed close behind, just in case.

"Dude, we can take her home. It's not a big deal." Presley came up beside Kim and put his arm around her. She spotted me behind him, and her eyes softened.

"Okay, dude-bro. I didn't ask your opinion on it."

"Don't talk to him like that." The fire was back in Kimberly's eyes now. I hadn't seen it all weekend.

"He's a big boy. He can handle it." Chris scoffed.

"It's okay, Kim." Presley patted her back and turned back to Chris. "I'm not trying to get in the middle of whatever this is, I'm just trying to help."

"No." She crossed her arms. "You don't get to talk to him like that. I think you should leave."

"You're embarrassing yourself. Come. On." Chris reached for her arm again, but Presley pulled her back a step.

This time, Chelsea stepped in while Monica flanked her. "Don't fucking touch her."

There was a crowd now, and people turned at the volume of Chelsea's voice.

I stepped in next to Chris. "I think you should cool down. She said she wants to stay."

Chris studied me, and for a minute I thought he might try to punch me, but he didn't.

He turned around and left without a word.

Presley steadied Kim, who swayed on her feet. "You didn't have to do that."

Despite the crowd watching her, she smiled. "No one's allowed to be mean to you on my watch."

Chelsea caught my attention and motioned to Kimberly like it was supposed to be obvious what she meant. When I didn't immediately get it, she motioned to the stairs and rolled her eyes.

"Come on, Kim. Let's get you upstairs." Without waiting for her to respond, I picked her up and threw her over my shoulder. "Say good night to Chelsea and Monica."

"Good night! Call me!" Then she erupted into a fit of laughter as we made our way upstairs.

"How drunk are you?" I laughed as she jumped onto my bed.

"Probably not as drunk as I should've been to be able to do that, but damn, it felt good."

"You're quite the rebel."

"Yeah, I don't really care what he thinks . . . only what you think."

There was a long silence, but it wasn't uncomfortable. She scanned me up and down without a word passing through her soft lips. Just like before in the kitchen.

"Tell me what's on your mind, Burns."

She giggled again. "I don't know what you're talking about."

"Oh, you're thinking about something, you just don't want to tell me."

"Maybe . . ." She gave me a playful smile, and her eyes lingered on mine for far too long, and my heart rate picked up, and almost instinctively, hers did too.

"You need to go to bed." I forced a laugh. I went into my closet and threw out some clean clothes. "You can sleep here tonight if you want. I'm gonna go back downstairs and try to enjoy what may be the last party of my life."

I didn't want to go back down, but I needed to. It was nonnegotiable at this point.

"Are you sure you want to do that?" She lay back on my bed with a sigh, still giving me that damned look. My blood ran cold, and I let myself take in the length of her perfect legs—just one second. Maybe two.

I cleared my throat and rubbed the back of my neck. "Yeah, I'm sure. You need to get some sleep. But I'll see you tomorrow morning."

She sighed softly and grabbed the clothes on the bed. "Okay. And Aaron . . . Thanks for taking care of me."

There she went again. Thanking me for things she should never have to.

I ran across the room in a flash, and she didn't flinch when I appeared in front of her. "You never have to thank me for that."

I leaned down and kissed her forehead. The pink rolled to her cheeks, and before she could say anything, I bolted for the door and shut it behind me.

Friends kiss each other's foreheads sometimes, right?

ELEVEN

AARON

The night wound down slowly, and unlike our previous parties where we'd let anyone stay for as long as they wanted, we shoved people out the door around 3:00 a.m. The plan was for us all to have an after party with The Legion, and the deal was no one started cleaning up till tomorrow, but we did all change back into more comfortable clothes. All the human members had either left or crashed for the night.

"Well, that was a crazy night," Presley said as we all gathered in the kitchen. "We're definitely gonna have to do that again."

William ran his fingers through his hair while plopping down on one of the wooden chairs. "That's unlikely."

"Why? Nobody got hurt, there was only one small fight, nothing big."

"We'll see."

"Well, Dom and I had a great time scaring people in the haunted house. Didn't we, Dom?" Thane was next to Presley, smiling ear to ear.

"Most fun I've had in weeks." Dom still wasn't smiling though.

Conversation broke out, and we shared stories of the night. Thane had the best stories from the haunted house, and we made more money than we'd anticipated. We were starting to feel like a unit now. How much time did we waste by fighting each other all summer?

Just as the night threatened to escape us completely, the lights went out.

My first thought was a power surge. They happened sometimes in Brooklyn, but we'd never had one here. Noise faded until there was only dead silence and darkness. The only light coming from a few real candles laying around lit the room. Most were fake and the batteries had died.

"What the hell?" Zach sounded more annoyed than anything.

"Do you think it's Sigma Nu getting back at us for dying their pool pink?" Presley said.

William was already up to his feet with Thane. "Everyone stay close."

"What's happening?" I asked.

"Shut up."

Zach and Luke were instantly there, pressed up next to Presley and me, completing a weird circular huddle. There wasn't any more talking. Just complete silence.

"There's someone outside." Skylar's voice startled me when she came into the room. She peeked out the window to confirm. "Just one."

"You're sure?"

"Felix is double-checking the perimeter."

The shrill ring of the doorbell cut through the air. I froze from being way more scared than I should have been. I think it was solar.

We didn't move an inch. Zach and Luke were pressing Presley and me tightly together. We were practically on top of each other.

Presley opened his mouth to speak, and I covered it with my hand.

The door clicked and creeped open. A set of footsteps I hadn't recognized were coming toward us. I hoped to see a drunk classmate begging for a ride home. Or to see our foyer ambushed by a fraternity and confirming this was just some Halloween prank.

Instead, we saw a pale man dressed in a black blazer and a black button-down. His brown hair was slicked back and perfectly combed. He looked like royalty. Not in the expensive way, but he was put together and wearing sunglasses inside. When he made his way into the darkness, he removed them.

"Connery?" Luke and Zach said at the same time.

That's when I realized who this must be; he was part of The Family. The Family was here.

In Blackheart. In my house.

We were at a disadvantage. Many of The Legion members were off giving rides. Other than the core four: William, Thane, Dom, and Skylar. Instinctively, I went for the stairs to protect Kimberly. My body just moved, but Luke grabbed my forearm to steady me. He'd read me in an instant.

I'd gotten the message. This guy wasn't here for her. He was here for us.

"There you are. My brothers." Connery's voice sounded odd. Like nothing I'd ever heard before. Not because of an accent but an odd faraway softness. Like he was a walking corpse—only his heart rate beat against his rib cage like the blades of a helicopter.

His eyes were black, and he eyed Zach and Luke like they were presents under the tree on Christmas morning. "I've been looking everywhere for you."

"What . . . happened to you?" Zach said.

"She finally accepted me. S-She cares about me. She really cares about me." He stepped forward with an unsteadiness in his legs. "She sent me to find you. To bring you home where you belong."

"No," Luke said.

"I know that you feel it too. Our family doesn't exist without you. Y-you're important. You must come back. She wants you to come back."

"We're not coming back," Zach spat.

"I'm sorry for hating you both. I get it now. I've seen the light, and I understand . . . the connection."

"What did She do to you?" Luke said.

"I've come as a gift, and I have a message for you. We will all be together again. Soon. Drink in Her splendor. Dream of Her."

He pulled out a long silver dagger from underneath his blazer, and in a split second, he shoved the knife deep into his chest until only the handle was visible. I gasped. It shouldn't have done anything to his skin, but he dug the blade in a diagonal slice across his body. Black blood spilled to the floor, and his clothes became drenched in the black tarlike substance. My brain didn't catch up with what happened. I could do nothing but hold on to Presley.

The twins were gone in an instant, running toward the body on the floor. William reached out to touch Zach, and he went limp and fell to the floor.

It took me too long to figure it out. Was it the body? No. It was the blood. He was headed for the blood.

Luke lunged forward, and William and Thane grabbed him from behind, but Luke flipped them over his shoulder and dropped them to the hardwood below.

That's when I noticed Luke's warm-brown eyes were gone and now they were solid black. He barreled toward the blood, and the remaining Legion scrambled to stop him. Presley and I were frozen in our spots.

I snapped out of my trance and ran in front of Luke, pushing on his chest to stop his momentum, but he was solid and fast. In less than a second, he pushed me to the side and covered his hands in the black blood and poured it into his mouth.

I ran full speed at him and used his lack of attention to my advantage. We fell into the wall, and he snarled and turned on me like he was about to tear me apart, but he stopped.

"Aaron don't." William's voice was far away. "It's not safe."

"He won't hurt me," I said. I placed my hands on Luke's shoulders, pushed him back, and looked into his eyes, praying he could still hear me in there.

"Luke, you have to stop."

His eyes stayed trained on the blood seeping into the cracks in the floor. He tried to pull away from me, and I dug my fingers into his skin to keep him in front of me.

"Let go." His words were ice cold. The dark pools of ink stared back at me.

"No." I forced my feet into the ground, refusing to move. I didn't understand what was happening, but I knew I couldn't allow Luke to reach the blood on the floor. He couldn't drink any more.

"A little help here." I jumped on Luke's back from behind to keep him in place.

When someone else came to help secure Luke, I expected my brother to return, but he didn't. It took all four to wrestle him to the ground. And even then, he tried to crawl to Connery's body, and the blood stained the floor in a mess of what looked like oil and spiderwebs. William finally put him under after a few minutes of trying.

"What's wrong with him?"

William was on his feet, working like a well-oiled machine. "We need to take him to Kilian. Now. You guys need to pick up Zach and put him in the back of the car and follow us." He pointed to someone behind me, but I didn't look. "Secure the humans upstairs and make sure they stay in their rooms until we clean up this mess."

"Someone needs to stay with Kimberly. If they know where we are, there might be more," I said. I was shaking again, but this time it was fear.

"I don't think so. They could have sent more. They didn't. Skylar, maybe you can wake her up and take her somewhere . . . public. Safe.

Everyone else here should be fine."

"I'll stay too." Presley squeezed my arm. It was a relief. I trusted Presley more than I trusted The Legion, but it still made me uneasy to leave her. But Luke wasn't staying under from the power of William's compelling. He jerked around like any second he might wake, and Zach was still out cold. He needed me there.

"Okay, let's go."

Kilian wasn't far away. I half expected us to go back to the old church. Instead, we pulled into a rural area at the end of campus, down a back road that led deep into the tree line. A small A-frame cabin looked well-kept despite the leaves piled in the yard. In different circumstances, I might have even been comforted by the warmth it gave off. It was like the nice ones Kimberly liked to point out to me as we drove around in the summer, but I had to think of my squirming older brother in the back seat.

Thane drove so William could be close to Luke to keep him under, but he'd whimpered and groaned, sometimes even opening his eyes completely. His eyes were still black as coal. I wanted Zach to wake up. This was something Zach was cut out for. I wasn't ready.

We pulled my brothers from the truck. Zach was still and easy to pull up the wooden porch stairs, but William and I were having a hard time keeping Luke stationary and secured as we entered the house. The inside was warm and covered in lush ornate rugs. The walls were lined with logs from floor to ceiling, and cedar burned in the fireplace. Kilian was at the door waiting and quickly ushered us into what appeared to be a guest bedroom.

"Did he drink any of the blood?" Kilian asked while we laid Luke down on the bed.

Luke stirred again; this time awakening. William and Thane took his feet, and Kilian and I took his arms.

"I need it. I need it," Luke mumbled over and over with trembling lips.

"A little. I tried to stop him but . . . he's been like this," I said.

"He won't stay down," William said.

Kilian placed a hand on Luke's forehead like he was some sick child. "Because he's suffering. Locked away in his own head. This addiction runs deep."

"What does that mean?" I asked.

I was lost. Nothing he said ever made any sense.

"It means that it's worse than I thought. I didn't realize how far things had gone for Luke. His blood needs to be cleansed."

"What do you think, Aaron?" William looked at me like I knew what that meant. Like I was the one calling the shots.

"I have no idea what that means!"

Luke lurched forward, almost knocking us to the floor,

"You need to ask Zach. You need to wake him up!"

I motioned to my brother still out cold and lying on the pleated armchair that sat in the corner of the room. I wasn't prepared to make decisions like this. I couldn't advocate for Luke. I was just his brother. Zach was his twin. More than that . . . I was alone—a feeling I'd only encountered once before, and it didn't end well for any of us.

"I don't need him flying off the handle and making this entire situation much more dangerous than it needs to be," William said.

"He won't. If Luke is hurt, he'll be calm. I promise."

"Fine. Hold him down." William was gone in an instant and then appeared next to Zach.

With the softest touch across his skin, Zach awoke gasping and frightened. In those short few seconds, a weight lifted, as if I saw the responsibility fall back on my brother's shoulders.

Before he was even on his feet, he asked, "Where is Luke?"

William motioned him forward to the bed where we were still struggling to keep Luke down.

"Please. Help me. I *need* it." He lurched forward again.

Zach placed a hand on Luke's chest. "How bad is it?"

"His blood needs to be cleansed." Kilian said that thing again. I still didn't understand.

"How am I supposed to trust you?" Zach's jaw was set and serious.

"Luke is hurting. The thing I want the most right now is to relieve that suffering." Kilian's eyes softened. It didn't suit the hardlines in his face. "Surely you can trust that truth."

"Fine, do it."

"Someone needs to drain the tainted blood from his body. It cannot be me. My blood must remain pure of Her blood."

"I'll do it." Zach stepped forward.

Kilian placed a hand on his chest. "No. His blood is tainted with Hers. You may suffer the same fate."

"I-I can do it." I cleared my throat. I hadn't realized I stood in the corner until I noticed the distance between us. I couldn't pull my eyes off Luke as he writhed on the bed, muttering and clawing to get up. I'd do anything to make him better.

"Absolutely fucking not. That's the last thing I need," Zach growled.

I opened my mouth to protest, but Thane spoke up. "I'll do it."

There was a pleading in his voice, like he wanted William's permission.

"No," William said. "It's better if it's me. I'm older. I can handle it."

"You've already tasted their blood before . . . it could be risky." Kilian's attention flickered to me, and his iron brow furrowed.

"You can trust me." William talked only to Zach now.

He scanned William like he was inspecting for any cracks in his armor, but William was dressed in confidence.

"Alright, hold him down." William stripped his coat and walked to the head of the bed.

I grabbed Luke's hand, forcing his fingers to bend in my grasp.

"It's gonna be okay." I don't know who I was trying to soothe more, myself or Luke, but I knew my brother couldn't hear me. He was lost in darkness.

William sunk his teeth into Luke's neck and drank. All my senses were on high alert as the threat neared Luke. I could hear everything. The scuffs on the floor, the bed creaking, the fire cracking. The strength in Luke's body waned, and his squirming slowed. Every tick from the antique clock on the wall felt like a year.

Kilian nodded to Thane, and he disappeared to the kitchen. When he returned, he had at least five blood bags.

Kilian watched me. "They were for you, just in case."

I nodded. Thankful I hadn't needed them since the start of the summer.

William pulled away, and Kilian pierced a bag with his teeth. Red droplets peppered onto the white sheets. He held the bags up for Luke, and after the fourth one, Luke's eyes opened and his brown irises glowed from the light of the fire. I sighed in relief. My brother was back.

Luke pulled away, smudging the sheets in a deep red in the process.

My mouth watered. *Shit.* I hadn't realized watching Luke drink that much blood would make me thirsty. I sucked in a breath and held it, refusing to make myself a problem.

"W-what happened?" Luke grabbed the bed as he took in the unfamiliar surroundings.

I squeezed his hand again. "It's okay. It's safe here. Everyone we care about is safe."

Luke looked straight through me at first, like I was a stranger, but the recollection flickered on his face, and he leaned back against the headboard still holding on to me.

"A member of The Family became Her vessel to lure you. It appears they had been allowed to drink Her blood. Lots of it in order to expose you to that blood . . . probably to coax you to them."

"She's here . . ." Luke shot up again, with panic breaking his voice, but Zach was there to help him lay back.

"No, She's not here. I promise. I'd know if She was . . . I'd feel it."

"They know where we are, though. We need to get away from here, right?" I said.

The fear was getting to me. Everything that had been laid out before me was now uncertain. The thin illusion of safety shattered. For Kimberly. For my brothers. For me.

"I do not think that's the best course of action," Kilian said.

"Why the fuck not?" A rare vein popped in Zach's forehead while he comforted Luke.

"Because, even if they know where you are, we are well established here. You are safer here surrounded by our well-laid systems and procedures. If we flee now, we risk being overwhelmed and losing what little leverage we have. This has been the plan all along." He leaned in. "The Family may be powerful, but they must still adhere to rules. They will not expose themselves in public."

"You're saying we just need to go about our business?" I asked. "And, what? Go to class?!"

This was always the plan, but now when it was thrown in my face, I could see how ridiculous it was, and dangerous. How was I supposed to go to class and return to OBA like someone hadn't killed themselves in the foyer? And how was I supposed to protect Kim . . .

"Yes. During the day. That will be when you will be the safest. It's at night when the public is asleep that things will be harder. We must figure out the full extent of what is happening here." Kilian's eyes shifted to Zach and Luke. "They have crossed the country to find you and to bring you back with them. That shows how valuable you are. This is the closest we've ever been to bringing this coven down. Thanks to your invaluable insights, we know how many of them there are, therefore, we can plan what we think their next move will be. This changes nothing. The plan stays the same."

Kilian and Zach shared a moment that was completely their own.

"Fine. Almighty leader, how are you going to make sure my brothers' safety is the highest priority?" Zach said through clenched teeth.

"You are all going to be accompanied by at least two members at a time. You will be shuttled together when possible."

"What about Kim?" I said. "She gets protection too, right?"

Luke squeezed my hand.

Kilian straightened the jacket on his corduroy blazer. "I may be able to pull some strings and get her lodgings changed. She will be safer staying in the house where security will not need to be spread thin."

"She needs to be a priority," I said.

"She will be." Luke was back to reassuring me again, even though he still looked to be on death's door.

"I promise." Kilian nodded.

I thought seeing Luke back to normal would give me relief, but I knew this was the start of something bigger. We were no longer hiding. We'd been found.

TWELVE

AARON

"I can't believe I'm having this conversation at an IHOFT." Zach pushed his hair back as he leaned into the squeaky blue booth.

IHOFT used to be one of my favorite places to go eat. As the International House of French Toast, they could make some mean French toast. It was one of the only places open twenty-four hours in Blackheart.

The smell of syrup and the sound of sizzling bacon brought me back to those rare Sunday mornings as a kid. Since my mom had four boys that could each eat their weight in French toast and pancakes, it was more of a treat. The last time we'd all gone was on my mom's birthday. I remembered it all vividly, and I half expected to look over and see her sitting there at the table. My heart ached to hear her comforting words and for her to tell me everything would be okay. I wanted to drown in the blueberry syrup sitting in front of me.

I squeezed Kimberly's hand under the table. Not allowed, but I didn't care. Neither did she. She pressed up against my shoulder in the booth, so close her breath warmed my neck. I think we both needed comfort, and my brothers didn't comment on it. All our eyes were still on Luke, who leaned his head back on the wall with Zach's shades on. Every couple minutes his head would fall and he'd reawaken. He looked ridiculous in Kilian's spare clothes because they were way too long for his body, but the arms were snug around his biceps. I was certain the waitress thought he was plastered because she'd offered him water three times. I think he'd much rather have been.

"It's the safest place until we can secure every area and return to campus. It shouldn't take long." Kilian was with us in the largest booth in the restaurant. The early morning darkness greeted us from the window that overlooked the parking lot. Thane, Skylar, and Dom took a booth by the door. They'd all ordered pancakes they would not eat.

"Now, tell me . . . why didn't you mention anything about Luke's condition?"

"Wait!" Presley interjected. "I want to order food before we get into that."

"You're just gonna waste it." I peeked around Kimberly to glare at him.

"No, I need something to do with my hands so I can focus!"

I turned to Kimberly. "Are you going to get anything? You should probably eat."

I felt especially bad for Kim, as I anticipated the hangover she was having. She had to be wiped, but her eyes were wide as she picked at the skin on her lip. I was thankful to have her close again, as the fearful loneliness I'd felt earlier in the night was long gone.

She groaned in protest. "I might throw up if I do."

"Come on, it will make you feel better."

After more coaxing and arguing, Kimberly and Presley got their pan-cakes. The waitress set them down on the table, and the sweet, sugary scent overloaded my senses.

Zach sighed, finally ready with his answer. "It's complicated. I thought . . . he was better. I didn't think he could be triggered like that."

"I don't get it. What happened to Luke, what made him like this?" I said, more eager this time.

I was tired of being out of the loop. We were out of time. How many secrets and stories did they have buried?

Zach looked down and fiddled with some sugar packets. "You know, you weren't the only one who had a hard time with the change. Luke and I got into this huge fight when we realized we made a mistake and were . . . different."

Zach and Luke hadn't had many fights growing up, but the ones they'd had were marked in red in my mind. They were long sullen days when neither of them would speak to each other. It affected everyone in the house, but they were so rare we named them according to the offense. My least favorite was the "Great Fist Fight of Year Ten" when they got into a fist fight at school. To this day, they won't tell us what it was about.

"We both dealt with it differently. Luke went to Her. I didn't realize there was even a problem until I visited home and realized Luke hadn't been picking up Aaron and Pres from school, because we didn't talk for almost two weeks."

"Wait, that's why? I thought that was because you guys were settling into your new place," Presley said while cutting his pancakes into little pieces and stacking them.

I did too. I'd told myself Luke just got busy after graduation, but I think even then I knew it wasn't true. Luke never forgot.

"When I found him with Her, he was different. Acting strange and . . . jittery. I tried to get him to get in the car with me, and he wouldn't do it. He wouldn't leave Her side. That's when I knew something was wrong. I went to Ezra for help . . . he's the one that helped me get Luke back to normal. Luke and I made up, and I realized I could never leave him alone with Her again."

"For clarity, Luke was allowed to drink the queen's blood, *and* Ezra—a member of The Guard sworn to protect Her and Her will—helped you cleanse his blood?" Kilian's brows knit together.

"I know it sounds like bullshit. But that's how it happened, alright?" Presley raised his hand in the air. "Is this a sexual thing?"

"What?" Zach said.

"I'm not judging. I'm just trying to get the whole picture. It sounds like it could be kinda sexual."

William leaned in front of Presley and the mess he made on the table. "Why would a member of The Guard help you? Especially if this was something She did on purpose and it sounds like She did."

Luke stirred, and we all grew silent. He groaned and buried his head in his arms on the table. Kimberly had barely touched her food, and I encouraged her with a little extra syrup on her pancakes.

Kilian leaned back, lost in thought for a moment. "Maybe the conditions weren't right. Or maybe he saw that Luke was getting too far gone and needed to intervene."

"What does that mean?" Kimberly was finally perking up a little more after her second cup of coffee. "Too far gone?"

"Queens use their blood as a tool to manipulate their followers. But it's not used often, and if used too much, it can have dire consequences. Too much blood and they can't exist without Her. They can't stand to not be in the same room. There are stories of that happening to other covens. She gave them too much blood and they devoured Her."

Kimberly dropped her fork and took my hand again.

"Shit." Zach looked to be two seconds away from lighting up a cigarette in the booth.

Luke had had too much of Her blood and it made him obsessed. There must be residual effects from it. It explained why he talked about the queen the way he did and why he missed Her. There was still something I didn't understand. Something I needed to know, and having Zach cornered in an IHOFT might be the only way to ever get that information out of him.

"Why did you stay when you realized they turned you and what She did to Luke? Why didn't you leave?"

Zach sighed. "We tried, Aaron. More than once. The first time . . . that's when they took Sarah. But the queen made us forget everything. Sarah's death. All the horrible shit they did. We weren't acting . . . we had no idea where Sarah went. We even helped her family look. Until . . . She gave us our memories back when we tried to leave for the second time. To punish us. Again."

He held a butter knife and dug holes in a napkin as he spoke. Each jab was a little harder, and I was sure he was leaving marks on the table. The familiar ache of hearing Sarah's name almost made me stop asking questions, but I needed more. I needed the full story.

"How did you figure it out again? What happened that made you send Mom away and take us with you?"

Zach groaned and pressed his palms into his eyes. There was something he didn't want to say, but that's exactly why I needed him to say it.

"Come on now, we don't have all day to hear your sob story. Out with it." William sighed.

For once, I was thankful for his impatience.

Zach sucked in a breath through gritted teeth. "She started offering us Her blood regularly, and it became harder and harder to resist, and one night, we just couldn't resist anymore. Things got very weird after."

"I knew it was sexual," Presley said before he stuffed a whole forkful of pancakes in his mouth and then immediately spit them out on his plate. "Eh, still gross."

"What the hell are you doing?" William's eyes were wide and horrified.

"They looked so good! I wanted to make sure they still tasted like dirt."

"It's not sexual," Zach snarled. "I mean . . . not really. It's complicated. I can't even explain it to you. It's like an addiction. It's totally different from drinking human blood . . . and being around Her . . . I can't describe it."

I scanned the restaurant to make sure no nearby waitresses were eavesdropping on our blood-drinking conversation. Other than us, there were only one or two other tables being served.

Luke stirred again.

Kilian's eyes grew wider, and he leaned over his cold coffee. "She allowed this?"

"Yeah, She baited us. It started with Luke . . . again." Zach turned to me, Presley, and Kimberly. "The queen doesn't drink human blood. She has to have the blood of the lower members to survive. Donating to Her is considered a great privilege. Everyone and their dog wants to fucking do it, but it's on rotation. No one gets picked multiple times in a row—you're lucky to be picked every couple months—but Luke did because She was fucking obsessed with him. She kept picking him, and I got fucking sick of it. So I volunteered. She knew I would. Pretty soon, Luke and I were sucked into donating to Her every week. Somewhere in there . . . us donating turned into Her donating to us."

Kilian's eyes sparkled, like he'd been told the greatest story of his life, and I could almost see the wheels turning in his head. "This case is truly fascinating. I've never heard anything like it."

"How did you stop? How did you get away from Her?" Kimberly had stopped eating and was alert in the conversation.

"I only drank Her blood one time. And I knew I couldn't ever again, or I'd never be able to come back. Luke couldn't take anymore. When we tried to leave again, that's when She made us remember everything." Zach shuddered. "She thought it would break us, but it strengthened our resolve. We knew what they were, and we thought our family was next. There weren't any other choices but to escape and leave Brooklyn. Ezra caught us, but he ended up helping us. I don't know if it was fucking genuine, but we would have never been able to get this far if he hadn't."

I leaned back into the booth. This was what we were up against. All the pieces of the puzzle had started to make the picture on the box—Mom loved puzzles. No wonder The Family never stopped looking for my brothers. I might have been slower at understanding the point nine times out of ten, but this flashed at me in big white letters like the IHOFT sign outside. The Family would never give up on finding us because there was something they wanted from my brothers, and possibly from me. Something big. I was taught blood was the only thing that mattered. Not that I ever agreed with it, but that lesson had taken on a new meaning. Her blood was powerful, maybe even more powerful than the blood I shared with my brothers.

When I looked at my brothers again, I saw them in a different light. Like I finally understood. After the church, I thought I did but sitting in that booth, everything changed. Instead of me begging for them to save me, I wanted to save them. I wanted to be the one to save them from their fate and from everything they'd ever run from. Especially from that place. Guilt washed over me like a fresh rain when I remembered all the times I froze. All the times they needed to come and save me. Not anymore. I could save them from this.

I caressed Kimberly's knuckles with my thumb. I could save everyone.

THIRTEEN

KIMBERLY

The bathroom of an IHOFT wasn't where I expected to have my first mental breakdown, but I was sweating and needed to be anywhere but that hot leather booth that smelled of the gobs of butter Presley left on his mutilated pancakes.

How did Luke and Zach manage it? How? How did they ever stay so . . . normal? No wonder they never wanted to talk about it. We were in deep, and now this invisible darkness wasn't miles away like I wanted to believe. They were here in Blackheart. The safest place I'd ever known.

I pulled out some paper towels, wetted them in the cold water, and retreated to a stall to place them on my neck and gather my thoughts.

My head was pounding, my stomach was turning, and I couldn't tell if it was the panic attack or the hangover. Probably both. The urge to count the blue tiles on the bathroom floor crowded my brain. If I did, maybe I'd feel better. If I counted just enough, then maybe everything would be fine. I could prevent the tragedy that felt inevitable. The Family barging in and taking everything away from me. *No.*

I breathed into the cool air hitting my neck. I'd gone to therapy for that exact reason. I didn't have the money to continue, but I still had the skills. I needed to feel my way through this. Even if it was all new and terrifying and felt like uncertainty of it would eat me alive.

There was a certain beautiful fog of ignorance I had when I'd met Aaron and learned about vampires. I had no idea what that meant. All I knew was a handsome blonde boy with beautiful eyes wanted to make up for his mistakes. That was different. He also had that same ignorance that prevented us from freaking out. Like there was this certain time in the universe that was meant for us. Our own hiding place. Our own spring.

Ignorance was better. Now we couldn't hide. We were exposed in every sense of the word.

I receded from my hiding place and went to the sink to splash my face. My pulse slowed, and the room wasn't foggy anymore. *Get it together, Burns.*

Funny enough, I never referred to myself by my last name until Aaron came along. He was the reason for the exposed nature of my heart. For this worry. That stupid, beautiful boy.

I used a wet paper towel to clean up the remnants of makeup melting down my face. My muted chuckle echoed in the bathroom as I remembered the night and how everything had seemed so important. My fight with Chris was the least of my worries now. It was better that he was mad at me. That meant he'd stay away from me. He wouldn't call, and The Family could never touch that part of my life.

When I was finally done cleaning myself up, I sighed and attempted to make my hair look like anything but a tangled mess.

The Family was here for the people I cared about most in the world. How the Calem brothers became the most important people in my life, I didn't know. I was too invested. I cared far too much to run away to New York and leave them here to deal with this fate. How was I—a human girl—ever going to help? I could think of one thing, but I wasn't ready to add that to my list of possibilities yet.

I left my shelter in the bathroom and returned to the booth where they appeared to be waiting for me. It looked like Presley had been filling the void with random questions Zach was less inclined to answer than the ones before.

"You're back! Did you throw up? You'll feel a lot better if you throw up," Presley said.

Aaron got up to let me into the booth, and I scooted between them. He gave me that look again. Like he was waiting for me to say enough was enough.

"I didn't throw up."

William rolled his eyes and laid his head back on the booth. He was the one who trapped himself in the back, not me. Kilian didn't look to be paying attention to us at all anymore. He rubbed his beard while staring at the napkin rack in the middle of the table. I wished I could peek into his mind to uncover whatever new thoughts Zach's story had recalled, but it didn't look like he cared to share.

I nuzzled into Aaron and wrapped my arm around his. I cared little what it looked like or what anyone thought. Aaron was warm. Holding onto him felt like someone coated me in the finest steel, and no one could touch me there. He was safe.

"What are we going to do?" I broke the silence this time. "How is this going to work?"

I'd already been told about my pending living situation. I couldn't say I minded. Being in OBA would help me get better sleep, anyway. I'd become a light sleeper, where every sound in the hallway would wake me up. Like my body knew I had some target on my back.

William spoke this time. "Well, for starters, we need the boys to be a lot more helpful. No more going off and making annoying plans behind our backs."

"Hey, we've been good lately! The mixer was a one-time thing," Presley said.

"You all will need to be at one of three places only. Class. Work. Or home. That's it. No midnight strolls. No day trips. Unless we're all going, you're not going. The theater often gives you shifts together, so that shouldn't be a huge problem."

Presley placed his head on the table. "No, I forgot I have to work today."

"Luke's on the schedule today too," William said before sighing as Luke groaned again in his sleep.

Zach leaned back, barely listening to us. "I'll cover him."

"No. I'll do it. You stay with Luke," Aaron said.

"What else?" I leaned forward, trying to catch Kilian's eyeline. "This keeps them safe for now, but what else is there? How does this help us take down the coven?"

I was tired of that faraway look in Kilian's eyes. There had to be more to the plan than being shuffled around like precious cargo. Kilian was unknown in my book. Some mythical figure who said nothing but knew everything. I wasn't sure why the Zach and Luke trusted him, but I didn't like the way he regarded them. Especially Aaron.

He raised a brow at me and straightened himself. "We integrate them into our systems. We have the knowledge. We have the resources." He met the eyes of all the Calem boys. "We can teach you how to fight."

"I know how to fight," Zach said.

"That's what this all leads to . . . one big fight?" I said.

Aaron rubbed my arm. I hadn't realized I'd been squeezing his.

"Yes." Kilian's jaw hardened. "And you know how to fight . . . but not how we fight. There are many things we can teach you."

"When do we start?" Aaron asked with an eager light in his eyes.

My stomach sank. *No.* I couldn't imagine Aaron fighting. I didn't want to. Or Presley, for that matter. And Zach and Luke couldn't take anymore.

"This week."

Aaron was the only one who appeared to be excited about that. Presley was tearing up a napkin with a firm line between his brows, and Zach looked tired. Unbelievably tired.

Luke awoke gasping and nearly took out the salt and pepper shakers. It was loud enough to startle everyone in the restaurant. Even Skylar and Thane turned around.

"Are you okay?" I asked. Luke was directly across from me.

He scanned everyone at the table. The seconds ticked by, and the panic drained from his face, the only hint of it left was in the way he pulled his hands through his hair.

"I'm okay." His voice shook, and he placed both hands on the table. "I need some air."

"That's my cue." Zach followed Luke out the front door, and they stayed out of sight from the window.

Soon after the sun was up, we returned to OBA. It was trashed with SOLO cups and spiderwebs cluttering the floor, but there was no longer blood in the hallway. Skylar had tried to shield me from it on our way out the door, but I think it was still stuck to the bottom of my shoes.

I felt obligated to help clean the remaining decorations, but I was dead on my feet. Luckily, the humans lingering in the house most likely wouldn't be up for hours. I followed Aaron, Zach, and William as they helped Luke to his room to get some rest. He'd fallen back to sleep in the car without saying a word.

As we turned to descend the hall, Zach's voice echoed.

"William, hold on a minute."

I turned around in time to see Zach pushing William up against the wall.

The tremor shook the painting and then it landed on the floor with a crack. William wasn't cowering. He let Zach hold him to the wall by the collar of his shirt.

Zach's voice was sharp and low. "Do not put me under like that again. Ever."

A chill rushed down my spine. He didn't threaten him, but it was implied. Zach never implied.

He pushed him away and walked past us on his way down the stairs without glancing in our direction.

William straightened his collar and wiped his vest. "Here I thought he was starting to warm to me."

"It's not your fault." Aaron motioned toward the door to Luke's room. "Zach always blames himself when Luke gets hurt."

William raised his eyebrow, like he wondered if he wanted the whole story. "Do tell."

"Just . . . every time Luke's gotten badly hurt. A broken arm . . . A fight. Zach wasn't there. Whether it was because he was sick or they were fighting, it doesn't matter. He just thinks it's his fault."

To my surprise, William didn't scoff or roll his eyes. He nodded and descended the stairs.

Aaron led me to his room, and we collapsed on his bed. The smell of fresh laundry and his mint shampoo lulled me further into the sheets.

He rolled over to face me. "You should sleep. I've got a day full of cleaning, and working, apparently. Will you be okay?"

"I'm fine. Seriously, with everything going on, please don't worry about me."

"I'll always worry about you."

I stole a glance at his lips as he did mine.

It just kept happening. I'd be a liar if I said I hadn't kept thinking about that night in his room despite my best efforts. Why was he inevitable? Why were his lips something I'd never be able to fight? No matter what, we always ended up in the same place.

I inched closer to him. Our hearts drew like magnets in our chests.

He sighed while still looking at my lips. "I should go."

"Probably," I said, closing my eyes and wishing he'd stay. Sharing a bed with him when I had my concussion was the best sleep I'd had in months.

His hand grazed my cheek. "I'll protect you."

"I don't need you to."

"I know."

Something stirred in my mind, and I had to ask before the moment was gone. "Do you trust Kilian? Really, truly trust him?"

"I trust my brothers. And they trust him . . . so yeah, I guess."

"I just want you to be careful."

Aaron was too good for them. Trusting and kind. I was trusting The Legion more with things like ensuring we weren't all murdered in broad daylight. I didn't trust them with that light of optimism in Aaron's eyes.

"Always."

His lips were close to mine again, and all my worries floated away. It was just us in his room. A place we'd been many times before, but now things were different.

There was a brief silence and then he spoke again. "I think I messed up your timeline. Like you were supposed to be doing something else right now but met me instead."

"Or maybe I messed up yours."

He shook his head. "Impossible. I'm pretty sure, in every reality, I'm the one that comes crashing into you."

I smiled at that thought. Vampire or not, Aaron Calem would always find a way to crash into my life. I imagined all the people he could have been and all the ways he'd find me. I bet I always had a choice, because Aaron always gave me one. And maybe I chose wrong every time, and a choice to stay with Aaron Calem was always my downfall.

Aaron pulled away first and left me to sleep in his bed.

If this was the wrong choice and I was supposed to be doing something else, why did it feel like my heart was swelling twice its size when he was near? And why did I want him to stay?

FOURTEEN

KIMBERLY

H ad I become a complete coward? I'd confronted a vampire and threatened him. I'd run headfirst into a dark room of a creepy church to have a chance at saving Aaron. I'd started to accept my death to a vampire cult might very well be on the horizon. So why was I imagining what would happen if I shoved all the Calem boys into my car and just drove away?

If we just kept driving, how would anyone ever find us? We'd only have to stop for gas and food for me sometimes. The boys were immortal. They could literally drive forever or until my car gave out. My car had over 150,000 miles on it, so scratch that—maybe we could take someone else's car.

Presley would be the easiest to convince. I could lure him into the car with Taylor Swift music and the promise of fun. Aaron too. Zach and Luke . . . that would be a hard sell. Especially since they'd tried that exact thing and still ended up here. Trapped. I couldn't help but think if I just thought about it long enough, I'd be able to find the solution we needed.

As I poured another fountain drink for a customer, I thought the scenario over one more time to see if I could think of something better.

"And then he was like 'You will be mine, body and soul,' and he plunged the dagger in his chest." Presley told me the story from the Halloween party for the fiftieth time today, but he'd had to start and stop between customers.

"That's not what he said. What did we say about being overly dramatic?" Aaron rolled his eyes. He sat on the counter now that the crowd for the last movie had disappeared into the theater. He tired of Presley's storytelling quickly, but I didn't. I wanted to analyze it from start to finish, as if thinking on it over and over would be helpful. I had to find some way to be *something* useful.

Presley sighed. "Try to keep it to Tuesdays and Thursdays only."

Being the fifth wheel to the Calem brothers' life-changing events bothered me. Maybe it shouldn't, but the very real knot in my stomach told me it did. How come I was always involved but never actually helpful?

Mondays were our night to close with our manager present, but Presley had taken an extra shift to fulfill The Legion's wishes to be together as much as possible. I think Aaron was more upset about it than I was.

Things were different, but life around us moved on the same. The theater was bare except for Skylar sitting on the bench by the double doors. She was on her second book today. Another romance novel. I'd never seen someone read that much, but she had a lot of time to kill. Thane and Dom were outside doing most of the surveilling.

Presley banged his fist repeatedly on the counter, shaking the cardboard movie displays.

"Presley . . ."

"I can't help it! This is boring. Why is the reaction to the killer cult finding us to work?"

"Because it keeps us out of trouble," I said.

"And because it's what Luke wants," Aaron added while he plopped down from the counter and pretended to sweep the lobby.

I covered a cough with the sleeve of my uniform and then popped another cough drop. Someone at the Halloween party got me sick.

"Are you sure you're okay?" Aaron asked. He'd run out to get me medicine as soon as he heard an inkling of a cough.

"It's just a cold. I'm fine."

"I see why The Legion hates us now. They have to do all the unexciting stuff with us. They're probably used to doing all sorts of fun stuff like traveling to Puerto Rico." Presley's voice was muffled as he rested his elbows on the counter and held his face in his hands.

"I don't think they get to choose where they go, Pres. It's not like vacation. They're working," Aaron said.

"Doing?"

"I don't know. Kicking ass and taking names." Aaron winked at me, and we shared one of our first smiles since Halloween night.

Aaron had been gone most of the day Sunday, and the rest of the night we'd spent moving some of my stuff from my dorm to the frat house and taking care of Luke. He was still shaken and couldn't sit still. We'd helped steer him away from another panic attack by pure distraction.

"Do you think they kill people? I bet they have. At least by accident."

"Presley," I warned while stealing a glance at Skylar, who was engrossed in her book until Thane came in to talk with her. It looked to be a complete social endeavor.

"Do you think they're a thing?" Presley wiggled his brows, not even trying to hide his snooping.

I, at least, pretended to be disinfecting the register.

"Is this really the most important thing right now?" Aaron asked.

I gave Presley a look that said he should do some digging and give me details later.

He smiled and went onto another topic. "What do you think members of The Family will look like, anyway? Will we be able to tell? That one guy was wearing a suit."

"Doubt they'd dress in suits on a college campus," Aaron said.

"What about that guy over there? He looks suspicious." Presley motioned to a guy our age walking to the men's restroom.

"Now you're just trying to make trouble." Aaron smirked.

"Well, we gotta be able to pick out who is who. How do we know a member of The Legion isn't secretly working for The Family?"

"That's not possible," Aaron said. Of course he'd think that.

I added it to my list of possibilities I could mull over in my head while I lay in bed.

"Could be!" Presley was clicking our register pen repeatedly, and Aaron slapped it away from his hand.

I already evaluated every relationship I had in fear of them being targeted. I'd wanted to invite Chelsea to study sometime this week but thought better of it when I realized it may not be a good idea to be seen with her too much. It was hard enough trying to explain to her why I was moving into one of the campus apartments midsemester. Even more difficult when I wouldn't let her help me move. I couldn't hide from her with the theater being a prime place for entertainment in Blackheart because students got good discounts. She'd seen me earlier when she came in with Monica, and I tried to be busy in the back so Presley could get her snacks instead. Lying was hard.

"What are you guys doing?" Thane's shadow loomed in front of us, and we all jumped.

"Nothing," we said simultaneously.

"They've got cameras in here, dude. You should be careful," Presley said.

"Please, give me a little credit." Thane leaned over the counter like he didn't have a care in the world. "You know we can hear you, right?"

"We knew that . . . maybe you shouldn't eavesdrop, it isn't nice." Presley pretended to go back to cleaning the popcorn off the ground.

"I like it. You're like your own little Scooby gang! Like a brain trust."

"You say that like we're kids or something." I crossed my arms.

"I'm more than a century old. You're all kids to me." Thane laughed but kept his tone light. "I was just talking with Sky about something, and she loathes texts."

"Anything that would cure our boredom and satisfy our curiosity?" Presley said.

"Just work stuff."

We all perked up, listening more intently. We were "work stuff." Our seemingly mundane college lives had become their encumbrance.

"I'm not supposed to say anything."

"Now you gotta say it," Aaron said.

Thane opened his mouth to say more, but Chelsea came walking down the hall with what I guessed was her empty drink in hand. I poured him a small drink, and he left for Skylar's side.

"Hey."

"Hi." My voice croaked.

"Are you sick?" Chelsea passed me her drink, and I could tell by the color she wanted more fruit punch. Her favorite.

"Just a cold."

"Well, you'd think one of these gentlemen here would have offered to close for you."

They did. Aaron did twice, but I couldn't. I needed something to do to get my mind off things.

Presley opened his mouth, probably to argue, but Chelsea cut him off.

"I'm not in the mood today. Did you hear what happened?"

We shook our heads.

"Mrs. Henry went missing. She never came home Saturday night."

Blood ran from my face. "From Sociology?"

"Yeah, I just saw it on the news."

I put the straw in her drink and passed it back to her. "She's the one with that tutoring program you've been going to, right?"

"Yeah, she's amazing. I've been there every week this semester."

I swallowed the spit caught in my throat. "Well, I'm sure it's nothing. She'll be okay."

I'm not sure who I was trying to convince more—me or her.

Presley, Aaron, and I added little to the conversation. I think we were all dazed and processing that information. Blackheart wasn't safe anymore. Not just for us, but maybe other people too. Innocent people.

When Chelsea left, we pounced on Thane.

"Dude, that's what you were hiding!? You have to tell us stuff like that," Presley said.

"That's it, then? They're killing people in town on purpose?" I said.

Thane's eyes softened. "Please don't worry until we have a little more information. Not everything means something. More importantly . . . this is not your problem. It's ours. You don't have any control over what they do."

"You sound like my brothers," Aaron grumbled.

"Well, they're pretty damn smart. Panicking and assuming get us nowhere. That's something you learn the older you get. You have to stay calm."

Thane tried to be reassuring, but it still felt patronizing. I gave him a pass for sincerity.

"I get it. You're still learning to trust us. But you can lean on us. We all want the same things."

Maybe Thane was right. Trusting The Legion and their word was crucial in this scenario. We *needed* their protection. They knew more about The Family than maybe even Luke and Zach. Shoving us all in a car wouldn't make our problems go away, but working with The Legion might. It could solve our problem.

We all shared a look. Worry, fear, but there was hope swirling in there too. I hoped that maybe Thane was right and we were worried for nothing, but hope would not help me sleep at night.

FIFTEEN

AARON

K ilian hadn't claimed a room. Instead, he could be found in the small library on the first floor of the OBA frat house. Since the Halloween party, he'd been there every day that week. I would have to get used to prying eyes.

Kilian was extremely old. He never told me how old, but I guessed it had to be centuries older than William. He just acted differently than everyone else. Even though his body was perfectly primed and ready for anything, his motions were slow. His talk was slow, and even the way he read books in his study seemed slow. I didn't like the feeling I got around him. Like I would become as old and slow as he was someday. Guilt punched my gut at that thought, and I wondered if I would even make it a fraction of the time he had on this Earth. With The Family still out there, the jury was still out.

Zach and I walked into the study—a warm room that looked way too modern to be housing someone like Kilian—but he was there sitting next to a pile of books in a leather armchair, whispering something to Luke. William loomed in the corner of the room giving us a nod as we entered.

Luke had started a few "sessions" with Kilian since the incident. He said he rarely talked during. It was more exposure therapy, where Kilian would help Luke work through hard memories. Still too early to tell if it helped. From my view, it had only made things worse, but Kim told me it would probably get worse before it got better. I wished she'd come, but it wasn't a group event. Zach had only invited me. What fell under their umbrella of secrecy was now being offered to me. I took it as a good step forward.

The grandfather clock chimed. It was just after two in the morning, and I was getting used to the weird silence that lingered in the house after hours. Tonight was exposure therapy of a different kind. That's all I was told. I think Zach liked being cryptic to piss me off, though. This had Luke's idea written all over it.

We took a seat next to Luke on a long sofa nestled by an open fireplace. Last year it was never touched, but now the fire stayed lit and carried the smell around the house.

"I'm glad you guys are here. Let's begin."

One thing I liked about Kilian was he was swift and to the point. The man didn't mince words or waste time. It was a nice contrast to my brothers, especially Presley who could tell me a story for thirty minutes and still not arrive at the conclusion.

"What do we need to do?" Zach tapped his foot.

"Just being here for support is enough. We're going to start slow." Kilian reached into a wooden box and pulled out a vial filled with black liquid. Both of them shifted their weight on the couch.

"Is that . . .?" Luke's eyes were locked with the vial.

"Yes, it's Her blood. We saved a sample from Halloween night."

"Why the fuck would you do that?" Zach said.

"For reasons just like this one. After seeing Luke's and *your* reaction to the blood, we thought it might be good to save it."

Zach sat up straight. "I would have been fine. I was just caught off guard is all."

William scoffed. "You didn't see your face."

"Well, this will be good practice for you both." Kilian placed his hands on the top of the vial, it had a rubber seal that made it airtight. "I'm going to open this. Luke, I need you to try to hold your breath and then take a very small inhale."

My whole body was alert now, ready to hold Luke back if needed. *Is that why he asked me to be here?*

The bottle opened, and Luke shifted forward and then Zach pushed him back to the couch. Luke's entire body was rigid. He hadn't taken a breath, yet his body moved forward as if some invisible force pushed him out of his seat.

"Release him. Try to make him do this on his own," Kilian said.

"I don't fuckin' like this." Zach let go and clenched and unclenched his hands.

"Stay focused." Kilian kept the bottle grasped between his bony fingers.

Luke squeezed his hands so tight I imagined he could bend thick steel. He keeled over, pushing into the couch, and a crack of wood split the air, and his side of the couch caved in a few inches, pushing me and Zach closer.

He shook his head, and the black returned to his eyes. "I can't do it. I need it."

I didn't like the sound of desperation in Luke's voice. In my eyes, there was nothing my brother couldn't do, and yet this tiny bottle of blood threatened to overtake him.

That's when I realized why he wanted me to come.

"Come on, Luke. I know you can do it," I mumbled. "It's just a small thing. Nothing you can't handle."

A thing Mom used to say to all of us. There was no way he wouldn't remember. She said it for every cut and scrape. For every trivial disappointment and argument. This was much bigger than any of that, but it worked the same.

His eyes locked with mine, and the darkness in his eyes faded. Luke buried his head in his hands, and a low groan filled his throat. William was alert and staring a hole in the back of Luke's head.

"Take a breath. Prove to yourself She doesn't have power over you," Kilian said.

"Luke?" Zach's voice was desperate too. He unraveled watching Luke suffer his invisible battle.

Luke stopped moving, and I watched his back carefully. His posture stilled and his breathing moved his chest.

He lunged forward and was caught by Zach on his left and William on the right, but he didn't advance farther. He shrugged them off while still staring at the bottle.

"That's enough! Please. Enough," Zach said. It was rare to hear desperation in his voice.

Kilian closed the bottle, and the room quieted, besides the crackling of wood.

"You did well, Luke, you kept your composure. For the most part. It's a good start."

Luke nodded. His eyes settled on me, and he slumped into the couch. I gave him a reassuring thumbs-up, and his face twitched into a small smile for a second. I took it as a win.

"Zach? You good?" William hit him on the shoulder.

"Fine." Zach shared that same faraway glare Luke did for a moment before he shut his eyes and shook his head.

"Good, now fuckin' sit down before ya fall over."

To my surprise, he did and didn't complain about it.

I never thought I'd see anyone who could deal with my older brothers, but William got the hang of it in his own way. And I might have been wrong, but it looked like he might care about them.

Zach flipped him off as he fell back into the couch, and William did the same.

Maybe not.

Kilian placed the vial back in the box and set it on his desk. It stood at the center of the room, capturing all our attention without making a noise. That lingering curse between us that bound us all together.

I was constantly looking over my shoulder, pretending I was ready for whatever was coming. Last year, I wanted to be Aaron Coleman. Just a normal college guy. I chatted up all my desk mates. We studied together. I'd even pretended to eat food in the cafeteria a few times with some guys from OBA.

Now, I couldn't walk down the hall without checking over my shoulder. Everyone was a threat. I'd stopped trying to talk to my classmates. My brothers and I were the poison leaking into the campus grounds and infecting everything with the things that followed us.

That's why Mrs. Henry was missing.

"What is The Family waiting for?" I asked.

I hadn't seen or heard anything suspicious. It was maddening. I couldn't do anything without wondering what lingered in the shadows.

All eyes were on me again.

"They have all the time in the world to wait."

"We're just going to let them keep taking people?"

"No one's doing that," Zach said.

"Patience. We will be ready for whatever comes."

I could see why The Family had used Her blood as a weapon.

I didn't know exactly how I felt about any of it.

But I knew one thing—I didn't want to suffer the same fate as my brothers.

SIXTEEN

AARON

"**A**gain!" Zach yelled through clenched teeth. It echoed into the rafters of the old gym.

The Legion may not have been loaded, but they had a few tricks under their sleeves. And that included an old boxing gym that smelled of sweaty feet and mildew. From my limited knowledge from movies, it looked like it used to be an old butcher shop. The metallic smell of animal blood was embedded in the caulking in the tile. It reeked. And I hated the way it stayed on the bottom of my shoes. The dirty white walls were saturated with peeling paint and large water spots that signaled a severe leaking issue. I was surprised the fluorescent lights overhead were still working.

Zach and William had been sparring for hours, both in their spandex long sleeved shirts and fighting shorts. Their bare feet were black from the dust. I had come less prepared in my simple slouchy T-shirt and sweatpants I wore as my pajamas. The rink was dirty and bathed in dim blue lighting. I could hardly keep up with their movements. I had seen Zach spar with Luke many times, but this was way different. There wasn't an ounce of hesitation in Zach. He wasn't holding back, and with no humans around, he didn't need to be careful.

Zach's punch narrowly missed William, and with the lightest touch by William to his shoulder, Zach collapsed to the floor. He was at the disadvantage of William's psychic ability. In less than five seconds, Zach was on his feet again and bouncing from foot to foot.

"Again." Zach's iron eyes never left William.

"I can knock you on your ass all day long." William grinned, holding out his palm and motioning him forward for another round. He'd been looking for any opportunity to knock Zach down a peg.

Presley was next to me rubbing his eyes. "Ugh. I'd rather be at work."

I had to admit I would too. It was the end of the week, and Kimberly finished out her school day and then got stuck covering a shift at the theater. Friday was the day my classes ended early and I got to spend the rest of the day bugging Kimberly and trying to get her to skip her last class. She never did. That's why I loved the challenge.

Luke was still recovering from his encounter with the blood, but he seemed to be getting better. He'd skipped his classes all week, but Presley and I were expected to start our first training session. The Family would come for us, and we were deadweight. We needed to learn to fight. I didn't hate the idea. I'd be excited if Zach wasn't my teacher.

Zach was great at teaching martial arts. I wouldn't be surprised if he ever opened his own gym. I'd told him plenty of times it might be the only job in this world he'd actually enjoy. He taught some of his friends at our house back in high school, and even Ashley, his high school sweetheart, but he was horrible at being *my* teacher. He'd attempted to help me learn to ride a bike in kindergarten, and it left me with tears and a broken bike. We maintained the same power struggle when we played baseball as kids and he tried to teach me how to swing.

"Come on, guys, it will be fun!" Thane hit my shoulder and walked onto the gym mats as his long hair brushed past his shoulders. I was thankful for Thane's can-do attitude. Presley and I were notoriously lazy and needed someone to light the fire under us.

Presley followed first. "Alright. Teach me to be cool."

Thane chuckled and the fluorescents gleamed in his brown eyes. "Well, first you need to loosen up. You can control almost every muscle in your body with extreme precision."

Thane ran straight toward the wall and used his momentum to rise a few feet and do a backflip that knocked Presley to the floor. He slid across the ground and tripped me in the process. It was parkour but faster.

He popped up, leaning over me with a smirk. "Cool, huh?"

I'd never put a lot of thought into moving my body in that way. I'd given up sports after freshman year of high school, and I'd been a couch potato ever since.

"Teach me. Teach me," Presley said, rising to his feet before I could get a word in.

"Alright, try it. Use your body to the fullest extent and then push harder. Don't let gravity move you. You move gravity," Thane said. He'd trained people before. I wondered what kind of training was required to be a member of The Legion, if any.

Despite me still being confused, Presley understood his language. He was off, jumping from wall to wall and bouncing back to his feet. He ran full force up the wall—the ceiling was about twenty feet high—and did a backflip.

I finally realized how much we'd had to keep hidden. There was never a day we were able to go wild and feel every bit of our new bodies. Since we left home, we'd been in a constant state of hiding, concealing, and running. No wonder I'd never even considered it.

Of course Presley was a natural, and once his feet were on the ground, Thane went after him.

"Whatever you do, don't let my hand touch you," Thane warned.

They were a steady blur as they shot across the room, running past the rink and on top of shelves. The room had plenty of things to jump on: tables, chairs, old lockers. It didn't look like The Legion minded any mess here. Thane never went for the obvious course. He used his environment to give him an edge over Presley. When Thane would catch him, Presley would be knocked unconscious, fall to the floor, and awaken seconds later and start again.

"It's your turn." Zach motioned to me while he wiped his chin, obviously still aggravated from his sparring with William. William ducked out of the ring with a smirk still painted on his face.

I moved into the ring without a word, wondering why Presley had gotten the much easier first assignment.

"Aren't you going to teach me to loosen up?" I held my hands in the air, awaiting the hell sure to follow.

Zach smirked. "I'm going to teach you to toughen, sure."

I groaned and was on the ground. The scent of sweat overpowered my senses, and a layer of dust clouded around me.

"Lesson one, keep your hands up and your eyes open."

I jumped up, swallowing the anger already moving up my throat.

"There. Now you're a little angry. Hit me." Zach bounced on his feet, and his hands stayed covering his face, casually waiting. I was convinced Zach liked seeing me struggle.

"What do you mean?" Any attempt to punch Zach would land me on my ass again. Was he going to teach me anything or just use me as his punching bag?

I contemplated how to position my body. I thought back to my first childhood lesson from Luke about throwing a punch. Power comes from the back leg, use your whole body—

Zach pushed me to the ground again. "Fucking hit me!"

This time when I got back to my feet, I lunged forward, but Zach countered and pushed my face into the mat. "Now we're getting somewhere. You gotta learn how to get angry and throw a hit."

I flung him off and took a swing, Zach dodged me and kicked me to the ground. It didn't hurt anything other than my sliver of pride being held on by a thread.

"See, you're not teaching me. You're just pissing me off." As if I expected anything else from the brother who most easily got under my skin—and he always had. He was notoriously hard on me in a way he wasn't with Presley. Presley always got the free pass if he didn't understand something or didn't want to learn, but not me. Zach would make me stay until I was red in the face and shaking from anger.

"You need to get pissed off," he said, his eyes following me as I struggled to my feet once again.

"No, I don't, I need to learn to fight." I spoke through gritted teeth.

"That's how you learn!"

"Not everyone is angry all the time," I said. Anger had never helped me. Not one moment in my life was better because I got angry, especially when I changed into a vampire.

"Okay, Your Royal Highness, stop being such a baby and hit me," Zach said, growing more bored by the second. He continued to circle me like an animal in the ring.

William and Dom were in the corner talking in barely a whisper. Dom had come from outside, probably wondering what took so long. I didn't blame him. He'd often taken to shifts that involved being outside and staring out into the woods. I couldn't imagine the torture of discipline. Maybe that's why he hated us.

I caught them in a laugh directed at us. They loved watching us unravel. It fueled the anger overflowing. I wanted to sock my brother in the face, but more than that, I didn't want to play into his game.

"No, this is why I don't let you teach me anything. I'm not doing this." I moved toward the edge of the ring, about to duck under the rope, when the door opened.

"I'll teach him." Luke appeared with a glowing smile despite the dark circles around his eyes. His hair was more unkempt, but he came dressed and ready. He stalked over to join me in the ring.

His smile enveloped me. I knew then he came for me. He knew I needed him.

The worry was back in Zach's eyes, and he clenched his jaw as he spoke. "You're supposed to be resting."

Luke shrugged him off and cracked his knuckles. "And miss the family fun? Not happening."

Zach's previous anger melted, and he left me and Luke in the ring, but not before he bumped my shoulder on the way out. *Asshole.*

Luke smiled. "Everyone fights for different reasons. You have to figure out what fuels you . . . for me . . . I've had someone to protect since birth. When you have people that depend on you, it changes things. It fuels you. There's no such thing as giving up and throwing in the towel. People like you and me can't afford to lose."

We can't afford to lose.

I nodded and let his words wash over me. I had a lot of people I wanted to protect. I was sure I'd never be as strong as Zach and Luke, but I wanted to be even an ounce of how strong they were.

"Okay, let's do it." A new fire had started under my feet.

Luke laughed. "That's the fighting spirit!"

His words pulled me into a memory. Luke's laughter carried through our tiny house. I was around eight when he suggested we wrestle in the house while Mom was at work. Though he was the most responsible of us now, when we were younger, he had his moments. We'd loved spending the evenings watching wrestling on the TV, and sometimes we'd makeshift our own wrestling pad with couch cushions and blankets.

We'd spent the entire day trying to copy our favorite wrestlers, but one flip over Zach's shoulder had me careening into the coffee table and onto the hardwood floor. The impact left unexpected tears in my eyes.

"I don't want to play anymore," I said, rubbing the ache in my shoulder.

"Don't be a baby. Come on." Zach held out his hand to me.

"I'm not a baby." I remember his word choice hurting more than my shoulder.

"If you're going to cry about it, then you can't wrestle with us anymore. Come on, Pres."

Presley jumped on a cushion—his blond curls were much brighter back then. "Ding. Ding. Ding!"

And they ran at each other.

I remembered the feeling of lead in my stomach when I slammed the door to my room. I thought of all the ways I could get back at Zach later that evening, then Luke came in and sat on the edge of the bed.

"He's lying, you know. You can still wrestle with us." He nudged me, and I didn't respond. "Is your shoulder okay?"

"It's fine." I groaned, inspecting the floor in my very dirty room.

My grumpiness didn't make him falter. "Come on. What do I have to do to get you back in there with us?"

There was a brief silence before I answered, "Why is he so hard on me?"

Luke moved the long pieces of his hair from his face. His hair was always wild back then, never styled. "Because . . . you're an older brother like us. He wants you to be tough."

I was soft. I knew it. Softer than Zach and Luke, at least.

"I'll never be like you guys."

Luke fell back on the bed with a wide smile, looking as carefree as ever. "Sure you will. You're already tough."

"You think so?" I asked, even though I knew Luke never lied.

"Yes, now come on!" He'd hopped off the bed and dragged me back to the living room.

We used to have fun together. It was a side of him I wondered if I'd ever see again. A form of him that didn't exist anymore. But the memory was still there as vivid as before. It lived on in his smile and laughter. I wasn't sure if he even remembered what it was like before The Family, and I was confident he could never go back after what happened to Sarah.

An unthinkable tragedy, yet he carried it far better than I ever could. How he ever smiled again, I'd never know.

Sparring with Luke was easy. He taught me where to focus my attention and everything I needed to be aware of. We then shifted to proper form and how to land a punch. I needed the recap. Hours passed as we danced around the ring, and even though I was nowhere near Luke's level, I felt stronger. I felt . . . tough.

The sun would set soon. I didn't run out of breath, and my body didn't hurt. There was no reason to take a break. I could have kept going, but I wanted to check my phone. Kimberly was probably on her way back to the frat house by now.

> **Me:** How was work??

> **Kimberly:** Way too busy and I feel like I'm sweating the popcorn butter. I'm gonna get in the shower right when I get home, will you guys be long?

> **Me:** No, I think we're wrapping up. Skylar with you?

> **Kimberly:** Of course. Don't worry.

I couldn't wait to get home and tell her all about my time with Luke. There was something about going home to her that made me giddy. I had to remind myself constantly it was only temporary and for safety purposes.

"Let's go again." Zach ducked back under the ropes and into the ring.

"No, I'm tired from kickin' your ass all day." William leaned against the wall, picking at his fingernails.

Zach scoffed. "Oh yeah? What if I make it interesting? We fight the way I was taught to fight. No mind control."

William sighed and pushed off the wall. "This should be good."

"Zach," Luke cautioned him. He had a darkness in his eyes I hadn't seen before. He was more tired than he'd led on.

"He can handle it. Right, Will?" Zach said.

"What exactly do I need to handle?" William joined him in the ring, rolling his shoulders.

Zach smirked and brought his lips to his wrist and bit down. Black blood gushed to the floor, and he spit blood on the ground. Despite it contrasting with the white floor, the dirt helped it blend in.

Presley and Thane stood by Luke and me, and even Dom looked intrigued.

"Uh-oh. Looks violent." Presley's eyes lit up, waiting for the carnage.

Luke's jaw was set and serious as he watched Zach and William pace around the ring.

"We'll see how strong you are without that power," Zach said.

William smirked, accepting the challenge by biting his own wrist. Minutes passed and their blood littered the floor. Blood loss was how they were taught to fight? How would that help anything?

Black voids of ink leaked into the torn padding in the ring. I remembered my own experience with losing blood. I was instantly weaker and then I lost control of my limbs. I was slow. Everything hurt. It was like being human again.

Zach didn't look fazed; he was calm, exhilarated even. He circled William as they waited for their blood levels to lower.

"This is how we were taught to fight. Fight when you're at your weakest. This is where it really comes down to how well you can fight. Life or death. It makes you fight your hardest."

It sounded sadistic, but I was intrigued. Zach hopped on the balls of his feet while bringing his hands up to cover his face, and in one breath, he was still—completely focused and ready for a fight. I shouldn't have been surprised. The more I learned about The Family, the more real my terror became. Of course they would battle in blood.

Zach and William lunged forward at the same time, only Zach was faster. Much faster. He dodged William's advance, moving away from his outreached hand and directing him into the ground. Black blood smeared beneath him, and he wasted no time pulling himself up. This time, he wasn't smiling.

William advanced again, but Zach was a millisecond ahead and bent his arm behind his back and kicked him in the leg. It was just enough time for him to lock William in a chokehold and bite his neck.

My chest tightened, and I looked to Thane beside me. He, too, was unusually serious. William grabbed Zach's arm and flung him over his shoulder, but Zach had more strength in his limbs. He planted his feet and threw William on the ground.

"Come on. Fight harder." Zach kicked him in the back, but William was up again sparring, blow for blow. William fought harder, but it wasn't enough. Zach was calm despite the blood loss. William's movements were sloppy.

Zach grabbed William's arms and bent them behind his back before taking another bite of his neck. "Submit."

More blood littered the floor around them and soaked their clothes. William said nothing but strained to get up off the ground. Zach kept a firm hold of his arms. I wasn't sure if it was possible to break our bones, but ripping limbs off was definitely on the table, and Zach looked like he was trying to tear off William's.

"Submit!" Zach said with a crazed look in his eye.

"Will, come on!" Thane said, his voice unnaturally strained.

"Stop," William said through gritted teeth.

William screamed in pain, and Zach let go and pushed him to the floor. "You may have more than a hundred years on me, but I can still kill you."

It was a threat. Leaving a stale dark aura lingering in the air. I wanted to be mad at Zach, but I couldn't deny this was something he'd been taught to do. It was bred into his very being. I wasn't mad at him. I was mad at The Family for making him hard. How old was he when they started teaching him to fight? And once they were made into vampires, how often did they train? From the looks of it, my guess was every day. Everyday training to kill your opponent and bring them within an inch of their lives. Maybe those fights weren't as tame . . . maybe not submitting meant losing one of your precious limbs. I gulped.

Zach's eyes met Luke's, and his body softened. Sparing a moment for their twin telepathy, he seemed to come back to his senses. Luke had to have known this would happen. That's why he cautioned Zach. They were trained to kill. Even Luke. Looking at William sitting in a puddle of his own blood, I wondered if he, too, had been through the same training. My answer came when I saw his expression. His eyes were full of pain.

William dug his fingers into his palm, clenching them into a fist, and black blood oozed from his wounds. He used his elbows to hoist himself up. Zach offered his hand, but William waved him off. William wasn't my favorite person, but I got the sickest feeling in my stomach watching him.

The Legion underestimated them. It was written in the blood on the floor. Something told me bloody fights were not something The Legion normally witnessed. How long had it been since they battled anyone or anything?

When he finally made it to his feet, his dark eyes settled on Zach. "Well, it looks like we've both got something to learn from each other."

Zach smiled. Loving that answer.

SEVENTEEN

KIMBERLY

It was late when I rested my head on my hand and the sleepiness settled into my body. At least I tried to study. My classes that semester weren't challenging, but focusing was nearly impossible. I looked over at the vanity mirror on the corner of my desk I used for makeup. A permanent stress line had formed at the corner of my brow, and I sighed. My desk in my dorm had been meticulous, but every day since I'd been in the frat house was chaotic. Only a week and half here and I'd rarely gotten a moment alone. If it wasn't Presley coming in my room every second to tell me stories about his day, it was other things like keeping Zach from killing William because he wouldn't let him turn down the thermostat. I couldn't blame him. There was a weird smell when the heater was on.

I put my book away and hopped into bed. The frat house was oddly quiet for a Friday. As I laid my head on the pillow and my eyes grew heavy, my heart leaped into my throat when a knock sounded on my bedroom window.

Aaron stood on the balcony with a grin spread across his face and a bouquet of peonies in his hand.

I opened the window, and he thrust the fluffy bouquet in my hands, and the sweet scent filled the room in a flash. I quickly went to work throwing out the old withered bouquet on my desk and replacing it with the new. Peonies were no longer in season, and it wasn't as easy as getting them in the school garden anymore.

"Where did you get these?"

"Doesn't matter. And no, before you ask, I didn't steal them."

"Aaron, peonies are expensive."

He shrugged. "What's a couple extra dollars? You deserve nice things."

I knew exactly what he could use that money on. Including their collective family pot. Presley called it "The Calem Cash Stash." It was a secret they kept from The Legion for emergencies. I wouldn't have been surprised if he'd already mentioned it to Thane.

I buried my face in the velvet petals and took in the smell. They were lovely. He was lovely.

"And what are you doing outside my window?" I couldn't hide the giddiness I felt despite the late hour. "You could have used the door, you know?"

"Coulda," Aaron said right before he shot in front of me, getting close enough for our chests to touch. He leaned down to whisper, "But then I couldn't come and steal you away."

I wiggled my eyebrows while keeping my voice low. "You have that look on your face like you're about to say something that's going to get me in trouble."

"No. Never. I just want to take you somewhere . . . alone."

"You want to sneak out?"

He nodded as his gaze panned to my lips. Which made my whole body heat up. We hadn't had a real moment alone since before the Halloween party, and something in me was craving the adventure in his eyes, but it was too risky.

"Have we not learned from our past mistakes? We shouldn't be sneaking around alone. Especially now that The Family knows where you live."

Aaron tilted his head. "True. But what if I told you I had learned from my past mistakes, and I already got . . . sort of permission? I told Thane where I'd be during a certain timeframe, and he agreed not to tell the others. Except Skylar. I had to tell her. I don't think I'd be able to sneak you out of here without a specialized SWAT team with her around."

"That's still sneaking."

"Yes, but they'll be close by. Plus, the place we're going is right on campus. Not far at all."

I crossed my arms, contemplating why I'd considered another reckless decision. Aaron was still close. His smile pulled me in. He knew I'd inevitably say yes.

"I know how stressed you are. I'm feeling it too . . . Come away with me. Let's be reckless just one more time."

I doubted it would be the last, but I dropped my hands.

"Okay, let's go."

"Yes!" Aaron exclaimed, still whispering. He walked to the window and held out his hand to help me out.

"Wait, I have to change first," I said.

He eyed my pajama shorts and T-shirt. "No, I think that will work. You don't even really need shoes. I'll carry you."

I ignored him, putting on my fuzzy cat slippers and slinging a jacket over my shoulders before I followed him.

We stepped out onto the balcony together. The sky burned with too many stars to count. One of my favorite things about Blackheart was how secluded it was. The night sky was always filled, though the lights of the campus dulled them more than anywhere else in town. There was a chill in the autumn air. As we moved into November, I couldn't ignore the cold wind blowing on the mountain. That was typically when we'd get our first snow, but I guessed it would come late with the drought.

Aaron crouched down, signaling for me to jump on his back. I obliged, snuggling into his warmth and taking the backpack he'd brought and placing it over my shoulders.

On my next inhale, we were off. Being on Aaron's back when he ran felt like teleporting. It was too fast for my eyes to see and made me dizzy. My hands tightened around Aaron's neck and, in less than a minute, we were there, staring at the gym in the moonlight.

"You want to hang out in the gym?" I grumbled as my slippers hit the grass, and my teeth chattered due to my lack of pants.

"You'll see." Aaron grabbed my hand and guided me to a small window on the side of the building. It had privacy glass, which made it impossible to see what was inside. He bent down in front of it and pulled on the bottom of the window.

I grabbed his arm. "Are we breaking and entering right now? What if it has an alarm . . . or cameras?"

"No cameras on this side of the building. I already scoped it out. And there's no alarm . . . I think."

"You think?" I said, my stomach turning. I wasn't looking to add vandal to my college transcript, but I trusted Aaron. He knew how important school was to me, and he'd never do anything to jeopardize it.

The window opened, and Aaron dropped inside first. I looked down into the dimly lit room.

"I'll catch you. Jump." Aaron's voice echoed.

My chest heaved at the height, but I leaped anyway. Aaron caught me, squeezing me to his chest and erasing all the tension I held.

His master plan came into view as I stared at the dimly lit pool. A cool wash of blue against the warmer tiled walls. I hadn't been here since our encounter with William earlier in the year. Steam lifted from the cold into the air, and the smell of chlorine hit me like a freight train.

"We have a pool," I teased.

"Yeah, but this is secluded." Aaron stood over me—close enough to smell his mint shampoo. In the blink of an eye, he ran around the pool. "No cameras here either."

He stared at me with that big goofy grin I loved and peeled off his shirt. "You don't have to swim if you don't want to. But I'm in need of a cooldown."

He said it casually while unbuttoning his pants, and they fell to the floor, leaving him in nothing but his donut boxers. I couldn't help admiring him for a second. Aaron trained with The Legion every night that he wasn't working. He'd been gone all night, and I saw evidence of his hard work in the veins in his forearms and added width from the swollen muscles in his shoulders and chest. I swallowed, and my whole face got hot.

"Admiring the view, Burns?"

I bit the inside of my lip, contemplating. It was absurd to be sneaking away and swimming at a time like this. But if I let go of that little snippet of logic for a few hours, what would it really hurt?

"I did bring you some extra clothes if you wanted to—"

I pulled off my top. If I was going to be reckless, I wasn't going to chicken out halfway. If we were breaking and entering into the school pool, I would go all the way.

"W-what are you doing?" Aaron's mouth hung agape.

"Going swimming," I said matter-of-factly, fighting the warmth in my ears at Aaron's gaze.

"Right." Aaron coughed as I pulled off my pajama pants and revealed my matching pink underwear.

I didn't need to hear his heartbeat to know it was beating as fast as mine. He was the nervous one now, and I liked that. I flung my clothes to the end of the pool, and Aaron's eyes sparkled from the glowing pool lights.

"What's wrong? Never seen a girl in her underwear before?"

He opened his mouth to speak but stopped. I never thought I'd see Aaron Calem speechless. I placed both hands on his chest, and as the anticipation caught in his breath, I pushed him into the water. I dove headfirst toward the deep end. The water washed away every bit of doubt and fear I had and awoke my tired body. When I emerged at the top, Aaron was there with that smile I loved.

He splashed me. "You think you're so funny, huh?"

I moved my hands through my hair, feeling as light as a feather, and I glided through the water. "Don't act like you weren't going to push me in first, given the chance."

His eyes narrowed, and he disappeared under the water. There was no way it was fair; he didn't need to come up for breath. His shadow came closer, and I shrieked when he grabbed my legs and lifted me up out of the water. Our laughter echoed to the ceiling and lingered in the air.

"Isn't it great? We can be as loud as we want." Aaron winked at me through wet lashes. He'd released me, but I still felt him on my skin. Every place his hands had been.

The chill of the night air was long gone in the heated pool. The condensation built on the foggy windows.

"Meet me at the bottom of the pool," Aaron said before his head disappeared beneath the water.

I followed him farther and farther down, opening my eyes to the slight sting of chlorine before they adjusted to the pool lights, then I let out a steady stream of air to sink to the bottom.

Aaron held up his finger, prompting me to wait. Then he opened his mouth and let out a yell that got crushed under the pressure of the water. A genius idea.

He rolled his hands forward to signal my turn.

I squared my shoulders and thought of everything I'd been holding in, and I screamed it into the water. The string of bubbles took the last of my oxygen to the surface and my worries along with it. When we surfaced, peace lingered in the air. We'd finally found a place for just us. Ours. No Legion. No vampire cult. And even though I loved them dearly, none of Aaron's brothers.

Aaron peeked up at me from under the water, and we moved closer together. He had his arms on my elbows, helping to keep me afloat. I was an okay swimmer, and I didn't need the help, but I was drawn to every touch of his skin on mine.

The sounds of my breathing and dripping of water from my hair was the only noise. That invisible tether tightened that connected Aaron and me, and I pulled my arms around his neck at the same time his arms wrapped around my waist.

"Do you wanna do something else a little reckless?" He leaned in close to my lips, and I closed my eyes, enjoying the rising heat as his lips almost touched mine. "I'll warn you, it's probably a bad idea . . . and you should definitely say no."

I smiled and nodded, taking that challenge.

"Can I kiss you?"

His warm-brown eyes took me in again. Only, this time, he was perfectly and blissfully happy, and so was I. I'd never dreamed someone would look at me the way Aaron was.

"Yes."

My head spun when his lips met mine. Every kiss from him left me lightheaded as we fell into the water. I didn't care about sinking. Our kisses didn't stop until Aaron pulled me up for air. I held onto his shoulders and let him drag me to the shallow end. This time when he pulled me in for a kiss, it was slower. He gingerly pulled the pieces of wet hair from my face and lifted my chin to meet his.

I wasn't used to the care in which he held me. I'd never felt something so strong yet so fragile. His hands were sure as they moved over my face and tangled in my hair. Now I was scared. Held captive by one internally optimistic man that kissed me like everything in the world would turn out okay. I was enamored by that light, and with every kiss, I believed it too.

Friends don't kiss, I reminded myself yet again. If they did, it wasn't like this. With tongue and heat, and a longing blistering and threatening to overtake me. Aaron moved to my cheek, kissing across my jawline. I was only briefly aware of my abnormal breathing when he kissed down my neck and to my shoulder. My bra strap had fallen. Any other day, I'd be irritated by it, but not today.

He pulled me tighter to his body and kissed my collarbone, slowly making his way lower. My brain was off, and I liked it that way. I leaned back and threaded my hands in his hair, inviting him closer—ready to open myself up to him further.

He must have gained back the sense I'd given up because he stopped. His lips found mine again and he kissed me one more time.

"For the record, this isn't why I brought you here." He held my face tenderly as water dripped from his hair, and I drank in the sight of him. Pure radiant sunlight.

"Oh, it was definitely your master plan to get me here in my underwear."

"No, I brought you extra clothes! You're the one who wanted to strip."

I smiled to relieve him of the guilt gathering in the lines of his forehead. "Don't worry. Let the record show I made my own choices with no coercion."

He laughed. "I wanted to take you away from everything for a night. It was truly supposed to be a friend thing, but I . . . I needed to see something."

"You wanted to see if the kiss in your room was a fluke?"

I knew the answer because I'd asked myself the same thing every night since as I lay in bed and remembered the feeling of his lips on mine. He'd kissed me like he meant it, but he pulled away—like he had before.

"I needed to see if this is . . . real or if I've just made it up in my head. I probably shouldn't have asked you to kiss me, though."

"Since when do we ever do what we're supposed to be doing?"

He smiled and kissed me again. Long and slow, and my head was up in the clouds again. I savored every taste of him.

One thought lingered on the tip of my tongue. "I was worried you might . . . not like me like that at all, and you never wanted to kiss me. That maybe I embarrassed myself over and over again by wanting to kiss you."

I never thought I'd tell him that. Not in a building where our breaths echoed.

A line settled between his brows. I hated it. He pulled me closer and kissed me again. This time deeper than before. He was everywhere at once, and he felt like mine. When he pulled away, his lips stayed grazing mine, and our chests were pressed together. I placed a hand there to steady myself. His heartbeat was smooth and steady underneath my palm.

"Does that answer your question?"

"Definitely," I said, still breathless.

"I can't kiss you like this and just be friends," he said before kissing me again and pulling away a few seconds later. "And you're my best friend. That's why I've been trying to actively avoid it. Or stop it. I can't lose you."

His best friend. He couldn't lose me . . .

I tried to process the words, but I was still reeling from his kiss. From the moment we'd met, I'd felt drawn to him. Something unexplainable. Unavoidable. Inevitable.

"Maybe we don't have to be just friends tonight . . . just for a night."

What was I saying? The words tumbled out. I just didn't want it to end. For one night, I wanted Aaron to be mine, and I could be his.

He smiled from ear to ear and playfully kissed my neck again and again, making me giggle.

"You have the best ideas."

"I know," I chimed.

It was a bad idea. I knew that. But I cared less and less about bad decisions and more about what I wanted to do. And oh, how I'd wanted this. I didn't think I'd even realized how much I did until his lips were on mine again.

He released me and took my face in his hands. "Then tonight I can finally tell you how beautiful you are. So unbelievably beautiful."

"Tell me more." My cheeks were hurting from smiling.

He moved his hands to my waist, but they were lower than ever before, placed just under my hips. "Should I tell you . . . how long I've wanted to do this?"

His fingers were cool against the heat of my skin when he brushed my hair to the side and kissed my shoulder. "Or maybe . . . I could tell you you're the bravest person I know . . ."

He spoke in a whisper along my skin between each soft touch of his lips. "Or how incredibly brilliant you are."

I felt drunk again. Wobbly and free. Only, the poison was Aaron Calem shirtless and wet with his puppy dog eyes.

His kisses didn't stop till he was at my neck again. "You're funny . . . compassionate . . . warm."

Every word that poured from his lips felt like honey sticking to my skin. Aaron was flirting with me. Like, *really* flirting with me. I'd asked for it, but I wasn't ready. Where did this man come from?

"You're . . . quite the . . . gentleman." I could barely talk.

"This isn't the half of it. I could make you so happy, Burns." He exhaled on my neck and brought his lips to my ear. "I'll be so good to you."

I giggled as goose bumps raised on my arms, and then splashed him with water. "You've been holding back on me."

I wasn't sure what surprised me more. That Aaron Calem was a huge flirt or that it was overcoming me in a matter of minutes. My uneven breathing made me lightheaded and, compounded with the steam rising from the pool, I had to pull away before my resolve melted completely.

"Of course I have. You don't know how hard it is not to flirt with you."

"But you do flirt with me."

"Yeah, but you've basically given me free rein now. And I'm pulling out all the stops."

Aaron was solid. A lifeboat in my sea of uncertainty. He was sure. I'd never been able to turn my brain off and let someone else take the reins, but here I wanted to. And I knew if I did, I'd be just fine. Mind, body, and soul; Aaron wouldn't let me drown.

We'd floated over to the side of the pool, and my back rested against the ladder.

"Are you okay?" His wet hair fell in his eyes.

I smiled and licked my lips. "I don't think I've ever been happier."

That made his eyes light up again, and he grabbed my hips and placed me on one of the steps. With both hands on the ladder rails, he stepped between my legs, and my heart fluttered. I cursed myself for how easily I fell at his mercy and radiant smile.

"You're really good at this. You must have seduced a lot of girls."

"No, just you. Always you."

"I can't keep kissing you, Burns. I feel like I'm going to murder a small village if I keep going."

He laid his hands behind his head, looking up at the ceiling, and I joined him, lying beside him and scooting a little closer for warmth. There was peaceful silence between us as we worked through what lingered in the air. I found Aaron's hand and grasped it.

After another half hour of playing around, swimming, and kissing—lots of kissing, we wrapped ourselves in two big fluffy towels from the locker room. Aaron brought some from home to lay on the heated tiles, but the ones the swim team used were way better.

Without the blanket of the water settling all our worries, they started to pop up again.

"I have to go hunting with Zach tonight." Aaron wrinkled his nose. His eyes were faraway.

"Is that why you ran away with me instead?"

He turned back to me, perking up. "It might have been one reason."

His gaze returned to my lips, and the heat returned to my face. Despite being as vulnerable as I'd ever been with someone—almost naked and wrapped in a towel—I'd never felt so exhilarated. Like nothing could touch us in the cover of the night.

"What's it like . . .? With that Thing in your head."

His thumb caressed the back of my hand, and a minute passed before he spoke. "It feels like someone in my head that's constantly bugging me. Telling me how much easier things would be if I just gave into it. It's been better but when I kiss you, it gets loud. I feel . . . crazed. Like I can't tell what's me and what's It."

I turned to face him and he turned too. He was a sight to behold with the blue pool lights glowing in his brown eyes.

He continued. "It's like It knows how important you are to me."

This time Aaron didn't smile, the line in his forehead signaled something much larger on his mind.

The burden of his inner demons was always there. He'd struggled for the better half of the summer, and only now did it seem like he had a good routine with hunting. He was touchy on the subject, though.

If I chose to be a vampire, I'd also have the same thing in my head taunting me. Could I handle it? That same thing had threatened Aaron's very being. I almost lost him, and now it was a constant battle. His smile was a miracle after what he'd endured. Something came to mind that I was almost too afraid to speak.

I pushed past my hesitation despite the tightening in my chest. "Can I ask you something? It's something I've been wondering about for a long time, but I wanted to wait till the right moment to ask you."

"Okay . . ."

"I know I wasn't the first . . . the first person you bit. What happened your first time?"

I never asked Aaron about hunting. He always brushed over it in conversation, preferring to talk about anything and all else, but as we drew together, I wanted him to know I could be his safe place too. He didn't need to be afraid.

He moved to turn away from me, and I stopped him with a reassuring squeeze of his hand.

"The first time was somewhere in Wyoming on our road trip here. But it wasn't like the fun kind of road trips . . . I wouldn't talk to any of them. I was so angry. My older brothers took me and Presley to this small town, and we parked next to a pub. I just remember how cold it was . . ."

He chewed his lip, and I nodded for him to continue. Worry built in his eyes. "I don't want you to think differently of me."

"I know you . . . it's okay."

He nodded. "We waited in an alley by the pub. It was snowing. Presley went first. He made it look easy. When it was my turn, I didn't even think. I just grabbed this guy and bit him. He was drunk, of course, but I lost it completely when I tasted blood for the first time. I don't know how long I drank, but I remember all three of them hauling me off him. Before I could say anything, they dragged me away. Someone was coming down the alleyway, and we couldn't be caught. I didn't check for his heartbeat. I still remember his face . . . I don't know if he survived."

I rubbed the back of his hand. I couldn't imagine that cold dark place in comparison to where we lay now.

"I ran away that night and went to the only place that was open . . . a church. Catholic, I think. I would have confessed to anyone within arm's distance but it was just me in there. My brothers found me. They always do." He half smiled, but he still refused to look at me.

I placed my hand on his face, and his shoulders settled. "I'm sorry."

"That's why I don't want you to rush into anything. Don't let my brothers pressure you. I know what turning really means. It's hard. It's really hard."

Aaron's cautionary tale made my stomach turn. He was right. Turning meant much more than giving up my old age. It meant agreeing to harbor something dark inside me. Something that was hungry for blood. But that was the price of having this night last forever.

We sat up, our hands still intertwined. It was effortless. So normal.

Aaron's chocolate eyes twinkled in the pool lighting. "And it makes this harder . . . because I don't want to sway your decision. I want you to get a choice. One I didn't have."

He was right. I knew he was right.

A creaking of the window broke our conversation.

"Shit," Aaron said as he stood to gather our things. William stepped through the double doors, catching us off guard.

Aaron wrapped his towel around me to further shield me while fumbling for the extra clothes in his bag.

"Oh, God." William averted his gaze while Aaron helped me to dress.

"It's not what it looks like." Aaron chuckled as he pulled his T-shirt over me, and I couldn't help but laugh with him.

"Enlighten me." William lifted his brow in amusement.

"Swimming."

Aaron's radiant smile was back, and I bit my lip, trying to fight the laughter that kept coming.

Thane plopped through the window. His boots echoed through the room. "Sorry, Aaron. I tried."

"I can't believe you're making me come back to this place," William grumbled. "Isn't it bad enough I had to join the swim team last year to keep tabs on you?"

"Guy hates water in his ears," Thane joked, but his smile faded when William didn't laugh.

"You're still being reckless, I see." William spoke to Aaron this time.

"It was just a little fun. You should try it some time," I said.

As soon as the words left my mouth, I wondered what came over me, but we deserved a moment alone, and Aaron shouldn't take all the blame.

William's eyes darkened. "They're rubbing off on you, Kim. I liked you better when you were quiet."

I rolled my eyes. "And I liked you better before you tried to kill us."

He cracked a smile before moving farther into the room. He surveyed the whole building with disdain.

I'd given up on William and me having a friendly relationship. He seemed to hate me the most out of everyone. Even Zach. At least he talked to Zach and looked like he'd jump in front of a bus for him. He was indifferent toward me.

Aaron grabbed my hand, and his gaze darted to the door. I knew a plan brewing when I saw one. I squeezed his hand as an acceptance to his invitation.

"She's got a point. At least you used to be dark and mysterious. You've lost your element of surprise. Without being menacing, you're just a dick."

"Well, maybe if I didn't have to babysit a bunch of children who do nothing but cause trouble, I'd be a little nicer." He leaned up against the wall, pulling out his lighter and cigarettes.

"Don't worry, we'll get out of your hair. Meet you back at the house."

And we were off. Aaron threw me on his back, and we zipped through the gym lobby the way William had come. A few dizzying seconds later, we were on the steps of the frat house. Both of us grinning ear to ear.

"That was worth it." Aaron laughed.

That night was exactly what I didn't know I needed.

Within seconds, William and Thane were next to us. William grumbled and shoved us through the front door. "Made me waste a cigarette."

Skylar also appeared. She must have been waiting outside. "Glad you're all right . . . both of you."

She inspected us before nodding and retreating into the house. I thought I detected a little smile on the way in, but I could be wrong.

"Luke! Deal with your brother," William yelled in the foyer and left toward the kitchen. Thane followed but not before giving us an apologetic look.

Luke strolled down the stairs, and Aaron and I waited. Dark circles stood out on his normal radiant face. He took us in at once. Wet hair, damp clothes, and guilty expressions on both of our faces.

Luke crossed his arms and stepped to tower over Aaron. "Did you have fun?"

Aaron nodded and his smile beamed.

Luke grinned and nodded toward the stairs. He winked at me and shook his head. It was nice to see him smile again.

Aaron and I held each other's hands up the stairs until we had to part in the hallway. Neither of us wanted to let go but knew we had to.

EIGHTEEN

AARON

I should have kissed her one more time in the hallway. I didn't think
I'd ever been so happy. Ever. This night was one of those nights you'd
remember for the rest of your life, and since I was immortal, that meant
forever. Well, if I lived that long. I replayed it over and over. Everything I'd
wanted. I checked the time and sighed. It was past midnight. Our night
as more than friends was over. I wanted just one more kiss.

"You look happy," Zach said as we walked through the night.

I was over the moon. Actually, in orbit in outer space, and didn't know
if I'd ever come down from the high.

I shrugged. Happy to keep it all to myself.

Hunting at night was scarier when I thought someone might pop up
out of the trees like a scary sheet ghost and try to recruit me into a cult.
But Zach had the collar of his jacket up and was smoking a cigarette, like
he'd challenge anyone and anything that got within a few yards of him.
He hadn't said many words. He just chain-smoked on our way down
the mountain. It was still very much a group endeavor, but our group
followed us in a car down the road. Which now consisted of Felix and
two others, in addition to Thane and William. It looked like we were
about to be abducted, so maybe that would make our actual pursuers
stay away.

This time we'd picked one of the trails in a park. It was normal for
people to go up and get drunk at all hours of the night. I snuck another
glance at Zach.

When I didn't answer, he spoke again. "Luke told me that you got
caught with Kimberly at the pool today."

My focus shifted. "It's not what it sounds like. We were just swimming."

The smoke fell into the air as he laughed. "We have a pool."

I sighed. The last thing I wanted to talk to Zach about was Kimberly. He wasn't good at talking about girls. At least with me. He was bad at empathy. He used to make fun of me for picking out the perfect Valentine's Day card for my crushes at school. Imagine my surprise when I found out he wrote Ashley poems in high school.

I decided changing the subject was better. "How was Luke today?"

"He's getting better. I think work helps."

Luke was a ticket taker at the theater and got to stand all day greeting people and scanning their movie tickets. I think it got his mind off things. He preferred busy shifts with lots of people, and he'd traded all his night shifts with Zach because he couldn't sit still. Luckily, he wasn't taking many classes. Technically he was a part-time student. Zach too. When Presley asked if he could be a part-time student, Zach threw a popcorn bucket at his head—we were all on a late shift.

"It's my responsibility to worry about Luke. Not yours." He watched me closely. "He'll be okay."

I should have protested, but I was thankful. Luke was my constant. I probably relied on him way too much, but something deep in me quaked when Luke wasn't well, like I, too, might break if Luke ever did. I shivered at the thought. I had too much to worry about already.

We walked along, and I could smell a campfire ahead despite everywhere near us being on a burn ban. Something about the fall air was quiet. Zach and I weren't often alone, and now that we were, I remembered I'd wanted to ask him about the Halloween party. Only, I was sure I was going to chicken out.

"What?" He took a long drag of his cigarette, somehow detecting my gaze in his peripheral vision.

"Can't a brother just hang out with his older brother?"

"You want to ask me something. Tell me what it is."

"Why didn't you tell me you struggled with drinking blood at first?" I chose a slightly easier question first.

"Honest?"

"Yeah, be honest."

"I just . . . didn't know what I was doing. I was so focused on keeping you fuckers alive I just did anything I could to make that happen. Being a good brother and making sure you guys liked me and felt happy about the whole thing was the last thing on my mind."

"It was your idea to change us?"

He huffed. "Yeah. That was my golden-ticket idea. There just wasn't a better way. At least immortal, we could hide you. No need for food. Water. Now you know who you can blame for the worst parts of your life."

He said it with a smile, like he'd already accepted that fate.

Only it wasn't. Maybe most parts, but not all.

"There is one other thing . . ."

I tried to summon the courage, knowing I was about to get my head bit off. "Did the queen . . . do . . . something to you?"

Zach didn't answer right away, then his brow furrowed. "Why are you asking me that?"

"Because I overheard something I wasn't supposed to at the Halloween party, and I was too scared to ask you at the time. I guess it's none of my business, but I'm trying to put the pieces together and get a clear picture of who She is."

Zach nodded, looking out into the night and taking another drag of his cigarette. "She's an evil lying bitch."

"I've gathered that." I waited, wondering if that was the end of our conversation or if he would tell me more. Personally, I was shocked I'd gotten that far. "I need to know what we're up against here. Tell me something."

"Remember that story I told you about the queen picking Luke to be Her donor over and over again?"

I nodded and forced my mouth shut. I didn't want to ruin a once in a lifetime chance to get Zach to open up by asking something that would set him off.

"Well, when I volunteered in Luke's place and told Her what I thought about it, She showed me exactly who was in charge."

I frowned, wondering what he meant.

"I woke up with no clothes and these bite marks all over me. I could barely walk from the blood loss. Ezra said he'd never seen Her so . . . possessive."

"Oh."

The pieces snapped together, and I felt the weight of his words.

"She just wanted to teach me a lesson. Bitch." He exhaled his cigarette smoke into the night.

"You and Luke talk about Her so differently . . ."

"It's not his fault, he's had too much of Her blood. He can't help it. Hence why I got pissed when She was trying to make him Her permanent little blood bag. She does it just to mess with his head . . . and mine."

"I'm sorry . . . I'm sorry that happened."

I braced for Zach's wrath. He hated pity more than anything else. Small or big. He didn't want it. But I had to say something because I wanted him to know how sorry I was for everything he ever went through.

To my surprise, he scoffed and took another long drag. "Now do you see why I don't want Her near you or Pres?"

I nodded.

That was all he said, and somehow it was enough. Zach was our protector, and he always had been, but he needed me to be stronger. I got the message loud and clear. I had to get stronger to endure whatever was needed of me. That way I, too, could protect the people I love.

"I think it's good. You and Kim." His lighter tone caught me off guard.

"Really?"

"Yeah, she's a keeper . . . you'd make her happy. I know that for sure. She's good for you. You're good for her."

I stopped walking, fear kicking me in the ribs. "Are you dying or something?"

"No. Can I not be nice?" He stopped and rolled his eyes like I was the outrageous one.

"Not to me. You're only nice when something is wrong."

"This is exactly why, because you worry too much."

My shoulders relaxed. "That might be true."

The sound of laughter came from behind a thin covering of trees. We'd found our targets, now we'd need to wait out the evening. We stumbled upon pieces of cut wood and sat down.

The silence between us continued.

"Listen, about the gym thing—"

I shook my head. "No, I get it. You were right. I was being too soft."

He watched my face and his brow lowered. "Nah, not too soft."

My cell phone ringer cut the air like a knife.

Zach and I cursed, and the humans at the campsite shrieked. Zach grabbed my jacket and pulled me back the way we came. He flung me against a tree out of walking distance from anyone at the campsite.

"Really?"

"Sorry," I said as I checked my missed call. It was Kimberly. I redialed immediately. Kimberly knew where I was, and she should have long been asleep. "It was Kim. I think something is wrong."

My heart hammered as I waited for the ring. I bolted back toward the car without anyone else's permission. Luke and Kilian were there when we left. She was probably fine, but I still felt sick.

"Aaron?" Kimberly answered. Her voice was laced with urgency and concern.

"What's wrong?"

"They found her. Mrs. Henry. She'd dead. Chelsea just called me crying. They're going to announce everything tomorrow . . . they think she was murdered."

"Oh, God."

Zach looked away from me and into the trees with gritted teeth. He'd heard.

"Can you come home? Please."

I hated the fear in her voice. I was already in the car where William was on the phone with someone. I knew then we'd all received the news at the same time. Our worst fears were confirmed.

"I'm coming."

NINETEEN

KIMBERLY

"We'd like to take a moment of silence for a treasured member of our staff. Jessica Henry was with our university for more than twenty years. She was a kindhearted person who brought a smile to everyone she met. Her memory lives on in her children, husband, and the students she dedicated her life to. Jessica believed in a world where everyone should have the opportunity to forge their own paths and see a bright future ahead of them. No matter the circumstances, she fought for her students. She will truly be missed, and we hope the police will soon be able to shed some light on the investigation."

The intercom squealed behind us, and we all cringed. Nothing said in plain sight more than at the top of the bleachers in front of the announcer's box. The Legion wanted us all together and very public. The Saturday BFU football game was the next best alternative to locking us all in a cage.

Chelsea sat beside me. Her perfume gave me a headache, and her long nails were leaving an impression on my arm.

Aaron was on my other side. I fought the urge to hold his hand. Not that I'd adhered well to our friends-only rule when I'd all but begged him to skip hunting and come lie in my bed with me. He did it. Of course he did. He held me all night, and that was the only way I was able to sleep. I'd feel more guilty about that if it wasn't for the wall of guilt I'd run straight into over our missing professor.

After the moment of silence was over, a dull roar of whispers ran through the bleachers in waves. Mrs. Henry was all anyone talked about. In the frat house. At the ticket gate.

"I still can't believe this is happening." Chelsea was abnormally quiet. "This is supposed to be a safe place."

It used to be. Chelsea had told me one reason she and her mom chose this university was because of the low crime rate on and off campus.

According to The Legion, we were the victims, but it didn't feel like that. It felt like I'd handed the weapon over to the killers of Mrs. Henry. Surely, I could have prevented this somehow?

Aaron leaned into me. He took it hard. Though, there was no confirmation it had been The Family. The Legion had been milking their sources for any information on the investigation. The only thing revealed was foul play and blood loss.

I coughed. The slight tingle in my throat lingered and the cold air made it worse.

"Are you still sick?"

"Barely."

"I'll get you a hot chocolate." Aaron stood, and Thane and Skylar looked over. They were only a few seats away along with Dom. It wasn't just them; other members were spread throughout bleachers. Even Kilian had come to the game, though he remained to be seen. Something happened behind the scenes. I could feel it. He knew something. We'd been instructed to call out of our work shifts, and I awaited word that we would all get written up for it.

I grabbed Aaron's hand, not wanting him out of my sight.

"I'll do it!" Presley jumped up. He'd been fidgeting all morning, looking for any excuse to move. "Zach, Luke . . . wanna come? Chels, you want any food? I'll bring snacks."

"Sure," Chelsea replied without a snide comment, and my guilt deepened.

They left with William and a few others. William didn't grumble, but I imagined the look on his face. If it were up to him, I was sure he'd have preferred the cage.

Our mascot was walking through the bleachers trying to get the excitement back in the crowd. A white dog with big, animated eyes and a dark-green Black Forest University shirt on. He wasn't nearly as popular as our live dog mascot, Pretzel.

It was almost criminal to see someone having fun on such a somber day, but life went on, and at the sound of the whistle, any talk of Mrs. Henry seemed to fade away. Our pom squad and cheerleaders were peppy as ever, and the crowd got lost in the game.

Chelsea didn't take her eyes off Monica, who was front and center on the pom squad. The mascot danced to the beat of his own drum around them to what looked like a completely different song.

"How are you and Monica?" I wanted to lighten the mood, and Monica was her favorite subject. I suspected Chelsea was still angry at me about moving, but she didn't bring it up once. I think she was lonely.

"She wants to meet my mom at Thanksgiving."

"That's huge."

"Yeah, I know. But oddly enough, I'm not scared. I think my mom will love her. It's kind of soon, but I feel good about it, you know?"

"Yeah, sometimes you just know . . ." I knew Aaron could still hear us, but he was trying to make himself look busy and engrossed in the football game.

"I just want to get out of here. Thanksgiving can't get here soon enough. I feel like I'm suffocating. After everything that's happened, it's like there's a black cloud hanging over Blackheart."

"I couldn't agree more," I said, and my attention returned to the sky. It was cloudy and faintly smelled of smoke. Because of the wind, the wildfires felt a little closer than normal.

"I hate mascots," Chelsea said as our mascot danced next to Monica.

He wasn't close enough to hear, but I swear he did because once he was done dancing, he walked up the bleacher steps.

"Oh, God, he's coming up here."

And she was right. Like he had a radar, he'd walked up the stairs right to where we were sitting. He sat next to Chelsea and pretended to yawn and put his arm around her.

"Okay, very smooth. I'm not in the mood," Chelsea grumbled.

He peeked around her and looked straight at me, and I froze. I could not take the embarrassment. He stood and motioned for Chelsea to scoot over, which she protested, but our mascot didn't take no for an answer.

I looked over at Aaron for help, hoping he wouldn't let me get dragged down to the field or something. He grabbed my hand and winked.

The mascot put his arm around Chelsea and me and tried to get us to stand up and follow him despite our protests.

But Aaron was up on his feet too. "I don't think they want to go, dude."

The mascot turned to face him with us under his arms and cocked his head. He released us and pretended to wipe dust off his shirt and then he brought his hands up in a boxing stance. Aaron took his challenge and put his hands up, and I finally saw the carefree smile return to his face. They pretended to fight for a few seconds until the mascot stopped and bowed to Aaron.

"Hey!" Presley was back with hot chocolate and hotdogs. His eyes went wide as he took in the sight of the big fluffy mascot. "You're the coolest, man! Good work!"

The mascot high-fived him and turned back to me, placed a small stuffed dog in my hand, and patted me on the head. He saluted us and danced his way back down the stairs.

"Dang it! Why did I always miss all the fun?" Presley frowned.

"I never thought I'd say I was thankful for Aaron Coleman being here but thank God," Chelsea said as she smoothed her hair.

"He looked handsy," Zach grumbled.

Luke agreed and then plopped next to Aaron. "Did we miss anything with the game?"

At the end of the third quarter, I think we were all over the game. Even Luke seemed distracted. Aaron and Zach were arguing about random things, and Presley kept standing up every few minutes. Chelsea left at halftime because she was too cold, and the hot chocolates only helped a little. It was the sitting around that was killer. The constant stewing in my thoughts made me restless, and I think I could say the same for them too.

The bleachers were still full of a sea of dark green, white, and black, but it had thinned as the game went on and the air got colder.

"What do we do after this? Please, there's got to be something better than holing up in OBA." Presley stood again. "I know we're all sad, but I feel like I'm going to explode if I have to sit here anymore. We should do something. Something active."

"What do you suggest?" William's Irish accent was peeking through a lot today.

"Why don't we play a game? Right, Luke? Maybe we could play football or something?" Presley was laying the puppy dog eyes on thick.

"I don't know, Pres," Luke said.

"I know a place. There's an old, abandoned football field not too far from here," Thane said.

"There is. The university built this one only a few years ago," I said. It was easy to remember facts like that in a small town.

"I was instructed to keep everyone together and in sight," William said. Enough people had cleared the bleachers for him to stretch his legs.

Presley said before the crowd behind him roared. "How is it any different from OBA right now? It's completely dead. Plus, if we all go, it's like the same thing."

"He's kinda right. I mean, it's not that far. You can see the old goal posts from here," I said, not knowing why I was encouraging Presley, but I didn't want to go back to OBA either. It felt like a prison.

"You really want to go?" Aaron said.

"It's better than sitting here and thinking about everything even more than I already have."

He nodded in agreement.

"Luke? Please?" Presley frowned like a sad clown.

Luke sat up with his bright smile and ran his fingers through his hair. "It might be nice to get some distance for a little bit, especially while the sun is up."

Presley erupted into cheers that got muffled in the crowd. It took a little more convincing to get Skylar and Dom on board, but they came around eventually when Thane promised to do their laundry for a week. We all headed for the field that was almost entirely encased by the tree line.

"Aren't you going to call Kilian?" Zach nudged William as we walked.

"Thirty minutes won't kill him. I can't sit through more of the fuckin' football game with everyone screamin' every five seconds."

"Doubt Kilian would approve. Aren't you all sworn to be all eternally holy or some shit like that?" Zach pulled a pack of cigarettes from his pocket, and William took one too.

"Uh, Kilian isn't as religious as you think, and neither are a lot of us,"

Thane chimed.

Zach scoffed. "You're kidding? What the fuck was all that in the church?"

"Only for trial when the fates of others are being decided. He still likes to pray . . . he just doesn't know who or what he's praying to." William blew the smoke from his cigarette into the cool air. "Then he seals it with water blessed by his own hands."

"And you all go along with it?" Presley said.

The crunching of leaves sounded as we walked from the sidewalk and headed for the trees. The colors of fall were fixed in with the evergreen leaves.

"If it pleases him, yes. I do not know or care where they go when they die. If it takes a little longer to bring him peace, I'll do it," Skylar said with Dom towering next to her and nodding in agreement.

Something in her tone caught my attention. She spoke about Kilian with respect. I hadn't seen a lot of their interactions, but it made sense. She'd come at his call, on a job that was dangerous and more than a little annoying.

"You guys gotta remember that we came from all around the country to see you die. Might as well make it interesting." Thane tousled Presley's hair. "Glad we didn't have to, though."

It was a weird dynamic. Going from nearly killing us to protecting us like we were the most important people on the planet.

"What about the creepy robes?" Aaron said as he pulled off his hoodie to give to me.

I'd worn a warm sweater, but as the sun fell lower, it had gotten at least a degree lower every hour. I thanked him and put it on, savoring the warmth it gave me.

"Oh, those are just because of the blood." William grinned at Zach's unamused face. "Didn't want to stain our clothes."

I leaned a little harder into Aaron's shoulder, and he rubbed my back. I'd tried hard to get the image of Aaron covered in blood out of my head.

"Sorry to disappoint you, assholes." Zach scoffed and exhaled a puff of his cigarette next to William. "Will, you seem to be his little pet. Tell us more. Where does the dude come from?"

William gave Zach a death glare, but answered, "Kilian was alive when the first queens were made. He used to be Roman Catholic . . . but from the things we've seen, there's no book or scroll that explains any of it. He's seen too much to believe in God anymore, but . . . he still prays."

Hope. Kilian hoped. He was a mystery to me, but I wanted to know the things he'd seen and the places he'd been. Maybe he wasn't as bad as I had thought. The Legion had followed his requests to be here. They believed in his purpose.

The fact that we were able to sit here and talk about it like a distant memory spoke volumes for how far they'd come in trusting in each other.

We reached the field covered in dead grass and tree limbs. The rusted goal posts stood on either end, along with a few abandoned brick buildings. The old bleachers were gone, and a large dirt patch sat in its place. An overcast sky made everything seem gray and muted.

Presley ran in front of everyone, tossing the football he stole from the sidelines. "Come on! Let's all play V-ball."

"V-ball?" Thane said.

"Yeah, vampire football!"

"I would, but you'd just be disappointed when I wipe the floor with ya," William said, crossing his arms.

Presley threw the ball to Luke, and he caught it with one hand.

"I don't think you could take me or Zach in a football game." Luke smiled and dusted off the football.

"We've got centuries on you. We can." William raised a brow. "What do you think, Thane?"

I was shocked to see William being so lax. He had as much pressure, if not more, on his shoulders from Kilian. Playing a game might be what they needed. I know the pool with Aaron was what I needed. Even if it made everything else harder.

"I think I haven't played a lot of football, but it can't be that hard." Thane smirked. "As long as the other Calem boys play fair."

"We won't cheat! Promise." Presley burned energy by running around on the abandoned field.

"Not like you do at poker?" Skylar smiled and stood next to me.

I nudged Aaron with my elbow. "You should play."

He'd been quiet all day, and it was making me nervous.

He smiled. "Might be time for me to impress you with my physically fit prowess."

"We'll see if he can keep up." William pushed Aaron to the center of the field.

"Skylar and Dom, are you in or out?"

"Do I have to?" Skylar sighed before scanning me. "This wasn't part of the job description."

"It's not a job, it's called *fun*." Thane laughed.

Skylar looked up at Dom and shrugged, and he nodded in confirmation.

"Fine, we're in."

They all gathered in the middle of the field. The Legion in one huddle, and the Calem boys in the other. The Calem boys buzzed with energy while the huddle of Legion members kept their heads down in quiet mumbles. Luke had found a large stump and placed it on the edge of the field for me to sit on.

"Wooo! Let's Go!" Luke clapped and took the position of quarterback, and Zach was center.

Aaron and Presley stayed on the outer edges, and I wondered how their game would work with The Legion having a combined more than a century of age on them.

Zach hiked the ball, and bodies were instantly on Luke, but he'd already thrown it across the field to Presley, who was swarmed again. He spun and threw the ball to Aaron, but it was intercepted by William. It was fast, and sometimes I'd blink and miss things.

I watched their back-and-forth. The constant movement made it hard for my eyes to keep up. It made me tired just watching, but neither their muscles nor their energy ever faltered. I realized that this may be the first time I saw them laughing together.

Our time with The Legion was often painful. A constant strain, but at this moment, everything was still. They weren't pulling against each other in a battle. They were working together against a common goal. To beat each other.

I thought of Mrs. Henry again, and how she'd probably have loved the boys if she'd met them. She could see what I saw. A future of hope.

Luke made the first touchdown, and the boys erupted in overexaggerated cheers. Zach picked Luke up and spun him around. I remembered Aaron telling me this was Luke's element. He was a natural in high school, and I saw how. There was an extra spring in his step as he bounded across the field. I wondered what younger Luke had been like before he had to be this Luke.

Luke did a touchdown dance, and I laughed. Thane found it hilarious along with the Calem brothers, but William did not.

The game proceeded, and I hugged myself as the wind blew through the trees. My eyes always returned to Aaron. I admired the cute look of determination and the funny way his hair bounced as he took a pass. His wall from earlier was down, and the light from the sun reflected in his smile.

It didn't take me long to discover Skylar was the second-best player on the field, and I wondered when she learned to play.

"Whoa, Sky," Presley said. "You're good. Maybe you should teach Dom how to throw a pass."

Dom wrinkled his nose before he grabbed the ball from Skylar and threw it to the other side of the field where William caught it and made a touchdown. I bit my lip to hold back my laughter.

"Come on!" Aaron flung Presley back into the chaos.

After about thirty minutes, my toes started to go numb and my teeth chattered. My arms were warm, but the cold seeped into my jeans and my boots.

There was a brief intermission in which Luke came to sit by me. He had his brothers running drills in his absence, considering they didn't need the rest.

"Here." He pulled off his jersey, revealing a tight shirt underneath. "I know you gotta be cold."

I thanked him and wasted no time pulling it over me and let the soft warmth thaw my ice-cold legs.

"Play it again!" Luke yelled and then looked at me and smiled. It had been a while since I'd seen that smile on him. "Run it through without me."

"They'll get killed out there without you," I said. After thirty minutes of watching them play, it was apparent how much they all listened to Luke. It was a constant back-and-forth of questions and reassurance.

"Now, if I just told them everything, they'd never understand the plays."

"What do you mean?"

"They need to work together alone. If they're always looking at me, they'll never see where they need to go. I teach them the play and then let them work it out."

"Won't The Legion see your plays, though?"

"No, you'll see."

Luke admired them with a proud smile. I wondered what he saw when he watched his brothers. Chaotic children who desperately needed guidance? Something told me he loved nothing more than to be their guide. But I wondered what Luke would be doing if he wasn't here now. If he wasn't the oldest and had been allowed to do anything he wanted. I could think of at least five professions at the top of my head he'd excel in. He had that natural gift and talent everyone wished they were born with.

He moved his hand to his cheek, almost as if to wipe a tear, and his brows knitted in worry, but there were no tears. His gaze lingered on his clean hand.

"Are you okay?" I said.

His head snapped up at my comment, and the smile was back as easily as it had left. He pushed himself up to his feet. "Never better."

The game didn't drag on much longer because the Calem brothers got their act together. Luke was right. All they needed to do was to work together. They worked like a well-oiled machine while The Legion had brief intervals where things got moving only for a wrench to be thrown in the cogs a few plays later. The game ended with the Calem boys scoring the final touchdown and jumping up and down as they celebrated by running the field.

Aaron spotted me from across the field, and within seconds, he was back in front of me.

"Hey, let's go warm you up," Aaron said before backtracking. "You know . . . like hot chocolate or something."

My heart fluttered, betraying me again.

"Right." I wasted no time grabbing his arm, craving his warmth, and he happily obliged.

"Say it." Presley fluttered around William as they walked from the field.

"No."

"Say we win. Or I'll pour bleach in one of your bonsais."

William scowled at Presley. "You wouldn't."

"Could be an accident. You know, cleaning the windows and then *bam*."

"Fine. You win." William pinched the bridge of his nose, but Thane patted him on the back.

"Losers have to stay behind and clean up!"

"Someone needs to walk with them," Skylar warned.

William lifted his hand in the air as tribute.

We looked back at the tattered old field. It looked like a tornado had come through. Their game left the goal posts bent, and some of the old buildings now had holes in their roofs. We headed back to the original football field with the cold wind blowing us forward. The crowd in the distance cheered, signaling the end of the BFU game. I gave Aaron his hoodie back, and he put his arm around me. I took that as an opportunity to press my face into his side and enjoy his touch. That got me a few smiles from his brothers.

"Great choice with the hoodie today, Aaron. You just look so good in hoodies." Presley snickered, and I was sure I missed an inside joke.

"Doesn't he just look *so* good in hoodies, Zach?" Luke nudged Zach.

Zach smiled too. "Totally. The man should live in hoodies."

Aaron sighed with a smile. "Shut up."

TWENTY

KIMBERLY

The breeze was soft as we waded through the tall pine trees. A few yards ahead I saw an opening in the brush, and I thought about how we would all spend the evening with much less stress on our shoulders than before. Everything felt okay again. Not great but bearable because we were all together.

A twig snapped overhead, and the twins quit moving, causing the rest of us to run into each other. The breeze stopped.

Zach and Luke were frozen, staring at a shadowed figure in the trees.

Above us, sitting with his legs dangling over the branch of a tree, was a man with slicked-back black hair. He wore a long coat with rolled up sleeves, and dark tattoos covered his pale forearms.

"Didja miss me?" He smirked like a kid who'd found his favorite toy.

I blinked and then he was there in the dirt in front of us, landing with ease. The dirt swirled round him, and he cocked his head to the side. I couldn't see Luke's expression, but I could see Zach's wide unblinking eyes.

"Long time no see, boys."

"Who are you?" Presley blurted. He was to my left, huddling into my shoulder.

"The second highest-ranking member of The Guard . . . Her guard," Luke said.

He said it like a warning to show us how serious this was, but I could already feel it in my tiny fragile human body. It was nothing compared to the feeling of blood lust radiating off Aaron and William at the campsite. This was different. Immense power radiated from him. The way he spoke and carried himself made the spit catch in my throat.

"Name's Akira." His dark eyes settled on Presley. "Ah! Littlest brother! The afterlife suits you. Tell me, how are you liking it? How's it been?"

"I've been better . . ."

"And, Aaron! Glad to see you teaming with life. We're all connected now. You're practically my brother too."

Aaron scoffed and put his hand on my forearm like he might try to bolt with me any second.

"Let's see, who else do we have . . . the boy scout." He scanned William. "Who cares about you, and oh! Kimmy is here. Aaron, you really are a lucky guy."

I was frozen. My blood pumped with adrenaline. It told me to run, but there was nowhere to go, as we were surrounded by trees. I squeezed my palms, trying to dethaw from my body's freeze response. We were in trouble.

"Kimmy, I've heard you've made quite the addition. It's a shame I'll have to kill you."

Aaron's hand tightened on my arm. "You won't."

"Did you just come to bore us to death with your pleasantries?" William said as he rolled his shoulders. I didn't have to see his face to know he was ready for a fight.

"Altar boy. Please. I'm talking." Akira rolled his eyes. "I can't believe you guys decided to work with The Legion. It just makes everything so . . . complicated. Because of you and your little friends poking around, we had to relocate."

Akira's eyes burned into William's. "Pity, isn't it? You thought it might be easier to find Her but just like always you're one step behind."

The vein in William's forehead was about to burst.

"Anyway, Kimmy, how did you meet the boys?" Akira was back to focusing on me for reasons I didn't understand.

"You don't have to answer that," Aaron said.

"It's fine." I cleared my throat. "Aaron and I met when he bit me in the forest while I was camping."

That story lacked the fairytale of our hallway story, but despite my stomach doing somersaults, my gut told me telling the truth was a better option.

"No shit? All is good now, and you just love hanging with the vamps, huh? Let me guess. They were going to turn you." Akira smirked again.

"I was still deciding," I said.

"Well, that's a good thing. Don't want Her blood mixing with yours.

That would be a trip."

"What do you mean?"

"Kim—" Aaron started to say.

"No, I want to know."

"She wouldn't want it. Only Her chosen. It has nothing to do with you, I assure you. It has everything to do with them. Particularly those two, I might add."

He pointed to Zach and Luke. "I guess I can tell you guys now. Even with my added audience of two since I'll kill you both anyway. Zach and Luke—"

I flew backward toward the clearing, with a hand firmly wrapped around my waist. As quick as it started, it stopped, and Aaron dropped me.

Akira stood at the edge of the clearing. "Come on. You're not taking the girl anywhere. She dies here. But that doesn't mean we can't all have a little more fun. This is a family reunion, after all."

"You call this fun?" William said.

"Altar boy! Shut up before I come over there and kill you right now. Killing tends to make everyone a little angry and then no one will want to talk to me. So, I'd appreciate it if you shut the fuck up before I lose my temper."

Akira ran both hands through his hair. "Where were we? Oh, right! Big bro and bigger bro. Your favorite twins. I bet you're wondering why . . . why would we care? Why haven't we killed you for your disloyalty yet? Why would we come all the way over here to fetch you *alive*, I might add. It's all because of a little . . . prophecy. You see. The Guard. We last for centuries. But all good things must come to an end. Our time serving the queen is ending, and I've got four vampire boys here that would be perfect for the role."

"Wait. What?!" Presley said.

"Zach and Luke have been destined to fulfill that role. She's seen them coming for at least fifty years now. The other two are . . . practice. She sees a great amount of potential."

"She can see the future?" I whispered.

"Yes! She can. And guess what? She's seen every single one of these boys wrapped around Her little finger. I'm sure you thought they were all innocent little snowflakes."

"You're lying . . ."

"Nope. Not even a little bit." Akira appeared in front of Luke and Zach, and his speed was effortless. "Why do you think She's been obsessed with you two? Since Ezra found you both on the side of the road, we knew. That's why we've been taking care of you and waiting for the day when you'd be ready. It's time to come home. Let's stop this madness. Let's get to the good part."

Akira's eyes darkened. "Hey, maybe I'll take the girl as a snack, and we can all feed on her for fun on the way home!"

Zach and Luke rushed him while William grabbed the rest of us, and we headed for the trees.

For the second time, Akira stood in front of us. Blocking the way. He was way too fast.

"You know . . . I was mad at first when Sirius told me he'd found you guys and you were using *them* for protection but then I realized it just shows me how desperate you really are. The Legion are nothing compared to us, and I'm sure you've figured that out by now."

Akira advanced on us, inching forward with a little shuffling of his feet while we stepped backward into our huddle. He turned his attention back to Zach and Luke.

"Did you really think they were going to save you and your brothers? I don't really get what all this running away was for. Your brothers will live on with us. We don't even care about your mom. We let that go too. We can provide you with the protection you need. The safety you crave. The thing you've always wanted most in the world. To keep your brothers safe."

There was a sincerity in his voice and a glistening in his eye as he spoke. Every second he peeled back the layers, the years of practice in manipulating came shining through. He was good.

Akira walked back slowly into the middle of the clearing with his coat flaring at his turn. He carried extreme confidence, and for all I knew, he had a reason to. My fingers hurt from clenching my fist, and my forearm ached from Aaron pulling at my arm. I couldn't tell if the shaking in my muscles was from me or from him.

"Now your little brothers are family too. Which means their protection will span the ages. Centuries. Isn't that what this is all about? The Legion can't give that to you. I can."

Neither Luke nor Zach were moving. They were frozen and held captive by Akira's words. I wanted them to say something . . . to say anything.

"Don't listen to him." I forced the words out, hoping it would thaw them from their shock.

"Kimmy, you gotta stop it, or I'm gonna fall in love with you." Akira looked at me longingly with pieces of straight black hair falling into his eyes.

"You love listening to yourself talk, don't you?" I faked a smile.

"Of course! God, you're the most interesting addition of all. We didn't see you coming. You're lucky it was one of the little brothers you fell for, or She'd want your head on a platter."

"She sounds lovely," I said.

I had to keep him talking. The Legion weren't far off. They'd be there any minute, and we'd have the numbers. And that would be relatively easy to do since he had been monologuing since he got there.

"Oh. She is. As a human, you can't imagine the bond that blood gives you."

He was right. I turned my attention to Aaron, who still held my forearm in a death grip. His brown eyes were hazy with a darkness creeping into his irises, and his brows lowered. He was the one shaking.

"Cut the shit, Akira," Zach warned, stepping forward.

Akira smirked. "I will if you will. What's so radical about what I'm saying? You're looking at me like I'm the bad guy here. When I've done nothing but keep you safe your whole life."

Akira turned back to me and threw his hands in the air. "He forgets! Who was the one who came to Luke's aid when he was shot and lying bloody in the street? Who made sure he didn't die before the ambulance arrived and rode with him on the way to the hospital? Oh, right. That was me. Where were you?"

Zach's shoulders dropped as Akira circled closer to him.

"Who was the one who stood in the operating room making sure that brainless on-call surgeon didn't kill him on the operating table? Oh, I remember now. That was me too. And that's not even the tip of the iceberg here. The reason you're alive and didn't starve in that little shitty house in Brooklyn was us. Your real family."

I waited for Luke or Zach to challenge him. For any sign what Akira said wasn't true, but their silence confirmed what I think I already knew. The claim The Family had over them was larger than I'd ever thought possible. They were deeply interwoven and twisted in something much bigger than themselves.

"There's only one way this can end. Their futures have already been written. They come with me. And unfortunately, Kimmy, that means I must kill you. And no name over there."

There was a brief glint of sadness in Akira's eyes, and for a moment, I almost believed his words.

In a blink, Akira was in front of me, his hands inches from my face before Zach and Luke tackled him from the side. My human eyes couldn't keep up with their movements. Each swing and kick were a mix of tumbling and jumping. They had complete control of every muscle, which made their movements something out of the action movies Aaron made me watch. But nothing landed. Every single blow, he dodged. Akira was too fast. William joined the fray, and Akira's eyes grew wild. He simultaneously pushed the twins into the dirt while getting his hands around William's head.

"God, I could crush your head like a grape right now."

Presley ran to help get him off, and Aaron followed, but not before Akira sunk his teeth into William's neck.

He pulled away with black blood staining his mouth, and spit it on the ground. "Disgusting."

They all rushed him again, but with one push, they flew off him and landed in the dirt and leaves, muddying their clothes. This time he was more serious and calculated.

"We're only a minute in and you guys are already losing. That must be so embarrassing for you." Akira's laughter echoed in the trees.

Zach groaned and rushed forward, nearly knocking Akira to the ground. Akira must have been thinking a step ahead because he pinned him under his arm without flinching. "You used to be able to spar with me, now you can't even keep up. You haven't been training."

Luke went in next, and Akira used his momentum to push the two together. Their heads collided, and they fell into the dirt.

"Not nearly hard enough." Akira pushed William into the ground with his foot. "Did you think you could just come and live a normal life here? You're getting weaker by the day."

Akira grabbed Presley by the collar and sunk his teeth into his neck, and a shriek left my throat. I couldn't help. I couldn't move.

"See? You've left him here all helpless."

He handled them all simultaneously, swatting them away like flies. He flung Luke into a tree, and Zach flew back into the brush where I couldn't see.

Aaron rushed forward, but Akira grabbed William by the neck and flung them both to the ground.

Nothing stood between Akira and me any longer.

"Aaron, take Kim and run!" Luke yelled. But he was too far. He wouldn't make it in time.

"Alright, Kimmy. I think this is your final stop."

Akira was in front of me again, reaching toward me. This time his expression was void of any humor. I braced myself for whatever pain followed.

But then Aaron was there.

Standing between us.

He'd moved swiftly. I hadn't felt myself shift back a few inches.

Aaron stopped Akira's hand with a death grip on his wrist.

Excitement grew in Akira's eyes. "Ooh. Aaron, you've gotten interesting. If I'm honest, you used to be my least favorite brother."

Aaron's knuckles were white. His back was rigid, and everything went eerily still.

"Damn, you're hurting my arm a little bit. It feels good to have power, doesn't it? It's too bad what you're doing rots your brain. But I know how you can get real power. Come with me, and I'll show you real power you can control."

Aaron pushed him with one arm, and Akira careened into a pine tree a few feet in front of us. The branches cracked and splintered, leaving a few falling from the sky.

Akira popped up on his feet and wiped off his coat. "Finally, a challenge."

Everyone watched as Akira rushed Aaron, and he countered, ducking as Akira swung above his head. Akira was the better fighter. But Aaron was as fast and strong.

Akira grabbed Aaron in a headlock, and Aaron took out his footing and slammed him into the ground.

Akira's crazed laughter sent chills down my spine. He rolled in the dirt, holding his stomach like he'd heard the funniest joke. This time when he got to his feet, his brow lowered, fear shot through my chest. I couldn't let him hurt Aaron.

"That's enough." Kilian's voice cut the air. Alongside him were the other members, and they'd dispersed to the twins, who were already up on their feet.

"Well, well, well. Kilian himself is gracing me with his presence. Come to wrought me of my sins?" Akira's voice had hardened, and the smile slipped from his mouth.

"Akira, nice to see you're doing well. You're much more trained since we last met." Kilian walked in next to me, dressed in his routine blazer and slacks. Next to Akira, he wasn't intimidating but as he moved closer, his height made up for it.

"You don't know the half of it," Akira said.

"Aaron, you can come back." Kilian placed a hand on Aaron's shoulder.

Aaron said nothing. He watched Akira with his fists clenched at his sides.

"He won't. Aaron's one step into the void." Akira stared Aaron down. "Don't worry. You'll have all the blood you need with me. What are they teaching you? To suppress it? You can use it. Feel it. Let it fuel you. You can have all the power without any of the risk."

Kilian pulled Aaron away from Akira, and the rest of The Legion members surrounded him.

Akira flipped up the collar on his jacket and smoothed his hair. "This has been . . . enlightening. Be careful, brothers. Feel free to come crying to me when Kil tosses you to the curb. It's only a matter of time."

He walked backward toward the trees before pivoting on his heels and disappearing into the forest. "I'll be around."

The Legion rushed in. Skylar was the first to my side, surveying me from head to toe.

"I'm sorry. I should have been here."

I shook my head. "I'm fine."

I wasn't. I couldn't feel anything and wasn't even sure I was still breathing. But I couldn't stop staring at the back of Aaron's head a few feet away from me. I reached for him, but Skylar stopped me.

"Aaron . . ."

Kilian was in front of Aaron, who was soon followed by Luke. "He needs blood. Now."

I tried walking closer to see his face, but Zach and Presley were next to me, pulling me backward. They forced Aaron to his knees on the forest floor. Pools of black ink filled the whites of his eyes. That Thing had taken over and wasn't letting up.

A few seconds passed and then a guttural surging of pain escaped his lips. Slowly he unraveled, and his humanity dissipated. He became more rigid and defensive, pushing off anyone who tried to still him. His fingers dug into the soil as he tried to crawl out of their grasp. One minute he was looking at me like I was the thing he was trying to get to, and the next, his hands were in his hair pulling and straining with his chin tucked to his chest.

Blood flooded my cheeks when I peered up at the surrounding vampires all gawking back at me. Their faces said what I already knew was true. I was the only available donor.

"How bad is it?" Luke said through gritted teeth.

Kilian was straining to keep Aaron on the ground. "He can't wait for the house."

"I want to help."

Aaron made his way to his feet again and grabbed Dom by the throat and flung him to the dirt despite being half his size. Dom struggled beneath his death grip, but Aaron was crazed and strong. When members of The Legion tried to drag him off, Aaron had no trouble flinging them with a vicious snarl.

Luke tackled him from behind and with pure willpower, muscled Aaron's arms behind his back. William, Dom, and Kilian all came to his aid, but it was barely enough to counter Aaron's violent thrashing. Like a petulant child, he kicked the earth, leaving deep indentions in the dirt. His face twisted into a mixture of rage and pain.

"Let me help!" I tried to push Zach out of my way, but his body was stone.

"Hell no!" Zach grabbed my shoulder, and I shrugged him off.

Presley had his hands over his ears, and his fingers were shaking. "He's right! You can't. He's going to take your arm off."

"No, he won't. He's stopped before. He'll stop again."

"I'm not taking that risk," Zach said.

"It's not your decision." The words poured out, and I squared my shoulders.

"The fuck it isn't. He's my brother."

"Exactly, and he needs help! I'm helping."

"And what if he kills you!? Who's going to take the blame for that, then? Oh, right, that's fucking me." Zach's words echoed Akira's. He wasn't going to budge.

"Guys. Please stop fighting," Presley said while he swayed. Black blood stained his neck and the front of his shirt. Despite his hands still covering his ears, he jumped every time Aaron let out another bloodcurdling scream.

"I can make sure he doesn't kill her. I'll put him under if it comes to that, but I can't guarantee much else. Broken bones are possible." Kilian was on Aaron's left with his hands pressed firmly into Aaron's shoulder.

"Can you just put him under now?" Zach snarled.

"No. Aaron is fighting for control. Locking him in his head will do the opposite of what we need. We need him to gain control again."

"We don't have any other options." I rolled up the sleeve of my sweatshirt, revealing my scarred wrist. The same wrist Aaron bit not even a year ago. My body surged with adrenaline, readying itself for the pain.

"I can help with the pain. Come over here and grab him." William motioned to Skylar, and she took his place. Aaron shifted and almost pulled her off the ground.

William eyed Zach and me. "We doin' this?"

I stood in front of Zach. "Yes, it's my choice. No one else's."

Zach peered over to Luke, who was still busy trying to keep Aaron on the ground, but he gave me a reassuring nod.

"Fuck it. It's your funeral. Literally."

A nervous laughter left my lips as I held my arm out for William, and my heart kicked my ribs. He'd done it before. In the church, my arm didn't hurt.

William's eyes were set and serious. "This won't hurt. But if he breaks your arm, it won't be enough to help."

I nodded in agreement, and William brought my wrist to his lips and bit down. It didn't hurt. Not even a little.

Aaron pulled himself to his feet at the smell of my blood, nearly knocking everyone else over, but they wrangled him back to his knees.

"Any day now!" Thane yelled.

I crouched in the dirt, and all feeling was gone in my wrist. There was no moving my fingers. At the proximity of my bloody wrist, Aaron pulled away and crawled back toward Luke, but there was nowhere for him to go. He was still in there. Fighting.

I moved my wrist to his lips, and his eyes met mine. I longed for the burning amber to come back.

"It's okay. You won't hurt me."

He bit down with more force than I'd anticipated. William was right. The numbness, though seemingly impenetrable, wouldn't save me from the pressure in my wrist. I exhaled in an attempt to breathe through the pain.

The numbness crept from my wrist and into my arm. My entire body was on fire. Zach and William both had a hand on my shoulder, ready to pull me back at whatever cost. I didn't want to think of what that could be.

After three seconds, Aaron's shoulders dropped and the muscles in his face loosened.

My pulse pounded in my head, but my attention was on him, hoping it would work and every second of pain was worth it.

I probably should have been scared or disgusted. Perhaps all the above, but I wanted to help him, and I wanted it to always be me—his lifeline in the dark.

I shivered. My head felt heavier and heavier, and my fingers were cold.

Aaron pulled away, and when his eyes opened, they were beautiful pools of honey.

He groaned, blinking a few times to get his bearings.

"Aaron!" I cried out, then grabbed his face to make sure it was really him.

His head shot up, and his eyes softened. "It worked. You're okay."

"You chose to do that?" I was still breathless.

"Well . . . kind of. I had to do something, and now I see what a bad idea it was because it was hard as hell to get back."

His arms were freed, and he wiped the blood from his lips. He moved slowly until he spotted my bloody wrist.

"Wait, did I hurt you?"

Luke had torn a piece of his shirt and wrapped my wrist in the most pristine bandaging I'd ever seen.

"No." I shook my head. "You saved me."

TWENTY-ONE

AARON

"Aaron. You risk yourself every time you allow that thing to take over." Kilian's voice amplified the ringing in my ears.

I squeezed out the rest of the blood in what had to be my tenth blood bag and flung it on the ground. A pile of bloody plastic crinkled at my feet, and I wiped my mouth while resting my elbows on my knees. Which was useless because I was covered in blood. Thick, dried blood was caked under my nails, and my chest was sticky.

We were all in my room, and I leaned over in my computer chair. That's all I knew. All my brain would let me comprehend. It felt like I'd been hit by a semi and then promptly backed over for good measure.

"He did what he had to." Zach had his arms crossed and propped himself against the windowsill. "Because of him, Kimberly is alive."

I dared to make eye contact with Kim across the room. Not wanting to face the fact I'd turned feral and downed at least five of those blood bags with no memory.

She was quiet again, sitting on my bed and holding her bandaged arm. I was sure I felt guilty about that, but all my remaining brain cells were trying to keep my eyes open.

It lasted two seconds before I closed them and let the voices in the room fill the space. I wasn't even sure who was in my room or who was speaking. I wanted them to leave so I could lie across my bed, and maybe see if Kimberly would rub my head.

"What are we going to do now?"

"Did he mention how he found you?"

"Does it matter?!"

"He said it was Sirius. He never mentioned Ezra."

"Ezra kept his word to you, then . . . interesting."

"Fuck Ezra, what's your plan? Akira is too strong."

I fell forward and a firm grip on my shoulder stopped me from falling out of the chair. It was Luke.

He smiled halfheartedly. "You okay?"

I nodded in agreement and leaned my head back on the chair.

"He needs to rest for his body to heal . . . and his mind." Kilian stroked the salt-and-pepper stubble on his chin.

"Question. What did he mean about all that prophecy stuff? Is that even real?" Presley's voice grated on my eardrums. He had to be close.

"Many believe it to be. Yes. But historically, it's hard to confirm or deny. You didn't know about the prophecy?" Kilian's voice lowered.

I didn't care about prophecies. I needed to sleep and then I might care.

"Of course we didn't know," Luke said. "Why would we be here if we knew that?"

"Why the hell did you not tell us you knew Akira? What the fuck was that about?" Zach spat while glaring at Kilian.

"It wasn't pertinent to our situation at the time. I've been alive for centuries. I've had a few run-ins with the coven before. Nothing that would concern you. Akira's arrival was unexpected, but it doesn't change things. Our course of action is still the same as it was."

"That's not for you to fucking decide," Zach said.

Presley spoke again. "Wait, I want to go back to the prophecy thing. Who's going to be a part of The Guard, and what exactly does that mean?"

"No one is going to. That's not happening." Luke's firmness made me turn to him. The room went quiet. "Kilian, can we talk to you downstairs? Alone. Everyone else. Out."

Luke wasn't asking. He walked to the door and motioned everyone through the door. His tight-lipped expression made even me want to get up, but his eyes softened when he saw me.

"Kimberly, will you help Aaron get to bed?"

She stood. "I'm on it."

No one else said anything. Presley didn't even make a joke. Luke could be downright scary when he needed to be. Even scarier than Zach. When he lost his cool, it was for a good reason.

I was thankful for the silence when the door shut behind them.

Kimberly came up beside me to put her arm around me and walk me to the bed.

I sighed. "I think I wanted to hear that."

I'm sure I did. Maybe they would tape it for me or give me the cliff-notes version after my long nap.

"Me too." She sat me on the bed and leaned in front of me. "But this is good too."

My eyes were threatening to close again. Betraying me. But she was still there watching me with those cool-blue eyes. I couldn't sleep yet.

"God, you're beautiful, Burns. Did you know that?"

"You might have told me." The corners of her lips tugged but fell just as fast. "You really need a shower."

"The only way I'm getting in the shower is if you're coming with me."

Most of my brain cells were already asleep, and the only ones left awake wanted to flirt with Kimberly. *Or did all my brain cells want to flirt with her?*

Her cheeks pinked. "I think you're delirious."

"Deliriously in love with you."

I said it like a fool, covered in blood. Because I was a fool covered in blood.

She blinked slowly and sucked in a breath.

Oh no. It wasn't how I wanted to tell her. I wasn't sure I even wanted to tell her.

I shook my head. "It's nothing for you to worry about. Can we just ignore me? Do I get a pass for being the hero?"

She laughed at that, and I relaxed.

I wanted to know what she was thinking. To understand why her heart was beating so hard. To know if that glimmer in her eye was longing for me or just fear.

"Stay here."

She disappeared, and my eyes closed again. What only felt like seconds passed and then she was there again, shutting the door behind her and scooting close with a rag in her hand.

"Here." She grabbed my hands and started toweling them off with the wet rag.

"No shower, then?"

She laughed that bright beautiful laugh. "Hush. Let me take care of you."

This woman. This brilliant, extraordinary woman. It felt like a sin to have her helping me, with that bandage on her arm.

"Lift your arms."

I did.

She pulled my shirt off and threw it in the carnage on the floor. Her hands warmed my chest, and she moved the towel to wipe the blood from my neck. Thank God I had black towels.

I rested my hand on her neck and stroked her cheek with my thumb. Her pulse raced at my touch.

Kimberly grabbed my hand and placed it in my lap. "No touching."

This time her smile widened, and she moved the rag to my cheek.

"Yes, ma'am."

Dishes clashed and the sound of yelling followed. I was too tired to check.

Kim stopped to watch the door. "Should I go down and spy?"

"I wish you'd stay."

She did. And I tried to keep my eyes open by staring at her face. Her long lashes. The little beauty mark by her eyebrow.

"Your pants need to come off too."

"Are you going to take them off me?"

She shook her head. "Off. Now."

I groaned as I peeled them off and threw them on the floor, and she motioned for me to lie down. I hadn't realized how much she had held me up till she let go and I fell into the blankets.

The weight that settled in my chest pulled me under and my eyelids closed.

"Burns, you can boss me around anytime. When are you free next?"

The bed shifted, and her lips touched my cheek. I felt warm. So warm.

"Go to sleep."

Her fingers raked through my hair.

She didn't leave. *Thank God.*

TWENTY-TWO

KIMBERLY

I awoke alone in the night. The soft pitter-patter of rain knocked on my windowsill. Not enough to satisfy our drought, but maybe enough to keep the fires at bay. A sharp pain traveled down my arm when I moved my fingers. One glance at the clock told me it was hours before it was time for me to wake, but my body stayed fully alert. I concluded it was too much adrenaline for one day.

After taking some pain pills, I made my way down the stairs. The house was quiet, and every step I took creaked the hardwood. A lamp glowed in the middle of the living room, but no one was there. The Legion must be at every exit.

By the time Aaron fell asleep, everyone had dispersed downstairs, and Presley hadn't been able to get any more information. My fix-it mode could wait until the sun came up and I wasn't groggy and alone.

I rounded the corner and met Zach, who sat with his legs propped on the dining table, nursing a drink.

"Couldn't sleep?" Zach asked without looking up at me. He was in his sparring uniform, and I wondered if he'd already gone for the night or was waiting to go.

I shook my head and grabbed a chair at the edge of the table. Zach was deep in thought. His mind seemingly elsewhere.

There were a lot of things I could ask him. I could demand to know what they talked about with Kilian. Or ask a million questions about Akira and the prophecy. I could even argue with him about what happened in the forest with Aaron.

Instead, I asked, "How's Luke?"

Zach's eyes met mine. "He's all right. He's supposed to be taking some time to rest in his room. I doubt that's what he's doing in there."

Zach seemed less confident than before, as his fingers traced the rim of his glass. They'd both been quiet when Akira appeared, but they didn't need to say anything for me to see the fear and burden that came crashing into them at that moment. We were supposed to be safe but may never be, and I still hadn't fully processed that.

"He'll be okay. He's got you guys, after all."

He smiled and then after a few seconds of silence, he spoke again. "You know you remind me a lot of Sarah."

There was a brief silence as the autumn air settled around us.

"Shit. Sorry, I just meant that . . . you're kind like she was. She was also very smart, and she loved Luke. Really truly loved him for who he was. I can tell you care about Aaron the same."

This time I didn't protest, something about the witching hour made it clear it was time to be honest.

"I do. I never thought I'd ever care about a person as much as I do him . . . it's scary."

Zach smiled. "Love is scary."

"Can I ask you something kinda personal?"

"I'll allow it." Zach took a deep breath, awaiting my heavy question. The house was still. No music. No TV.

"Why Sarah? Why just her? If the queen is obsessed with you both. Why not kill Ashley?"

I'd silently been racking my brain trying to find the code. Was Zach not worried about Ashley? Would they come for her like they did Sarah?

"Because of Luke . . . because he's good and innocent and She gets jealous . . . because She wants his innocence. Don't get me wrong, I worry about Ash, but I warned her, and she's got the family means to stay safe. Sarah didn't. The queen just wants Luke. She wants him all to herself. Luke is everything good in the world, and She needs him . . . his humanity. Not people like me."

I couldn't help but imagine Aaron. He was the spitting image of Luke at heart. Only Luke had grown up much different. He was harder. Tougher. More responsible. Aaron had never seen the pain Luke had. The thought was normally a comfort, but this time it was a knife twisting in my belly. What would the queen think of Aaron? His soul overflowed with pure light. Would She see the same thing She saw in Luke?

"People like you?" I pressed in, resting my elbows on the table.

"There are people like Luke who are meant to be good. So much so that it literally tears them apart to be anything but."

"Like Aaron."

He nodded. "Yeah, exactly. They have always been good and then there are people like me who have always been bad. It doesn't hurt me to be bad and to do bad things. It doesn't matter to me as long as my family is safe."

"You mean, to protect them, right?"

His dark eyes beamed through me. "Kim, if you knew half the things I think every day . . . what I thought of you the first time I met you. I'm confident you wouldn't like me very much."

I let that threat settle. I hadn't thought highly of them when I met them either. I was still unsure if they would freak out and kill me at the time.

"I can take it. Tell me." It was a rare occasion to get to pick Zach's brain, and something told me if I passed up the opportunity to ask, I'd lose my chance forever.

He placed his drink down, staring past me for a moment before speaking. "I thought . . . who is this annoying, naive girl coming to make my life harder? I could tell just by the way Aaron was looking at you that he was head over heels."

Butterflies circled my stomach at the thought. At the time, I'd scarcely thought of Aaron more than someone that could help me out of my poor situation. I never noticed.

He continued. "I was already thinking of what I could say to make him forget about you or where I could bury your body if he slipped up and killed you. I wanted you gone before you could cause us any more trouble."

I remembered Zach breaking Presley's chair, and now I understood the anger behind that kick and what had been brewing beneath his dark eyes. His jaw tightened as he waited for me to reply.

"I'm surprised you weren't meaner to me, then."

He grabbed his drink again, downing the rest. "I'm not really into making girls feel like shit. Even if they're going to end up fucking up my life."

"And what made you change your mind?" I kept my tone soft, though nothing Zach said had hurt my feelings. I'd always known how protective he was of his brothers.

"You don't utter a word of this to anyone." He pointed at me.

"You know I can keep a secret."

"You didn't see him before. For those two months after we changed them, Presley seemed completely fine, but Aaron just had this look on his face. He smiled but it wasn't him. I was convinced I'd really fucked him up. Truly. I know I've done a shit job at being a good role model, but I'd prefer not to fuck up my brothers and their lives. But when you left the house that day, Aaron wouldn't fucking shut up. I'd barely gotten him to speak to me and suddenly all he wanted to do was talk. Talk about you . . . school . . . everything. He was his old self again. He smiled again."

I hadn't expected to be surprised. Partly by Zach's vulnerability but also by his words. My heart ached to go back upstairs. I'd always known I'd been the wrench in Aaron's life, but I hadn't realized the good. The parts that weren't him being forced to protect me out of guilt. Even from the beginning, there was good too.

He shrugged. "I still wasn't convinced I liked you until I realized you didn't rat on me and my brothers."

I knew there was a hidden compliment in there somewhere.

"You do what you have to, to protect everyone. I think I can understand that."

"That's what makes people like me incredibly dangerous. We're selfish. I love my brothers, but it's different from Luke's love. His is . . . better."

And that's when I finally understood the way Zach saw himself. In his eyes, he'd never be a good person like he imagined Luke was. Almost as if he had to be one or the other.

"So, which type of person are you? That's the real question." Zach poured himself another glass of whiskey.

"I . . . don't know yet."

I didn't. Could I consider myself good like Luke and Aaron if I considered becoming a vampire? They were both changed against their will. A choice to turn was a choice to harm and potentially kill people. Then how could I ever be considering it? How could that be the way my heart was leaning? A life with Aaron was selfish.

But there was one thing I knew about Zach—he was the opposite of selfish. Presley came to mind next. He too might be considered a selfish person. His only real meaningful relationships were with his family members, everyone else was disposable to a certain degree.

There was a clear line in the sand between the Calem boys, and I wasn't sure what side I fell on in terms of morality.

I walked up the hardwood steps and stopped at my door. Tonight of all nights, I didn't want to be alone.

I turned my brain off and found myself standing back in Aaron's room. The glow of the TV was the only light.

He'd already turned and covered the corner of the bed. I moved in, pushing him over just enough for me to slip in.

As I reached up to pull the covers over me, his arm gripped me by the waist and hauled me close to him, cradling me from behind. Our bodies fit together effortlessly.

With his sweet, tired voice, he said, "Is this okay?"

I blushed under the cover of the dark. "Yeah."

His warmth covered every ache in my body, including my wrist. There, in the dim light, heart to heart, I knew I'd found it. The thing I had always been searching for. In Aaron's arms, I'd felt the safest I ever had. I didn't know how I'd be able to sleep with my heart beating out of my chest, but I didn't care. I wanted to savor it.

There was no more hiding. I was in love with Aaron Calem.

TWENTY-THREE

AARON

*S*he was everywhere. She was everything. She was mine. All mine. Her pulse synced with mine. Her blood was my blood, and what was mine was hers. She was mine. All mine. Mine. Mine. Mine.

My lips touched the sensitive skin on her neck, and she sighed. How long had I waited for this? How long had I wanted her? Her skin on my skin.

I pulled away to see her. Kimberly. My best friend. Her red hair sprawled across my sheets. But there was no red. No life. No smile.

Just Her. White eyes, void of any hope, staring at me with strands of snow-white hair laying on my pillow. Black blood stained Her mouth as She smiled. Her hands caught in my hair, and She beckoned me closer. Her lips were soft. They were everything. She was everything.

But why did I feel sick? Why did I feel so cold? Why was my heart not beating?

Why? Why? Why?

This wasn't right.

This wasn't how it was supposed to be.

I woke up gasping. The birds chirping outside and the light cascading in my window brought me back to reality. A dull ache pulsated behind my eyes. *Damned nightmares.*

Sleeping as a vampire wasn't as great as I remember as a human. Human me would wake up and stretch, light as a feather. Waking up now felt heavy, not just my body but my mind. I didn't remember my dream, but I felt as if I had lived a thousand lifetimes wherever I was.

All of it hit me at once. Akira. The prophecy. Biting Kim . . . Telling Kim I was in love with her. *Oh, God.*

I moved my hand to touch the other side of the bed. She was gone. Her scent still filled the room. Roses. How could I ever let this go if I kept finding myself in the same bed with her? I had to let her go now, didn't I?

I stared up at the little crack of paint where I'd thrown my tennis ball way too many times late at night while I listened to Luke pacing in his room. I replayed yesterday's events in my head. The fear of seeing Akira. The feeling of losing control of my body to save Kimberly. The voice in my head wasn't hard to convince.

I was right. I couldn't believe I was right. The Family would never stop searching for my brothers because they believed we were meant to live in some weird fantasy world where we were . . . bodyguards of a vampire queen? That sentence couldn't be real. As if the vampire thing wasn't a trip, now there was someone claiming prophecies about my brothers. It didn't feel real, but my splitting headache said otherwise.

I shot up, and my body was slow and groggy. My hands tamed my hair, and I tugged on a pair of new sweatpants and a clean shirt before heading into the hallway. The carnage I'd expected to be on the floor of my room was gone. Kimberly had cleaned it in my sleep. I sighed. More guilt.

"Aaron, how are you feeling!?" Thane came out of Presley's room holding a gaming controller. The battle music coming from the TV blasted through the hall. Presley was hot on his heels.

"I'm okay . . . groggy."

"Well, Kilian wants to see you." Thane snuck a glance at Presley.

"Is it a lecture?"

Thane scrunched his nose and held up his fingers an inch away from each other. "A teeny, tiny bit."

Presley watched me with a wide smile, not saying a word.

"What?"

"Nothing."

I shifted, fighting the annoyance of my headache coming back. "Spit it out."

"You just smell good. What is that floral scent wafting off you and your bedroom?"

My eyes narrowed. "I'll go see Kilian in a second."

Presley motioned toward the hallway. "She's in her room."

I knocked on the doorframe and greeted Kimberly, who sat on her bed next to the window. She wore that checkered dress I loved with the long sleeves and stockings. It never ceased to amaze me how she made the place look like home. It was larger than her previous dorm room, and she'd made up the difference with various colored rugs. I admired the way she made it feel special, and asked her to help me with mine.

Since her arrival, she'd helped me get pictures on my peg board. She also convinced me to buy my first ever desk calendar to help me remember my assignments. And to get a huge BFU wall banner to sit above my bed. She said to remind myself of anything that made me happy. And it did. I was finally letting go of the past. It wasn't about replacing the old ones of my mom and our childhood home. It was about making new ones, even in the worst circumstances.

She turned, and my eyes went to her wrist wrapped tightly in gauze. The sinking feeling in my stomach was back. How could we be back here?

Suddenly, I was angry. Angry at the one person I could blame. Me.

She smiled at me and moved over for me to sit. The silence grew while indie music played in the background.

"Are you okay?" The only words I could think of tumbled out of my mouth.

"Yeah, it doesn't really hurt. I've been taking some painkillers. I did need stitches, though. Luke did them."

Mom taught Luke to do stitches at a young age. Mostly because he wanted to learn, but I think she knew he'd need it someday. He had good practice with all of us growing up.

"Can I see?"

She hesitated. "Why would you want to do that?"

"Are you afraid I'll freak out?" I leaned on the bed.

"No . . . I just know you, and I know what you're going to say."

I cracked a smile I wasn't expecting. She knew me, and it felt great to be known.

"You don't want to hear me being a broody mess for the month? Is that what you're saying?"

Her eyes softened. "You told me you were sorry every day for weeks." She grabbed my hands in hers, and my heart responded.

My fingers caressed the softness of her hand. She watched me more closely than usual. Her heartbeat elevated as I ran my fingers across her warm skin to find the edge of her bandages. The gauze was rough, and I fiddled with the tape for a few seconds. Her eyes flickered from me, and she bit her lip, only watching my hands. Was she nervous? Fear took the front seat, and it gave me the answer. She feared me. Afraid I might snap.

I peeled back the bandages to reveal her bruised skin. The faintest dark spots rested next to the stitches where my teeth had ripped her flesh. It was still red and irritated, and I guessed the worst coloring of bruising was yet to come.

Saliva filled my mouth, and I swallowed. *It* remembered the taste of her blood. I was freshly full and yet, the Thing in my head was still reminiscing under the surface. Though I couldn't hear its distinct voice, I could feel it. Waiting in the back of my head. Wanting more.

"This was my choice. I know I didn't have to, but I wanted to. You saved me. I saved you. That's how it should be."

I tried to hold her gaze but the weight of it was too much. This Thing in my head was getting stronger. And my feelings for her along with it. Our proximity had the hairs on my arms raised. Every time she glanced at me, I was one step closer to kissing her. She was everything I wanted, but I couldn't have her.

"Kim, we can't do this anymore. Your blood has to be off-limits to me at all times. You're already in enough danger. We don't need to add me to the list."

"What if it's to save your life?"

"Not even then. If this Thing in my head thinks for a second there's a chance I'm going to taste your blood again . . . It's going to take it. And maybe I won't be able to stop It. So, no more blood."

She'd taken too many risks for me. Every day a piece of the girl I'd met was changing. I felt like Peter Pan dragging Wendy into the darkness of Neverland. She was never supposed to be here, but I brought her here, and like Peter, I didn't want to let go. I wanted her to stay forever.

I rewrapped the bandage tenderly over her skin.

"And we probably shouldn't . . . be kissing either. It's just making this harder and it's risky. I don't want you to choose anything because of me, and if we keep doing this, then we're just going to be doomed to repeat history over and over. I kiss you, and I can't control myself. And I can't stay away from you."

Her eyes glistened, and I wondered if I hurt her. Our argument in the forest came to mind. The words she said had punched me through the chest, even then when everything was new. Only now I knew why she'd said them. Sometimes being together made things harder. I clouded her judgment, and I wanted her head to be clear about all of it. We were already repeating the past.

"You should go to New York."

Her eyes widened. "What?"

"You shouldn't be here, Kim. This is only getting worse, and maybe if you go with Chris, then you can get out of this, and leave me and my brothers to deal with this ourselves."

She pulled her hand away. "You said you wouldn't leave."

"Technically, I'm not leaving. You are . . . or should."

She stared past me. "Chris is furious. He won't even talk to me."

"He would if you told him that we got you drunk on purpose, and you need him to come get you. I bet he'd get you the first plane out."

"I'm not doing that." She shook her head, and her pulse hammered under her skin.

I wanted to kiss her and see the smile return to her face. Kissing her always did that. But every word I said pushed her away and felt like having to pull my own heart out of my chest. But I had to. Ventricle by ventricle. Because I might be doomed . . . and I refused to let her go down with me.

Her nostrils flared. "I fail to see how me running off with Chris would make me safer than being here with you."

"Because Akira wants *us*. My brothers and me. He's not going to follow you. This might be the last chance I have to get you out. You saw how strong he was. It's nearly impossible for me to keep you safe. But Chris, I know he could look after you. Maybe I can even convince Kilian to have Skylar go with you."

If I asked my brothers for help on hiding Kimberly, they would help me. No matter what.

"Well, you can't tell me what to do." She shook her head when she said it. Her hurt was tangible.

I moved a piece of hair from her face, and everything in my chest still hurt. "I wouldn't dream of telling you what to do. I made you two promises I intend to keep. I promised I wouldn't leave you, and I meant it. I'm not going anywhere . . . but I also promised to protect you. I'm trying to keep my promise."

Her breath hitched in her throat as my hands grazed her cheeks and then fell into my lap. It was time to let go. No touching.

She sat up a little straighter. "Okay . . . I'll think about it."

She left me there on the bed while she straightened up her desk. The peonies in her vase were wilted, and she chucked them in the trash bin before continuing with wrappers and old papers. With my hand on the doorframe as I left, I wondered if that was the last bouquet I'd ever get to buy her.

Kilian waited at his desk, a book in one hand and supporting his head with the other. He barely looked up to acknowledge my presence as I sat down. He reminded me of my high school principal waiting in his chair to tell me I had detention. Which was an unfortunate curse that plagued all the Calem brothers.

This would be interesting.

I was never alone with Kilian, and that was something I did on purpose. I liked to bring a buffer, usually Zach or Luke, but I didn't pass either of them on my way to the library and wasn't in the mood to deal with Presley's carefree attitude.

"Aaron, how are you feeling?"

"Fine."

He studied me, as if trying to read my mind, and his steel-gray eyes bored into me. "Tell me what's on your mind."

"Uh, what's on my mind is that you wanted to talk to me, and I'm here waiting for you to talk to me."

His stone gaze softened. "I'm in your corner, you know? I understand you have a . . . drinking problem that caused your current plight, and I thought you might benefit in talking to someone who has . . . experience."

Was this therapy? I was *not* in the mood for that. But I answered.

"I've been doing everything I'm supposed to be doing."

"Hm," he said, closing his book for a moment and inspecting the spine.

What was his deal? I was starting to understand why Zach didn't like him.

"Has this been made easier with our help?"

"Uh, yeah, I guess . . ." I fought the urge to bolt for the door. "Can you just lecture me for a few minutes so I can go?"

This time he smiled. "You and your brothers share that same restless spirit. I wanted to express my concerns to you but also let you know I'm here to help. I don't want to further push the subject . . . but I must caution you. If you keep letting It take over, you will not be able to find your way back. I've seen many brave, honorable men fall prey to the same trap in my lifetime. I do not want the same thing to happen to you."

I was stunned by the conviction in his voice and averted my attention to the floor. "I know. I just didn't have a choice. And I felt . . . strong."

"The strength It lends you comes with a price that you are already paying for each time It seeks out your weakness, looking for the thing It wants most." The flames of the fire flickered in his eyes. "It wants you to believe It is the strong one. But It is the one that needs you. It wants what you have."

I thought back to the power I felt surging in my body when I held Akira back. Darkness pooled in my gut and the voice in my head told me everything I wanted to hear. I could keep them all safe if I just gave into It.

But the thing I remembered most wasn't that strength—it was fear. I'd been afraid I wouldn't be able to force my way out once It took control of my mind. It felt like sitting in a dark room with a TV at the far end. I knew what was happening, but my hands were tied. Nothing would budge. I screamed into the void until I heard it—her heartbeat. The soft thrum pulled me from the back of my mind and into the driver seat. It wasn't just her blood sacrificed to that Thing inside me, it was her. Her heartbeat awoke something in me that pulled me back into our best memories and reminded me how much I cared about her. That I'd do anything to keep her with me. I needed to make it back to her.

No wonder that voice in my head never shut up when I was around her.

"I want to get stronger. I have to."

It was the only way to save her and them. If using that Thing wasn't an option, then I'd need to try harder. To do whatever it took.

This time Kilian smiled, actually smiled. "You know . . . a boy once sat across from me and told me that exact thing."

I thought for a minute. "William?"

He nodded. "Yes, he was quite the ambitious one. He was a bright child who went through a tragedy. I'll leave the details for him to disclose, but he was just a child when he wanted to grow strong, just like you. I told him if he waited till he was old enough, I'd show him, and he's become stronger than I'd ever hoped."

He talked like a proud dad, his eyes faraway, as if he were reminiscing on his favorite memory. I imagined a young William pleading for Kilian's help. What kind of childhood did he have?

"You can be strong all on your own, Aaron. We'll help show you."

"How long does it take?"

Kilian shut his book and gave me his full attention. "What makes you think you are out of time?"

"Akira being here kinda speeds things along. That's what you were arguing with my brothers about, isn't it?"

"It was unexpected that a member of The Guard would expose themselves in such a manner. I'll admit I didn't account for it. That led to some disagreements, but it does not change what we are doing. This new development puts us at a greater advantage. Understanding the why behind it changes everything. We know how valuable you are."

"Let me guess . . . you're not going to elaborate."

I couldn't tell if he was talking in circles, giving me just enough information to stop me from asking questions but not enough to tell me anything. It felt a lot like all the times I'd tried talking to my older brothers.

"I've got time. Ask me. Whatever you want."

I leaned back in my chair and let the fire warm my back. "What can you tell me about the coven? The Guard? All of it. I want to know all of it."

"You're talking to the world's leading expert on the matter. I'm one of the last alive who has any information on the remaining covens."

He pointed to his book, a half-written page of that fancy writing I'd bet they used to write the Declaration of Independence. He'd been transcribing. The writing on the spines of the books stood out to me.

All labeled with various dates.

"Of the few covens left, I've been studying this one for more than three hundred years. The queen, as you know Her, was the daughter of a Chieftain in Northern Ireland more than five hundred years ago. She took over his reign after he died and was loved by many. She married shortly after. Only, She was said to have died just three years later of an unknown illness, according to Her death certificate." He leaned back in his chair, and it creaked. "There isn't much written about Her other than Her marriage and Her untimely death. Cecily Dooley was Her name. Any mention of Her disappears after that, but it's likely She was moved to a monastery to hide Her identity. I believe She inspired a few stories in Irish mythology. Tales of a woman so beautiful that young poets and musicians became enthralled with Her and they no longer cared about eating or sleeping. Their yearning for Her would bring them to an early grave."

"This is a person?"

"All of the queens were people at one time. Some believe their souls are still trapped inside their bodies, and they're just a vessel for the demon. But it's only a theory."

"If She's from Ireland, how did She end up here?"

"The first were created in Europe, but the ritual and the information spread. Once created, the queens were often smuggled from country to country for various reasons—war, shifts in power. It was not always a stable environment. Without a fully formed Guard, their dynamics become volatile. I believe She was moved sometime in the late 1800s, and they were able to interweave themselves into the fabric of New York City. Thanks to some information your brothers gave us, we were able to gain a better understanding of how they work internally. They're able to work closely with crime families as underwriters for their crimes, providing them confidence, occasional funding, and influence to carry out their criminal activities. Not that they're spotless in manner, but it explains how they've eluded detection. They're main objective is to guard Her. They do that by ensuring Her protection."

"So . . . The Guard. It's important to them."

"The Guard is the most important component that makes up these families. Queens don't pick just anyone. They'll wait centuries for their chosen to be born. Someone who is compatible with their coven."

Chosen. My older brothers were chosen before they were even born. Maybe before my mom was. What did they have that couldn't be found for centuries? What did *we* have?

"W-what about Presley and me? Akira said we were . . . practice."

"Some roles only certain people can fill. Others have more leeway. It doesn't mean you are any less important to them. Sometimes they just need . . . to feel that connection. Your relationship with your brothers is special. She felt that when She touched you."

A fact I liked to forget. That memory still didn't feel like mine. I liked to imagine it had been a dream. No way I met Her. I was still trying to convince myself She was real. She was; my brothers knew Her. Yet I couldn't wrap my head around Her being real. She might as well be a fictitious cartoon villain because, other than the impression She left on my brothers, I had no evidence of my own of Her existence. Only the blood in my veins that turned me into a monster.

He continued. "Queens will wait centuries for their Guard, and when that balance is disrupted . . . one dies, for instance, it leaves a hole. Sometimes the new can't forge with the old, and the old Guard will pass away."

He clenched his jaw as he spoke. I guessed he wasn't talking about them peacefully falling asleep.

"Why? Why do they go willingly?"

"All for Her. Because when their Guard is solidified, it's nearly impossible to find them or take them down."

Kilian's voice sped up when he talked about The Family. Like there was nothing in this world he'd rather talk about. A strange excitement in his eyes reminded me of the way Presley looked when he talked about winning poker games last year—back when they let him play.

The door opened and Luke peeked in. His hair was disheveled, and he had a bandage on his wrist. They'd been sparring. He glanced between the two of us.

"I was told I could find you here. Come on." He motioned me toward the door, and I followed.

"Don't worry. I'm here whenever you want to know more."

I nodded and prepared myself for the real lecture I was sure Luke would give me.

He led me outside where the pool had seen better days. No matter how much we cleaned it, the leaves blew in there, and whoever was supposed to be putting the chemicals in had stopped.

Luke towered over me. "How are you feeling?"

"Okay. I think. I had shit dreams, but I'm okay."

He wrapped me in a hug, and I froze. His muscles constricted, and after the shock dissolved, I melted into his shoulder and patted him a few times on the back.

I managed a muffled, "I'm okay. Really."

When he pulled away, he smiled. "I know. I . . . I'm sorry—"

"Don't do it."

"Just let me say it."

"No. I got to save you for once. We're still not anywhere close to even from all the times you've saved my ass. Can we just leave it at that?"

He crossed his arms and let out the biggest dad sigh I'd ever heard. "Fine."

Akira came to mind when I least wanted him to. My brother was meant to be a member of The Guard. Destined. He didn't fit the mold. He was too kind. Too good. What did they want with him? Why him?

"What did Kilian tell you?"

"We just talked about The Guard. Just histories and stuff."

That was enough to make the joy leak from his features. "I know you're curious and I won't tell you not to be, but you don't need to be learning that stuff. I don't want you to worry about any of this."

"I know."

I nodded, but doubt had settled in for permanent residence. I needed to know more. I needed to be ready.

"LESSONS"

PRESLEY

"Kim?" I knocked on her door. "Hello?"

The only thing I could hear was Taylor Swift's *Red* album playing. And sniffling?

"Kim, open the door," I said, waiting exactly two seconds before throwing around dramatics. "I'm going to break down your door, dude. You better open up. You know I'm totally serious."

I was a little serious.

There was a shuffling around, then she appeared, with her face red and her eyes wet from tears. An absolute snotting mess. Not her best look.

"What did he do?" It had to be my brother. No one died or anything. I mean, I guess she almost died yesterday but still. I didn't think it warranted *that* much crying. Certainly not a skipping-dinner affair.

She grabbed my shirt, pulled me inside, and shut the door behind us.

Used tissues littered her bed, and she had *The Notebook* playing on the TV. She was *really* going through it. Before plopping down on her strawberry bed spread, I moved the tissues.

"He—Aaron. He wants me to go." She wiped her melting mascara with a tissue.

I didn't have the heart to tell her it was a lost cause.

"Huh?"

"He didn't say anything to you?"

"No, of course not. No one tells me anything. I've got to find it all out myself."

It was relatively easy with Aaron. The twins were a different story.

The tears welled in her eyes again, and she tried to hide her face. "I can't stop crying. It's ridiculous. I know. I—"

"Kim"—I grabbed another tissue from her ceramic cat tissue hold-er—"pull yourself together, woman. You're Kimberly Burns. You don't cry over stupid boys. Come on, that's our rule, remember?"

She nodded, taking the tissue with her good hand. The other was wrapped in gauze.

I knew as well as she did, my girl had gotten soft. She wasn't the girl I'd met on the front steps of OBA. Aaron had that effect on people, making them weepy and caring. Some might call that sensitivity a weakness, but it looked good on Kim. She wore it like a thousand-dollar dress.

I thought back to when she'd shoved me in the car after nearly dying in that church. Her arm was wrapped up then too, but she had been more worried that I'd need a coat later.

I'd wanted to stay. To go to the church and find my brothers, knowing I'd get captured and that would be the end.

"No. That's not happening. We're sticking with the plan," she said, all fiery.

"Why?"

"Because if you go, then you're all gone and it's all over. And I can do this. I know I can. We can do this. I'm going to take care of you. I'm not good at this kind of thing, but I'll learn." Kimberly gripped the steering wheel hard. *"I promise."*

"Kim, you just met me."

"Yeah, but it doesn't matter. We're ... family."

"Yeah. Okay."

She looked so determined, with the kind of courage only brave people had. Not me. People like Luke. Or Aragorn, maybe.

"Okay." She'd nodded like she was trying to believe a little bit too.

I knew I liked Kimberly the first time I saw her on the doorstep. She was guarded, spikey all over like a little sea urchin, but add a little heat and cook up the insides, and it was a delicacy. Okay, my metaphor didn't quite make sense, but point being, my little urchin had shed all her spines, and now she had no protection from things like my brother.

This was all his fault. That's what I would run with, anyway.

"Tell me what he said."

"He said he wanted me to go to New York to be with Chris."

"Like *be* with Chris?"

"No. Yes. I don't know. It doesn't matter. I don't think I want to go. He said I should leave everything here behind. But I ..."

"You . . .?" I waited for her to speak, but she was hesitant. This whole conversation was taking too long for me, and I was already rightfully annoyed with my brother.

"I love him." Her eyes welled. "And it doesn't matter because he wants me to leave, and I couldn't tell him."

"Oh, Kim. I know you do. He's an idiot." I opened my arm for her to cry on my shoulder. Poor thing, she was being subjected to Aaron's fatal flaw. His good-boy routine was, without a doubt, the most annoying thing about him. Seriously. He was about to ruin everything, all because of his stupid conscience. He had the perfect girl and was on the verge of blowing it.

Lucky for him, his cunning, smart younger brother was more than willing to help him see the error of his ways.

Oh, was I going to make him pay for this one.

"Okay, here's what we're going to do. We're going to make him rue the day he ever mentioned leaving as an option."

"What does that accomplish?"

"He apologizes, wraps you up in his arms, and asks you to stay."

"What if he's right?"

"That's crazy talk, Kim. No. What's a safer place for you to be here than with your family?"

She wiped her eyes, and finally, her tears were stopping. "How do we do it? Make him . . . rue."

"Oh, don't worry. I can handle that part. You just try to sit in her and compose yourself. Take a bubble bath or something. Jeez. And you're not allowed to listen to this album or watch this movie anymore."

"Fine." She sniffed. "Thank you."

I smiled. "Nothing I wouldn't do for you."

I shut her door behind me and was already thinking of all the ways I could make Aaron hurt for this. Through the door, I heard the music change. She's switched it to Taylor Swift's *Midnights* album instead. I rolled my eyes and pounded on the door.

"Not better. Pick something else!"

Once the song switched to something less depressing, I let her be.

Sure, we objectively had bigger problems with the cult and Akira, but I had the superpower of compartmentalizing it all with ease. It was simple. That was a problem I could not solve, and my older brothers, per usual, were already going at that problem with a hacksaw. I had to let them. Plus, they were great at hacking at that, and I wouldn't be able to make a dent.

Kimberly and Aaron being in a fight. Now, that I could fix. That was a problem I was well-versed in because I knew them both well. It was classic. Two star-crossed lovers too afraid to admit they loved each other, so they pushed each other away. They needed me.

Their problems practically had my name spray painted all over them.

I went down to the kitchen and passed Aaron on my way for a beer.

"Can you pass me one?" Aaron said, objectively less peppy than usual.

"I'm not talking to you."

"Why, what did I do?" What didn't he do?

"Uh, I don't know, why not ask the crying girl you left upstairs?"

"She's crying?" Aaron's expression dropped. I was happy he looked utterly shocked and equally devastated at that news.

"Of course she is."

"I'll go talk to her."

"No, she doesn't want to talk to you. *I'm* bringing her dinner."

"What's going on?" Luke entered the kitchen with Zach behind him.

"Aaron made Kimberly cry." I grabbed a beer from the fridge and handed it to Zach.

"Kim never cries. What the hell did you do?" Zach gulped his beer.

"I-I just told her I didn't know if this was the safest place for her," Aaron said, his head hung low. He was already spiraling. *Good.*

"He told her to leave and go to New York," I said.

"With what's his name?" Zach snorted and chugged the rest of his beer. "Oh shit, you guys are top tier entertainment."

"I was just trying to do the right thing. I wasn't trying to make her cry." Aaron was pacing now. "Did I mess everything up?"

"Everything will be fine." Luke soothed him. "Your heart was in the right place. Maybe just give her some space."

"I just want her to choose what's best for her, not because of me."

I rolled my eyes. Little late for that.

"I-I'm going to my room." Aaron sulked away, and I went to follow and maybe pester him some more.

"Wait." Luke narrowed his eyes at me.

I raised an eyebrow, waiting for him to speak.

"I know that look. What are you going to do?"

"Leave this problem to me. I can fix this. You worry about the, uh . . . large cult problem we've got going on."

"You'll go easy on him?"

"He made her cry. Can't I let him suffer a little bit?"

He held up his fingers. "A tiny bit. Careful, though."

"Aye aye, captain."

An empty SOLO cup on the counter jogged my memory and gave me the best idea I'd ever had.

"I think I'm going to take her to the Sigma Nu party next weekend."

Zach scoffed. "I'm not letting you out of my sight."

"I guess that means you'll have to come too," I said.

"No. No way."

"Yeah, and we can just bring Will along."

"No fucking way!" Will called from the other room.

"Come on, we have to make this happen. Luke?"

"It could be good for you. Get your mind off things." Luke cleaned the kitchen, including taking a toothbrush to the oven. I think he needed the distraction too.

"We can all go," I said.

"No, someone's gotta make sure Aaron doesn't blow off the handle with whatever you're planning."

"Kilian will be here. And it's across the street."

Zach frowned. "Is this really the time?"

"It's the perfect time to spend time together. Right, Luke?"

If Luke said it, then it would happen.

He nodded, then I knew it was set.

I couldn't help myself. What could I say? Watching Aaron squirm was my favorite thing, and I needed him to learn this lesson and never have to be told again.

"Presley, this dress is too short."

"*Kim*. It's not short enough. Stop pulling it. We need him to see your legs and die a little inside. In fact, you need lotion and glitter stat."

"That's too much." She pulled her black mini dress again.

"Nope. Come on." I tossed some glitter I had in my pocket for this very occasion. She needed to be sparkling.

"Why do you have this?"

"Wouldn't you like to know. Put it on!"

She complied, mixing a little of it with her rose-scented lotion. Personally, the scent of roses made me sick, but I'd endure anything for Kim.

"Aaron will be absolutely feral when he sees you walk out of here. Even better when he won't be able to stop you walking out with me." I wrapped my arm around her and turned her toward the mirror, taking in the sight of us. Both in black, I'd painted my nails and decided black eyeliner was appropriate. She was in a painfully short spaghetti strap dress, black heels, and her hair was pin straight. I wanted her to hit him where it hurt, and I couldn't wait to see his face.

She frowned. "It's not his fault. He's just trying to protect me."

"Remember, we're set on revenge right now? No logic. We need to show him what he's going to be missing if you get on that plane."

She wasn't going. Not if I could help it.

"This seems unimportant with everything else going on." She frowned.

"If it's important to you, we consider it important. Everything is important. Even the little things. This is your future we're talking about."

"Okay." She nodded. "I'm following your lead."

"Good." I opened her door and offered my arm, which she clearly needed to walk in those heels. She wanted to go shorter, and it just wouldn't do. Even if it made her much taller than me.

Eyes were already on her. The boys in the hallway, and even a few members of The Legion, stopped to give her a double take. *Perfection*.

"Okay, we're leaving!" Zach and Will were waiting by the door with the exact same scowl.

Zach fought a smile when he saw her. Will shook his head.

Aaron waited by the entrance to the foyer with Luke. I relished it all.

His mouth dropped, and the complete awe of her washed over his face.

Oof. That one had to hurt. I actually almost felt bad. Then I remembered everything was going according to plan.

"Y-you look b-beautiful," Aaron said.

"Thanks . . ." Kimberly was going to cave. She tugged on my arm, moving toward him. It was the puppy-dog eyes—lethal to women.

"Do you want a jacket in case you get cold?" he asked.

They were full on Rose and Jack'ing it in the foyer, eyes locked with so much longing I felt dirty watching it.

"She can have mine." I pulled her away.

"Please, can we go? Let's get this over with," William grumbled while pinching the bridge of his nose. It didn't surprise me that Luke convinced them both to come. I didn't know how he did it, but I was thankful he had.

I reached up to put my arm around Kimberly and pulled her toward the door.

"Don't wait up! Have fun, Aaron."

"I feel sick," Kimberly said as we walked outside and into the cold.

I rubbed her arm. "It's part of the plan. And it's working."

"Presley, you get two hours. Tops. I'm counting. I can't believe Luke is making me do this." Zach lit up a cigarette.

"Just long enough for you to get a few drinks and relax."

He grunted. He'd been drinking less. I guessed it was because he wanted to be on full alert. Everyone was, and I was helping. Taking Kimberly to this frat party was objectively the best thing I could do to help everyone. I had to get our family back together.

What was the alternative?

Watch Aaron sulk and let Kimberly cry in her room? Let Aaron's flaw of being unselfish ruin everything while I waited around and watched my older brothers spiral out of control. No. This was good. Positive progress. Plus, fun. Win-win.

The yard was packed, and the buzz of the party pulled me in. That feeling alone made me want to stay all night. We walked through the door, and the familiar feel of the bass engulfed me.

Kimberly's heart hammered faster and faster.

"You need a drink, huh?"

"A small one." She was glued to my arm.

Everyone was looking at her. Probably shocked to see her with just me since Zach was finishing his cigarette outside with Will.

It was phase two of my mastermind plan. People talk, and they'd be talking about this. Talking about her. A few social media stories of her twirling around in that dress would circulate, and Aaron would be listening. I'd bet about a million bucks he was trying to get information right this second.

We moved toward the kitchen for beer and shots, just enough to prevent Kimberly from bolting. The house was smaller than ours and had no foyer. The front door led to the living room, and a fireplace was going in the corner. I swear every house in Blackheart had a fireplace.

After our shots, I dragged her back to the living room where people were dancing.

Chad from Sigma Nu wore an abysmal tank top despite it being like thirty degrees outside. He reached for Kim's hand. "Come on. Come play with us."

He motioned toward the beer pong table.

I pushed him away with my hand to his face. "Not interested."

I didn't acknowledge the finger he gave me as I ushered her away. He wouldn't do anything. Everyone was too afraid of my older brother, which I was used to. I'd heard whispers they thought he killed a guy and buried him somewhere on campus. It was now one of our favorite inside jokes.

We made it out to the dance floor, and I got to see only a sliver of the girl I saw on Halloween. She wasn't nearly as relaxed, but she danced with me while I twirled her around, and it was easy to make her laugh with my dancing.

She kept her eyes on the door, and I guessed she hoped her Romeo would show up.

Jess grabbed my arm in the middle of the crowd.

She was drop-dead gorgeous with long black hair and a tattoo sleeve—and taken by some loser. She gave off black-cat energy, and that was my personal poison of choice.

"Hi. I didn't know you'd be here." She hooked her arm around mine.

"Yeah, I'm here with Kim."

"Where's your brother?" she asked.

"He's being a dick so I'm teaching him a lesson and trying to get her mind off it."

"Such a gentleman." She smiled, displaying that beautiful tongue ring.

"Always. Dance with us."

"I'm waiting for Josh."

"Is he officially your boyfriend again?"

"We broke up again yesterday. But I think he forgot."

Men everywhere must be collectively losing their minds.

"Well, you'll be all warmed up for him when he gets here."

She danced with us for a little bit, and her and Kimberly got along well. I knew they would. It was all innocent fun. Okay, I might have danced *on* Jess a little bit, but it was consensual, and she was the one sticking her ass on *me*.

Josh entered the room, ending my fun.

I turned to Jess. "I can't stop staring at your lip gloss. What kind is it?"

"It's cherry."

"Can I taste?"

"Uh . . . I . . . yeah." Her heart fluttered, and her blue eyes filled with hopeful anticipation.

I leaned in like I would kiss her, meeting Josh's eyeline.

Stopping short of her lips, I wiped some lip gloss from the corner of her mouth, then licked it off my thumb.

"She was just telling me about her new lip gloss. Cherry. Very good," I said.

It wasn't.

She said nothing, her cheeks flushed red.

"Yeah, yeah, Calem." He put his arm around her shoulder and steered her away.

She would probably end up marrying that jackass and having his babies. *Tragic.*

Zach shook his head at me from across the room, and I couldn't resist shimmying over to hear his scathing opinion.

"You got something to say?" I asked.

"I'm not helping you when her boyfriend slugs you." He smirked.

"You would, you can't resist a good fight."

"You'll never learn otherwise."

"Come on, all I gotta do is fake a few tears and you'd come running." I pretended to wipe tears from my eyes. "Please, big brother. People are being mean to me."

"Shut the fuck up." He threw his empty cup at me.

"Like you don't do the same thing. I've seen you, dude."

"That's different."

"It's not. Admit it, we're the same. Only I'm more fun and better looking."

He shook his head. "Whatever. While you've been flirting, I had to send Will to save Kimberly from the herd of drunk bros in here."

"I told him if he steered them away, we could leave early."

"Genius."

"Please tell me that's a possibility."

"Yeah, I think my job is about done here, just let me get another shot and say bye to a few people."

I went to the kitchen and poured myself a shot while being entertained by the three drunk girls attempting to cook mac and cheese.

"So, you and Burns?" Chad was back, slurping his drink loudly.

"Oh, no. She's not my type. She's way too nice to me."

My taste in women consisted exclusively of girls who liked to treat me like shit. No in-between.

Besides, this wasn't an episode of the Vampire Diaries. It was to piss off my brother. There was no actual—almost—girlfriend stealing here. Not to be dramatic—it wasn't a Tuesday or Thursday—but I'd rather tear my own heart out of my chest than betray my brother. Especially over girls. Kim was more than just a girl but still. We'd never liked the same girl at the same time, but even if we had, it would never be an issue.

"So she's free, then?" he asked.

"Nope. Actually, she's engaged."

"To who?"

"My brother, Aaron."

"No way."

"Yes way. Tell all your friends to steer clear."

"I don't see a ring."

"Because she's getting it polished. That rock is huge. Needs special care."

That might have been an overstep, but I wasn't sure it mattered. My brothers hadn't said anything, but I could see the writing on the wall. Our time in Blackheart might not be as long as I'd hoped. As much as I wanted it to last, I was okay with where'd we go next, no matter how far or horrible, as long as we were all together, and that included Kimberly.

I left him to find Kimberly again, and in the hum of conversations, I caught the tail end of Will and Zach's conversation.

"This shit doesn't bother you as much as you act like it does," Will said.

"I like that the only thing they're worried about right now is how to make my brother jealous. It's fuckin' absurd. But it's how it's supposed to be for them. Easy."

I didn't have time to unpack that because I couldn't find Kimberly, but unlike my brothers, I didn't always think of the worst. Instead, I searched for the scent of rose, and it brought me out on the empty patio where she looked up at the night sky.

I pulled off my jacket to wrap around her shoulders.

"I miss him. Is that pathetic?"

"No. That's how it's supposed to be." I leaned over the deck railing, breathing in the smell of the pine.

"Aaron isn't someone I think I can live without anymore. I never thought I'd ever say that about anybody."

"Tell me, what's so great about my brother?"

"I love that he's so . . . soft. And calm. I feel hard around the edges. I don't know how to not be that way. But when I'm around him I feel like putty. Soft and moldable. It's changing me. But I like it."

"Oh, Romeo, Romeo." I chuckled.

"Stop." She smiled. "I used to think people in love were . . . well, kind of ridiculous. Now I'm ridiculous too."

"Welcome to the club."

"Thank you for tonight. It helped give me some things to think about. I think I realized a few things too. Can you take me home? My feet are killing me."

"Our chariot awaits. And by that I mean our guard dogs William and Zach will be happy to escort us. But I need you to do one more thing, which is let me carry you back in the house on my shoulder so Aaron can see. He'll hate that."

She laughed, and it echoed in the night. My job was done. If tonight didn't teach Aaron a lesson, I didn't know what would, but the light was back in Kimberly's eyes. She was giddy again and probably aching to see my brother. That was all I needed. Everything was right. If only for one night.

TWENTY-FOUR

KIMBERLY

T hink about it. He wanted me to think about it. It was a horrible idea to split up. That's what I thought. Go to New York and do what? Go to college. Let them all get recruited into the vampire cult and get themselves killed? And I would just go on pretending they didn't exist.

No. Absolutely not.

Smoke lingered in the musty car air because of Zach's cigarettes and the wildfire smoke sneaking its way into our cozy town. The fire was too far away for me to worry about, but a strong wind had set in, making it impossible to ignore. It was Friday, which meant there was a traffic jam of cars in town.

Two weeks. Two weeks with no sign of Akira or anyone else from The Family. Two weeks of me agonizing over my life's decisions. Two weeks of silence between Aaron and me.

I wanted to give myself an authentic experience of what it would be like if he wasn't in my life anymore. Only, it was impossible when every waking moment I was forced up next to him. Aaron, Presley, and I were in the back seat. This time I made Presley sit in the middle. I welcomed his warmth in contrast to the cool fall breeze outside. It was a rare occasion that we were allowed to ride in the car together.

Akira's appearance changed everything. I became aware of how naive I had been earlier in the year. The Legion weren't a threat. The danger we were in back then was nothing compared to what was happening now. The "hiding in plain sight" was much harder than it sounded. Kilian had called in more recruitments to shuffle us around and watch us from the background. If Luke was a king and Zach a knight, that meant Aaron, Presley, and I were all pawns. We all served our time on the chess board.

Everyone was training. Zach's days of sweeping floors at the theater were over. The day after Akira showed up, the twins quit. Zach was constantly there, which meant Luke needed to be there too so William didn't need to split his time. Luke still trained for resistance to Her blood. He was weaker and worn out most days, but he kept training Aaron. Even Presley was being more cooperative than usual and complained a lot less about splitting his time between the gym and the movie theater.

And then there was me. The biggest cliché. I was doomed to be the victim. I couldn't protect my newfound family. Though I had convinced Skylar to give me lessons, I just wanted to do something to make myself seem useful. My mind was never at ease. Always pulling me in two directions.

One held on to the present, to Kimberly Burns, the college girl. The orphan who would single-handedly pull herself up by her bootstraps and graduate college. All with a newfound skill of popcorn making. The girl who had finally made some good friends she'd happily carry through life with. In the last two weeks, I'd tried to find her again. I locked myself in my room at night and did all the things I used to do. I watched the same movies and read the same books. I'd pulled my hiking backpack out of the closet to pack for New York and even typed a text to Chris, but the bag went back in the closet, and I deleted the text.

The other side of me screamed and gnawed under the surface. Someone who barely thought of her schoolwork and was instead focused on what was next—beyond the brick of BFU. And that girl needed the Calem boys to be okay. It kept her up at night staring at the ceiling. Thinking. Calculating what The Family's next move might be and what she could do to help.

I wasn't sure which girl was winning the game of tug-of-war in my mind.

"I'm surprised William agreed to separate cars this time. He's usually attached to you guys at the hip." Presley's voice cut my concentration.

"He said they'd already be there by the time we got there," Luke said, lying back in the passenger seat, but his foot was tapping. It was always tapping.

"Don't get me wrong, I like having the guy around. He's not bad to look at either."

Zach drove which meant nineties rock blared from the radio.

He spoke over the music. "Presley . . . don't start with that shit right now."

"What!? Come on. I have eyes. Kim, back me up. William is hot, right?"

My cheeks went hot, and I tried not to look at Aaron leaning forward and staring daggers at Presley. William was attractive. That was a fact, but I honestly hadn't given it another thought since we'd suspected him a vampire in the spring.

"Well . . . uh . . . yeah, I guess so."

I felt guilty for admitting it. Though, I had no reason to. Aaron and I weren't together, and he'd made it very clear we should go our separate ways.

"Sorry, Pres, he's way too old for you . . . and for Kim, for that matter," Luke said matter-of-factly but with a softness in his voice.

"I'm right here, guys," Aaron said.

This time Zach turned to Luke. "Uh, yeah . . . too old, and, I don't know . . . he tried to kill us all, and he's Legion. What are we even talking about right now?"

Luke held up his hands. "I'm just saying, I don't approve."

Zach one-handed the steering wheel while he pulled a cigarette and lighter from his pocket. In a flash, the lighter clicked and he pulled in a long drag. It was his second cigarette in ten minutes.

Presley snickered in the back seat as the back-and-forth continued. He nudged, which confirmed my suspicion that he wanted to get a rise out of everyone and lighten the mood.

"You're right. Sorry, Aaron, I wasn't being a bro. Say, I've been meaning to ask, how does the whole vampire-human thing work for you and Kim? There's got to be some interesting kinky biting action going on there."

I sucked in a breath before the chaos ran loose, knowing I didn't need to say a single word because the boys would do enough talking.

"Presley!" Luke and Aaron said at virtually the same time.

"Right, right, I forgot you guys have that totally platonic thing going on right now. Maybe you wouldn't care if she dates someone else, then? Maybe I should tell Will she's free game? Or, hey, maybe I'll steal her."

Presley winked at me. I'd told him everything. He'd come in my room to check on me when I skipped dinner, and to my own disdain, I couldn't hold back the tears when I told him what Aaron said. I didn't want to cry. I didn't even know why I did. I knew the day would come. I should be thankful Aaron was smart enough to say what needed to be said. To do the thing I knew needed to be done. It should have been a relief. But I kept crying about it, and that made me mad. Who replaced all the logic in my brain and left me with all these . . . feelings?

Aaron shook Luke's seat from behind. "Luke, make him stop."

Luke turned, still serene and calm like he'd done it a million times. "What did I say about making girls feel uncomfortable?"

"You're right. Sorry, Kim." Presley batted his eyelashes at me.

"What about me!?" Aaron said.

"Oops, I missed one. Sorry, Aaron." Presley snickered and turned his attention back to Zach. "Hey, can I paint your nails?"

"Does it look like this is a good time, Pres? I'm driving."

Presley leaned over the armrest. "Come on, you said I could, and I brought it with me."

"Paint Luke's nails."

Luke smiled, holding up his hand with black nail polish. "Already done."

"Aaron, then."

"No way. We've got beef right now."

"No," Zach said.

"But you promised."

"Will you shut up if I do?"

"For at least five minutes."

"Fine." Zach swerved the car while he steered with his cigarette hand and moved the other behind the seat. "You get one hand."

I marveled at Presley's ability to wrangle his brothers. On the surface, it was purely unhinged behavior, but he knew his brothers well and exactly how to help them with their stress levels. Except for maybe Aaron.

It wasn't long after Presley finished painting Zach's nails and filling the car up with the stench of nail polish that Zach turned into the gym parking lot. There was no warning and I fell into Presley, pushing him into Aaron.

"Everyone out of the fucking car."

Before I could open my door, Presley had crawled out the other side and was at my door.

He opened it with a cunning grin. "For you, my lady."

I accepted and straightened the oversized T-shirt I wore over my leggings. He grabbed my hand and kissed it and then wrapped his arm snuggly around my shoulder. I was thankful I'd chosen my sneakers because of the height difference.

Zach shook his head and rolled his eyes before throwing his cigarette in the dirt. "You're all giving me a fucking headache."

The laughter that fluttered in my chest surprised me. The first laugh I'd had in those two weeks. Presley was trying to make Aaron jealous. And judging from the scowl on Aaron's face, it worked. I'd be lying if I'd said that didn't make me a little happy.

Aaron was getting good. An unending determination radiated from him as he dodged Luke's swing and shuffled his feet. He grinned, enjoying the challenge. Long gone was the nervous, unsure boy who followed every whim. No, Aaron had matured, that much I could see. With that maturity came a confidence that only made his steps more solid.

Everything he learned brought me comfort. And he looked pretty good in the tight shirt and basketball shorts.

Heat rose in my cheeks as he danced around Luke with a smile plastered on his face. With one motion, he ducked around Luke's punch and landed his own across Luke's jaw.

He jumped up. "I finally got you!"

Hair in his eyes, Aaron spotted me watching him from across the room, and Luke tackled him to the ground. They laughed as Luke pulled him back to his feet.

"Distracted?"

"Yeah, sorry."

"Alright, I think that's it for me, anyway. I've got a meeting with Kilian." Luke ran his hands through his hair.

"Did you say home? Because I want to go too. I'm over this." Presley hung upside down from the pullup bar; he'd been done sparring with

Thane for thirty minutes and was having trouble entertaining himself. I'd occupied most of my time with homework.

"Alright, fine." Zach pulled away from William and left the ring.

"I think I want to stay for a little bit . . . if that's okay, Thane?" Aaron said.

"Hell yeah, let's do some drills!" Thane was naturally full of energy and swaying on his feet at the mention of more training. Aaron, Presley, and Thane had become their own little club. They were always together talking about training or places Thane had been.

It all felt right. Everything was falling in line for them. I'd heard whispers about the future. Kilian had made plans that spanned twenty years at a time. Blackheart was just temporary, and every day they took one step out the door, and I felt . . . alone—a side quest on their bigger story. I didn't belong in their world.

As everyone packed up to leave, Aaron took a seat next to me.

"You should stay."

He meant the gym. But it still made the butterflies flutter in my stomach.

"No, I've got stuff to do."

"Stuff sounds important." He smiled, knowing it would make me smile.

I'd made a fatal mistake. Aaron Calem was my kryptonite. He'd found an undeniable way around my cold shoulder—bugging me until I cracked a smile.

Couldn't he just let me be miserable?

"So important."

"What if I told you staying would be infinitely more fun than being at the house?"

He didn't need to convince me, I already knew that.

"Let me guess, because you'll be here?" I kept my eyes on the crisp pages of my textbook.

"Totally. And maybe we can get you some ice cream on the way home? Your favorite . . . orange sherbet?"

Food must have been the way to his heart when he was human because he'd offered to cook me everything under the sun. Which I replied by thanking him and declining. I did miss his grilled cheese sandwiches, though.

"Ignore him, Kim. I can get you that sherbet, and you can eat it in my room. I've got a sweet bedspread that's way comfier than Aaron's."

Aaron gritted his teeth, and I swear I heard him growl. "You're pushin' it, Pres."

He put his hands in the air and patted Aaron's shoulder on the way out. "Love you, brother!"

I stayed, but it didn't have anything to do with Aaron in his tight shirt or the fact he wanted me there. No. It was quiet and perfect for studying. I had a big test coming up and it gave me time to make flash cards. After all, that's what I should have been focusing on. If I was going to be college-girl Kimberly, that meant refocusing.

Skylar sat next to me, with her hair pinned up at her ears by the sparkly barrette I let her borrow, while I ate my dinner. A cold-cut sandwich from the deli in town.

"Thanks for the sandwich. You didn't have to do that."

"I did. You need to eat." She watched Thane and Aaron spar as closely as I did.

Skylar's calm demeanor had become my new favorite thing. She was sure of everything. When asked if she wanted to go or to stay, she'd replied immediately.

I tuned into the boys' conversation. "Now, what to be careful of . . . not only do you need to be in control of their arms, your main objective in a fight is to keep them from grabbing and biting you. Only the venom in our teeth will pierce skin. Once your opponent loses blood, you will be able to pierce their skin with other objects. Our bones stay solid, but our skin can be torn." He tapped Aaron in the chest. "Always protect your head, but more importantly . . . your heart. You must have blood in your heart."

Aaron nodded, and I was thankful. That's the information I wanted him to know. He had all the right people to guide him. Thane would protect him. I trusted that.

I tried to focus again on my book and ignore the ache in my chest as they continued sparring.

After another half hour passed, and Thane's voice echoed in the empty building. "Kim, do you want to learn anything?"

Thane vibrated with energy despite having been pinned to the ground by Aaron.

Skylar shook her head. "Thane. Don't. Her wrist is still recovering."

"What? I'll be careful. I've heard you know some moves, let's see them." He grabbed striking pads.

"No, Skylar's right. You shouldn't." Aaron looked at me like a lost child with nothing but pity and worry.

Suddenly, I was hot all over. I didn't want to hear that word ever again. I slammed my book shut. "No, I think that sounds great, actually."

I moved into the ring and flexed my hand. I'd just had my stitches taken out and was way too sore to hit the bag, but I could go through the motions and move through his instructions.

Skylar and Aaron stayed at the edge of the ring while Thane ran me through a few moves. Most I had forgotten, but his teaching jogged my memory of my classes at the W. It was like riding a bike. All the muscle memory was still there. We danced around each other playfully for a few minutes.

Just when I was starting to loosen up and get into a rhythm, Thane moved around me too fast, and my head careened into his shoulder. The pain rocked me back to my heels, and I covered my eye from the sharp pain.

A string of cuss words followed, not by me.

But Aaron was there before I could move, with his arm protectively around my waist, and his soft scent wrapped me in comfort. His warm-sunlight eyes greeted me, and he touched my face with urgency. "Are you okay?"

Before I could answer, the darkness pooled into his irises. The tension building in his shoulders was directed at Thane.

"Aaron, it's okay. It was an accident," I said as I wiped away what I thought was my nose running, but a small smudge of blood stained my hand.

Thane was next to us, checking on me. Too close.

"I'm so sorry. I just slipped."

But Aaron was gone.

He grabbed Thane by his shirt and took him to the ground hard enough to crack the beams underneath us, and Skylar held me up and pulled me away from their scuffle.

"Sorry isn't good enough."

Aaron pinned one of Thane's arms under his leg and used his hands to immobilize Thane with ease. His fingers dug deep into his skin. He went for Thane's neck, spewing black blood over the floor.

Skylar and I rushed over to pull him off.

"Stop! I'm okay." I tried prying Aaron's stone arms from Thane's neck.

"He could have given you another concussion." He stopped, his eyes still hungry with rage and destruction.

"I'm okay." I leaned in, rubbing his back. I probably should have felt more scared than I did.

No matter which way Thane thrashed for leverage, Aaron was stronger.

Aaron leaned closer, with his thumb and pointer finger nestled under Thane's jaw. "There better not be a next time."

"Come on." Skylar grabbed Aaron, using all her strength to get him to his feet. Then she went to work helping Thane recover. It was the first time I'd seen her even slightly frazzled. She used her jacket to cover Thane's neck while he comforted her like she was an overbearing mother and he was a child who'd just gotten a papercut.

I steadied Aaron with both hands. As soon as the warmth returned to his eyes, he stumbled into me.

I called for Skylar, unable to hold him up on my own. I must have appeared terrified because she soothed me.

"He'll be fine. We just need to get him home. Both of them."

Thane immediately took up Aaron's other side as he became dead-weight.

"No, Thane. I can help."

He shook his head and smiled. "Nah, I got him. He's kind of the ball to my chain."

"What did I just do?" Aaron rubbed his eyes, still not registering the black blood smeared on his clothes.

"Don't worry about it, brother, it's all right," Thane said.

He mouthed his apologies to me as they headed for the door.

I nodded in acceptance, but my face felt hot where I'd been hit. It would bruise. For reasons I didn't understand, Chelsea came to mind. She'd worry. How was I going to explain yet another injury to her? I couldn't tell her the real reason. Being a human in a vampire's world was dangerous, and it didn't matter how protected I was. Somehow, I always ended up in the crossfire.

TWENTY-FIVE

AARON

"You should take Kimberly to homecoming," Luke said. Before last night, I'd been enthused by the idea. I was willing to try anything to get her to talk to me again. Only, now she was injured again, and I'd gone feral in front of her. Not great topics.

I'd explicitly gone out of my way to prevent Zach from finding out what happened at the gym last night. He was in a shit mood, and I didn't want to be the thing that pushed him over the edge. Luke, I told right away, and Presley . . . Presley was just good at finding out things he wasn't supposed to. I was surprised when he didn't blackmail me to keep the secret.

He'd mentioned taking care of Kim in his room, and I had to have Luke put an end to his fake flirting before I accidentally killed him in a fit of rage. Ever since that day with Akira, I couldn't trust myself anymore. That Thing was too close to the front of my mind, and now I had to evaluate if I'd kill my little brother if he took one of his jokes a little far. I knew he was joking, and even though it was annoying as hell—okay, I was a little jealous—the real me would never let that stuff get under my skin. But the monster in me was prepared to rip someone's heart out for touching her.

I'd profusely apologized to Thane when it all came rushing back. It was an accident. He took it like a champ and told me to forget about it.

I wish I could.

I'd tried to apologize to Kimberly too but like every night since Akira, she'd cut me off by shutting her bedroom door in my face. Of all the things happening in my life, her not talking to me was bothering me the most. I was a complete ass for admitting it, but Luke was constantly telling me to focus on school and the future when I brought up anything to do with The Family.

He'd say, "Think about five years from now. What do you want to be doing?"

And I'd say, "I just want to not be dead . . ."

And then I'd think for another minute and add, "I want us all to not be dead."

He'd just sigh and tell me to think of more things.

Homecoming could now be scratched off the list. The whole stadium was painted in deep green and white. Every inch of the bleachers was filled for home and away. We were safe. For the first time in weeks, we weren't sandwiched between my older brothers.

Presley busied himself by being my buffer, sitting between Kim and me, talking nonstop.

First, it was his thousandth mascot story. Then, it was a tangent about how he thought the fraternities and sororities needed to have some huge festival in the spring. He had all these ridiculous ideas, but she listened to all of them with steady enthusiasm, laughing and giggling. Proving the fact *I* was the third wheel and, once again, I was in danger of killing my little brother.

If I had a moment alone with her, maybe she'd talk with me. We were still friends, right? Or did she hate me and never want to talk to me again? I couldn't figure it out no matter how many nights I spent staring up at the ceiling. I couldn't let things end like this.

Presley slurped his monstrosity of a cocktail he'd snuck into the game. His BFU jersey swallowed him, and he'd stolen one of Luke's hats and put it on backward.

"Pres, did you down that entire thing?" I asked.

"Possibly. Maybe. No, wait. Yes."

He was drunk, and I wanted to be too, but I needed to be alert, just in case. I think Presley was having party withdrawals. We were the only frat that didn't put up a tent for homecoming. Zach and Luke had to make their rounds to all the tailgating parties to save face.

"Do you guys ever think there are other universes out there where we are allowed to just be ourselves and do whatever we want?" Presley said, wrapping Kimberly and me in his arms. "I'd want us to all be together."

"We're together now," Kimberly said.

"I know. I know. I just want this to last forever." Presley turned and rubbed his face on mine. "I love you, man. Even if I'm still mad at you for trying to break up our happy family."

"Jeez." I pulled away and pulled the cup out of his hands. "I love you too, but no more drinks for you."

"Halftime is about to start! Zach wants me to meet up with them over by the entrance. I'll be right back." Presley shot to his feet. "Don't worry, I'll be fine."

"Skylar, can you go with him? Please?" Kimberly was watching him with worried eyes.

She agreed despite the hesitation and followed Presley with a sigh. I guessed she was probably cursing Dom under her breath for offering himself up for extra protection detail for the twins due to the crowds.

"You have the coolest hair! Do you do it yourself? You have to teach me. Start right now from start to finish. Tell me every single step," Presley said as they descended the stairs.

I whistled to Thane who was a few seats away. They preferred to stay by the exits. He gave me a thumbs-up. Presley was really drunk, and I needed someone who knew how to handle him from point A to B.

I stole a glance at her. Her red hair stood out in the cloudy November sky. Half of it was pulled up and a few tendrils framed her face. Her lips were flushed with a vivid red. The space between us felt hollow. I could live with being friends. That was better than being nothing. Minutes passed as I struggled to string a sentence together. Every second that passed, she felt farther and farther away. Maybe that's what I was supposed to do . . . let her go.

"And you say I talk a lot." Akira's voice was next to me. He leaned against the bleachers with popcorn in his hands. He chomped a few pieces while the crowd cheered around us and I wondered how he was able to do that without throwing up. "I thought he'd never leave."

Every muscle tightened, and I gripped Kim's wrist.

"Where are you gonna go?" Akira smiled. "No one's looking at us right now."

He was right. The crowd thinned in anticipation for halftime, and my brothers were across the field. Of course, I sent our last bit of help away.

"Kimberly, go," I said.

"No."

I knew she wouldn't.

"Yeah, Kimberly, stay." Akira's arm was around my shoulder with his hand inches from Kimberly. "I doubt you could flinch before I'm able to drop you. Plus . . . it's game day. Woo!!"

Akira threw a few pieces of popcorn in the air as our team scored a touchdown.

"I see this isn't some casual fling. You really care about this girl." Akira squeezed my shoulder. His breath was too close to my ear. "Maybe, I'll even let her live."

I blinked and then he was next to her. Had he used his mind control? We were in trouble.

He grabbed her hand. "Such beautiful delicate hands. Hm, I've seen better."

She yelped as he squeezed her fingers. A second was all it took for me to see red. Red everywhere. I stood up. Ready for a fight. Guard be damned. As for the people in the bleachers around us, I wasn't opposed to a show.

He leaned over, put his hand on my knee, then I was sitting—not my doing.

"I forgot you were the crazy one. My bad. Look, she's fine." Akira kissed her hand, and she yanked it away.

"What do you want?" I said through clenched teeth.

"I need you to come with me. Alone. I can't risk Kilian seeing me here." Akira surveyed the crowd. "Say, Kimmy, did you like my gift I gave you last time we were here?"

The color drained from her cheeks. "You . . . you were the mascot."

"Yep. What a blast! You college kids really know how to party."

This was bad. He had the upper hand and likely some plan.

Kimberly tried to wriggle his hand off her knee. "He's not going. Right, Aaron?"

I shouldn't, but if I had the opportunity to get him to take his hand off her, I needed to take it.

He sighed. "You're going to make me do the thing? Fine. If you don't, I'll snap her neck. Okay, now will you come with me?"

"Kim, stay here." I stood, and she grabbed my arm.

"Aaron. No. Don't."

The desperation in her voice was like a sedative shot into my vein. It hit with enough force to knock me right on my ass. But it was her or me. So, it had to be me.

"I'll be right back. I promise."

"Don't go for help. Or, you know. Death," Akira said while he gripped my arm and pulled me down the bleachers. Everything was a blur. He had all the control. He led me to a gate underneath the bleachers—he'd already broken the lock—then he shut us inside.

"You gonna kill me . . . or are you going to talk me to death like last time?"

Maybe he wanted to after last time.

I waited as he sauntered toward me. He could pass as a student with the clothes he had on. Baggy black jeans and a leather jacket.

"Let me guess what they told you . . . we're all liars . . . manipulators." He pushed his hand into one of the steel beams, and the metal creaked and tore in his grasp. "But how could that be true? I'm strong enough to take all of you home right now but I won't because I want to wait till you're ready to come home."

Home. The way he said it tickled my spine. He truly believed—in his own twisted way—we were family.

He grabbed me by the collar and pushed me against the beam. Everything was still blurry.

"What about your older brothers? All we were doing was protecting them. We helped them so they never had to experience any of the hurt of our world. We shielded them."

"To manipulate them," I spat.

"No. No. Because they're family. They are special. Just like you." He leaned in closer to my face. "You of all people know how important family is, don't you?"

I said nothing. My body stayed firmly pressed against the beam. The way he carried himself mirrored Zach's cold stare, and the desperation was an echo of Luke. That look on his face in the church. The way he talked about Her . . .

"Loyalty and family values. That's what you'll find. What does The Legion value except our demise . . . revenge? Most Legion members are filled with hate. That's all they know. But you see it . . . the holes in their armor. They want what we have. They're weak because they cannot fully work together like family."

He grabbed my hand and held it to his chest with a wild fierceness in his eyes. "But we're already bonded. Can't you feel it? It's Her."

I pulled away, but his fingers dug into the flesh in my palm. "It's all love for Her, and when you meet Her, you'll finally understand."

"Stop."

"Don't push it away. Tell me you don't feel it even now? The connection between you and me . . . The Family . . . Her."

I swallowed. I wanted to punch him, but another part of me knew exactly what he was talking about. It was a feeling that couldn't be explained in any human capacity. It felt like a strong rope tied to my heart, pulling at every mention of Her. I should have hated him. But I didn't. He felt like someone I knew—a long-lost relative.

He craned his ear to the side with a chuckle. "She didn't listen. She went for help."

"Yeah, she does that."

He released me and straightened his jacket. "You can't trust them. You know I'm right."

In the blink of an eye, Akira was on the ground, and Luke towered over him.

"There you are. Finally, I can get in a word with just the three of us."

"What did he say to you?" Luke growled. He was a hulking mass compared to Akira.

I was taken aback by the anger in Luke's features. A stark contrast to the faraway state of shock when we'd first met Akira in the forest.

Akira popped up and dusted off his jacket. "Oh, you know, just family stuff."

"I'm going to kill you." Luke moved forward.

"You and I both know that's not true." Akira rolled his eyes. "Luke, you're tired. I can tell how run down you are. You need rest. We can help."

Luke stepped back. There was real fear filling the air between us.

The sounds of drumming and tubas echoed in the mountain air. Another world rested beyond the bleachers.

"Don't worry, I'm not here to mess with your memories. Just deliver a loving message . . . She misses you."

Luke's body stilled and his jaw clenched.

"She's devastated without you."

"Don't."

"Luke, I know how you feel about Her. You think you're the only one that's had a taste of Her blood? I've had just a fraction of what you've had. I can only imagine how you feel being away from Her. Actually, I don't need to imagine. I can feel it. Your pain has been tormenting me every day since you left. I don't know how you stand it . . . but I guess it affects us all differently."

Luke didn't deny it. His chest heaved.

He put his hands on Luke's shoulders. "This place has nothing for you. You know it. I know it. This isn't where you're meant to be. Why do you think no matter how hard you try, you can't escape that feeling? Because you're working toward something impossible."

We were fucked.

I grabbed Luke's arm. "Luke, come on."

"Yeah, come on. Let's go back. Right now. We can leave the others here. She just wants you home." Akira pulled a plastic bag from his pocket. It was a blood bag filled with black blood.

He moved it in front of Luke's face. "You can have this right now. Just come with me."

"Luke! He's lying!"

My words fell on deaf ears; like a dog with a ball, his eyes were trained on the bag, watching every splash of the black liquid.

"This is your chance to be the best big brother. Save your family. Do that sacrificial martyr shit you love and still get exactly what you want. What your body is craving."

There was a shuffling of feet and voices coming toward us. Help was on the way, but with the crowd, it was slower than I wanted.

I squeezed Luke's shoulder. "Think about all the training you did. Don't let it be for nothing. You're not Hers . . . you're my brother."

Luke turned, and I finally saw it. The mirror. Not in size or looks but in every other way possible, we were the same. Only his inner demons were stronger than mine.

Akira's gaze poured through me. "You're going to love Her. One day soon you'll understand. You'll never want anyone else . . . or anything."

"No. He's never going to meet Her. And I'm not going with you." Luke's voice was stronger this time.

The boredom returned to Akira's face, and he frowned. "You guys are starting to piss me off. I'm trying everything to make this easy for you. I've been nice. I can't guarantee it will continue to be that way."

Akira's threat sunk into my stomach like a stone.

Luke didn't budge. "I'm ready when you are."

A wicked smile snuck onto Akira's lips, and he grabbed the back of Luke's neck to whisper in his ear, and I couldn't make out the words.

Akira pushed him away, and in a second, he disappeared into the crowd.

"What was that? What did he say?"

His stare hardened while locked on the place Akira left. There was a give in his voice, and his eyes glistened. "Nothing."

TWENTY-SIX

AARON

"She's not going to be able to hide that shiner for long," Presley said, with his legs dangling over the counter as we watched Kimberly disappear to get the mop and bucket for the restrooms. I tried not to curse at his lack of help with closing duties. "Zach is going to flip his shit. Please, I want to be there when he sees it."

"What can I do to help? Kimberly won't let me apologize to her any more," Thane said, standing next to us in the lobby.

"You don't have to do anything. It was an accident," I reassured him.

"I don't know. Maybe you should grovel at her feet some more. She's been having a rough time." Presley snickered.

He wasn't wrong.

In less than a year, she'd gained a black eye, at least four bite marks, stitches, and a concussion. If she wasn't injured, she was sick. Sick from the party I threw and made her come to. The common denominator in these issues was me.

The scattering of popcorn and stale candy across the floor paled in comparison to the cataclysm of my life. The twins were freaked. Zach was back to being protective of Luke and refused to go anywhere without him. And The Legion reeled from their lack of defense. Their explanation was shit, and tensions were high. Work brought me little relief. The only good thing I had going was fall recess was later this week, and I had only one class today. Work and home were the only places I felt safe . . . the only places I could keep her safe. But Kimberly was still mad at me. Why else was she still not saying anything?

We'd spoken briefly when the others reached us under the bleachers, but that was days ago. Her not wanting me to die didn't mean much of anything. Akira was closing in, and I didn't know how much time I had with her.

"I can do that! I'll clean the bathrooms." My voice echoed in the empty theater.

Our manager loved Kimberly, and I was pretty sure that was the only reason we could close together.

"No, I got it." Kimberly pushed the bucket and broom through the door to the men's restroom. Like I was some random coworker she'd never cared about. Some random person she'd never kissed. Her bandages were gone, but I knew her wrist still had to hurt.

"She's pissed at you, dude." Presley was lying on the counter, and I pushed him off.

"I've gathered that, Pres."

"She told me everything you said. It was pretty harsh."

"She told you everything?"

"Uh, yeah, Kim and I are besties."

I hung my head. "How do I fix it? I can't take the silent treatment anymore. Two weeks is way too long."

I needed something to happen. Closure, pain, whatever awaited me. It was a special kind of hell having been close to her, only to watch her shut me out of her life like it was nothing. It was justified. I'd hurt her in more ways than one.

"Yeah, well sending her to New York would feel a lot worse than that."

"I just said it was a good option!"

"You basically friend-zoned her and told her to get as far away from you as possible."

"Is that what she thinks?!"

He shrugged.

"Help me!" I grabbed his shoulders and shook him.

"Why don't you guys catch a movie together? What's her favorite one?" Thane sounded eager.

I thought for a minute. "Well, she loves *The Princess Bride*."

"Perfect. I can convince Sky to watch a movie with me and Presley." Thane smiled.

Presley hit his hands on the counter. "On it! You just got to get her to agree to stay here in the same theater with you for a few hours."

Alone time with Kimberly could work. Surely I could get something out of her.

Like a creep, I walked into the bathroom while she cleaned. The psychedelic tile patterns always hurt my brain, and the smell of bleach was enough to take down a horse.

"Hey."

"Hey." She kept her eyes on her task, but she struggled to move the broom with her nondominant hand.

"I'm begging you to let me clean the floor."

"I can do it."

"Kim." I grabbed the broom handle, and she stopped. "Please talk to me before I implode."

She smiled, but it did nothing to dissolve the worry lines in her forehead. "Aaron. I'm trying to make this easier for the both of us."

I stepped closer to her. "I know, but I don't want easy. And you're obviously way better at staying away from me than I am of you. I'm sorry . . . for so many things."

She stared at the floor. "I was just trying to . . . make this hurt less."

It was worse than I thought. She pitied me. I was sure of it. She'd only stayed around these last two weeks because I wouldn't stop bugging her.

I stepped in closer and put my hand on the wall above her head. "I think this is going to rip my heart out full and proper. Whether that's today or tomorrow, you're gonna leave a scar, Burns. But I need you to go ahead and get it over with because I can't take it anymore."

Her eyes glistened, and the redness that gathered in the whites made the blue brighter.

I loved her. I had to make this easier for her. How?

"Kim, I'm the entire reason all this horrible stuff has happened to you. Maybe you need to hate me . . . because I'm the person who ruined your life."

That day I saw her in the cafeteria, I could have just let her get her food. I'd seen her. She was alive. But it wasn't enough for me because seeing her was the hope I needed. Only now was I able to finally understand how selfish I'd been. Because now that I loved her, I could see the burden I'd placed on her from the beginning. The hard choices I made her make, and the ones she still had to make because of me.

She shook her head and leaned back into the wall. "You didn't ruin my life."

"I did, and you should hate me for it."

Her eyes hardened. "I should, shouldn't I? Seems like there's a lot of things I should and shouldn't be doing. Go ahead. Tell me what it is you want me to say here."

I'd broken through the wall. She was finally fighting with me.

"Say you hate me. Tell me all the ways I messed up."

"I'm not doing that."

Why was she still trying to spare me?

"You have to. I need you to tell me."

"Why?"

"Because. I want to hear you say it."

"You . . . want me to . . ."

"Yes."

I couldn't tell what emotion flashed across her face. Her ironclad wall worked overtime on keeping me out and hiding her feelings.

"Fine. We were never supposed to meet. I was never supposed to be a part of your life. You shouldn't have talked to me. We shouldn't have been friends. We shouldn't have been in that church together, and we definitely shouldn't have kissed. Without you, I would have the highest grade point average. I would be safe and sound in my bed, and no one would be trying to kill me."

"Good. Now, come on. Just say you hate me and tell me to leave you alone. Break my heart, right here." I moved in closer.

I needed her to say it. Then I could stop thinking about her and put her on that plane and never look back. I couldn't wait any longer for the inevitable pain and disappointment of losing her. Not when I loved her like this.

"No."

Was she going to make me beg and make a bigger fool of myself than I already had?

I towered over her, and she moved her chin up to meet my eyeline.

"Why not?"

"I-I can't . . . I can't hate you, Aaron."

"Why?"

I expected her to argue with me again, but instead, she let out a breath. A long slow breath that raised the hairs on my arm. Her lips were perfectly plump and covered in gloss.

Oh.

She blinked a few times and squared her shoulders. She was definitely looking at mine too. And for a split second, I wondered . . . did she love me too?

Neither of us were moving, and I should, but she was staring at me. Her pulse grew louder until I could practically hear it echoing in the bathroom.

She couldn't. There was no way.

"Uh, am I interrupting?"

Presley was leaning up against the wall with a bottle of cleaner and a rag in hand.

I wanted to scream, *Yes you fuckin' are*!

"No. Nothing." Kimberly huffed and moved under my arm and back toward the lobby.

I had to resist the urge to shake him much harder this time. "I'm going to kill you for that."

"I could hear you guys arguing!"

"We were working it out."

"Don't worry. I'll fix it. I'll finish cleaning. I already set up your guys' movie . . . in the VIP room. Can we be even now?"

He was trying, and he wouldn't be if he didn't care.

I sighed. "Fine."

Finally, alone. Thane, Skylar, and Presley were in the theater with the longest run time, hoping they'd get the hint. Skylar reluctantly agreed to the plan despite it interrupting her time at home reading.

Kimberly chewed another piece of sour candy. Her hair was pulled into a messy ponytail, and despite being at school all day and then working, her eyeliner was untouched. She leaned into the red velvet recliner that we shared. The only good thing about working at the theater was getting an all-access pass to the VIP room. The only place with spacious recliners and a foldable table. It was a smaller theater with only ten tables, and we had the whole room to ourselves.

She'd agreed to stay for a movie, but only after Presley assured her it was worth it and Skylar said she needed some relaxation. Our fallout from the bathroom lingered in the air.

"What are we watching?"

"Oh, only your favorite. *The Princess Bride*."

"What?! No way." Her eyes lit up in that way I loved, but it was muted compared to its usual brilliance.

"Yep. Made it happen just for you."

"And it's not even my birthday."

I admired her long lashes and the warmth in her cheeks.

She couldn't love me . . . but what if she did?

I'd never seen it as a real possibility. Sure, I'd imagined, but I imagined a lot of things. Like how beautiful she'd look in a wedding dress with my ring on her finger. Or all the ways I could burn up the time in eternity to make her eyes light up and see her smile. Those were things I never thought would come true. Only things I wanted.

She did kiss me—more than once—but wanting to kiss me didn't mean she loved me.

Kimberly side-eyed me. "You're doing it again. You're giving me that look."

"Can you blame me? You're nice to look at."

Why was I flirting? It was like a reflex.

A smile caught in the corner of her mouth. *Noted.*

"Are you going to tell me what to do some more, or are you just trying to seduce me?"

She was flirting. Flirting didn't mean love, but combined with everything else in our situation, it might. The possibility struck a match and lit up everything I'd hidden away and refused to let myself believe could happen.

I raised a brow, taunting her. "Seducing you? Never. I'm a gentleman."

"Right . . . sure." She crossed her arms and chewed her bottom lip.

I tried to refocus, but we were watching a love story, and they were kissing.

It was a dangerous game. I'd been wrong before.

"You know everything now, Burns?"

"Definitely." She said it so matter-of-factly.

Maybe she did love me, and if she did, I had to know, and there was only one way to ask her.

"You know . . . I do need you to tell me one more thing and then we can drop this."

She flipped her hair over her shoulder and raised her brows. "Oh? What's that?"

In the glow of the theater screen, I held out my heart to her, hoping and fearing the words.

But I had to know.

"Do you love me?"

Her heart skipped, and her lips parted. "What?"

Our shoulders were touching. Burning. She leaned into me. Despite being in the theater with the best surround sound in the county, all I could hear was the sound of her heartbeat steadily kicking her ribs, made worse with every twitch. A minute passed, and yet her heart still hammered. She hadn't said yes. She could have run, said no, but she didn't.

Did she want me to make a move?

The thought made my whole body warm. I never thought I'd see the Kimberly Burns I knew appear shy, yet there she was trying not to look at me and doing a poor job of it.

I admired the flush in her cheeks. "Your heart is beating really fast . . ."

Her blue eyes met mine and froze me.

I focused on the rise and fall of her chest. Every breath was shallow and fast. Heat flushed my body from head to toe.

Her innocent doe eyes begged me to kiss her. *I couldn't touch her*, I told myself as I trailed my fingers up her arm. Her body responded with goose bumps that sent a chill up my spine. A breath hitched in her chest.

"Do you want me to stop?"

"No . . ."

I shouldn't kiss her, yet there I was leaning closer to her lips. The heat of her body against mine was intoxicating. Everything fell away, and all that was left was the smell of her perfume clouding my judgment. Those damn roses.

She shuddered as our lips touched.

"Do you love me?" I asked one more time. There were a million reasons not to.

She should say no. She should run. She should break my heart.

"Yes," she whispered as she gripped the collar of my shirt to pull me into her.

At the taste of her, every bit of control I had flew out the window. I grabbed her all over. Her face, her hair, her arms. Anything to have her closer. The way she tasted . . .

Shit.

No part of me wanted to stop kissing her. Ever. It was intoxicating. She loved me.

What happened at the pool was all happiness. Light. Freeing. Every kiss now felt deeper than that. All the hurt and pain we'd endured burned with each touch of our lips. This was need. Fast and ravenous. More than the lust. Though, I felt that too when my fingers wrapped themselves in her hair and she whispered my name. I'd do just about anything to have her keep saying my name like that.

All the pain and frustration from the last two weeks melted away in our urgency. There was no more longing, not with those three little words hanging on her lips.

And there was no way I would be able to stop.

The table was gone in seconds, and I pulled her under me. Our lips effortlessly found each other, and every sound she made felt like a demand to give her more. More pressure. More touch. More everything.

"Tell me." My lips grazed her ear.

A fluttering laughter escaped her. "I love you."

I groaned into her neck and continued kissing under her chin. Now I was laughing too.

"Tell me." Her delicate hands pulled my face to hers.

"I am madly in love with you, Kimberly Burns."

I think I could die happy. I didn't know what could top this in my five-year plan.

She pulled at my shirt and then my hair. I begged for some sense of control, but the taste of her on my tongue made my brain turn to mush. All I wanted was her and everything she would give me. My hips pressed deeper into hers, and our kisses slowed. I'd wanted it for so long. The night in the pool only scratched the surface of what I wanted. I *needed* to devour her.

Her fingernails scraped along my back. I obliged by kissing her jaw and then her ear and neck. I hung on her every breath, savoring the desire in her sighs. My hands moved down her body, hesitating at her chest and then moving to her outer thigh. I hooked her leg around me, lifting the side of her skirt just enough to where the tips of my fingers grazed her bare skin.

I didn't notice when I tuned into the sound of the blood pumping beneath her skin right beneath my lips.

It remembered the taste of her blood and the warmth coursing through my veins.

Ours.

For once, the voice agreed with me. I felt my resolve slipping. I was giving into it.

The desire for her danced around with the need for her blood until it melded into nothing but red. Deep red. The blood pumping next to my lips left me salivating and eager, and I imagined what it might feel like to bite her for just a second. My teeth at the edge of her skin and the feeling of her pulse radiating in my veins. Red. Everything was red.

The room was a blur when she pulled away.

"Aaron, you're shaking."

The sound of her voice pulled me back into the theater.

She was right. Another thing I hadn't noticed. My palms were shaking, and I willed myself to stay glued to my seat.

"Shit. I'm sorry."

I pressed my palms to my eyes, shielding myself from her. I had to go before I hurt her. I couldn't trust myself to keep her safe like this.

"It's okay." There was no fear in her voice.

She grabbed one of my trembling hands and placed it on her chest, just over her heart. I tried turning away, guilt filling up like bile in my throat, but her soft hand grazed my face, and she smiled sweetly.

"You're in control."

Her heart drummed in a steady rhythm beneath my fingertips. That beautiful symphony. I'd never loved a sound so much, and I loved nothing like I loved her.

The movement of her chest grounded me, and after a few minutes, the shaking in my palms stilled and then it was just me and her, with my hand on her chest and the realization of what we had just done.

I pulled my hand away, still lost in her blue eyes. "You . . . this . . . was

. . ."

She shook her head. "We didn't . . . we just . . ."

There was no denying it. Every touch and kiss were still there, urging us to fall back into their natural rhythm.

"Okay, okay. Let's think about this. If you love me, and I love you . . . then that just leaves us with one real problem. I'm immortal and you're not."

She nodded. "You're right. That is a problem."

"And the last thing I want is to have you choose between actually living and being with me."

"Right."

"We can't do this . . ."

"It doesn't change anything," she said, watching my lips, and I stared at hers.

"It's settled . . . we have to stop this . . ." I moved closer to her.

She gave me that look again, waiting for me to kiss her. "For sure . . ."

The heat built in my chest, and I knew if I kissed her, I wouldn't be able to stop this time. Therefore, I did the one thing I could do.

My coward ass started picking up all the snacks and trash we left in the chair.

"I think it's time to go home."

Kim was already heading for the door, pulling her hair back up and smoothing her clothes to appear presentable. "Agreed."

Thane and Skylar would be pleased, but Kim and I were nowhere near satisfied.

The ride home was mostly in silence. Well, other than Presley. No one asked about our decision to leave early. I was thankful for their lack of care in my personal life. Kimberly offered to drive and made small talk with Skylar on the way home.

I stared out the window as my mind replayed the night over and over again. My hands in her hair. The warmth of her body. Her lips pressed against mine. There was no denying what I wanted. Not now that I'd had it for a few minutes.

I felt like some lovestruck teenager, unable to think past anyone other than myself and my wants. I did what I always did when I thought about Kimberly too much, I thought about my impending doom and possible death instead. Here I was imagining kissing Kimberly while my older brothers were probably training or doing something helpful. They were preparing.

Luke's words came to mind. *"I don't want you to always be running. I don't want that life for you. We never wanted that."*

I'd have to tell him the new additions to my five-year plan.

When we arrived, Kimberly and I said our good nights in front of her door. She hugged me, then I was floating again.

"You're not going to stop talking to me again, are you?"

She smiled and reached up to kiss my cheek. "No."

I walked to my room with that relief and flipped on the light.

Presley knocked on my doorframe seconds after. "Okay, spill."

He creeped into my room holding a silver can and slightly closed the door before popping the top.

"Well, it—"

Zach peeked his head in the door. "Did I hear beer?"

"You fuckin' alcoholic." Presley chuckled while handing him a beer he had stored in his pocket, for some reason.

"Not like it even matters for us."

"We don't technically know that. It could still morph our brains or something," Presley said.

They shrugged and took a sip.

Presley smiled wider. "Anyway, how was your totally platonic movie date?"

I rubbed the back of my neck. "It was good . . . great."

Zach and Presley shared a glance.

"Came back a little early, didn't ya?" Presley said.

"Yeah . . . uh, Kim was feeling sick, so we thought it would be good to come home."

"Right. Right." Presley was still snickering and sharing that shit-eating grin with Zach.

I huffed. "What? Why are you looking at me like that?"

Zach took a large sip. "You got a little . . ."

He pointed to the side of my face where Kimberly's pink lip gloss was smeared on my cheek.

"I . . ."

They waited for me to speak while batting their eyelashes.

"You know, I think I'm turning in for the night. Get out of my room."

Assholes.

TWENTY-SEVEN

KIMBERLY

I needed to clear my head, and like many times before I found myself in my sacred space . . . with Skylar. I needed to run. Like really run, run till my toenails felt like they would peel off and my chest was sore. Run till I felt like I would die and then go one more mile.

My wrist throbbed for the first hour but then it was numb compared to the pain of everything else. Skylar ran alongside me as we made another lap around the town square. We were challenged with elevation, so we stayed on sidewalks to avoid stopping at crosswalks. She didn't complain. Not even once, and she didn't ask me what was wrong.

The night before was on repeat in my head. It was everything I'd longed for, but I couldn't fully enjoy it. Aaron had made a promise to protect me. But they couldn't protect me. Not like this. I'm the only human in this scenario, and I was starting to understand William's words and the rage behind them. You either die young or you turn. There was no in-between. I had to choose.

This I would miss—the feeling of my blood pumping in my head. The runner's high and absolute euphoria. The sense of accomplishment every time I hit another goal. If I turned, I'd never have this feeling again. My most tried-and-true hobby would be nothing but a memory. Where else would I go to vent my frustrations and wonders?

We passed a family in a stroller, and I ran harder, willing every aching muscle to give me more energy and more power. I'd never thought about kids. I knew it wasn't something I cared about now, but how would things change in a few years? Would I feel differently? I wasn't convinced either way, but what I knew was I had mom issues, and growing up, it made me never want to consider kids until I was at least in my thirties.

Still, I had a choice to make. I didn't have to make that choice right away, but I had to choose someday. And that choice meant the difference of the relationship Aaron and I could have. How long could I hold out in Aaron's presence while loving him? Could I go years watching him and separating myself from him? My heart ached at the thought. I never imagined what love would feel like, but I never thought it would be painful.

I never imagined I would be in love with a vampire either.

I knew what I wanted, what my heart was telling me, but my brain wasn't convinced. I wasn't convinced of anything anymore. Not with The Family or The Legion.

There hadn't been a sighting of Akira since the football game, and everything was on high alert. I had to practically beg on my hands and knees to get out of the house. I had nightmares of Akira's dark soulless eyes. I was confident I never wanted to know the things he had seen.

We had rounded the corner to the main street when Skylar passed me a water bottle.

"I think you should rehydrate and take a break."

My wobbly feet stuttered to a stop, and I took small sips of water between rapid breaths. My ears were ice cold. The morning air on the mountain was cold, and the sunlight peeking over the building was barely enough to kiss my face.

We walked side by side. The cool air was getting to me as my body slowly cooled. She peeled off her coat and handed it to me. A strong, expensive perfume rushed my senses in the cold misty air.

"Just take it."

I did, and the faux-fur collar warmed my cold ears.

Skylar had this way of saying things that made me soften and listen despite her seriousness. Despite her appearance and how young she looked, something about her was motherly like a big sister would be. We weren't that close, but I trusted her to protect me more than the other members of The Legion.

"Do you want to talk about it?" She kept her eyes ahead, and her expression was relaxed.

"Am I a fool? Seriously, I need you to tell me if I'm being ridiculous for even considering becoming like you. Am I just being a naive girl or something? Am I being selfish?" The words kept flowing. "I feel like I'm being so irrational about everything. I can't decide what I want to do."

"I think you'll know what to do when the time is right. You can trust your own opinions. You may be young but you're smart."

I eyed her, not saying a word. I let her words wash over me for a moment.

Skylar sighed. "You know . . . I wasn't much older than you when I turned."

I stopped walking. We'd reached the town square where a fountain sat in the cobblestone. There weren't many people around. "Wait, really?"

"My brother, Dom, was recruited by the same coven more than forty years ago. Only, he was a new lower rank. Lower members never meet the queens."

I gasped, sitting on the cold fountain. "And he got out?"

"Yes, my brother was manipulated just like the Calem brothers had been. They killed my mom . . . our mom. They probably would have killed me too, but since I wasn't blood and I was out of the house by then, I guess I didn't make the cut."

It was all starting to make sense. Why Skylar was the only one who seemed to tolerate the boys except William. Why she'd put up with this madness.

"When I found out what my brother was and what he was up against, I took matters into my own hands. I confronted Dom and made him change me, and together . . . we fled. We met Kilian soon after. He'd been lying in wait. That led us to the life we live now. It is not the greatest, but I have no regrets about my young woman's decision. I'd do it again."

My eyes were wide. "You escaped . . . that means it's possible. I'm sorry I never asked you all this before."

"It didn't need to be said then. When a queen's Guard is complete and they grow old together, they become almost impenetrable . . . that's why the boys are important. This may be our only chance to kill Her. And I want a shot at it."

It was official, Skylar was the coolest person I'd ever met. Her eyes spoke of many lifetimes that were far away. For the first time, I felt hope. Hope that The Family wasn't this all-powerful force we'd never be able to fight. Skylar defied the odds. She saved the people she cared about the most.

"Why? Why wouldn't you just want to run away and live somewhere tropical where no one will find you? I mean . . . you guys can do anything. You're free."

Free. That word caught in my throat.

She smiled without teeth. "I detest the sun. And . . . we aren't free. Not until she's dead. My mom . . . she was a hard woman, but she deserves justice. As do the Calem brothers. This coven has ruined the lives of many, all for the sake of their own agenda. That blood is poison that bleeds into the fabric of the world and corrupts good people. I want Her dead, and I won't settle for anything less."

"And Dom feels the same?"

"I think Dom would much rather be doing anything else than living in a frat house." Her laugh was light and fluttery. "But . . . he's the one who convinced me to join The Legion. He's always believed in the work we do."

She stood, her white hair mirroring the snowcapped mountains. "There's your answer. You can trust in whatever choice you make. Because it's yours."

I wanted to hug her, but she'd hate that.

"Kim!" Chelsea's voice cut the mountain air.

I gasped and pulled the sunglasses I had resting on my head over my still very-bruised eye and prayed the makeup would be enough to cover up what was still visible.

Chelsea was bundled in a puffy mauve jacket and thick-soled ankle boots, and on her arm was someone with their hand draped over her shoulder.

Akira.

I sucked in a breath, fighting the urge to bolt. He nuzzled his head into her neck, and she giggled. I didn't think I'd ever heard her laugh like that.

Akira was adorned in all black. A shorter coat this time but still long and a few sizes too big. The rings on his hand were all silver with black and green stones.

He couldn't have been much older than thirty when he changed.

"What are you doing here?" I spoke only to Akira.

Chelsea seemed unharmed and oddly far happier and less stressed than I'd seen her in weeks.

Chelsea spoke slowly. "You know him? Isn't he great?"

"Tell her where we met," Akira whispered to her.

"We met at school. Right outside OBA, actually."

"We're leaving." Skylar grabbed my arm, but I stayed planted on the cement.

"Calm down, Sky. We're just chatting." Akira hung his head to the side like a bored child.

I swallowed. Fear was my first instinct. It was the only thing I felt coursing through my veins, and it made me shiver, but his fingers were wrapped around my best friend's hair. There was no way I could leave her there.

"What do you want, Akira?"

His eyes sparkled. "You're cute when you're angry, Kimmy. I just wanted to let you know I've done my part of making this relationship work. I've learned all about you. Your friends. Your favorite places."

Chelsea wasn't paying attention, just watching the water trickle in a steady stream from the fountain.

"You're threatening me."

"No way, if I wanted to be threatening, I could have killed your friend here and left her dead, decaying body on your doorstep for you to find, and I promise that would have been a lot more fun than following you around town. No . . . this is me being nice."

"By not killing my friends . . .?"

"Exactly." Akira tapped on the crinkly material of Chelsea's coat.

"And you're hoping this will make the boys come with you or something?"

He flashed his teeth in a harmonious smile. "Maybe, truly I just wanted to have a girls' day with you. Maybe we can get our nails done?"

Skylar and I shared a horrified glance.

"You want to go to the nail salon . . .?"

"What better way for us to chat? Come on." He hugged Chelsea close. "If you humor me, I won't take a drink of your friend. And she smells *really* good."

We weren't the only people by the fountain. I could scream. Alert someone. Anyone.

"If you're thinking of screaming, I wouldn't. Her neck would be so easy to snap. Sky, go ahead and tell your two little friends watching us over in that car to send in the troops if that makes you feel better. With the traffic, we'll be done with our conversation before then. Why do you think I met you in public?" He looked right through me. "I won't hurt you."

Alone with Akira in a nail salon wasn't what I would have imagined in a million years, but we submitted.

Akira kept his arm firmly around Chelsea, whispering in her ear as we walked up to the town square to the only nail salon in town. A little shop that was bear themed with bear chairs for kids and old wooden floors that creaked under the scattering of rugs. I'd only come on special occasions, except for when one of my foster moms brought us every week so she could hide from her husband.

It was packed, but Akira leaned over the counter and greeted the front woman with . . . charm?

I watched his hands. One stroked the back of Chelsea's head, and the other brushed over the cashier's. The blood pumping in my ears was deafening. I had to focus on the revolving fan hooked on the desk. Methacrylate was the only thing I could smell, and it would be the death of me. I was going to throw up. My knees wobbled, and Skylar's iron grip steadied me.

He couldn't beat me here.

My jaw hit the floor as the cashier stood on her chair—a woman too old to be standing on a wobbly chair—and yelled for everyone to get out. After the horror registered, the guests complied, and as they passed, Akira touched each of them on their way out. He was showing me his power. How capable he was of getting exactly what he wanted. Clearing a room full of people was nothing for him.

He instructed the ladies to pull their tables together, while the other nail techs stayed in wait. Any protesting was silenced by Akira's soft voice and touch.

"You paying?" Skylar snarled.

She was more prepared for this sort of thing than I was. She wasn't even shaking.

"Yep, this one's on me, ladies. What color nails does your friend like?"

"Black."

"Oh, me too." Akira smiled. "Kimmy, I wanted to get you alone. But I knew that wouldn't be possible without a crowd. So, I'll settle for this."

The nail technician came up to me and placed a bottle of red polish on the table.

"Did you tell her I wanted red?"

"It suits you," he said.

"I want French tips, please." I wanted any semblance of control I could get. She went to get the white, and Skylar chose the red.

When she placed the polish on the table, her hands were shaking.

I placed my hand on her arm. "It's going to be okay."

I glared at Akira, which he thought was hilarious.

"You act like I've slaughtered a town. No one is going to die here! She'll make enough in these ten minutes to cover this shop's pay for the entire week so everyone can go home early." He pulled his hands through his long black hair. "Humans are hard to please. Your unfailing love for all of humanity. I'm always surprised how loyal humans can be even to strangers . . . it's what I love most, really. I once let a man live for defending some random girl I wanted to sink my teeth into. He had a wife . . . kids. And he was still ready to fight me to the death to keep me from killing someone he didn't know."

I didn't know what to say. There had to be a reason he told me that, but I didn't know if I could trust anything he said.

"I see that in you, Kimberly. Unfailing loyalty. I like that."

Almost nothing about Akira was soft. Not his edgy haircut, or the tattoos that went to his wrists. But his eyes were. Much softer than when I'd stared into William's eyes, where only anger stared back at me, but with Akira, there was something gooey and warm.

"How would you know anything about me?"

"I know lots, babe. I know that you were an orphan. You got in trouble a lot as a kid too—"

"How? How do you know that?"

"Anything I can't coerce out of people, I can steal."

Talking to Akira differed from William. Akira was straight forward. Direct.

"Why would you need to know anything about me?"

"Because I need to see what type of relationship you have with the boys. I've been watching you for a while. Good job on finishing that marathon, by the way, but . . . sorry about that tumble you took." He watched Skylar. "I quite enjoyed that little story. Cute."

Skylar's eyes could kill, but I grabbed her arm. *Keep it together.*

"What I really loved was your reckless little sneak-off to that pool. You and Aaron must be close."

I straightened my hands as the girl painted my nails, and willed them to remain steady. He watched my every twitch and breath. Akira said he liked me, and I only had a few guesses as to why that might be.

He'd been watching us the whole time. Waiting to pull the rug. The more shock value, the better. He wanted theatrics. Tears. Well, he would not get it from me.

"We are."

"Just Aaron?" Akira blew on the nails of one of his hands. One coat of black was enough.

"What are you implying?"

He leaned forward. "I'll be honest. Your answer determines when and how I kill you."

I clenched my jaw. "It's just Aaron."

"Would you show me?" He reached out to me, revealing his palm.

That was the last thing I wanted to do. But what choice did I have? Him taking my hand would not make him any more likely to kill me than sitting across from him. If he wanted me dead right now, I'd be dead.

"Fine."

Skylar's chair squeaked. I placed my hand on his palm, and he wrapped his fingers around my hands and wrists. He was cold.

I expected the pain Aaron told me about. The forcing into my head with gnawing intrusion, but Akira didn't push. He waited for me. He wanted my most recent memories of each of them, and I showed him. My face was hot when I came to Aaron and relived our time in the theater with an intruder. The memory was so real. I could feel everything. Breath, lips, tongue.

He let out a slow whistle and pulled away. "Wow, what a show."

I squeezed some of the hand sanitizer in my hands. I wanted no feeling of Akira left on me. Our most intimate moments weren't safe from them.

"You and Aaron are forbidden lovers. It's kind of poetic. Something for the storybooks."

The nail technicians finished their finishing touches on Skylar's and my nails, and I wondered how long we'd be there. There was no clock in sight, and I couldn't glance at my phone. We were trapped in a timeless void with Akira, and I didn't know how long I could keep up my act.

"Kimmy, I'm going to give it to you like it is. I've been ordered to kill you."

"By who?"

"The queen, of course."

The queen knew about me? My blood was turning hot. This wasn't real. It couldn't be real.

I could barely force out the words. "And you're sitting here getting your nails done with me because . . ."

If that's what She wanted, why was I still alive, why the hesitation?

"Because, personally, I don't think killing people is the best way to get things done. It just creates unnecessary drama. Bodies start dropping and then everyone is shaking like a little deer, screaming, running. It's annoying."

"That didn't stop you from killing Mrs. Henry."

I threw out my accusation, hoping it would pick up something.

"The teacher? Okay, the teacher was an accident. I mean, they're all kind of accidents. Controlling everyone in the group isn't my specialty. Leadership is a shit gig. Ezra is much better at that than I am. The boys get . . . restless. Sometimes they get drunk or ravenous and kill people. It happens."

He wasn't alone. Rage. Pure rage took over. I sat back in my chair to glare at him.

"Then why haven't you killed me?"

"Because. I have another option I think everyone here would prefer. You leave. Go . . . I don't care where. But you leave. We won't follow you. I won't mess with you. Just like the boys' mom. You can live."

I was missing something. Something crucial.

"What about the prophecy?"

"The boys will be Hers. You're not changing it." His brow lowered, and pieces of his hair fell into his face. "You can't save him. I'm sorry, babe. Best take this last train ticket out of town. You're young and beautiful. I'm sure you'll find someone normal to grow old with. Next time, stay away from the ones who bite."

Our girls' day was over, and I didn't leave unscathed.

You can't save him.

He'd found the chip in my armor. My Achilles' heel. Those four words would be the nail in my coffin. I felt it as soon as he said them.

After tending to the nail technicians, he walked us back toward the fountain, and Chelsea was still silent and tucked under his arm. I think

I was numb. Everything in me shifted from self-preservation to self-destruction.

When we reached the fountain, he spun on his heels to face me. "Well, I truly hope I won't be seeing you again, Kimmy. If I do, I'll finish what we started in the forest."

He winked and then he was gone, disappearing into the bustle of people in the town square. I stayed frozen. Maybe I was supposed to die in that forest when I met Aaron. I was never supposed to be here. Akira was right. I couldn't save him. I couldn't save any of them.

Chelsea was the only thing to shake me from that dark place. I pulled my sunglasses back on and grabbed her shoulders, checking her for any marks. "Chelsea . . . are you okay?"

I had no idea what she'd remember from any of it. My guess was very little. With Akira constantly whispering in her ear and touching her arm, I assumed he'd kept a firm grasp on her version of the story.

She blinked a few times before her eyes settled on the ground. At least that's what I thought she was focusing on, but she grabbed my wrist and held it up.

"Uh, what the hell is this? This is the same hand you hurt before! What happened?" She looked at me with a furrowed brow.

I stared at her, curious as to why her first thought after being mind-wiped by a vampire was to be worried about me.

"Hello? Answer me," she said, waving her hand in my face.

"I got bit by a . . . dog. It was like a week or ago on my run. It will heal quickly."

She sighed, dropping my hand and fluffing her hair. "Well, I'm surprised you still wanted to come get your nails done with me today."

That's what the story was going to be. Skylar shot me a tentative glance.

"I'm glad I did. It was nice to hang out." My mind was still going a million miles per minute and small talk was useless.

"Yeah, well, it would be *nice* if you'd let me come see your new apartment. I can't believe you haven't invited me over." She eyed Skylar, and I knew exactly what she thought.

I'd replaced her with another friend. We'd scarcely talked since I moved out.

I wanted to say something—anything encouraging to let her know I hadn't—but what could I say? She needed to stay away from me, and this was the strongest warning I'd ever been given. Akira surveyed my every move. She was lucky to be alive.

"I'm sorry. I've just been busy. It's not that I don't want you there. I'm just getting it put together first." I coughed out a barely acceptable answer.

"Right." She sighed but held her head up as she pulled her purse over her shoulder. "Well, I'm just saying. You're missing out because I'm great at interior design."

She was. I remembered how perfectly she'd put her room together. We'd thrifted together, and she'd picked out things and transformed them in ways I'd never thought about. She had a distinctive dark-academia style I admired. I thought about all the things I wished I could say and then let them go. They turned to dust in the cold, mountain air tainted with the faintest scent of smoke.

"I know. But I'll see you at school?"

She nodded and then got in her car and drove away. The dread Akira left behind lingered.

TWENTY-EIGHT

AARON

Zach stopped the car in the middle of the road.

My brothers and I jolted forward, and I gripped the headrest in front of me. A list of expletives filled the car, along with the sound of screeching tires.

"Get the fuck out."

I'd have protested more, but I saw her. A flashing of red hair among the few lingering autumn leaves. Skylar pulled over next to the tree line, and Kimberly found me instantly. I closed the distance between us.

For a second, nothing mattered besides the floral scent of her skin and that steady beat in her chest. She buried her head into my shirt, and I wrapped my hands around her like it was the last time.

I kissed her head before pulling away and moving her sunglasses so I could see her eyes. Bright blue and burning amid the tears threatening to spill down her cheeks.

I should have been there.

"You're okay," I said.

I couldn't stop myself from kissing her forehead, the bruising by her eye, her lips.

"I'm okay," she said in a breath. She encircled her hand in mine and stayed glued to my side.

When everything came back into focus, I realized we were in some type of standoff. On a backroad surrounded by trees except for one lone street sign. I'd been here before when we'd taken Luke to Kilian's cabin.

A large SUV stopped in front of our car, and Kilian, Thane, William, and Dom poured out and were followed by another car driven by Felix and filled with more Legion.

They looked pissed—well, except for Thane. He made direct eye contact with me. His unflinching jaw told me that we'd fucked up, and it was only partly justified. When Skylar sent out the SOS text, we argued all of five seconds before we grabbed the keys to get Kimberly. The Legion wanted to think, plan, talk. We wanted to go get her, so we did.

Luke was the first person Skylar called and told she was on her way to Kilian. Which made me feel safer standing next to her.

Kimberly, Skylar, and I stayed on the side of the road while my brothers stayed near our car. I held Kimberly closer. I would not let her out of my sight. Not again.

Zach barreled toward Kilian with fists clenched. "You're supposed to be fucking protecting her."

Kimberly's grip tightened on my hand.

"You're supposed to follow orders. You jeopardized everything by leaving." Kilian's nostrils flared and veins were popping in his forehead and arms, but he was still eerily calm.

"Fuck you. She could be dead."

Luke stepped next to Zach. "The deal is you protect them. If you don't, we will."

"This is the second fucking time, Kilian." Zach's anger was boiling over and threatening to spill over onto the road, and I didn't want to be there when it did. "How many times are you going to let this fucker through your supposed ironclad defense before I start finding body parts of my family on the front lawn?"

Jesus. What did he know? What things had my brother seen?

But Luke was calm and firm. "He's right. You haven't kept your end of the deal."

"There was a breach of protocol. She shouldn't have been allowed in town without proper protection. We'll double up. We'll—"

"Not fucking good enough!" Zach's voice echoed in the trees.

Luke crossed his arms. There was no smile. He was all business.

"He never should have been able to get to her or to Aaron at homecoming. Something has to change."

"What did he say to you?" Zach pivoted to Kimberly, and his jaw was clenched. "Wait, what the fuck happened to your face?"

Shit. Shit. Shit.

Thane was studying the back of Kilian's head, avoiding any eye contact with Zach. "It was an accident. I was teaching Kim some stuff when we were sparring, and she bumped into me."

"She bumped into you?! What the fuck does that even mean?" Zach stepped forward, shoulders back. I'd seen that look before. That shadow that passed over my brother's face, leaving everything around him dull. My brother was a tornado when he was angry. All hell was about to break loose, and Zach would be the center of the calamity.

William and Dom stepped in front of Thane.

"Dom, please don't," Skylar said, still hovering next to us.

"He said it was an accident," William said. I knew he'd back up Thane no matter the circumstance.

"Hide behind your little groupies like a coward. It won't help."

An eye for an eye. Zach's only true moral compass. There wasn't room for accidents.

William stepped forward and rolled up his sleeves. "You won't fuckin' touch him."

"Choose your words wisely, Will," Zach spat. "Do we need to have a replay of what happened back at the gym?"

"Will, stop. It's fine. It's my fault," Thane pleaded.

Dom followed, and the others closed in. "Skylar get over here."

"No." Skylar said.

"I wouldn't." Luke stepped close to Zach.

Luke would never let Zach fight alone. I spotted Presley hovering beside the car, and I prepared myself to grab Kim and get us all in the car.

"Do not engage," Kilian said, but it did nothing to stall the resentment in their eyes.

His colder outer exterior had cracked.

"Yeah, listen to your master like the little puppets you are. If you had half a brain, you'd leave this asshole behind before he gets you all killed."

I didn't want this. We weren't supposed to be fighting. There was power in numbers, and we were seconds away from chipping away at that body count.

"He said I needed to leave . . . and if I go, he wouldn't kill me," Kimberly yelled. They stopped.

"He confirmed that he wasn't alone . . . he brought some guys with him and that they're behind the missing people around town."

That got everyone's attention. All eyes shifted to her.

"He looked in my head. He wanted to see the relationships I had with the boys . . . our last interactions. I think he was fishing for information on the twins."

My blood ran cold. No way he touched her. No way he pushed himself into her head—

She peered up at me, anticipating my question. "I'm fine. It was brief, and I agreed to it."

Their voices ran together in a steady blur, but I was only thinking of her. Their previous quarrel moved to the back burner. Now they were talking among themselves and making more plans. Where they thought she should go and more arguing, whether it was worth the hassle, and it most definitely was. All I was thinking about was how much safer she felt next to me. How much longer I had . . . days . . . minutes.

My chest hurt. It wasn't time. How was I going to say goodbye?

"I'm not going." Kimberly let go of my hand and stepped in front of me. All their arguing stopped.

"Told you, she has a death wish." William's jaw hardened.

Kilian walked in closer. "We have people up North. Skylar can go with you."

"No. I'm not going. I've made up my mind."

"I wouldn't advise it."

"I don't care what you advise." Kimberly's voice was firm and unwavering. "Nothing you say will change my mind."

Damn. I could do nothing but stare at the back of her head and admire her. Her bravery. Her sureness.

She turned to Luke. "I know it's a lot to ask . . . but will you guys protect me?"

Luke beamed with confidence. "Hell yeah, we will. You don't have to ask."

He turned to face the rest of them. "It's settled, then. Kimberly is staying. No else's opinion matters. We're going back to OBA. Kim . . . Aaron. Get in our car. Everyone else feel free to follow us back to the house. We can hash out the rest there."

"You need to follow protocol." Kilian's voice burned with something new. Impatience.

"No, I don't. You need us. From now on, we choose where we go and when. I'm not waiting around to have your approval. I suggest you stick close by unless you want Akira picking you off one by one."

There was silence when the doors of the car slammed shut and we were all inside.

Presley was the only one smiling. "Holy shit, Luke, you're kinda badass."

"What do we do now?" I said after making sure Kimberly was buckled in.

"We're leaving." Luke stuck the key in the ignition and the engine started with a sputtering. The car was stolen and running on fumes.

"Fucking finally!" Zach said while he rummaged through his pants for his lighter.

"Now!? Like today?" My stomach turned at that thought.

"No. They'd never let us go. We have to be smarter than that. This time, when we disappear, we're disappearing for good."

"Are you sure . . . because they said they have more people. Maybe once things cool down—" Presley started.

Luke's foot tapped again, and it shook the car. "I know. I know what they said and what I said, but . . . they can't stop them. They aren't going to stop looking for us."

"So, we just run forever?" I said.

"However long it takes." Luke met my gaze in the rearview mirror. "It wasn't supposed to be like this. I wanted it to work. I wanted them to protect you, but it's just not working. I can't risk Akira having access to you guys."

Kimberly squeezed my hand, and I leaned into her shoulder. I desperately wanted to know what she was thinking.

"What about school?" Presley said.

"Fuck school," Luke snapped, and we all recoiled and sank into our seats.

The hum of the car was the only lingering sound, and the green fuzzy dice Presley bought blew around from the hot air coming from the air vent.

Luke pinched his nose, and his eyes softened. "I'm sorry, Pres. I know I've done nothing but tell you where to go and what to do. One last time . . . I need you to trust me. We'll start this all over if we have to, but I promise I'll make sure you guys are safe."

Presley nodded, and I squeezed his shoulder.

"What about Kim?" I asked.

Luke turned to address Kim. "I wish I could say you had a choice . . . but I don't think you do. You're not safe staying or going. Even if you want to stay—"

"I'm going." Kimberly leaned forward. "Wherever you guys go, I'm coming."

I wanted to savor the relief in my stomach, but I couldn't. She wasn't safe. Not by a long shot. None of us were. But at least she'd be next to me.

Zach's lighter clicked, and he took his first drag of a new cigarette. "How are we going to do it?"

Luke kept his eyes on the road. "It's not going to be easy. It will likely lead to a fight."

"Then we'll fight," Zach said.

"We're not going to hurt them, are we?"

"A little pain won't kill them, Pres," Zach said.

Presley and I shared a look. We liked them. Thane especially. He was our friend now. Many of our late nights were spent playing video games or listening while Thane told us random stories about his life before becoming a vampire. He kept them light, only mentioning happy memories. Mostly his mistakes. Things he wished he'd done differently.

"We'll have to ditch the bodyguards," Luke said.

"That's four people . . . four vampires, at least. If they don't send more," I said. "Maybe I could convince Thane to step aside. Or maybe I could convince him to be elsewhere on the night we go."

"Yeah, maybe it won't have to lead to a fight. It's possible Skylar would let us leave . . . and Dom would listen to her," Kimberly said.

"That only leaves Will. That's doable." Zach had rolled down the window, but his smoke was blowing back into the car. I hoped they'd find another car to steal if we were going to be traveling again. Preferably from someone with another who wouldn't miss it too much.

We were stuck in the wake of my brothers' problems all along. A fact I knew but now realized was futile to get out of the waves. It kept taking us further and further out. And it didn't matter how close we appeared to shore, we'd always get pulled back under.

Where would we go? Where wouldn't The Family find us? I didn't know if that place existed.

"What about money? We don't exactly have a stack of cash to go gallivanting around the country," Presley said.

"He's right. We'll need gas. Kimberly needs food." Zach took another drag of his cigarette. "We've got some that we siphoned off the haunted house, and a little in our fund, but it's not going to get us that far. We need more. Quickly."

"Ooh! Oh! Pick me! I have an idea!"

"Just say it," Zach grumbled.

"What if we did a car wash . . . a shirtless car wash?" Presley leaned forward, shaking the seats in front of him. "A guy I know in Sigma Nu told me they did one last year and it was a huge success. They raised like five thousand dollars . . . only, technically, they did it for charity."

"That could work, what if we said we were donating to a local animal shelter? Girls love that shit," Zach said.

"That's so fucked up." I didn't hide my disgust. "No living things. It's bad enough we'd be stealing the money."

Zach put his hands up in the air to mock me.

"Aaron's right." Luke's knuckles were white as he gripped the steering wheel. "It's got to be something that won't have a lot of impact. That way if the money goes missing, it's not something they couldn't replace."

"What if it's something that everyone on campus loved? Particularly the other fraternities and sororities . . ." Kimberly was deep in thought and then her eyes lit up. "The Spring Break thing! The festival you were going on about, Presley. What if OBA offers to host it for start-up funds? We could frame it in town as a revenue for them in the spring . . . maybe get extra support."

"I like that. They'll probably end up doing it anyway, even if we bail," I said.

Some of the bigger fraternities were loaded compared to ours, and they had the bodies to make something like that happen.

Presley sat back in his seat. "Well, I don't like that because it's going to be the best party of the century and I won't be here."

"Perfect. Now, how are we going to plan it without The Legion poking around and asking questions?" Zach sighed.

"We could make it exclusive? Or . . . frame it that way. Start it with a secret text chain. More people will show up if they think it's cool. Chelsea is good at that kind of thing. Plus, if we have it for one day only . . .

Sunday, the day after everyone is back from break, we could catch some parents too," Kimberly said, and I sat in awe of her brain.

There was a collective silence, and I think my brothers and I were all thinking the same thing.

"Kim, where the hell have you been all our lives!? You're a genius." Presley was excited again.

Yep. Bingo.

With the five of us, things felt complete. Like it was finally right.

"Luke doesn't have to be the only smart one. We finally have some more brain power," I said.

"There may be hope for us after all." Zach smiled and nudged Luke, which made him smile.

"It's settled. Sunday night. We're leaving with whatever cash we have," Luke said.

My fingers found Kimberly's on the seat beside me, and she wrapped hers around mine. Everything was changing, but I had *them*. All the most important people in my life were safe. That's all that mattered.

If leaving Blackheart would save us all, I'd try anything, yet I couldn't help but think back to The Legion. All our time together had to mean something.

I'd spent all that time trying to bond with them, hoping it would be our salvation. In a way, they were. They'd allowed us more time and put their lives on the line for us. Leaving them and leaving their mission felt wrong in a way, but sometimes being selfish was required for survival. At least that's what my brothers would say.

That's all we were doing—surviving and protecting what was ours. I waited for that thought to bring me relief, but as we continued to drive and plan our escape, it never came.

Our relationship was transactional, and we learned everything we needed to. That's all this was ever supposed to be. Maybe if I repeated it enough, I'd believe it.

TWENTY-NINE

KIMBERLY

*I*t was pitch black. Dark pools of ink overtook my vision. Leaves crunched as something was dragged across the forest floor.

The clearing in the trees was familiar. No noteworthy trees or interesting bark formations, but my blood scattered on dead leaves and dry branches. I was back in the forest where Aaron had left me. The darkness pressed in around me, and a shiver ran up my spine. I wasn't alone.

In the clearing, a long white draping of hair and soft fabric appeared. Delicate hands with long dainty fingers grabbed the flaking bark of a redwood with long pale nails. A woman appeared. One look into her eyes and I knew who it was. The queen.

A scream curdled in my throat, and a strong set of hands gripped my neck. I struggled to swallow.

"Quiet now." Akira's breath was hot on my ear.

As the queen appeared and stood in the middle of the clearing, Her eyes bore into mine. Despite Her white eyes, they were void of any light. The hands on my neck tightened, and tears streamed down my cheeks. I was alone.

Aaron rushed through the tree line and fell to his knees. "Please, don't hurt her."

I froze. Any movement only tightened Akira's grip on my neck. Aaron's dirty-blond hair brought me relief, but the comfort was short-lived.

The queen walked closer to him, and Her thin fingers brushed through his hair. My chest lit with rage. I didn't like the way She was gazing at him, touching him as if he was a long-lost lover.

Aaron spoke again, "Please, I'll do anything. Just don't kill her."

My heart sank as a smile curled on Her pale lips. With long, pale fingers She tilted his chin to look up at Her. "You'd do anything?"

Aaron nodded. His body shook.

She brought Her wrist to Her lips and bit down. Streams of black blood dripped onto the ground below. Akira's grip slipped. His whole body shifted forward, nearly knocking me off my feet.

"Drink."

Aaron hesitated.

"Commit yourself to me. To us." Her voice was laced with venom.

I wanted to scream, but all I felt was a small hum in my throat. Aaron grabbed Her wrist and brought it to his lips. His touch was soft at first but turned forceful as he drank. Leaning forward, his sneakers smeared the blood in the dirt. When he pulled away, his shoulders were drawn back, and he was alert. The queen whispered something too low for me to hear.

Aaron turned around, his eyes black and filled with malice.

This time when I screamed, it ripped through me.

I awoke in my room. The soft mutterings of *The Princess Bride* were still playing on my TV. My chest was tight, and with each shallow breath, I melted back into my sheets and grabbed my phone. Aaron had been out hunting with Zach, and I hoped he was home.

> **Me:** Hey, are you back home?

> **Aaron:** Yeah, what's up? Everything okay?

> **Me:** Maybe . . . why do you ask?

> **Aaron:** Um, because it's like 2am and you're the most grandma person I know. You lay in bed when the sun is out.

> **Me:** I just can't sleep.

> **Aaron:** How can I help?

> **Me:** Wanna come to my room?

> **Aaron:** Yeah! Give me like two minutes.

His two minutes felt like an eternity. Aaron softly knocked on my door and let himself in, towing a glass of milk and cookies. My heart melted. The fear lingering in the air dissipated with his ear-to-ear grin.

"Thought you could use a pick-me-up. My mom used to bring me warm cookies and milk when I couldn't sleep. Only, hers were home-made."

His hair was a disheveled mess like he'd also been lying down, and he was dressed in baggy pajama pants and a baby-blue cotton T-shirt.

Without a word, I raised the blankets, signaling for him to join me. There was a tinge of hesitation in his eyes. He barely laid the plate on my nightstand before I fell into his chest. I wanted his comfort and warmth to stop the creeping darkness from taking over. I needed him to save me.

"Whoa, hey. Are you okay?" Aaron's voice was more worried now.

He pulled his arms around me and held me on his chest. His gentle heartbeat calmed my nerves.

"I just had a bad dream."

The scene replayed in my head. The feeling of strong hands crushing my windpipe. The queen manipulating Aaron, determined to take every bit of innocence left in him and turn him into something he was never meant to be. The rage turned into sorrow. I'd had bad dreams before but none that felt real. A part of me wondered if it could be prophetic. That maybe everything we were doing was futile, and soon, Aaron would have to choose, and I knew he'd save me.

But that meant losing him. Every good thing about him. He'd be tethered to The Family and forced to do God knows what. He'd never bring me cookies again, and I'd never have my sunlight. It would be dark forever, not just because he wasn't near but because I was confident if he gave in and drank Her blood . . . he'd never come back to me.

Tears filled my eyes, and I buried my head into his chest, savoring his smell. His arms tightened around me, and he held me for a minute.

"It's okay. I'm right here. It's just a dream." He rubbed my back and buried his head into my hair.

That only made me cry more. I couldn't lose Aaron to those monsters. I couldn't let him become a shell of himself. He was supposed to be in the world. He was meant to give other people the sunshine he'd given me. His reassuring smile. His never-ending optimism.

"Hey." Aaron tilted my face to meet his gaze. "What is it? What can I do? Please stop crying."

Through the dim light and tears, I met his amber eyes. Soft. Worried. One hand grazed my face while the other held my head. And I kissed him.

He didn't pull away. For a moment, we melted into one another. Two pieces finally melded together. We didn't hold back. I savored the way his hands felt tangled in my hair. His lips parted between mine, and every movement lit my body on fire.

He was freshly fed, but with the way he grabbed and tasted me, I'd have called him a liar. I wasn't a want to him, but something so deeply needed it threatened to kill us both. When we were that close, I had a hard time caring about anything other than never letting his skin leave mine. Everything was hard and fast, yet gentle. He wasn't taking anything from me other than my breath. Giving me all he had.

It wasn't enough.

I pulled his shirt off and threw it on the floor. I wanted to memorize every plane of his chest with my lips and engrave the pulse in his neck onto my tongue. He gave me more. More tongue. More pressure.

When I struggled to catch my breath, he slowed down. Taking his time kissing my neck and mirroring my exhales with hot breath across my skin. My body tingled when his fingers teased their way up my stomach and along the thin material covering my breasts.

I whispered his name. My best attempt at a quiet invitation for more of him. For all of him.

He pulled away, leaving me cold again. His muscles trembled.

"Stay . . ." I said in silent desperation.

Stay now. Stay tomorrow. Stay forever.

His eyes darkened, and he rolled on top of me, forcefully but carefully. It was the right amount of everything. Strength and gentleness playing tug-of-war. His forearms were still quivering when he pressed his hips into mine and guided me where I needed to go. I bit back a moan as he peeled off my T-shirt, leaving me in only my bra and underwear.

Still not enough. Not nearly enough.

With a fist full of his hair, I pulled his lower lip into my mouth and bit down. He growled, sucking my lower lip between his teeth. A metallic taste lingered on my tongue, tainting the taste of him.

He pulled back, but I tightened my legs around him. I wasn't afraid. It didn't hurt. At least not in a way that made me want to stop.

"Are you okay?" He said it with his hips still pressed into mine. In the dim light, I could see his eyes. Careful. Thoughtful.

"Never better."

My breaths deepened when his fingers grazed my lips to open my mouth. I complied, and he traced the inside of my bottom lip with his ring and middle finger.

Everything inside me turned scorching hot.

There was darkness in his eyes when he licked my blood from his fingers one by one, but it was equal to the light. Burning and blending.

I stroked that worry line between his brow, waiting for him, until the shaking stopped.

He kissed my fingers, my hand, down to my wrist. Every touch was softer when he reached the sensitive skin still healing, confirming what I already knew was true—I was safe with him.

When his lips met mine again, the kiss was stronger. A gentle suction on my lower lip made my head spin, and with his tongue, he circled the edge of my lips, cleaning the blood.

"You have no idea how good you taste," he said against my collarbone.

I arched my neck, giving him greater access.

Heat gathered in my core as a groan tore through his throat, and he used his teeth to play at the straps of my bralette.

He burned me, filling me with the most radiant aura anywhere he touched. The sunlight that encapsulated his soul left fingerprints scorched onto my skin. He wasn't the sun. He was brighter. So much brighter. A star in the darkness that threatened to overtake him.

"Aaron," I moaned.

"We're in a house full of vampires, you have to be quiet."

He nestled his head into my neck and caressed me like I was the most important thing in the world. And when he looked at me like that, I believed him. He beamed. Enjoying how much I wanted this. "Can you be quiet for me?"

The words caught in my throat as his fingers trailed down my chest. Tickling. Teasing.

"Or . . . should I stop . . ." He removed his hand, just before reaching my underwear, and talked achingly slowly.

"No—" He touched me again, and I spoke in a strangled whisper, "I'll be quiet."

"You're such a bad liar, Burns."

I gasped when he pinned me down by my forearms. The light flutter of his lips followed the middle of my breastbone and went lower, stopping just below my belly button. My body vibrated and squirmed with every second that passed. I needed him like I'd needed nothing before.

I'd been able to keep quiet until he tugged at the edges of my underwear and tossed them to floor.

I couldn't hold in the whimper when his kisses went lower. My stomach. My hip. My knee.

Now I was shaking.

There was a soft pressure on my inner thigh, followed by teeth. He bit down, not enough to hurt and not enough to break the skin. I didn't care either way. The need to have him closer fluttered in my stomach.

His mouth reached the apex between my thighs, and my breath hitched. I didn't know what I was doing. A million thoughts ran through my mind at the same time. Too many to keep track of. But he was there. Soft and gentle. I trusted him with my life. My body. Everything. So I let go.

Aaron knew exactly what I needed. The right pressure. The right speed. The right place to touch. I couldn't stop saying his name.

This was all uncharted territory, but my hand was in his, and the other was wrapped in his golden hair. We navigated it together. Through every wave of pleasure that threatened to leave my mouth. Through every stroke of his tongue that sent me to places I never thought I'd go. I'd never *felt* so much. So much pleasure, so much love. So much of absolutely everything everywhere all at once, and I wondered if it would destroy me.

I welcomed it with open arms.

Gilded tears gathered in the corners of my eyes with each slow and pulsing movement that got faster and faster until everything in me shattered and came alive again.

He made his way back up to my chest, teasing me on my collarbone, my jaw, then my ear. A soft kiss turned into a light suction that made my breath falter. But there was no pain and no bite, just euphoria. I gasped.

Aaron was alive. So very alive. And I'd never been. Not really. Not till now.

"Aaron," I said with a sigh, still reeling from the pleasure that ripped through me.

A soft laughter accompanied his touch on my face. His eyes met mine with a wide grin.

"What's funny?" I said, waiting for my breathing to slow.

"I like it when you say my name like that."

My body hummed, and my face was still red-hot.

"At least you're not crying anymore." With one thumb, he wiped the wetness from my eyes. For a moment, we stayed tangled up in my blankets. He was on top of me, but that wasn't why I was having trouble breathing. "We gotta stop meeting like this. I'm trying to be good."

A giggle escaped my lips. "I know. I know."

I hadn't told him yet. That I was tired of running. I'd been fighting his gravity for almost an entire year, and I was ready to lay down my weapons. No more war. No more bloodshed.

All I wanted were barefoot nights by the fire while curled up in his arms. Ones where we never had to say goodbye. I imagined us arm and arm in a flower field enjoying spring. Every spring.

He thought he was the problem. A boy that ruined everything with his gilded touch. But it was me who'd made every choice. At every turn, I'd reached out to him.

I think I always knew I was the problem. Standing in the way of my own happiness. I saw him like a single star in the night. Burning. I couldn't look away. From that moment, my fate was sealed. I would be searching, reaching, and clawing my way toward it until it was mine. Beating and pulsing in my hands.

Aaron's heart beat steadily under my fingertips. I wanted to feel it forever.

"I promised myself I wouldn't ask you this . . . But I feel like it would be my greatest regret if I don't, just once." His golden eyes softened in the glow of the TV, and he pulled me in tighter.

"Ask me what?"

His fingers traced my face slowly. "Will you stay with me . . . forever? I'll build you the most perfect A-frame cabin you've ever seen, with one of those huge wraparound decks. We can travel whenever you want. Get like a million degrees—"

"Do you know how to build a cabin?" I teased.

"No, but I bet there's a degree out there that will teach me something like that." His nose nearly touched mine, and I wondered if I'd die if he stopped touching me. "After all this is over, we can do whatever we want. And I want to do it all with you. I don't know what the world will be like in a hundred years, but I can guarantee you I'll find something for us to do. I can make you happy. I know you don't need me . . . but it would be a mistake if I never told you how badly I want you."

He actually thought there was a world in which I wouldn't say yes. I could see it in the way worry hung in brows. He wasn't asking for a day. Or a lifetime. Something more. Something I didn't think either of us could fully imagine. And I wanted it. To whatever end. For however long, I would hold on to him with everything I had. I savored that final moment. The last moment I had any semblance of control.

I grabbed his face with both of my hands. "Aaron . . . you don't get it. You're the only thing I've ever fully chosen for myself. I *do* need you. More than anything. Of course I'll stay with you."

Excitement flashed in his eyes, and he kissed me. Everywhere. Tickling and light. Absolute euphoria enveloped me. Aaron was mine.

Everything he'd given me, I gave back to him. This time, I kissed him. First his neck and then his chest. His hips pressed into me, and I moaned, pulling his earlobe between my teeth.

He pulled away, his muscles quivering, but the smile was still wide on his face.

"You gotta stop biting me."

I reached up to playfully bite him on the shoulder. "Why is that?"

He pinned down my forearms. "Because I'm going to bite you much harder, and I won't be able to stop."

"I don't think you'd hurt me . . ." I ran my fingers down his chest, cherishing the warmth and the feeling of having him all to myself. My own ray of sunlight. I couldn't bottle it up and keep it in my pocket, but I could have him. Forever.

His thumb grazed my lips as each staggered breath escaped me. The need in his eyes grew larger with each passing second. A dark intoxication. Greed.

"I gotta stop, Kim. Or I'm going to hurt you. I can feel it." He chuckled. "A slight problem for the time being. But I'll work on it. I promise."

I wanted to protest, but the hunger in his gaze told me his words were probably correct.

He grabbed my hands and kissed them. "Slow down, Burns. We have forever, right?"

"Forever," I said, my heart bursting and bruising my ribs with its rhythm.

He smiled from ear to ear, and his cheeks became flushed. I'd never imagined a lifetime with anyone, but I couldn't imagine another minute without him.

I laid my head on his chest, marinating in his warmth and smell.

"Do you *want* to tell me about your dream?"

I considered it for a moment, but the thought of bringing The Family into the safety of my room again wasn't appealing. In the sheltered room of the frat house, protected by The Legion, it felt like our safe space.

"I'd rather just eat one of those delicious cookies you warmed up for me."

Aaron grabbed one off the plate and held it in front of my face. "Anything for you."

THIRTY

AARON

"Yeah, I think you'll probably have to go with the turtleneck." I brushed her hair back over her shoulder to hide the huge red mark I'd left on her neck.

I thought I was being gentle, but a clear bruise from a bite mark on her inner thigh said otherwise.

The bright morning sun poured into her room, casting everything in a haze. A perfect idealistic world that nothing and nobody else could touch, and it was new and undiscovered.

I rubbed her bottom lip before I kissed the top of her head. "Are you sure you're okay?"

She was glowing. Her skin, her hair—she said it was too messy, and I respectfully disagreed. That content smile widened when she peered up at me. "I'm a big girl, Aaron. I can handle it."

I laughed, remembering exactly where she'd told me that before. Oh, how different things were. Back then, I'd never thought I'd be here in her room, and I'd never believed something like last night would ever be possible. But there she was walking over to my closet, still in her red bra from last night. She turned toward the closet and shredded it for another, then pulled on her shirt and a sweater to cover it.

I could get used to this.

She threw me my shirt that was still crumpled on the floor. "You should wear this one today. I like the way it looks on you."

She'd never told me anything like that before. Other than the hoodie thing, and since I'd heard those words, I'd worn one every chance I could get.

"Oh, really? Do tell."

"It's the color. It compliments you. Blue is the opposite of yellow on the color wheel."

"Yellow?"

"Yeah, you're . . . yellow. Your smile. Your hair. You're bright like the sun."

"Is that because I'm sitting directly in front of the window?"

I smiled. If I was the sun, then she was the moon. My anchor that tethered me to the best parts of myself, and she was never afraid of the dark. Kimberly was fiercely brave, and I needed to be too.

She kissed me. I'd happily be the sun for her. Any day, for the rest of forever.

We walked down the stairs and awaited the barrage from my brothers. They promised to be cool, but I knew better.

In the night, I'd gotten up to get Kimberly a glass of water. That was my first mistake.

They were all gathered at the dining room table, and they quieted as I came in. Presley shielded himself from me to hide what I guessed was a bombardment of questions. He was squirming, bursting at the seams to ask me something.

They'd heard. There was no way they couldn't.

I sighed. "Just say it."

"We didn't hear anything." Luke scratched the stubble on his face to hide his smile.

Zach didn't hide his wide grin. "Not a peep."

Presley kept his lips firmly shut and shook his head.

Of course they did. I'd tried to keep things quiet . . . but it kind of became less of a priority as things progressed.

"You guys better not say anything."

"It's official!?" Presley sprinted in front of me. "Tell me it is and I don't have to keep watching you both suffer."

"Yeah, it is." I couldn't stop smiling. It was like I was back in kindergarten telling them I talked to my crush.

They all shouted with their congratulations and mentioned for the thousandth time it was about time.

"But you have to be cool, okay? No weird comments. Presley, let her bring it up. Luke, give it a minute before you tell her welcome to the family. And Zach, keep it PG . . ."

"That falls under no weird comments," Zach corrected me.

"I know! But there can be no record of this. You guys heard nothing.

You know nothing."

"That five-year plan is looking pretty good right about now." Luke winked at me, and I resolved to tell him my additions later. He didn't make fun of things like that. Not like Presley and Zach.

Zach snickered. "I guess now we know your secret."

"It's the cookies." Luke chuckled.

"What the hell did you put in those things?" Zach had said.

"Definitely the cookies," Presley had said. "You'll have to tell me what your secret recipe is."

"I hate you all."

I had no choice but to hope for the best. Presley came skipping out of the living room and was waiting for us by the time my foot hit the bottom step. He nearly took out one of William's prized monsteras from its pedestal.

"Wait . . . something is different here."

Subtle. I fought the urge to roll my eyes, and Kimberly narrowed her eyes at me.

She cleared her throat. "We're dating."

"Holy shit! It's official!" Presley picked her up and spun her around. "Tell me you guys heard that!"

"Hell yeah! Welcome to the Calem club," Luke said, smiling from ear to ear.

"It's about fuckin' time," Zach grumbled, but there was a smile on his face as he leaned against the wall.

I wanted to burn this moment in my brain forever. I never thought I'd get to see it. I was afraid to even think about it. Wherever she went, I'd follow. I kissed her hand, and I knew she was all mine.

"We need to celebrate! Let's have a party. Kim, what do you normally do for Thanksgiving?" Presley said.

"I don't really do Thanksgiving."

"What do you mean you don't do Thanksgiving?" I said.

"I mean . . . as sad as it sounds, I just get one of those little frozen dinners and call it a day."

My mom would have had a meltdown if she'd heard that. She'd told us every Thanksgiving to invite anyone we wanted and then she'd cook for them. Even if she had to work on the actual day, she planned for it every year.

"Wait . . . what?! No, no, no. We need to do Thanksgiving! We can make a big meal with all the old recipes."

"You don't have to do that," Kimberly said.

Zach frowned. "I mean, not to be the asshole here, but we have bigger fucking things going on right now."

He had a great point, but I liked the idea of us all at the table together. There were many things I wanted to share with her.

"No, it's perfect timing," Luke blurted, sharing that twin telepathy I loved so much, "Thanksgiving is in, what? Three or four days? We can make Kim some of Mom's favorite recipes. Show her a real Calem holiday."

"You and your sentimental shit." Zach shook his head.

"Some things need to be celebrated. Regardless of circumstances." Luke grabbed my shoulder. "Plus, it's a nice distraction."

We all circled together as William, Thane, Skylar, and Dom entered the living room.

Zach was staring daggers as Thane.

I gave Thane a sorry expression. I felt bad for him. I'd had my share of accidents as a vampire too.

"We come in peace, asshole." William licked his teeth. "We need to talk."

Skylar walked forward. "We know that things are strained, and your faith in Kilian is faltering, but we are committed to you. Whether you believe that is up to you.

Dom nodded. "We will see it through."

"We don't need you around. We'll figure out our own protection."

"We'd still be around." Thane rubbed the back of his neck. "I've been hashing it out with Aaron, and honestly, no matter what you say, I'm committed to protecting him. I made a promise to myself that day after the church. We all did."

"So, you're all saying you want to be invited to Thanksgiving?" Presley said.

"Oh, fuck. I don't want to be lumped into that." William ran his hands through his hair, and Skylar elbowed him. "But, yes. We will be there protecting you asshats because . . . we want to. Not because we have to."

"Did Kilian put you up to this?" Luke said.

"No, Kilian is very . . . unnerved by recent events. We just know you're all bound to do something dangerous."

"Well, the more, the merrier. You can help us get groceries." Luke winked at me before grabbing a pen and paper to make the grocery list.

The mood lifted. We might salvage things if we could keep Zach from killing Thane.

"I'll steal some money so we can splurge on a turkey," Presley said before getting a death stare from William.

"Maybe we can all cook her something? Our favorite foods?" I said, nudging Thane.

"What a brilliant idea. I think we could probably swing it, right, guys?" Thane said, "Skylar?"

"Yes, me and Dom can prepare a dish."

William sighed. "I feel like this will be a total waste of time, but yes, I will make a dish. Something classic from Ireland you've surely never tried before."

"It's settled, then. We're giving Kim the best Thanksgiving she's ever had," Luke said.

THIRTY-ONE

KIMBERLY

The doorbell rang.

"I'll get it!" Presley almost knocked me over, and a flurry of flour and dough flew from his apron.

Luke was very particular. Presley could make the pie and only the pie. I think it had something to do with not trusting him with the open flame on the stove. My only job was to supervise Presley and help him cut apples. Zach clinked glasses with William in the corner, and I smiled at the lingering hope for their friendship. Aaron was busy helping Luke, and his hair fell into his eyes as steam poured from the boiling pot that smelled of starchy potatoes. A sly smirk rested at the corner of his lips, and I tried not to stare at the veins in his forearms as he grabbed the skillet and tossed the onions. That didn't stop me from imagining the feel of his lips on my neck again.

"Oh, hey, Chelsea's here!"

I inhaled. My sense of calm shattered as I bolted toward the front door. The frat house was one place I didn't want her. Not with Akira watching our every move. I hoped a week wasn't too long for him to wait for my answer. The firm 'no' would undoubtedly end with him coming to kill me.

She was dressed in an all-black sweater dress, and the first thing I noticed was her freshly done manicure. Black acrylics replaced the uneven paint.

Her smile faded when she saw my black eye I forgot to cover.

"Holy shit, what the hell, Kim?!" Chelsea said with a mixture of horror and shock in her voice.

"I'm fine." I grabbed her shirt to pull her in the door, but she had other plans. She grabbed me by the sweater and pulled me out the front door.

"Okay, what is going on?"

I stared at her, trying to gather my thoughts, and trying to construct a lie that would make sense to her.

"I was . . . sparring in the gym, and my partner hit me pretty good, it's not a big deal. It was an accident."

Her eyes narrowed. "What are you not saying? You can tell me. I didn't peg Aaron as the type, but if he's hurt you—"

"No way! That's not it. I promise. I would tell you. This was an accident. Really."

She let out a long breath. "You've had a lot of accidents this year. I'm starting to get concerned you won't make it to graduation."

Her tone was lighter, but she was still surveying me with a fine-tooth comb. She didn't believe me.

I needed to shift the conversation. "And miss what might be the greatest day of our lives? Never."

I used to believe that. That graduating would somehow bring me all the happiness I'd ever wanted. I had no plans for after, as if life ceased to exist. Now everything was different. It was still something I wanted, but it wasn't the end all for my hopes and dreams. Maybe my path there would look a little different, but I'd get there.

"Exactly. Anyway, come on. Let's go get something to eat. I'm going home to see my parents for break, and I'm trying to enjoy the silence for a few more hours." She wrapped her arm in mine and pulled me toward the stairs, but I stopped.

"I-I can't. I'm sorry. I've got plans."

Internally I cringed at my inability to think of any better excuses on the spot.

"Oh. That's fine." She let go of me and brushed off her dress. If she had any disappointment, she didn't allow me to see.

"I did bring you something, though." She picked up an insulated bag on the step. "I have no doubt the boys will do something over-the-top, make you some measly Thanksgiving dinner and make a huge mess in their mancave, but I wanted to bring you some from our sorority dinner, just in case. I made the mashed potatoes."

Without another word, I embraced her. I didn't deserve her kindness. I longed to linger with her in a world that was no longer mine. I'd hoped for a friend like her all last year. If I had met her even a few months earlier, things might have been different. I imagined it as clear as day. Waking up alone in the hospital bed but this time with someone to call. Someone who would have never let me near Aaron. I might have been less inclined to hear Aaron's words and more willing to turn him in to the police. Then who knows what would have happened to them and their family. I shivered at the thought.

But I would have still been here. Still striving for the one thing I had always been missing.

"Thank you. This is really sweet." I took the bag. The smell of sour cream and cheese wafted in the air.

"You're welcome. Now, don't let any of those boys have any. This is for you only. They can make their own."

I laughed, and we said our goodbyes. I watched her disappear, this time with peace.

The time for faltering between the two sides was over. There was no would've or should've anymore. I'd chosen what I wanted. On my own terms.

The sun was almost gone when we found ourselves at the firepits in the square. String lights were interwoven in the branches above our heads. There were a few other groups of students at the pits, and I relaxed. A semipublic area and our closest Legion members helped. I longed for a day with no running, but as I searched the faces of the Calem brothers, I knew my journey was just beginning. My race had just started, but they'd already been around the track a few times. Yet, they smiled. Every. Single. One.

Aaron put his arm around my shoulder. "Hope you're hungry."

"This feels weird being the only human here. You guys made way too much food."

"Oh, don't worry about that. We'll bring it over to the other house-mates. Someone will eat it."

I had already texted Chelsea, who would be back in just two days, that I had some food waiting for her. I didn't have the guts to ask her to help me assemble the car wash yet. I was blissfully holding that bomb until after tonight. Nothing had registered yet.

I wouldn't be coming back. Nothing would ever be the same when I stepped out of Blackheart, and Presley started preparing me for how little I'd be able to take with me.

But it could all wait for one more night. Tonight was for celebrating.

I tried to take it all in. The sheer amount of people, the warmth of the fire. A peach and lavender sky filled with stars while the tastiest-looking Thanksgiving meal was set on my lap. A plate filled to the brim and smelled of turkey breast and thyme.

This time last year, I was eating my lukewarm Thanksgiving meal from the freezer and watching every Thanksgiving episode from my favorite TV shows. I never felt sad, or at least I didn't notice it if I had. It was just what I did on holidays. I didn't decorate, and I didn't accept invitations to go anywhere. I told myself it was because I liked my routine. But staring at the group, my heart felt like it might burst, and I realized it was just a mask. One of the many I'd shed. Here in the light of the fire, I was fully exposed.

"Are you okay?" Aaron stared at me with his warm-honey eyes. He was a little too good at reading the sound of my heart beating in my chest.

"Yeah, I'm just really excited to eat all this food."

We all moved around the fire. The licks of the flames teased the cool autumn air, and I scooted a few inches closer to Aaron. His hand rested on my leg.

The Legion sat on one side, and we sat on the other. Skylar was bundled in a sherpa hoodie and pulled her legs up in the chair while she shared a quiet conversation with Dom. She laid a plaid blanket over his legs, and I swore he cracked a smile.

William and Thane were sharing drinks with the rest of the boys. I'd declined one. Tonight, I wanted to remember every single second. Despite me being the only one eating, everyone was full of smiles and laughter.

"Let's tell scary stories," Presley said, warming his hands.

Aaron and Zach booed while Luke egged him on.

"I've found real life is much more terrifying." William held his glass up, and Zach clinked the necks of the bottles together in agreement.

"Why don't you tell a good story, then?" Skylar laid her head back on the chair. "You can't possibly be gloomy all the time."

"She's right, Will. Crack open that shell," Thane said.

William sighed. "I'm not drunk enough for that."

"Oh, got it." Luke passed down a bottle of liquor and shot glass.

"We're all really fucked up, huh?" William snickered as he poured liquor into what was the biggest shot glass I'd ever seen.

"Yep," the twins said in unison, and they all took a shot at the same time.

Aaron put his arms around me while I shoveled the best food I'd ever had in my mouth.

"Fine. I'll tell one fuckin' story. But 'tis not that interesting." William's accent came through with each drop of alcohol. His fake persona at BFU involved him growing up in California, so he always had to hide it.

"In my country, there was a ghost story of an abandoned house on a hill. Tales of banshees that lived in hills and screamed in the night. My sister and I . . . we always played together, and we'd play there in the yard. She wasn't afraid of things like that . . . ghosts and spirits. But I was. She was younger but much braver."

We all listened in silent attentiveness.

"It was her idea to spend the night there. She wanted to sneak out in the night, unbeknownst to my mother, and look it in the face and see if it was true. She was hard to convince once her mind was set on something."

Aaron nudged me, and I wrapped my arm around him.

"We went, and I was fuckin' terrified. Every creak. Every blow of the wind. But I couldn't back down. I was supposed to be the strong big brother. The night came and went and there was nothing. No banshees. No cold chills. It was just a house."

I never believed in ghost stories growing up, but I imagined if I had a little sibling, I might do the same. Help them conquer their fear.

"It would be a few more years before I learned there was far more to fear than made-up ghost stories and haunted houses. Life is that ghost. But even more terrifying."

Silence accompanied the cool breeze rustling through the trees.

"What was your sister's name?" I said.

I didn't even know if he'd answer, but he'd told me about losing his sister once. He didn't have to tell me the truth then. He could have told me any story.

"Eilean." William's eyes softened in the light of the fire.

"You've never told me that," Thane said.

"You never asked." William poured himself another shot and downed it.

The others continued with a few stories. Thane told the story of his drunken stupor in an Irish pub that led him to William and Kilian. Skylar shared her and Dom's first time meeting Kilian, which involved her trying to kill him for tracking them down a few years after their escape. I wasn't surprised by any of it.

They were knit together, but in a much different way than the Calem brothers. Not quite a family but close. Caring. Thoughtful. Individuals coming together for a common cause that just happened to like each other's company.

I would miss them. Even William. They'd undeniably kept their word in keeping us safe. A part of me felt sad for what awaited our newfound friend group.

But that one night under the starlight, we were all family.

As everyone prepared to go home, The Legion started picking up and walking to the house, which was visible from the firepit. I drifted back toward the fire.

"You and Aaron made it official, I hear." William's cigarette smoke wafted into my face.

"Yeah. Come to tell me some obscure insult?" I said, crossing my arms.

He laughed. "No, love. Actually . . . you two are good together."

I turned to him. That was the first nice thing he'd said in months.

"See, I can be nice. Bit of advice, though . . ."

"Here it comes." I waited. I never cared for unsolicited advice, especially from him.

"Turn. As soon as you can. They're gonna tell you to wait till you're ready. All that shit. No. You need to turn soon, or guaranteed . . . they'll be burying you before spring."

My stomach knotted. It sounded almost like a threat. But the muscles in his face were relaxed. He was being sincere.

"Thanks. I'll keep that in mind."

He clicked his tongue. "Until then, I guess sunglasses and turtlenecks will be your new best friends. At least they're fashionable."

He walked away and joined Thane. There was a story there, and I wondered if I'd ever know what it was.

"Did you have fun?" Luke was next to me, and Zach followed behind him.

"Yeah . . . it felt nice to be a part of something." It was a more vulnerable thing to say, but I embraced the discomfort.

Zach and Luke shared a look. That "telepathy" Aaron swore was actual magic.

"Uh-oh." Aaron was behind me with a smile. "I know that look."

"I think it's about time we officially inducted Kimberly to the Calem family."

The fire illuminated all our faces, and Zach pulled a pocketknife from his joggers.

"A blood pact," Zach said with a toothy smile.

"Only if she wants to," Aaron said.

"Finally." Presley was beside us instantly.

"Wait, what exactly am I agreeing to?"

"It's just a pact Luke and I made with Pres and Aaron when they were younger. Talk is cheap but blood is forever. You're one of us now. Let's make it official," Zach said.

"Aw. Someone does have a heart," Presley said before Zach pushed him.

"What? I can be sentimental sometimes. What do you say, Kim? It's just a little blood. Not like you'll turn or anything."

"Speaking of, when are we doing the thing?" Presley asked.

William's words were seared on the back of my skull.

"I-I . . ."

"Kim will tell us when she's ready," Aaron said.

"Let's give her more than a few days to decide," Luke said.

The Calem boys all stared back at me, and their eyes were heavy with anticipation. I didn't have words. It wasn't a question I expected being asked. My whole body felt hot from excitement. I hadn't realized how much I wanted to be included, to be considered one of their own.

"Well, in the meantime. Let's make another life-altering commitment." Zach smiled.

"What do I have to do?"

Zach brought his thumb to his lip and bit down. A small dot of black blood appeared. He handed me the knife. "Just a little pinprick."

Aaron's arm grazed my shoulder, and I gave him a reassuring smile.

"I can handle a little blood," Aaron said tentatively.

I pressed the blade into my thumb, the pain stopped me from making more than an indentation in my skin.

Aaron placed his hand in mine, steadying the blade. "Are you sure?"

I knew what he was asking me. Something much more serious deep down. To be a Calem, marked with their blood, was to be family. To be their family meant being marked for death, but it also meant being greatly loved and protected. This was the final seal. Their final promise to me, and in return, my promise to them.

"I'm sure."

My mind flashed back to the old church and the crack of thunder. William's proposition to forget. I'd already made my mind up long ago.

"You're the only other person who's been inducted. This is special stuff." Presley's eyes glistened in the fire. "Sarah and Ashley were going to . . . until . . . Sarah went missing."

Zach's hand raked through his hair. "Ash didn't want to do it without her."

I expected to see a solemn Luke, but when he finally tore his gaze away from the fire, he smiled that million-dollar smile that told thousands of stories all at once. The kind where the heroes always get back up no matter how beaten and bruised.

"Alright, let's do this." He clapped and stood.

The smile lingered when he bit down on his thumb, and Presley followed suit.

Aaron's warmth was blazing hot in the cool of night. With his hand on mine, we pressed the blade into my skin, a small dot of red appeared on my forefinger. His eyes drank me in as he bit his thumb. Fear and hope smoldered together and floated into the night like the crackling embers.

"Repeat after me." Luke pulled his shoulders back. "With earnest, I swear to . . . protect, to love, and to fight for this family. Until my last day."

The words hummed in my throat after I said them. A secret song.

We placed our hands over the fire, joining our thumbs under the light of the moon. Our blood meshed as one. They belonged to me, and I belonged to them.

My heart surged with pride and love. A vow to my new family. Forever.

A strange feeling tickled my spine, and I scanned the darkness hidden in the trees. If Akira didn't know then, he knew now. I wasn't running.

"JUST A LITTLE BLOOD"

AARON

"Did you enjoy your Thanksgiving?" I asked as I placed down a dish on the counter.

My brothers weren't back yet, and all the members of The Legion were with Kilian in the study. Our kitchen was oddly calm and quiet for once.

"More than I ever thought possible. Is this how it always is for you?"

"Chaotic? Loud? Blood rituals? I think those are all becoming part of the Calem family traditions."

She pulled her hair over her ear, displaying her neck, while she cleaned up the pie dough.

It hadn't been long since I'd fed, but I focused on the pulse there, the rush of blood running through her veins, and—just for a second—thought of running my lips over the warmth of her skin.

"What?" She blushed.

"Nothing."

She returned her attention back to cleaning, and I helped. "I just meant . . . it's full. Full of everything. Holidays for me have always been complicated. I didn't celebrate them more than I celebrated anything else in my life. You guys celebrate *everything*."

"There's a lot in life to celebrate. Birthdays and holidays were my favorite days of the year."

"And my least favorite. Not because I wasn't happy or bitter, but because everyone crowds the grocery store. It means more traffic, and everything closes. It was so inconvenient."

"What does it feel like to know you don't have to spend another holiday alone, like ever?"

"I feel like I've missed out on a lot of things. Like the Calem tradition of 'who eats the first buttered roll'? What's that about?"

"Oh. That's easy. We ate all of my mom's homemade rolls every year before dinner started, so we had to instate the honor of the first roll to the most deserving to ensure it was fair. This year that was you."

She rolled her eyes with a smirk. "I'm the only one who could eat it."

I moved to wipe the flour from her chin and held her gaze. Not a drop of alcohol in my system, and yet I was falling into her.

"Can I help you?" She jutted her chin out, and I brushed it with my thumb.

"I wanna try something."

"You have that look."

"Like the big bad wolf coming to devour his prey?" I joked.

"More like you have a bad idea, and I'm going to end up going along with it."

I grinned. She was right, but she made no attempt to move away as I leaned into her neck. She gasped. The soft drumming right under her ear called to me, and I grazed her sensitive flesh with my lips and nearly groaned.

She was pinned against the countertop with nowhere to go.

"Would you like me to bite you, Burns?" I asked, still taking pleasure in the pace of her pulse racing. I nudged my face into her neck. "Come on, just a tiny one."

She giggled as my nudging turned into light kisses.

"Sorry, blood bank's off-limits."

"Oh? Where are you gonna run off to?"

"I've got a plan." She scrunched her nose up with the challenge in her eyes.

"Oh yeah?" I challenged back.

She leaned in and I did too. It was just enough of a distraction for her to duck underneath my arms, but I grabbed her from behind and sat her on top of the counter.

"Do you think there's a place you could hide from me? Now that I know your scent . . . your heartbeat. I could track you for miles if I wanted to." I leaned in to savor her smell.

A playful taunt, and with her labored breathing and the way she held my gaze, I knew she was into it.

"*Now*, you're looking at me like you want to eat me." She snickered.

Oh, she had no idea. Such a strange feeling that didn't exist in a human capacity. I used to love to eat. Anything. Everything. Salty or sweet. Didn't matter. Now, the only thing that got me salivating was the woman in front of me. It was overwhelming how much I wanted her. Me and the monster playing a game. A terrible, messed up game.

"Oh definitely. Every last bite."

"Aaron . . . your eyes," she said, with more strength than before.

I quieted her with kiss on her neck. She arched into me.

Savoring the surrender of the rise and fall of her chest, I dragged my teeth across her carotid. I hated but also loved it. She wasn't prey, but to the voice in my head she was. A human willing to let me get this close to her. Willing to let me do a lot of things.

She was also my *girlfriend*. I would not tire of saying that any time soon. I gripped her waist, taking my attention back to the softness of her lips, and forced myself to think past the want, screaming for my attention and her. Her breath in my throat. The softness of her skin. I loved this woman. I'd protect her. Even if that was from myself.

"Whoa," Presley said, standing in the doorway. "Don't you guys have bedrooms?"

He'd propped himself against the wall, smiling.

Kimberly and I exchanged an equal look of horror. Somehow, we'd gotten a little carried away in the kitchen, and it didn't look good with her skirt hiked up by her waist.

I helped Kimberly off the counter, and she averted her gaze as she moved past my brother.

"Don't say another word," I warned.

He pretended to zip his lips, then waited till we were at the top of the stairs to add, "Use protection!"

Speaking of protection. I'd already had to have that painful conversation with William, of all people. I didn't want to ask, but I had to know, and since my older brothers didn't know, it was him or Kilian, so I picked the lesser of two evils.

"I have to ask you something. And I need you to not be a dick about it." I'd cornered him in the hallway one day.

"That's a tall order. But go ahead."

"Can vampires . . . can we—" I'd stopped to double-check Presley wasn't around because I'd never hear the end of it.

"Spit it out, Calem."

"Can we procreate? Like is there any chance of that happening?"

"You and Kimberly are moving a bit fast, are ya?"

"No. It's just in case. You're the only one except Kilian who might know, so please don't make this painful for me."

"No. You can't. No life can come from bodies like ours. I could get into logistics if you want to have a sex-ed conversation right now."

"Nope. That's enough. Thanks."

He nodded but added, *"Aaron, just be careful before she's changed."*

"I will."

"Good. Let's not do this again."

Kimberly disappeared into my bedroom, and I shut the door. Everything was dark as I reached for the light, simultaneously pinning her to my door.

I stopped to feel her instead. Her heartbeat was the only noise in the room, constantly reminding me to be gentle.

Pull but don't *pull*. Grab but don't *grab*. It distracted me from the very thing I wanted. All of her. So maybe it was a good distraction, then.

She wasn't being gentle with me, though. Not that I wanted her to be. My bottom lip slipped between her teeth, and the pulling of my hair was enough to make all my blood rush south.

Like before, I struggled under the weight of the need for her. A confusing twist of pleasure and concentration battled each other.

"Should we try again? Are you okay?" Kimberly whispered as I moved my lips down her throat.

I wasn't. I wasn't even okay when I'd fed the same day, and it had been a few days.

"I-I don't think I can. But just let me enjoy this for just a few more minutes."

We weren't close enough. It was never enough.

I peeled off her shirt so I could have better access to her collarbone.

"Okay . . ." she said, panting. It was good. *So good.*

I nipped at her skin, and the soft whimper that escaped her lips urged me to please her. Nothing could stop me from stripping her further before leaving the room.

Gentle.

I grabbed her, as gentle as I could, with my blood pumping in my ears, and laid her over my bed. Everything felt hot and urgent.

I enjoyed peeling her leggings off more than I should have. I'd wanted to so many times, and now I *could*. It was all spectacular new territory.

As my own pulse spread, I became more aware of how much I couldn't handle it.

Maybe if I didn't know what her blood tasted like or felt her heartbeat in my veins. If I fed right before, then maybe.

I started by her ankle, savoring her heat and the salt of her skin as I kissed up her thigh. Every touch of my lips made her squirm and buck beneath me. My teeth grazed the tenderness of her skin, and I shook with need.

Come on, one little bite won't hurt.

I let the thought in for half a second. If I'd ever be able to control the venom enough to bite her without it hurting. I'd had a lot of practice in the last few months . . .

No. Focus.

I didn't want to bite her. *It* did.

My tongue followed the pulse in her leg until I was at the apex of her thigh. I ached to sink into her.

"Do you need to stop?" she asked.

"No, I'm okay. Just a little more," I whispered, with my cheek resting on her thigh.

Stroking her core, she arched into me. Wanting me. Relaxed and calm. I needed to give her more. More pleasure. More of me.

Moving her underwear to the side, I paused to ask, "Is this okay?"

She let out a slow breath. "Yes."

I eased into her. One finger slowly.

"Oh," she breathed out. I could hardly hold myself together. Thrusting into the edge of the bed did nothing to take the edge off.

We stayed in a rhythm that had her inching closer. How could I stop?

I added another finger, gently stroking her deeper this time.

She let out a half gasp, half choke. "Aaron. Please."

"Shhh. I'm here. It's okay."

I kissed the tendon on the inside of her thigh. The pumping of the blood in her artery set my heart ablaze. I traced it with my tongue. My entire body shook harder.

This wasn't helping that need to devour her, but it helped relax her.

It was painful that I couldn't have her, but she could have me. That was enough to focus my thoughts.

She opened herself up to me, spreading her legs and relaxing into me as I moved within her.

I would not get tired of this, and my body physically would not. I could give her whatever she wanted for however long.

She tightened around my fingers and dug her nails into my shoulders until I leaned over her.

"Just don't go. Don't stop touching me."

I eased in another finger. A silent assurance I wouldn't.

"Better?"

She nodded into my chest, pulling at me as if she let go, I'd disappear.

I moved my attention back to her core. I couldn't taste her blood, but I could taste *her*. Warm, sweet, and perfect.

That's what she needed.

As soon as I took her in my mouth, a deep groan left her lips. She tugged at my hair and worked her hips while she rode out her orgasm.

I kissed my way back up her stomach with a grin. Her heartbeat was wild and relentless. She held onto me like she thought I might get up any minute.

"I like this. Being this close to you."

"I *love* it," I said.

From friends to this. It made everything we did feel just that much more important. That much more real. "It's pretty much the best thing ever."

I didn't want to stop touching her, tracing her lips with my fingers and feeling her warmth, but I probably needed to.

I kissed her forehead and tried to pull myself up, but she stopped me.

"Wait."

She yanked me by my shirt till I rested on top of her with my hips crushing her. "Stay close to me."

Nevermind.

"Always." I kissed her cheek. Why had we waited so long for this? "We should probably stop while we're ahead, though."

"You're right." She sighed, then smiled. "I'm happy I'm staying."

"Me too. We don't have to hold back anymore. And I don't ever have to say goodbye."

Then, like magnets, we were falling into each other again. She kissed my chest as she peeled off my shirt. Then . . . bit my ear and my neck.

"Not fair."

I pinned her with shaky arms. My blood instantly boiled over with need, and the hunger twisted in my gut.

"Maybe we don't need to stop yet," I said, kissing her neck again. "I just really love this."

I stopped to look at her and revel in our foreheads touching while drinking in the feeling of her breath slowing. The pumping of her blood underneath her skin grew louder, quick and powerful, and I fought the urge to trace her veins with my tongue. *A dangerous game*, I reminded myself.

But I couldn't stop touching her. I wasn't done.

I traced the line down her stomach, and she let me, watching me with careful ease.

"I love that sound you make." I eased my fingers back into her, stroking her.

And there she was again. Back to clinging to me. Her nails dug into my back. *Mine. All mine.*

"Aaron, I can't."

"You can. You're such an overachiever."

She gasped as I curled my fingers, strumming faster and circling my thumb around her most sensitive skin. This time, I groaned.

"I need you," she breathed out. An admission to something much deeper.

"Don't worry, I'm here," I said, watching her come undone for me, showing her I wasn't going anywhere. I could handle this. She said my name again and again while writhing beneath me.

That's where I focused my attention. On loving her. Being there for her. Forever.

"You're doing so good, Kim."

"It's too much."

As she got closer to climax, I pulled her closer. Chest to chest. Every attempt she made to squirm, I held her tighter and gave her more. Her body was good at showing me what she needed. Her attempts to get more friction or more movement.

The sounds she made were driving me to the edge.

"I've got you," I whispered as she came for me again, clenching around me and laying her head back.

It was amazing how clear my head got when I focused on her pleasure instead of mine. When I thought of how much I wanted it for her.

For two people who should avoid sex, we weren't doing the best job at it, but there was something so natural about it. It was easy to love her and touch her and make her feel good. I'd pull my heart out of my chest to make her happy.

So Kim and I were bad about doing things we should do? What was new?

"Feel better?" I asked.

Her hands were in my hair, and I was still hungry for her, every inch, but I'd have to wait till I could ensure I had enough control.

"Do you . . . want me to touch you?"

The blood raced from my brain. *Be good, Aaron.*

"No. I mean. Yes. Hell yes, but I can't. I really, really can't. This does so much more for me than you know. We'll get there."

She smiled up at me. "This is good practice."

"Yeah." I held her close, squeezing her before I finally let her get her clothes back on.

"How's that finger?" I asked.

"It's a little sore," she said as she pulled her shirt back on. "But it was worth it."

I grabbed her hand. "Want me to kiss it?"

I kissed her finger softly, and the faintest taste of iron lingered on her cut. The kiss turned into a light suction. It was brief but long enough for me to *taste* her.

All my thoughts were gone. Everything was red again.

She gasped.

I pulled away. "Shit. Sorry. I'm so sorry—"

"It's okay." Her voice felt far away.

Just a little blood. Humans don't need all of it.

The voice had a point. Humans gave blood all the time. If I only took a little, she'd be fine.

That's it. She'll let you take it. She has before.

If I had a little, then, maybe, I could focus. The memory of her blood in my mouth filled my mind.

I could clear my head and—

I moved to stand up. To run.

She stopped me with a hand on my cheek. "It's okay. It didn't hurt. I think it comes with the territory of having a vampire as a boyfriend."

She placed her finger in her mouth, sucking off the remnants of blood. "See, no biggy."

There was no hint of fear in her eyes, as I pulled her to me in an embrace. Our lips met, and I slid my tongue into her mouth. I savored the remnants of her blood still coating her tongue. So faint but still there.

I pulled away. "We should go downstairs."

"Okay." She smiled but stopped me from getting up. "Hold on. Just sit here with me."

Taking her hand in mine, I leaned into her until our foreheads touched. My palm rested right over her heart.

"I was just waiting for your eyes to return to normal."

"Oh."

"We have all the time in the world, right?" she asked.

"Right."

I wondered if I'd ever be able to have her like I longed to. She smiled and kissed my forehead. We would figure it out eventually.

"You're really good at this . . . you've had to have done this before." She looked up at me through her lashes. It was a hidden question.

"I've been with some girls. Yes."

I watched her process that slowly. A frown set on her lips. "I figured."

"It doesn't compare to this. I've never had or felt anything like this."

There were two defining parts of my life. Human Aaron and vampire Aaron. At one point, I'd have said I liked human me better, but that wasn't true anymore. Kimberly didn't exist in that world, and in this one, she was radiant and real. And she made me better. Everything we'd gone through made me better.

"Me either," she said.

She was still far away from me, looking at the door.

"Let me in, Burns. Tell me what you're thinking."

"You're the first person I've ever let this close to me. This is all new for me. But I like it. I like how intimate it is. I like how you touch me. You make me feel so safe."

I smiled, stroking her cheek. "Monster and all?"

"Yes, all of it."

"I'm so in love with you."

She smiled, leaning her head into me. The smallest glimmer of a tear rested in the corner of her eye. "I'm so relieved. Relieved that you love me the same way I love you. There's gotta be a statistic somewhere that says how unlikely that is for people."

I was in awe of her. This beautiful woman, who was afraid to open up to the world was bare before me, and I knew what it meant for her. It only made that call to protect her grow. I'd protect her tenderness. That part of her she let no one else but me see. There was a level of responsibility I had now, but that didn't scare me. When I looked at her, everything seemed possible.

"I won't let you down. Even with the vampire thing and this being new territory, I can handle it."

"I get monster you and you." She chuckled.

"Package deal. And when we're finally able to do this, it will be new for me too."

"Together."

I smiled. "Yeah, together."

THIRTY-TWO

KIMBERLY

On the grassy lawn of OBA, the morning breeze rushed through the trees. The redwoods stayed evergreen while the maples had long shed their leaves, and only a few oak trees held their fall leaves. I grabbed a large, thick black marker and wrote "Car wash" on a piece of poster board Chelsea had stored under her bed.

"Have you lost your mind?" were the first words out of her mouth when I asked her to help me organize a frat car wash in just a few days. I was reluctant to have her help, but I desperately needed it, and she had connections. Not just in her sorority, in which I knew she could guarantee every single one of them would attend, but even up to the school board. Over the summer, she had told me about how she'd made great friends with the woman in the dean's office. Black Forest University loved their fraternities and sororities because they brought in the most traffic.

Chelsea was next to me using her marker like a magic wand, and every sign looked like a professionally printed sign. She sighed and flung her marker down, making that our tenth sign. We still needed to put them up all over town.

"Can you pass me the glitter?" I said, contemplating every life choice I'd ever made.

She flung it to me, and it rolled to my knee. "First you blow me off and then you come pleading on my doorstep asking me to help you put this huge event together in one day—"

"I haven't been blowing you off! I promise. I've been busy."

I was being a horrible friend. If only I could come clean. If only she could see I was probably saving her from getting killed by a cult.

She glared at me, then her brow softened. "I know. I know. You're in love. But the Coleman boys are not that interesting. I don't get how or why you want to hang around them all the time."

"They're fun."

"They're cavemen, but I digress." She held up a pink glitter sign, and little piles of loose glitter fell into the grass. "You're lucky just about every girl on this campus will be clawing their way over here to see the Coleman boys shirtless . . . Aaron included."

My stomach turned. Envy was a dear friend, but jealousy was new.

Chelsea smiled from ear to ear as she pulled her hair back into a high ponytail.

"You're happy about my pain, aren't you?"

Chelsea held up her fingers close together. "Just a tiny bit."

I could not believe we'd once been at each other's throats over Aaron.

We walked arm in arm toward the door of the frat house, where William had clearly figured out the plan for the car wash, considering there were already people piled on the lawn. Even the other fraternities wanted to come and support. Probably to drink too. Our secret text went out the night of Thanksgiving, and as expected, the sororities and fraternities went wild.

"I'll be right back. Then me and Skylar will help put signs around town."

I hadn't asked Skylar yet, but I assumed she'd protect me.

Chelsea turned to leave, but I stopped her. "Chelsea . . . thank you. I don't know what I'd do without you."

I'd never be able to fully thank her for her friendship. I was going to disappear, and I'd just be a memory to her. I hoped she would forgive me after a few years. Maybe time would heal my abandonment, but I knew that feeling well. Time helped, but the scar never went away.

She smiled and rolled her eyes.

I couldn't believe I would probably lose one of my first friends at college because I was too busy running around keeping vampire secrets.

Behind William, the Calem boys came strolling out of the house, all shirtless and wearing swim shorts. Except Zach who had voted for compression shorts. They were laying it on thick. My attention lingered on Aaron. His chest. His arms. That smile. The sun warming his skin made everything about him light up. When he ran his hands through his fluffy hair, I imagined those hands. The lines. The strength. The way they felt on my skin. All the places they touched . . .

William pointed to the steps and motioned for them to sit. They all did. I walked in slowly behind, hoping I could avoid the wrath, but Presley spotted me and waved.

"Oh, perfect. You're all here," William said with flared nostrils. "Do any of you want to tell me what the hell you're doing?"

Presley raised his hand. "It's a car wash."

"Yep. Gathered that. Now, why the hell are you having a car wash on our lawn?"

"We wanted to make money for the spring block party," Luke said.

"Really? *You're* so concerned with the spring block party, then?"

"Totally." Luke smiled from ear to ear. "What else could I possibly be concerned with right now?"

"Bullshit. You fuckin' bastards." William paced in front of them. "I know you now. You're up to something. I can smell it."

"We just want to flaunt our bodies. Honest." Presley snickered.

Zach and Aaron nodded.

"You wanted us to make money in an honest way," Luke said.

"Yeah, that's why you had fuckin' jobs! You're tellin' me none of ya are scheduled to work today?"

"We moved everything around so we could do this!" Presley said.

William turned, only now noticing the glittery sign still in my hand. "That fuckin' poster. You're all in on this?"

I hid it behind my back as if it would help.

"Cool poster, Kim!" Presley gave me a thumbs-up while the other boys snickered.

"You all think is fuckin' hilarious, don't ya? How do you think Kilian is going to feel about a shirtless car wash in front of the fuckin' house!?"

The mental image of Kilian sauntering to the front lawn to see the boys wet and topless was enough to make us all squirm and hold our tongue to keep from laughing. The boys all stared down at their feet, not saying a word until Zach broke his composure and threw a hand over his mouth to smother his laughter.

"Maybe he could join us." Aaron bit his lip, still fighting a smile.

"Oh. I know you're up to something. I'm going to figure out what it is. Fuck."

He turned around, still talking to himself, and threw his hands in the air. "I'm tired of fuckin' babysitting."

"Wow, he is pissed." Presley laughed as he left.

Zach stood up and patted Luke on the back. "I like this plan more and more."

I'm not sure it had set in for any of us yet that tomorrow night would be our last night on campus. I think we were all savoring it. Soaking in our last moments as regular college kids. Luke and Zach said they never planned on going to college. But even though they struggled through the classes, as they walked next to each other, I couldn't help but think how happy they were together. Almost like it was what they were meant for. Connection.

They grabbed their buckets and sponges and headed toward the road. Presley worked the sorority girls, playfully grabbing their hands and beckoning them to grab their friends. To my surprise, Zach and Luke were doing the same thing. Usually both very coy, they were flirting, subtly flexing, and playing every bit of the charming frat-boy persona they could.

Aaron nudged me. "Think you'll be jealous when the ladies are eyeing me?"

I smiled. "Nope."

Aaron pinched my chin and tilted my face. "You're sure?"

I stuttered, my breath stopping in my throat. "Mhm."

He put his hand above me, our stolen moment just out of sight, while his chest pinned me to the porch pillar. Soft lips grazed over my ear, and I shivered.

"I kinda love this," he said, his breath still hot on my neck while his fingers grazed my breastbone. "That little kick in your heart every time I get close to you . . ."

I swallowed. My mind blanked for a second, and I forgot where we were.

"You're just teasing me now."

He smirked. "A little."

"I don't like it."

"Are you sure?" He leaned in to kiss my cheek and whispered in my ear, "Your heartbeat says otherwise . . .."

It did. I pulled away and tried to regain my composure.

"After the hold you've had on me from the moment you walked away from me in the courtyard, it's nice to have some . . . control." He laughed.

But I wasn't ready for him to move away from me. "Tell me what you're thinking."

He seemed surprised by my question at first, then his chest pressed into mine. The light danced in his irises.

"You couldn't handle what I'm thinking right now." A shadow cast over Aaron's eyes and warmth flashed in my core.

He was probably right. It was the same look he gave me when he'd had me pinned down in my bed, but there was a part of me . . . a part I wasn't ready to admit to yet, that wondered what exactly that might be.

I straightened myself, determined not to bend. "Oh, really? Because you're the one who's blushing."

He sucked in a breath, losing his composure, and the smile returned. "Am not."

But he was a mess of blushed cheeks and blond hair, and I savored that shy smile that appeared when I said it. I didn't know where we were going next, but I'd be next to him and that made me feel okay.

"Okay, love birds. Come on. Aaron, we have our bodies to sell for money." Presley appeared next to us.

"What the hell, Pres?" Aaron grumbled.

"Sorry, as your little brother, it's a core part of my life's mission to be a cockblock. I don't make the rules."

We followed him toward the road, weaving between the growing number of students.

"Kimberly, feel free to join if you wanna put on a bikini," Presley said. It was way too cold for that.

"I'm okay."

"Just wanted to ask in case you felt left out."

I'd always been scared to leave Blackheart. There was something holding me back, but with the Calem brothers, there was freedom. It lingered on the horizon, and for the first time, I wondered what else was out there. I was ready.

"TWILIGHT MARATHON, ANYONE?"

PRESLEY

✱ Author's note

This scene is dedicated to mom, who took me to watch nearly every Twilight movie in the theaters.

I'd played matchmaker, and now I needed to assume another role. Helping my older brothers relax amid their shitstorm. They wouldn't tell me their past. They didn't want to talk about their traumas. Which was fine. I wasn't sure I wanted to know. Not that I didn't care. It was a lot to process, and me processing, hindered them keeping their heads above water.

I hated seeing them so miserable. Luke couldn't sit still, and Zach was constantly worried about Luke. It made me dizzy watching their dance over and over again.

"Let's do a Twilight marathon," I said, watching Luke pace in the living room yet again.

"Fuck that," Zach said. "No fucking way."

"You're fighting this too hard. It will be fun."

The quickest way to get Zach to do anything was to get Luke to do it. It was twin magic. Zach would do literally anything Luke was on board for. Even if it involved something embarrassing like joining the ballet and counting butterflies in a flower field. Somehow, if Luke was involved, so was Zach.

That's why we called them the twins. Not just because of the fraternal thing or the whole grew in the same womb thing. I'm sure there were twins out there who were not as close as my older brothers. Zach and Luke had always moved around each other like planets orbiting the sun. I mean, I was close with my brothers. I'd die for them and all that, but I could tell it was different for them somehow. Since I could remember, they did everything together.

Naturally, I used this to my advantage.

"Luke, I need a pick-me-up. Please."

Luke frowned, analyzing me in the way big brothers do. He'd know I was lying. I didn't get how he knew. I wasn't like Aaron with the most painfully obvious tells. Like his voice raising and avoiding eye contact. I swear he only got away with lies because of that puppy-dog eye thing. At least, I knew how to deliver a decent lie with a straight face, but Luke still knew somehow.

I batted my eyelashes at him. "Pretty please."

"I don't know, Pres. I can't sit down and focus on movies right now."

"But we don't have to just watch, you'll have my commentary to help you stay focused."

"There's a lot to do."

We were leaving tomorrow night. I wasn't completely on board with the move because I would miss this place a lot, but I guess it didn't matter. It didn't matter where we were. As long as we were together, we'd make fun memories. Even if we would forever be on the run from a vampire cult.

"Even better because they're not going to suspect a thing if we're in the living room all night watching vampire movie."

Zach shook his head, mouthing a firm, *No*. He was afraid to have fun I think.

"It will be a great distraction. Please Luke, I haven't gotten to hang out with you in a hot minute and we're not going to be able to steal the streaming services from the guys here anymore."

"Fine. How many movies are there?"

"Luke," Zach said.

"Five."

"I can't think of anything else I'd rather be doing," Zach said.

"It will be good family bonding," Luke said.

"How much family bonding do we need? I'm stuck in a house with you all twenty-four seven."

They call me dramatic, but Zach was way more dramatic than me.

"I'll get the beer!"

I rushed to the fridge and grabbed our seemingly never-ending supply of beer. I didn't know who put it in there, but it was constantly stocked.

I jumped over the back of the couch and planted myself next to Luke. The house was quiet because of the holiday break. Which also meant we could turn the surround sound on to full blast.

"Why is everything blue?" Zach asked as the title screen came on and the misty little forest came into view.

"It's the iconic blue filter." I hit the top of my beer on the edge of the coffee table, and the cap flew off.

"I don't get it."

"It's cinematic. Creative." Luke nodded.

Luke got it. Like he got everything. He made everything fun and exciting. He used to be my dedicated movie buddy because I could get him to watch anything with me. Rom-Coms, documentaries, you name it. I hated that he couldn't enjoy them anymore.

They both listened to my lesson on Bella. How I thought her mom kinda sucked and Bella suffered from hyper-independence. I never read the books. Mostly because me and books just didn't mix. But I was in enough fan groups to get the gist of what I missed.

"Edward is such a dick," Zach snarled. "Why is he the favorite?"

"He's a broody vampire. He's the shit," I said. "You have to pick a team. Edward or Jacob."

"Which one is Jacob?"

"The childhood friend that was in the truck with her," I said.

"He was on the screen for five seconds."

"He plays a bigger role in the second movie."

Zach looked at the TV with a curled lip. At least he was distracted. "Definitely him. Literally anyone but Edward."

"I like Bella. She seems nice," Luke said.

"Okay, Luke is team Bella. Zach is team Jacob, and I'm team Edward." Edward could gaslight me any day.

They were getting into it. Luke wasn't shaking the couch with his leg bouncing, and there was no mention of tomorrow. It was just us and our teenage vampire movie. Poetic.

"You're never telling anyone I watched this with you."

Zach was more invested than before and wouldn't shut up about how much he wanted to fight Edward. He could take him. Edward didn't have enough anger. My brother was a ticking time bomb of rage, and though I'd been with him all his life and had seen him explode many times, I think there was more bubbling under the surface. He would inevitably erupt—like that huge volcano we all learned about in school would bring upon the apocalypse. I wanted to be there to see it.

"Why would she rather die than stay away from him?!"

Zach was nice and buzzed now, so he was having a good time.

"What the fuck are you all doing?" William stepped in to the living room.

"Watching Twilight. Duh."

"It's a teenage vampire love story," Luke added.

Edward's best scene played in the background. The one where he corners Bella in the woods and yells at her to admit he's a vampire.

"What are you up to now? There's something. I know it."

"Will, you're starting to sound like a little cartoon villain every time you speak," I said, not bothering to hide my laughter.

"What the fuck is that?"

"Did you not watch cartoons?"

"Will's too old for that." Zach snickered into his beer.

Will cursed under his breath and left for the kitchen.

"You sure you don't want to watch?!" I yelled.

"Fuck no!" Will yelled back.

"I want to watch," Thane said from somewhere in the kitchen.

"We've got stuff to do."

I felt bad that Thane couldn't watch with us. He worked hard to keep us safe. He deserved to relax and watch two dudes fight over Bella as much as the next guy.

"Take a sip of your drink, every time Bella bites her lip in this movie."

The twins were laughing. Lying back onto the couch with their feet on the coffee table. My mission was well on its way to success.

"Presley, please stop singing 'Flightless bird.'" Zach begged.

New Moon was already a hit. It wasn't my favorite because there was no Edward to look at, but Jacob was shirtless the whole movie, so that was great.

"Oh shit. Bella is getting dumped." Zach snorted into his beer.

"He leaves her in the woods?" Luke did not approve of Edboy's decision. "Who does that?"

He got progressively angrier as we watched the extra long shot of Bella crying and then lying in the dirt. *Thank you, extended editions.*

"Okay, I don't want to watch this anymore."

"Dude. It's fine. She gets saved by wolves."

My current psychoanalysis of Luke was that he only liked Bella because he wanted to help her. Bella was the equivalent of a lost little lamb, and Luke had a savior complex. He did it for everybody. Going out in the world with Luke meant we needed to add in extra time because he'd make us help someone. Last time, we stopped to help some guy on the side of the road whose tire had blown, and not just to change their tire. We had to take them to and from the tire shop. I tried to be good and not complain about it. He enjoyed it. So I tried to enjoy it too.

"Uh-oh. Luke, look away," I said as I noticed which scene was coming up.

Bella started her bike and would be headfirst into a rock in a couple seconds.

He took a worried sip of his beer.

It didn't take long into the movie for Zach to change his mind.

The rain scene where Jacob dumps Bella played.

"Wait, Jacob sucks." Zach threw the crumpled-up label from his beer at the TV.

"Who's your new favorite, then?" I asked.

"None of them."

"You gotta pick."

"Fine. Bella's dad."

"Charlie."

Footsteps sounded in the foyer as Aaron and Kimberly descended the stairs. I was surprised Kim was still up after all the work that went into the carwash.

"It's the love birds," Luke said, smiling.

"What is this?" Aaron said.

"New Moon," I said. Aaron took one look at the screen and shook his head.

"No, I'm not getting sucked into this again."

"Come on. Kim hasn't seen them!" I motioned for her, opening my blanket for her to sit between Luke and me. I tried to resist the urge to gloat when she accepted my offer and Aaron had to sit in the armchair next to Zach.

"What's it about?" she asked, laying her head against the couch. She looked tired. It had to be late. That, and they were probably tiring each other out up there. Good for them. They both deserved it. Plus, not going to be a lot of alone time for them when we got on the road.

"Wait. Why is the sad guy not in this one at all?" Aaron asked.

"Edward. And remember he left Bella in the forest when he broke up with her because he was being a total idiot."

Aaron stared daggers at me from across the room. "Oh yeah, I remember. How could you let me forget?"

I was glad Kimberly and Aaron joined us. One, because Kimberly was warm. Two, because she seemed completely engrossed. I caught her up on all the details she missed.

Toward the end, the Volturi scenes were making the twins nervous. Luke was involuntarily shaking the couch every time Edward went on trial in Italy, and Zach had gone from laid back and relaxed to both feet on the ground, watching the TV with too much intent and attention for a Twilight movie.

I needed to adapt.

"Does this call for shots?" Since there were no house members around, I got the liquor and shot glasses from the kitchen in two seconds.

All three of my brothers were game.

"Come on, Kim. Just one"

"Don't pressure her," Aaron said.

"Aaron, you don't have to protect Kim from me. I respect her boundaries." I turned to Kim. "I'm just pleading my case. One shot will just liven this party up. Only if you want to."

She thought about it for a minute, then smiled. "Alright, let's do it."

"Atta girl!" I said, pouring the first and handing it to her.

By the time we were done with our round and my quick trivia to make sure everyone was straight on their Twilight facts, Bella and Edward were back together happily safe and sound.

"Why doesn't Bella have any goals?" Luke rubbed his hands over his eyes while we watched Bella talk to Renee.

"I thought Bella was your favorite?"

"She is! I just wish she had some goals for herself other than being with Edward."

"Your dad is showing." Aaron joked.

"What would you suggest for Bella at this point?" I asked.

"Go to college or get a job. Give it a year or two at least before turning."

"She'll never do that. Bella wants to get laid immediately. It's clouding her judgment."

Renee's thong flashed us, and we collectively cringed.

Kimberly hated the lover triangle, and she'd groan every time Bella couldn't make up her mind. I loved the drama of it all. Two dudes fighting over Bella. Jake warms her in the tent, with Edward having to watch. There was nothing more entertaining. Well, except for maybe Bella kissing Jacob, and Edward having to mind-watch the whole thing. That scene was gold entertainment.

"I like this one," Zach said as the Cullens mowed down newborn vamps.

"You just like it because there's fighting and death."

"Exactly. It's finally getting interesting. I'm waiting for one of them to die."

"Why would you want that to happen?"

"That's just the way the world is. People die."

"Try to imagine a happy ending for once, maybe?"

We took more shots when the Volturi showed up again. Because fuck them.

The Breaking Dawns were my favorite. What could I say? I was a sucker for an overly extravagant wedding and a killer baby plotline.

I didn't think anyone else shared my sentiment, though.

"I'm so happy for Bella," Luke said as he took another sip of beer. Bella wobbled in her heels with Alice like a little lamb.

Except maybe Luke. He wasn't going to love the demon-baby story-line, though.

"This is what we need to do for your wedding, Kim," I whispered to her.

"What if I want to elope?"

I saw that one coming a mile away.

"As long as you're not selfish and decide to do it without me there."

We continued to watch. No one cried at the wedding except me.

"You're telling me you don't want to have a Cullen-sized rager for a wedding?" I nudged her again.

"I know like five people, and you're one of them." She chuckled with a sleepy smile.

"We could make it work."

My favorite part of the movie was the honeymoon. I wondered what it would be like to have that much money so we could have our own island. My brothers and I would have a fun time in Rio. Now that we were moving on, I watched and wondered where we'd go next. I hoped it would be warm and tropical. Hiding out in the Bahamas sounded like a trip.

Everyone maintained their attention except Zach, who I think was dying from too much pregnancy drama. Lucky for him, there was plenty of violence and blood during the birth of Renesmee.

"What the actual fuck is happening?" Zach was wide-eyed during Bella's labor. And that was saying something.

Luke looked concerned by Bella's seemingly imminent death.

"Ratatouille is killing Bella. Edward has to bite her out."

"I don't think that's her name," Luke said.

"No, sounds right to me," Zach said.

Kimberly had left me and taken all her heat to go sit on Aaron's lap, so I had my blanket pulled over my ears. As satisfying as their collective shock and disgust was at the birth and the imprinting of a child, what I was waiting for was the grand finale. The final battle with Alice's vision.

I leaned away from the TV to face them and watch their reactions. Aaron had seen it, so he didn't count, but he was now holding Kimberly as the horror of watching Carlisle Cullen get his head taken off washed over her. I couldn't hold back my smile. Zach smiled too, finally, and nodded like he knew it would happen all along. Luke rubbed his hand over his mouth and chin and was also shaking the couch again.

Once the dust cleared and the happy ending was revealed, I asked, "So, what did we learn?"

"Don't get pregnant with a vampire baby," Kimberly said, clearly feeling that second shot.

"Hear that, Aaron?" I snickered.

Aaron narrowed his eyes at me.

"Kill the bad guys when you have the chance," Zach said.

"Okay, dark. Wouldn't expect anything less from you. Luke?"

"Things always work out. Eventually."

"Poetic as usual. Closing thoughts, Aaron?"

"Uh. Don't let you make us watch these movies ever again?"

"Please, you'll all forget them in a couple of years, and we'll have another marathon together."

And I couldn't wait for that day to come.

THIRTY-THREE

AARON

There wasn't much packing to be done. All my belongings fit into my school bag. Only a few sets of clothes, but I'd made sure to put in the rock Kimberly gave me. I stood at the foot of my bed and faced the wall. My Black Forest University flag stared back at me.

I couldn't believe this was the end of our journey at BFU. I'd started to like it here. I remembered the first time I'd set foot in my dorm room. Lifeless and dull. I'd sat on the edge of the bed, full of anger and resentment for my brothers.

But everything was different now. I didn't want to leave, not when we'd set up such a good lie. Even I had believed for a second that I could be Aaron Coleman. A guy who gets the girl, parties with his brothers on the weekends, and has a normal future. Someone who only has to worry about school and his family. I liked being him, even if it was only for a little while.

I made my way to my headboard and decided the flag needed to come with. BFU would be a nice memory.

As I stared at some polaroids, Presley's camera came to mind. He'd taken one singular object with him when we left home—Mom's camera. She loved taking our picture and always had her head buried in that old scrapbook. A thought I usually tried to push away, but this time I kept it close, savoring the sadness. She was still out there. I didn't know where we were going, but it might take us even farther from her. I was happy she was safe, but I missed seeing her in our photos.

A knock on the door startled me, and I kicked my bag under the bed.

Luke appeared with a towel in his hand as he dabbed his hair dry. "Don't worry. Just me. I wanted to check in on you. The Legion are all on the other side of the house right now talking with Kilian."

I didn't want to think if that was good or bad news. My guess was they were discussing the events of this afternoon. We'd earned about four grand, which was enough to get us started on our journey tomorrow night.

Luke sat on the edge of my bed while I took down the flag. His gaze burned a hole in the floor.

"You're checking on me . . . has anyone asked you how you're doing?"

His head popped up, and his automatic response kicked in. "Don't worry about me."

Luke would never tell me how he felt. The only thing that ever brought me comfort concerning that was knowing he'd probably told Zach.

I plopped down next to him, bouncing for a moment. "You don't have to do that, you know? I know you're not all right."

"You seem sure of that." He watched me for a moment before changing the subject. "How was Kim with everything?"

I got up, scanning the room and picking up some old towels and readying them for the laundry. I didn't want to leave too much for anyone to do in our absence.

"She seemed okay. I think she's just as good as any of us right now. Maybe a little worse . . . this is her home. I think she's sad. More than she lets on."

I knew that feeling. She was about to leave her home as I had mine. I wished it didn't have to be that way.

"I guess she's like you in that way . . ." I rummaged through the papers on my desk, double-checking it wasn't anything I'd need.

I let the silence between us settle. Something nagged at me. I was finally ready to ask him.

"How'd you do it . . . keep going after Sarah. I mean, you knew you loved her since you guys were in kindergarten. I've known Kimberly less than a year, and I can't imagine losing her, let alone losing her the way you lost Sarah."

Luke frowned. "Why are you asking me this now?"

"I don't know what I'd do if something happened to her. I promised I'd protect her."

She chose to stay with me, and that meant keeping her safe. I was ready for it, but I wasn't Luke—someone who made carrying his burdens look easy.

His eyes softened, and he patted the bed next to him. "Nothing's going to happen to Kimberly. I'm sure of it."

I joined him. "How can you say that?"

"Because I have a feeling."

"And with Sarah you didn't?"

"With Sarah . . . I had a lot of warnings I didn't listen to. Sarah was never meant to be in my life. I don't think I can say the same thing for Kim. I think she was meant to find us. Maybe not in the way it happened, but she's a missing piece or something. I just couldn't let Sarah go. That's what it comes down to."

It was still achingly close to my relationship with Kimberly, but I agreed. Things with Kimberly felt right. Like a scratch you finally get to itch.

I let in the pain of hearing Sarah's name. Though my pain was nothing compared to Luke's. I couldn't imagine it—living in a world where Kimberly wasn't. Even worse, a world where I'd be directly involved in her death.

"How do you . . . deal?"

Luke's shoulders were hunched as he leaned onto his knees. "I never had the choice not to. I keep living and suffering . . . that's my punishment."

I didn't like that answer. Luke didn't deserve to suffer or be punished. Would he ever forgive himself? I wouldn't if it were me, but I still wanted that for him.

"Aaron . . . she'll be okay. She's got us."

A sick feeling washed over me, and I got up and continued to pack, only faster this time. Something brewed under the surface of our little charade. I wanted to believe Luke's words. But I couldn't. Not until we were on the road, and even then, I wasn't sure if the feeling would go away.

"I just . . . worry about you, and I don't want you to have to go back. You're always protecting us but who's protecting you?"

He wasn't the brother of my childhood. Luke was the fun one. Even more than Presley. He got us up off the couch to play sports in the street. I never remember him frowning. Not once.

Luke smiled unexpectedly and laughter escaped his lips. "You've always been the sensitive one."

"Uh, I'm not!"

"You are. It's not a bad thing but not something I've ever had to worry about with Presley. That's a good thing."

I still failed to see how it could be a good thing. If Zach was here, he'd be commenting on it.

"It means you're a good leader. You understand the emotions of others."

I let go of a breath. "Oh."

I never considered myself the leader type. I paled in comparison to Luke. His cool attitude in times of trouble. His ability to always make me feel like I could do anything. I wasn't sure if I'd ever be able to give that kind of hope to anyone. How could I ever fill the big shoes of my older brothers?

"I have something for you." Luke handed me a small piece of paper. "I want you to memorize that. Know it forward and backward. Okay? Starting now. Memorize it, then burn it."

It was a bunch of numbers and symbols written in pencil.

"What is it?"

"Just memorize it."

"Now?" I said, still skeptical and wondering how good my memorizing skills were.

He nodded and headed for the door. The weight on his shoulders seemed a bit lighter.

"And you're not gonna tell me why, are you?"

He smiled. "Nope. Just trust me."

I did. With my life. With her life. Like always.

THIRTY-FOUR

KIMBERLY

"**A**re you sure you're okay?" Skylar said as we pulled into the movie theater parking lot. Dom turned down the music so I could reply.

My palms were sweaty, and my heart was pounding against my ribs.

Presley put his arm over me to silence me. "We'll be quick."

On my last shift, I'd stashed some of our bags in the lockers in the employee break room. It was the perfect excuse to get some of us out of the house and split up our security. It also prevented suspicion. It was my plan. A good one, but I still felt dirty about the whole thing.

Skylar put the car in park and leaned over the seat. "I'm coming in with you."

"It's okay. We won't be long," I said, trying not to avert my eyes.

"I know, but just in case." She opened the door, there was no reasoning with her.

Presley shook his head, signaling me to not reply. I promised to let him do the talking.

"Thanks again, buddy." Presley patted Dom's arm as he left.

Dom only replied with a grunt. He had a weird way of showing it, but I think Presley had grown on him.

It was only thirty minutes to close, and the staff was light. One was our manager, and the other was a twenty-two-year-old guy fresh out of college. We almost never had shifts together.

Cary, the manager, spotted us beelining for the back. "Just what are you two up to?"

"We just forgot some stuff in our lockers, and we need it for school."

"Uh-huh. Come here. I have a bone to pick with you." She pointed a finger at Presley and signaled him over.

Presley didn't show up for his shift today, for obvious reasons, and was likely in for a tongue lashing.

Skylar and I shifted from foot to foot in the lobby as we waited. Christmas music played in a soft cadence. *I wouldn't miss that.*

"Are you going to go and get your stuff?"

"Uh, I think I'll wait for Presley." My heart hammered again.

"You know, you can tell me if something is wrong," Skylar whispered. "Maybe I can help."

The guilt was like liquid sloshing around in my stomach when I drank too much water on a run.

How was I going to tell her? *"This is it. This is our last few minutes together because we're leaving Blackheart."*

All the time she put in would be for nothing. She wasn't any closer to the queen than when she started if we left, but she'd understand why we had to go. Or maybe she'd hate me for it.

"I know . . . you've helped me so much. I'll never be able to repay you for it. Thank you."

She frowned. *Uh-oh.*

I was blowing it. She was catching on.

"Come on, Kim!" Presley wrapped his arm in mine and skipped me to the staff room.

"Did Cary just fire you?"

"Nope, she's in love with me, I think."

We entered the breakroom. The only employee room that didn't smell like stale popcorn. I never spent my breaks there. I'd go sit on the bench outside and talk with Skylar, or Aaron would talk my ear off in the hallway. I would miss this. This tiny moment in my life was almost at a close, and I wasn't sure I was ready to say goodbye.

"We have to stall for a few more minutes. I just got a message saying they're delayed a little bit at the house." Presley typed in his code for his locker. "Can you keep it together?"

"Yeah, I'm just . . . sad all of a sudden."

Presley pulled out our bags. "This is the hard part. Like standing in line for a roller coaster for two hours. But it's worth it in the end. This will be worth it."

Presley's soft smile brimmed with optimism. Nothing could penetrate that unbreakable wall.

"Were you sad to leave Brooklyn?"

He stopped and handed me my bag. "Yeah, I was . . . but every time I thought about being sad, I just remembered I had everything I needed and that made me feel better."

His story differed from what I'd heard from Aaron and Zach. To them, he'd remained completely unfazed, but he didn't look undaunted to me. He knew exactly what we were up against. He chose happiness.

My phone buzzed in my pocket. Aaron sent me a message.

Aaron: I'll be there soon. I miss you already. Good thing we'll be crushed together in a car for who knows how long.

Aaron: I love you.

I smiled. This was the right choice. My choice. I had everything I needed.

We walked toward the lobby, and I prepared myself for what I would say to Skylar. I'd practiced at least twenty times in my bedroom mirror. I'd prepared for the good and the bad, but as I walked, none of it was coming to mind. It would all have to come from the heart, then. I'd tell her a proper thank you for everything. How I would have never been here without her, and how she'd inspired me to finally choose my own path.

"Wait, where did everyone go?" Presley's voice echoed in the hall.

The lobby was empty, but I could hear the last movie playing in the theater down the hall.

Where was Skylar? The parking lot outside was bare with only the streetlights, and there was no sign of the headlights of Dom's car.

We went up to the door and pulled. It was locked.

"Kim . . . I smell blood."

I turned around to see a paralyzed Presley staring at a dark figure sitting on the counter.

Akira sat with his hands dangling over the front counter. Blood stained his hands and the countertop as he jumped to his feet.

"You both seem surprised to see me. What'd you think? This is a little too public for ya? You see . . . you underestimated the body count I was prepared to make in this place. Your little ticket booth friends are already dusted and in the dumpster." I wanted it to be a bad joke, but he was more serious than he had ever been. His eyes were black under the glow of the neon lights overhead. "Along with the straggling customers in the theater one."

"You're . . . joking . . . right?" Presley spoke slowly.

"No, I'm really not, not this time. Sure, I could have compelled them to leave early, but I was feeling a bit pissed off. Someone didn't listen, and I'm tired of waiting."

Presley grabbed me by the arm, and we walked backward. "What the hell are we going to do?"

"What *are* you going to do? You can't outrun me. You can't fight me," Akira said.

I was confident it didn't matter how fast we ran, we weren't making it. My first instinct was to protect Presley, but he wasn't the one Akira was here to kill.

"Presley, whatever you do, you need to tell the others," I said. "They need to know this is happening right now."

"Yeah, Kim, I gathered that. What do you mean?"

"I have a plan. Don't follow me." I took off toward the showrooms. I had one shot—not to escape or outrun him—to buy myself enough time to figure out how to get him to not kill me. He wouldn't kill Presley. That I knew.

"What!?" Presley's voice echoed as I ran closer to the theater hall.

"Trust me!" I called to him, pushing faster.

"Oh! I was hoping you'd run." His soft snickers turned into an echoing of laughter that threatened to immobilize me.

My body was numb as I tore through the lobby. The classical Christmas music meshed with my footsteps in the empty building. There was no use going for the door. I had to make time. A quick glance behind me, and Akira was gone. I turned down the theater hall and was met with the plush red carpet and then I stopped.

A muffled sound came toward me, but it wasn't behind me. It was directly on top of me. Something or someone was rummaging through the ceiling. As I went to run, one of the tiles crashed to the floor along with a blur of white and black.

My throat went dry. It was Skylar. Her skin was translucent and pale, and her eyes were black, and little streams of black blood trailed onto her cheeks. *She's dead.*

I couldn't scream or feel as tears blurred my vision.

Akira's muffled laughter resounded again. I couldn't outrun him, and I couldn't fight him. I was going to die like Skylar. I'd never felt such terror or hopelessness. Not even that night in the forest with Aaron. I always found a way to fight. But in the cold theater, I was alone again.

I quieted my sobs and made a turn toward the back storage room. A room permanently stained with the smell of popcorn. While stifling sobs with one hand, I steadied myself on the floor with my other.

What would happen to Aaron if he found out I had been killed this way? Would he be able to move on? Would they all be? My life would be a mist on this Earth to them in the grand scheme of their long lives. Would it even matter?

My body shook with each new surge of adrenaline. Nothing other than the music playing in the lobby could be heard. Akira was toying with me. Whatever spectacular display I could give him, would no doubt be what he wanted. He wanted me to feel like a cornered animal all alone.

I dared to think of Aaron again. Of us alone in his room safe from this place. I may never see Aaron again. The fear washed over me, almost turning me into a weeping mess on the floor. A blur in the corner of the room caught my attention. I willed myself to stand, but before I could, a hand was placed over my mouth and a strong arm held me to the floor.

It was Dom crouched next to me.

He motioned for me to be quiet and removed his hand. Staring into his eyes brought a wave of pain. I knew then I had to tell him.

I kept my voice in barely a whisper. "Skylar . . . she's . . . she's—"

"I know," Dom said too matter-of-factly, but his body told a different story, it was cold and unwavering, but I could see the desperation and fear streaming from his eyes.

"Why are you here, then? You don't like us."

"I made a promise to protect you." He pulled me to my feet. "So, I'm going to make sure you get saved."

Skylar had given her life for this and Dom was too. Not necessarily for me, but for what they believed in. I couldn't give up. No matter what, I had to make it out of this theater. Her death couldn't be for nothing.

Hopefully I bought Presley enough time to reach his brothers. I wasn't naive enough to think he got to escape.

"Let's go." He led me out of the storage room into the hall that faced an exit door.

"I can't leave without Presley."

"Let me worry about him."

Before I could protest, the lights flickered off, the music stopped, and everything was eerily silent. The only sound was my ragged breath. The generator kicked on, leaving a few overhang lights on. The dim-lit hallway suddenly seemed a few inches colder.

"Kim, run toward the front."

As I went to round the corner toward the front door, I ran right into Akira's chest.

"No, babe. You're going to want to stay."

Our eyes met for the briefest of seconds. His bloodlust bolted my feet to the floor. His cologne engulfed all my senses, and he went to brush my cheek.

Dom pulled me from behind and shielded me.

Akira sighed. "Sorry about your sister. She wasn't exactly reasonable. But you . . . it took me some time, but I remember you."

Dom said nothing, but backed me up until I touched the wall.

"You were one of us. Connected. I can't imagine how you must feel now. Alone. No little sister to protect. You feel it . . . the void returning to you."

"You don't know me."

"Of course I do! I was you till I found Her. Till I discovered the true meaning in life. Your journey was snuffed out long before it could truly begin. I could help you. You could join me, and I can take that pain away forever."

I gripped Dom's arm.

"I don't want that life anymore."

"Ask yourself, what would you do if I wasn't going to kill you right now? Would you go back to them? What do they have for you there? Nothing. They don't give you anything of value. All they do is take. With us . . . your family, we never take. Only provide." Akira stalked closer.

Dom's shoulders stiffened, and he pushed me backward into the hall. "I'd rather die."

Akira peered up at him with a furrowed brow. "That can be arranged."

They slammed together. Akira grabbed Dom in a choke hold, but he wiggled free.

"Run!" Dom called, his voice echoing with the sound of his struggles.

All the front exits were closed, the only other option I had was the auditorium. I ran as fast as I could. My mind reeled. There was no guarantee. These could be my last moments on Earth. My last breath would be here. In some old movie theater that smelled of stale popcorn. I didn't run outside. If I made it out, I doubted I'd be able to scream for help, or worse, someone would try to help and he'd kill them too. We were caught.

Think. Think. Think. Why did he tell me to leave? Why is he here now?

One glance behind me, and Akira was there, skipping down the hallway with black blood drenching his shirt. He stayed close behind me, pausing to watch me run and snicker in silent delight. It was as I suspected—he liked the game of cat and mouse. I ascended the stairs to the projector room of our largest auditorium.

I wondered if my heart would burst from my chest, and I forced myself to focus.

This all had to do with the boys and that ridiculous prophecy. Aaron. He wasn't part of this until that day. That day She touched him.

I pulled open the hidden door to the projector room. The pattern of the door blended in perfectly to the wall, where no one thought it existed.

The projector room was frigid and dark. Only with the sounds of the last projector rolling.

I pushed everything I could find against the door. The desk, the chairs, everything the last bit of adrenaline would buy me, and as I stared at the empty auditorium below, I remembered Aaron's and my moment together, and I found my answer.

Touch.

Akira broke the door in seconds and slammed into me from behind. It knocked the wind from my lungs and sent me to my knees. I gasped for air as he spun me around and pinned me to the floor with his body. He pushed his hips into mine, ensuring I couldn't squirm away, and his fingers tore into my skin, and I squealed.

He smelled of thick leather and sandalwood cologne. The little front pieces of his hair dangled above me. "That was fun, Kimmy."

I tried to look anywhere but his face, but his darkness overtook me. I had one opportunity. One last resort.

His hands trailed along my skin. "You're shaking like a frightened animal. Don't worry. A promise is a promise. It will be quick. No pain, barely any pressure. It won't hurt like when Aaron bit you. I'm well practiced."

I took a deep breath in and let it out slowly. "I have a question."

"Yes?" He pressed into me more firmly and brushed a piece of hair from my face.

"You said . . . She can see the future. She saw them as Her Guard. But She has to touch them to know their future."

"Still yes."

"How do you know the future hasn't changed in the last half year?"

"What are you driving at?"

"I think you know that you can't go around killing people close to the boys, or it ruins your plans. You didn't stop pursuing their mom out of the kindness of your heart. You did it because you *need* them, and they aren't committed to you. That perfect future She saw can change. That's why you wanted me to leave, because you saw and knew the truth. I'm their family now. Not you. If you kill me now, I promise you they won't go with you no matter what you do."

I hoped it was enough—it was the only card I had left to play. A single match lit in the dark.

"Oh, you know that for a fact, huh? I think you're just trying to stall. It was nice meeting you, Kimmy." He leaned in farther, and his breath was hot on my neck.

"Then why don't you take me to Her!? Because once I'm dead, it's over. And I know you'd hate for Her Royal Highness to be pissed off with you. Plus, wouldn't it be more fun to take me along? I'm sure She'd love torturing me, even if She couldn't kill me."

He sat back up, his eyes searching mine. He waited for me to break. To cry. To show any sign of weakness. But with every ounce of energy I had left, I refused.

He picked me up off the floor. "Stay here."

In the time it took me to catch my breath, he brought Presley beside me. Everything was a blur. He was weak and covered in black blood, and I was shaking so hard I could barely stand.

"Kim! I've never been so happy to see someone in my entire life." He wrapped me in a weak hug. "I'm getting my blood all over you, and I don't even care. Also, sidenote, I'm never setting foot in this place again. Total nightmare fuel now."

Somewhere in his arms, the dam broke, and tears streamed down my face. I clutched him closer, wanting to bottle up all his innocence and keep it forever. His bloody shirt was the only semblance of comfort I had in that dark space, and I clung to it.

"Kim, you can't cry." Presley whined, and a stark frown appeared on his face. "I'm the only one in the family allowed to cry because I have the youngest privileges. It's not your fault . . . I haven't given you all the rules yet."

His voice broke, and we fell to the floor in tears.

"Get up you two sorry saps." Akira watched from the stairwell with a bored expression. "You're both coming with me."

Presley and I helped each other up with a death grip on each other's clothes.

Akira stopped me. "I wouldn't get too excited about your life extension. I was doing you a kindness of a painless, swift death. I promise She won't be as kind."

Presley and I walked arm in arm following him while Akira's words danced in my head.

THIRTY-FIVE

AARON

The nausea came in waves but, I kept myself from freaking out by pacing the library. The wood in the fireplace wasn't burning. Everything was cold and way too quiet.

Zach buried his head in his hands. Luke's eyes were void of feeling as he watched the video footage on his phone. Blackheart was burning. The movie theater was up in flames, and the local news station covered it. The monotone drone of the news anchor was the only sound. I'd been glued to the footage, but when I saw the flames grow higher and higher, the nausea got too intense. My mind was at war between feeling way too much at once and then nothing at all.

I wasn't even sure I was awake. No, just stuck in one of my horrible dreams.

Kilian would come back any minute and help. It would fix everything. They weren't dead. No. They—

Kilian entered the room. Everything was dark.

"Presley and Kimberly were taken. Dom is the only survivor and says he saw Akira take them. It appears Akira killed everyone left in the theater, including Skylar, and then set it on fire to cover his tracks. Due to how fast the fire engulfed the building, it seems to have been planned."

The lights came back on. I could think again. I could stop moving.

A halfhearted relief hit me first, followed by anger. At myself. Akira. Kilian.

Then sadness. For Skylar. For everyone that cared about her. For the people's lives shattered tonight, and the more that were watching it go up in flames.

Kimberly and Presley were alive. That was something.

"Holy fuck." Zach was up on his feet closing the distance between us.

Luke wiped his face, regaining composure and moving next to me.

"What can we do?"

"Yeah, how do we track them?" Zach said.

Presley's and Kimberly's location on their phones was off. Whether Akira was smart enough to turn it off or their phones were burning, I didn't know.

"They're calling for an evacuation of the school any minute now. We won't be able to track them. The amount of people moving off the mountain means, even if we wanted to—"

"We fucking want to! I'm not listening to this shit again." Zach moved toward the door.

Kilian squared his shoulders. There was no emotion in his features, just blank numbness.

"Akira is baiting us. He's baiting you. Giving in and looking for him is exactly what he desires. *You.* We've come too far to give in now."

"You don't care about us. You only care about your mission," Zach spat.

"Zach, please. There is a far grander story at play here. We have the potential to stop the suffering of many. All the people this coven has hurt. Those lives mean something too. Just as much as your family."

There was sincerity in Kilian's voice which made me angrier. How could he say that? How could he expect us to listen to him?

"Debatable."

My hands were shaking. The lines drawn in the sand were blurring. Kilian was blocking the door.

"Move." Luke's voice was the only thing anchoring me.

Red. Everything was turning red again and pulling me out of the room.

Why was Kilian blocking the door?

"I'm sorry, I can't let you do that."

I couldn't go berserk here. I had to find Kimberly and Presley. I had to get out of the room, but Kilian was in my way and I could move him.

I went for the door, but Kilian's arm was immediately on mine, pulling me away from the door and pushing me up against the wall. Hard.

Let me help.

The voice in my head was loud. Like It was real. Like It was in the room with me.

No, not like this. Losing control here meant I'd never make it out of the library.

I was being pulled in all directions. There was a shuffling about the room, and I was trapped between the wall and Kilian's hand on my throat.

"I'm sorry."

The red was gone, and everything turned black.

I was jolted from the darkness. She was the first thing that popped into my brain. Her smile. That distinct laugh when I said something that really wasn't that funny.

Kimberly could be hurt.

He could be torturing her and my brother.

I had to get out of this room.

Luke and Zach were sitting across from me. I couldn't move. A firm hand was placed on the back of my neck. Judging by the pressure, it was William, and Thane was next to him. I could hear his distinct squeaky shoes tapping the floor beside me.

Luke must have seen the panic on my face because he said, "Aaron. It's okay. It's just been a few minutes."

The grandfather clock in the study chimed, signaling midnight. Minutes. It was too long. They could be anywhere. Akira could do anything to them.

I tried to stand, and the hand tightened on my throat.

"Don't move," William warned.

The worst type of Déjà vu was resurfacing. We were repeating history yet again.

Only, I thought we'd been a step ahead this time, but we never were. If we were a step behind Kilian, that meant we were two steps behind Akira. There wasn't time to argue.

I moved again, and my vision blurred.

"Don't. I promised I wouldn't mess with your memories. I'd hate to have to go against my word."

My brothers weren't restrained, but they wouldn't move. Not with William's fingers digging into my flesh.

Sirens sounded outside along with the sounds of frantic movement and talking. Everyone was evacuating except for us. We were still trapped in our eternal prison while the world was burning.

"Kilian will be back with our travel arrangements shortly."

"You don't want to do this. Come on. We're wasting time." I groaned.

William kept his tone neutral to any feeling. "This isn't a democracy."

"He's been lying to you. He doesn't care about any of you. The only thing he cares about is getting to them." Zach had no soft approach. He was hard all over, with his arms crossed and death glare.

"Did he tell you about our deal?" Luke was more delicate and calculated. "Has he told you anything?"

"You guys won't let me have a moment of peace, will you?" William said.

Thane spoke up quietly, "You made a deal . . . with Kilian?"

William sighed.

"Maybe . . . we should hear what they have to say?"

I knew Thane cared. Everything we went through couldn't be for nothing.

"Fine. What deal?" William said.

Luke looked at me this time. "Me and Zach were going to go back to The Family. That's been the plan we agreed upon with Kilian the night of the church. He told us he would protect us until the time was right. We were going to try to take them down from the inside. We traded information and our compliance for the protection for Aaron, Presley, and Kimberly. It was all done in secret."

I felt like he'd punched me in the face. That would have hurt less. They were doing it again. They couldn't go back to that place. Back to Her.

"And why would he make a deal and not tell me?" William didn't sound convinced, but I knew Luke wasn't lying.

"Because I don't think he ever intended on keeping his end of the deal. Everything changed when we learned about the prophecy. We lost all the leverage because we all became more valuable."

"No. We did everything we could. All of us were instructed to protect you with our lives. Kilian is an honorable man. He doesn't do back door, shady deals with . . . with kids. Criminals."

"Oh, fuck this." Zach threw his head back. "He told you anything to keep you busy and to keep you from asking questions. His *security* never worked. He just wanted to use us as bait to draw them out, and he used all of you to keep us here like prisoners. We knew what was happening, but we couldn't do anything. Every time Akira came out of the woodworks, Kilian was waiting for it to happen. This has always been his plan. He fucked you over. Get over it."

William's grip tightened on my neck, and I signaled for Luke.

"He wants to take down the coven and we were willing to help. We still are, if that's what it takes. But right now, we need to get our brother and Kimberly . . . and Kilian is never going to let us leave here." Luke's eyes were pleading.

I couldn't sit in the chair anymore. Everything was taking too long.

"I don't know why he wouldn't just tell me . . ." There was finally a hint of something in William's voice that might get us somewhere.

"I've known Kilian for a long time . . . And I've never seen him react the way I saw him react when he finally got you all in that church. He was entranced. It kinda makes sense," Thane spoke slowly.

"You believe this bullshit?" William spat.

"I'm just saying when have you ever seen Kilian invested in anyone with The Family. He'd have killed Dom and Skylar when he tracked them down if it wasn't for you."

Zach sat up straighter, his tone more controlled this time. "Think about it, Will. How else was he able to get into the games? Almost kidnap Kim in broad daylight? He wanted him to take one of them. He's the only one who can even match Akira in strength, and he's never around. He was constantly sending Skylar, Dom, and Thane on suicide missions."

The realization hit me harder than I expected. Skylar should be alive right now. There was never a bigger mission or picture. Just us sitting in Kilian's perfectly plotted scheme, and when Akira threw his wrench in, he put his money on Zach and Luke.

"He's always with you, and he put you with us. It's obvious he cares about you. Maybe he was trying to protect you too." Luke turned his attention back to me. "Maybe he just didn't know how to tell you."

I wanted to be mad at him for keeping secrets again, but it would have to wait.

I squirmed. "We don't have time for this. We have to go."

"Sit." William's fingers dug into my neck.

"Use that big fucking head of yours, you asshole. He did everything he could to ensure we were never alone because he wanted to control us. Skylar would be alive right now if it wasn't for Kilian."

Thane's voice lowered an octave. "I didn't agree to this. Skylar deserved better. She trusted us . . . she trusted me."

"Fuck. Just let me think for a second," William said. He was almost drowned out by the siren going off outside.

"We don't have a second." I didn't care how desperate I sounded. "Please. You have to let us go save them. You don't even have to help, just let us go."

He was our deciding factor. The only thing left standing between me and that door. Every minute felt like an eternity.

Kilian walked into the room, and we all quieted. "Dom has arrived. He's in poor condition. We'll tend to his wounds and then we are moving. Will you two be able to secure them for travel?"

He didn't look like some villain. There was pity in his steel eyes, and I wondered if he cared. If maybe this was what he needed for his own survival.

"Yeah," William said. "I'll keep them quiet."

William let go of me to lock the door behind them, and slowly turned. The air in the room went stale.

As I contemplated my next move and how I would have to wrestle him to the ground despite him being more experienced than me, he brought a finger up to his lips and pointed to the door.

We all stood speechless for a moment. He held up a hand and cautioned us, listening for the footsteps in the hall.

"Me helping you now means nothing. We get them. That's all I'm helping with."

I was instantly on my feet and spared only a moment for relief. Thane was beaming. Finally, we agreed on something.

He motioned for the door, and I stopped. "Shit. My bag. It's got all our money in there."

Either my bag was going to get toasted by the impending fire or we wouldn't be able to come back, and it was the only money we had to escape. We had to get it.

"Bag? Money? You plan a trip or somethin'?" William cocked a crooked brow.

I was face-to-face with him at the door.

"Uh, I don't think I want to answer that."

"We'll tell you later. Let's just fuckin' go." Zach was pushing toward the door.

"Wait, I can get it. Aaron, it's in your room?" Thane said.

I nodded.

William shook his head, but Thane smiled. "I can do it. Don't worry. I'll meet up with you."

William agreed, and after a few minutes, he signaled us to move. We followed him close behind and made quick work of sneaking out through the hallway and to the side door by the pool. The humans were long gone, and The Legion seemed to be pooled in the living room. The only thing I could make out was a few urgent words and a muffled sobbing.

We were silent until we were in the street. We blended into the chaos of students running around us. The midnight air was cold and smelled of bonfire. The light coming from the fire lit up the night sky behind the stadium.

I pulled out my phone to check again if Presley's or Kim's location was on. Emergency notifications buzzed for my attention, and I pushed them away.

I gasped. "It's on! I know where they are! It looks like a . . . farm? It's down the mountain a couple miles, and there's traffic the whole way."

"Then we'll go on foot," Luke said.

I hoped they'd be together. There was only a little bubble on Kimberly's face. A picture I'd taken of her eating ice cream over the summer . . .

The nausea was back. "What's the plan?"

Zach was right on my heels. "We'll think of one on the way there."

For once, I agreed with him.

My phone rang—barely registerable amid the noise and yelling surrounding us.

Kimberly's picture flashed across the screen, and I answered.

"Aaron!" Kimberly shouted on the other line and then muffled clamoring.

"Hi, Aaron. There's your proof of life for your little girlfriend." Akira's voice was giddy and high-pitched. "I'm sure you were awaiting my call. Hopefully you got my . . . what's it called? Location. Location what? Pin. Location pin I just sent you."

"Where's my brother?"

"Oh. Right!"

There was more shuffling and then I heard Presley's voice clear as day. "Hurry, this guy is really weird."

I pushed down the emotions fighting for my attention. Kimberly wouldn't let her emotions overcome her. She'd followed me into the altar room without a second thought. This time I would save her and my brother.

"You better get here quick before I tap a vein on this little redhead. Let's get the whole family together for one last time."

He hung up before I could speak. My ears were ringing, and my muscles were quivering.

I'm going to kill him.

"Let's go." I barreled toward the tree line.

"Wait." Zach stopped in the middle of the road, and the streetlights cast a shadow over his face. "Before we go anywhere with you, I need to know why."

"Does it matter?" I said, eager to find the others.

"Yeah, it matters. I need to know if I can trust you." Zach's eyes were locked on William. "Tell me why you're helping us."

William turned to face us all, and I saw a softness in him I'd never seen before. "Because I was a big brother once . . ."

His little sister. Only, he lost her somehow. He was a big brother too, and that meant we understood we had responsibilities others didn't have.

"Still are. Once a brother, always a brother." Luke patted him on the back, and we wasted no more time disappearing into the night.

THIRTY-SIX

KIMBERLY

"We're not going to die, are we?" Presley had pulled his knees to his chest, shielding most of the blood on his shirt, but there were still black smudges all along his jaw and cheeks.

My body shivered as I counted the drips from the broken air conditioner hanging over our heads. Presley had mangled it enough to stop blowing cold air despite his condition. We were in a freezer. White buckets lined steel shelves filled to the brim with various produce. Apples, vegetables, even some flowers. It smelled of dirt, and every breath brought more cold into my lungs.

Akira was trying to kill me, or, at the very least, make it so I wished I was dead.

The only sound was the chattering of my teeth in the dimly lit room. I'd found a cardboard box to sit on, and we huddled together in a corner. It all helped, but my body still quivered despite it only being ten minutes since we were locked inside. Any minute, Akira could walk through that door and kill me.

"Kim, you haven't said anything in like five minutes." Presley rocked back and forth with his hands on his knees, knocking into me every time.

He told me he'd been mauled back at the theater. According to his story, a group of no less than fifteen guys in black suits wrestled him to the ground. He'd almost defeated them all but the last one was "like Superman on steroids" and that was the reason he'd been unable to escape.

He was probably trying to get me to talk.

I couldn't take my eyes off the shelf in front of me. My body was numb, but my brain was going a million miles a minute. I had to find a solution. Anything.

Presley shook me. "Hey, you're scaring me."

The way Presley stared at me brought me back to our car ride after the church. His hands were shaking so I offered to drive. Back then, he was the oddly quiet one, and I was trying to get him to talk. I had come up with a plan A, B, and C, and steadily working over the details of D—provided we weren't able to get out of the state. I'd made a silent promise to myself then that no matter what happened I'd make sure he was safe.

And as I looked upon his curly blond hair, all I could think about was how loved he was since birth. Every single hair on his head was marked in the love of his mother and brothers. I loved him like that. Their love for him was powerful. I felt it back then, and I felt it now, burning inside me and calling me to protect him as if he were my own blood.

I turned to him. "I'm here. I'm sorry. I'm just trying to think about how to not get killed and for you not to get taken back to a mind-controlling vampire queen."

Nervous laughter escaped his lips. "Okay, let me help. Maybe . . . maybe I can catch him by surprise and . . . and hit him . . . over the head with something?"

I stared at him till my eyes dried out and I had to blink.

"Or . . . I can . . . distract him with my ultra-charming jokes. I don't know, Kim! What do we do!? Truthfully, I was kinda waiting on my brothers to come and save us."

I shook my head. "No, if we do that, you and all of your brothers are going to be captured and taken away, and I will be killed before you even make it there."

Presley leaned his head back against one of the steel shelves, and it shifted under his weight. "You're saying we're screwed?"

I closed my eyes to focus my concentration. There had to be something else I could do. I had bought us some time, and now I had to follow through. Aaron and his brothers would know where we were taken by now and would be searching for us. They would find us. I knew that for sure. Presley and I were outnumbered and outgunned. But on second thought, I hadn't heard anyone else in our current location. Only Akira.

"Pres, can you listen to see if we're alone? Have you been keeping tabs on what is going on in the building?"

"Uh, kinda. I just hear him clambering around in his boots. But I can't hear him now, I don't know where he is."

"But he's not talking to anyone?"

He had people with him, but they weren't here. I didn't know why that might be, but I took it as a win.

"I don't think so. I think this building is pretty big. He keeps walking out of range and then coming back."

There was one thing I hadn't thought of. Something that kept popping up into my brain like a little gnat bidding for my attention.

I thought it over for just another few seconds. I didn't have time to meander back and forth between two decisions. I had to choose. There would never be certainty. I could think of every possible good and bad scenario, but no amount of planning or thinking would give me a perfect answer.

I needed to choose.

"I have an idea."

Excitement sparked in Presley's eyes. "Yes! I knew you were the smart one. Hit me."

"I need you to change me."

I waited for it to settle in. There was a brief silence as Presley contemplated my words.

It was the only card we had that made any sense. The element of surprise.

"Uh . . . what?"

"You're going to turn me into a vampire. That's the one thing he isn't expecting. Why else would he put us in here together? He doesn't think you'd change me. If you turn me, then maybe we can give your brothers a chance. Small, but it's better than nothing."

"Whoa, are you crazy?! He'll just smell the blood."

He had a point. I scanned my body and found a scrape on my leg from where Akira tackled me in the projector room. With the edge of my shirt, I started rubbing. With my cold skin, I barely felt it.

"Whoa, stop! You're freaking me out." Presley scooted away from me like I was an axe murderer.

"If I'm already bleeding and he's somewhere else, we'll have a small window, but it could work."

"No way am I doing that! I don't know if my blood is even strong enough to change you. I have to drain your blood and basically kill you, and what if I feed you my blood and it doesn't work?"

"Then . . . I won't be any worse off."

"Kim! I can't risk killing you. If I killed you, I'd never be able to forgive myself."

"You bite people all the time!"

"Yeah, *people*. You're not people. You're family. Not to mention, Aaron would kill me. Do you even want to be a vampire? What about all the stuff Aaron's always going on about?"

"Presley. I'm ready to make my own decision. Whether it's the right one, I don't know, but I do know if I don't at least try to do this, all of us are as good as dead. If you guys get taken to The Family, they're going to turn you guys into the queen's guards, and who knows what that really means, but to me, it means that none of you will be yourselves again, and I won't allow that to happen. I just won't."

Presley stared at me with wide eyes.

I held out my wrist. "We don't have a lot of options here. This is our best bet. How long does the transformation take?"

"I don't remember! I was passed out for half of it, and you would be too. What am I supposed to do if he comes back?"

"Maybe . . . try to convince him I'm asleep."

He tried to scoot back again but the shelf behind him prevented it. "Kim, I can't do this! What if I kill you!? And he's going to come back, and I don't know what to do! I can't. I won't."

For some reason, I thought of Luke and his sureness. It was all hope hidden under the disguise of his confidence. All the boys had it in their own way.

Then I thought of Skylar and how all her decisions, good or bad, led her to a place. And even if that place wasn't what I wanted or what she'd imagined, she chose every step of it with sure decisiveness.

I wanted to be both. Confident and hopeful.

"Come on, Pres, think about your brothers and every time they've ever stuck out their neck for you. This is us doing the same for them. Do it for them. Be brave."

I could barely grab his hand; my fingers were stiff.

Presley buried his head in his hands and groaned. He was silent for a minute, and I imagined our window closing. I had no idea what I was getting myself into, but one thing I knew for certain was that it was the right move. It was our only move.

"Fine. I'll do it. But you better not die or I'm going to be pissed at you."

I chuckled, holding out my wrist. "I won't die. Promise."

The air around us grew still, and Presley concentrated hard on my wrist. "This is gonna hurt."

I squeezed my eyes shut and waited for the pressure and the pain. Presley tore into my wrist, and I dug my fingernails into my palm. It wasn't nearly as painful as my run-in with Aaron in the spring but still felt like being stabbed in the wrist.

Truthfully, I'm not sure what I expected for my turning into a vampire. I thought it might be a few years, or at least until I was of legal drinking age. But that's not what life had planned for me.

I imagined the boys would make a big deal of it, probably throw me some party. Luke would bake a cake. Something over-the-top, knowing them. It would be a fun night and then my turning would be something to celebrate. A long-awaited venture.

As my body grew weaker, my head got heavier, and my death got closer, I realized all my struggling and trying to be logical and planned about it was futile. It was always going to turn out this way. I would never wait and do the logical thing. I would never choose the other path to grow old, have kids, and turn into a little old grandma. Not because I didn't want those things, it was too early for me to tell, but because they weren't logical or calculated. The Calem brothers just lived. And now they were my family.

A group of people I'd never want to part with, and one I'd follow even into death.

Aaron came crashing into me. But I chose this, and that was enough for me.

My body shook from the shock, and my eyes were slowly closing. I'd never felt so cold.

"Kim, okay. Here." Presley set my hands up like a cup and poured a tiny bit of his blood into my hands. "Please, let this work. Please."

And I touched my lips to the blood. It tasted of iron, and a wave of nausea ran over me. It didn't stop the curtain of black from suffocating me and shutting my eyes for good.

I hoped it would save him. I hoped it would somehow save them all.

THIRTY-SEVEN

AARON

"This is a suicide mission if I've ever seen one." William was staring at the same building I was with the exact same expression.

Dark and dim, a large industrial building sat in a large field of dirt between rolling hills and redwood trees, a farm in the moonlight. But there were no animals from what I could see or smell, just dirt and rows of apple trees. I scanned for any footsteps lingering.

"Okay, let's talk this out." Luke gathered us all in a circle. "Here's how this is going to work. We aren't strong enough to beat Akira outright, but if we play our cards right, we might be able to get the jump on him. All we need is an opening."

"Can't William put him under or something?" I said.

William was our greatest advantage. The oldest and more experienced. I wouldn't dare say that in front of Zach, though.

"No. Akira is ancient compared to me. I'm not going to be strong enough to hold him under."

Of course, there was a limit, and it always happened at the most inconvenient times.

"We'll need to weaken him. Somehow, we have to bite him at least once," Luke said.

Zach stood in front of us, arms crossed. "So, one of us will need to drink his blood?"

"Right . . ." Luke's eyes glossed over, as if he was entranced in thought.

"I'll do it." William clenched his jaw. "None of you should be drinking Her blood. Too risky. And don't fuckin' argue."

"But you did it last time," I said.

"And I'm fine. You might not be as lucky. End of discussion." William dug his heels into the dirt.

"Fine. Will bites him. Is that the crux of our plan?" Zach said.

A shit plan. I focused on the building, listening for her heartbeat. I couldn't hear it. I couldn't hear anything. Everything was taking too long.

"Maybe I could do the thing again . . . seemed to work pretty well the last time," I said.

"No," they all said.

"Let's not think about it or anything."

But they were already ignoring me, talking about ways we might be able to play on Akira's weaknesses. From what I'd seen, Akira had no weaknesses. Even with their extra training of a few months, it would never compare to the years Akira had.

"We could use ourselves as bargaining chips," Luke suggested.

"No, I'm tired of that always being the plan," I said.

Zach crossed his arms. "We're the only important thing that we have and they want."

"This would be different from last time." Luke nodded like he was agreeing with his own plan. "We can act like we're making some type of decision . . . maybe one of us pretends to go with him."

"Okay, I'll do it," Zach said.

"No, it should be me. He'll believe it more if it's me."

"I don't give a shit."

A scream echoed off the side of the mountain, muffled by the aluminum building in front of me.

Kimberly.

My feet were already moving under me at the sound of her cries. Panic. Pure fear and panic pumped into my veins.

The door slammed open and echoed through the tall ceiling. Dirt and old leaves scattered on the concrete floor.

Akira stood with one hand wrapped around Kimberly's neck, and the other knotted in her hair. She looked pale, sick. Weak. Presley stood with his back pressed against the wall, soaked in his own blood. His eyes widened when he saw me.

"I knew if one squealed, you'd come running." His lips grazed the skin at her neck.

Kill him.

It had the right idea. Everything was bathed in crimson, and I had to clench my fists to gain composure. One wrong move and she was . . .

I couldn't even think it.

The others gathered at my sides, and I stepped forward. I didn't want to listen to another long monologue from Akira. Everything he said was confusing. And I think he did it on purpose. Saying just enough to make sense, but not enough for it to be the truth.

Akira's fingers pressed farther into Kimberly's neck. We all froze. Her heartbeat soared in her chest. She watched me, her chest heaving unevenly.

"Uh-uh-uh. Poor Kimberly's vertebrae might snap out of place if you take another step."

"You don't have to do that," Luke said, and I mimicked his movements. The alert shoulders, the set jaw.

His lips pulled into a smile. "I don't get you all. Why for this girl? She's just this weak, little human girl."

I needed to be beside her. The urge to snatch her from his fingers was all I could think about. I was back in the same spot I was before—helpless while Kimberly was dangled over me like bait. Only, things were different now. I was ready for whatever fate awaited me. My knees weren't shaking, and I wasn't scared. This time I would fight.

"She's stronger than you give her credit for," I said.

Luke took a step forward. "Let's end this now. I'll take you up on that offer. I'll come with you."

That wasn't happening. I wasn't letting him go back, but I didn't protest.

Akira's eyes sparked in the fluorescents. "Really? Are you hurting that bad you're finally willing to leave your little brothers behind?"

"He's not going. I am." Zach stepped forward.

"No, you're not." Luke stepped next to him.

"Would you just shut up and let me do this?" Zach said.

Akira's laugh echoed. "Having you guys back home is going to be a blast. Watching you tear each other limb from limb for Her attention will truly be the highlight of my three hundred years."

He sighed with joyful anticipation and then it all melted away.

"Too bad that option isn't on the table anymore. I want the whole set"—his fingers moved to Kimberly's chin—"including the little redhead."

"I don't get to be included?" William said with a dry laugh. "I'm disappointed."

"Sorry, I forgot you existed." Akira's eyes darkened. "Where's your great mentor now? I'm a little surprised he didn't come with."

William said nothing. The dripping from an air conditioner was a slow clock that filled the silence between us.

Akira tightened his grip on Kimberly, covering her mouth. "Oh, didn't he tell you? Too hellbent on his own revenge to be a leader. To make . . . a family that really means anything."

"What are you talking about?"

"Kilian has a secret. The reason he is *enthralled* with all of you." Akira put his face next to Kimberly and whispered, "Because we killed his little brother."

"What?" William's voice was softer, unguarded.

"In our defense, they attacked first and he took a member of our Guard with him." Akira's dark eyes burned with intensity. He liked inflicting that pain. "I'm surprised he never told you. I tried to warn you. The only thing he cares about is his own vendetta."

William said nothing.

"He didn't tell you that . . . did he?" The corners of Akira's mouth grew wider. "I get it. It's hard to learn that everything you know is a lie. You've been playing on the wrong side of the field this whole time. Kilian has been using your hatred to fuel his own desires. Filling your head with all these tales and lies about who we are and what we do. We survive. That's it. We don't want the world. We have everything we need. It's *you* that's lacking."

"Good thing I've got enough hatred for you lot. I don't need his. I never did."

"Oh, interesting. What happened? We kill someone you know? That's always what it is. Don't worry, I'm sure it was quick."

William stepped forward. We needed an opening, or it would be an easy fight for Akira. I surveyed the room, but we couldn't wait for something. I had to be proactive this time. No waiting for someone to save me, I needed to be the one doing the saving.

The tighter his grip on her neck, the stronger my resolve became. I could see the whites of his knuckles. How was she breathing?

"It's settled. I kill you, and we finally go home, right? Or are we thinking we take the redhead as a little snack?"

I could be that opening.

Yes.

The voice in my head answered me. I knew the risks, but I would take them. Even if it meant not coming back. The trembling was already starting in my hands. I was stronger now but not strong enough, but that didn't mean I was useless. I would save her this time.

I'm ready when you are, the voice mocked me, and I prepared myself for the complete loss of control.

To lose myself and the chance of ever seeing her again . . . and my brothers.

I was ready to give them everything they'd given me.

To love them completely in my sacrifice in the way my brothers always did for me.

And then it happened.

The one thing I'd never contemplated for even a second.

Kimberly bit into his wrist.

Her teeth turned to fangs, and she bit him.

A stream of black blood littered the floor and then there was a collective pause among us. All our faces mirrored the same confusion, then spark of hope.

She was our opening.

Luke's smile got my feet moving, and we sprang into action.

Akira cursed as he threw Kimberly to the floor and put her to sleep. Her body was lifeless and unmoving. I had so many questions, but for now, she was safe and unharmed.

He hadn't expected it. She did it. She surprised him.

Luke and Zach went for his arms while I slid on the floor to grab his legs, and Presley joined me by wrapping his arms around Akira's waist to immobilize him.

Avoid the hands, I repeated to myself. Akira's body was strong, but one bite was all it took to give us an edge. An opening just large enough for William to come up behind him and bite him on the neck.

It was a bloody scene as William used every bit of his power and strength to stay locked onto Akira.

Akira's muscles tightened, and with one large push, we all fell to the floor. He grabbed William's collar from behind and threw him over his shoulder. His body colliding with the ground cracked the concrete under our feet.

As he went in to bite him, we all rushed again. Our momentum was enough to knock Akira from his feet.

Akira laughed. "Are we playing football or something? You guys are hilarious."

He wasn't going for any of us. He knew we were protecting William, and that's where all his focus was.

Despite his loss of blood, Akira kept up with our speed. Zach grabbed Akira from behind, attempting to put him in some kind of bear hold for William.

"Still not good enough."

Akira slammed Zach into the concrete. Hard enough to leave a small cloud of dust. But every second the exposed wound on his neck was dripping and filling the floor in a wash of gray and black.

He was holding back. I didn't know why. He could have put us under like Kimberly, but he wasn't. He joined us in an endless dance of knocking us back and continuing his advances for William.

In one fluid motion, Akira grabbed William from behind and sunk his teeth into his neck.

I was there trying to pry Akira's grip from William. Clawing, pulling, grunting.

Nothing would budge his iron grip as he drained William. His struggling was slowing, and his eyes were closing.

"Shit, he's going to kill him!" I screamed for Luke. "What do we do?!"

Luke went straight for Akira's neck.

"Luke! No!"

His advance worked. William dropped to the floor.

"You're going to have to try harder than that to kill me." Akira pushed Luke off him, but Zach grabbed him from behind and bit into his neck.

He was weaker now. It was working. We could do this.

Presley and I shared a glance and ran toward him.

I pried Akira's stiff hands from Zach's collar and bit down.

Mistake. I knew as soon as the first bit of his blood touched my tongue.

I was gone.

His blood seared through my veins and filled every aching part of me. Something inconceivably gaping I'd never known was there. Every gulp pulled me further into an inferno of longing.

Everything I ever wanted was there in his blood. It satisfied in a way human blood could never.

How could I ever stop?

Why would I ever stop?

Somewhere in the haze, we were all there, pulling and yearning for more. More blood. Once Akira was drained, I'd have to find a way to get more. Somehow I—

No. Her heartbeat. Find her heartbeat.

I searched, finding it next to me. So close. I pulled away.

My hands trembled, this time from the euphoria. I knew then my brothers felt it too.

Luke's eyes were black again, and Presley was still drunk with desire, pulling at Akira's arm along with Zach who still had him by the neck. Akira was growing weaker and weaker. Unable to push us off now. Only seconds had passed, but it felt longer.

I grabbed Luke by the shoulder and tried to force him off, but his muscles were stone.

"Zach!" I screamed, my panic growing.

Zach responded to my cries, and even in his dazed state, without me saying anything, he knew what he had to do. He grabbed Luke by the neck and pried him off while I yanked Presley by the collar, and Akira's faint laughter echoed.

"Yes, drink and dream of Her. We can only hope to be reunited in Her presence once again. Surely, we will all be brothers in the next life and be with Her." Akira smiled as his limp body crumbled to the floor.

Neither Presley nor Luke were speaking, just wobbling around lost in the same euphoria. This was Her blood.

Akira's hands curled into his body as he grew more lifeless and cold by the minute. A pool of black blood stained the concrete under my feet.

Zach helped William to his feet. His black pupils enlarged as he leaned over Akira's body.

He grabbed Zach's arm. "You know the bond we have transcribes blood. It's forever. Farewell my brothers. I can think of no more perfect fate . . . because all four of you have seen the light and tasted Her splendor. She waits for you."

A dull aching reverberated in my chest. I clutched my shirt, and tears

threatened to form in my eyes. A stranger, yet I couldn't shake the odd
sense of familiarity or grief as he withered away. It was stronger now. The
connection we shared. That thread under the bleachers was so faint I
wondered if it was even there, but there was no denying it now.

"Mox cum ipsa eris." That was the last thing Akira said.

Zach grabbed Akira's head and twisted it from his body with an
upheaval of anger. I had to turn away.

Luke's eyes were returning to normal, and he moved to his feet to
check on Presley.

They were still them.

My entire body was still buzzing. His blood made me feel faint and
sick, yet the best I'd ever felt in my entire life. Rejuvenated. Exhilarated.

I followed that trail of blood dripping from Akira's arm. When would
I ever get this chance again for more?

The black was blending into something red. *Kimberly.*

I snapped out of the trance and ran to her. Her hair was soiled with
spills of black ink.

Her skin still felt the same, her heart still sounded the same. She was
still her.

I pulled her into my arms and moved the hair from her face. "Hey,
Burns. You gotta wake up. It's over."

Her eyes opened, revealing the most beautiful pools of blue I'd ever
seen. I kissed her face. My eyes welled with relief. A few of my tears fell
onto her cheek, and I wiped them.

"Aaron." Her hands found my chest first and then my face. "Did we
win?"

A chuckle escaped my lips. "Yeah, we won. Everyone's okay."

I memorized every detail of her face, took in the sweet scent of her skin,
and listened for the best sound. The rhythm of her heartbeat.

Finally, It was silent. No voice in my head taunting me about the smell
of her skin or the taste of her blood. Her blood was like mine.

Finally, it was only her and me.

She was having trouble keeping her eyes open. Her body was still
transforming. I couldn't wait to get her out of here. Off the dirty, cold
floor and into a warm bed.

William helped Zach prepare to burn Akira's body while they argued
with Luke on whether to burn the whole building with it.

Her eyes glistened. "It wasn't how I imagined it . . . but it was the best I could think of."

"It was perfect. You're perfect."

And mine. Mine to protect. My love.

"Do I feel . . . different?" Her voice gave way to the emotion clouding her eyes.

Like maybe she was afraid after everything that I didn't love her. Like there was a possibility I'd reject her. But my heart was fastened securely with hers. It would actually kill me to ever leave her.

She still didn't understand. I'd always crash into her.

From the moment I met her, my fate was sealed. I didn't know how many other universes there were out there, but if there were more, I'd bet I tried to make her mine every time.

I didn't believe in fate.

But I believed in this. The love pouring out of my heart for her.

"I just feel you." I kissed her forehead.

She smiled. "Forever."

I took her face in my hands and lifted her chin. "Forever."

When our lips touched, every bit of fear and despair that had threatened to swallow me a few minutes before didn't exist anymore. I didn't care about where we were or the blood. I was lost in her.

"Jeez, get a room," Presley said with a sheepish smile.

Luke walked in next to him and placed his arm around him. They were propping each other up for support.

"How are you feeling?"

Kimberly sat up. "Tired and nauseous. I don't think I have any of the cool stuff yet."

"Hey, fangs are pretty cool," Presley said.

How Presley had seen a dismembered person and had almost seen us all die and still found a way to summon all that energy, I would never understand.

I rubbed her hand. "It goes away quickly. I promise."

"Yeah, we'll get you somewhere you can get some rest. Help you ride out the rest of it," Luke said.

I felt alone when I changed. I wouldn't let my brothers help me. Therefore, everything was terrifying. Especially when my hearing changed and I was pulling a door off its hinges without trying.

She wouldn't have to do it alone. She had us. We could ease the hard parts.

I helped her to her feet. The trail of black blood still stained the concrete beneath us where Zach and William had dragged Akira's body. He laid it on the wooden pallets and found some gasoline to pour over him.

I couldn't believe it. It was over. We'd done the impossible thing.

Presley came up to me still covered in blood. "You're not mad at me? Kim made me do it. I didn't want to, I—"

I grabbed the sides of Presley's head and pulled him close to kiss him on the forehead. "Always listen to Kim. She's always right."

I was proud of him, but I wouldn't tell him that, not at that moment, anyway.

He wiped it off. "Jeez, okay. I get it. You love me."

"What now?" Kimberly relied on me to hold her up. A job I'd happily do forever.

"We keep running . . . together," Luke said.

"I'll do the honors." William popped a cigarette in his mouth and handed one to Zach before lighting them both and tossing the lighter.

Dear Chelsea,

I shouldn't be writing you this letter, but I tend to not do things I should do. I didn't want you to worry about me. Please know I'm okay. Don't look for me . . . you won't find me. I heard they're going to have a funeral or a vigil of some kind for everyone at the theater. You should go, but don't use it as an excuse to buy another black dress. You have plenty.

I'm sorry I couldn't be the friend I wanted. I could never replace you. You were the best friend I've ever had. There were so many things I couldn't tell you. I'm sorry we couldn't graduate together.

For what it's worth. I'm happy. Finally.

Give Monica a hug for me.

With love,

-K.B.

THIRTY-EIGHT

KIMBERLY

The letter was tucked safely in the backpack sitting on my shoulders. Sunshine broke through the heavy canopy of the giant redwoods, and the early morning mist was dissipating.

I took it all in.

Everything was brighter. Even the far away streams were clear enough for me to see the colored stones underneath. The ache in my calves was nonexistent as we walked together in the wilderness. Every step was smooth like gliding through water. No gasping for breath.

This was the beginning of immortality.

Last night, we'd broken into someone's vacation cabin so I could rest for a few hours. It wasn't enough, but we had to keep moving. A strange gnawing bore a hole in my stomach. Almost like hunger, but the thought of eating anything made me gag. I was stuck between being human and fully being a vampire. Aaron had to carry me most of the way while we ran North, away from Blackheart.

A strange anxiousness settled onto my shoulders thinking about what came next, but I kept my eyes firmly on what was ahead.

Zach and Luke were in front of me talking back and forth with William while Presley walked backward trying to butt into their conversation. William was adamant on only escorting us far enough past the wildfires and then he was done because he couldn't wait to wash his hands of the whole thing. But he could have left us back at the farm . . . or at the cabin.

Aaron walked steadily beside me. His golden hair shined brighter in the sun, and he put his arm around me, hugging me close to his chest. Now, I could hear the steady beating in his chest. A soft flutter that was soothing and hypnotic enough to be its own lullaby.

"Wow, look at that view!" Presley hopped a little too close to the edge.

We all stopped and took in the scene in front of us.

An expansion of trees blanketed the snowcapped mountains in the distance, and smoke rolled into the blue sky, making a milky haze. The fire I was afraid would reach us, burned across thousands of acres. The original was long gone, but smaller ones popped up around it. It was a relief it would never reach my former home, but I might as well have held the match that made my town go up in flames. I didn't have my phone anymore. My room. My objects.

But I had them.

They'd each given up a crucial part of themselves to be here. Luke and Zach left behind every dream they ever had for themselves. Presley left behind his childhood and a little of that innocence his brothers fought hard to protect. And Aaron . . . he'd probably say he lost a piece of his humanity. Though I wouldn't agree with that statement.

And me . . . I left behind my home.

But we still had those things. They were never really gone. We'd make new dreams and new memories. Find a new home. We'd tell stories. The same ones over and over again, hopefully by the light of a campfire, until they were knitted into the fabric of our brains forever. Nothing could take away our humanity. Even if we could never be guiltless again.

"I've got places to be." William swayed on his feet.

"Why? Thane can't go a day without you?" Zach chuckled. "I thought you were supposed to be a good mentor."

"I don't want to be stuck with you all for another second of my life. You've wasted enough of my time." William's tone didn't match the softness in his features. "Plus, he's too much like you. Tends to get in trouble when I leave him too long."

Thane met us back at the farm shortly before we left. He was delayed in the evacuation, but luckily the fire was contained before it reached the school.

"What's Kilian going to do to you? That guy's got to have a dungeon or something where he . . . never mind." Presley was still peering over the edge of the cliff with his feet halfway hanging over.

To my surprise, William laughed. "Ha. No dungeons. You don't know him like I do. He won't do anything to me. Maybe argue about it for a few days, but he'll get over it."

"Aren't you mad he lied to you?" Aaron said.

"Yeah, but that's why I need to go and talk to him. I knew he had a brother that died, but I didn't know it was the coven. Maybe I should have been smart enough to figure it out, I don't know. Kilian isn't a bad person. He's done a lot of good . . . but he's flawed."

"We'll take your word for it on this one." Luke patted William's shoulder.

They smiled like actual friends.

William shook off the smile as quickly as it came. "Come on, assholes. You're slowing us up."

"We can't have one moment to take this in? Wait, hold on." Presley rummaged through his bag and pulled out his camera. "That's perfect."

He snapped a couple candid pictures of us. Zach was scowling. He disappeared behind us for a moment, and I grabbed Aaron's hand.

"Aw. Cute." Presley patted Aaron on the shoulder.

"Do I hear wedding bells in the five-year plan?" Luke nudged in closer to Aaron.

"Five-year plan, huh?" I cocked an eyebrow.

Presley spun around while simultaneously stuffing his camera back in his bag. "I want to be the officiant! Please, please, please."

"As long as I get to be the best man," Zach said.

"Oh, that's my job." Luke put his arm around Zach's shoulder. "We could share and become a super best man."

"Stop. You guys are going to freak her out." Aaron pulled his hands through his hair. "Sorry. That's too much. They're being too much. Don't feel—"

"I think you'd have to try a lot harder than that to scare me away." This time I enjoyed that worry line between his brows.

Aaron's cheeks reddened, and he let out a long breath before smothering me in another embrace. I couldn't feel the chill in the air, just warmth. Being with them felt like being eternally in the heat of summer.

If only Skylar could see us now. I wished I'd told her everything. Now I knew she'd have understood. She would have let me go because she understood me, even if we had different ideas of freedom. A lump formed in my throat. There would be time to mourn, just not yet. Not till we were safe.

"Hold on." William stopped and craned his ear to the row of trees on his left.

I searched for the same sound but only heard the steady chirping of birds. Every hour that passed, I could hear more and more. Birds, bugs, twigs snapping close by.

"Shit," Zach said before a figure appeared in the trees in front of us.

A man with gray peeking through his sideburns walked through the trees, and my every muscle froze. He held the same presence as Akira, but something about him screamed power. Everything was clean-cut. His hair. His brow. The beard.

A trickling of fifteen men followed him in black suits. Their eyes were locked on the Calem boys, and their faces were expressionless.

"Ezra?" Luke spoke in a strangled whisper.

"There's no way. The only person that knows where we are is . . ." William said under his breath.

Thane walked out from behind the trees. His mouth poised in a smirk.

"What the fuck is going on?" Zach spat.

"Sorry guys." Thane waved. "Akira showed me the light . . . he showed me what things could be like if I met Her."

William shook his head. "No. Fuck. This. When?"

"Does it matter?" Thane still appeared the person I knew. Polite dimpled cheeks. Soft eyes.

"It matters."

"The night after we escorted Aaron and Kimberly back from the pool. I had surveillance duty and . . . it just happened."

My heart sank. Thane was working with The Family. Questions mounted in my head, one on top of the other. But more importantly, why?

"But, Will, it's going to be okay. We're all going to Her. They promised not to hurt you." Thane was still smiling, his eyes filled with hopeful anticipation.

"What about all our training? All the times we talked about this . . ." William took a step forward. I couldn't see his face anymore, but there was real hurt in his voice.

"It doesn't matter anymore. I've felt it. Something you could never understand. She's the most important thing. I have to go to Her. I have to see Her. Come with me." Thane looked at him expectantly.

Luke pushed Presley back, and Zach blocked us from the other side. My heartbeat was in my ears. It would not be enough. There were too many of them.

Luke and I shared a brief glance, but somehow, I understood completely. Get ready.

Ezra sucked his teeth. "No more running. This ends now."

They pressed in from every side, creeping toward us.

"I'm very disappointed in you both. You killed a member of The Guard."

"Uh, he tried to kill us," Presley said before Aaron threw a hand over his mouth.

Between a small gap next to Luke's shoulder, Ezra's blue eyes found me. Two sapphire orbs against ivory skin stared back at me.

"You changed her?" Ezra ran his hands through his hair and spat on the ground, and I wondered how he knew. Akira had been wild and unhinged, but Ezra reminded me of a pissed off dad whose kids ran his car into a tree. "This is such a mess."

Aaron squeezed my hand.

"We're going home, and she can't come. But you and your brothers—"

"No," Luke said. "We're not going anywhere with you."

"Yeah. Fuck off," Zach added.

A spark reflected in Luke's eyes, and I followed his line of sight to a small opening in the tree line still unprotected by the men. It would be tight, and we'd have to go fast, but maybe just maybe we could make it. It was closest to me.

I'd need to lead the charge, but I wasn't sure my legs even worked like that yet.

"No, you listen!" Ezra's voice echoed in the canyon, and Luke and Zach stood straighter. "This isn't up for discussion. You've already made this harder than it was supposed to be. I mean, forming an alliance with The Legion? What were you thinking?"

"What were *you* thinking, you fucking asshole?! You told us nothing and sent us here. Why did you come back for us?" Zach shook with anger.

Ezra gritted his teeth. "It was always the plan to come back for you. You had to know that. I didn't think you'd screw it up so badly. You were supposed to get your brothers settled. You had time . . . and now you're out."

I grabbed Aaron's hand and motioned to Presley. Our opening was coming. I could feel it in my gut.

Ezra's eyes softened as he turned to Luke. "She misses you. She wants you to come home. No strings attached."

"I know what you're doing. Stop messing with my head." Luke pulled his shoulders back.

"I've only ever done what's best for you. You know now that you have a destiny. You can't get out of this."

"We're not going back to Her. I'd rather die."

Luke seemed sure this time. He said it with finality that ended any argument.

"Well, if I can't change your mind . . ." He motioned behind him. "I can make this harder for you."

Two men grabbed Thane from behind and restrained him.

Things were moving faster now. They were stirring, readying themselves for a fight.

While holding one arm, they bent Thane's other arm back behind him and bit into his neck.

William moved forward, and Luke stopped him. "Wait."

The wind picked up in a gust strong enough to hide the first crack of my footsteps, and in a split second, I was already in the trees, gripping Aaron's hand, and Presley's footsteps were right behind ours. My feet moved on their own. Faster than I even imagined possible.

The thick scent of smoke billowed in the air, and I pushed forward toward the source. It was the only sense of direction I had. The men in suits were pushing into my peripheral vision. Little black dots grew larger and larger.

"Keep running! Don't turn back, no matter what!" Luke was somewhere behind.

That was enough to keep us moving. I pushed harder. Every muscle in my body came alive, as if all my previous years I'd only been using a portion of what I was capable of.

A strong set of hands grabbed my shoulders and sent me flying sideways through the trees. My body smacked against a tree and knifelike pain ran up my spine. That would have killed me. It still hurt, but I stood and faced my attacker. A burly man with a crooked jaw and two other guys on his side. None looked much older than me.

I readied myself for a fight I couldn't win, but in seconds, Aaron and

Zach burst through the branches. Aaron tackled one while Zach took down two. It was fast, but I could see it. I could finally see it. Every twitch of muscle and determined scowl.

Zach pinned one against a tree and bit into his neck. "Go!"

We took off again. This time I paid more careful attention to my dodging. Every duck between the trees pushed us closer to the wildfire ahead. The ashes fell into my eyes, but it didn't slow me.

My legs weren't tiring. My lungs weren't burning. I was doing it. I was running faster than I ever had before, and it was invigorating.

I could get us out. I *would* get us out.

With a quick glance behind, I realized no one was following. I stopped and retraced my steps in enough time to see Presley trying to pull one hulking guy off Aaron. Fire ignited in my veins, and I barreled forward. Everything snapped into place. The guy went flying like I'd slammed into him with a car.

I spared only a minute for shock at my new body.

We were surrounded by another barrage. At least five more. How many were there?

"What part of 'don't stop' don't you get?" William came in fast, and pieces of his shirt were torn and muddy. "Move!"

Presley ducked, avoiding an attack from behind. When they came at us again, we scrambled. All we could do was dodge. They sparred with William blow for blow, never losing steam. One of them grabbed my arm, and Aaron went rigid. He took the guy to the ground and wrapped his hands around his neck.

"Aaron!" My panic grew. If he lost control, I didn't know if I was enough to bring him back.

The twins broke through the clearing and evened the playing field, but as the seconds ticked by, more came from the trees.

"I'll hold them. Go." William flipped one guy over his shoulder and absorbed the punch of another.

Luke shook his head. "No way."

"Just fuckin' go. Please." William's eyes flashed with anger and then desperation.

With a push from behind, all three of us disappeared into the trees again. Faster this time.

"Will!" Zach's voice echoed in the trees behind us, but we were already running again.

A never-ending series of branches snagged my sweater, and debris hit my face. None of it could hurt me. I thought firmly on what Skylar would do. Keep looking forward and—

"Shit!" Aaron was covering me this time, trying to stop my momentum before we came to a halt.

Ezra stood in the clearing. Unlike Akira, he said nothing before he lunged forward. His fingers missed Aaron's forehead by only centimeters. We stumbled into Presley and huddled together. We were fast, but he was faster. He lunged again, and we scrambled, barely avoiding his touch. If one of us went down, we'd all go down.

Zach appeared and grabbed Ezra from behind. I didn't register the scream leaving my throat when Ezra pulled him to the ground and went for his throat.

Black blood stained the warm dirt beneath our feet.

"You can't beat me." Ezra kept Zach pinned.

"Good thing I don't need to." Zach smiled, not moving an inch.

A crack sounded in the air. Loud enough to be thunder but there were no clouds in the sky. Leaves and branches fell over head.

Aaron pulled me before I even knew what was happening.

A large tree fell into the clearing. The vibration radiated into the soles of my shoes. I grabbed Aaron and motioned to Presley to follow.

"No, wait!" Aaron was frantically searching the clearing for them.

Luke stumbled out of the trees and put his hands on Aaron's shoulders. "Go."

"No, I—"

Luke leaned forward to look Aaron directly in the eyes. "You're ready. Trust me."

"Be good, Pres." Luke patted him on the head to silence any talking.

His eyes shifted to me, and he nodded.

I instantly felt heavier. He was leaving it up to me. The task of making sure they didn't plant their feet there in the dirt. We had to keep running. I grabbed Aaron, and Presley begged them to run with me. When they protested, I pushed them forward until we were running again and zipping through the trees.

"Don't look back!" Luke's voice echoed.

My eyes burned. We were getting closer to the smell of ignited wood.

Everything around me turned hazy and orange.

I snuck a look behind, and there were still a couple of men following us, but no Luke or Zach.

"Come on!" I yelled.

We'd reached the edge of the tree line, and the heat coming off the fire in front of us was intense. There was only one way to lose them.

I ran through the trees. The heat from the fire singed the hairs on my arm. I didn't care. I kept pushing. Harder and harder. We couldn't stop. The heat was harsh on my skin, but there was no sting like when I was human.

It was hot, but it didn't burn.

The boys were nipping at my heels as we peeled through cascading logs of fire. The air was sweltering and void of oxygen. Thankfully, I didn't need it.

We were going fast enough to keep our clothes from catching fire, swiftly dodging trees. The soles of my hiking boots were melting, but we couldn't stop.

Keep going. Keep pushing.

I didn't know how far we'd run, but it didn't matter. I'd run forever—until we were safe.

The sound of the helicopter was music to my ears. That was our way out.

I followed it. Only glancing behind me to make sure Aaron and Presley were still there.

Finally, we made it to a clearing. The helicopter circled overhead, and all three of us collapsed to the ground.

"They're gone," Aaron said, his voice breaking.

"We have to go back." Presley's voice was lost in the roar.

"We can't . . ."

Presley pushed past him, and Aaron tackled him to the ground. "Let go! We have to go back. We can't just . . . just let them take them!"

"I know. I'm sorry. I'm sorry." Aaron hugged Presley tight to him to stop him from bolting back into the flames.

There was no one left to protect us. The Legion was gone. The twins were . . .

As the ash filled the air and embers landed my skin, I sucked in a breath. The two remaining Calem boys were falling apart in front of my eyes, and I struggled to keep my composure. My body screamed for any safety or certainty. The helicopter made another pass. We'd been seen.

Safety was looming, but it was a hollow victory. Behind us in the blaze, nothing but ash and burning wood followed us.

I laid a hand on my chest to still my ragged breath and the tears threatening to fall. My brain wouldn't accept what I knew to be true. It wasn't the ash filling my lungs that made it feel like I wasn't breathing. It was the nagging pain of knowing the truth.

We made it, but they didn't. Zach and Luke were going back to The Family, and William with them.

We were on our own.

EPILOGUE

ZACH

Hello, Hell, you've been expecting me.

I always knew it was coming.

Blackheart was our purgatory. The in-between. Moving farther into hell was part of my destiny apparently. Limbo would never be my final destination.

The loud hum of the jet engine and the frantic buzz of the hair clippers filled the silence between Luke and me. There were no more restraints as we sat in the front of the plane. Black velvet seats hid the falling pieces of my hair.

Mine blended in perfectly, but Luke's blonde hair stood out. I couldn't look at him.

If it was Hell, then Luke would never have been there.

The buzzing was close to my ear, blissfully filling my head with a strange numbness. According to Ezra, Luke and I looked unpresentable. She liked Luke's hair short and his face shaved. Of all the fucking things they thought to do when they finally had us, a haircut was apparently right at the top of that list. My hair had always been long, and I didn't think She even cared what I looked like, but some goon in a suit started cutting, and I'd let him. It didn't matter. Nothing mattered anymore.

I guessed I didn't want Luke to be alone.

We endured our haircuts without a word. They made us change immediately. Our dingy hiking clothes were shed for pressed silk suits—all black from head to toe.

Luke hadn't spoken a word since we were captured. I spoke a lot.

I could still hear the echo of Ezra's words to us as we stepped onto their jet plane. It was waiting for us at a rural airport not far away. I didn't think it was theirs. Something borrowed or stolen, probably.

None of it was surprising. A meteor could crash into the ground and a crazy ass alien could pop out and shake hands with me, and none of it would budge the muscles in my face.

"Things are going to be different now. You had responsibility before, but now you're someone. You killed a member of The Guard. You'll train to take his spot." Ezra's eyes looked like they might pop out of his head. The thought usually made me crack a smile.

The gray in Ezra's hair was from Luke and me.

"Aren't you going to torture us for treason?" I said it so he could feel the loathing in my voice.

Ezra pushed me against the wall of the plane. "Trust me. You'll both suffer the consequences of working with The Legion. Including the torture of your little friends in there. She's got plenty of plans for them."

Fucker. William and Thane were stashed in the back of the plane. Thane was still on my shit list, but, Will . . . I couldn't get to him if I wanted to. I hadn't figured out how to help him or even keep him alive. But he sacrificed himself for my brothers, which meant he was now under my list of responsibilities. I was pissed at him for that. Hell was my thing. No one was supposed to follow me.

"And what about you? Now that everyone here knows that you helped us escape."

He slammed me harder into the wall. "Listen to me. That, along with your transgressions, never leaves this plane. Do you understand?"

"You gonna hit me, *sir*? Don't you need to be welcoming me like the prodigy I am? Haven't you heard? We've been foretold."

If only sarcasm could kill.

His grip tightened on my collar. "If you want us to stop hunting your brothers, then you need to take your role next to Her. No more running. Time to be a man."

Ezra released the grip on my shirt with a pained look on his face. I felt it too. The dull ache pulsing in my chest. Akira was his brother, by Her blood. They'd had hundreds of years together. It wasn't enough to make me feel sorry for the bastard.

He stared at Luke, who was near catatonic. The one who trusted Ezra to teach him growing up. The one that followed him around, ready for knowledge. He was the reason Luke was suffering. Fuck Ezra and any version of me that ever trusted him.

"You both need to be ready by the time we arrive. You will be regarded like a member of The Guard." Ezra grabbed the collar of some random guy standing next to me and kicked him in the shins. "Show some respect. You will bow in their presence from now on."

"Yes, sir." The boy shielded his eyes from me.

Ezra had spoke again. "Everyone on this plane knows you were working with The Legion, and they will be taking that secret to the grave with them. They are indebted to you forever. It's your job to protect them and lead them, so we can protect Her. Got it?"

Neither of us had said a word.

"Good. Now sit down and get your haircuts. You're going to want to rest before we arrive."

I jolted myself from the memory. The sound of the razor had stilled, and Luke was ready, wearing that same military cut he had once loved, but he didn't look like my brother.

"That's fucking short enough." I ripped off my cape and left it in tatters on the floor. To my surprise, the guy listened to my demand. He left me with a drastic undercut; the top was still a few inches long.

"Leave."

He disappeared through the curtain behind us, and I went to crouch down in front of Luke.

I shook him gently. "You gotta say something. Anything. Tell me the fuckin' sky is blue or some shit. Just please talk to me."

Luke's eyes met mine, and the stone in my chest turned into a boulder.

"I know what it means to be a member of The Guard. I know what they do. Who you have to become. I can't do it. I won't."

"What's our other option?"

"I meant what I said . . ." Luke's eyes softened. "I'd rather be dead than do the things they want me to do . . . than go back to Her. I won't be able to stay away from Her."

"Don't say that." I gritted my teeth.

I hated when he said shit like that. Even if it was true.

"I can't. I'm sorry." Luke's voice leaped with desperation, and he leaned forward to hug me. It nearly knocked me over.

I shook my head, fighting the lump in my throat. "No. No. No. You promised me not to give up."

Luke pulled away. "We were kids."

We'd made a pact a long time ago. Neither of us could pass on without the other. We were two humans made with the same blood. It made sense that we'd go together. Even younger me understood that concept clearly.

"Yeah, but you promised you would never leave me here alone. I-I can't do this without you. We have to keep going."

The cries of William filled the cabin, and Luke buried his head in his hands.

There was no peace in death or life for us. We were in hell. And I had to get him out somehow.

"We can do this. We can save him, and if we do what they want, then Pres, Kim, Aaron, Mom, they'll all be okay." I pulled my hands through my freshly cut hair, desperation leaked in my voice with the lingering of William's cries. "We have to try. Please. Try with me."

I knew it wasn't true. I was a selfish asshole for asking him while knowing exactly what awaited us. Luke didn't need me. I needed him.

Tears gathered in Luke's eyes. "How? I don't know how I can do it."

"I'll do it. Anything too hard, too much that you can't do. I'll do it for you. I can be your right hand. I'll get my hands dirty. Whatever it takes."

I'd ruin myself for my brother in a heartbeat. I was pretty far gone, anyway.

Luke shook his head. "No. I can't let you do that for me."

He always believed in me for reasons I'd never understood. I'd never given him a reason to. He got all the good parts in the womb. Like whatever the fuck was in the sky thought he needed it more than me or something. He gave him the hope, the optimism, the *good*.

At a young age, he cared about everything. Literally everything from the bugs on the ground to the neighbor's dog. I'd watch in awe as he'd give his toys to others, and I wondered if he thought they'd magically reappear to him or something. I'd even spy on him playing, thinking maybe some fucking gnomes or some shit were rewarding him with more. It wasn't till I was older that I understood he expected nothing back. He just gave with a smile.

I never cared about anything. Only things that were mine.

My brothers were *my* brothers. My family was mine. My stuff was mine. Why would I care about anyone else's anything? That was their problem. Their responsibility.

"It's easy for me. Just don't leave me here to do this alone. Promise me.

Again."

Luke sighed and held out his hand. "I promise."

Maybe that's why I'd always felt the need to protect Luke. Because he was good, and good needed to be protected.

My younger brothers all tumbled out with the same goodness I saw in Luke. With Aaron, the world was ending if he had to do anything even a little questionable. I used to find it annoying. The pranks Luke and I pulled didn't sit right with him, and he'd run and tattle on us. I finally realized there might be someone in this world filled with even more good than Luke. How was that fucking possible? Wasn't Luke the epitome?

I related to Luke despite our differences, but I couldn't see myself in Aaron. He was the golden boy . . . and kind of a dick. It's like he saw through me. Like he knew I was dirt compared to him. That there was nothing good in me. It was in that horrible look he'd give me when I had to protect what was mine. Luke never gave me that look.

If it wasn't for Presley, I'd have never believed there was hope for me. He was good too, but in a different way. Sure, he freaked the fuck out if I hurt his precious Earth, but he was the only one who ever understood my obsession with what was mine.

I think that's why we stayed as long as we did and listened to Kilian's nonsensical plan. Why I let Luke convince me outside the IHOFT to keep going with the plan . . .

We wanted more time there with them. And Luke was better. Not fixed but a lot better. We were all together, and for a moment, even I believed it might stay that way.

Past tense. I would never see them again.

And with that last thought, I let go.

Of my brothers.

Of what was mine.

Of my family.

Maybe God gave me all the bad parts to punish me. *Yeah, sounds about right.*

BONUS CHAPTER

"Bad
Decisions
and
New
Beginnings"

The flash of a camera marked the end of an era, and a flurry of red caps painted the sky with their golden tassels. The tiny strings blended into the colorful flurry of confetti and silly string. Zach and Luke, the undeniable rocks of the Calem family, embraced each other. The wide smiles on their faces overshadowed the cuts and bruises tainting their skin.

One of Luke's brown eyes was tinged red with blood. His lip was busted, and every breath hurt his broken ribs. Zach sported two shiners and a bandage over the healing gash on his nose. None of this stopped them from celebrating the greatest day of their lives. The day they'd been waiting for, for years.

"Ah, okay, Mom. Please, no more pictures," Luke said as he shut his eyes, shielding them from another swift flashing.

"Yeah, that fucking flash is giving me a headache," Zach groaned.

"Language."

A swift hand slapped the back of Zach's *very* sore shoulder, and he cried out, "Jeez, Mom."

"Just one more. Both of you get together, put your arm around each other." Vera smiled. She had waited for the day her eldest sons would graduate high school. Long nights were spent worrying if they even make it past eighteen—but there they were, finally graduated.

She knew raising four children alone would be hard, but she'd never anticipated the worry that had seeped into every cell in her body since she first held Luke in her arms. A worry that had only grown with the age of her two eldest sons. She watched them change. One eternally happy boy and the other soft and sensitive had become rough around the edges.

Though she had asked, they refused to mention the person or persons that hurt them, and the guilt felt so tangible she convinced herself it might as well have been her that caused it. But standing before her, they seemed happy.

Zach and Luke rested their arms on each other's shoulders for the picture. Their red gowns trailed the freshly mowed lawn of the football field. The stadium lights clicked on as the sun faded from the sky and the moon slowly took its place. Luke had played many games on that field. Countless practices of blood, sweat, and tears were spent in that very spot. His heart yearned for those days again. If only for a day to relive the sound of the crowd.

Zach could be found under the bleachers. He didn't care to look back at the field. Unlike Luke, he had never been emotionally attached to high school. It was something to do, and he was happy he'd never have to do it again.

Zach squeezed his eyes shut and threw up his index finger and pinky while Luke gave his mom his best smile and held his fist in the air. The camera flashed again. Graduation caps had fallen and littered the ground, creating the perfect backdrop underneath the glow of stadium lights.

Presley ran up behind them, followed by Aaron, who had his head buried in his cell phone.

"Wow, you guys made it. Gotta say, I'm surprised Zach isn't dead in a ditch somewhere. You know he does cocaine, right, Mom?" Presley's eyes glistened.

Zach stuck his middle finger up in the air with a grin still spread across his face. "You little asshole."

"If it's true, I don't want to know." Vera sighed, pulling a hand through her salt-and-pepper hair. Her natural long dark hair had been speckled with gray earlier than most. She attributed the stress of being a mom to four boys and her late-night shifts as an ER nurse.

"It's not!" Zach grabbed Presley in a headlock.

Luke eyed the high beams overhead. His mind drifted back to his days playing football. Just two years ago, he played on that field. He wondered how different his life would be if he had stayed on the team. He could have had more time on the field, more time with . . . her.

The long, warm-brown hair of Sarah Garanger broke Luke's train of thought. Her skin was freshly tanned and freckled by the sun since her trip over spring break.

Luke realized he'd never see her cheering him on from the sidelines again with red-and-gold pom poms pressed firmly in the air. Sarah had earned her popularity as "The Most Likely to Succeed" not only by being insanely brilliant but also from being kind. From the moment they shared a PB&J sandwich on their first day of kindergarten, they were inseparable.

"Sarah's looking for you, you know." Aaron nudged his older brother with a smirk.

Sarah wrapped her arms around her dad's neck. He was a short man with strong bushy brows. Her father always wrapped Luke in a strong hug when he saw him. At first it caught him off guard, but it was now Luke's favorite thing about him. Sarah's family was large. Her cousins chattered around her in a flurry of excitement.

A pang of guilt punched Luke in the gut, and a strange sense of worry glued his feet in place. "Yeah . . . but I don't want to—"

"Go on. Go talk to her." Aaron pushed Luke forward, and Luke took a step with his head down.

Sarah's green eyes lit up when her eyes met Luke's. "There you are!" Her hands lingered on his broad shoulders as she pulled away, and she moved one hand to graze his brow. "That eye is looking better."

"What's all this fuss about me? Look at you!"

Her eyes sparkled, and her warmth melted him where he stood. "You're too sweet to me."

He smiled. "Impossible." His eyes trained again on the crowd and a frown twisted on his lips. "Where's Marco?"

Marco was Sarah's boyfriend. He was a year older than her and rarely visited from his college upstate.

"Oh, I think he said he was going out with his friends tonight." Her confident voice faltered for a split second before returning to normal. "But it doesn't matter. We can party the night away."

Their conversation was interrupted by loud insidious laughter.

Ashley Park, Zach's long-term girlfriend, ran full speed into Zach's arms. They embraced in one long kiss as he spun her around. Ashley was a petite girl; her larger dark eyes complemented her short brown hair that grazed her shoulders. Like Sarah, she was also popular, but instead voted "Most Creative" in their senior class. She had painted the brightest mural in town on the side of their high school.

"We did it!" Ashley giggled as Zach finally dropped her onto the grass. He could feel Ashley's dad's gaze heavy on the back of his head. He didn't dare look at the only man he might actually be afraid of.

"Ashley!" Sarah grabbed Luke's arm and pulled them into the group.

"Oh my God!" Ashley said as she squeezed Sarah as tight as she could. "Can you believe it? The four of us made it out of this hell hole."

Her eyes darted to her father to make sure he was out of hearing distance.

"I tried to find you so we could sit together!" Sarah wrapped her arms around Ashley and admired her electric-blue eyeliner.

"Vera, I'm not sure who I should be congratulating more tonight. Your boys or you for getting them to graduation." Sarah's dad appeared and wrapped Vera in a hug.

"Keith. Thank you." Vera's hands rested on his shoulders as she pulled away.

Sarah and Luke shared a look. Their single parents had a lot in common. Keith reminded Vera of her father, and since they moved to Brooklyn and her mother died, every time she buried her head in one of Keith's hugs, she felt at home.

Keith smiled, his firm gaze landing on Luke and Zach. "Glad to see you're both doing better. Didn't know if you were gonna make it."

Luke met Keith's eyeline but couldn't hold it. His gaze fell to his feet, and he moved the grass off his sneakers. Zach nodded with his eyes averted. Keith's eyes held a mirror that they weren't ready to face.

"Hopefully that'll be the last time I have to worry about y'all getting into a . . . freak accident." Keith placed a hand on Luke's shoulder on his way back to his family. Luke's body went rigid. Their freak accident was no accident, and despite the twins' refusal to speak about what happened that night, everyone knew.

"Alright, Dad." Sarah's hand replaced Keith's on Luke's shoulder. "I'll be back over in a second."

"So, what are we doing tonight?" Ashley held onto Zach as she reached into his gown to wrap him in another hug.

"Party!" Presley yelled.

"I was going to go over to Enrique's," Aaron said, his attention was back to his phone. "But if you guys are gonna be home, I won't go."

"I could pick up some pizzas! We've got plenty of room at the house." Vera looked up at them expectantly.

"Mom, I told you. We have somewhere to be." Zach pulled a pack of cigarettes from his pants and went to light up.

Vera snatched the cigarette from his mouth. "You may be old enough to make your own choices. But you know better than to smoke in front of me."

"Come on. Can't you reschedule?" Sarah was still smiling, glowing. "For the first time ever, everyone's schedules line up. It's fate."

Ashley smiled. "She's right. How often do we get to be graced by all four Calem boys and their beautiful mom."

"Oh, now you're just sucking up." Zach scoffed.

"It's okay. Mom reacts well to that type of behavior. That's how I became the favorite." Presley puffed out his chest.

"What are you talking about? I'm clearly her favorite," Aaron said.

Everything was as it should be. The people they most cared about in the world were together and happy.

"Are you sure you guys have to go tonight?" Vera pleaded. She didn't know exactly where they were going but her intuition told her everything she needed to know.

They shared a glance. Every bone in their bruised body was begging to stay, but tonight was special for more than one reason.

They had gone through every initiation. The Family. And tonight, they could finally join them. Securing a good life for their family. The fresh tattoos on their skin burned with the spring air.

The determination resounded in their eyes, and they spoke as one. "Yeah, we're sure."

Luke pulled the car into a gravel road near the harbor. It was dark, and the ships in the water moved slowly in the night. He turned down the dial on the radio blasting nineties rock.

"I can't believe we're finally doing this shit." Zach smiled from ear to ear. Pride filled his chest. This was the one thing he finally got right. Something he'd done that would protect his family indefinitely. He could be proud of that. They'd never have to worry about money again, and his family would be safe.

Luke put the car in park and took a deep breath. He looked down at his wrist and felt the crushing weight of responsibility. If there was ever a time he could turn back and choose another path, that day was long gone. Unlike Zach, Luke wasn't as sure of his choices. He thought long and hard about what the future could have been like if he'd never met Ezra.

Tonight, he would have been at that party with Sarah. Better yet, he would have asked her to be his girlfriend years ago. He still wanted that dream. The harbor lights loomed in the pitch-black night. But he was finally ready to give it up.

He would give this everything he had. He had to think bigger than his own desires. To be in The Family was to think ahead. To be a part of something more important.

"I think I'm ready."

The boys pulled out a crumpled piece of paper. It had been delivered to them that day and was scribbled in red ink. Only a location and a time along with the word "faith" scribbled at the top. It was their last test. Their brush with "strength" is what led them to the hospital. A night that started the same way. A note and a dark place followed by a barrage of fists and weapons.

They walked into an open garage with the only light in the harbor. The night was cold, and since they came straight from the football field, they hadn't even bothered taking off their gowns. Both felt the uneasy turning of their empty stomachs, but they kept quiet in search of whatever was coming.

There was no one in sight and no sound other than the soft movement of the ocean and the buzzing fluorescent light. In the middle of the garage, stood a singular barrel and two silver goblets lay in wait.

Their last trial. The goblets were filled with a red liquid to the brim.

Zach picked up a goblet and smelled it. The sickly-sweet scent of cherry filled his nostrils. "Maybe it's poison."

"I don't think they'd bring us this far to kill us," Luke said.

Zach shrugged, not caring either way. "Together?"

Luke picked up his goblet and wrapped his arm around Zach's for a toast.

Luke started. "To new beginnings."

"And possibly more bad decisions." Zach finished.

Their smiles lingered, and with the clink of their goblets, they downed their drinks.

"Fuck." Zach threw his glass on the ground, and it tumbled with a loud crash on the concrete floor.

"Disgusting." Luke's lips were numb when they left the glass.

"I'm gonna be sick." Zach lurched forward, holding his stomach. Luke went to reach for him but found himself on the dusty concrete floor.

Their tongues were numb and could no longer form sentences. Within minutes, they gave way to their weak knees. Their consciousness waned in brief intervals. The world around them disintegrated into an endless spinning until they were surrounded.

Dark silhouettes pulled them from the cold floor. A woven sack scratched their faces as their world went black. Their feet fumbled around as they were thrown into the back of a van.

Zach couldn't keep his eyes open, but he willed himself to move his heavy arms to find Luke. Once he felt Luke next to him in the van, he relaxed, letting the car take them to whatever destination. Luke was more trusting. He couldn't see but he could hear a familiar set of voices, and that was enough to ease his fears.

There was no sense of time in the van. Every wild jerk reminded the boys that they were vulnerable. The van smelled of leather and sandalwood and radiated with a flurry of voices.

The vehicle stopped, and the door opened and then they were filed out one by one. Their feet barely moved as they were ushered into a red brick building. Laced within the brick laid gritted stone. Pure white that stretched to the night sky until it ended in point. Stone cherubs hid in the darkest corner, overlooking the scene, aged many years by the sun and the rain, but this was no church.

They were lifted over the stone steps and into a dimly lit basement that led into a common area. No sound was detected in the entire four-story building, only the scuttling of their feet against a hardwood floor. The smell was oddly familiar to them.

Once in the middle of the common area, their hoods were ripped off, and Zach and Luke found themselves face-to-face. Their pupils were dilated, and they could barely see. The warmth of the hearth fireplace beside them and the crackling of the logs did little to warm the monstrous building. Their world lagged like a video game, and they found another set of hands tugging on their clothes and pulling them off. The muscles in their faces were too weak to protest.

Firm hands pushed them to their knees in only their boxers. A Persian rug, made of pure wool, padded their fall but was little comfort to their growing nerves.

"It's time." The boys recognized the voice of their immediate superior and relaxed a little. Ezra was there, and if Ezra was there, that meant they were safe. This is what they had wanted. This was what they'd been waiting for.

Again, they were pulled from their knees and onto their feet. This time, the journey would be much harder. A spiral staircase lined with a dark-wood banister was thick and black ornate metal lined the railing. It contrasted with the red brick that greeted them with every step. The journey, seemingly impossible for two men who couldn't feel their legs, was made easier by three sets of arms carrying them up to the top.

The three guard members stood arm in arm with the boys until they reached the top. A strange silence filled the building. Despite being in central Manhattan, not a car could be heard outside. Everything was quiet as they waited.

With a strong push, two large wooden doors opened to the altar room. A room with concrete floors that still didn't lose its charm. A balcony window in the back of the room was covered with thick white drapes for the occasion. Candles lined the floor, shining on the faces of The Family. A group of no more than twenty men on bended knee waiting for Her arrival.

Zach and Luke were forced to kneel, this time, on red velvet pillows. As their knees hit the pillows, their heads swirled from dizziness. Luke caught himself before falling into the concrete. As he picked up his heavy head, his gaze landed on a stream of white.

A woman with pure white hair and skin walked to the altar in front of them. Every eye in the room was on her, but Luke couldn't understand why. He turned his head slowly, observing the unblinking crowd as they followed her every move. He had never seen anything like it.

Zach casually eyed the woman through hazy eyes. She was nothing special, but she was pretty, he guessed.

Her eyes met Luke, and he froze.

"It's a pleasure to meet you . . . Luke." Her voice sung the song of someone who yearned for him, but he'd never known she existed.

He tried to clear his throat to speak, but a groan was all that came out.

"Don't strain yourself. I only wish to speak directly to you both. To tell you how long awaited your arrival has been. I'm so happy to see you both home."

Zach's stomach stirred, something felt odd. There was never mention of any girl. Why would they keep her a secret? And why did she want to see them so badly?

"Valiantly. You have both shown your loyalty to our . . . family. In the secrets you've kept, the assignments you've completed, and by the final trials you've endured. Your bruised bodies will soon be made stronger. Our gift to you."

Nothing she said made any sense to the boys, and every word hung in the air like an echo. Whatever drug they took worked; there was no use in fighting anything. They weren't going anywhere.

Ezra and Akira stood at either shoulder, and at the nod of her head, they sunk their teeth into the neck of their twin. A pressure surged in their necks. It was deep and intense as teeth tore through their skin and into muscles. It didn't hurt, but when their blood was nearly drained, they were too weak to sit up. The faint sight of red blood littered the floor in droplets beside them.

"It's time," the woman said.

The room went dead silent.

Zach was aware of every breath in his chest. The woman grabbed his face and brought it toward hers. "Welcome home."

She bit her wrist and black blood poured down in front of him. As soon as the blood hit his lips, he was gone. His muscles seized, and he fell back against the concrete floor. Not in pain, in pure bliss.

The woman wove her hands in Luke's hair and whispered in his ear, "I've long waited for you" before feeding him a few drops of her blood. Luke's eyes went wide.

The room disappeared, and in that moment, She was the only thing that mattered to them.

Everything about Her was magnificent. Her hair, Her skin, Her nails. Everything She was, they wanted to be. Her blood coursed through their veins, leaving scars. And though they couldn't feel any of their muscles, their bodies were alive. Alive with a new feeling of belonging. Life was worth living if She was there. From that moment, they'd be forever tethered to Her. All fear they had was long gone.

They were exactly where they wanted to be. With Her.

S.L.Cokeley

Samantha Cokeley was raised in a small town in Oklahoma. Growing up, she always had an active imagination and an interest in crafting stories. She developed a love for writing after college when she discovered anime and fan fiction. If she isn't spending time painting colorful sea creatures, you can find her with family, including her pug named Kylo. The This Blood that Binds Us series ends this year. But you can expect many more stories with vampires, heart warming found family, and fluff to come.

Follow Me

Links to my newsletter so you can stay up to date.

Follow me on Amazon so you never miss a release

Facebook Reader Group

Instagram